Uritus and the Sword of Fire

"The Song of the Suvah" and "The Legend of the Adalos"

By Dove Segovia

A Letter From the Author

Beloved Reader,

Thank you for being here. This story is incredibly important to me. Its roots grow deep in the history of my life, an entanglement so intrinsic that putting it on paper felt like breathing—innate, intuitive, inevitable. Though I am a bottomless well of pretty words, I will always fall short when trying to describe the depth of the honor I feel for how you have chosen to take a chance on it too.

I've taken the liberty of including a couple of tools for you to utilize as you embark on your adventure into the Free World: the first, a map, a gorgeous rendering of the land you will soon discover drawn up by my dear friend, Anthony; the second, tucked into the book's back pages, a pronunciation guide to ease your experience with unfamiliar words. Use these as you will. They are my gifts to you.

As I am ever present in this story, so are many whose hands have graced my life. Everyone I've ever loved, everyone I've ever lost, everyone who has ever been gracious enough to offer me their exhortation. I am who I am because of the stories—breathing and paper—that have shaped me, and this book is no different. Here there is trauma and heartache and grief, but it is not without love and community and hope.

I hope you find yourself in here. I hope you find the people you love in here. I hope you laugh and weep and learn to recognize the pure and steady beating of your heart itself as something worth fighting for. May you find a steady path as you make your way forward.

All my love,

—D

The Frozen Sea
The Blessed Sea
N
W
E
S
Looming Mountains
Akmen
Snow City
Niramel
Cordish
Netha
Maresh
Alabaster Keep
Valley of the Sun
Sheth
The Little Wood
The Emerald Sea
White Mountains
The Academy
Myrell
OF Healers
Swamp of Sigmount
Tosh
Condir
Plentiful Lake
Trader's land
Port
Martella
Judi
Forest of Idor
MX Venadalis
Lorethh
Suscundos
Quabish
The Southern Mountains
The Holy City
Tila Forest
The Favored Plains
Vindellaria
Kanel
Cropidea
The Eldest Forest
Oacai
The Sea of Glass
The Free World

For you.

Table of Contents

<u>Prologue</u>

On a still, peaceful Winter night, Uritus and Erclidus slept soundly in the room they shared with their brothers and sisters. It was not yet dawn, fair fingers of frost still crawling their way across blades of grass, but a gentle rapping sounded on their door. It creaked as it was pushed open and a stream of light poured into the room.

"Uritus, Erclidus, wake up!"

Erclidus apprehensively opened one eye to see the light glowing from an old lantern in his father's hand. He obediently rose, climbed onto the bunk above his, and shook his younger brother awake. Uritus groaned, unprepared to rise before the sun. He eventually obliged Erclidus's insistence and the two boys followed their father outside.

"Why did you wake us so early?" Uritus asked, stepping through the threshold into cold moonlight.

"Come and you'll see."

The man—Odipar Subian—had the full trust of his sons despite his solemn urgency. He led them to the barn, and inside, the boys saw Quickspa, the mare, lying on the floor of her stall.

"She's birthing her foal."

Uritus looked up at his father with sparkling eyes. He had never before witnessed the birth of an animal. He was seven years old, and suddenly felt for the first time that he must be growing up. His brother—three years his senior—made a show of gloating two years prior after his own first invitation to the barn in the night. Erclidus was excited now to show Uritus everything he remembered from when he helped aid in Velatondra's birth. Odipar smiled to see his eldest son take on the role of the teacher.

Day broke as the colt was finally born. Odipar turned to Uritus and declared that this horse was his. "What'll you name him?"

The seven-year-old had deliberated about this. He had a sharp mind and a vivid imagination, so he often dreamed about what his horse would look like and fantasized about the journeys they would undertake. The small animal was gangly and silly-looking, a bold white star on his face shining against the black of his coat, yet the boy saw nothing short of glimmering promise in him. Someday, people would tell stories about the adventures they shared.

"Moonracer," he declared without hesitation. "When he gets old enough, he'll race the moon and win!"

Odipar chuckled and smiled at the vast confidence of his son. How fiercely he loved them, all six of his children and his wife. He was a fisherman by trade, training his two oldest boys to become the same. They dwelt in the small fishing village of Tosh, one of three like villages resting on the edges of the Plentiful Lake.

They had been caught in a drought for the past several years. The fisherman and his wife were diligent to keep their worries for their future out of the minds of their children. The eldest boys sensed their father's anxieties about the increasing lengths of time between rains. But all the same, they saw clearly the hope he carried with him at all times. If he—with a better view than they had—looked ahead and saw bright days, then surely they must be there.

Though he was good at hiding it, Uritus dreamed of one day leaving Tosh and doing something great in Myrell, the Holy City, or even Suscundos. His parents made it their mission to instill their children with courage and confidence, and it was because of this that Uritus was certain he was designed with a grand purpose in mind—something that the mediocrity of the fishing village would never be able to offer him. He knew it would be years before he could adventure out on his own, so he tried to remain happy in the state he was in, all the while quietly imagining a brighter future nonetheless. But then came a day, a mere few months after Moonracer's birth, when all of his dreams were shoved to the back of his mind.

Unanticipated by anyone, his mother fell ill with a strange fever, the likes of which no one in the village had ever seen before. The mystery of the illness made it difficult to cure. No one knew how to best help restore the fading light once carried by the wife of the fisherman, and Odipar soon came to understand, with sadness in his heart, that there was nothing they could do to save her.

When the children began to realize that they were spending their last days with their mother, Uritus refused to leave her bedside. He sat with her while she rested, listening fearfully to the ragged uncertainty of her breath. A lump grew in his throat as he considered her role: the figurehead, the inspirer, the one who so easily anticipated the needs of all those around her—in their family and the whole village—and filled them without needing to be asked. Uritus couldn't comprehend a future without her, and he sobbed as it grew clear that this very future stood at the threshold of their home.

Maja Lowwar had spent days searching her mind for words to comfort her grieving children. The sounds of the younger ones running about the garden could be heard above Uritus's sobs. She reached out a shaky hand and placed it atop his. "Uritus..."

The boy lifted his head to look at her through bleary eyes.

"Listen."

He wiped his nose and took in a few shaky breaths in an attempt to calm himself. He strained his ears, frowning when he heard nothing but the shrill voices of his siblings and the soft, gentle crashing of the waves upon the shore. He shook his head in frustration. "There's nothing."

"Not nothing."

Uritus listened again. "Nothing but the water and the kids. Maybe wind, I don't know..."

"That..." she drew in a shaky breath and let it out, "...is what hope sounds like."

"Hope?"

"Mhm."

Uritus gripped her hand, trying his best to be patient.

"Hope is—" A fit of coughing suddenly cut her off and she paused to recoup her strength. "Hope is... like the water," her voice cracked as she went on. "It's always there, in some form or another, whether we see it or not..."

Uritus swallowed his tears.

"Sometimes we lose it. And when we do, we must look to each other." She moved her hand to his cheek, feeling the softness of his youthful skin beneath her weathered fingertips. "You are that hope for me, Uritus. You and your siblings and your father. In you, I see the Magic that exists all around us, more clearly than in the hand of any Wizard, the heart of any Healer, or the mouth of any Prophet."

Uritus dissolved into tears as he began to realize that this was his mother's goodbye.

"If we exist for any reason, it is for each other. Don't ever forget that."

"But—" he choked. "I don't know what I'll do if you're gone!"

"No one is ever truly gone, Uritus." She smiled weakly and closed her eyes. "Not really."

Uritus buried his head in her sheets and wept, remaining by her side until she took her final breath.

***

The loss had been so sudden and unforeseen. The devastated family fell into a state of weary mourning. Odipar was forced to enlist the help of neighbors to care for the younger children when he returned to his boat. With his nets coming up only half-full on good days, he could not afford to remain with them while they grieved. He devoted himself to caring for them as best as he knew how, and after a time, they began to adjust to their new life. But it was not long before a familiar unwanted guest again darkened their doorstep.

Slowly, one after another, the younger children began to contract strange symptoms, unnervingly similar to those their mother had just before she fell ill. Ragged breaths, weakening limbs, sudden, shivering fevers. Uritus, Erclidus, and Odipar all seemed to be in good health, so tried to remain optimistic that the children were merely catching cold.

Tragically, they found themselves to be incorrect. They toiled in the fishing boat and at the children's bedsides every day until their bodies collapsed into their beds at night, praying that one of the physicians in Tosh or Martella would have a breakthrough and be able to provide the life-saving care that the children were in desperate need of. But their work would prove to be in vain, and it was not long before they found their small cottage feeling suddenly open and empty and cold.

Their devastation weighed heavy on their shoulders. They did not say it, but each held the fear in his own mind that to attempt to reclaim hope for the future would only result in further devastation. Eventually, the plague did pass on, and the two sons wondered why they stayed so strong and healthy despite how easily the disease seemed to be contracted.

Odipar constructed a theory that their immune systems were strengthened because of their constant physical labor and regular exposure to dirt and filth. He also explained that, far in the past along his family line, one of his ancestors had married a wood elf. The elves were far less susceptible to illness and physical ailments. Those genes must have passed on to his eldest two and over the younger ones.

The thought was hardly a comfort, and Uritus found himself burdened with guilt, rationalizing that if he hadn't been blessed with the elven genes, perhaps one or two of his siblings could have been spared instead. But Odipar comforted him with the knowledge that his lost family members were now free from their mortal frames, dancing in the Great Beyond. If the three of them were spared, they must find purpose here, now, in the Free World.

***

Years later, on a cloudy November day, the boys took the cart to the market on an errand for their father. Working the market had been Maja's duty until one of the other merchants had offered to take over the task for her when she became pregnant with her third child. Walking the dusty road with Quickspa's reins in hand reminded Uritus of when his mother would bring him along with her. So while he enjoyed aiding his father in the boat on the lake, market days were a welcome interruption to his ordinary routine.

They were just outside town when they happened upon an interruption in the otherwise consistent landscape—a large tent with a sign posted beside it. It boomed in loud letters bordered with gold,

"Come skeptics, come believers!
Witness the incredible power of the Magic of the West!"

Though his curiosity led him to slow down enough to look the tent over, Uritus did not stray from his intended path. His father had told him all he needed to know about traveling sorcerers. They were men who journeyed about from village to village conjuring small tricks, claiming to be Keepers of Magic. Sorcerers were not true Keepers, according to Odipar. They were Thieves. The practice of Stolen Magic was dangerous, difficult to learn, and forbidden East of the Looming Mountains. Anyone who claimed that he had found a way to steal from the Source for his own gain was more than likely a fraud. In either case, Odipar told the boys that it was wise to remain far away from them.

Erclidus, though, was fiercely curious and forever seeking to expand his knowledge of the world, and he was not as prone to unquestioningly trusting his father as Uritus was. He had a spark burning within him that Maja and Odipar had recognized since the day he was born. They had chosen his name for its meaning: passionate one. They made it a priority to nurture this side of him— something they knew would cause him to become headstrong and difficult to

4

corral. But they valued training their children to be independent thinkers and were willing to shoulder the burden of his stubbornness if it meant he would always stay fiery.

Now, standing there, mere paces from the market, he felt a tug as if on his sleeve and turned his head to regard the tent. The fabric shimmered when it caught glimpses of pale sunlight, a deep burgundy unlike anything he had ever seen. Frowning, he looked back at the humble town of Tosh and its market and felt a twinge of disgust for how drab it looked in comparison. It was almost always cloudy in Tosh, he observed, something he knew was because of their proximity to the lake and the White Mountains. But he suddenly felt, within his stomach, a growing feeling of disdain for the home he had always known.

Erclidus came to realize how he had never desired much for his life before. Uritus had always been the one who dreamed of dragons and quests and great victories, but Erclidus only ever wished to travel to Myrell for a time to further his education, after which he assumed he'd just return home. But the resentment began to grow as he considered how presumptuous his father had been to assume that he wished to spend his life as a fisherman at all.

He furrowed his brow and turned back to the tent and, almost unconsciously, took a step toward it.

"Erclidus?" Uritus realized he had now led Quickspa several steps ahead of his brother and called back to him, "Are you coming?" Noticing the reason for the delay, he frowned. "What are you doing?"

The eldest Subian looked to his brother and then back at the tent. He debated for a moment leaving with Uritus, having lunch as they'd planned, and then returning home to read like he always spent his afternoons on market days. But at that moment, the wind moved swiftly through the grass and lifted the flap of the tent just slightly, and Erclidus became steadfast in his resolve.

"I'm going to watch the show. Come on, we can drop the fish off after. I'm sure it won't be too long."

"I don't know…" Uritus shifted nervously on his feet. "I don't think Father would want us to."

Erclidus loudly laughed, startling his brother. "It's just a show. Father doesn't need to know."

Uritus frowned, suddenly frustrated and anxious. "No!"

Erclidus blinked in surprise and furrowed his brow. His brother was not known for speaking forcefully.

"I mean… please…" Uritus shook his head, purposely avoiding looking back at the tent. "Please, can we just go? I don't think Father would have told us to be careful if it wasn't actually dangerous. And besides, I'm getting hungry, and—"

Erclidus snorted.

Uritus blinked. This was not a side of his brother that he was familiar with. He hated feeling like Erclidus was upset with him. He admired him for his capability, his boldness, and his strength, but especially for his cleverness. It seemed there was never a snag that he wasn't capable of thinking his way out of.

Uritus did not tell him—as Erclidus was prone to boasting when his ego was fluffed—but the younger Subian looked up to the elder just as he did their father.

"What?"

Erclidus sighed agitatedly, rolling his eyes with such fervor that his head moved with them. "It doesn't matter."

"If it didn't matter, you would tell me."

Erclidus sighed again. For as long as he could remember, it was he who had been tasked with caring for his younger brother. Uritus was an eager worker and a fast learner, but he was also far too... *responsible* for Erclidus's liking. He never did wrong, not if he could help it, and as Erclidus grew older and hungrier for greater independence, he felt increasingly more burdened by Uritus's timidity.

"Please," Uritus's voice was small. "We're almost there. We can play duel when we get back if you want, I've been practicing, and I—"

"I don't want to *play duel* with you, Uritus, I want to do something real!"

Uritus took in a small, startled breath. Silence hung in the air between them, cut only by the shuffling of Quickspa's hooves.

"Father does not know everything," Erclidus said finally. "He is not a Keeper himself, who is he to tell us anything at all about Magic? You think you're doing right by being obedient, but there's more to life than that. Do you never tire of being so *good*?"

He spat this last word out with disgust. Uritus bit his lip against its trembling and said nothing.

"Of course not."

Erclidus turned on his heel and stormed off toward the tent. Uritus took in a shaky breath, returned his attention to the road, and led Quickspa on.

***

When they sat down to supper that evening, Erclidus seemed to eat more and talk less than he was ordinarily prone to. His father questioned him about this, wondering to himself if he needed to start sending the boys with a larger stipend for food when they went to the market to fuel their growing bodies. Between mouthfuls, Erclidus casually shared that he hadn't eaten since breakfast.

The fisherman frowned slightly. "Why not?"

Erclidus paused, realizing that he had unintentionally trapped himself. He slowly finished chewing and swallowed, all the while twirling his fork in the air as he willed the wheels in his brain to do the same. "I, um..." No convincing lie came to mind. "I just... didn't."

"I see." Odipar cleared his throat and turned to Uritus, "Did you skip lunch as well?"

Uritus stopped chewing and looked at his brother, wondering what he would do if Erclidus willed him to lie.

"Uritus?"

The younger boy tore his gaze away from the elder's steely one to look back at his father and then down at his food. "No, I ate." He felt the heat of Erclidus's stare beat down upon his head but refused to meet his eyes.

"I see," Odipar said again.

Silence filled the room and Erclidus shifted nervously in his seat. His father had no reason to become accusatory. Even if he had, it wasn't in his nature. Odipar knew he was not entitled to every thought that passed through the minds of his sons. But it was this very trust, this very *silence* that had Erclidus's stomach slowly coiling itself into a giant knot of guilt.

It was unclear in his mind if Odipar genuinely trusted him or was rather playing a waiting game, allowing the shame to build in the room until Erclidus couldn't take it anymore and confessed, unprompted. He clenched his hands into fists and glared across the table at his brother who kept his eyes downcast. How small and frightened he looked. He wasn't even the one who'd done something their father would disapprove of. If Erclidus didn't bend to the pressure of his father's mind game, Uritus's guilty look was surely more than enough to make it clear to Odipar that something was wrong. The knot in his stomach transformed into one of rage and made its way into his chest. *Who were they to decide what he should do, what he should think? Who were they to stand in his way?*

Finally, the silence was broken by Odipar, "Have I not been sending you with enough coin to the market? You'll have to forgive me, I did not know. Next time I'll be sure to—"

He was cut off by the clattering of Erclidus's fork across the table.

"I saw the show, okay?" And then, when he was met with silence, "The traveling sorcerer just outside town. And you know what? It was incredible."

Silence fell again. The fisherman calmly set his fork down on the table beside his plate. "Surely, I do not need to tell you again that men of his kind are untrustworthy…"

"He's nothing like you said, Father."

"Erclidus—"

"I'm telling you the truth! It was *you* who told me to keep my mind open. Well, now I have, and I'm telling you, he's not a fraud, he's not dangerous. He's just a man, and Magic is just Magic."

Odipar sighed. "I believe you are smart enough to know that is not true."

"How could you possibly know that? You too are just a man. All my life you've encouraged me to go where my mind beckons me. Now you criticize me for doing just that."

"I am not trying to criticize you, I am just—"

"Mother would have understood."

A cloud grew over the fisherman's brow. "Do not dare invoke your mother in your anger."

Erclidus looked down, feeling a wash of shame.

"She was and is more than a tool to be used to win an argument."

"I'm sorry," Erclidus met his father's gaze. "I didn't mean to."

"I know."

The boy shook his head. "But I feel like you aren't listening to me!"

Odipar's face softened. He reached his hand across the table to rest atop his son's, which was promptly snatched away. "I am sorry. I do hear you. And I understand. Magic can be incredibly enticing, but it is for that reason that we must remain diligent in our efforts to not let our fascination with it consume us." He paused. "I am not upset with you. I love you. And it is because I love you that I take very seriously my duty to keep you safe."

Erclidus snorted. "That's hardly encouraging. Your protection did nothing for the others."

Uritus gasped. Odipar sighed and leaned back in his chair. A wave of guilt rolled over the eldest Subian boy and he wished sincerely that he could take it back. He felt a nagging at the back of his throat urge him to apologize. Instead, he just sat, arms crossed, eyes cast solemnly down at his plate, now cold.

"Uritus," the fisherman cleared his throat. "Did you join your brother at the show?"

Uritus—who up to this point had been sitting silently, eyes darting back and forth between his father and brother, hoping desperately to stay out of the argument—violently shook his head. "N... no, I just... went to the market and then came home."

Odipar nodded and Erclidus felt the knot in his chest twist as if like a knife.

"Coward."

"What did you call him?" Odipar's voice dropped both in volume and in pitch, not harsh—he was never harsh—but firm and direct.

Erclidus shrank back, remembering his father's stance on wielding words with intent to wound. Odipar was a believer in the power of words. He knew well how the things spoken over one by others—as well as the things one spoke over oneself—had a profound effect on who they turned out to be. "A... coward."

"Erclidus..."

"It's the truth!" Erclidus cried out, frustrated by how Uritus always seemed to have his father's favor. "All he ever does is daydream and read and hang on your every word."

"Erclidus—"

The boy rose to his feet and leaned across the table to look his brother in the eyes, sparkling blue and glistening with tears. "You're a coward and a weakling and you're never going to become anything if you don't learn to think for yourself!"

"That's enough!"

Erclidus lurched back at the boom of his father's voice, knocking his chair down in the process. Uritus's quiet sobs were the only sound that filled the cottage for what felt like a lifetime.

Odipar closed his eyes and sighed deeply. "I reject those words, and I reject whatever is compelling you to behave this way. This is not who you are, Erclidus. You are not foolish and you are not cruel. I expect better from you." He took a breath, still trying to calm himself so as not to frighten his son. "Can I trust you to learn from this? To stay away from that man?"

Erclidus often found himself in a difficult position due to how his father raised him, never directly forbidding anything, but instead educating his children and expecting them to be smart enough to make wise choices. Ordinarily, it felt empowering, but now, the knife still twisting its way deeper into his chest, he could feel nothing but rage.

"I make no promises." He turned from the table and stormed out of the cottage.

Odipar sighed and shook his head, feeling sorrow for the heart of his firstborn. He turned then to his youngest, "Are you all right?"

Uritus sniffled, shrugged, and wiped his eyes. "I'm sorry," he said tearfully. "I should have tried harder to get him to come with me…"

"No no no." The fisherman reached out and took his son into his arms. "You are not his keeper. He is responsible for his choices and you for yours. I am sorry you had to witness all this."

Uritus helped his father clear the table and put himself to bed. When he woke, Erclidus still had not returned.

***

Eventually, he did, still quietly seething. He did his work and left when the sun went down and did not speak to either his father or his brother for the rest of the day. A week went by like that, with Erclidus sometimes opting to spend the night at home and sometimes gone when evening came, sometimes eating, though usually not, communicating as much as he needed to work efficiently and never more than that. Both Odipar and Uritus attempted the first few days to make peace, but were only ever met with scowls, scoffs, or more loud silence. The fisherman encouraged his younger son to allow the elder some space to return to himself again. Uritus reluctantly agreed.

At night, he lay up restlessly, plagued by fear for Erclidus. *Where did he keep disappearing to?* There was little but open grassland around Tosh and the tent was no longer set up outside town. In the day, he did his best to heed his father's instruction and allow his brother some space. But in the barn one afternoon, as the two boys mucked stalls, Uritus's desire for reconnection compelled him to speak.

"I fixed the crooked wheel on the cart yesterday."

He waited in silence for a response. He received none.

"It wasn't too hard, but I did it myself, so it took longer than I hoped. It should be a much smoother journey tomorrow…"

"I'm not going to the market with you."

Uritus bit his tongue, a sting in his chest as he returned to quietly scattering fresh hay on the floor of Moonracer's stall. Anxiety began creeping its way into his ears. He shouldn't have said anything.

"I don't understand you."

Uritus looked up. "What do you mean?"

Erclidus shook his head. "You used to have dreams of things you wanted to do away from here. You couldn't stop talking about them. After every new story you read—*I'm going to be a horseman*; *I'm going to be a Knight*; *I'm going to be an adventurer*. Then, one day, you stopped. What happened?"

Uritus was as surprised by the nature of the question as he was by the fact that his brother had elected to speak at all. "I don't know what happened…"

"I do."

The younger boy did not respond.

"The plague taught you that the world is cruel, and now, you're afraid to leave."

Uritus frowned. "I am not afraid."

Erclidus shook his head with a sigh and returned his attention to his task. One of the horses whickered.

"There's going to come a day when you will need to make a choice, and there will not be a clear right answer."

Uritus lifted his head, furrowed his brow.

"No one else will be able to decide for you. If you don't have some solid sense of who you are and what you want by then, you'll choke."

The younger brother looked up into the elder's inky blue eyes and saw there a profound sadness that he had never recognized in him before.

"I just hope, for your sake, that you figure it out by then."

"Have you figured it out?"

Erclidus hesitated. He leaned his pitchfork to rest against the wall. "Not yet. But I'm not afraid to try."

He turned then and departed from the stall and Uritus finished his work in silence.

***

Uritus endured another restless night alone in his room. He had chosen to keep his conversation with Erclidus to himself, and his brother's words repeated themselves in his mind. Too tired to sleep, he rose to fetch a drink of water. He came to a stop halfway to the water pump as he noticed a scrap of paper lying on the kitchen table. The gray light of dawn was just enough to read its scrawl,

Uritus raced out of the cottage and to the barn, relief crashing into his chest when he found his brother there, saddling his horse.

"What are you doing?" he cried, angry, devastated tears spilling onto his cheeks.

Erclidus closed his eyes and sighed in the manner that was so characteristic of their father. "You weren't supposed to read that until I had already gone."

"Where will you even go?" Uritus sobbed. "I know Tosh is boring, but it's a good home!"

"It's not my home anymore. It hasn't felt like home in a long time."

Uritus's vision blurred, his head throbbing with pain. He couldn't believe this was happening, he wouldn't...

"Goodbye, Uritus." Erclidus pulled himself up to a seat in his saddle.

"No!" Uritus raced to stand in the barn's open doorway, arms held wide. "You can't go!"

Erclidus sighed frustratedly. "Get out of my way—"

"No! Father and I need you! You cannot just—"

Suddenly, Velatondra rushed forward, kicked in the side by his brother's boot.

The younger boy did not move. "Erclidus!"

In an instant, he was yanked from the path of the galloping horse. He struggled to break free of his father's strong grasp, sobbing and screaming after Erclidus.

Odipar clung tightly to his son. "No, Uritus. Let him go. He will come back, I swear it."

Uritus buried his head deep into his father's shirt and wept. Odipar spoke naught. Instead, he held tightly to his boy and wept silently for his other as Erclidus disappeared over the horizon.

***

Something changed in Uritus the day his brother left. He was now the sole remaining family that his father had, the first apprentice in line to become a fisherman. In Erclidus's absence, he felt as though he had to prove something, prove that he could be as strong and capable as his brother who had outweighed him by at least forty pounds. He worked diligently in the fishing boat and in the market, doing his best to make up for the loss of the third member of their team. Because of this, he grew strong quickly, and dramatically increased his skill in his trade. He studied history and the elvish language and pored over books about archery and swordplay. He became a master in the saddle, and there was not a task he was assigned that he didn't complete perfectly and with great speed. He wished only to make his father happy again. Though Odipar maintained his calm, hopeful demeanor, his heart had broken in such a way that even when it healed, the scar that remained would always ache.

Almost two years had passed since Erclidus left, and Uritus still found himself looking to the horizon to see if he had finally decided to return home. The hope instilled within his soul by his father took root and grew, and he tried to nurture it with thoughts that his brother was smart, his brother was good. Surely, someday, he would make his way back to them.

The Summer before Uritus turned fourteen, Odipar suddenly began to tire. He still worked hard, often pushing himself far beyond his limits, but so much of the strength that he had once carried gradually started to wane. Uritus saw this happen but was hesitant to be concerned. His father was a hero in his eyes, capable of great, impossible feats. Perhaps Odipar only *seemed* to be fading because Uritus was growing stronger. Uritus wasn't sure how to ask his father if he was all right. Instead, he found subtle ways to take on more work, leaving the tasks for Odipar that were less physically taxing. Odipar didn't seem to notice.

The late August heat was particularly thick one day, white sun shining high in the pale blue sky. The boy and his father worked together unloading crates of fish to be peddled by the merchants, the fresh catch of the morning as well as the latest salted and cured batch. Odipar lifted crate after crate from the wagon and handed them off to Uritus to transport to the stalls. The fisherman would return to the boat in the afternoon while his son mended nets and tended to the horses. Though their routine had needed to change many times over the years, it was never long before the new felt familiar.

The people of Tosh were kind and generous, willing to offer assistance to one another during hard times despite individually struggling under the weight of the drought and reeling from the aftermath of the plague. Though they had been quick to offer help however they could when Uritus's mother and siblings had passed, still the boy hesitated to ask for anything more than he needed. He'd become particularly independent in this way. But this proclivity for self-reliance fell to the wayside as Odipar collapsed upon the ground beside the wagon.

"Father!"

The marketplace stirred with urgency. A townsperson rushed away to fetch a cup of water; two more hastened off in search of a physician. A merchant dropped to her knees alongside Uritus as he fearfully cried out for his father to answer.

"He's all right," she told him, pressing her palm to the fisherman's face. "He's still breathing, but he's warm. Let's get him into the shade…"

"No, he needs to go home. Help me get him onto Quickspa."

"I'm sure he's just—"

"Now!"

Another merchant moved to assist them and a third unburdened the horse from the cart. Odipar began to revive as he was lifted into the saddle.

"Send the physician to the house," called Uritus as he mounted Quickspa behind his father. "I'll be back for the cart this afternoon." The boy urged the horse into a gallop and rushed his father back home.

* * *

Uritus crouched to the ground on the shore of the Plentiful Lake, trying and failing to calm his breaths. Inside the cottage, the physician tended to Odipar, who had been well enough to stumble to bed with his son to help support his weight. He had tried to tell Uritus that there was nothing to worry about, but the boy was too frightened to take him at his word.

He could hear his heartbeat in his ears, the image of his father collapsing to the ground playing over and over in his mind's eye. *He was just tired, it's only the heat.* No amount of internal assurance was carrying with it any peace. Uritus's breath quickened and he clutched his chest, feeling suddenly like he was going to drown.

"Look at the water."

Uritus raised his head with a gasp and looked around. There was no one there, no source the voice could have reasonably come from. He returned his gaze to look ahead, and as his eyes fell upon the lake, an undeniable sense of peace washed over his shoulders. He did not understand it, but he did not fight it, drawing it into his lungs with a long, even breath. The White Mountains stood tall and steadfast in the distance. The light of the sun glimmered across the surface of the water, so simple in its profound beauty.

"Uritus?"

The boy turned, standing to his feet as the physician exited the cottage. "How is he?"

"Feeling much better. He wishes to speak with you."

Uritus's eyes drifted to the cottage and then back to the physician. "Of course. If you wait just a moment, I'll go fetch your coin—"

"There's no need," they replied with a weak smile. "I'm glad to help."

A knot of anxiety returned to Uritus's throat as the physician turned to depart. He swallowed it down, looked over his shoulder once more at the lake, and then made his way in to see his father.

Odipar rose from his chair with a smile as his son entered the room.

Uritus was too nervous to return it. "How are you feeling?"

Odipar did not immediately respond. He gazed at Uritus for a prolonged moment with pride shining in his eyes. But the sadness in his smile ultimately betrayed the true state of his heart.

"What did they tell you?"

Odipar sighed sadly. "Would you care to walk down to the shore?"

"Tell me here. Please," Uritus begged. "What did they say?"

13

Odipar sighed again but still relented. "There is… an unusual strain on my heart…"

Uritus felt his chest tighten.

"They said that in the time since the plague, they have seen this more and more."

"Seen what?"

Odipar smiled sadly. Night would be here soon. He wished only for a final moment of peace with his son before it arrived. "Won't you walk with me?"

Uritus would have flown to the moon. He took his father's arm and went with him to sit on the shore. The waves rocked gently up to greet them.

The fisherman turned to his son with a breath, "In the years since the plague, the physicians have observed a number of cases like mine. It would seem that the stress of the plague and the years since has proven too much for many of us."

Uritus frowned and shook his head. "What do you mean?"

Odipar met his eyes. He strived always to be honest with his son, but the truth in this case was a mighty burden. "I must tell you that of those whose hearts have been weakened like this… none before have survived."

Uritus felt as though a brick had hit him in the chest. Fear and grief flooded back into his body and threatened to choke him again. He would not accept this outcome. "Let me ride to Lorethh." He leapt to his feet. "I will find a Healer and bring them here. None have survived before, but there is no reason you cannot be the first. You stayed well through the plague…"

"All who have fallen victim to that which ails me now remained well through the plague."

Uritus fell silent, his eyes brimming with tears. "Let me do *something*…"

The pain in his son's eyes was felt in the fisherman's body. "You may go if you wish," he said, "But I must make sure you understand the reality that were you to leave tonight… I cannot promise you that I would still be here when you returned."

Uritus let out a heavy breath and dropped back down to a seat on the shore. He looked out across the water, at the orange glow of the sun as it sank low in the sky. His grief hit him with a crash. He let his tears claim him.

"I'm not ready for you to go."

The fisherman took his son into his arms, succumbing to his own sorrow. "I am sorry. I'm not ready to leave."

They remained that way for some time, neither noticing when a pair of the townspeople returned to drop off the cart. Eventually, Uritus sat up, slowly shaking his head.

"What am I going to do?"

Odipar sighed sadly. "That will be up to you."

Uritus hung his head wearily.

Odipar set a gentle hand on the side of his face, turning it to meet his eyes. "You are stronger and braver than any man I have ever met. I do not know what the future holds… but I know that whatever you do choose, it will be good. I have never been more sure of anything than I am of you."

The fisherman raised his hands to lift a piece of leather cord from around his neck. A fragment of shell hung from it, a treasured piece Uritus had never seen him without. Odipar brought the cord over his son's head and the shell came to rest against the fabric on his chest.

"I'm always here."

Tears returned to Uritus's eyes. "I don't know what to do."

His father took his face again into his hands. "You must cling to hope. Even in the darkest of midnights." He smiled, a tear traveling down one cheek. "Sunrise will always find you."

***

The next ten days felt agonizingly long, yet somehow passed in a blink. Odipar tried at first to return to his ordinary tasks, but it became quickly clear that his heart would not allow it. Uritus abandoned the boat to remain by his side. Though the physician did return, and the boy did his best to care for his father as well as he knew how, the fisherman's light continued to steadily dim. It went out the day Uritus turned fourteen.

Though he had done his best to prepare for this day, Uritus's heart was shattered. He buried his face into his father's bed and wept. Rain poured down upon the roof of the cottage and thunder rolled in the distance—a powerful downpour, the likes of which Tosh hadn't seen in years. He stayed this way for hours, the storm outside a melodic representation of the war that raged within him. It went against everything Odipar had ever stood for to spiral into depression and just *quit* like he so desperately wanted to do. But he couldn't find the strength to even lift his head, let alone get up and start rebuilding. So he did neither, instead lingering at the threshold of his new reality, wavering between heartbreak, anger, frustration, and guilt—guilt for ever daring to hope that he might someday get to leave this place.

He began to feel something he never had before, a feeling he could not immediately identify. At this moment, he didn't have the energy to try. So he sat in it, growing ever colder, not noticing that the fire in the cottage had burned out an hour before. The seemingly endless well of tears finally dried up just before the rain began to cease, and as numbness started to seep into his bones, he put a word to what he felt.

Hopeless.

He shivered as if to cast the feeling away. Depression he could relent to, anger, even, he could rationalize; but hopelessness was something foreign to him, so much so that in this moment, it felt like a sin. He shook his head, rattling his brain to erase the thought. If his parents had been there, they would have wanted him to embrace what he felt before shoving it aside, to hold it in his hand, observe it from all angles, and only let it go once he felt it no longer served him. But this particular emotion—cold to the touch and hollow—he knew in his heart didn't serve him at all. Hope was the glimmering star that had always kept his family afloat, that had inspired Heimar Vindella and the rebellion during the war, the sacred jewel at the heart of every story he read that moved him.

"Uritus, what are you doing?"

The soft Voice startled Uritus but filled the room with warmth. He turned his head to look around, though he was confident that it hadn't come from someone within the cottage. It felt almost as though it came from within his own head, yet simultaneously wrapped itself around him. And then, all at once, he understood.

"I'm always here."

"No one is ever truly gone, Uritus. Not really."

His parents had never once lied to him in life and it was clear now that they still hadn't, not even to comfort him as they stood at death's door. Whether they and his siblings rested now in the Great Beyond or as a part of the continuous cycle of energy that always moved around him, they were *here*. Peace settled into his chest, warming him from the inside, beginning at his heart and moving slowly through his body and settling into his limbs. He took in a deep breath and closed his eyes, listening to the pattering of the last raindrops against the window and allowing his parents' final words to fully take root in his heart and his mind. He turned to rest his back against his father's bed and opened his palms to the ceiling, a gesture intended both to release and to receive.

And in that moment, the Voice filled the room again, *"What are you going to do now?"*

Uritus took another deep breath and turned to look out the window. Thin, pale ribbons of sunlight glittered across the lake's surface. Reaching up, he clasped the shell hanging from his neck and nodded to himself. He knew not where he planned to go or what he intended to do, but it was clear to him now that his time in Tosh had come to its end.

He rose to his feet, dried his eyes, and chose to make his way forward.

***

He burned his father's body and scattered his ashes in the wind across the water as they had done with his mother and little siblings. He sold the boat and gave Quickspa to one of the village merchants who promised to care for her. But no one seemed to want the old cottage or any of the rickety furniture in it. So he packed up the few items that were his own as well as a bag of his father's, mounted Moonracer, and left the fishing village behind, headed North. He glanced back over his shoulder when he reached the base of the White Mountains and whispered a goodbye to his family, his past, and the only home he had ever known.

He traveled deep into the mountains, observing their sheer, glimmering faces and resting every so often at the banks of the skinny, clear streams that twisted their way through the range, icy rivulets that ultimately trickled down to feed the Plentiful Lake. The water was cold and energizing for both the boy and his horse, and the paths it carved through the smooth white stone of the mountains served as a navigational guide as they made their way further up and in. Thick fog met them in the mornings, dissipating quicker as they gained altitude, and vegetation was scarce but somehow provided enough sustenance that neither of them was ever undernourished. Uritus had heard of the Magic of the White Mountains. He would often stare wistfully at their sharp peaks and dream of summiting them himself one day. Now, amidst them, it was clear that their crowns were almost certainly inaccessible due to the smoothness of their rock, but he felt the thrum of their spirit all the same, both exceedingly humbled and honored to have found sanctuary here.

But still, despite the mountains' enchantment, the death of his father hung heavy on his heart. He rode as far away from Tosh as he could in a subconscious attempt to create distance between himself and the place that had caused him so much pain. He stopped here and there, trying to make friends with the people of the mountains, but most of them were stone miners, polite but cold, or young men making their pilgrimages through the peaks in search of the Magic they had heard lived there. Uritus had hoped that some of these spiritual wanderers could serve as temporary travel companions. But it soon became clear to him that the journeys these men took were, in almost every case, self-serving missions with a desire for personal power at the heart of them, so he never stayed in any one place for very long.

He had been journeying for several weeks and the arrival of Autumn had long since come and gone. Uritus knew the time would soon come when he would need to seek out a more permanent shelter to take refuge during the colder months. As it was, he and Moonracer slept every night near a stream and under the stars. They shone clear and dazzling against the velvet night sky and they captivated the fisherman. Of course, the stars could be seen from Tosh—though the clouds usually prevented it. But even the clearest night sky in Tosh paled in comparison to the majesty of the ether that shone above the White Mountains. Uritus felt as though he could reach out his hands and scoop up thousands of twinkling pinpricks of light, swirling endlessly in obsidian liquid. While he felt a monumental peace sleeping in the open air, he knew the stars, plentiful as they were, would not warm him when the snow came.

He brought Moonracer to a stop near a spring that bubbled up and then trickled down, winding its way across the fragments of ivory stone that covered the majority of the mountains' walkable surfaces. He unburdened his horse and came to rest beside the water, cupping his hand and dipping it beneath the surface to take a drink as Moonracer lowered his head to do the same. Leaning back against one of the larger boulders, he turned his face to the sun, and in the corner of his eye caught a glimpse of something shining in the water.

He tilted his head inquisitively. His time in the mountains had taught him that —while they were remarkably vast and striking to behold—their landscapes remained consistent no matter how deep into the range he journeyed. There was nothing but white stone, clear water, and dark shrubbery which sometimes bore pale fruit as far as he had seen. He climbed to his feet and stepped into the stream to investigate. There, nestled amidst the milky pebbles, rested a beautiful dark blue stone. He submerged his hands in the water and lifted it above the surface. Frowning curiously, he returned to where he had been sitting upon the bank. The stone was smooth and oblong, exactly the size of his hand from palm's heel to fingertip. It glistened in the sun, a deep shade of sapphire speckled with inky blots, and even though Uritus had just pulled it out of the ice-cold brook, it warmed his hands like sunlight.

"It's a dragon's egg."

Uritus looked up with a sharp breath, startled by the deep voice that came from his left. "I… I'm sorry?"

"A dragon's egg."

The man who had appeared was old and dark-skinned, clad in a gray robe nearly as pale as the landscape around them. Uritus looked around, wondering to himself where the man could have come from, as there was nowhere nearby to have been hiding and the crunching of footsteps on gravel should surely have given him away. From his face, weathered by time, hung a long, wispy beard. Thick eyebrows shaded his eyes, which were dark green and kind-looking, so Uritus was not bothered when the man moved a few steps closer and leaned against his smooth wooden staff to sneak a look at the egg. Carved into the top of the long piece of ivory wood was the figure of a perched owl.

The old man squinted at the egg. "It's a flyer, by the looks of it. The mothers lay their eggs and then move on somewhere else. The young take care of themselves."

Uritus's mouth fell open as he looked back down at the egg. "Should I… should I put it back?"

"No, no!"

Uritus furrowed his brow at the strange man and waited for him to explain.

He crouched down to be nearer to the boy. "Dragon's eggs… are hard to come by. Nearly impossible, actually… To sell one would net you a fine purse! They are cloaked with Magic, my boy. No one who is impure of spirit or who has selfish intent may find them. But you…" He looked at Uritus and smiled softly. "You must be a man of great character to be able to see through so strong a natural spell."

Uritus looked down, feeling a lump grow in his throat. "My father was better."

The man paused, stroking his beard for a moment. "Perhaps that is true—"

"It is true."

"—But the egg did not come to your father, did it?"

Uritus fell silent and looked at the egg again. "What am I to do with it then? I've never even kept chickens. I know nothing about hatching an egg."

"You needn't. It will hatch in time and the dragon will raise itself. But you must know, it will imprint upon you. You will be its rider."

"Its rider…" Uritus shook his head with a bewildered laugh. "No dragon has had a rider."

"Not since Heimar Vindella during the Hope War."

Uritus looked at the man again, intrigue in his eyes, "I… thought that was just a bedtime story."

The man shook his head. "Many do. But it is true. I know. I was there."

"What?" Uritus shook his head. "The Hope War was over five hundred years ago. That would make you… a…"

The word felt too mystical to be spoken.

"A Wizard, yes."

Uritus drew in an astonished breath. "Who *are* you?"

The man smiled. "I am glad you asked." He rose to his feet and removed his hat, revealing a head of short, stark-white hair. "My name is Uriah." He swept his hat across his chest and bowed dramatically. "Wizard of the White Mountains, keeper of the legends of the Free World, at your service." He straightened himself and replaced his hat atop his head. "And who would you be?"

"Ur… Uritus," the boy stuttered over his own name. "I'm a fisherman. Well… I *was* a fisherman…"

"And why not anymore?"

Uritus sighed. "I'm afraid that's quite a long story."

Uriah nodded slowly. "Well, I would love to hear it, if you wouldn't mind joining me for tea."

Uritus looked down at the egg and over at Moonracer and a smile grew across his face. "Yes. I'd like that. I'd like that very much!"

***

Uriah led the boy and his horse through the mountains to his home, the Alabaster Keep, where Uritus ended up staying for tea and for the next several years. The Wizard taught him history and language and literature and the defensive arts. Uritus spent hours in the grand library reading and soaking up knowledge about dragons and the Hope War and the legends of the Free World. The egg hatched six months after he arrived at the keep, and the little flyer bonded to Uritus as quickly as Uritus bonded with the Wizard. The boy named his dragon Milion after the elvish word for fearless, and learned their unique way of communicating before he sent him out to find a comfortable place to dwell in the mountains. The mighty creature could be summoned with just a thought.

Not long after the dragon hatched, Uriah began to open the castle to more lonely wanderers—craftsmen and artists and warriors, all unique in their loves and talents, all who deemed themselves to be alone. The coterie grew gradually over half a decade until one day, Uritus looked around their table and saw them clearly for what they were—a little patchwork family; two of them teenagers, the rest, young adults who felt directionless, older ones who'd lived multiple lives, the Wizard most of all. Each had faced heartbreak or devastation, but all found solace in the comforting knowledge that even at their loneliest, they never had to be alone. For now, they had each other, and that was more than enough to inspire hope.

Book One:

The Prophecy

Chapter One

"Adiadni"

The 27th of March in the year 4451, the 535th year of the Free World

Sit yourself down upon the rug beside the fire, my beloved, and I will tell you one of my very favorite stories. It is a tale of courage, about choosing to fight for the things that set your heart ablaze regardless of the obstacles you may happen upon. It is a tale of love, about how community and togetherness are amongst life's greatest joys. And it is a tale of hope, about how Shadow has no substance and can be chased away by a single spark. Your great-grandfather used to tell it to me often, as he lived during its happening. And now I think it time that I pass it on to you, Dear One, so that you may harness its morals and use it as inspiration to propel you forward on a journey of your own. It is filled with adventure, daring battles, ferocious beasts, harrowing confrontations, tragedy, victory, darkness and Light. It is about a young man who, much like you, did not understand his importance. But hopefully by its end, you will come to realize—as he did—that you are capable of more than you know.

It happened near the dawn of Spring, just over five hundred years into the New Age. Adiadni Vindella—the daughter of the king and heir to the throne—was readying herself to celebrate her twenty-first birthday. All of Suscundos was preparing for the grand affair that would begin at sunset and not end until two more had passed. They adorned the city with banners and silks, lanterns, thousands of flowers. Musicians and cooks and entertainers and vendors arose early in the morn to make ready for the celebration—one which seemed to grow more grand and extravagant each year.

The princess sat at her dressing table in silence as an attendant named Gwynn arranged her long hair into a fluffy dark braid and adorned it with flowers. Adiadni smiled softly to herself as she listened to the music and children laughing in the streets below. She closed her eyes and inhaled the scent of lilacs and cherry blossoms wafting from her balcony window. Her smile faded as her eyes returned to the looking glass. She let her gaze fall and folded her hands in her lap. Surely, she could will herself to find the energy needed for the next few days. They were celebrating her, after all. She could think of no reason why she should feel anything other than gratitude.

Adiadni was graceful and poised and smart as a whip. She was the only child born to her royal parents and was raised to be the ideal model of intellect, dignity, and compassion. She'd had tutors from each corner of the land, clothing tailored and cuisine prepared especially to suit her needs. Her education had a heavy emphasis on history and politics as her father deemed it most important to prepare her to one day become the leader and guardian of the Free World. She was taught how to dance and how to dine, how to greet dignitaries, and how to take criticism with grace.

As the daughter of a river elf and a wood elf, she possessed both a sharp intellect and a fierce compassion for all those around her, traits she inherited directly from her parents. She was the clear descendent of them both, with skin fairer in the Winter and golden when the sun returned, thick, curly hair that fell to her waist, full lips like her mother, rosy cheeks like her father, and deep, sparkling brown eyes—the sole physical trait she shared with both of them. And upon her right shoulder, swirling as though painted there intentionally, she bore a curious birthmark.

It was this birthmark for which the people of the Free World rejoiced when the princess was formally presented to the city of Suscundos a month after her birth. For five hundred and fourteen years they had awaited the birth of the one prophesied by the Seven Kings at the dawn of the New Age—the one destined to pave the way for the Hero who would vanquish the Shadow for good. Adiadni would grow up feeling both the weight of the birthmark on her right shoulder as well as the weight of the Free World on both.

Of course, she took very seriously her duties as future queen, for the line of Vindella was responsible for safeguarding all the kingdom's people. In her youth, she had possessed a spirit as if of fire, eagerly attending all of her lessons and especially liking the combative ones, her nimble body and quick feet offering her a unique sparring style that her educators nurtured. But as she grew, her parents pressed upon her the other crucial aspect of her title: to inspire and encourage the Free World's citizens. She had a natural inclination to this, as the destiny that walked before her had a way of stirring the people on its own. Even so, she made it her aim to act always out of grace, humility, and empathy, and the natural charm with which she moved enraptured the citizens of Suscundos to her all the more.

And yet, Adiadni was profoundly sad. She did not know why, and she often felt guilty for it. She had everything anyone could ever hope to have and more than she could ever need. She was intelligent and powerful and surrounded by people who loved and adored her. But she often felt… *empty*. Empty and lonely, as though there was a piece of her that was missing, though she had no idea what it could be. She never spoke of her sadness, as she didn't believe she had a right to it. Instead, she simply pressed on, smiled a lot, and continued to do what was expected of her. Her purpose was a sacred one, and that was something she did not take lightly. At the end of all things, she was grateful for the opportunity to give herself for the people she loved.

"Adi!" A small figure burst through her bedroom doors and barreled across the floor toward her.

The princess looked up and laughed when she met eyes with Fennispar. She thanked Gwynn and dismissed her and turned back to the dwarf child, "Fenn, darling, what can I do for you?"

Fennispar grinned up at her, a bright, toothy smile, "Are you ready yet? Winchells was asking about you."

"Oh, does he need me for something?" Adi rose to her feet. She desperately hoped he did. Spending time in the kitchen with the cook sounded far more amusing than adorning herself for the party that night.

"No... actually... that was a lie. He wasn't asking about you. I just wanted to know."

She laughed again and sat back down. "Oh? And why were you wondering then?"

Fennispar blew a single chestnut curl off his forehead and clasped his hands behind his back, swaying gently side-to-side as he always did when he wanted something. "Well... would you want to... go play?" He produced a small leather pouch with one hand and dumped its contents into the other—a set of six emerald-colored dice, two of which tumbled to the ground. He stooped to retrieve them.

The princess smiled at the boy's request and leaned forward to get a closer look at the dice. Fennispar was ten years old, carefree and vivacious and not yet expected to be anything more than that. He had been brought to the palace by her cousin, Pressio, who had rescued him when he was found wandering, alone, just outside the walls that surrounded Suscundos. The king and queen searched the city extensively for the boy's parents, but when a month passed without any luck, they chose to take him into their home and raise him as their son. Adi had been delighted to have another young person in the palace since her parents had not had more children after her. The dwarf boy kept her young and kept her wild, even though she would never dare be that with most anyone but him.

"A new set!" she enthused. "Where did you get them?"

"Press brought them for me. Said they're from Quabish." The boy frowned. "He also said that if I ever wish to beat him at Kepu, I had better get to practicing."

Adiadni bit her lip, willing herself to hold in her laughter and trying to determine if she would have time to grant Fennispar's request before she was expected to be ready. A voice cut through her train of thought before she could decide.

"Adiadni!" Queen Betina appeared at the open chamber door. "Are you ready to go down?"

Adi looked at her hands and back up again. "Not quite."

Betina entered the room and greeted the boy with a smile, "Hello, Fenn."

Fennispar returned her smile and made his way for the door.

"Another time, Darling," Adi promised.

The boy smiled and nodded and raced away to find another companion.

The princess cleared her throat and turned back to face the dressing table. "I'm almost ready. I'll be down in just a short while."

Betina furrowed her brow and crossed to stand behind her daughter, bringing her hands to rest on her shoulders, "Adiadni, are you all right?"

The princess sighed again. She contemplated for a moment whether she should be honest. She knew her mother cared for her deeply. Being a wood elf, Betina Alenvir possessed a tender heart and an intuition for the emotional needs of those around her that made her difficult to deceive. Of course, Adiadni had no true desire to hide anything from her mother, but as her sadness was so fully entwined with a feeling of selfishness, she found herself keeping much more inside than she ever intended to. Deciding against causing unnecessary concern on Betina's part, she looked up and smiled at her mother's reflection in the looking glass.

"I'm fine," and then, seeing Betina's slight look of uncertainty, "Truly, I am. I'm looking forward to tonight."

"Good." The queen patted her daughter's hand and picked up a string of jewels to fasten around her throat. "Your father and I wish to see you in the Western library before you greet the guests."

Adi nodded. "That's fine. I'll finish getting ready and meet you there shortly." She caught her mother's questioning glance in the mirror again. "I really am all right."

The queen sighed and nodded and left her daughter to finish getting ready.

Adiadni donned a new dress—azure silk cut in the same style as most of her wardrobe with long bell sleeves and a train that followed her as she walked— along with some jewels and a circlet. She stood in front of the looking glass and tried to will herself to go downstairs. Frowning, she pressed her hands against her stomach in an attempt to still its frantic fluttering. She knew she was in no trouble. She knew she had done nothing wrong. But she also knew, almost certainly, what it was that her father wished to discuss with her.

Basil. She shook her head tiredly. She didn't even *dislike* the man that her father had chosen to be her betrothed. But she wasn't particularly fond of him either. Surely, now that she had come of age, it was time for the betrothal to become an engagement. She had no real desire to go against her prior commitment. No, she knew her role and she knew it well, and she knew that to object to the match at this point would cause a rift too ragged to easily repair. Granted, her mother had asked her before she had agreed to the match if it was really what she wanted. Adi smiled and nodded—as she did with most things— and since then, her fate had been sealed.

He was a river elf of good stock, the first born to wealthy parents who hailed from Vindellaria, and he knew well what was expected of anyone in an authoritative position. While he wouldn't be reigning king—as he was not from her bloodline—he would still be given the title and the people would still look up to him just as they did her mother.

King Agamemnon was exactly what anyone would expect of a king. He was noble and just, strong-willed and commanding, but undoubtedly kind, and this made him well-liked. He was a river elf of the line of Vindella, thoughtful, intellectual, levelheaded, reasonable. He had gone against his father's wishes and taken a wood elf as a wife, sweet and gentle and driven by her heart above her mind. Such a match was frowned upon less in the modern day, though still there remained some elves of both kinds who felt their differing values were incompatible with one another. Agamemnon was unquestionably happy with Betina, but it hurt his heart to imagine his daughter subject to the same criticism that he had been.

He had offered to choose a suitor for her when she was fifteen and dreadfully overwhelmed by all those who came to call. He thought he might use his wisdom to find a man who would be favored by the people. Adiadni had conceded—not wanting the pressure of choosing the right one to be on her shoulders—but she regretted so when she grew older and Basil began to change. Agamemnon desired the very best for his child, Adiadni knew this well. She also knew that her father would never take action without considering what was best for her. The problem was that *his* idea of what was good for her so often differed from her own. And at twenty-one years old, she still wasn't sure which of the two of them was right.

Eventually, she breathed deeply enough to collect herself and made her way down to the Western library to meet her parents.

The king turned from the window where he had been gazing out upon the city when he heard his daughter enter, "There you are, my dear. You look lovely." He crossed the room to stand in front of her, took her hands in his, and kissed them. Stepping back, he looked over her face and cocked his head to one side, observing that something about her demeanor seemed unusual. "Are you well?"

Adiadni squeezed her father's hands and nodded with a slight smile.

"Good." He cleared his throat and gestured for his wife to come stand at his side. "Would you like to take a seat? There is something we wish to discuss with you."

The princess took in a shaky breath and obliged, perching herself delicately on one of the old armchairs. This had always been her favorite room in the palace.

Her parents settled themselves on the sofa beside her and shared a brief look before her father cleared his throat and began to speak, "Now... you know about the prophecies surrounding the birthmark on your arm... how you are the heir who is destined to strike the first blow at the heart of the Shadow that grows beyond the Looming Mountains."

Adiadni nodded slowly as she began to realize that she had misjudged what it was that the king and queen wished to discuss.

"Well, now that you are of age, we think it is time that you hear the rest of the story."

The princess frowned slightly. "There is more?"

Agamemnon nodded. "You may wish to settle in. There is much that you must know."

Adi said nothing, rather looking at her father and waiting for him to continue.

The king leaned forward and folded his hands in his lap. "After the Hope War, when the Seven Kingdoms of Arkenn joined together to form the Free World, the Seven Kings knew that the enemies who had fled beyond the mountains in the West would one day wish to return and attempt to take the land again."

Adiadni knew this much. She had studied the history of Arkenn and the Free World in great depth. She had read all about the Nameless Sorcerer who had laid siege on the Seven Kingdoms; how the seven heirs to the thrones of Arkenn had joined together to win back their land during the Hope War. She knew that the kingdoms were joined together and renamed the Free World after the Hope War had been won, and how Heimar Vindella was named king after defeating the Nameless Sorcerer in the final battle at Suscundos. And she knew about the prophecy of the heir with the birthmark. She had borne that weight from a very young age. She was uncertain how much more there could be that she did not already know.

Agamemnon rose to his feet, turned to cross the room, and brought himself to stand in front of an ornate chest—a beautiful, sturdy piece that had lain there for centuries. The chest was carved from redheart wood, featuring majestic, elaborate trees carved into all of its surfaces. It rested in the place Adi had always known it to, against the North wall of the library flanked by two tall marble statues—one with long, flowing hair, holding a lantern extended in its right hand, and the other posing nobly, a longsword clutched in both.

It occurred to the princess that she had never thought to question what the chest contained. There was so much in the palace and Suscundos that was considered sacred; she had always assumed it was the same and would therefore always remain sealed. But now, the king produced a key from his left pocket, unlocked the chest, and opened the lid. Turning back around, he motioned for Adiadni to join him. The princess slowly moved to his side and peered into the chest. Inside lay a beautiful sword in a sheath, smooth and shining and untouched for over five hundred years.

"This is Emipera." The king lifted the elegant weapon out of the chest and held it out to his daughter. "The Sword of Light. It is yours."

Adiadni hesitated and looked to her mother. Betina nodded encouragingly. Turning back to her father, she gently lifted the sword out of his hands, finding it to be much lighter than she had anticipated. She grasped the hilt and unsheathed it, revealing a cool silver blade, an ethereal glow radiating from it. She gazed upon it for several moments; turned her wrist one way and the other and found that it fit well in her grip. Suddenly, she frowned and thrust it back into its sheath.

"Why?"

Agamemnon hesitated. "Adiadni…"

"Why do I need it?"

The king opened his mouth but then shut it again and turned to look back at his wife. A moment passed as they silently communicated with one another. "Would you sit down again—"

"You can tell me as I stand." She dropped the sword back into the chest and closed it. "Why do I need it? What is coming?"

Agamemnon closed his eyes and pinched the bridge of his nose. It didn't matter how carefully he selected his words. There was no way to put it softly. "Nothing is coming. You must go to it."

"To *what*?" Adiadni looked from her father to her mother and back. "To what must I go?"

"To Dagamor."

The color drained from Adi's face.

"Adiadni, please, come sit down," Betina begged.

The princess obliged, joining her mother on the sofa, leaving her father to take a seat in the armchair. She folded her hands in her lap and looked at him, awaiting some sort of explanation.

The king paused a moment to organize his thoughts. Sighing slightly, he leaned forward and began, "Dagamor was birthed of Stolen Magic and set into the Looming Mountains—"

"To keep the Free People out of the West, I know. I've always known." The Dagamor was a horror story and much of the reason the Free World was more densely populated to the East. It had been created by the Thieves after their defeat when they fled beyond the mountains seeking sanctuary. The princess had often found herself haunted by nightmares of the beast robed in flame. She was horrified to learn that their fates were entwined.

Agamemnon paused again before continuing, "Emipera has been enchanted. The prophecy states that the one with the birthmark—the one who wields it— will slay the monster and open the door to the West."

Adiadni leaned forward and rested her head in her hands. She sat there for a long time, breathing heavily and shaking her head. "You cannot just expect this of me." Her voice rose in pitch. "I am not at *all* equipped to take on something like this…"

"This is why we've had you trained," Betina tried to console her. "This is why we've made sure that you've studied weaponry and defense—"

"Sweet Divine, fencing with a tutor is far different from going to war with a waking nightmare!"

"Adiadni—"

"I've never been in combat! I've never even left Suscundos except to visit the Holy City. I've never been further West than *the Clearing*." She looked back and forth between her parents as her heart rate began to rise, "I take it I am supposed to just… waltz into the mountains and slit its throat as though it were nothing? I cannot do this—"

"Adiadni, you must!"

The princess snapped her mouth shut as her father stood to his feet.

Agamemnon bit his tongue. He rarely raised his voice. It reminded him too much of his father. King Cereill had loved his son, but every breath he took was with the consideration of how the Free World might be impacted by it. This had manifested as a particular set of beliefs about the *right* way to do things; how to speak, how to dress, who was or wasn't an acceptable match. Though he had learned many valuable lessons from his father about the importance of the guardianship, Agamemnon never wished to impress upon his daughter the illusion that her choices were anything but her own.

Adiadni's eyes drifted to her lap. "I am sorry I grew hysterical," she apologized, attempting to still the tremor in her voice. "I know that was out of character and out of line. But certainly, you can understand my concern."

Agamemnon sighed and sat back down. "Forgive me." He took his daughter's hands into his own. "I know you are afraid. It would be unreasonable to expect you not to be. The weight you bear is a mighty one, and it is also incredibly unique. But you must not forget, yours is only half of the prophecy."

Adiadni met his gaze.

"There were two swords forged. One was of light and called Emipera. The other was of fire and given a sacred name." He paused. "The one who bears the first is the one who will slay the Dagamor, she who will pave the way for the Hero."

"The Hero…"

The mystical figure had been but an afterthought in her mind until now. She felt foolish and self-centered as she considered this. All her life, her focus had been to prepare *herself* for whatever fate awaited her. But it wasn't even about her, not fully. There was a whole other half to her destiny that she hadn't contemplated until now.

Agamemnon nodded and continued, "There is one, prophesied to be born around the same time as you, who is pure of heart and of spirit, who will bear the Sword of Fire and put an end to the Shadow for good."

Adiadni spoke hesitantly, "And the second sword… it is…"

"Beyond the Looming Mountains, hidden away. You must go with the Hero and a small company of companions to retrieve it." He crossed the room to the chest and produced a scroll from a compartment at the bottom. Returning to his daughter's side, he handed it to her. "The map drawn up by the Seven that will show you how to get there."

Adiadni took the scroll but did not break its seal. She set it in her lap, myriad questions swimming through her mind until one found its way to the front, "Who is the Hero?"

The king looked briefly to his wife. "We do not know."

The princess closed her eyes and took a breath, trying to slow her heart and organize her thoughts.

Agamemnon spoke again, "I am sending out word to all of the land that the time has come for the prophecy to be fulfilled and that we seek companions to accompany you to the West. We cannot hesitate, as every hour wasted, the Shadow grows. I know—I am quite certain—that the Hero will be among those who arrive. You must have faith, my dear." He crouched down before his daughter and took her other hand, looking lovingly into her eyes, "The hand of the Divine will be upon all of this."

The princess nodded solemnly and looked down at the scroll. "Is there anything else that I must know?"

Betina stroked her hair. "Nothing for now. This is already so much, we know."

Adi nodded again. "May I be excused then? I'd like a moment to myself before the celebration begins."

Agamemnon hesitated briefly. "Of course. You may take your time here." He rose and escorted the queen out of the library and left the princess with her thoughts.

Adiadni buried her head in her hands. She didn't know how to wrap her mind around these new revelations. The prophecy had always been something… not quite real. Not more than a story people had been telling since her birth as though they were imparting a blessing upon her. Of course she knew that one day, the story would play out, she and the Free World's Hero at the heart of it. But as much as her parents and her teachers had sought to prepare her, she saw now that they never truly could. How does one tell his child that they will kill the unkillable, bring light to the Shadowy place, lead the people through to their future? How does the child step into the dark knowing just what horrors lie in waiting there? A thousand thoughts and fears plagued her mind. She clenched her jaw to stop herself from crying, knowing that she couldn't possibly explain to every party guest why she was unwell. Her mind spun and she began to feel dizzy.

But just then, upon the window sounded the faintest of tapping, and the princess lifted her head to see a small bird—a sparrow—hopping about on the sill. The sparrow looked at her as she looked at it, utterly peaceful and unbothered. It hopped a few more times as if to allow her to admire it and then chirped once before flying away.

Adiadni nodded her head softly, took in a shaky breath, and rose to make her way to the celebration.

Chapter Two

"Uritus"

T he Wizard Uriah puffed thoughtfully on a pipe one misty morning and a lone black star streaked its way across the sky. He did not recognize this star; its arrival had not been scheduled in advance. It carried with it an air of profound importance, a pressing urgency—though, to the raven, it was merely taking a swift flight to visit a stranger in the White Mountains. It brought itself down to land on the balustrade beside the Wizard and gave a single sharp caw.

"Hello there," Uriah chuckled, reaching out to stroke the feathers on the bird's chest. "What have you brought with you?"

The Wizard clenched his pipe between his teeth and his fingers found their way to the small canister fastened to a harness on the raven's back. He retrieved its contents, unrolled the tiny scroll, and lit a cold yellow flame on his fingertip to serve in place of the sleepy sun.

"Hmm…"

The raven gave another caw.

"Very well. Thank you, Friend. May your return home be safe and swift."

With a final caw farewell, the star disappeared into the sky. Uriah tucked the scroll into his sleeve and returned to his chamber within the Alabaster Keep.

There were dozens of swift black stars that week making their own journeys across the Free World. The king had made haste to send word to the land's Keepers that the search for the Hero had begun. Uriah had been awaiting this news for centuries. Quickly, quietly, he began attending to his affairs. The coming days had many things in store, and though there was much still to be seen, the Wizard knew he was one of many who would have an important role to play.

***

"The bastard said that to yer face?"

"Every word."

"Swear it."

Perplexus stood from his chair at the dining hall table and set his right hand firmly atop his heart. Not every seat was yet claimed, but he made a dramatic show of waiting for the occupants of the room to cease speaking before he obliged the blacksmith, "On the sun and the moon and all of her stars. He looked straight into my eyes. Didn't even blink."

"Damn it, Lex, don't tell me you began sharing your tale without me."

Oripidus pridefully folded his arms across his chest and chuckled. "What can I say, Hav? The boy prefers me to ye."

Havian entered the room with Punznes at his side; the raven, Qibat, at his usual perch on Punznes's shoulder.

"I can start from the beginning." Truthfully, Perplexus was eager to do so. "Laiv, Darling, set the mood for me, won't you?"

The bard eagerly took up his lute and began picking a suspenseful tune as the remaining companions filtered in for their meal, "So there he was, our swashbuckler boldly staring straight up into the face of death—"

"Down, actually. The top of his head couldn't have touched the base of my neck if he tried."

"And what was it he said to you?"

"That I have a bridge on my face, a bean in my head, and a week-old sardine between my legs."

"Damn, Lex, he assassinated you," Mikka said, choking through a laugh. "Dead and buried. Why didn't you slink back to your foxhole when you had the chance?"

"Because then I wouldn't have had the opportunity to offer him my condolences for how all the hair on his head traveled south for the Winter and never returned."

A bout of cheers went up from the table, cups raised into the air.

"Who could have known the stouthearted thumb was the elder brother of the two largest oafs on the dock?"

"What did you do to get him so riled up in the first place?" Punznes asked.

"Apparently, Lex shared a couple dances with his mother last week at The Sleepy Seal and she couldn't stop talking about how charming he was."

The family dissolved into hysterics at the explanation Uritus offered. The fisherman shared a glance and a smile with his charismatic friend on the other side of the table.

"And how did ye manage to escape with naught but a tall tale?"

"Same way I always do. My hero appeared."

Uritus shook his head with a chuckle as Perplexus extended a hand toward him.

"He offered to repair their wobbly iceboat."

Punznes was skeptical. "That all it took?"

"That..." Uritus replied, "...and the promise that I would give this one a stern talking-to about conducting himself more appropriately in the future."

"And did you?"

"Tried my damndest, but if you haven't caught on, our swashbuckler isn't one for being told what to do."

Lex held out his arms with a playful shrug. "I am who I am and you love me for all of it."

"In *spite* of all of it."

"Love you too, Mik."

The Wizard smiled, gazing fondly across the faces that surrounded him. The family who called the Alabaster Keep home were a lively bunch who would give the blood in their veins for one another. Their assembly together at the table was not an uncommon one, but the reasoning behind Uriah's request for their gathering was unique, to be sure.

Uritus Subian sat to the right hand of the Wizard, chuckling to himself as Laivar improvised a number of verses about Perplexus's latest spat. For all of their quirks, he was grateful to call this place and people his home. Over nine years had passed since he left Tosh and journeyed into the White Mountains, and he had grown into a strong and attractive man. He was tall, with a lean muscular frame and hands calloused and hardened by the miscellaneous work he did for the fishermen of the Frozen Sea. He didn't fish much himself anymore, the ice fishing of the North a very different world from the lake fishing he did in Tosh. Still, he learned what he could, and ventured out a few times with the ice fishers to try his hand at it, but spent most of his time studying, sparring with members of the household, and fashioning lures and mending rods and iceboats for the Northern anglers. His hair, golden-brown and bleached in places due to years in the sun, and his skin, which easily tanned but never burned, were the only other physical clues as to his prior vocation.

He was intelligent and caring and unassuming, always willing to take on unpleasant tasks if no one else wished to do them, clad only ever in humble garments. And his eyes, usually a warm amber, took on a shade of dazzling sapphire blue whenever his body flushed with adrenaline or strong emotion—a genetic mutation rare in the elves and rarer still in humans. He had become just like his father had been: kind and understanding and hard-working and honest, and he was admired by all who lived in the keep and near it.

Uriah cleared his throat.

The tails of the last few sentences tapered off as they turned to regard their figurehead. Each individual there felt a personal sense of allegiance toward the Wizard for his immense generosity over the years. They'd come to know him to be incredibly wise, endlessly giving, and particularly private, so the event of his call to assembly and intended address intrigued and excited them.

"Most of you know by now that I recently received a raven. It has taken some time to get my affairs in order, as the message I received was one of great importance. But I am now organized well enough to share it, and I must tell you, one way or another, that it concerns all of us."

The companions perked up and leaned forward in curiosity.

"The raven was from Suscundos. King Agamemnon has requested our presence at the capital for the celebration at the dawn of the Summer."

Immediately, excited chatter broke out amongst them.

"The king wants us?"

Ilya's question drew the group back to the seat at the head of their table.

Uriah nodded. "I have been blessed to know many generations of Vindellas, and for this, Agamemnon trusts my judgment. He knows I have many brave and good-hearted souls living under my roof, and has asked me to extend the invitation to you."

"For what purpose, may I ask, does the king seek our bravery and good-heartedness?" Nadarum inquired. "Are boisterous vagabonds known for being especially desirable party guests?"

"The very best at this very table!" Zaphron raised her flagon of ale.

"Hear, hear!"

Uriah chuckled as the room settled down again. "I will not recall the many details of the legends I have already had you study in depth, but I will tell you that, after many centuries of waiting, the Vindella heir who bears the birthmark has come of age."

A silent air of reverence settled upon them. Uritus's lips parted as he considered the significance of this event and then came to understand what the Wizard was proposing.

"Her name is Adiadni, and the time has come for her to take her journey West. The king seeks a group of escorts to travel with her beyond the Looming Mountains so that she may slay the Dagamor and retrieve the Sword of Fire. Am I right to assume that such an adventure sounds appealing to many of you?"

The following bout of excited conversation livened the energy of the room more than Uritus had thought possible.

Havian triumphantly raised a fist. "The king has called and the people will answer! Frankly, Agamemnon was right to seek us out. There's no party better in the Free World."

Ilya shared a glance with her husband beside her and he raised his eyebrows with intrigue. "We *are* rather overdue for an adventure of our own," he said.

Laivar stood, lute in hand, and brought his foot up to rest on the seat of his chair.

"Let it be written,
Nay, let it be sung,
That folk from the Mountains
Have fire in their lungs.
Be it fear, doubt, or monsters
That stand in their path,
They'll conquer them swiftly
With a wink and a laugh."

Joyous applause arose.

"I do not wish to dampen the mood," spoke the ever-practical Robalto as it calmed, "But we must also consider the duty of the keep."

The others nodded seriously. The Alabaster Keep served an important role in the White Mountains as an organizer of goods and supplies for the stone miners.

"Surely, we cannot all leave."

Uriah nodded. "This is true. I encourage you all to consider this and discuss it with one another. I believe that the guidance of the Source will make it clear who should stay and who should go. It is quite a journey to Suscundos, so we must leave by week's end. Let me know in the morning what you have decided."

The companions agreed to this, quickly returning to their lively chattering.

"My boy," the Wizard addressed Uritus, "Will you join me in my chamber after you've finished here?"

"Of course."

Uriah smiled, rose, and disappeared from the dining room, the family too lost in their elation to notice. Uritus and Perplexus shared a glance across the table.

***

"Do you think you'll go?"

The fisherman pondered this silently, stacking dishes and putting them into various cupboards. "I don't know," he answered honestly.

Perplexus regarded him with a cocked head. "How is it even a question?"

Uritus shrugged.

"Have you not always longed for adventure?"

"Theoretically, yes. Don't all children?"

"You'd be surprised. I've met many a brat with neither a thought nor a wish. We need their kind of course, just as we do the wild ones. But I never pegged you for the *content with mediocrity* type."

"Do you find our life mediocre?"

"That's not really what I'm getting at."

"What then?"

There was a pause as the dark-haired man lifted his eyes to the ceiling. Perplexus Everstone was a wild and passionate being, and he had been since long before he sought refuge at Uriah's keep. He'd been orphaned at fifteen when both of his parents were killed in a stone mining accident. With no siblings and no place to go, he set off in search of the Wizard rumored to have welcomed into his home another lost boy about his age. He and Uritus had been fast friends ever since.

An outside observer might look at the pair of them together and make the natural assumption that they didn't have much in common. Uritus was reserved and gentle, an excellent listener who carefully considered each of his steps. Perplexus was nearly a year older than Uritus—with brown skin, dark eyes, and black hair that fell to his shoulders but was almost always tied up—and he was bold and loud, often doing things without fully thinking them through, and always striving to make people laugh. In an ordinary world, they may well have never found each other. But the few things that they did share in common—their love of the Free World and its people, their hunger to explore, and desire to affect their community positively—kept them in a tightly woven companionship from the very beginning. It was nice to have someone who meant it when they said that they understood your pain.

After a moment, Perplexus replied, "I only mean that I've known you for nearly a decade, Old Boy. We've talked in depth about the things you've desired for your life. I know you are content here and grateful for the stability you have now, but can you tell me honestly that if you were to pass up such a thrilling opportunity, you would feel no remorse?"

Uritus thoughtfully folded an old cloth and set it on the counter. "I suppose I cannot."

"What's causing your hesitation then?"

The fisherman considered this for a moment and then shook his head. "I'm not sure."

His friend nodded. "That's fair enough."

"Will you go?"

Perplexus looked back up at the ceiling and shrugged.

"After all that?" Uritus laughed. "What could possibly be stopping *you*?"

Perplexus was, by nature, an explorer—a trait etched into his bones due to the nomadic nature of the miners he grew up alongside. He had learned to navigate the uniform terrain of the White Mountains by the light of the stars, and dreamed of applying this skill to journeys across all of the Free World. He pored over Uriah's atlases in his youth, dazzled by artists' renditions of the land's many varying landscapes. Though his heart burned with an ache for adventure, he had found joy in applying his skills to helping those of the mountains he called home. Uritus could think of no one better suited to accompany the princess West than he.

"It is not that I am unsure if I will go; I don't think I am capable of turning down an adventure this grand. There is just something inside me that is willing me to…"

Uritus waited patiently for his friend to complete his thought.

"I don't know," the navigator sighed frustratedly. "It is almost as if I am being warned to watch my step." He paused, studying the fisherman's face for a moment. "You, however, have to go. I will accept nothing less."

Uritus smiled with a shake of his head.

"I mean it! The Free World needs you more than you know, Old Boy. You're going to go on that mission and retrieve the Sword of Fire, defeating countless obstacles along the way." Perplexus took up a knife and swished it through the air in mock combat.

"Ah, Lex. I think you see me as a far more majestic version of myself than I am in actuality."

"Nonsense. I merely see you as you truly are." A sly smile grew across Perplexus's lips. He flipped the knife in the air and caught it by the blade. "You know, I've heard many a verse written as a celebration of the princess's beauty…"

"Goodnight, Lex." The fisherman turned from the kitchen and departed for the corridor.

"I'm going to find *someone* who suits your fancy one day! Mark my words, Old Boy!"

Uritus chuckled to himself and made his way to meet Uriah in his chamber. Now that he had a quiet moment to think about it, he realized that he had, for some time, felt a growing sense that something historic was on the horizon. He had not, however, had any expectation that the event would have such a drastic impact on his life. He was more than content in the Alabaster Keep—he was profoundly happy here. The security of a home like this one made him feel safe to pursue the great desires of his heart: education and connection with those he loved and service to all those around him. But Perplexus had not been wrong to presume that to miss out on such a unique opportunity would leave the fisherman feeling… somehow incomplete.

Uritus knocked on the chamber door and entered when Uriah invited him in. The Wizard sat with his pipe in his hand in an old leather chair, one of two positioned beside a large fireplace inside of which a few logs always seemed to be burning. Uriah gestured to the chair beside him and Uritus took a seat.

Uriah smiled. "Thank you for joining me, my boy."

"I am always eager to hear what you have to say."

The Wizard puffed a few times on his pipe. Uritus had always loved the way the smoke curled so curiously. When he was young, he would lie on the carpet and watch the twisting haze and the logs as they burned for hours, bright flames waving playfully to catch his attention. He barely noticed them now, his mind far too preoccupied by his mentor's proclivity for suspense.

Uriah tapped the pipe in the stone ashtray atop the small wooden table beside him. "Tell me, my boy," he said as he began meticulously cleaning it, "Will you be coming with us to Suscundos?"

Uritus searched his mind for an answer and arrived back in the same place he had before. "I don't yet know."

"Do you *want* to come?"

He did not need to consider this for long. "I do."

"But…"

The Wizard had an uncanny ability to tell when there was more that Uritus was not saying. The fisherman leaned back in his chair and took a long breath. "But… I don't think I feel ready to leave the White Mountains."

Uriah looked up from the pipe in his hands. "Why is that?"

"I don't know…"

The Wizard set the pipe down and folded his hands in his lap. "Do you truly feel unready or are you seeking out an excuse because you feel afraid?"

Uritus chuckled. For all of the mystery and metaphor that shrouded the Wizard, he never had been one to stray from bluntness. "I am afraid, yes."

Uriah spoke naught, awaiting a more complete response.

"I am honored to even be offered the opportunity to embark on so sacred a quest," the fisherman explained. "But unlike my peers, I do not feel confident enough to think that such an invitation means that I am worthy of it." He paused, taking a silent moment to sort through his thoughts once more. Rising to his feet, he crossed over to stand in front of the fireplace and brought one arm up to rest on the mantel. "I fear that misplaced confidence in this case could have devastating consequences. There are many who are far better equipped than I am."

"What makes them more equipped?"

Uritus hesitated. "Wisdom. Experience. Age…"

"Age counts for very little," the Wizard reminded the fisherman. "It does often come with more experience, yes. But there are many of a greater age who would have floundered had they undergone the things you have in your years."

Uritus knew this was true.

Uriah sighed compassionately. "To age is a gift not granted to all. And, indeed, such a gift often brings with it wisdom and greater skill. But for many, there also comes greater fear and a stubborn certainty that one's way of doing things is the only way. Think not of age, my boy. Your destiny cares not about age."

Uritus frowned as he met the Wizard's eyes. He must have misheard him. "Destiny?"

Uriah did not elaborate right away, rather picking up his pipe and resuming its cleaning. Uritus shifted his weight from one foot to the other and turned his attention to the fire, contemplating his mentor's words all the while. The steady ticking of the grandfather clock mingled with the crackling of the logs, a soothing, quiet noise that the fisherman often got lost in. He tried for a moment to envision himself appearing before the royal family in Suscundos and accompanying the princess to the Looming Mountains and beyond. He was neither quick-thinking and rash like Perplexus nor as sage and level-headed as Uriah, but he did possess one trait that he felt may be of use on this quest, and that was his fierce instinct to protect all those he cared for. This was, unquestionably, a product of his tumultuous background, but he recognized its value all the same. Were it not for his intervention on more than one occasion, many members of the house (usually Perplexus) may have fallen to harm. Concern for his personal well-being be damned, it was simply not in his nature to elect not to intervene.

Uriah tapped into this line of thought as he finally spoke again, "You have far more to offer the Free World than you yet know."

Uritus drew his lower lip between his teeth as tears pricked his eyes. "I want to believe you…" He paused. "It is only that my history of seeking to protect those I love has not always been as successful as it is now."

Uriah immediately rose from his chair and crossed to wrap his arms around the fisherman. He saw before him a young boy plagued by loss and fearful of the world's harshness, but tenderhearted and resilient all the same. It was this boy whom he loved like a son and held a fierce conviction that his role to play in the Free World was one of utmost importance. Cupping Uritus's chin in one aged hand, he lifted it until they met one another's eyes, "There is far more to you than your past, my boy."

Uritus knew this to be true, but was unsure if this repeated correction would ever feel like the truth.

The Wizard waited a moment for his pupil to steady himself before speaking again, "There is something that you must know."

Uritus dried his eyes and Uriah gestured to him to take a seat. He did, this time not needing to wait in silence before the Wizard explained himself.

Uriah cleared his throat. "I know I needn't recount to you the legends of old. Surely, I must have bored you with them by now. I have thought long over the years since we met how I would one day share this with you, but as it is, the only thing I can think to do now is just tell you outright." He leaned forward, resting his folded hands in his lap. "The king seeks not only escorts for his daughter. He searches also for the Hero who may bear the Sword of Fire. I believe that Hero to be you."

A burst of laughter escaped Uritus's lips, dissipating as the Wizard remained solemn. "I am a fisherman from Tosh," he said, incredulous. "You cannot be serious…"

"But I am."

Uritus's mouth fell agape. Surely, his mentor was mistaken.

"I am not mistaken," Uriah went on. "Though, no doubt, there are many we will meet in the capital who will share my conviction for their own prospective heroes. But when I came upon you in the mountains, it was clear to me. You are the one we have long awaited."

Uritus sank deeper into his chair, his head falling back. He stared up at the ceiling for a moment that felt like hours. Uriah was fierce in his convictions, and rarely wrong about them, but even the fisherman's vast imagination was incapable of stretching to this degree. This could not be the truth.

"How could you possibly know this?"

"My boy, you know well, there are many things I know which I do not fully understand. But to give you a more satisfying answer… Milion was my initial clue. No truer test has there ever been for the state of one's heart than the dragon's egg."

Uritus nodded slowly, trying to comprehend.

"It is because of what I know that I cannot offer you the same choice to remain here as I did the others," Uriah continued. "Forgive me. I had hoped you would choose to join us on your own before I shared this with you. But time is short, as I have said. Your destiny will not wait for you… but if you would wish to evade it, I suppose it is true that not even I can stop you."

"No," Uritus spoke without thinking. "I do want to come. I *will* come, though I cannot promise that I am who you say I am. I see now the truth that I would regret it were I to remain behind." With the matter settled, excitement for this venture began spreading through his body. A smile bloomed on his face. "I *have* always wanted to see Suscundos."

Uriah smiled, satisfied. "Very well. Thank you, my boy. Now, get some rest. We depart in three days."

***

The dawn of the third day arrived in a flash. Uritus found himself in Moonracer's saddle outside the keep as the sun's first rays peeked over the horizon. With him was the rest of the journeying company, all of whom had been clued in on who the Wizard presumed the youngest of them to be. There was Havian Elix, the swordsman; the married couple Nadarum Cupetati and Ilya Sadieu, the horseman and the archer; Laivar Lethiel, the poet; Mikka Galinzen, the former soldier; Oripidus Vengar, the blacksmith; and Punznes Caen, the physician, who brought with him always his raven, Qibat; as well as Uriah and, to Uritus's joy, Perplexus. Remaining behind were the twins, Robalto and Zaphron Hammitt, a carpenter and leatherworker respectively who felt assuredly that the people of the mountains needed their services far more than Suscundos did. Uritus let his eyes drift across their faces, almost not hearing when Uriah prompted him to lead their way.

To lead.

Despite all the dreaming he had done in his youth, this was one thing he had never envisioned for himself. The very thought of guiding or commanding others tied his stomach in knots. It was this humility that Uriah assured the fisherman made him the perfect one for the job, though Uritus knew he would be relying on the group's confidence in him to supplement his own, at least for now.

"Uritus?"

He locked eyes with his best friend, who smiled upon recognizing Uritus caught in a web of thought. Perplexus nodded his head to the South-and-East sun in a gesture of encouragement.

Uritus aligned Moonracer with the light and briefly lifted his eyes to the sky. Regardless of his self-doubt, he understood that his responsibility to his companions outweighed anything he felt inside. They looked to him whether he felt deserving of their trust or not. It was clear that his duty, in addition to leading their way, was their inspiration. A gentle breeze ruffled his hair as he lifted his hand to his neck and traced a finger across the shell that had lain there for years. It was time. Turning over his shoulder to look at the group, he raised a proud fist above his head.

"To Suscundos!"

Chapter Three

"Gesturing"

The 21st of June

Adiadni's birthday celebration whirred by like the wind, a dim haze shrouding her for its entirety. Somehow, she had managed to mingle amongst the guests, to dance, to feast, to accept their toasts with grace despite the thunder that roared in her head throughout the whole of the event. As soon as it ended, she was whisked away to begin preparations for her journey. These primarily consisted of additional time with her swordplay, archery, and riding instructors, armor fittings, lessons and blessings from Suscundos's Keepers, and in-depth study of the map that would guide her West.

She withdrew into herself during this time, feeling somehow as if she was observing her body from the outside for much of it. So rapidly was everything changing. It seemed as though overnight she went from Agamemnon's heir, a youth who would one day take his seat, to the embodied hope of the Free World, the sole thing that could save them all from the Shadow. Of course, that was only half true—there was another yet to be discovered—and she had always been this, she'd known so all her life. But the prophecy became suddenly, violently tangible the moment the king announced to the city that the time for her journey had come.

The princess had always hated being doted upon, whether by her staff, her parents, her suitors, or the citizens of Suscundos. She felt unworthy of their admiration, especially considering how, up to this point, she hadn't really *done* anything to be deserving of it. The Vindella line had been adored for centuries, this she knew, but she considered herself merely another link in a long chain, not a hero, not even yet a ruler or a victor. Still, they looked to her as a leader all the same, and despite her fears of the Looming Mountains and whatever lay beyond, she knew she had to make peace with this role she had been appointed.

So she attended her lessons and readied herself however she was asked to, all with her soft and carefully crafted smile upon her face. And when asked, genuinely, by her close friends, Jasch, Kristefani, and Friya, how she was feeling about all the sudden changes and did she feel ready for her commission, she told them, dishonestly, that she did. The words pricked her throat as she spoke them, almost as if something in her body was willing her to share her true feelings with them, these loving three who had walked beside her since early childhood. But still, she felt disconnected from herself and could see no benefit to being honest in this case. She was setting off on her journey in a few short months whether she felt ready or not. She may as well feign self-confidence, if only in the hope that the real thing would appear in time.

It was not quite confidence, but rather acceptance of her fate that plated her heart like pseudo-armor as the Summer reached her doorstep, and she acknowledged that this would have to do for now. Thick, lush canopies of green had grown in place of the blooms of Spring and the city labored for weeks to prepare to celebrate both the arrival of the new season and that of the travelers who sought to accompany the princess on her quest. Celebrations were a fundamental aspect of Suscundos's culture, with citywide festivals held at the dawn of each season and on the anniversary of the final victory of the Hope War, and smaller community and family gatherings taking place every new and full moon. The people of Suscundos revered the passage of time, viewing themselves as temporary visitors in the land they called home, and this manifested itself in their celebrations, honoring of traditions, and sacred views of birth, aging, and death. Most families who dwelt in the city had been there for generations, passing down history and legends, and now, with the prophesied one having come of age, new energy fueled their bodies and excitement took root in their minds, and they poured this into their preparations for the coming days.

Colorful banners and silks adorned the prominent buildings in the city and lined all the streets, strung along on poles twelve feet high. Intricately patterned paper lanterns were hung in all the trees, lit with cold, Magical yellow flame at night which never burned out, but rather faded as the sun rose and reappeared as it set. Tents and stalls were erected by vendors around the edge of the city square—an inaccurate but unquestioned name for the open circle of stone-laden ground just before the steps of the palace. Popping up all over town were flower and fruit carts and street performers; and taverns boasted terraces blooming with Summer roses, each one complete with musical entertainment and barrels of ale, mead, and wine.

Adiadni loved this time of year. The Spring was always overshadowed by its proximity to her birthday, but the Summer—its cloudless ocean of sky, the smell of the sweetgrass and ripe stone fruit, the hot sun on her skin which made her look ever so slightly more like her mother—it was the Summer that she awaited all year. She felt freer in the Summer, more frequently allowed to shirk her studies and yet still routinely finding herself lost in a book beside the falls or in the orchard. It seemed to her that Suscundos truly came alive in the Summer, and as she grew, she realized that she did too.

She felt a twinge of sadness upon the arrival of this particular Summer, realizing that it was the first time she encountered the season with anything other than excitement and joy in her heart. Those feelings were still there—mingled with a squeeze of anxiety—but as she gazed from her balcony across the city she loved, she chose, at least for the duration of the festival, to keep her attention turned toward everything she loved about this place. She knew too well how long it would be before she would see it again.

"Adiadni!"

The clear, melodic voice danced across her ear from the garden below. It was one she recognized well, the notes of her name oh-so-familiar in that sing-song tone.

"Press! You're early!" She leaned over the balcony and smiled down at her cousin. "I didn't think you'd be here for the festival's opening!"

Pressio Alenvir raised his head to smile up at her, shaking his shiny black waves out of his eyes, "I thought I might surprise you!"

"And Crys?" Adi scanned the group of passing soldiers for Pressio's sister.

"Crystella won't be making it back before you leave, I'm sorry." He began to remove his gauntlets as he crossed to the balcony, dropping them to the ground one after the other. "She's sorry too. She'd been hoping to make it back by now but got caught up in Quabish. Something about reinforcing the structural integrity of the mines or some heroic shit like that. She sends her love, though, and her congratulations."

"Congratulations?" Adiadni frowned down at her cousin who had reached the palace wall below.

He paused and looked up at her before he could begin to climb, both hands and one foot already secured in the trellis. "For… your journey, of course."

"Mmm." The princess nodded slowly, taking a few steps back so her cousin had room to lift himself over the balcony and then embrace her.

"You don't sound very enthused."

Adiadni tamped down her disappointment in Crystella's absence. "No, I am. You know how I love the Summer festival."

"Ready to meet the prospective companions?"

Adi shrugged. "Adda met one group already. They arrived yesterday, from Judii. There are… three more, I think? Each one led by a Magic Keeper certain they've found the Hero." She sighed and shook her head. "Hopefully one of them is right."

As if on cue, a deep horn sounded from the city's Western gate announcing the arrival of a traveling party, quickly followed by the same sound from the East.

Pressio chuckled at the coincidence. "I'll leave you to prepare yourself then. I suppose I should get cleaned up as well before the festival."

The princess laughed. "Yeah, you fucking stink." Her smile faded as she frowned slightly. "Are you not meeting them with me?" She bit her lip. She had dearly hoped to have one friend at her side when she greeted the strangers.

"I'm afraid not." He took her hands in his and kissed them. "You'll be all right, Birdie. You always are." He departed back down to the ground, leaving Adiadni to steel her nerves on her own.

***

The city of Suscundos was unlike anything Uritus had ever seen. He gaped at it as he and his party approached the outer wall.

"The Clearing here is one you may have heard of before," Uriah snuck a look at the fisherman beside him. "It's the battleground where the Free People reigned victorious at the end of the Hope War."

44

Uritus let his eyes fall to the grassland they traversed as they drew nearer to the city. He led his party slowly, reverently across, feeling his heart pulse with elation for having made it this far. The past days they had spent journeying had led them across miles of varied terrain which only deepened his love of this land, but something about being *here* at the epicenter of so much rich history felt… *sacred.* Much like it had felt journeying into the White Mountains as a boy.

The city itself was massive, circular, three tiers high, towering on grassy hills above the open valley below. The wide river, Tuvibati, snaked from the West around the city's Northern edge until it poured down, a raging waterfall off the stony cliffs on the other side. Suscundos was surrounded by two thick walls with both a Western and an Eastern gate, and the palace, stretching to the sky from the highest tier, was made of shimmering, pearlescent stone that gleamed in the sun as if it were glass.

Mikka furrowed her brow, a curious smile on her face. "Can we truly hear them in there from this far away?"

The companions ceased their conversing to listen, grinning at one another when it seemed that she was right.

"Suscundos is called *home of celebrants*," Punznes reminded them. "They threw an extravagant party upon their great victory and it never truly ended."

"Ha *ha!*" Havian laughed triumphantly and raised an open palm above his head. "Friends, we are home!"

A wall of sound—loud horns—hit them, sending a shock through their bones as the outer gate began to slowly swing open. Uritus urged Moonracer into a canter, prompting his companions to do the same. When they reached the city's entrance they were greeted by a squadron of guards led by a Cropidean troll.

"I am Digtrision," the commander introduced himself. "May I be the first to welcome you to our fair city."

Uritus had never before met one of the cropidus. They were short, muscular people with tough, thick skin and rusty-colored hair. There weren't many of them left in the Free World, and those that were dwelt mostly in Cropidea to the South, but some remained in Suscundos, having contributed to the city's safekeeping for hundreds of years. The trolls had played a pivotal role in the Hope War, their fearless hearts and cunning traps serving as a crucial asset to the rebellion, and they had remained allied with the Vindella family ever since.

Digtrision was gruff but courteous and he welcomed the traveling party generously, immediately instructing his troops to unburden their horses.

"Would you care for any food or drink? You are surely famished after your journey."

"I wouldn't say no to a cold ale," replied Oripidus.

"Of course."

Digtrision gestured and a number of attendants stepped forward to serve refreshments to the travelers. They graciously accepted, taking up cups and figs and bunches of grapes. Uritus politely declined their offerings, his senses overwhelmed by their enthusiastic welcome.

Digtrision conversed briefly with Uriah while the others looked around, taking in the scene before them. A crowd had gathered atop the inner wall—dozens of people who simply could not wait to catch a glimpse of the visitors. Nadarum and Ilya shared a look. They had been here before—multiple times on their travels—but the warm receptions they had received in the past far paled in comparison to this one.

The commander identified Uritus and then informed Uriah that they were expected at the palace. The Wizard thanked him and led their way on through the city.

Moving through the second gate, they were met with uproarious cheers and applause and the clanging of handbells. The citizens of Suscundos lined the streets, waving joyously at the strangers and casting flowers on the ground before their horses. The trek to the palace was slow and winding, with more cheerful faces around every turn. Children shrieked and giggled when their eyes met those of the foreigners, and clear, upbeat music embraced them from every direction. The party was touched by this welcome. None of them had expected their arrival to prompt this much merriment. The travelers took in all the sights, sounds, and smells of Suscundos with glee, pointing out to each other the city's gorgeous buildings, fountains, and copious amounts of flourishing trees.

Perplexus leaned back in his saddle and raised his goblet of wine with a whoop.

"Enjoying yourself?" Laivar teased.

"If I was made for one thing, it's being celebrated."

"You are rather good at it."

"Thank you, I've had a good bit of practice." The navigator touched a free hand to his mouth and blew a kiss to the onlookers.

The bard turned his head to regard Uritus and saw him appearing utterly bewildered. "They're a rather jovial people, are they not?"

Uritus met his eyes, his mouth half-open. He had not anticipated this. The crowd seemed to grow even thicker as they ascended the levels of the city to the palace. Never in his life had the fisherman seen this many people in one place. He did his best to acknowledge them graciously as his friends did, but felt his mind become an unstoppable rushing blur.

"You deserve to be here, Old Boy."

Uritus looked to Perplexus and gave him a quick nod. The people certainly seemed to think so.

They dismounted as they reached the circular square and their horses were promptly led away to the stables to be watered. The people approached them, adorning each one with a garland of greenery to hang around their necks. Uritus felt a dull, throbbing headache behind his eyes, his sole indicator that they had changed their hue. Uriah looked down at his pupil and shared a smile with him before leading their party to the base of the wide palace steps.

They were joined there by two more groups. The travelers waited patiently, the cheers of the crowd softening in anticipation of the royal family.

Trumpets sounded as the palace doors swung open. King Agamemnon and queen Betina were greeted with the same enthusiastic noise as the traveling parties. They descended the steps hand-in-hand, waving to the crowd with gracious poise. The king was tall, clad in crimson velvet, with wavy, shoulder-length brown hair crowned in gold—the majestic headpiece twisting as if made of vines. The queen was nearly a foot shorter than him, her own thick, dark hair piled on top of her head, wearing a violet gown and a crown that matched her husband's. They came to a stop atop the third and lowest flight of stairs and Agamemnon raised his hand and waited for the crowd to settle.

He began to speak once they did, his voice loud and confident, first thanking the parties for making the journey and pausing between each sentence to allow space for the citizens' enthusiasm. He went on for a few moments, detailing the purpose behind their assembly. Uritus did his best to keep his attention turned to the king, but it was torn away when, in the corner of his eye, he caught a glimpse of a flurry of sage-colored silk at the top of the first flight of stairs.

The gown was worn by, he could only assume, the princess Adiadni, who hurried down the steps and stopped when she reached her mother's side. Agamemnon paused his speech, reaching over to take his daughter's hand in his own and proudly presenting her to the city while moving her to stand on his right. The cheers that met her in response were noticeably louder than any Uritus had heard up to that point.

She smiled sweetly, extending her hand to greet the crowd and receive their admiration. She was graceful and poised, and she stood with her shoulders back and head high, her silver tiara resting atop a mass of long, dark curls. The neckline of her gown scooped across her shoulders, partially revealing the intricate birthmark on her right. Her movements were elegant and purposeful, her smile soft and bright. But in her eyes, Uritus saw something he could only describe as unease. He shook his head, certain that he must be wrong. She was a Vindella, the prophesied one. An event like this surely wasn't foreign to her.

He tore his gaze from the princess as Perplexus stuck an elbow in his side. Perplexus smiled and raised an eyebrow as they met eyes, "Captivating, eh?"

Uritus shook his head with a light laugh and returned his attention to the king, all the while willing himself to ignore the fluttering fabric that continued to dance in the corner of his vision.

***

"I appreciate each of you for the work you have done to prepare our city for tonight." King Agamemnon moved his hand from where it had been outstretched in front of him and brought it to rest against his sternum. "The Summer festival is a favorite of my daughter's, and I can think of no greater way to begin the festivities than by celebrating our new friends."

Again his hand reached out, gesturing to the newcomers as the crowd turned their cheers to them. The king always moved this way, Adiadni observed, whether he was addressing thousands or just her, alone in the palace. It was genuine, driven by what he was feeling inside, but it occurred to her now just how… *political* it looked. As if he'd been king his whole life. He *had* married young; his father having fallen ill suddenly, Agamemnon had needed to step into his role sooner than he had anticipated. But looking at him now, Adiadni saw a man who was born for this, a man better suited than anyone she could imagine to inspire and protect his people. *Her* people. She could picture no one on the throne but him. Though she knew that one day his seat would be her own, she felt inside that, somehow, he would be the Free World's guardian forever.

Once more that hand raised coolly, proudly above his head. "The festival begins at sundown! I look forward to celebrating with you all tonight!"

He leaned over as the crowd roared once again and whispered a few words to his wife. She looked up at him admiringly and he kissed her forehead. As she turned to descend the steps to speak with the travelers, a smile crept across Adi's face, for it was only then that her father's other hand released her mother's.

The king turned to his daughter, "You were late."

"I know. I am sorry. I was…" She looked up at him, and any instinct that she might have had at that moment to lie to him faded away as she saw nothing but genuine care in his eyes. "Nervous." She looked down at her hands clasped before her.

"I understand," the king gently cupped his hand under his daughter's chin and lifted her eyes again to meet his. "I appreciate you being here anyway."

The two shared a smile.

"Do you think you feel well enough to say hello?"

The princess nodded assuredly. "Of course. I'd be happy to."

Agamemnon nodded, turned, and descended the steps to welcome one of the groups that Betina hadn't yet. Adiadni let her eyes drift over the few dozen visitors, wondering if she should join one of her parents or move on to another group. This was the first time the king and queen had expected her to greet guests on her own. The party that arrived the day prior had joined the waiting masses below, and she was suddenly struck by just how many people she was expected to get to know over the coming days. Her heart began to pick up its pace and she was all but overwhelmed when her eyes fell upon a vaguely familiar face. She gasped and smiled broadly as she recognized it.

"Uriah!"

Down the steps she ran where she was caught up in the arms of the Wizard.

He laughed as he embraced her. "Hello, my dear!" They held onto one another's arms as she stepped back. "Let me get a look at you. It has been a long time."

"Far too long!"

The princess beamed up at the Wizard. Uriah had visited Suscundos several times in her youth before he settled in the White Mountains, returning when she was about thirteen and then never again until now. She wrote to him via raven occasionally, and he to her, and it was her letter, sent the day after her birthday, which initially informed him of the journey she would be taking West. In his preparations to equip the keep for his departure, he had been unable to return her note, and she was overjoyed to see him now.

"I didn't realize we'd be expecting you!"

"Yes, I thought I might surprise you," the Wizard winked. "Now, Adiadni, may I introduce you to my family?"

The princess grinned. "I would love that."

Uriah showed her to each member of the party and she welcomed each of them warmly, conversing with them for a few moments before turning to the next. She was intentional with her questions, Uritus observed, spending nearly all of her time with each person trying to learn everything about them that they were excited to share. She stayed a while longer with Mikka after learning that she had once served in her father's army.

"I was fairly young," Mikka explained, "...and didn't hold my rank for long. I felt inspired in my youth to use my strength for something positive. Never saw combat, of course. I spent most of my time out East, primarily in the Holy City repairing the walls after the heavy rains. You and I never got the chance to meet."

"Oh!" Adiadni's face lit up as the pieces of Mikka's story fell together in her mind. "You knew my cousin!"

Mikka smiled and raised a hand to brush her short blond hair out of her eyes. "Stell, yes. I could never forget her. That was her first assignment."

Adi nodded enthusiastically. "Crystella always spoke so highly of you. I am sorry she isn't able to be here to greet you herself. But I can tell you assuredly that she sends her love."

The princess seemed genuine in her interest, Uritus noted, and collected and casual in a way that made one feel both seen and recognized. She had a natural charm about her, a melodic laugh that melted away any anxiety one might have about conversing with a person of her rank. Uritus wondered how he could have thought she looked anything other than regal and serene.

And... beautiful, undoubtedly. He tilted his head back slightly and raised his eyes to the sky, releasing a long, slow breath in an attempt to recenter himself. By the time he returned, Uriah and the princess were standing in front of Perplexus, and then...

"Uritus?"

Uriah told her his name and she repeated it to confirm. She reached out both hands to take his as she had with everyone before him.

He cleared his throat and returned the gesture. "Adiadni." Her hands were soft and surprisingly cold. He felt as if the cracks on his own could cut her.

"Uritus is, in my humble opinion, our Hero." The Wizard winked at the fisherman this time.

Adiadni stiffened slightly, her mouth and eyes briefly widening before she spoke again, "You're the... first one I've met." She blinked, her gaze softening.

"It's an honor. If you're the one we're looking for, *they'll* look to you," she nodded to the crowd, "…just as much as they look to me."

Uritus's stomach flipped. Since Uriah had told him who he suspected Uritus to be, the revelation had settled into Uritus's mind as if in waves. The first, during their initial conversation in Uriah's chamber. The second, during the journey to Suscundos, upon officially designating Perplexus as their navigator after encouragement from the group that he needn't bear this burden alone. And the third, just now, the murmurs of the citizens of Suscundos still around him and the voices of the king and queen slowly approaching. His prior assumption that this was a potential quest that he may embark on and then return home from may not have been correct. No, there was more to this unfolding story than he knew.

His gaze met Adiadni's again and he squinted slightly, blinking back a few times against the thrumming in his temples.

The princess smiled and tilted her head curiously to one side. "You have…" she paused for a second, but only a second, "…trustworthy eyes."

Uritus returned her smile, his heart pounding. She opened her mouth to speak again but was promptly interrupted by the sudden whinny of a horse.

They dropped each other's hands and she took a step back as the crowd split to make way for a group of a half dozen river elves on horseback. Their apparent leader dismounted before his horse could fully stop. His long white-blond hair was tied low on the back of his head, a glossy plait that fell down his back. His armor was pale gold, gleaming and polished, a sword strapped to his waist, no helmet on his head. A velvet, olive-colored cape completed his ensemble. It swished behind him as he rushed to the princess, hugged her tightly, and planted a kiss on her cheek.

Adiadni recoiled slightly, as much as she could without betraying to any of the eyes watching her that the kiss was unwanted. This was Basil Dagious, the princess's intended, and the public loved to catch a glimpse of the two of them together.

"Basil…" She took his hands in hers, an action intended to create space between them. "I… didn't know we were expecting you."

"Well, I got your father's raven! I'm here to accompany you!"

Her eyes flicked to Uritus and then briefly looked over the riders Basil had arrived with. "I… um…" She took a few steps back, leading him up a couple of the stairs. "I… didn't realize you had a Keeper with you…"

"Oh, I don't. But I figured what's the harm in sitting in on the council? I'm going to be king someday. Wouldn't it be perfect if the Hero had been with you all this time!"

Adiadni bit her lip, eyes scanning the crowd below and then locking with her mother's. Betina immediately noticed her daughter's distress and hastened to her side.

"Basil, darling!" The queen embraced him, leaving Adiadni free to release her hands and clasp them together. "Why don't you freshen up before the festival? I can have Dijonas show you to your rooms."

Adi's eyes drifted again as she heard Basil tell her mother that he *felt adequately fresh but all right*, and then her eyes met her father's, a questioning glance. The king nodded, freeing her to leave. She looked once more to Uriah and Uritus and smiled, nodding her head to her hands in a prayer position, and then turned to ascend the steps to the palace. Uritus watched her fluttering skirt and sleeves as she departed, all the way up and through the door, and he felt the dull aching in his head subside.

Chapter Four

"A Pitch or a Six"

In the heart of the palace, the kitchen bustled with activity. Winchells, the head cook, stood at one of the central counters adding garnishes to various dishes which were immediately picked up by kitchen staff or festival organizers and rushed out to the tables in the square. The sun was making its slow descent in the sky and all of the city dashed about to complete the final preparations for the festival. The palace supplied the majority of the food for the celebrations, with the city's bakeries, butchers, and some households also electing to provide dishes of their own. The traditional sustenance this time of year consisted primarily of fresh, raw fruit and vegetables and always, of course, *lethaa*, a crispy, flaky, square-shaped flatbread paired always with a duo of sauces—one, heartier, lightly spiced, and made of an assortment of seasonal vegetables, the other, creamy, buttery, zesty, and bright. The bread and the sauces provided a lovely neutral base for pairing with an assortment of produce and proteins, and never was there a meal of significance in Suscundos where it did not make an appearance.

The princess sat perched upon the counter beside the cook, a piece of this bread in her hands, tearing off small bites and eating it slowly, unaccompanied by sauce. She had preferred it this way when she was very young, feeling its perfect crunch was dulled when introduced to moisture. Now a young adult, she had come to enjoy it both ways, regularly sneaking a small piece with the cook as he brought it to the counter fresh from the clay ovens, something he always did barehanded to Adi's amazement. A flurry of bodies hurried around them now, their quick steps and efficient communication with one another melding into a buzzy ambiance as the two conversed.

"Anyone particularly notable amongst the newcomers?" Winchells asked, plucking greens from their stems and sprinkling them over the trays piled high with lethaa.

Adiadni shrugged. "I've hardly had any time with them thus far. Didn't even have the chance to greet them all before lord Dagious arrived."

Winchells nodded understandingly. "The elder or the younger?"

"The younger, though I'm certain his father is not far behind." The princess sighed wistfully. The cook was one of a select few she trusted enough to be honest with her feelings concerning her intended; the kitchen one of a small number of spaces in the city where she felt fully free to relax and express herself in a way that was not at all performative. "He thinks himself to be the one we are looking for." She grimaced as she met Winchells's eyes and he returned her expression.

"Ah, yes. I suppose if I possessed a similar nature of self-importance that I may think the same of myself." He chuckled and Adi joined him before casting her gaze down at her few remaining bites of lethaa. The cook searched his mind for words to comfort the girl he loved. "Don't worry, Darling," he brushed a lock of hair from where it had fallen across her forehead and tucked it behind her ear. "I am sure Basil is not merely pompous and pigheaded. He may well surprise you."

She clucked her tongue at him and he promptly straightened and went back to garnishing the stacks of flatbread, a playful gesture mocking the subordination he knew she detested. She rolled her eyes at him. "I wish you wouldn't do that," she pouted. He chuckled and relaxed and the princess lifted her eyes to the ceiling and sighed deeply. "I suppose you may be right, though."

The cook shrugged.

Adiadni studied the face of her friend. "I envy you, you know." And when her admission was met by his laughter, she shoved his arm playfully. "I mean it! I've had my whole life laid out ahead of me before I could even speak. All anyone expects of you is to tell your jokes, bake your bread, and only spit in the food when you are truly at your wit's end."

"Adiadni!"

The princess gasped and whipped her head around, only to sigh with relief when she saw Exstarferus enter the kitchen bearing two bowls piled high with edible flowers. Winchells's husband's impression of her father had only grown more uncanny with time, and both cooks found it amusing how flustered the princess became whenever she thought she had been caught by the king behaving irreverently.

"Damn you, Star, you wretch," Adi cursed at the tall, thin man as he crossed the room to stand beside them and greeted Winchells with a kiss.

She softened as she watched the two of them together, quietly discussing the few tasks that remained before the festivities could begin. They had been a pair for as long as she could remember and were as complimentary as the lethaa and its sauce. Winchells was a wood elf, shorter and stouter than his partner, with rosy cheeks and nose, and Exstarferus was a human, decidedly lankier with a head of curly black hair which he boasted made up for Winchells's lack thereof.

The love the two cooks shared and the love shared by the king and queen were Adiadni's two shining examples of lifetime partnership, and she felt herself wilt ever so slightly every time she tried and failed to envision herself sharing similar moments of intimacy with Basil. Of course, she knew that comfortability would grow with time, she just needed to be patient. But fear sunk its roots deeper in her heart every time he touched her or spoke to her or looked at her and left her feeling... nothing.

***

Elsewhere in the palace, Uritus meandered the halls, somewhat lost in his attempt to return to his room. He had stolen away for an hour, having the attendant who had led him and Perplexus to their shared chamber show him to

53

the library before he left. It was one of two large libraries that could be found in either wing of the palace—identical ones, he presumed—the one he visited in the Western wing the grandest and tallest room he had ever seen. Two levels, with a balcony on the second, towered high with three slightly curved walls stacked to the roof with books. Rolling ladders leaned against each, wide and sturdy, caringly carved of redheart wood, with two framing each a large fireplace on the lower-level Southern wall and a pair of noble stone statues to the Northern. In front of the statues lay a beautiful chest, made of the same wood as the ladders. And to the West, a wall entirely of windows that stretched to the ceiling bathed the room in sunlight—the steadily deepening tone of which had been Uritus's initial clue that he should find his friend and make his way out to the festival.

He hadn't intended to read anything, and he didn't. He wandered along the shelves looking to spot any titles he recognized and finding only a few. He imagined it would take days, *weeks?* to sort through all of them. Most of his time in the library, though, was spent standing below the two statues, studying them and the chest lying below. He couldn't summon the courage to touch most anything in the palace, save for the contents of his room, but he crouched down to bring his eyeline to the rim of the chest, observing the strange and unique but somehow familiar markings carved there. He hadn't ever *seen* them before, nor, he thought, anything quite like them, yet he felt strangely that if he squinted his eyes just so, he should be able to read them.

He stopped trying when he noticed that the sun had dipped low in the sky, and he hurried away in search of his room. He had done a poor job, he realized, of keeping track of the path they had taken to get there. He had been captivated by the scale of everything in the palace, particularly the stone which made up the walls and most of the floors. Its shimmer was also profoundly familiar to him, and it did not take him long to realize that *this* was the stone mined from the very mountains he called home.

The Alabaster Keep was made of the same, but it was rectangular, with a turret erected at each corner, and didn't glisten nearly as much as the palace did. Uritus had known the stone was not only used to build the burroughs carved into the White Mountains that were utilized by the stone miners. Havian and Punznes had told him that the Mirrored Cities of Judii and Lorethh were made entirely of it, and he had seen sketches of them in books. But never until now did he consider that the stone was transported out East as well. Knowing these pieces of his home met him all the way here in Suscundos settled his nerves tremendously, and recognizing their invisible vibrations which pulsed with energy all around him brought him profound peace.

This peace was shaken, just a hair, as the clanging of bells met the fisherman's ear from the square outside, and he determined that he would need to make his way out to the festival and look for Perplexus there.

He made two more turns through the winding halls of the palace's first floor and then breathed a sigh of relief as he came upon a wide set of wooden double doors, as certainly here he would find a way out. He hurried to one, grabbed its handle with both hands, and pushed, finding the door not quite as heavy as its size would suggest.

On the other side, Adiadni shrieked with laughter, then gasped and leapt down from the counter when the door to the kitchen opened and she saw...

Uriah's chosen, Uritus, who looked surprised and deeply embarrassed to have accidentally stumbled upon the princess. A burst of laughter again escaped her lips, one of both amusement and relief, and she promptly clapped her hand to her mouth to quell it. The two cooks shared a glance behind her and a silent moment passed, the fisherman and the princess staring at one another with wide, panicked eyes.

The princess spoke first, "Excuse me, I was... you, you surprised me." She giggled, trying to relax herself.

He hurried to apologize, "Princess, I... I was just trying to find my way outside—"

"No, no," she waved her arms in the air. "You needn't apologize, and you *mustn't* call me *Princess*." She laughed and he relaxed, a nervous chuckle escaping his lips.

"Forgive me... Adiadni..."

She smiled at him and his heart did a flip. She opened her mouth to speak again, but behind Uritus, a small but loud voice called her name before she could. Uritus looked down, a rush of fabric moving around where he stood with one hand still on the door. A small boy, presumably a dwarf, slid on his knees across the kitchen floor, stopping right in front of the princess.

"It's time!" he cried out. "Festival time!"

The chiming of perfectly timed bells rang out and Adiadni reached down to help the boy to his feet. "That it is, Fenn. Shall we make our way out?"

He rolled his eyes at her. "Obviously!" He took her hand and began to pull her to the door that led outside, but paused and turned to look at the fisherman. He cocked his head, studying Uritus's face, and Uritus bit his lip to stop himself from laughing at being so shamelessly examined. The boy craned his neck to look up at the princess. "Can he come?"

Adi laughed down at Fennispar and looked over to Uritus, that radiant smile still alluringly splashed across her face. "Of course he can. That is... if he wants to." She tilted her head gently over one shoulder, a warm invitation in her eyes, and Uritus swallowed hard.

Fennispar let go of her hand and crossed the room to Uritus, who took a knee to meet his eyes.

Adiadni smiled. She had such a soft spot for the boy, fiercely protective of him like any older sister would be, and it made her feel warmed and at ease to see him so comfortable with the stranger. Fennispar stood there for some time, hands holding onto each other intentionally behind his back, looking Uritus up and down, and then planting his hands on the fisherman's shoulders and staring intently into his eyes. Uritus returned his gaze, softly smiling, waiting patiently for the boy to complete his analysis.

Finally, Fennispar turned over his shoulder to look at Adi, "Is he the Adalos?"

Her lips parted, a smile gently tugging at one corner of her mouth. She looked from Fennispar to the man who still knelt in front of him and he met her eyes. They held each other's gaze for a moment and she furrowed her brow slightly. She could have sworn his eyes were blue before.

She looked back to Fennispar, realizing that he was still awaiting her answer. She shrugged. "We don't know yet. What do you think?"

Fennispar looked once more to Uritus and nodded confidently. "Yes. I trust him."

The princess giggled at his solemn tone and Uritus spoke, "Thank you, young sir. I trust you too."

Fennispar rolled his eyes at his new friend. "Of course you do. Everybody trusts me."

The fisherman and princess laughed in unison and Fennispar gasped upon hearing the tolling of the bells for the third time. "Come on!" He grabbed Uritus's hand and dragged him to where Adi stood, taking hers as well. "We're going to be late!" Adi and Uritus shared one more look, the fisherman's smile fully loosened this time, and Fennispar dragged them outside the palace.

***

They arrived in time to catch the majority of Agamemnon's speech, stopping at the edge of the square, hands still holding tightly to each other. They finally let go as the speech reached its end, throwing their arms up in the air as the sun kissed the horizon and Suscundos's people tossed thousands of rose petals into the sky above them. The people cheered, the joyful sound of their voices one that would not subside for many hours. Music filled the air. Some people immediately began dancing in the Southern half of the square where the performer's stage was positioned. Others made their way to the long dining tables that sat in rows in the Northern half. The two sections were divided where a tall, circular, three-tiered fountain made of that same cool white stone stood proudly in the square's center.

Fennispar abandoned his companions shortly after the music started, far too elated by all the sensory offerings of the celebration to remain in any one place for very long. When the raucous energy of the people had subsided to a level hum, the princess and the fisherman realized that they were alone together amidst the crowd that moved like water around them.

It was this moment—the official commencement of the festival—when Adiadni felt free to take the first full breath she'd had time for in months. She was off-duty, not a thing expected of her by her parents or any of the partygoers until she resumed her responsibilities once the festival ended. She knew she'd need to make her rounds to greet the remaining visitors she had not yet been acquainted with, but standing there with Uritus, noting how out of place he looked, she felt in her soul a desperate longing to *pause* everything, just for a few moments, and bask in the love that ricocheted through every nook in the city around her. She wanted now, more than anything, to show him what it was about this place that set her heart ablaze.

"Would you walk with me for a while?"

The fisherman looked to the princess, his overwhelm subsiding as he allowed his focus to fix on her. Her request was soft, gentle, unassuming, and it quelled any desire within him to seek out the familiar faces of his party and cling to them all night. He had thought she was surely just being gracious when she had welcomed him along on her jaunt to the square with Fennispar. But looking at her now, her hands toying with each other, her head tilted just a bit over one ear, he saw in her eyes a certain hopefulness that indicated to him that she felt comforted—warmed, even—by his presence, the same way he was by hers.

"I would be honored to."

She lit up with a smile that reminded Uritus of a fresh spring on a hot day. He fell into step beside her as she turned and began a slow circle around the perimeter of the square. They walked that way in silence for a while, her taking in the ambiance of the event, him watching their feet crush rose petals beneath them as they went. He didn't know how to process the fact that he was truly here, after so many years of quiet dreaming. The city was gorgeous, its people kind, but with so many sights, sounds, smells, and things to experience, the fisherman could not help but feel like he was struggling even to tread water.

His overwhelm was quickly apparent to the princess. She knew such a feeling well. As much as she enjoyed disappearing into the chaos of the celebration, she too had experienced the strange sensation of feeling alone amidst a crowd. In similar moments, she had learned that it was helpful to expand her perspective, so her eyes searched the city around them for a point to draw his attention to.

"It's hard to see beyond the stalls, but the stables are just down that road."

He followed the line of her arm to where it pointed.

"There are some also on the Eastern side," she went on, looking over her shoulder. "I suppose I don't actually know which might be housing your horse…"

"Thank you." He smiled, appreciative of her attempt to help him feel more at ease. "I'll walk down to find him in the morning."

Adiadni touched her fingertips to each other as her eyes scanned their environment again. His attention fell to her hands and then returned to her face, her lip as she drew it between her teeth. Here was a side of the princess he had not expected to see. Less sure of herself, more… vulnerable. The fisherman was struck by a profound desire to alleviate her uncertainty however he was able.

Again, her gaze settled on something familiar nearby and her hand stretched to point it out to him. "This stall here is one of my favorite weavers. She has a method of dying cloth that produces the most stunning, vibrant colors. I always have my tailors go to her first when they're setting out to fashion something new. She was kind enough to prepare the silk for this very dress."

Uritus paused his walk and took a step back to regard her. She looked back at him with a small smile and her hands found their way to each other again. The long train that had trailed behind her during their first introduction had since been gathered up and pinned into a bustle at her hips to allow for greater freedom of movement. The fabric at the hem of her skirt and ends of her sleeves rippled with the breeziness of her motions like the leaves in the lush canopies above them. This soft shade of green perfectly complimented the Summer tan of her skin. He felt a dryness catch in his throat as he met her kind brown eyes again.

"It's lovely," he said, clearing his throat. "She does great work."

Adiadni's smile brightened, a slight blush coloring her cheeks as she returned to leading him around the square. "Just beyond the garden there is the greenhouse kept by our chief Healer, and down that road are the Western barracks…"

He listened intently to the melody of her voice, noting all the details of the decor, architecture, and assorted sights she pointed out to him. She grew visibly more excited as they continued to walk. Her fondness for this place was undeniable, her enthusiasm growing more palpable with each new piece of Suscundos she brought to his attention. He shared in her joy, laughing when she did and asking questions to make clear his interest in both the city and her perspectives of it. Her company brought him a profound peace, and it was not long before his body released the tension it had built up trying to remember how to swim and stretched out on the surface to float. This place was somehow even more spectacular than Uritus had ever dreamed, and he felt especially honored to be seeing it now through the eyes of someone whose ancestry was built into its foundations.

"And you?" Adiadni looked at her companion, her interest turned toward his roots now. "Are you from the White Mountains? Is that how you know Uriah?"

Uritus hesitated. He felt no shame in his humble upbringing, but he knew that this conversation would almost certainly take a turn for the sorrowful if he let the princess pry too deeply. "I live there now, yes, but I'm from Tosh originally."

"Tosh…" Adi raised her eyes to the sky, envisioning a map in her head. "On the Plentiful Lake?"

He nodded.

"Are you a fisherman?" A clearer picture of who this man was began to form in her mind, his humble clothes, his rough hands…

"Yes. Or rather… I was. I do more work on tools now than on the water."

She nodded, smiling at him. "I don't know much about fishing. Surprising to no one, I'm sure. Perhaps you'll have to teach me?"

Uritus swallowed and returned her smile. He could think of no words at this moment, having been caught again in the warm sincerity of her eyes. He nodded instead.

A look of sheepishness moved over the princess's face. "Forgive me," she said, "I've been going on for quite some time."

Uritus shook his head. "Not at all. You're lucky, I happen to think I'm a pretty good listener."

She nodded definitively with a light laugh. "Yes, you are very gracious. Thank you for that." She giggled and leaned toward him slightly and the scent of her filled his nostrils. Juniper and rosewater, simple, elegant, understated, yet enamoring all the same.

After a few moments of silence, his mind settled on a question he knew she could answer, "The boy earlier... Fennispar?"

The princess nodded, encouraging him to go on.

"He used a word I don't know when referring to me..."

Adi thought back to the conversation in the kitchen. "Oh, Adalos?"

The fisherman nodded this time.

"It's *arkennish*, the old tongue. All but dead now. It's the tongue the prophecy was written in so I'm familiar with a bit. Uriah knows more, I think. He's been around since it was spoken."

Uritus pondered this, remembering the vaguely familiar markings on the chest in the library.

"But anyway, the Adalos, it's the Hero. But it's more than that... It's also a leader or savior. But definitely one who is brave."

Uritus nodded slowly.

"It's the counterpart to me, the Suvah. The Way-Maker." She frowned, recalling something. "Your name. Uritus. It means *brave*, does it not?"

He smiled, surprised at her knowledge. "Courage," he told her. "I'm impressed that you know that."

She giggled, tucking a loose lock behind her ear. His eyes lingered there for a moment, the curl of her hair, the carve of her jaw...

Just then, a man appeared beside them—the same man who had made such a show of his arrival in front of the palace before. He bore a flagon of ale in one hand and a goblet of wine in the other and promptly inserted himself between the fisherman and the princess.

"There you are, my darling." He looked solely to Adiadni, ignoring Uritus. "I've been looking all over for you. Come, the festival is nigh! We must celebrate!" He offered her the goblet, clunked his flagon against it, and took a long drink.

Adi took a small sip of her wine. "I suppose it would be wise for me to eat a bit before I take to the dance floor." She looked at the fisherman and felt a pang of compassion for how he again looked not quite at home. "Basil, this is Uritus, one of our visitors. He's from Tosh."

"Tosh?" Basil turned to finally acknowledge the man who stood to his right. He looked him up and down, noting how the stranger's rugged garb surely meant he was no one of importance, and feeling a twinge of resentment upon noting that they met each other's eyeline even though the stranger had no significant lift to his boots. He cleared his throat and stuck out his hand in a greeting. "Basil Dagious, of Vindellaria," he curtly introduced himself, and then, insecurity itching at the back of his throat, added, "Adiadni's betrothed."

Uritus took his hand and shook it, feeling his heart slam into his stomach. Surely, Basil's greeting of the princess in front of the palace should have been a clear indicator that the two were attached. He felt suddenly foolish for the way he had allowed his mind to wander as he watched her lips while she spoke. Her captivating nature was not a flirtation. He was here to offer her his sword. Nothing more.

Adiadni watched their hands grip one another and then separate. She resented the way Basil spoke about their betrothal as if he was pulling rank. She didn't know how to address it and almost certainly wouldn't have had the courage to if she did. The moment she spent identifying what she felt swiftly came to an end as Basil turned to her again.

"Come now, my darling. The feast awaits!" He took her arm and began to drag her away.

Uritus caught her eyes briefly as she left—a note of apology shining in them —and he gave her a brisk nod to indicate that he understood. He scanned the crowd as she disappeared, searching the masses for a familiar face. Spotting Perplexus seated at one of the long wooden tables with Oripidus, Mikka, and Laivar, he made his way to them.

"There he is!" Perplexus greeted his friend enthusiastically as Uritus took a seat beside Laivar.

Oripidus pushed a pint of ale across the table. "Drink up. Yer fallin' behind."

Uritus tipped his head back and took a long drink, letting the rich, frothy liquid warm him from the inside.

"Where have you been, Old Boy?" Perplexus questioned playfully, puffing on a slender wooden pipe. "Already stealing away with the princess?"

"Adiadni is betrothed," Uritus informed them, certain they already knew.

"Ugh," Mikka groaned loudly. "To that gent from the East? All talk, no substance. He's never seen a day of combat in his life, but he carries himself as if he's already a general."

"Come now, I think he's rather funny," Laivar countered, and Mikka raised a suspicious eyebrow at him. "I do! Every now and again you come across a man who hasn't a modicum of self-awareness. It's the perfect fodder for a good story, if nothing else."

Mikka snorted and rolled her eyes. "Set him face-to-face with the goblins then. *That* would be a good story."

Oripidus chimed in, "Aye, he'd be excellent fodder for them."

They laughed uproariously, the drink already mingling with their blood, and Uritus waited for them to settle down before he spoke again, "Well he *is* the future king, whether seemingly fit for the job or not."

Mikka and Perplexus shared a glance across the table. "That is merely a title and a seat to Adiadni's left," Mikka countered firmly. "He'll demand our respect, yes. That doesn't mean we owe it to him."

The conversation fizzled out and Uritus realized he had reached the bottom of his ale.

"I'll get ye another." Oripidus snatched up the empty vessel along with his own and drunkenly hobbled away.

"Here," Mikka picked up her plate, still half full, and set it in front of the fisherman. "Eat up. Ol' Rip'll have you drowning in liquor before you get a chance to stuff your face, and by then it won't stay down."

Uritus thanked her and took a bite of the crispy flatbread.

"We wouldn't want that. You'd be hard-pressed to convince the princess to run away with you with the stench of vomit on your breath," Laivar teased, batting dark lashes which framed deep emerald eyes.

Uritus shook his head at his friends as they laughed but said nothing.

"Come on, Friend, it's all in good fun." Laivar clapped his hand on Uritus's shoulder.

Uritus patted Laivar's hand affectionately and turned to Perplexus, "Where is everyone else?"

"Nadarum and Ilya haven't left the dance floor," Perplexus answered.

"Typical, those lovers," Laivar gazed wistfully at the bodies that hopped and spun atop crushed rose petals beyond the fountain. "Always dead-set on reminding us that they're the happiest of us all."

"And Havian and Punznes," Perplexus jutted his thumb out to where the swordsman and physician stood with a trio of amiable elvish women who fawned over the raven on Punznes's arm. "They sought out fairer company. Can't say I blame them. No offense, Mik."

Mikka laughed sarcastically. "None taken, Lex. You know you're always welcome to insult me just so long as you insult yourself with the same breath."

Perplexus took Mikka's hand in his and planted a loud kiss upon it.

"And Uriah?"

Perplexus shrugged. "Fuckin' about, uncovering the mysteries of the universe somewhere." He puffed a few times on his pipe. "But you never answered my question. What held you up? If I recall correctly, we were supposed to make our way to the festival together." He raised a knowing eyebrow at his friend.

Uritus chewed his food slowly and swallowed. "I was with Adiadni."

"Ha *ha!*" Perplexus slapped the table with satisfaction and Laivar and Mikka clunked their drinks together.

Uritus looked to the sky, chuckling at his friends. "Surely, I don't need to tell you that it wasn't like *that.*"

"Yes, of course. Such a man of honor you are," Perplexus smiled slyly. "But surely, you cannot blame *us* for letting the wine go to our heads a bit."

Mikka clutched her hand to her heart. "Our boy fancies someone! We were beginning to think the day might never come."

"I haven't said I fancy her," Uritus protested.

"Well… do you not?"

Uritus stuffed the last sauce-covered piece of lethaa into his mouth in response to Laivar's question and the table howled with laughter again.

The noise subsided and, as if on cue, the princess appeared at the end of the table beside Mikka, crouched down, and splayed her arms out across it. "I need to ask a favor of one of you."

Perplexus, Mikka, and Laivar shared a wide-eyed glance before bursting into laughter again, and Uritus lowered his head, blushing furiously.

Adi tittered as the group composed themselves. "Forgive me, I've interrupted something, haven't I?"

"No, forgive *us*, Princess." Laivar reached across the table to touch her hand. "It's been a long time since we've had this much drink of this quality. What can we do for you?"

Adiadni raised her arms to interlace her fingers together and rested her chin on top of them. "Just a dance." She batted her long eyelashes pleadingly. "Just one dance and I promise to leave you be. I've had my fill and made my rounds and I desperately wish to sneak in a couple before the wine has my head spinning without guidance from my feet. I'd ask my intended but…" She rolled her eyes. "He's even more inebriated than the lot of you."

Her request was met with quiet initially, with each of Uritus's friends silently allowing him the space to speak first. His vocal cords tied themselves into a knot and Perplexus kicked his boot underneath the table, urging him to say something. But as the seconds ticked by, Uritus could not find the words, and so the navigator spoke instead.

"I'll join you, Adiadni, if you can forgive my missteps." He rose, tapping his pipe on the table and tucking it into his belt, and then took the princess's hand in his and twirled her away.

Uritus watched them depart and Laivar gave him a gentle smack on the back of the head. "Come on, Man. She came here for you!"

Oripidus returned then, setting a flagon of ale in front of Uritus. The fisherman brought the beverage to his lips and took a long drink.

***

Adi shared not one, but three dances with Perplexus and she was grateful for his companionship. He was a fine dancer, despite his insistence otherwise, and his degree of mirth matched hers. But with every spin, she found herself searching the crowd for Uritus. She was intrigued by him, she realized, at how… steady he seemed, grounded, and curiously multi-faceted despite having supposedly led a fairly humble life up to this point. She knew she should try to be impartial with her time over these next few days, as surely her father and the council would want her input as they sought out the chosen one. But something in her heart implored her to find him again. And so, her third dance with

Perplexus coming to an end, she was pleased when he led her to the square's edge to reunite with the fisherman.

Uritus had left his table when Laivar and Mikka disappeared in search of sweets and Oripidus struck up a friendly conversation with a table of fellow dwarves. The fisherman wandered along the perimeter of the square until he met up with Nadarum and Ilya, and they stood there together and watched the partygoers prance in time with the lively music. Uritus spotted Adiadni with ease, her uncommon grace making her easily identifiable. Every step she took was elegant yet strong. She laughed brightly as Perplexus spun her around him, holding tightly to his arms as they moved in unison, and Uritus kicked himself for not being quick enough to grant her request earlier. Laivar was right, she *had* been looking for him, and no doubt had addressed the whole table to allow the fisherman his freedom of choice. He hated the idea that he had let her down, and he vowed to himself that he would not let it happen again. Before he knew it, she stood in front of him once more, still arm-in-arm with Perplexus.

"You dance beautifully, my lady," Ilya complimented her, handing her a goblet of sweet red wine. "No doubt something you've been doing your whole life?"

The princess nodded graciously and took a large gulp. "Dance is one of life's greatest joys. I saw the two of you out there as well. Surely, you've been partners for a long time?"

The couple gazed lovingly into each other's eyes. "Yes, quite long, and yet still not long enough." Nadarum kissed his wife and Adi smiled dreamily at them and then straightened herself a bit and clutched her goblet with both hands, realizing she had still been leaning heavily on Perplexus.

The navigator cleared his throat to bring the married couple out of their amorous haze. "What say we take a bit of a walk? I think our bodies would thank us for it."

Nadarum replied first, "Speak for yourself, Lex, I've not yet drunk nearly enough."

Ilya rested her hand and head against her husband's chest, his arm encircling her waist. "I would sell my very soul for a cottage pie."

Adi grinned. "I think I know a place that can satisfy all your wishes. That is…" she looked to Uritus, "…if it would fulfill yours as well."

All eyes turned to the fisherman and he searched his mind for a request that was neutral but also honest. "I think I'd be happy doing anything next, just so long as it's good fun."

The princess clapped her hands together, delighted. "Perfect. It's just down the road, this way."

They moved together from the square along the street and down to the city's second level, chatting and drinking and laughing and admiring the lanterns in the trees. Nadarum and Ilya led them, arms wrapped around each other, and the fisherman, princess, and navigator followed behind, walking side-by-side. Adiadni swooned every so often as she observed the subtle showings of love between the two in front of her. They were beautiful, she an elf and he a human.

They were both deep-complected, muscular, and tall—though he still head and shoulders above her—with rich brown eyes and close-cropped black hair. They hailed from the Valley of the Sun, Northerners who grew up on adjacent farms and fell in love in their young adulthood. Their parents had never approved of their union and rejected them when it became known that the couple did not wish to remain on their family farms. So they left their homeland together, traveling across all of the Free World, her hunting to keep them fed, him doing occasional work training horses and offering riding lessons in the cities where they stopped. They lived like this for a long time together until Uriah welcomed them into his home for a brief stay. While there, they realized that the love of a close-knit community was the thing they had been missing, so they never left.

Uritus watched Adiadni as she listened intently to his friends' story. Her empathy moved him, her eyes growing ever glossy as the tale traversed its sadder parts. She carried in her hands two halves of a ripe yellow peach that she had Perplexus cut open for her. She had snatched it from a fruit cart where she abandoned her empty goblet as they left the square. One half still had the pit inside, the other she munched on freely, messily, its sticky-sweet juice smeared across her mouth, covering her fingers, and trickling down one side of her wrist. She melded seamlessly into their group, laughing loudly as her companions joked with her and leaning into Uritus as she did. Her scent of juniper and rose mixed with that of peach juice and red wine and in her sloppy inebriation, her careless steps, and her hair growing ever more unkempt over the course of the evening, he saw a different beauty in her, somehow more iridescent than that he had observed upon their first meeting. Her radiance was enrapturing, and he found himself pulled toward her a little more each time she squealed with glee or brushed her arm against his.

They arrived shortly before a tavern—The Gilded Rose—a wooden sign swinging above the door emblazoned with the image of the thorny red flower covered and dripping with liquid gold. Adi entered the tavern with Nadarum and Ilya in search of their refreshments, leaving the other half of her peach with Perplexus. He removed its pit, cast it upon the ground, and finished the piece of fruit in two bites as he and Uritus meandered to the patio. A pergola covered it, purple wisteria and tangerine roses climbing its pillars and growing across its beams. The paper lanterns also hung overhead, glowing with warm light. A couple dozen people sat at the tables beneath the blanket of perfumed flora and quiet flame, most of them eating, drinking, or smoking, but a few gathered around smooth, square boards that rested upon the tabletops, playing rousing games of dice. The two friends watched the players for a while, observing their quick movements and sharing an exhausted glance upon spotting—or rather *hearing*—Basil Dagious amongst them. They did their best to ignore his loud, drunken jeers as they studied the game, but were unsuccessful.

"The game is called Kepu," Adiadni appeared between them bearing two mugs of ale which she handed to her companions. "It's fun. Most in Suscundos and some other cities out East grow up playing it but I never got very good, I'm afraid."

The married couple arrived on the patio shortly after Adi did, Ilya carefully, reverently carrying her cottage pie with both hands, Nadarum with two mugs of ale in one and a goblet of mead in the other. He handed the goblet to the princess before taking a seat at a nearby table with his wife.

"Talk us through it?" Perplexus asked.

Adi took a big gulp of her drink, holding the goblet with both hands and swaying gently. "Certainly. It's rather simple."

She moved to the side of one table and they turned their attention to the game being played there, Basil versus a Suscundos citizen.

"There are two players," she explained, "...the Challenger and the Thrower. The Challenger, naturally, is the one who challenges the Thrower to a game. The game is played using the Thrower's set of dice and the winner traditionally keeps the set. Other bets can be made as well, of course."

Basil gathered up each of his dice and placed them into a smooth leather pouch. They were ruby in color, carved of real gemstones from the looks of it, with gold paint emphasizing each dimpled pip.

Adiadni went on, "The game consists of three rounds, with the object of each being to capture four of the six dice in play. The Challenger must begin each throw by placing a single hand on the table with fingers outstretched to indicate the number on the dice that they will attempt to capture that throw, called the Pitch. The Thrower and Challenger may try to capture either dice of the same number as the Pitch or sixes, but at the end of each throw, the Challenger keeps only the dice that match the Pitch, and the Thrower keeps only sixes. Any sixes the Challenger captures as well as any Pitch dice captured by the Thrower are returned to the pouch and rolled again on the next throw."

Uritus and Perplexus kept their eyes glued to the playing board as the Challenger who sat opposite Basil held out two fingers with his left hand and set them on the table, the first Pitch of the third round.

Adi took another drink and continued, "Once the Pitch has been determined, the Thrower takes all the dice in play into his pouch and casts them upon the board. Either player may then attempt to capture the dice by placing a hand over one and moving it toward himself, but only one die may be captured at a time, and it must be done with a flat hand to limit one's ability to cheat."

The trio watched this play out on the table in front of them, Basil throwing the dice and then capturing two sixes, his opponent capturing none.

"So it's a blend of both luck and skill," Perplexus nodded thoughtfully as the players set up for the next throw, none of the dice capturable this time.

The princess nodded as well. "A game ideal for those with fast reflexes. I can never manage to read the dice quick enough to capture one in time."

Uritus regarded the board as the third throw took place, with Basil capturing one more six and his opponent capturing one of the Pitch. "And if a die is captured that is neither a six nor the Pitch?"

"That die goes back into play, as well as one of the offending party's captured dice. The same is true if you knock one off the board or disturb it so that its number changes."

This scenario played out in front of them as if prompted by their conversation, with the Challenger accidentally capturing a four instead of a five and begrudgingly pushing it back toward Basil along with the die he'd captured on the previous throw.

Basil took the remaining three dice into his pouch, shook them up a bit, cast them upon the board on the next Pitch, and captured not one, but two sixes, surpassing the requirements for victory. He cheered and gloated, a few of the bystanders clapping him on the back with praise, and his opponent rose from the table, cursing angrily, and stumbled away in search of a drink to comfort himself with.

"Anyone else?" Basil asked, his haughty demeanor causing Perplexus's ears to grow hot with annoyance. "Anyone at all?" He brought himself to his feet and spread his arms wide. "Come on now, you certainly can't *all* be a lot of cowards!"

Perplexus removed the satchel that had been slung across his chest and passed it to Uritus, handed his half-finished ale to Adi, shook his dark hair free of its knot, and began tying it up again as Basil taunted the crowd around them. He took the mug again, throwing his head back and taking several long gulps to empty it.

"I'll take that challenge."

Basil whipped his head around, surprised to hear a response.

"Or rather, I challenge you, if that's how this thing works."

Basil glared at Perplexus who smiled with one corner of his mouth. "Fine. I suppose you'll do." He reclaimed his seat at the table and gestured for Perplexus to do the same.

The navigator turned briefly to the princess, handing her his empty drinking vessel again. "Darling, might I trouble you to fetch me another?"

Adi smiled curiously at him, surprised at his request and unable to recall another time in her life when someone so casually asked something this ordinary of her. She nodded to him, happy to be treated in the same manner as he would any of his other friends, and hurried away.

Basil blinked at this interaction and glared at Perplexus as he lowered himself to the opposing bench, angry that this new Challenger had stolen his chance to make a show of having Adiadni wish him luck.

Uritus felt his pulse quicken as the two got set up for their game. He knew all too well how Perplexus was prone to egging people on, to countering the rage that met him with jokes and banter—something that did not always go over well. He remembered the first time his friend returned to the keep from one of his journeys working as a navigator with a black eye and a bloodied lip but bruiseless knuckles, insisting his jesting had been all in good fun and his attacker had just gotten a bit too heated. Uritus turned his head to look over one shoulder and met Nadarum's eyes. The horseman rose with Ilya and moved to the fisherman's side, not needing to be told Uritus's concern that Perplexus's drunk witticism may lead to worse than just a heated game of Kepu.

"What do you care to wager?" Basil asked coolly.

"Let's say your set of dice…" Perplexus reached his hand down to his waist, "Against my knife."

The hem of his shirt lifted slightly as he produced a beautiful dagger with a gleaming, bone-white handle. The blade was long and curved; its hilt he had carved from the rock of the White Mountains when he was a teenager. The dagger had also a polished silver sheath engraved with the twisted roots of a tree which lined up with the carvings on the handle of the tree itself.

Basil nodded once. "That will do. I trust you know how to play?"

Perplexus nodded curtly. "Adiadni was kind enough to give me the gist. I'm confident I can figure it out as we go."

Basil narrowed his eyes again at the Challenger, casting the dice immediately once Perplexus set his hand down on the table with two fingers outstretched. When the dice settled, Basil moved first, clapping his hand over the solitary six. Perplexus quickly followed, capturing a single two.

The dice were rolled again with a similar outcome—Basil netting another six and Perplexus his chosen five. On the third roll, both Perplexus and Basil moved swiftly, capturing one each of the Pitch, a one this time. Perplexus took the lead. Basil huffed, returned his captured die to the pouch, and rolled immediately as Perplexus held out two fingers.

The die was rolled again and again, with neither a six nor Pitch appearing for some time. Finally, Perplexus's chosen was rolled—a five—and Basil snatched the die a split second before his opponent could. He returned it to the pouch, chuckling to himself.

Adi returned then and set a pint of ale in front of the Challenger. Perplexus held her wrist gently for a moment, thanking her and all the while feeling the heat that rose in Basil's face radiate across the table. He returned his attention to the game.

The next throw landed quickly on the Pitch, a five again, and Perplexus moved in a flash, capturing it as well as the first round victory. Half of the bystanders cried out in approval, Adiadni letting out a small squeal of her own and then immediately becoming silent and withdrawing as Basil shot daggers at her with his eyes.

Uritus noticed this and felt his head grow hot, pain moving across his brow. He clenched his fists at how the princess's intended made her wither with a single glance. The whole night up to this point, the fisherman had watched her blossom, and seeing the bud try to fold back in on itself made his pulse quicken. He softened one hand and brushed it against hers. She returned the gesture.

"Just a bit of luck."

Basil downed the last of his ale and tossed the dice to begin the second round. Two sixes were rolled as well as one Pitch, and Basil swiftly claimed them all before Perplexus had a moment to think. The Challenger nodded to himself, ignoring the Thrower's smirk, and took a slow drink.

On the next roll, he pitched a two. No two appeared, but rather two sixes, which Basil captured with ease. The Challenger grunted his frustration, finished his drink, and set the empty mug aside.

The third round began with Basil netting two more sixes again. Perplexus sighed agitatedly and felt one leg begin to bounce under the table.

"Lex."

The Challenger did not look up but took a deep breath and settled his leg, his friend's voice grounding him, reminding him to focus. He moved quicker on the next throw, and both he and his opponent captured a die each. Perplexus moved his head to the side, cracking his neck. He could not lose another.

Two more throws passed with neither a Pitch nor a six appearing. The onlookers stood with bated breath. Then, Perplexus pitched a four and captured it quickly.

Basil also captured a die which he presumed to be a six, but when he raised his hand, it was revealed instead to be a five. The crowd murmured and the Thrower's eye twitched as he returned the incorrect die to the pouch along with another of his captured ones. His head was growing foggy.

He cleared his throat obnoxiously on the next throw as Perplexus captured a third pitch and no sixes appeared. He would not be humiliated by this over-confident foreigner. Basil cast the die again, several times in a row, growing ever more impatient each time.

Then, Perplexus pitched a two, and as the die fell from the pouch, a loud crackling sounded from outside the patio. The patrons of the tavern turned their heads, startled and then relieved to see firecrackers sparkling beside the fountain in the street. But Perplexus did not flinch, and, spotting the two he needed, captured it immediately.

Everyone's attention returned to the board. The Challenger raised his hand to reveal the winning die and the Thrower flew to his feet.

"You damned cheater!"

Perplexus leapt up too and moved around the table to come face-to-face with his opponent. Both Uritus and Nadarum immediately sprang to action, Uritus placing a hand on Perplexus's chest and Nadarum setting one on Basil's shoulder. Ilya moved her hand, subtly placing it on the knife strapped to her thigh, and Adiadni called Basil to stop.

"He had the perfect moment! That was more than enough time to move the die, I call bullshit!" Throbbing veins pumped hot blood through Basil's face and neck.

"Lex, breathe."

Perplexus glared down his nose at the man who quivered with anger before him and did not take his friend's advice. "Don't worry, Uritus. Our lord is just upset that his beloved would rather see him lose."

Basil lunged at Perplexus. The navigator stood his ground despite Uritus's attempt to pull him out of range of Basil's fist, which was ultimately caught by Nadarum as Ilya began to unsheathe her knife.

"Enough!" The entire patio fell silent as the princess's voice rang out, loud and gritty and forceful. "It's a fucking game, you damned fools! Play another or let it go, but you will *not* ruin the night over *this*."

The tavern's patrons gasped at her harsh tone and language, having never before heard the princess raise her voice. Adiadni clenched her fists and her teeth, knowing that word of this outburst would certainly make its way to her parents who would no doubt chide her for it. There was silence for a moment; none dared to speak until Perplexus finally shook himself free from Uritus's grasp.

"The princess is right," he loudly proclaimed. "I, for one, let my drink get the better of me tonight." He turned to look her in the eyes and brought a hand to rest against his sternum. "Forgive me, Adiadni."

She swallowed hard and nodded to indicate that she did.

"As for you," Perplexus turned back to Basil whose face was still beet red, "I'll happily relinquish my title if it would please my lord and restore peace to the evening."

His use of the title *lord* was an attempt at both mockery and flattery, and Basil saw this clearly. It stirred up a rage from deep within his belly, but he knew he could not allow his opponent to walk away appearing like the better man. "Fine," he shrugged his way out of Nadarum's grip. "I shall let this go. But only if we can act like civilized people and try this one more time."

"Sorry, Man, I'm out." Perplexus swiped his knife from the table and tied it to his belt, turning to depart.

"You cannot just walk away from a challenge you initiated!" Basil spat, moving toward him. Nadarum stepped into his path again as he shouted, "Be a man and finish what you started!"

Perplexus stopped walking and sighed up at the sky through the slats of the pergola but did not turn.

Uritus moved into Basil's line of vision, desperate to calm the man his friend had provoked. "I'll play in his stead. No rules against that, are there?"

"None," Adi spoke quietly, shaking her head. Perplexus turned around.

Basil scoffed. "You? And what do *you* have, Uritus of Tosh, worth wagering against my dice?"

Uritus looked down at his person. "I haven't much, I'm afraid."

"Hmm." Basil stepped around Nadarum and slowly walked toward the fisherman, one arm across his chest, the other tracing his cheek as he looked him up and down. "How about that?" He gestured to the shell that hung from Uritus's neck—an appealing whorl cut right down the middle with a gleaming, pearlescent sheen on the inside. "*Amonii*, no? That'd fetch a pretty penny where I'm from."

Uritus gripped the shell. "Not that."

Perplexus spoke up, "He can still bet my knife."

Basil shook his head. "Has to be something of his own."

Silence fell again, Uritus and Perplexus not knowing how to satiate their opponent.

And then, Adiadni moved without thinking, snatched her tiara off her head, and shoved it into the fisherman's hands. "Here."

He looked down at it, stunned, then back to her, "Adiadni—"

"I'm giving it to you!" They held each other's eyes and the princess shrugged. "I have a hundred of them. What's one more? Never liked that one much anyway."

She pulled her hands away from his and crossed her arms over her chest so he could not try to give it back. He stared at her, still wide-eyed, and she gave him a subtle nod of assurance. She was trying to help.

"Come on now—"

"Basil." Adiadni's voice was flat as she stopped him from interjecting.

He clenched his jaw. "Fine." He returned to the table and Uritus followed suit, setting Perplexus's bag on the bench beside him and shaking his head at Ilya when she offered him the rest of her drink.

"Let's begin then."

Uritus pitched a one on the first cast and Basil swiftly captured the sole Pitch as well as two sixes. Uritus blinked and shook his head, feeling he had underestimated what he had gotten into. On the second cast, three sixes were rolled. Uritus captured one, but was briskly defeated in the first round as the Thrower captured the others.

"Come on, Old Boy."

Uritus drew in a long, even breath as Basil replaced the dice in the pouch. The fisherman pitched a three on the first throw, and he and Basil each caught one at the same moment the dice settled.

This happened again on the second throw as well as the third. Basil cleared his throat in annoyance and made up a bit of ground when he captured two sixes on the fourth throw. Several more throws happened after that, a half dozen and then a dozen, laces of anxiety being tightened ever so slightly around the room with each one.

Then, finally, a Pitch was rolled—a five. Both hands lurched for it, Uritus's hand landing atop the die and Basil's on top of Uritus's. The Thrower ripped his hand away and grunted at his loss. The crowd began to hum excitedly. Adiadni subtly found Perplexus's hand and clutched it.

The final round moved slower, with the Thrower capturing one die first, then the Challenger, back and forth until they had each captured two dice, with several uneventful throws between. Uritus pitched a three next, and when two of them were rolled, Basil thrust his hand at both, jostling the board and knocking them from it. He swore in anger.

"Settle down, Man," Nadarum warned.

Basil huffed hotly, swiped the two dice that Uritus had retrieved out of his hand, and placed three dice into the pouch. The next cast would yield a die for each of them with only one remaining. The Thrower cracked his knuckles.

One cast, with neither a six nor a Pitch.

A second cast, the same.

Uritus pitched a three on the third. The die tumbled across the board as if time had slowed, coming finally to rest at the corner of the board beside the fisherman.

A three.

He placed his hand atop it before Basil had the chance to think.

The Thrower leapt to his feet again, each of Uritus's friends instinctively moving their hands to their weapons as he did. He huffed at the Challenger for several seconds. Uritus met his stare, unmoving. Finally, Basil looked to Adiadni, her glare hot and sharp. He took one breath, a bit deeper than the last, and the blood drained from his face, returning his skin to its natural pale color. His demeanor changed as this happened, shifting so rapidly from enraged to peaceable that those who witnessed this change were unsettled by it.

He looked again to the fisherman and stuck out his hand in mock congratulations. Uritus took it apprehensively and gave it a firm shake. Basil turned then to address the room, leaving the dice still scattered across the table, the pouch lying nearby.

"Ah, what a night it's been." He crossed the floor slowly, arms wide, his onlookers still tense. "The Summer festival is always a lovely one and I feel… *elated* to have gotten to spend it with each of you."

Adiadni frowned as he moved closer to her, knowing he was building to something but not sure what.

"Now, I know that celebration is an intrinsic part of this city—my love's city," he arrived beside the princess, snaked an arm around her shoulders, and squeezed. "And I've been trying to think of a way to match your celebration. To expound upon it. Well, I think I've come up with just the thing."

He turned Adiadni around and guided her off the patio and into the street where more people had gathered for the evening's closing. The princess's new friends and the tavern patrons followed close behind, the tiara and dice abandoned on the table.

Basil stopped them beside the fountain and spun around to face the tavern once more. "Adiadni, my darling," he addressed her but did not look at her. "I have been waiting for this moment for a long time." He turned to her finally and produced a ring from somewhere on his person, a long, silver, diamond-shaped face with a large chartreuse stone inlaid in its center. "Will you do me the honor…" he descended to one knee, "…of making this betrothal official?"

Adiadni's pulse pounded in her ears and her head grew heavy. She felt sweat start to form beads in her palms and upper lip, her mouth growing drier the longer it hung open. She felt the thrumming of her heart, her fear pulsating through each vein in her body out to her fingertips. She felt she was going to become sick.

"My dear?"

Several moments had passed and she still had not given him an answer. Her breath quickened, growing shallow. She thought back to the events of the night, her moments of joy and anxiety, her time spent with new friends, her outburst at the tavern...

Without thinking, she found her head nodding yes and Basil rose to embrace her. He placed the ring on the third finger of her left hand and held her to him again. The crowd around them cheered and Adiadni squeezed her eyes shut as fireworks sounded in the sky above them.

Chapter Five

"Sparks"

The door to the room Uritus and Perplexus shared in the palace shut firmly behind them as they returned. The short walk back had been silent, pensive, with Uritus replaying the events of the night in his head continuously and Perplexus racking his brain for how he might bring solace to his friend. Now, back in their chamber, the silence persisted, only occasionally interrupted by the deep booms of the final fireworks that sounded above their heads.

Perplexus lay on his back, one knee crossed over the other, chewing on the end of his pipe and occasionally taking long drags, staring at the bed's canopy above him. Though Uritus moved through the room unpacking his belongings and saying nothing, Perplexus sensed his friend's annoyance with him. He knew he had behaved foolishly by carelessly teasing the man he knew was certain to explode if brought to his edge. He just hadn't stopped to consider that the explosion could cause anyone harm.

He had always loved to play with fire as a boy. The rubble that naturally fell from the mountains as they rose to the sky yielded perfectly sized and shaped stones whose natural energetic current caused them to spark when struck against one another. He would often strike them repeatedly, with no intention of allowing the cool blue sparks to catch on to anything. Just to watch them. Sometimes of course, like many children do, he would burn small piles of twigs or single leaves, holding them up to the sun and watching them with fascination as they curled and turned black in the crackling heat. But it was the sparks, the tangible representation of the Magic deep-set into the earth of his homeland which captivated him and made him feel the most connected to the Divine.

It was unfortunate, he considered now, how his fascination with things that burned hot and wild regularly singed him, and, after tonight, also the people he cared for. He had truly just been having a bit of fun, imbibing as he had been encouraged to. And he had seen the note of self-importance in the man who lorded his dice over everyone at the tavern and sought to snuff it out. But regardless of his intentions, he had put his friends in harm's way, and he knew that it was his responsibility now to own up to it.

"I'm sorry," he finally said as his friend sat on the neighboring bed and removed his boots.

Uritus did not reply.

Perplexus went on, "I know it was my fault, the conflict. I shouldn't have provoked him to begin with and I shouldn't have continued after he became upset."

The fisherman moved behind a dressing screen and began to remove his clothes.

"I didn't like what I saw in him. The haughtiness. I took it upon myself to quell it. Forgive me. I know it is not my responsibility to bring every arrogant shit to justice." Perplexus sighed. "I just never considered that he might try to hurt you. Or me, or any of us."

"I am not upset of my own accord." Uritus emerged from behind the screen in his nightclothes, a loose-fitting linen shirt and pair of trousers that cinched just below the knee. He moved to the washbasin lying adjacent to the screen and splashed his face with water.

Perplexus nodded slowly. "I ruined the night, I know. And Adiadni's fate is sealed now, but surely that was also true a long time ago. I couldn't have predicted that he would use her in his attempt to reign victorious..."

Uritus dried his face with a towel, sighed, and rested both hands on the edges of the washbasin. "And that is different from *your* using her, how?"

Perplexus blinked abruptly, removed his pipe from his mouth, and sat up on his elbows. "I can assure you that I don't know what you mean."

Uritus sighed again, then slowly moved to retrieve his clothes from where they hung on the screen and began folding them. "The affectionate name-calling. The intimate touches. Having her leave to get you a drink? You knew exactly what you were doing. You invoked her in an attempt to break him." He gathered his folded clothes in his hands and crossed the room to kneel before the chest at the foot of his bed. "You knew it would infuriate him to see her accept acts of tenderness from someone else. You found his weakness and sought to exploit it. *You* used her in pursuit of *your* victory, just the same as he used her for his." He paused before opening the chest. "We are here *for* her, to accompany her. To protect her on her journey. Not to put her in harm's way and not to treat her like a weapon to be wielded."

Perplexus sighed. His friend spoke the truth. He *had* seen sparks in Adi that night when they were dancing—before that even, when she freely approached their table in a bold search for Uritus. He had watched the tiny flame within her ribs grow—just a little—whenever they made her laugh or treated her as one of their own. He had toyed with it, blown on the embers to see how hot they could burn, observed the way the laces of the invisible corset that restricted her freedom loosened progressively over the course of the night and wondered to himself what might happen if he gave them a gentle tug. In the moment, he had interpreted their playful affection as merely a product of their growing comfortability with one another. But he would have been lying, he realized, if he said that the way the princess's attention on him brought so much fury to her intended hadn't at all fanned the flames of his persistent agitation. He brought himself to a seat, one foot dangling off the edge of the bed. "You're right. I'm sorry. But it is not merely *her* journey that we will be undertaking. You also have a role to play in all of this."

"That still remains to be seen," the fisherman replied. "But I am not the one to whom an apology is owed." He shut the lid of the chest firmly.

The navigator nodded. "I will find her tomorrow. I promise. I *am* still sorry to you though."

The fisherman rose from the ground and looked to his friend.

"I pestered you about her all night. I meant it in earnest, you're not one to be forthright about what you're feeling. You know that I believe love... or even just... new friendship paired with attraction should be celebrated. Always. In all its forms." He paused. "But in my attempt to open you up to feeling its joy, I... forced her into the arms of someone else." He swallowed, blinking back tears. "Forgive me."

Uritus sighed sadly at his friend. "I do. Always. And I didn't mean to make you think of Lys, I'm sorry."

"Ahh," Perplexus waved his hand in the air dismissively, but his eyes remained wet. "Love and pain are lovers themselves. On a lighter note though..." He returned his pipe to his mouth and held it between his teeth as he leaned across the bed to retrieve the set of dice in their leather pouch and tossed them to Uritus. "In the madness of the evening, you nearly forgot the spoils of your first victory."

Uritus caught the pouch and looked down at it. "I'm not sure I care much to carry a memory of tonight around with me," he said, "...but thank you anyway. I'm sure I'll find some use for these." He placed them in the trunk and moved to sit on his bed.

"Well, this one I'm sure you'll know what to do with."

Uritus looked up as Adiadni's silver tiara landed with a soft thud on the mattress beside him. He took it up and turned it over in his hands. "I'll return it to her tomorrow."

***

But much to his dismay, he would not find a moment the next day or the day after that to speak to the princess, whether alone or amidst a group. The festival raged on around them, as spirited and lively as it had been the first day, and he looked for her at every turn. She was easy to spot, dazzling, entertaining her citizens diplomatically, always with a nearly imperceivable glowing haze around her that lit up the faces of everyone she interacted with. He knew she would not care to have her tiara back, that she likely didn't even miss it. Nonetheless, he felt himself *pulled* toward her, as if by some invisible, magnetic force. Perhaps Perplexus was right and this force was merely an attraction, fascination with her effervescent beauty. Whatever it was, it caused a stinging sensation in the fisherman's chest as he observed her smile return to the perfectly polished porcelain one he had seen upon his first arrival in the city. Her distress was apparently evident to no one else.

Adiadni waded through a sea of congratulations from the moment Basil finally released her from his grasp beside the fountain, to her father's announcement of her engagement to the city that night, and through the the remainder of the festival. Basil stuck himself to her side and refused to leave it so she could not find even a moment alone with her friends or her staff or

75

anyone save him as long as they were in public for the length of the next couple of days. She resented him for this, for taking a celebration that was meant to be enjoyed by the whole city and centering himself in it, centering *her* in it, when all she ever wanted from the seasonal festivals was to become one with her people; to not have every eye in the city watching her intently with bated breath, just waiting for her to stumble.

She knew that they did not actually want this, that her people's love for her was true and that they wished for her happiness as well as her success during her reign. They had watched her since her birth in joyful expectation of her victories to come. The problem was that they and her parents viewed this moment in her life—the commencement of her betrothal—as one of those victories. But she was brought face-to-face with her true feelings concerning the matter the moment Basil presented her with his ring. She did not have the words nor the courage to articulate that she felt, by accepting it, that she had locked herself into a cage—one that could not be opened except by fracturing her familial connections with the Dagious house. Her sense of responsibility, as usual, defeated her sense of self-preservation in this case. Her only moments of connection for the remainder of the festival would be the fleeting ones when she caught and held eyes with the fisherman briefly across the square.

By twilight on the third day, the festival had drawn to a close and she retreated to her room to find solace in solitude. She sat on the floor, leaning her back against the chest that sat at the foot of her bed. Her feet were bare, her indigo gown pooling around her, her jewels abandoned on the dressing table. The doors to her balcony stood open to her left, allowing a gentle breeze to ruffle her curtains and the sounds of the whispering trees to fill her ears. Her arms rested on her knees, slowly turning Basil's silver ring over in her hands. A knock sounded at her door, along with her mother's gentle calling of her name, and the princess hastily thrust the ring back onto her finger and invited the queen to enter.

Betina shut the door softly behind her. "Hello, Love," she greeted her daughter. "Are you too tired for a short visit?"

Adiadni shook her head. Betina moved across the room and brought herself to a seat on her right, the skirt of her golden gown rustling as it settled alongside her daughter's. The two sat in silence for a while, listening to the leaves brush together and the few birds who still chirped in the cold, fading light of the disappearing sun. Adi began to fear that the time had finally come for her mother to confront her about the aggression she displayed at the tavern. But time continued to pass, scored by a peaceful quiet, until the queen took her daughter's left hand in her own to observe her ring.

She held Adi's hand like that for a moment, tilting it to see the smoothness of the stone in the cool light that poured in from the balcony and the light from the few enchanted candles that brought warmth to the room. Finally, she spoke, "Will you be terribly hurt if I tell you that I find it quite ugly?"

Adiadni burst into surprised laughter at her mother's candor, laughter which Betina met with her own.

"Oh good, I had been so terrified to tell you when you first showed it to us. Your father insisted I keep quiet about it but I just couldn't bear to lie to you."

Adi shook her head at her mother, always straightforward regardless of the potential consequences. "To be honest, I don't really care for it either." She pulled her hand back into her lap and swallowed down at the ring. "And it's a bit too small." She struggled to remove it, the skin of her finger pink and slightly inflamed due to the force with which she had thrust it on.

She finally freed it from her hand, letting out a relieved sigh as she did, and Betina held out an outstretched palm. "I can have it sent to a silversmith. Don't worry, I'm sure they can have it adjusted before you meet with the council tomorrow. How are you feeling?" She studied her daughter's face.

"About…"

Betina shrugged. "Everything."

Adiadni clutched her hands to each other, trying and then failing to blink back the tears that pooled in her eyes and fell in her lap.

Betina wordlessly moved herself closer to her daughter, wrapped one arm around her shoulders, and set the other against Adiadni's cheek to bring her to rest against her chest. Adi's tears fell freely, soft sobs causing her body to gently shake. The queen held her as she cried, saying nothing, instead closing her eyes and silently speaking words of love over her daughter. The sky had grown dark by the time the princess straightened herself and dried her eyes.

Betina touched a compassionate hand to her daughter's shoulder, tracing the swirls of her birthmark with one finger. "This is heavy for you, I know."

Adiadni sighed shakily but did not reply.

"And I imagine this is too?"

Adi sighed again, nodding sadly when her mother held the ring up in her hand.

Betina returned the nod with understanding in her eyes. "To partner with another is no small thing," she spoke slowly, thoughtfully. "I remember being nervous and overwhelmed as well when your father gifted me with my own."

The queen's ring encircled the third finger of her left hand, golden, delicate, appearing as leafy vines entwined with one another. It matched her husband's wedding band, their crowns similarly designed. The symbol of the interwoven flora was sacred to Suscundos, the golden ring appearing against a bright blue background emblazoned upon its city flag. The depicted image changed just slightly each season, featuring buds in the Spring, acorns in Autumn, and thorns in place of leaves when Winter came. The bands of the king and queen also changed their forms without prompting as time continued to move, each of them having been enchanted so they warmed the finger of the wearer just slightly whenever their partner was thinking of them. As it was, they were almost always warm.

Adiadni studied the piece of glimmering gold on her mother's middle finger and shook her head. "It was different with you and Adda."

"And how is that?"

Adi locked eyes with her mother and then dropped her gaze to her lap.

Betina nodded pensively. "I see."

She rose and began wandering around the room to light the few remaining candles. Adi watched her. She had always found her mother to be deeply beautiful. The golden light of the match she carried solemnly from candle to candle illuminated her smooth bronze skin. Her own curls were tighter and darker than Adiadni's, and even greater in quantity and volume. The queen's face was ever soft, radiant, understanding, the corners of her mouth turning upward just slightly so that even when her expression remained neutral, one still felt safe and comforted by her. She spoke again, continuing to bring light to the room as she did, her match burning continuously until she put it out of her own accord and replaced it in its tray with the others.

"I am sure you know that a requirement for love is patience…"

Adiadni shook her head. "That's what everyone keeps telling me!"

"Everyone?"

The princess ignored her mother's query. "You've told me many times the story of how the two of you met. You *saw* him, you met his eyes in the Eldest Forest and you knew. You *knew* that you loved him, or at least… that you would. And the same was true of him when he saw you." She looked to her hands again. "I've never felt that. And now…" Tears welled in her eyes. "I'm beginning to see that I never will."

"Oh, Love," the queen moved to crouch in front of her daughter and took her hands in her own. "Not all love is as sudden as the strike of a match. Some… *most* blooms over time. But it is no less valuable for that. If anything, it allows us to better appreciate the journey that it takes to get there."

Adiadni nodded, tears subsiding. "I do not believe you. But… I do trust you."

Betina smiled sadly at her daughter and brought one hand to rest against her cheek before standing to her feet to pensively pace. After some time, she spoke again, "There was… one other reason I wished to speak with you tonight."

Adi swallowed and sat up straighter.

The queen paused her walk, touching her fingertips to each other, and eventually crossed the room to sit on the chaise opposite from where her daughter still rested, legs crossed, on the floor. Betina moved one leg to cross over the other, folded her hands, and brought them to rest upon her knees. She leaned forward wordlessly, gazing into Adiadni's face for a few moments. The princess shifted her weight anxiously under the intensity of her mother's dark-eyed gaze.

After some time, Betina spoke again, "You know we value your input?"

Adi blinked and nodded, unsure where her mother was going with this.

The queen continued, "Your opinion in regards to whom the Adalos may be… it is just as important to us as the other aspects of the deciding process."

The princess chewed on her lip, again nodding slowly.

"I know this is all very new…" Betina paused, tapping her thumbs together. She leaned closer to her daughter, "Are you… drawn to any of them?"

Adiadni's lips parted softly as an image of the fisherman materialized in her mind. She *was* drawn to him, this was clear to her, and probably, also, to him. But she hesitated to share this with her mother. Uritus had been the first of the prospective heroes that she had met, the only one whom she had gotten to spend significant time with. She didn't know if her immediate connection with him was merely because he was humble and kind or rather something more mystical. "I'm not sure yet…" she spoke hesitantly and then nodded firmly and straightened herself where she sat. "But I am quite confident that it is not Basil."

The queen sighed. "Your father and I feel this as well, though we have invited both Dagiouses to sit in on the council anyway."

Adi nodded. Of course they had. Potential Hero or not, Basil *was* now, officially, the future king…

Betina went on, "May I ask where your certainty comes from?"

The princess sighed. "No one has told you, have they?"

The queen blinked curiously.

Adiadni sighed again, looking to the ceiling. She then brought herself to her feet, crossed her arms over her chest, and moved to gaze out over the shadowy garden from the doorway of her balcony. "The first night of the festival… at The Gilded Rose… he became… aggressive. Violent. Over a game of Kepu." She turned again to face her mother. "He tried to hurt someone."

Betina rose to her feet and crossed to stand in front of her daughter. "I did not know." She rested a hand on Adi's face, concern in her eyes. "Is everyone all right? Are you all right?"

Adiadni nodded, a single tear slipping down one cheek. "There were some who tried to restrain him, but… he was *so* angry…" She shuddered. "I had to shout at him, at the room to get them to settle down." A second tear fell. "I am sorry. I was afraid. I didn't want anyone to get hurt."

Betina wiped Adi's cheek with her thumb. "Love, I am just glad you are okay. Thank you for telling me. I will have to discuss this with your father. A violent outburst in a public forum on a night of celebration is hardly a good look for the future king." The queen turned to depart.

"Are you not upset with me? With my outburst?"

Betina stopped at the door and turned to look at her daughter, "Of course not, Love."

Adiadni shook her head. "Neither you nor Adda has ever had to become forceful to maintain peace. It is not the Vindella way." She hung her head, vision blurring again. "I am sorry."

The queen sighed sadly. "You needn't be. You did what needed to be done." With that, she departed, leaving Adiadni alone with her thoughts.

***

The sun rose slowly, unceremoniously, the following morning. Cool beams of light illuminated the pale stone of the palace, gently awakening the birds, the livestock, and then the residents of Suscundos. Uritus had risen before all of them, including the sun, and brought himself to stand in the cool mist of the early morn on his balcony, Perplexus still sleeping soundly in the room behind him. He watched the sky shift from charcoal to slate gray to icy blue and only lowered his eyes when a gentle rap on the chamber door broke him from his meditative state. Wood knocking against wood. The Wizard had returned.

Uriah pushed the door open quietly, stuck his head into the room, and smiled when he saw the fisherman on his feet and dressed. "Good, you have already awoken," he said, "Would you care to join me for a stroll around the garden, my boy?"

Uritus nodded and wordlessly followed him outside the palace, pulling on his boots as he left.

The two moved about the Western garden in silence, observing the abundance of multicolored flowers covered in dew and the trees of all shapes and sizes that no longer bore festive lanterns. The Western and Eastern gardens were similarly laid out but still unique from one another—long, wide strips of land brimming with impeccably manicured yet still free-growing vegetation. Each garden stretched for the width of the palace and came to meet a sprawling, half-moon-shaped orchard to the North which filled the entirety of the space behind the palace in the highest tier of the city. The dawning light of the new day sent a long, cold shadow over the fisherman and Wizard as they walked, and the light of the sun caused a halo to shine around the glittering stone of the palace.

After some time, Uritus elected to speak first, "I haven't really seen you since we arrived here." It was both a statement as well as a question.

"Forgive me, I had hoped my absence would mostly go unnoticed. I have taken the past few days to convene with the other Keepers in anticipation of today's council." The Wizard paused his walk. "Do you feel adequately prepared?"

Uritus shrugged. "As adequately as I can, considering how little I know."

Uriah nodded solemnly and moved to sit at the edge of a fountain, leaning on his staff as he lowered himself down.

Uritus joined him.

"I am sorry, my boy, to have kept you in the dark for so long," the Wizard apologized. "Surely, you have many questions."

Uritus nodded his forgiveness. He did have many questions, but somehow felt not at all agitated by their mysteries. He felt safe under the guidance of the Wizard, protected and empowered so that even when he was uncertain, his feet remained steadfast. Uriah had walked this land for longer than the fisherman could comprehend. He trusted his methods, even when they appeared to make no sense.

"I will say that my faith in you has only continued to solidify since we have arrived," Uriah went on. "Word reached my ears of the events of the festival's first night."

Uritus looked up. "You needn't chide Lex. I've spoken with him concerning the matter already."

"Yes, I rather thought you might have." The Wizard rested a hand upon his pupil's shoulder and studied him for a while. "Do you know why I believe you to be the Adalos?"

Uritus took a slow breath, turning the weight of the word over in his mind. "Before, you had said it was because I found Milion…"

"A crucial clue, yes," Uriah replied, "...but not the only one."

Uritus waited patiently for his mentor to go on.

"I searched the land for you when I received news of the birth of the Suvah. I did not know it was you I sought, of course. I knew only that it was my responsibility to find you, and that you would be born not long before or after she was." The Wizard moved both hands to hold his staff and lifted his eyes to the sky. "I followed my instincts and the guidance of the Source. I traveled across all of the Free World over many years and observed everyone I met, looking for signs of you at every turn. I spent time in all its major cities and smaller villages, staying also with the peoples of the forests and the mountains. I even came to Tosh…" His eyes lit on the fisherman who met his gaze, frowning, surprised.

"You would have been a very young boy at the time, not yet five. So I missed you." The Wizard smiled sadly. "But ultimately, it was *you* who found *me*."

Uritus shook his head. "I don't remember it happening that way. You came upon me at the stream…"

Uriah chuckled. "But what you do not know is that I had paused my search. Twelve years I had spent traveling the land and I felt it of great importance to find a place to settle down for a while. I could not ignore the Voice which implored me to rest." The sun had now traversed the horizon and lit the few fluffy clouds in the sky with shades of pink, peach, and lavender.

Uriah went on, "I returned to the White Mountains, a place I had settled before, and in return for my pledged allegiance, they offered me my home."

Uritus nodded, slowly taking this in.

"I was not looking for you anymore," Uriah stated seriously. "I walked amongst the mountains in search of their guidance and that day, they led me to you." He locked eyes with the fisherman, "Had you not come to the mountains of your own accord following the death of your father, you would not have found Milion, and I would not have found you."

The fisherman sat back. Each time he felt he had begun to grasp the gravity of the story he found himself at the heart of, a new incomprehensible layer appeared. He allowed his eyes to trace the golden outlines of the clouds as these new revelations settled into his bones.

"You were so gentle. So gracious. You carried yourself upright, proudly, despite the burden you still carried, and always with that shining thread of humility that I so love about you." Uriah's eyes became misty. "In all your years, amidst all your hardships, you have not once let your fear lead you and you have never allowed your spirit to be broken." He looked intently at his chosen. "*That* is why I believe you to be the Adalos. That is how I *know* you are him."

Uritus smiled graciously. "I must thank you for your faith in me. It has carried me to heights I never fathomed for myself."

The Wizard chuckled as he rose and the two again began to walk through the garden, wafts of misty, evaporating dew wisping around them. The shadow of the palace had grown shorter and they made their way North, towards its edge.

Uriah spoke seriously again, "Uritus, I was there when the prophecy was written. I knew Heimar Vindella. I see the same sparks in you that he harnessed within himself to set the fire of the revolution. I implore you to look for them yourself."

Uritus considered this, coming to a stop. "Did you fight in the Hope War?"

The Wizard paused as well, nodding sadly. "Yes. I did." He cleared his throat. "Though I, like the Free World, have not seen a battle since."

Uritus nodded thoughtfully and the two continued walking. The fisherman floated another query, "May I ask why you waited so long to tell me? About all of this..." He hesitated. "One might think I'd have been far better equipped to undertake this journey had I more time to prepare myself for it."

"I've taken it upon myself to prepare you anyway, though you did not know. Surely, you understood that I chose your paths of study with intention."

Uritus nodded. "Yes, I suppose I did. Though, I may have believed that intention to be merely a soft spot for me which manifested by allowing me to explore my passions." He laughed. "You *have* always had my best interests at heart, I just did not realize to what degree."

Uriah laughed as well. They walked quietly for a moment, approaching the garden's edge. The Wizard spoke again, "I suppose the reason I waited is similar to the king and queen's reason for waiting to tell Adiadni the whole of her own destiny."

Uritus frowned to himself. He had thought up to this point that certainly the princess knew what she was destined to face, that she had always known. He felt foolish for not considering that she may have been just as surprised by this unfolding of events as he was.

Uriah continued, "We wished to allow you to live relatively unfettered lives. We recognized the weight of your burdens and sought to shield you from them, just for a time. So you might grow up in peace."

The two reached the edge of the garden and stepped beyond the wall of the palace that shaded them into the warmth of the morning sun. The orchard spread out in front of them, rows upon rows of fruit and nut trees. The princess could be seen several yards away resting amidst them.

Uritus's eyes lit on her as he replied, "It's gotten less heavy over time. And while I suspect it will not always follow that same pattern..." he turned to Uriah, "...it is bearable for now."

The Wizard nodded, smiling down at him, chuckling to himself as Uritus again fixed his attention on Adiadni. "The Suvah and the Adalos are linked. If you feel pulled toward her, allow yourself to be." The fisherman met his eyes. "You will rely on each other heavily, and look to one another for help on your respective journeys."

Uritus turned again to Adiadni.

"Thank you for walking with me, my boy."

Uritus nodded and said nothing and made his way into the orchard.

***

Adiadni leaned against the trunk of a mature apple tree, a book of poetry open in her lap. She felt the heat of the morning sun warm her bare shoulders as it climbed into the sky above her. She wore a simple lilac dress, her curls piled on top of her head, held in place by a single silver pin. The gentle breeze that whispered through the orchard ruffled her skirt and caused a few fallen locks of hair to tickle her skin as they danced. She lifted her head upon hearing footsteps and a soft-spoken greeting.

She met eyes with the fisherman, clad in the same simple white shirt and brown trousers as he always was, the amonii that Basil coveted still hanging around his neck. She gave him a welcoming smile.

"Uritus, hello!" She tucked a single fallen curl behind her ear, still gazing up at him. "I am pleased to see you. I'm sorry to not have gotten the chance the past couple of days. I've been a bit… preoccupied." Her eyes fell to the book in her lap.

He nodded understandingly, noting that Basil's ring was missing from her finger and electing not to mention it. He turned his eyes instead to the book, "What are you reading?"

She smiled down at its pages. "Poems." She lifted her eyes without lifting her head, peering at him through thick, dark lashes, "Can I read you one?"

He returned her smile. "Please."

She bit her lip and turned a few pages in search of the right one. Uritus could not tell if she was actively seeking out a specific piece or rather waiting for one to make itself known to her.

She cleared her throat when she found it, sitting up as she began,

"In my dreams, I count flowers
I can name every one
Small ones, like dewdrops, bright ones, like the sun
And I take them all back
To my lover at home
Then I wake and I sigh to find myself alone

She's hard to remember
Yet hard to forget
I feel like I know her, though, in life, we've not met

But were I to hear her
Or glimpse her kind face
I'd know her at once, any time, any place

She's soft like the Winter
And sweet like the Spring
Freer than Summer, just as breathtaking
She's tender like Autumn
As deep as the sea
And I like to think she might also know Me

We'll collide when we do meet
In a rush, in a flash
Perhaps we'll go gently, more a wish than a crash
But I think no matter
The way that we fall
Before long, we'll forget we had to meet at all

We'll know one another
Like blood of our blood
Sinking ever deeper in ravishing love
I'll count all her freckles
I'll name every one
Small ones, like dewdrops, bright ones, like the sun

It may be some time yet
Until sparks are lit
But my heart is open to all phases of it
I'll wait here till she comes
Feet ready to run
To her blood and her breath and the light of the sun."

Uritus smiled softly as the poem reached its end. "That's beautiful."

"I think so too."

Peaceful silence settled between them and the fisherman shifted his attention to look around at the orchard. "It's beautiful out here too."

She smiled at him, a curious look on her face. "You know it's a graveyard?"

He cocked his head, looked to the tree nearest him, and furrowed his brow in confusion. "They seem healthy to me…"

"Not for the trees," she giggled softly, shaking her head. "For the Vindellas. And their partners. We are buried in the ground upon our deaths and our bodies fertilize the trees." The princess lifted her eyes to the swaying boughs above her. "The trees bear fruit, the fruit feeds the city. Circle of life and all that. We're rather fond of circles."

Adiadni watched Uritus take a step toward the tree in front of him and stretch out his hand to rest upon its trunk. One calloused finger reverently traced the pattern of the bark. He inhaled and closed his eyes for a moment, raising his face toward the sky. "This is a sacred space," he finally spoke, lowering his gaze again to the tree and then to her. "I am honored to be welcomed here."

The princess felt understood by how the fisherman moved through Suscundos with intention, paying special attention to each detail that she drew his eye to. She slid her bare feet forward along the earth so that they stuck out past the hem of her dress. "If you really want to feel it, you have to take off your shoes." She giggled awkwardly. "The Magic of this place exists either way, I just… connect to it better like this."

Uritus promptly brought himself to a seat against the trunk of the tree opposite Adiadni and removed his boots, setting them to the side. He pressed the soles of his feet to the ground, leaned his head back against the tree, and took three long breaths, feeling the breeze kiss his face as he did. A subtle yet steady hum traveled from the dirt and into his bones. A smile spread across his lips and he nodded his head, eyes closed. "I feel it." Another deep breath. "It's like… a heartbeat. A wave."

Adiadni beamed at this descriptor, understanding exactly what he meant. The wind moved through the rows of trees, causing their branches to rustle and stirring the wispy green grass to dance and sway softly around them. The princess observed the fisherman where he sat with one arm resting across his knees, the other palm-to-earth. His loose-fitting shirt fell open slightly, exposing the shell on its leather strap lying against his chest. It gleamed peach, gold, tangerine when caught in beams of sunlight cast between leafy shadows. She watched him there for a while, his restful demeanor, the corners of his mouth lifting in a peaceful smile, the wells of his collarbones deepening with each steady, even breath. She swiftly dropped her gaze when he finally opened his eyes.

He regarded her for a moment before he spoke again. She was backlit by the morning sun, golden highlights crowning her tresses and warming her soft skin. His attention was drawn to her birthmark as the sun and shadows danced across its surface. He hadn't specifically studied it before, but looking at it now, he recognized that its curling pattern did bear a striking resemblance to the darkened silhouettes of the leaves above her. She chewed absentmindedly on her bottom lip, gaze fixed on the open book still resting against her legs though she did not appear to be reading it.

"Can I ask you something?"

She raised her head. "Of course. But I do want you to understand that you are always welcome to. You needn't ask for my permission. I do not wish for you to think of me as your leader."

"Understood," he paused. "You *are* my leader though…"

"Yes…" She nodded. "But if you are the Adalos, you will be mine as well. Would I be correct to assume that you would not have me regard you only as such?"

"You would be," he replied. "How, then, do you wish for me to regard you instead?"

The princess sighed and lifted her eyes to the sky. Eventually, she shrugged and returned her gaze to the fisherman, "As a friend."

He nodded, smiling. "All right... Friend."

She returned his smile.

He continued, "It only very recently occurred to me how... overwhelmed you must be amid such great happenings. How are you feeling?"

Her lips parted and she allowed herself to bask for a moment in the warmth of the fisherman's empathy. She shrugged again. "Waves of anxiety quieted sometimes by peace when I can focus on the present." She sighed. "I only learned of the expectation that I will vanquish Dagamor in recent months and... mostly, I fear that I will fail. That I will let everyone down and never get to see this place again." She hung her head, swallowing back tears.

"I understand," he said, pausing to think of how he might comfort her.

She looked to him again, "How do you remain so... grounded? So steady despite everything. I feel as though I may drown at any moment and you..." She took in a breath. "Your half of the prophecy is far vaguer than mine and yet, since you arrived here, you've been the solidest thing I can see. How do you do it?"

Uritus rested his head against the trunk of the tree behind him. Her perception of him was far more generous than he felt he deserved. "The faith of others helps float me. The faith of Uriah, and my party..." He paused. "And of you."

Adi tilted her head over one shoulder.

"You hardly know me, yet you see in me something that you trust. I feel I should thank you for that."

She smiled.

"But I suppose the main reason is my trust in the prophecy itself. It says not that we will attempt a journey but that we will succeed. That you will not merely seek to defeat the Dagamor, that you *will* do it." He lifted his head and looked at her, "Whether I am the one who will go beside you or not, wherever I may end up next, I am certain that the Divine will guide my steps. I do not really understand Magic, but it has yet to lead me astray. I lean on that."

"Mmm." The princess tilted her chin to the sky, feeling the breeze move around her. "I feel Magic here in the earth. But mostly in the wind." The whispering zephyr rose to greet her. "Where do you feel the Divine?"

Uritus considered this as he watched the dancing leaves above them. "I listen for it most often amidst silence."

"Ahh." The princess nodded slowly and the wind brought itself to a still around them. "Like that?"

"Huh." Uritus regarded the peace which overtook the orchard. "Yes. Quite like that."

"What is it saying?"

He closed his eyes, fixing his attention on the quiet. A peaceful smile grew over his face. He opened them again to regard her before he spoke, "That I'm going to be okay. That you are too."

They held each other's eyes, suspended briefly in time, scooped up into the palm of a loving quiet that identified this moment as the sacred thing it was and sought to preserve it. As it dropped them back down, the princess began to laugh, a gentle hum at first, then growing into loud peals of joy which were caught up by the wind as it again rushed around them. Uritus smiled broadly, a quivering breath sucked out of his chest. Her smile was as bright as the sun. He joined her in her laughter, the moment prolonged only by them this time.

Eventually, they settled again into silence and he watched her raise her hand in search of one of the ripened pieces of fruit that hung heavy over her head. His brow creased when it appeared that the branch moved down on its own to meet her hand. As she grasped one of the speckled apples, plucked it, and brought it to her lips to take a juicy bite, the branch raised itself up again, and a realization dawned on the fisherman.

"You are a Keeper."

Adiadni shrugged dismissively. "Perhaps. Though not in the traditional sense by any means. I am certainly not a Wizard or a Prophet or a Healer. Though I do sometimes have dreams."

"But you are connected to the Divine..." he countered. "You manipulate the world around you. The wind. The trees..."

She nodded slowly, chewing another bite, and then swallowed and shrugged again. "Perhaps it is in my blood," she considered. "But I believe that anyone could keep Magic if they tried. If it is in me, it is in you as well. You hear the Voice in silence. Most never learn how to do that."

Uritus nodded thoughtfully, eyes drifting up and down her face as she spoke.

She closed the book in her lap and set it to the side, wrapped her arms around her knees, and looked intently back at him. "Uritus, I am your friend. And as your friend, I must implore you to regard yourself with the same esteem as you do me." She swallowed under the intensity of his gaze but still held it. "You possess just as much power... Magic... *hope* as I do. I have not known you long and I do not know you well, but something tells me your road to get here has been far more tumultuous than mine. And yet, still, you remain soft." Tears welled in her eyes as she dropped her gaze to her knees.

"Do you not consider yourself soft?" Uritus questioned her. "Even with those silken hands of yours?"

Adiadni let out a burst of surprised laughter and then quieted and gazed sadly at the grass in front of her. "I used to."

Uritus didn't understand. "Why not anymore?"

The princess hesitated. "Three nights ago... at The Rose..."

Uritus thought back to the night of the Kepu game.

Adiadni shook her head. "I shouted at you. At Basil mostly, but at all of you. In an attempt to maintain control of the patio, I lost control of myself."

"I hardly think that's—"

"No." She shook her head, tears stinging her eyes. "You didn't see the way they looked at me."

He still did not fully understand, but recognized all the same that this particular burden was heavy for her. He remained silent, allowing her the space to go on.

Hot tears spilled onto her cheeks. "They were afraid of me. The people in the tavern. They would not even speak for fear that they might upset me further." She breathed shakily. "My sole responsibility, my family's entire purpose in the Free World is to keep our people safe. The title of *guardian* holds more weight than *king* ever could. We do not rule, we provide for and we protect. And the people grant us their allegiance as their thanks."

He nodded slowly, his chest squeezing with frustration for his inability to help.

She shook her head. "If I cannot make myself heard except by force, I do not deserve their love. And if I cannot even protect them from myself… then I have already failed." The princess rested her forehead against her arms and allowed her sobs to overtake her.

The fisherman rose to his knees and crawled the length of grass to her side where he pushed away the half-eaten apple that she had dropped and brought himself to a seat. He turned himself toward her but did not touch her, and she brought her head to rest on his shoulder while she cried. The boughs of the trees swayed in gentle time with Uritus's breaths as the princess attempted to calm her own. His heart broke for her. The path she trod had not been paved by any of her ancestors before her. He was intimately familiar with loneliness, but hers was profoundly sad in a way he had never imagined. He waited for her sobs to quiet and her breath to calm before he spoke again.

"As your friend…" His voice was gentle, barely more than a whisper. "…I implore you to have grace for yourself."

She let out a sound that was half surprised laugh, half residual sob.

He went on, "I cannot imagine the weight of your position or what it must have been like to have carried it your whole life. But I know that everyone— even every great leader—fails at some point. You cannot allow yourself to dwell upon it when you do. You can only learn. It is how we carry on." He reached up absentmindedly to brush a curl away from her face.

"Huh." She let out a tiny relieved sigh and held the fisherman's gaze for a moment, resting her head against the trunk of the tree that shaded them, noticing that her breathing now also moved in time with its swaying branches. "You may be right," she finally said. "I suppose it would be much more difficult to appreciate and be grateful for our gifts if they simply came to us like that." She snapped and a flash of blue sparks lit around her fingertips.

Uritus's mouth fell open and Adiadni laughed at him. "That's something I'm certain you can do." She moved to sit on her knees in front of him and held out both hands to take one of his between them. "Look at me. Breathe with me. Center yourself."

He obeyed, looking deep into her eyes.

She swallowed nervously. "Then, um… when you're there, when your mind is quiet, just… snap. With intention."

He followed her instructions and snapped. No sparks appeared.

"Now, take your own advice and press on through your failure."

They laughed together and he snapped a second time, still no sparks.

"Sometimes it helps to talk through it so you don't hurt yourself by focusing too hard," she giggled.

"What would you have me talk about?" A third snap sounded without a flash, but the fisherman felt as though heat was beginning to grow between his fingertips.

Adiadni thought for a moment, feeling warmth rise in her cheeks as she looked at Uritus and realized his gaze had not faltered since she had asked him to look at her. She blinked twice, drinking in the inviting brown of his eyes until her mind lit on a question. "This may sound strange…" she began hesitantly, "…but I am all but certain that when we first met… your eyes were… blue?"

He laughed and she blushed. He continued snapping periodically, pausing to rub his fingers together between each attempt.

"It's ridiculous, I know…" she backtracked.

"No, not at all. They change sometimes."

She blinked at him, lips parting just slightly. "*Viraglas?*" she breathed. "That is rare even amongst the elves. I don't think I've ever seen it before."

He smiled. "Because of it, I have both my father's and my mother's eyes."

She smiled. "They must be very beautiful."

"Yes…" He hesitated. "They were."

Adi's smile faded as she felt a pang of sorrow for her friend. Then it returned to her face, empathy in her eyes. "Well, wherever they are now, I am sure they have just as much faith in you as I do."

And at that moment, sparks flashed around Uritus's fingertips—bright pinpricks of light that matched the blue of his eyes—and both the princess and fisherman gasped as they watched them fade.

An echo rang out through the orchard then. Perplexus calling for Uritus. The fisherman hastened to his feet. The sun had risen high in the sky by that point and both companions knew it wouldn't be long before the council would commence.

"I should probably go…" Uritus said hesitantly.

"Yes, of course…" Adi bit her lip, hands toying with each other as she attempted to manage her bitter disappointment that her time with the fisherman had come to an end. "Thank you for visiting with me."

"Of course… Friend." Uritus smiled, turning to leave.

"Wait!"

He turned around.

Adiadni hesitated as she looked at him, having called after him without thinking. "My mother asked me if I was drawn to any of the heroes and I could only think of you."

He blinked, lips parting slowly.

She swallowed her nerves. "I saw your face. Your eyes..." She stood to her feet and he regarded her in silence. "You may not see yourself as the Adalos yet, but I do. As does Uriah..." She paused. "I hope that in time, you will also learn this to be true."

Uritus smiled at her, his grateful surprise plain on his face. He brought his hand to rest against his chest in a wordless gesture of thanks before turning and departing after Perplexus's call. Adi watched him leave and then returned to her seat beneath the tree and picked up her book, trying and then failing to focus on its words. Twenty minutes passed before the princess realized that the fisherman had left without his boots.

Chapter Six

"Temperance and the Lack Thereof, for Better and for Worse"

The 24th of June

Uritus came to the realization that he was still barefoot when his feet left the grass and touched the cool stone that surrounded the palace. He looked down at them and then up at Perplexus who also noted what was missing from his friend's ensemble and raised a playful eyebrow at him, his pipe held in one corner of his smiling mouth. The navigator did not comment on the fisherman's curious lack of footwear but rather informed him that he had missed him at breakfast and that it would be wise for Uritus to eat a bit before the council convened at noon. Uritus took his friend's advice, and would later find his boots waiting for him at the door to his chamber with a familiar book of elvish poetry resting beside them. Uriah found him not long after, and the two made their way to meet with the royal family and the rest of the travelers.

The council was held on a half-moon-shaped veranda on the palace's second floor to the North. It was accessible only via the courtroom, which boasted a pair of tall, noble wooden doors with two wide, curved staircases leading up to it on either side. The palace had no throne room, just the courtroom on the second floor, the grand ballroom below it, and the king's study above, on the third. The courtroom had two sets of windowed doors on each end of the Northern wall that opened to the veranda. The roof of their meeting place was thick with crawling vines and blooming flowers which hung down from its edges, partially enclosing them from the world. Uritus and Uriah found a pair of seats on the veranda's curved edge alongside the other Keepers and their chosen ones, and the royal family sat opposite them, with Pressio Alenvir standing to the right of the princess and Digtrision to the left of the queen. Lining the wall of the palace between the two sets of doors stood a trio of Keepers—a Healer, a Wizard, and a Prophet respectively—who did not speak for the duration of the council but rather stood silently behind the royal family and observed.

King Agamemnon greeted his guests warmly as the midday bells sounded and thanked them again for making their journeys to the capital. He presented Adiadni to the group—donned in a maroon gown and no longer barefoot with Basil's ring again on her left hand, now a perfect fit. He spoke briefly about the purpose of their gathering before requesting that the duos rise and formally introduce themselves. "Before you proceed though…" The king reached a hand into his deep red garment and produced a weathered piece of parchment. "I wish to do a reading of the full prophecy in the translated common tongue. To remind us why we are all here."

The king's guests nodded solemnly and Uritus leaned forward in anticipation. Agamemnon cleared his throat.

A soft breeze made its way across the veranda, tousling the hanging vines and brushing Adiadni's hair behind her shoulders to make her identifier clearly visible. She held her head high as her father spoke, breathing evenly and allowing the words of the prophecy to wash over her. Uritus was right, the Seven Kings wrote assuredly of her victory. She allowed this revelation to fully set itself into her heart, emboldening her. Uritus smiled upon seeing a slight look of assurance in her eyes rather than one of fear.

Uritus reached a hand to his neck and gently touched the shell that hung there, a subconscious action that grounded him and made him feel secure. The heads of those on the veranda bobbed up and down in acknowledgment of the sacred words and Agamemnon gestured for the first of the visitors to make his introduction.

Kensus of Mount Venadalis rose from his seat nearest the queen, a Keeper who wished to be referred to only as such. He was clad in a simple, worn brown robe with nothing upon his bald head. He presented his chosen, Dustafes Elbon, and recounted the circumstances of their first meeting, "My spiritual practice keeps me most often in solitude. The cave within the mount that houses me is simple, modest, and free of distractions. This allows me to best connect to the Source in peace," he began. "But when word reached my ears of the birth of our beloved princess, I, of course, could not pass on the opportunity to seek out the prophesied one. I left my home and traveled North to the Trader's Land which I explored for some time before I found him. Dustafes was four years old at the time, the only child of a pair of humble merchants. Despite his youth, it was clear to me that he was remarkably generous and good-spirited. I journeyed alongside their convoy for a fortnight and then felt within myself a pressing urgency to begin to prepare the boy for his future. I shared my thoughts and intentions with his parents who, after a bit of deliberation, allowed him to return with me to the mount where I have sought to educate him ever since."

Kensus returned to his seat and Dustafes rose beside him, a plain-looking man in simple armor with a small sword hanging from his belt. "I must say how grateful I am to Kensus for finding me and plucking me out of the mediocrity of the trader's life before it became too intrinsic a part of my identity." A few soft chuckles met him in response. "I have had the opportunity to learn much under his guidance, and was able to avoid the same grisly fate met by my parents later that year when they were slain by bandits."

A small gasp escaped the lips of the princess. She briefly met eyes with the fisherman across from her, sorrowful expressions tracing their faces.

"Because of Kensus, I have been blessed with a new chance at life, and I very much look forward to demonstrating what I have learned for all of you over these next few days." Dustafes sat again and Uritus was struck by the brevity of both his and his Keeper's words, by the casual nature with which Dustafes spoke of his family's murder. The fisherman had not yet considered that he would no doubt be expected to touch at least vaguely on his own family history, and he did not anticipate that he would be able to do so with the same relaxed demeanor as the man from Mount Venadalis.

Next rose an elvish woman in a smooth, blue-gray cloak from her seat beside Dustafes, her hair neatly tucked into her hood. "I am Meladashing of the Holy City, Prophet of the Divine," she introduced herself. "And this…" she swept one hand around to gesture to the elvish man dressed all in white who sat beside her, "…is Iladder Qinna, the one we have been waiting for." She paused briefly before proceeding, "Iladder was, like many children, brought to the Temple when his parents recognized his gifts. Our doors are always open to spiritually sensitive young ones and we willingly devote our time as Prophets to training and guiding them on their quest for Divine connection."

Uritus regarded Iladder as his Keeper spoke, intrigued by the stoic nature of the man who sat beside Uriah. Iladder sat upright, completely still, hands on his knees, eyes cast straight ahead of him, never moving, hardly even blinking. Uritus knew that restraint and composure were common traits amongst the Prophets, but try as he might, he could not shake the feeling that Meladashing's chosen was wrestling with something unseen, just beneath the surface.

The Prophet continued, "Nearly ten years had passed since the birth of the Suvah. Iladder would have been just about nine at the time that I had my first and only clear vision about the whereabouts of the Adalos. I did not see much, but strongly felt the warmth and softness of his being, and came away from the vision with a clear image of his eyes, shining the most radiant blue I have ever seen."

Adiadni let out a small breath and looked again to Uritus, whose attention remained fixed on the Prophet.

Meladashing went on, "Night and day, this vision remained in my head, and I began to search the faces and hearts of the children in the temple who were about the right age for signs of the Adalos. I knew that if the Divine had entrusted me with such crucial details, it was my duty to utilize my knowledge for the good of the Free World. Iladder immediately stood out to me. His meekness and willingness to serve others paired with the startling sapphire of his eyes made it clear to me that he is the one we have long awaited. I trust this will soon become clear to you as well."

The Prophet again brought herself to her seat and waited a moment before clearing her throat to urge her chosen to speak. Iladder hesitated and then raised himself to his feet and turned his head to make eye contact with the king, "I owe much to Meladashing and the Prophets who raised me. I humbly come before you now and present my name for your consideration. I thank you for your generosity and your hospitality." Iladder sat again.

There passed a brief moment of silence before Uriah stood and began to speak. Uritus blinked, taken aback again by the unusual nature of the man from the Holy City, but he quickly turned his focus to his teacher as Uriah shared a story with the council not unlike the one he had shared with Uritus that morning in the garden. Bringing himself to his story's end, he turned to look down upon his pupil.

"I have lived in this land for over seven hundred years, since before it was known as the Free World. I have known many people of many vocations, of all ages, races, classes, and creeds. But none since Heimar Vindella have inspired me to become juster, kinder, or more courageous in the same way that Uritus has. He leads with compassion where others are cruel, seeks peace where others would quarrel, and always turns his face toward the sun where others would lose hope." He smiled down at the fisherman. "But I am certain no words that I may have could convince you more of his worthiness for this calling than merely spending an hour in his presence."

Uritus returned his teacher's smile and nodded his thanks. Uriah returned the nod and gestured for Uritus to stand as he brought himself down to his seat. Uritus rose and looked around at the faces that regarded him. "As Uriah said, I am no one of importance," he began, and Uriah chuckled. "I am from a village most of you have never visited and likely never will. I was trained as a fisherman, raised by the greatest people I ever knew…" He paused as he made eye contact with the princess, took a deep breath, and continued, "By the time I was fourteen, I had… lost all of my family. Parents and siblings. Mostly due to the plague."

Adiadni gasped and the mouths of the king and queen opened as they shared a glance. "Plague? In Tosh?" The princess frowned at the fisherman. "When was this?"

Uritus looked from Adiadni to the king and queen and then back, observing the upset expressions they wore. "It took my mother first, when I was seven, over fifteen years ago now."

Tears formed in the princess's eyes. "And you alone remained well?"

"Adiadni…" Betina reached across her husband for her daughter's hand.

"It's all right," Uritus addressed the queen. "I stayed healthy, yes, along with my father and older brother."

Adiadni nodded, met eyes with her mother briefly, and then cleared her throat. "Forgive me, I do not wish to make you relive your tragedy. The plague is just... I did not know."

Uritus nodded. "It passed through the town quickly, only lasting about a year. I would, uh... lose my father and brother on separate occasions a few years later."

The fisherman looked to his feet, shuffling for a moment before looking to Uriah who nodded encouragingly. He straightened himself and again turned his gaze to the royal family, "I do not tell you this to garner your sympathy, nor for any reason other than to paint a clear picture of the boy who stumbled upon a Wizard in the White Mountains. I was no one, I had nothing, save for my horse and my father's dying commission to always keep my eyes fixed on hope. I am still no one, though I have a bit more now, and while I cannot with confidence stand before you and call myself the Adalos..." He moved his eyes from the king to the princess and they locked with hers, "I can promise assuredly that if you choose me to go with you, no harm shall befall you. I would never allow it."

The fisherman and princess lingered for another second in their eye contact before Uritus again brought himself to his seat. Adiadni pressed her fingertips together and gently lowered her head to him as the Wizard to his left stood and began to speak.

"I am Erephus, Wizard of Judii, Keeper of the Free World's tongues, both dead and living." He removed his pointed hat from his head—forest green, like his robe—and swept it across his chest as he bowed gracefully, a greeting not unlike one frequently offered by Uriah. In his right hand he held a long wooden staff with a bronze ornament on top, fashioned to look like the head of a stag, a broad pair of antlers crowning him. "To my left is my chosen, Shrigmut Olar, a man of great strength and greater conscience. I found him in a similar manner to that which my comrade, Uriah, found his own chosen—by happenstance."

Uritus moved his eyes from the Wizard to the man who sat beside him. Shrigmut was tall from the looks of it, and broad-shouldered and barrel-chested. His clothing was slightly worn, he had a heavy broadsword strapped to his waist, and his expression was stony, still. Along his forearms and the right side of his face twisted several deep-set scars.

"Two years ago, I made the short trip to the neighboring city of Lorethh, a visit I make several times a year. Shortly after departing from my home in Judii, I felt struck with a pressing and undeniable sense of urgency. I did not know what for, only that the urgency demanded my attention, and upon arriving in Lorethh, I quickly saw why. A fire had broken out on the outskirts of the city and was rapidly consuming the homes there. I, of course, called upon it to cease, which it did, and while sorting through the aftermath over the next several days, my attention became fixed on Shrigmut. He was always there, clearing rubble, rebuilding homes. From dawn to dusk he worked tirelessly to help those of his community. I inquired about him, naturally curious as to who this selfless stranger may have been, and I learned that he had sustained burns when pulling victims from their homes and yet continued to volunteer in the repair efforts nonetheless.

"At that moment, it became clear to me: this must be the princess's counterpart. I would come to find out he was around the right age and that he had been this way—hardworking and good—since his youth. All who knew him or merely knew of him spoke ceaselessly of his selflessness. Never before have I met someone as willing to sacrifice himself for the good of those around him as Shrigmut is. I have taken it upon myself to educate and train him since then, but there is much which he has also taught me." Concluding his introduction, Erephus sat, and his chosen stood to his feet.

Shrigmut cleared his throat and held his hands behind his back as he spoke, "I am not a man of many words…" his voice was loud though he made no effort to project, "…but I do wish to thank your majesties for welcoming me into your home."

Adiadni shifted uncomfortably under the weight of the hefty title.

Shrigmut looked briefly at the Wizard beside him and then continued, "To be honest… I do not believe I am the one you are searching for. I know nothing of what it is to be a hero, but I do believe that there is more to it than simply wishing for and working toward the good of others. I believe that is something that each of us must do."

He looked to his feet and the princess was struck by how… *sad* he seemed, appearing before her as one so small despite the size of his frame.

He lifted his head. "I am very honored to be here though, and I sincerely hope you find who it is you seek." He sat, casting his eyes down at the floor.

"Surely, most heroes do not immediately believe themselves to be so," Adiadni spoke, and Shrigmut lifted his gaze to meet hers. "But I can tell you certainly, Adalos or not, you come before us today a hero all the same. Thank you for the care you have offered to the Free People. I cannot be everywhere, and knowing that there exist some like you who look after them with the same intention that I do makes the challenge that I will one day face as queen feel far less daunting."

Shrigmut smiled at her and briskly nodded. "Thank you, my lady."

The king and queen shared a proud smile.

The man next to Shrigmut loudly cleared his throat and abruptly stood. Patience did not appear to be one of his treasured values. "I am lord Suprafalo Dagious, and this is my son, Basil Dagious, the princess's betrothed and future king."

Adiadni swallowed and sat up a bit straighter as the younger Dagious brought himself to his feet beside his father. Suprafalo was about six inches shorter than his son and sported heeled shoes with a large brass buckle on each to make up for some of the difference. He wore loose-fitting, cream-colored pantaloons which cinched at his knee, with eggplant-colored tights beneath. A long tunic adorned his top half, dark red and elaborately embroidered with gold thread, with a wide brown belt—also sporting a large brass buckle—slung low across his hips. Draped asymmetrically around his shoulders was a velvet cape, also eggplant in color, and held in place by an eye-catching bronze brooch in the shape of a boar's head. Atop his head of shoulder-length, light brown waves was a hat, wide-brimmed, its brim pinned on one side, a pair of fluffy peacock feathers protruding from the band. And in his right hand, he held a smooth wooden cane with a spherical bronze ornament on top. Basil was clad in the same pale gold armor he had worn every day since his arrival in Suscundos, with a dusty purple cape this time to coordinate with his father. He remained standing as the elder Dagious continued.

"I, as you have certainly observed, am not a Magic Keeper, but rather a humble businessman. I oversee the jewel mines in Vindellaria and Quabish, and am a longstanding friend and ally of king Agamemnon and queen Betina."

Uritus nodded to himself slowly, beginning to better understand how Basil became... *Basil.*

"I come before you today and eagerly present my son for your consideration as the Adalos. I believe him to be someone of great capability, and his established connection to the princess is, in my humble opinion, a striking piece of evidence in his favor, as we know that the Suvah and Adalos are tied to one another."

Adiadni fidgeted with the ring on her hand and forced herself to offer Suprafalo Dagious a small smile as he motioned for his son to take the floor.

"Thank you, Father." Basil gestured with one hand as he spoke, leaving the other to rest on the hilt of his sword, which occasionally caught the light and momentarily blinded those on the veranda for how brightly it gleamed.

Suprafalo nodded at his son and took a seat. Basil looked around at those who surrounded him, "And thank you all, for being so generous as to include me in this deciding process. I, myself, was blessed to solidify my betrothal to my princess on the first night of the festival, and personally feel there is certainly no one better suited to escort her West than I."

He chuckled and his father joined him. Adi shifted nervously in her seat, crossing one leg over the other. She glanced at the faces in front of her, noticing a few of them sharing mildly irritated looks, and swallowed nervously. She blinked several times in an attempt to remain focused, but all the same felt as though a layer of her being was attempting to peel itself up from the rest out of a desire to no longer be there.

At that moment, a small gust of wind floated across the veranda, and it caused something to glint in the corner of Adiadni's eye. She turned her head and found herself looking at the shimmering piece of amonii that rocked gently back and forth in the breeze against the chest of the fisherman. She lifted her eyes to look at his face and he turned and met her gaze. He smiled, nodded to her softly, and took one deep, exaggerated breath to encourage her to find her center. She returned his smile, nodded just a touch, and followed his example, taking several long breaths as she returned her attention to Basil.

"...That said, of course, I will respect the results of the deciding process and will eagerly await my betrothed's return should I not prove to be the chosen one. But I do believe I may yet surprise you." He winked at Adiadni as he returned to his seat and she slowly released a breath she realized she had been holding on to.

Agamemnon rose beside her, opening his arms to the half-circle in front of them. "Thank you all for your thoughtful introductions. We may now proceed to the next phase of our gathering."

He swept his right hand around to the door on that side. It opened, and two palace guards stepped onto the veranda, each holding one end of a smooth, round, white stone pedestal which they placed in the center of the veranda before departing. Pressio moved from where he stood beside the princess and produced from behind him a weathered scroll. He unrolled the piece of parchment with care and placed it atop the pedestal, oriented so that the visitors could see it from where they sat.

He stepped back a few paces as he spoke, "What you see before you is the map drawn up by the Seven Kings which leads to the location of the Sword of Fire beyond the Looming Mountains."

Uritus sat up and leaned slightly forward to get a better look, an action mimicked by those around him.

Pressio continued, "Adiadni has studied this map in depth and knows well the path ordained by the Seven Kings as well as several alternate routes to take in case of hindrances or obstructions. The land was different when the map was drawn up, so, while it is of great importance that the Suvah follow carefully the steps preordained by the Kings, she will also rely on her intuition to do what she deems best for herself and the party that goes with her. Much of the path this side of the Looming Mountains will be easily traversed, but the main path does travel through the Forest of Idor and the Swamp of Sigmount."

Hushed murmurs arose and fell. Uritus chewed on one cheek as he contemplated this. The Forest of Idor was a large wood that stretched for several miles on the other side of the Clearing opposite Suscundos. It was not governed by the Vindellas, but rather a large swath of land that belonged to the fae. He did not know the present state of the treaty between the royal family and the Fae Court but knew it had been, at least for the last hundred and fifty years, that the fae dwelt only in their territory and the Free People left them be.

As for the Swamp of Sigmount, it was a mostly deserted wetland scattered with short, skinny trees. Uritus knew it to be on the far side of the Plentiful Lake, near Condir. It was difficult to navigate, and there were rumors of a strange breed of creatures who dwelt there called *entroleps*. Very little was known about them, but there was a consensus amongst those who believed in their existence that they were not to be considered safe.

"It will be the chief responsibility of the Adalos's party to see to it that the Suvah arrives safely to the Looming Mountains, by whatever means necessary. When the time has come for her to slay Dagamor and leading up to that point, her every word should be considered an order. Once she is victorious and the Looming Mountains are behind you, the burden of leadership will pass to the Adalos, who is the only one capable of bearing the Sword of Fire. You will locate it, retrieve it, and return to Suscundos." Pressio paused to allow the listeners to absorb this information. "Now, what comes after the retrieval remains to be seen. The Kings foresaw the growth of the Shadow in the West and prophesied that the Adalos would banish it, but we still are not certain what that may look like. King Agamemnon's council of Keepers have seen little regarding this, but anticipate that the Shadow will continue to grow in size and potentially make its way East."

Uritus looked from the soldier to the silent row of Keepers along the wall of the palace and back.

Pressio went on, "What we do know is that there is a great likelihood that there remain some Thieves beyond the Looming Mountains. If they wish to lay siege upon the Free World, they have certainly had time enough to build an army. While you are gone, the king, myself, the cropidus, and the rest of the king's armed forces will begin to fortify the city and prepare a defense plan should the time arise when we may need one. The responsibility of the Adalos and the Suvah, both on your journey and once you have returned, will be to inspire the people to action. The Free People have awaited the fulfillment of the prophecy for some time, and we are confident they will rally around you when the hour comes. They will look to you for hope. So, as important as it is that you are physically capable of the task ahead of you, we will also be looking for the one amongst you who is steady of heart."

Uritus nodded pensively as Pressio concluded his speech, retrieved the map from where it lay, and returned to stand beside Adiadni. The journey he felt prepared for, even the weighty task of seeing to the princess's protection he was not daunted by. But a war? One where he would undoubtedly be expected to lead troops… He could not fathom a world in which he felt prepared for this.

Agamemnon thanked his nephew as the palace guards returned to retrieve the pedestal and gestured then to Digtrision who took a few steps forward. "Over the next few days, the prospective heroes will participate in a series of physical trials to assess your readiness for the journey ahead. First will be an archery tournament, followed by a race on horseback, and finally, a swordplay match. Each will be closely monitored to ensure the safety of the participants. We will look for the one who is most accomplished across all skill categories, though the physical trials are not the only basis on which the Adalos will be chosen. Once the physical trials have concluded, each of you will appear before the king's council of Keepers for a Magic-led character assessment."

Uritus looked again to the Healer, Wizard, and Prophet who stood behind the royal family.

"The results of these trials, as well as any other observations made about you over the coming days, will all be taken into consideration in the search for the Adalos. You will have the rest of today and all of tomorrow to prepare yourselves as you will." Digtrision returned to stand beside the queen.

King Agamemnon rose once more from his seat and addressed the travelers, "Thank you, Digtrision. And thank you, again, to each of you for your patience as we undergo this process. We know that we are asking a lot of you. But the search for the Adalos is no small thing, and we hope you may understand our desire to do so thoroughly and efficiently."

Uritus nodded as he made brief eye contact with the king.

"We see much promise in each of you and are quite confident that the Adalos sits amongst us now."

A cool zephyr wafted across the veranda and Adiadni again looked to the fisherman. She wished, as her father did, to be intentional and meticulous in her considerations of which of the men before her may be the Hero they sought. But it was clear to her that she would be lying to herself if she said that she believed it could be anyone but Uritus. She resolved to remain open-minded over the next few days nonetheless.

Agamemnon brought himself to the end of his speech, "I do not wish to take up any more of your time, but I would be remiss if I did not allow the Suvah herself to take the floor before we conclude and depart." He returned to his seat and nodded encouragingly to his daughter.

The princess hesitated a moment before rising. Her father had not informed her that he wished for her to address the council and she had not prepared any words. Even so, she took a deep breath as she rose and let her eyes drift across the faces before her. "I have known myself to be the Suvah my whole life," she began. "I have been educated, trained, and prepared in every way possible to embark on the path that lies ahead of me. But if I am honest... I am afraid still, despite my apparent preparedness."

The king and queen shared a glance, uncertain of their daughter's purpose in sharing this.

"And if I am afraid," Adi went on, "I can only imagine that this is true for you as well, having had far less time to process who you may be than I have."

Uritus nodded to Adiadni as she briefly caught his eye, communicating her correctness and offering his reassurance.

"But as someone wisely encouraged me, we go not toward a potential victory but an assured one. I do not seek a second-in-command amongst you, but a partner, one who will go alongside me on a quest for the continued freedom of my people... *our* people." She allowed the corners of her mouth to lift into a soft smile. "I am certain as my father is that my counterpart is here. I greatly look forward to identifying you as such." The princess looked once more to the fisherman and returned to her seat.

***

Perplexus lounged, carefully carving a small piece of white stone, at the bottom of one of the staircases in the palace's grand foyer, and smiled and rose to his feet upon seeing Uriah and Uritus emerge from the courtroom on the second floor. Uriah informed the two younger men that he had some business to attend to and departed before Perplexus asked his friend if he fancied a walk.

The two made their way out of the palace and began leisurely wandering the streets of Suscundos. The excitement of the Summer was still alive in the city, with children running through the streets and playing games and the sound of laughter and joyous conversation wafting on the wind from the homes and taverns and other establishments they passed. Perplexus purchased a trio of apples from a fruit cart, stowed two in his bag, and retrieved a small knife which he used to peel the third, freeing a single, long strip of skin from the apple's flesh, spiraling as it grew longer. "How did it go?"

"The council?"

Perplexus chuckled.

Uritus thought for a moment. "Well enough, I think. It was mostly an introduction, though they also offered us some more details as to what comes next. Some combative events and a Magical test."

"Do you feel equipped for them?"

Uritus nodded. "I may have my doubts about whether I am fit for the title of Adalos, but I am confident in my abilities as a sportsman. I do suspect, though, that those of us in consideration have been observed since we first entered the city."

Perplexus nodded as well. "Certainly so. The king seeks the one who will go with his daughter on one of the most dangerous journeys the Free World has ever seen. Were they not scrutinizing you at every turn, I'd question if he truly loved her." He finished removing the peel of the apple and dropped it in the street. "Any true competition amongst the others?"

Uritus considered this. "Certainly, there must be at least some of them stronger or more skilled than I. One in particular who could undoubtedly best any of us in a fistfight."

"But any who appears to be the Adalos?"

Uritus hesitated. "It would feel particularly arrogant to say no. But I cannot deny that my confidence in Uriah's assumption has steadily grown since we left home, as has my confidence in myself. I have all of you to thank for that, really."

"Atta boy!" Perplexus cut a slice from the apple which he offered first to his friend, who accepted. "I knew it was only a matter of time before you saw what the rest of us do."

Uritus smiled, still chewing, smile fading as he swallowed. "I do foresee one potential hurdle, however."

Perplexus looked questioningly at his friend, biting into his own piece of fruit.

"Lord Dagious sat in on the council today."

Perplexus snorted. "Keeper or no?"

"None. Just his father."

"Horse shit."

"Lex…"

"I am not wrong." The navigator stopped walking and turned to face the fisherman. "The man is an insolent git!"

"*Lower* your voice."

Perplexus blinked. "Tell me I'm wrong and I'll take it back. But you will not make me respect him."

"I would never dream of it." Uritus took a step closer to his friend, his tone softening. "But I hardly think it is a good look for me, one of the king's candidates, to be heard talking shit about one of my competitors. Especially when that competitor happens to also be the future king."

Perplexus sighed and rolled his eyes but nodded understandingly. "You're right. As usual. The last thing I would wish is to jeopardize your destiny." He lowered his voice to a whisper. "Though I do fucking *hate* that man."

Uritus chuckled at the intensity of his friend's emotion and continued walking.

They moved in silence as Perplexus again cut a slice of the apple, held it out to Uritus, and ate when the fisherman declined. "Well regardless of... *the Obstacle*," Perplexus began, and Uritus chuckled again. "I can say assuredly that I believe in you, Old Boy. Always keeping everyone focused on their course. I would sincerely worry for the safety of the princess and the Free World should anyone other than you be determined to be the Adalos."

Uritus nodded but said nothing and the two friends continued on their walk.

***

Meanwhile, back in the palace, the royal family and their council of Keepers gathered in the king's study. Adiadni paced the perimeter of the room thoughtfully, half listening, half contemplating many things as her parents and their Keepers discussed the events of the gathering. Agamemnon and Betina sat together on a teal settee against the Western wall, across from which stood two plum-colored armchairs. On the wall behind them hung a large mirror with a golden frame which cast the afternoon light across the rest of the room, light reflected from the curved Northern wall of windows and glass doors that opened to a wide balcony. In front of the windowed wall was a sturdy redheart desk that faced the center of the room, with the king's burgundy leather chair sitting behind it and a pair of shorter, brown leather chairs on the opposite side. The Eastern wall—Adi's favorite—was lined to the ceiling with tall bookshelves and featured a moss-colored chaise in the South-and-Eastern corner which sported a soft, sky-blue blanket—Adi's favorite place to do her studies in her childhood so as to be near her father while he worked. The ceiling was ordained with patterned copper tiles, a large, sparkling chandelier suspended in the middle. The design of the room was tied together by several colorful patterned rugs and flourishing potted plants.

Adiadni turned her attention back to the conversation at hand, listening to the observations shared by those gathered. They spoke solely of the five potential heroes, but when they questioned the princess about her own opinions, her mind could light on only one question, "Did you know about the plague?"

Agamemnon and Betina looked at each other. The queen responded, "We did not."

"Do you not find that strange?" Adi questioned. "Is it not our responsibility to know such things?"

102

"You heard Uritus," said the king. "It moved swiftly. Surely, we do not receive word of all that goes on in the land…"

"That feels like a pretty significant thing to miss."

"Adiadni…"

"No." The princess shook her head. "We could have offered aid. Medicine, Healers. We could have done *something.*"

"*You* were but a child," Agamemnon reminded her. "You could not have done anything. Of course, I regret deeply that I could not help. You are correct, that *is* my duty. I wish the people of Tosh had known they could have requested aid, but they did not. We must now be grateful that Uritus was spared."

Adi nodded and the conversation returned to the topic of the travelers. The princess contemplated her father's words. She felt guilty for coming across as accusatory. She knew her father loved his people and would go to any end to care for them. But even so, a fear began to grow in her heart, for if the royal family could not even save the Free People from disease, what chance did they have at protecting them during a war?

"Adiadni?"

The princess's attention snapped back to the ongoing conversation. Her mother had asked her opinion. On what exactly, she did not know. "Hmm?"

"Do you have any thoughts? On the council? The Adalos?"

Adiadni lifted her eyes to the ceiling and her mind drifted again to thoughts of the fisherman—a place it had spent much time that day. She considered whether it would be more helpful to their ultimate cause to share her immediate suspicions about him. Her mother had asked if anyone was standout amongst the visitors and she had a clear answer now, clear enough that she had gone so far as to tell him that morning. But she also wished to have patience, be *certain*, and above all, to refrain from potentially impeding the deciding process due to her own favoritism.

"Love?"

Adi looked again at her mother and shrugged. "There is much to consider." She chewed on her lip contemplatively for a moment. "If I may speak freely though…" Her eyes moved from her mother's to her father's and he gave her a supportive nod. The princess took a breath. "I fear that continuing to entertain lord Dagious in our considerations without a Keeper to back him up may appear…" She trailed off, unsure how to finish her thought.

The king nodded understandingly. "Yes, I have also considered this."

"I certainly do not consider him seriously, though I did hesitate to say so due to the… political nature of the manner. Forgive me for withholding my thoughts," the Wizard who stood opposite the king and queen admitted.

"As did I," seconded the Prophet.

"And I," said the Healer who turned to the princess. "Thank you, Adiadni, for having the courage to say what we did not. The integrity-driven leader in you shines."

Adiadni nodded her thanks.

"Well, we must then consider a way to tell the lord which will lead to minimal… disagreement," the Wizard spoke gingerly.

"It is true," replied the king. "While I am sure that Basil will bow out of the running if I ask it of him, I do not wish to damage my relationship with his father. Suprafalo Dagious has much influence out East and it would be beneficial to have him as an ally with all that is to come over the approaching months."

Adi considered this, fidgeting with the ring on her hand as the others in the room continued conversing. Up to this point, she had personally felt as though she was the one who had much to lose should the situation with her betrothed turn sour. But it was her father and, she realized, the whole of the Free World who would suffer if lord Dagious rescinded his allegiance. There were potential enemies already looming to the West, and Suscundos certainly did not need more in the East as well. It was the responsibility of the Suvah—and the Adalos —to unite the Free People, not to cause division amongst them. This responsibility weighed heavily on her shoulders, and in that moment, she knew what she had to do.

"I will talk with Basil."

The room fell silent and all eyes moved to the princess.

"Are you sure, Love?"

Adiadni nodded. "He may be… hot-headed, but he has also pledged himself to me. He will listen if I am firm. And if I am the one to tell him, it will not reflect poorly on Adda. Even if the Dagiouses take issue with me, it should have no significant bearing on our relationship with them."

Agamemnon and Betina shared a glance. "Very well," said the king, "But it can wait until after the physical trials have concluded. Allowing him to compete may soften the blow. Thank you, my dear. You will be a wise queen."

Adiadni nodded but did not respond and the conversation continued as she again began to pace the room.

Chapter Seven

"The Arrow"

The 26th of June

Uritus spent the rest of that day and the majority of the next in the company of Ilya, Nadarum, and Havian, who were happy to utilize their respective skills to help the fisherman prepare for the upcoming trials. None of them believed he needed much help, as he had spent just shy of ten years devoting himself to the study of the defensive arts. But he was encouraged by their presence, so they offered it to him all the same. The rest of his party took it upon themselves to make sure that he did not forget to eat or rest, though he declined their offerings of various inebriants, feeling that they were more likely to impede his abilities than help him relax. The last thing he needed before so imposing an endeavor was an unfamiliar substance making him feel not quite himself.

The day of the trials arrived in a flash and Uritus rose early in the morning. He assembled with his trio of tutors in the courtyard of one of the city's swordsmanship schools where they offered him any final tips or words of encouragement that they thought may be useful. The noisy bustling of the city could be heard from outside the courtyard as Suscundos's citizens made their way to the arena which had been temporarily constructed in the Clearing. Uritus adjusted to the rising noise level as he fired arrows into targets and practice dummies dispersed throughout the space.

"You're certain the recurve and not the longbow?" He looked to Ilya for her opinion.

She nodded confidently. "I'm not sure exactly how your archery skills will be tested, but I'd wager that your ability to fire quickly will be of utmost importance. I'd be surprised if they didn't include some sort of moving target aspect—as that'll be the most applicable skill for the coveted job—but I cannot guess how they would design that other than by letting a herd of game loose in the arena."

"Rather dastardly of them to send you into a sporting match without telling you a thing about how it will play out," Havian remarked. "Though… a fitting simulation of the journey, I suppose. They could be planning to have you fight to the death in there for all we know."

"I hardly think the king would be stupid enough to risk killing the Adalos before he may even take his journey," Uritus replied, letting loose an arrow that hit its target with a dull thud.

"Perhaps not, but we'll be at the ready to back you up just in case."

Nadarum winked in jest and Ilya and Havian laughed as Uritus struck another bullseye.

***

Elsewhere in the city, Adiadni walked arm-in-arm through the streets with her own trio of companions. The girls laughed and joked as they chatted with one another, all the while speculating as to what the results of the day's trials may be. Adiadni, for the most part, elected to listen to her friends' excited voices rather than offering any opinions of her own, and she was grateful that in their merriment, they did not seem to notice.

That is until Friya decided to ask her directly, "Do you have a frontrunner in mind, Adi?" She tapped her elbow gently to her friend's side. Friya's blonde waves rivaled Adi's in length and caught the morning sun's light, shining as if she wore a halo.

Adi shrugged her shoulders up to her ears and her friends loudly voiced their disappointment.

Jasch pressed her, "Come now, Darling, you can*not* tell me that you've spent days with these men and not a single one has made an impression." She clucked her tongue suspiciously. "If that were true, I'd doubt the Adalos was   truly amongst them."

"He is," Adi countered without thinking. "I just do not think it wise for me to decide without having all the necessary information first."

Jasch shook her head, her fiery mane moving like a waterfall against the soft, sea-green silk of her dress. "I didn't ask you to make a decision. Do you *like* any of them?"

Adiadni hesitated.

"I like the fisherman," Kristefani remarked suddenly from where she stood beside Jasch. Adi bit her lip.

"Oh, Tefi, you *would*," Friya teased. "You do love yourself a quiet, brooding man. Though I'm still partial to his friend."

"The doctor or the swordsman?" Kristefani leaned forward to see Friya's face as she awaited her answer.

"Well, if I had to pick between the two of them, I'd say the swordsman, though I was speaking of the navigator, Perplexus. He showed me his knife," Friya said with a playful grin.

Adi laughed loudly with surprise. "Did he now? When was this?"

"An *actual* knife, Adiadni." Friya shook her head as her friends laughed at her expense. "He carved the handle himself! It was quite impressive."

"I'm sure it was, Fifi," Jasch joked. "But I am glad it was him to whom you were referring because *I* have already laid claim on the swordsman."

"Oh, that's right, you made a *connection* with him the first night of the festival when Fifi and I were still preoccupied with the bird," a coy smile spread across Kristefani's face. "Tell us, Bluejay, did anything ever come of that?"

106

"Oh, Tef. A lady never does." The girls took several moments to laugh before Jasch spoke again, unweaving her arms from her friends', picking up the hem of her skirt in both hands, and turning to walk backward for several paces to look Adi in the face. "But would you look at that? Our fearless leader manages to effortlessly weasel her way out of answering a question yet again." She raised an eyebrow at the princess who recognized that she had been caught.

Adi sighed contemplatively. "If I *must* make a choice now..." she considered her words carefully, gazing at the sky above her, "...then I would say that I see the most promise in Uritus."

Her friends shrieked with excitement.

"I fucking knew it," Friya squealed.

"Sorry, Tefi, looks like you'll need to rescind your claim on the fisherman," Jasch teased, returning to walk between her and Adiadni.

"Oh, that's all right. I *am* quite fond of the physician as well..." Kristefani lifted her eyes dreamily to the sky, her mind wandering to imaginings of the children they would have together, his auburn hair, her deep skin, his way with animals...

Adiadni halted her walk, causing her friends to do the same. "Need I remind you ladies that I am already engaged?"

Jasch chuckled. "And you easily could have told us that you see potential in lord Dagious but... you didn't."

Adi sighed, caught again.

Friya affectionately brought a hand to rest on the princess's shoulder, the sunflower yellow of her sleeve beautifully contrasting the cornflower blue of Adiadni's. "Come, Darling, you know how we live to tease you. Who would the future queen grow to be if not kept humble by her most trusted advisors?"

Kristefani's head bobbed up and down in agreement, her jet-black ringlets exaggerating this. "And we certainly do not mean to speak ill of Basil..."

Jasch snorted. "I did. The man's a brute." Adi clucked her tongue and Jasch shrugged and smiled slyly. "But there's no reason you couldn't take a lover."

"Or multiple!" Friya laughed and Kristefani blushed.

"Exactly!" Jasch went on, "The kings of old did it. I see no reason why our future queen couldn't revive the tradition."

Adiadni shook her head at her friends but smiled as they laughed.

At that moment, a round of excited cheers sounded from the building to their right. The girls shared a curious look before Friya crept toward the pair of wooden doors and leaned down to peek through the space between them.

"What *are* you doing?" Adi looked at the sign above the doors—no words, just the image of a pair of crossed swords.

"Ladies, you are not going to believe our luck!" Friya exclaimed.

"What is it, Fifi?" Kristefani moved to the doors and Jasch followed close behind. Friya took a step back so her friends could press their eyes to the door, each of them gasping as they did.

"What is it then?" Adi remained in the street, arms crossed over one another in mock protest of their delay.

Friya batted her cool blue eyes. "Why, it's your fisherman."

"And Jasch's swordsman," Kristefani added without turning her head. "Looking… rather dashing, I must say."

Jasch nudged her and Kristefani let out a surprised shriek.

"May we help you with something?" a feminine voice questioned loudly from behind the doors, and Adi recognized it as Ilya's. Her friends squealed and retreated from the door, giggling as they held onto each other, their amusement only growing louder when Kristefani tripped on the soft pink hem of her skirt.

Adi rolled her eyes and laughed at them, taking several steps forward to open one of the doors just enough that she could stick her head inside. She spotted Nadarum also in the small courtyard as well as what appeared to be an arrow stuck through an apple protruding from one of the wooden columns on the far side of the space. She hesitated for a moment as she met eyes with the fisherman —whose face broke into a bright smile when he saw her—and then turned her head to address Ilya, "Pardon the interruption, you will have to forgive my friends. They are curious to their own detriment sometimes."

Nadarum and Ilya shared a glance and a chuckle as the titters of the princess's entourage could be heard from behind her. Uritus kept his eyes on Adiadni, his heartbeat picking up speed as she returned hers to him.

Havian also chuckled, nervously looking over his shoulder at the arrow and the apple. "And you'll have to forgive us for *that*, Princess. We were making Uritus show off a bit."

Adi looked again at the apple and nodded, putting the pieces together. "It's hardly a worry. I *am* sorry for the intrusion, though…"

"Not at all, Adiadni," Nadarum sent a crafty look to his wife and she returned it. "I am sure our Adalos wouldn't mind a bit of a respite. And your friends are welcome to sate their curiosity as well."

Adi nodded and fully opened the door, sweeping her hand dramatically toward the courtyard, and her friends entered, single file, still giggling. Friya and Kristefani apologized as they made acquaintance with the archer and horseman. Jasch made her way straight for Havian, who chuckled when he saw her. Adiadni paused in the doorway and then took a few slow steps toward Uritus. He mimicked this action.

"This is a pleasant surprise," he said, looking her up and down. "I don't think I expected to see you till the feast tonight."

Her scent filled his nostrils as they arrived before one another and he noted how the blue of her dress beautifully complimented the deep brown of her hair and eyes. Her curls were tied behind her head, a long tail that moved as she did, with a few soft tendrils framing her delicate face. From the lobe of each ear hung a large, teardrop-shaped pearl, and the circlet on her head featured a similar one that hung against her forehead.

"Would it be too forward of me to say that I missed you yesterday?"

She shook her head fervently. "Certainly not." Her lips and cheeks were an appealing shade of rosy pink and the gentle melody of her voice stirred something within him as she went on, "I did not intend to disturb your practice, though I suppose I would be remiss if I didn't at least try to wish you luck before the events of the day proceed." Adi held her hands behind her, gently swaying back and forth as she looked up into the golden brown eyes of the fisherman.

"So you're saying I'll need luck then?"

The princess giggled. "Not at all! Just..." She lowered her voice a touch and took another step closer to him. "If I offer it to anyone, know that it is you and you alone."

His heart did a flip. A burst of laughter sang from behind him, but neither Uritus nor Adiadni broke their gaze from one another.

"Thank you, that means more than you know." The fisherman brought his right hand to rest against his stomach—his left still holding his bow—and also took a step forward.

She swallowed hard, looking down at his boots and then back up again. He appeared before her the same as he always had and yet... *different* somehow. He was clad as he usually was—in the same brown boots and trousers and billowy white shirt which opened just enough to show off the shell on his neck as well as the bit of skin beneath it; with no sword upon his belt but a half-full quiver of arrows on his back. His hair was tousled, his face clean-shaven, and his smile warm and inviting. And try as she might, the princess could not identify what it was about him in this moment that piqued her curiosity so, though she could feel a warmth rising in her cheeks as she realized now just how close they were standing to one another.

She nodded in acknowledgment of his thanks. "I do mean it."

His smile widened. "I know. I have grown steadily in my self-assurance since arriving in Suscundos and I do not doubt that your encouragement has contributed much to that. If I walk away from this week declared the Adalos, I will be indebted to you."

"Hmm," she considered this. "I am certain you will make it up to me in due time."

"Meaning you will hold me to it?"

She laughed. "Meaning..." Her eyes moved across his face intently, lips slightly parted as she contemplated her answer. "I trust you."

"Hmm." He let out a short, deep chuckle and she felt its vibrations in her chest. "Well then, I swear to you that I will do everything in my power to remain worthy of that trust."

She smiled with a corner of her mouth. "I know."

He looked then from her eyes to her mouth and she let out a soft breath. Before either of them got the chance to speak again, the sound of trumpets met their ears from the Clearing, and Adiadni gasped and leapt a step backward in surprise. The companions in the courtyard turned their faces to the Western sky.

Adi cleared her throat. "Girls, we should... um... probably be going." She looked from her friends to Uritus's. "Thank you again, Nadarum, Ilya, Havian, for your patience and for entertaining me and my friends." They nodded to her and began saying their goodbyes, Jasch and Havian lingering for a moment longer than the rest.

"Is that to say I have not entertained you enough?" teased the fisherman. "My apologies. I will be sure to take lessons in witticism from Perplexus so as not to disappoint you again." He winked.

She giggled nervously. "Not at all." Without thinking she again took a step toward him, reclaiming the ground she had lost in her surprise a moment before, and lowered her voice, "I would tell you to look for me in the stands but... there is no doubt something far more pressing I would have you focus your attention on instead."

He chuckled and then swallowed, admiring the tiny, curious, star-shaped bead of light that adorned each of her irises. "Well... knowing that you are up there will make that focus come far more naturally, I think."

They smiled at each other, lingering where they stood.

"Adi?" Kristefani's gentle voice snapped the princess out of her haze, and she turned quickly to look at her friends where they gathered by the open door. Jasch nodded her head toward the street and Friya lifted both hands to her mouth as a giggle escaped it.

"Right." Adi began to make her way to rejoin her friends, but then paused and turned back to Uritus, pressed her palms together, and bowed her head to them gently, walking backward toward the door. Jasch reclaimed her place on Adi's left arm and the girls departed, dissolving again into giggles before they made it out of earshot.

Uritus kept his eyes fixed on her as she left, his hand still resting against his torso, and only returned his attention from the open door to his friends when Havian loudly cleared his throat. The swordsman, horseman, and archer all gave the fisherman amused looks. He shook his head at them.

Adiadni's friends linked arms with one another and squealed with excitement when they returned to the street. Adi looked to the sky and sighed with exhaustion, but still smiled.

"Goodness, Dear, when I encouraged you to take a lover I meant after your coronation..."

"Jasch!"

"Gracious Mother, the two of you *do* look beautiful together," sighed Friya dreamily from where she stood to Kristefani's right.

Kristefani nodded eagerly. "Any desire I may have personally felt toward the fisherman simply melted away when I saw the way you looked at him."

Adiadni shook her head in protest. "I can assure you ladies that I do not know what you mean." Even as the words left her mouth, they did not feel convincing.

"Whatever you say, *your highness*."

Adi clucked her tongue at Jasch and the girls shrieked with amusement again, continuing to the arena as the horns sounded for a second time.

* * *

Uritus was retrieved by a palace guard not long after his interaction with the princess. He was escorted to a holding area inside the arena where his competitors were already gathered. The room was large, tall, and windowless, with two towering wooden doors on one wall which he guessed opened to the arena. He was impressed by the size of the mostly wooden structure in the Clearing, noting that there were seats enough for several thousand and that, from the sounds of it, all of them seemed to be full. He looked around at the others in the room, noting that all of them had opted to appear in armor of varying degrees of protectiveness, and he briefly wondered if he would regret not doing the same. He had with him only his bow and now-full quiver of arrows, but he reminded himself that the royal family would never intentionally put one of their people in harm's way and allowed himself to relax.

A handful of guards entered the holding area as the third clear round of trumpeting rang out and began moving amongst the competitors and tying different-colored strips of fabric around their non-dominant arms. Uritus looked down at the blue cloth being tightened around his left bicep as Agamemnon could be heard beginning his address. The guards departed as quickly as they came and Uritus looked again at his competition.

They stood several paces away from one another, wearing mostly neutral expressions lined with a bit of nervousness, except for Basil Dagious, who stood, hands on hips, facing the tall doors with his back to the rest of the room. Uritus momentarily wondered if he should attempt to make conversation with any of them. Before he could make a decision, the roars of the spectators sounded and the doors began to swing slowly open.

He took a few steps toward them along with his competitors and lifted his hand to shield his eyes as morning light flooded the room. Basil stepped into the arena before the doors had fully opened, waving one hand at the crowd, the other resting on the hilt of the sword still strapped to his waist. The others followed suit, Dustafes and Iladder stringing their bows as they walked. The ground they traversed was mostly dirt with some grass and shrubbery popping up here and there. Several targets were set up randomly around the space, and a small number of practice dummies, along with a few boulders of varying sizes.

They were met by the enthusiastic cheers of thousands of Suscundos's citizens who excitedly speculated and shared predictions, some of them placing bets on their desired outcomes. Wine and ale flowed freely, and many in the stands snacked on slices of fresh vegetables, spiced or candied nuts, and vibrant-colored squash blossoms stuffed with soft cheese and spices and lightly battered and fried. Vendors moved up and down the stairways peddling refreshments as

111

well as small, rectangular flags which were available for purchase in the same five colors worn by the competitors.

Uritus noticed a few of these waving vigorously as he looked across the stands and was surprised to see several blue ones among them. Word had traveled in the city since the prospective heroes had arrived, and many in Suscundos had already chosen favorites. For the most part, it seemed that the different colors were evenly dispersed among the crowd, though the fisherman noticed that red—the color worn by Basil Dagious—seemed to be the least coveted.

"Welcome, brave competitors!"

They turned to regard the king as he spoke. The queen sat beside him on a platform high in the stands above the doors they had entered through.

"We will soon begin your first trial of the day: the Trial of the Arrow. By now, you have no doubt noticed that you have each been designated a color. This will remain yours for the day, primarily to make each of you identifiable to your spectators, though they serve an additional purpose as well."

Uritus briefly allowed his eyes to drift across the masses in the stands around Agamemnon, feeling a twinge of disappointment when he did not spot Adiadni amongst them.

"This particular trial will assess your proficiency with your bow. You will be judged on your accuracy as well as the speed of your reaction time. Behind you are various targets as well as the natural landscape of the Clearing which may be utilized as you see fit for better viewpoints or cover."

Cover. Uritus and his opponents turned to look at the field that spread out behind them, their anxiety growing at the king's implication that there would be something firing at *them* as well. Basil Dagious again was the sole exception to this, keeping one hand on his sword and the other on his hip as he continued to face the king. Uritus scanned the arena as he returned his eyes to Agamemnon, noting no mounted archers in the stands or apparent windows in the walls where some could be hiding.

"You needn't worry for your safety," the king assured them, "...as we are not pitting you against one another, nor us. But you will be allowed to move freely throughout the field for the duration of the trial, so we implore you to be mindful of your opponents. We also have Healers and physicians at the ready, should any of you sustain injuries during the match."

Uritus began to feel a pressure in his brow and he blinked several times as his vision momentarily blurred and returned to normal, his eyes shifting from brown to blue.

"Now, we will be utilizing the help of some Magic today to simulate enemies." The crowd broke into a cheer and Agamemnon waited for them to settle before continuing, "As you will all be competing at the same time, there will appear colored projections throughout the field to indicate to each of you which targets you are to attempt to strike. Some will be stationary, some will be moving, and all will remain for a duration of three to ten seconds, providing various levels of difficulty. Some also will fire projections at you, but you needn't fear, as these are only projections and will not cause you any real harm. That said, if you are struck by one of them on an area of your body that would ordinarily lead to a critical injury, you will be considered out for the round."

The competitors nodded understandingly as this was explained, relaxing a bit more now that the rules of their match were clear.

"Basil."

"Yes, your highness."

"Would you be so kind as to demonstrate for us?"

Basil gave the king a short nod as he grabbed his longbow from his back, fitted it with an arrow as he turned around and fired into the sky at the red projection that materialized in the field. It appeared as a small cloud of red smoke which disappeared into thin wisps as it was struck, causing the arrow to vanish as it did.

The crowd gasped and cheered delightedly at this. A small smile of amusement crossed the fisherman's face. The setup of this particular match was remarkably different from any training he had done in the past, and he was intrigued by the clever way it had been designed to invoke the feelings of a true battle. He moved his head to stretch his neck one way and then the other and circled his shoulders, allowing his body to loosen up as he noticed he had been unintentionally tensing his muscles in his state of anxiety. He reached up to his neck and tucked the amonii into his shirt so it was out of the way, tightening his shirt's strings to ensure that it stayed there.

"Prepare yourselves," Agamemnon said as the crowd again quieted, "...as the rest of you will now be allowed a single practice shot as well."

Uritus pulled an arrow from his quiver, intently scanning the field for the next projection as he fitted its nock to his bowstring and lifted the weapon to anchor at the corner of his mouth. He flinched, nearly releasing as it appeared, but relaxed when he saw that the Magical cloud was deep purple rather than blue. It was struck a second later by Dustafes's arrow.

The next one, green, was promptly hit by Iladder, and Uritus observed that the man from the Holy City was left-hand dominant, something he had not noticed before. Between each practice shot were a few moments of pause for the competitors as the audience cried out with their approval, and Uritus utilized each of these pauses to take several slow breaths to fully remain present within himself.

The apparition that followed Iladder's was mustard yellow and positioned in front of one of the targets in the field. Two seconds passed after its appearance before it was struck by Shrigmut, swirling on one side where the arrow hit before it disappeared.

Uritus realized that the projections were not without sound, but rather quietly roared like the flame of a small torch while they were visible, and emitted a soft puffing noise like a flame extinguished when met by an arrow.

Not a second after he made this observation, he identified the nearly imperceivable sound on the far side of the arena to his left. He turned immediately and released his arrow, recognizing as it hit his target and vanished that he had only actually seen the projection for a fraction of a second before his arrow left his bow. He let out a breath as the crowd roared around him.

"Let the Trial of the Arrow commence!"

Uritus pushed the enthusiastic sounds of the audience to the back of his mind as he spotted a blue puff of cloud on the far side of the arena. He promptly fired at it. The apparition barely dissipated before another appeared, moving steadily through the sky above him. He tracked it for a moment before sending an arrow up into its path, where the two collided.

His opponents also sprang to action, firing at their respective targets, and the competitors began to move through the field, heads whipping back and forth to not miss any targets. It wasn't long before the projections began to change their forms, with some still appearing as clouds but others morphing to look like charging goblins, soaring birds of prey, or riders on horseback.

Uritus hesitated upon recognizing this change before shooting an arrow through the brow of an advancing projection. Never before had he needed to shoot at something that appeared to be alive. He shook off this sense of discomfort as the first of the projections fired at him.

He dodged to the side, narrowly avoiding the arrow-shaped apparition, and watched it explode in a cloud of blue dust as it hit the ground behind him. He looked back in the direction the shot had come from, releasing an arrow and striking his target before the goblin-shaped projection had the chance to nock another.

Dustafes cried out from a few yards to Uritus's left. The fisherman instinctively turned his head. Bright purple dust covered the upper sleeve worn by the man from Mount Venadalis, and he clutched his hand to his arm though no wound could be seen.

He looked at Uritus, his brow furrowed with surprise, "It burns…"

Uritus snapped back to attention as he heard a rapidly approaching hum. He barely had time to drop to the ground to avoid the Magical projectile before it exploded against the wall of the arena behind him.

The trial raged on, each of the competitors quickly adjusting to their challenges, efficiently utilizing the terrain of the arena for aid, hitting most of their targets dead-on but occasionally just missing.

Basil initially elected not to seek cover at all, relying on his speed to fell his projected enemies before they had the chance to fire at him. But as the challenge continued, the apparitions grew more aggressive, and he was brought to his knees with a loud cry of pain as a cloud of red dust struck his right thigh. He returned to his feet in time to fire at his target before he could be struck again. Limping behind one of the larger boulders in the field, he aggressively swore, realizing that the impressive height of his bow was providing far more difficulty than aid.

Uritus continued making quick work of the targets that swirled around him, noticing that his quiver was now less than half full. His opponents also made an impressive show of their accuracy, causing colorful clouds to burst throughout the arena. There were, however, still some misses, and rather than disappearing upon hitting their marks, the arrows that were under- or over-shot littered the ground, a few protruding from the wood of the arena's walls.

The fisherman shot an arrow into the chest of a projected gryphon that dove for him and gasped as the cloud dissipated, seeing an arrow flying steadily past a moving yellow target and headed straight for the crowd.

His entire body sighed with relief as it struck an invisible shield and slid down to the ground, the faintest blue wave rippling out from the place the arrow hit.

He heard a similarly relieved sound from Shrigmut near him. But Shrigmut's sigh was cut off and drowned in a startling cry of pain as Uritus watched the large man fall to his knees, golden dust now covering the front of his breastplate.

The fisherman snapped to attention, seeing his target appear several feet behind where Shrigmut knelt clutching his chest. Uritus nocked his arrow with impressive speed and fired into the blue cloud ahead of him.

No sooner did his arrow leave his bowstring than another whizzed past his head, narrowly missing his left ear and disappearing into a cloud of red dust a few inches off from a bullseye.

Uritus whipped his head around, feeling irritation and anxiety grow in his body as he met the eyes of Basil Dagious. The man from Vindellaria glowered at the fisherman, an all-too-self-aware smirk on his lips. Uritus felt a chill move through his body, but his mind snapped back to attention as he dodged another incoming projection.

He shot it out of the sky as Basil Dagious cried out. The fisherman looked his way only briefly as his competitor clutched his heart, red dust coating the upper corner of his breastplate.

Uritus returned his focus to the match, noting that neither yellow nor red targets had appeared since his two opponents had last been hit. The remaining contenders made quick work of the apparitions that followed, spending far more time dodging and ducking than firing. Colorful spots were scattered along the field and walls of the arena.

They were running low on arrows. The projections had begun to overlap with one another so if one enemy was not felled quickly enough, another would join them from elsewhere in the arena. This added level of challenge nearly got the best of Iladder when an arrow grazed his left hip, leaving a faint green stripe across his side.

The man from the Holy City did not flinch, but rather swiftly fired at one target and then the other, striking them both dead-on. It was not long after that both Iladder and Dustafes ran out of arrows, their respective colored targets ceasing to appear as they did.

The fisherman artfully dodged a blue arrow as it rushed past, fired by a projected man on horseback who barreled toward him from the far side of the arena. Uritus sprinted to higher ground, ducking to avoid another speedy apparition. He reached for his quiver as he arrived at a large boulder, grasping what he realized to be his final arrow as he leapt atop it.

He touched it to his bowstring, dodging to the right to avoid a third shot. As he brought its feathers to touch his cheek, he realized there was a second projected enemy rushing toward him, this one on foot.

He aimed first at the one on the horse, recalculated, shifted his aim to the left, and released his arrow as the riding projection fired its own at him.

The world around him seemed to grind to a halt as both projectiles soared through the air. The fisherman tracked his arrow with a pounding heart, watched its elegant spiral as it soared, paid no mind to the blue projectile making its way straight for him.

In an instant, the fisherman's shot collided with the first apparition, piercing through it to strike the second as their paths crossed. The projected arrow that rushed toward Uritus vanished into a puff of blue smoke inches in front of his face as his two enemies and his arrow did the same.

The crowd roared their approval and Uritus allowed this sound to again flood into his ears.

Several guards rode onto the field, dismounted, and rushed to the sides of those who had been struck, helping them to their feet and checking to make sure no medical aid was required. The cheers of the spectators raged on, and the guards had the competitors return to the Eastern side of the arena where Agamemnon rose to address them.

"Well done, each of you! I believe I can speak for the whole of the city when I say that you have greatly impressed us!"

The crowd cheered again, and Uritus watched as the same Wizard who had observed the council two days prior appeared on the platform beside the king and handed him a folded piece of paper.

Agamemnon waited for the crowd to quiet before he continued speaking. "Before I announce the winner, I wish to remind you all that these trials are merely a part of our considerations for the Adalos, and that each of you should be greatly proud of yourselves for what you have accomplished. But without further ado…" He unfolded the sheet of paper, pausing as he read its contents. "In the areas of speed, accuracy, and self-preservation, I am pleased to announce that the winner of the Trial of the Arrow is…"

The crowd waited with bated breath. Uritus reached for the amonii and clutched it.

"Uritus Subian of Tosh!"

The fisherman let out a breath and a small laugh. The audience made clear their approval of this victory. As surprised as he was to be named the victor, Uritus felt a surety settle into his stomach. He deserved to be here.

Basil Dagious swore and cast his longbow upon the ground.

Shrigmut gave Uritus a congratulatory clap on the shoulder. "You've done well. Your accomplishment is rightfully celebrated."

The tall wooden doors beneath the king began to swing open.

"Feel free, each of you, to go now and eat, rest, and prepare yourselves as you best see fit. The Trial of the Saddle begins promptly at noon."

The competitors began to make their way to the doors, Basil marching ahead of them, leaving his longbow behind. A guard appeared beside Uritus and raised one of the fisherman's arms in the air to allow the crowd a final moment to cheer for their victor. Uritus scanned the stands a final time.

Suddenly, a loud crackling sounded, accompanied by several bright flashes of blue light. Fireworks. They sparkled just above one section of the crowd, and as they vanished, Uritus saw that they had been set off by Uriah, who sat low in the stands with Perplexus and the rest of their party.

He broke into a smile when he saw them. Perplexus raised a strong, closed fist in the air which Uritus met with his own.

The audience went mad for this. A sea of small blue flags waved vigorously throughout the arena. Uritus smiled as he moved to exit through the doors. He felt an unfamiliar flush of pride, as well as profound satisfaction, but both emotions paled in comparison to the fisherman's quiet joy to have seen Adiadni cheering in the stands where she sat alongside his friends.

Chapter Eight

"The Saddle"

Uritus was presented with his bundle of disappeared arrows upon his return to the holding room. Ilya met him once he arrived outside the arena, caught him up in a warm hug, and gushed about how proud she was of him. The two made their way back into the city to meet up with the rest of their companions for a bite to eat and an hour of rest before beginning to prepare for the second trial of the day. Nadarum had chosen the tavern appropriately named The Horse and Rider as their designated meeting point, not far from the city's Western gate. But Uritus and Ilya found their journey to be surprisingly slow-going despite the short distance they traversed to get there, as every several yards they were stopped by citizens who wished to congratulate the fisherman on his victory and offer him their votes of confidence for the day's remaining trials.

Uritus found himself somewhat overwhelmed by this, by both the constant barrage of flattery and also the strange experience of being known on such a grand scale. He did his best to be gracious and communicate his gratitude to all who took the time to offer him their kind words, but he found himself far more exhausted than he had anticipated by the time they finally arrived at the tavern. He wondered how Adiadni managed to navigate this degree of attention in her daily life and made a mental note to ask her when he got the chance.

The tavern's patrons were also excited at the arrival of the arrow-slinging victor but allowed him the space to relax and dine with his friends all the same. They ate and joked with one another, some of them imbibing freely and others engaging in rousing games of Kepu with the sets of dice won by Punznes, Mikka, and Perplexus since their arrival in the city. Perplexus also took this time to regale the group with a dramatic retelling of Uritus's Kepu victory earlier that week, accompanied by Laivar strumming on his lute to set the mood. Uritus shook his head as his friends loudly sang his praises, laughing at their ever-present enthusiasm. When they finished their meal and the time came for them to depart, the innkeep refused payment, claiming that the opportunity to serve the travelers was payment enough. Uriah made sure to forget a small pouch of coin on their table all the same.

Perplexus caught Uritus by the arm before the fisherman could depart for the stables with Nadarum, rifling through his bag for something he wished to give him. Finally locating it, he took Uritus's hand in his and placed a small piece of stone into his palm. Uritus smiled, bringing the gift up to his face to get a better look at it. It was rectangular, about an inch tall, ivory in color, with a piece of leather cord looped through a tiny golden ring that ran through a small hole at the top of it. Uritus immediately recognized this as a little piece of their home—

rubble from the White Mountains. He ran his thumb the over the delicate scales on the fish that swam across its face.

"A talisman of sorts," Perplexus explained. "I had intended to give it to you upon your official declaration as the Adalos, but I already know you to be him, so I see no reason why it can't begin providing you with a bit of luck now."

Uritus closed his hand around the piece of art. "I wish I had words enough to thank you…"

"Ahh forget that," Perplexus waved his hand in the air. "I make you a little token, you save the whole of the Free World from eternal Shadow. Seems a fair trade to me," he joked, smiling with a corner of his mouth.

"Even so… I am grateful for you, Lex."

"And I for you, Old Boy."

The two friends embraced and Uritus departed with Nadarum, slipping the talisman over his head to rest alongside the shell.

***

The fisherman was filled with joy upon seeing his horse, having had few opportunities to visit him since their arrival in Suscundos, and Moonracer happily whinnied his approval of their reunion. It was clear that the horse had been well taken care of by the stable keepers, having been fed, watered, and groomed in anticipation of the day's event.

Uritus affectionately stroked the shiny black hair on Moonracer's neck and brought his forehead to rest against the star-shaped white patch on his face. "I missed you, Boy. I'm counting on your help for this next trial if you'd be so generous as to offer it to me."

Moonracer whinnied again and moved his head up and down.

"That horse would travel to the moon and back for you," spoke Nadarum. "Surely, you know this."

"Of course," Uritus replied, running a hand down the length of Moonracer's face. "But I like to ask him anyway."

"Is that the same reason you never summon that dragon of yours?" Nadarum moved around the large stall that housed the horse, readying Uritus's saddle and tack.

The fisherman shrugged as he moved to pick up a horse brush. "Milion doesn't belong to me. Neither does Moonracer, for that matter. They offer me their aid out of the goodness of their hearts. I feel it would be exceedingly self-centered of me to think myself entitled to their service."

Nadarum chuckled with an approving nod of his head. "That is but one reason you will make an honorable leader one day. And already are, in the eyes of our family."

Uritus nodded his thanks, running the brush along Moonracer's body with short, swift motions.

119

"No doubt the reason why they offer their assistance so willingly to you as well," the horseman remarked, pausing for a moment. "Have you ever ridden Milion?"

Uritus hesitated, lifting his head as a handful of men entered the stables via the door opposite the one adjacent to Moonracer's stall.

Nadarum lowered his voice, "Uriah encouraged you not to speak of him?"

The fisherman also nodded, returning to brushing his horse. "To answer your question though, a few times, yes, when I was a teenager. Uriah told me it was useful to complete the bonding process. To build trust between us. I haven't summoned him many times since sending him away to find a home, just on occasion. I check in with him when I can, to make sure he's still doing all right."

"How's that?"

Uritus paused as he considered this. "I… go into myself." He let out a slight laugh. "Close my eyes, think of him. If he's open to being perceived I… feel what he feels."

"Well, I'll be damned."

Uritus smiled.

"And what does he feel?"

"Hmm." The fisherman raised his eyes to the wooden slats of the roof. "Serene, mostly. Fervent joy when he flies. If I happen to tap into him when he's above the clouds, my eyes change."

"What a thrilling life he leads!" Nadarum let out a hearty laugh. "Have you any idea if he checks in on you?"

Uritus frowned thoughtfully. "You know, I've never considered that. Though, if I had to guess, I'd say the matters that concern him are far more noble than my own."

"You speak too humbly of yourself, my friend. Have you already forgotten who you are?"

Uritus chuckled. "I have not."

"Well, I have. Who are you then?"

Uritus laughed louder at this prompt and turned to face Nadarum, bringing his left hand behind his back and his right, still holding the brush, against his heart. "I am Uritus Subian of Tosh," he declared proudly.

Nadarum nodded and gestured with one hand to encourage him to continue. "And you are…"

Uritus smirked and rolled his eyes before returning to his formal upright posture. "And I am the Adalos."

Moonracer whinnied approvingly and Nadarum laughed, the deep, rich sound warming Uritus from the inside. "That you are."

A distressed neighing sounded from the other side of the stable. Nadarum and Uritus turned to see a horse rearing in the center aisle, its lead rope held in the hand of a very anxious man whom they quickly identified as Dustafes. Nadarum looked to Uritus and Uritus nodded, encouraging the horseman to offer his aid. The fisherman moved to Moonracer's other side to continue brushing him as Nadarum exited the stall and asked Dustafes if he would like any assistance. Uritus heard Dustafes accept the offer, then Nadarum's suggestion that he drop the rope and step back a few paces. A few seconds later, the neighing quieted down.

"He has quite a way with them."

Uritus felt a wave of goosebumps travel across his body. He quickly looked around Moonracer at the one whose tonic voice always captivated him. A surprised smile moved across his face. "It's you!"

The princess laughed rapturously and Uritus felt its every peal in his own throat. "It *is* me!" She stepped into the stall curiously. "This is your horse?"

The fisherman nodded. "Have you one of your own?"

She nodded too. "I call her Swadalla. She's smaller than this one, and brown. She's not here today, but she resides in this stable usually. When I was little, I'd climb up to sit in the rafters of the cupola to read. She was a bit nervous when she was younger, and I think it comforted her to have me nearby."

He smiled at this.

"You impressed me today."

The fisherman felt warmth grow in his cheeks. "I'm pleased to have pleased you. Performing for your benefit was the only thing on my mind."

She laughed. "I mean it though. Two targets with one arrow! I don't think I realized it was possible."

He smiled and shrugged dismissively. "Neither did I. Just figured it was worth a shot." He raised his arms up as though he was drawing his bow.

Adi laughed again and the two stood in silence for a moment, the brush against Moonracer's coat and the breeze through the rafters adding to the peaceful atmosphere.

The princess took a step closer to the tall black horse in front of her, hands held behind her back. "Is this the one who will race the moon?"

Uritus's face took on a surprised expression as he tilted his head to one side. "However did you know about that?"

She smiled. "Uriah told me. A long time ago." She took another step forward and brought her hand to rest on Moonracer's star. With one finger, she gently traced its pointed edges as she went on, "He visited Suscundos last for my thirteenth birthday. It was recently confirmed to me by my father that the milestone in my life was only part of why he had come here. The primary reason was to tell my father about you."

Uritus looked at her curiously, returning to brush Moonracer's left side.

"He had just found you… or rather, as he tells it, *you* had just found *him*."

Uritus smiled. The Wizard's way of storytelling made the fisherman sound like the legendary hero of a folk tale. Hearing the story repeated now by someone who first heard it long ago compounded his strange sense of separation from the version of himself that everyone else in his life seemed to see so clearly.

"I, of course, did not know this at the time," Adiadni went on. "But I recalled yesterday that Uriah *did* grace me with a tale of a boy he'd recently met, of how he came to the White Mountains in search of his future and how Uriah believed he could help him... *you* find it. He spoke of both of you," she addressed the fisherman and the horse. "And..." she hesitated, "...of a young dragon."

Uritus looked over his shoulder. Nadarum conversed still with Dustafes, a few others meandering through the stable.

Adi watched him, nodding slowly. "Ah, well, our friend does have a love of a good story."

"That he does..." Uritus lowered his voice and took a step closer to Adiadni, "...but all the best stories grow from a seed of truth."

Satisfied with this answer, she nodded again, smiling understandingly and turning to address Moonracer. "You really are quite beautiful."

Moonracer whickered happily and moved his head up and down in agreement. The princess and fisherman laughed together.

"But to think..." Adi turned again to face Uritus, "I've known about you all this time."

Uritus chuckled, dropping to one knee to brush Moonracer's leg. "Perhaps that is the explanation as to your effortless comfortability with me."

"Perhaps... And what of yours with me? Unless you would tell me that you do not feel that way..."

He chuckled again, rising to his feet. "I would never say that."

Moonracer whinnied again as the two smiled at each other, dipped his head, and moved it quickly to the left, forcing Adi several steps closer to the fisherman. She stopped when she bumped gently against his chest and laughed, turned, and planted a kiss on the horse's cheek as he again lifted his head. She took a step back as she turned again to face Uritus.

His eyes traced the features of her face, noting the thickness and curl of her long, dark lashes. "To answer your question though," he began, "I would say it is your intentionality that initially drew me to you. You listen to people. And creatures. See them as they wish to be seen. You remember things."

She nodded and then shrugged. "I think everyone deserves to be recognized."

"I know," he replied, "I love that about you."

Adiadni blushed and let her eyes fall to her feet.

The fisherman spoke again, his voice low, "I also like how you managed to find a way to subtly show your favoritism in today's proceedings." He took hold of her right wrist with his left hand, raising her arm so the cornflower tail of her sleeve fluttered in the breeze, the strip of blue fabric around his own arm doing the same.

She giggled, feeling a wave of tingles move up her arm, across her scalp, and down her spine. "A coincidence, albeit a convenient one." He smiled, releasing her arm, and she lowered it slowly. "On the note of wardrobe though..." She took a step toward him and traced her finger along the piece of stone that lay against his chest, its lower half falling beside the top of the amonii. "This is new. It's lovely."

Uritus smiled, looking down at her sweet face, his lungs filling with juniper and rosewater as she admired the little piece of art. "Lex's handiwork. His own embodied vote of confidence in me."

She smiled, still looking at it. "That's thoughtful of him. You have delightful friends."

"As do you. I appreciate the way you've fallen into step with mine. None of them have anything but positive things to say about you."

"Hmm," Adi sighed contentedly. "They're an easy bunch to fall into step with. And..." she lowered her voice a touch, "...it seems wise of me to spend time getting to know those who will go West with me."

Uritus smiled softly, feeling a rush move through his body.

Adiadni looked over her shoulder suddenly as a round of loud voices were heard entering the stable. "I suppose I've held you up for long enough."

"Adiadni, your presence does nothing if not energize me."

The princess felt heat in her chest. She swallowed hard as she looked up into the eyes of the fisherman. "As does yours to me."

They shared a brief smile. Adi turned to Moonracer to offer him a farewell pat and a few words of affirmation, the horse nickering and scraping one hoof against the dirt to communicate his readiness. She laughed at him and turned once more to the fisherman. "Well... for now." She pressed her palms together and bowed her head to him.

He repeated this action. "Till we meet again."

They lingered in their eye contact for a final moment before she vanished in a wave of blue fabric and Nadarum returned to help Uritus saddle his horse. The fisherman moved through the stall pensively, the image of the princess still fresh in his mind until the sound of trumpets shook him from his daydream and reminded him to remain focused.

Adiadni clutched one hand to her stomach as she departed in an attempt to still its fluttering. It was becoming clear that perhaps her friends were more accurate with their observations that morning than she had previously been willing to admit.

***

The second trial of the day was organized to take place in the strip of land between Suscundos's inner and outer walls. Uritus and the other competitors gathered at the Eastern gate when summoned for the race. The onlookers assembled atop the walls, their cheers intermingling with the roar of Tuvibati Falls just outside the city. The visitors and their horses stood in a row facing

North, and the king and queen sat again on an elevated platform atop the inner wall, just above its gate.

Agamemnon stood and raised a hand to quiet the excited crowd as the third round of trumpeting ceased. "Welcome, all, to the second trial of the day: the Trial of the Saddle. This trial will assess your skill on horseback, both your speed and your ability to navigate the terrain."

Uritus turned to look over the landscape that stretched in front of them, noting some boulders and shrubbery not unlike in the arena, as well as a few constructed wooden obstacles. He blinked against the headache that grew behind his eyes as he returned his attention to the king.

"Your goal is to travel one full lap around the city swiftly and efficiently. The first to return here to the Eastern gate will be crowned the victor. The track is just over three miles long. Be mindful of the needs of your horse and of any other obstacles that may appear along the way. Prepare yourselves…"

Each competitor brought his focus from the king to the track, gripped tighter his reins, and leaned forward and down just slightly.

Uritus reached a hand to stroke the side of Moonracer's neck. "This is all you, Boy," he whispered. Moonracer neighed, a low sound to indicate that he understood.

"Let the Trial of the Saddle begin!"

A loud horn sounded as a palace guard waved a large black flag. The racers sprang to life as the roars of the spectators met those of the falls. Basil immediately took the lead, his strong horse barreling straight ahead with Dustafes close behind. Iladder moved to ride along the length of the inner wall. Shrigmut traveled a bit slower, paying close attention to the terrain in front of him and carefully guiding his horse through the smoothest path.

Moonracer broke into a gallop before Uritus could prompt him to. The fisherman let him keep pace with the two frontrunners for a while before pulling on his reins to slow him a bit. His horse was incredibly fast and agile, and while Uritus knew that Moonracer was more than capable of winning an ordinary race, he felt something in his gut prompt him to slow down and be mindful, the king's vague warning of additional obstacles still humming in his ears.

It was not long after the race began that he observed, several yards ahead, colorful flashes of cloud appear in front of his competitors, red and then purple apparitions that forced the riders to divert course. A green one materialized just above Iladder, prompting him to duck; seconds later, a blue cloud on the ground in front of Moonracer. The horse cleared it with ease.

Uritus kept him moving at a steady canter, his eyes darting around the terrain ahead of them, their color matching the obstacles that periodically took shape in their path. The other competitors followed suit, maintaining the speed they had initially set out with, distance gradually growing between the front two and the rest.

The first mile or so passed quickly, uneventfully, the volume of the crowd seeming to increase as that of the falls faded behind the racers. As they rounded the Northernmost edge of the city, Basil and Dustafes's horses began to grow fatigued. Dustafes let up on his speed a bit. Basil did not, instead continuing to kick his horse's sides, urging him forward, leaping over nearly every bit of uneven terrain that he came upon. He remained in the lead, though the other four steadily gained on him as they kept pace with one another. Iladder's strategy of hugging the inner wall proved the most efficient, and it was not long before he found himself on the heels of the frontrunner. Dozens of green and red flags waved frantically in the hands of the spectators as it seemed that Basil would finally be overtaken.

Suddenly, as they rode past the Western gate, a colorful wall of cloud appeared, blocking the whole of the track and forcing the racers to come to an abrupt halt.

Basil—either out of a desire to reign victorious or simply due to being the closest to the new obstacle and having the least time to react—elected to ignore it, plowing straight through the apparition and leaving wisps of cloud swirling in his wake. The wall vanished and the others rode on again almost as quickly as they had stopped.

But Uritus hesitated, hearing a horse's distressed shriek and the gasps of the observers. He looked to his left just in time to see Iladder's horse rear, casting her rider to the ground.

Uritus leapt from Moonracer's back and rushed to Iladder's side. He held his hands out to the horse, still visibly spooked by the sudden appearance of the wall, and she calmed almost instantly. The fisherman dropped to his knees when he reached Iladder's side.

"Are you hurt?"

Iladder groaned and Uritus gently reached a hand behind his opponent's head, feeling for blood and finding none.

"Can you stand?"

Iladder grunted uncertainly as the creaking of the Western gate met the concerned muttering of the crowd.

"Can you try?"

Uritus held out a hand and Iladder grasped his arm and the fisherman helped the injured man to his feet.

"Are you all right?"

Iladder shook his head. "I'll be fine. But what are you doing? You'll finish dead last at this rate."

Three soldiers appeared on horseback, leading a physician and a Healer to Iladder's side.

"You're far more important, Mate."

"Even so, I'd much rather see you first cross that finish line than that bastard. I'd hate for you to lose because of me."

"Hey, who knows?" Uritus hurried back to Moonracer and leapt into the saddle. "This old boy may yet surprise you."

Moonracer reared excitedly with a loud whinny and took off.

Uritus let his horse gallop ahead at full speed. He kept his head and body low to Moonracer's back, feeling the wind rip through his hair as they flew. Moonracer expertly navigated the terrain, jumping and dodging his obstacles with ease.

A sea of blue flags rose atop the walls, creating a wave-like effect as the horse and rider barreled by. Moonracer's hooves pounded the earth with thunderous force. Uritus felt their vibrations in his chest where they met the steady beating of his heart. It was not long before the tails of their competitors appeared ahead.

The three racers traveled at a steady canter, keeping pace with one another, Basil still ahead by a nose. Just off in the distance, the Eastern gate appeared.

"Come on, Boy. Just like the fields around Tosh. We're nearly there."

Moonracer picked up speed. He and Uritus overtook their competition with a furious gust of wind, taking a note from Iladder and moving along the inner wall.

Basil swore and angrily kicked his horse's sides, forcing him back into a strained gallop.

Uritus kept his head down, moving away from the wall as a blue cloud appeared in their path. Behind him, he heard the labored breathing of Basil's horse on Moonracer's heels.

He did not turn his head. The Eastern gate grew steadily nearer. Despite Basil's persistent urging, his horse began to lose speed.

"No! Fuck! We're nearly there, you stupid animal!" A red cloud materialized as Basil was overtaken by Dustafes and Shrigmut, and he cursed violently as his horse brought himself to a full stop.

At that moment, Uritus looked to the inner wall, seeing the waving of the black flag and a multitude of blue ones as he passed the Eastern gate.

Basil's cries of anger were drowned out by the joyous cheers of the crowd.

Uritus slowed Moonracer to a halt as his eyes drifted over the masses on the walls, quickly spotting his party along with the princess and her friends atop the inner. He raised a fist as Perplexus did the same and the crowd went wild.

"Well done, Chap."

Uritus turned to see Shrigmut smiling as he dismounted.

"With a horseman as skilled as your friend in your corner, I'm not surprised things turned out this way," Dustafes said. "Congratulations. That's a fine horse you've got there."

Uritus laughed. "That he is!"

Moonracer whinnied happily and reared as the king declared the victor to be Uritus Subian of Tosh. Suscundos's citizens cried out their approval.

Basil cursed as he dismounted and marched through the gate's opening doors, leaving his horse still panting on the track. Uritus collected the tired beast's reins along with Moonracer's. His eyes lifted once more to the masses as he departed and their fluttering blue flags greeted him in return.

Chapter Nine

"The Blade"

Uritus reclined in the grass beneath a tree after the race and began to feel a soreness creeping through his muscles. His party gathered around him, drinking and snacking and smoking in the afternoon sun—minus Nadarum, who had volunteered to groom Moonracer so the fisherman could have a few moments of rest. Uritus had been disappointed to find that Adiadni and her trio of companions had parted ways with his group by the time he reunited with them, but the rounds of excited congratulations that followed—as well as the assurance that he would see her again that evening—quickly drove the thought from his mind.

He regarded the dancing leaves in the boughs above him, his left arm cradling the back of his head and his right holding a wooden cup, resting on his stomach. The merry voices of his companions and the melodies of Laivar's lute filled the air, and every few minutes, soft cheers sounded from the passersby in the street. They waved their blue flags upon spotting the victor and called to him words of encouragement for the final trial of the day. One Healer stopped for a moment, bringing herself down to sit in the grass beside the fisherman where they conversed for a brief time. She gifted him a small pouch of herbs as she departed, informing him that they would help his growing aches and dwindling energy. He thanked her, and Punznes steeped the herbs to make a tea which Uritus sipped on as the physician who leaned against the trunk of the tree beside him periodically plucked large grapes from their stems and popped them into his friend's mouth. Uritus was not particularly hungry and did not wish to become too full and sluggish before the sword match, but the physician insisted that he consume something small anyway to keep his energy up and counter any feelings of jitteriness potentially caused by the tea.

The beverage was warm, floral in both its fragrance and flavor, and mildly bitter, and it caused Uritus's tongue to tingle lightly as he sipped on it. He considered the generosity of the Healer, the gracious affirmations freely given by the citizens of Suscundos, the hospitality he and his party had been offered at every turn since arriving here. The warmth of this place was tangible, its goodwill palpable, and every glimpse of kindness offered from one to another made his heart thrum with a profound peace that was uniquely different from the one he found alone back home in the mountains. The culture here, the overarching sense of community, seemed to be a world away from the more reserved natures of the peoples of Tosh and the White Mountains, yet Uritus never felt anything but wholeheartedly loved by Suscundos's people. He closed his eyes and breathed in deep the perfume of flowers and fruit and baked bread that swirled around him and sent up a silent prayer of thanks to the Divine for having made it here, a childhood dream fulfilled somehow tenfold.

Opening his eyes, Uritus found himself looking up at Uriah now above him. The two shared a smile.

"Will you come with me, my boy, before you depart to prepare with Havian? I have something I wish to give you."

The fisherman nodded, finished his tea, and handed his cup to Punznes as he rose, the physician offering him the remaining grapes in return. Uritus bid his party farewell and they sent up cries and whoops of encouragement as he departed with the Wizard.

Uritus was surprised when Uriah led him through the palace and into the fisherman's own room. He paused upon walking through the door, a smile creeping across his face as his eyes lit on Uriah's gift.

In the center of the room, near the dressing screen, stood a mannequin adorned with several beautiful pieces of leather armor. The torso pieces caught his eye first—the glossy dark brown breastplate and backplate appearing sturdy but still flexible. The suit was complete with a pair of gauntlets, chausses to protect his legs, and a pair of sturdy leather boots to match. Attached to the pauldrons was a wool cape in a stunning shade of blue.

Uritus approached the gift open-mouthed and ran a hand along the smooth breastplate. "It's beautiful."

"Zaphron sent it," replied the Wizard. "It arrived yesterday. She had hoped to complete it before we departed, but also wished to spend the care and attention on it that would be deserving of the Adalos."

Uritus's eyes continued roving across the mannequin, dazzled by the detail of his friend's craftsmanship. "You'll have to send her my thanks. And to you as well." He turned to face his teacher, "I wouldn't be here without you. For that, I owe you the world."

"Ah, my boy. You deserve all this and more."

Uritus chuckled at the similarity of the Wizard's words to those of the Voice. He crossed the room to embrace his friend and Uriah encouraged him to try the armor on.

He employed the Wizard's help to fasten the bronze buckles, and then turned to regard himself in the looking glass against the wall. He noted he was about an inch and a half taller in the durable pair of boots. He found the armor to be heavy and tough though not at all restrictive.

"How's it fitting?"

Uritus nodded confidently. "Quite well. There's somehow even space for these." He hooked his finger beneath the two leather cords around his neck and pulled on them to reveal their ornaments.

"I may have enchanted it to be sure that was the case," Uriah winked. "And to give you a bit of a protective edge."

Uritus glimpsed the Wizard in the looking glass and saw that his eyes grew misty.

"I am rather proud of you, my boy."

Uritus turned to face him, placed his hands on his hips, and raised his chin in an exaggerated heroic posture. "Well, I swear that I will do all I can to net a final victory so that your pride is not misplaced."

Uriah chuckled and took a step closer to the fisherman, placing a gentle hand on his shoulder. "There is nothing you could do to convince me that my pride is misplaced. And trust me, my boy, today's next victory will be far from your final one."

***

Havian did not take it easy on Uritus during their sparring. He made sure to come at him with every quick trick and bit of impressive footwork he had up his sleeve. The swordsman was thirteen years Uritus's senior, and they had been sparring together for the last eight since the swordsman had found a home in the keep. He had gotten on well with both Uritus and Perplexus from their first meeting. He would grow to consider the boys to be akin to younger brothers or rambunctious nephews, and for that, he made an excellent swordplay tutor as they grew into adulthood. The competitive nature with which he laced all their lessons lit a fire within each of the students that drove them to seek improvement with their blades and ultimately led to their becoming incredibly proficient with them; though, of course, still not quite so as their teacher.

That playful game of fight continued into their young adulthood, and even now, with Uritus readying himself to face his greatest swordplay feat thus far, Havian persisted with his exaggerated antagonism. This was an unorthodox though efficient way to make sure that the fisherman remained light, both on his feet as well as in his mind, seeing to it that he stayed sharp, quick, and well aware of his surroundings. It took Uritus a bit of time to adjust to combating in such different garb than he was used to, but by the time the trumpets sounded and a guard arrived in the courtyard to lead him to the stadium, he had found his place in his suit of armor and managed to best Havian in their last three matches. The swordsman declared with pride that Uritus was ready, and the fisherman gave him his thanks as he departed, identifying that the effects of the tea were becoming recognizable in his body.

His muscles still ached, he observed upon entering the holding area, but his joints felt open and loose. He was alert though not at all jittery, and his vision remained clear save for a brief moment when it blurred and then returned to normal. He moved his head from side to side and raised his arms to stretch his shoulders as his eyes drifted across his opponents.

They appeared in the same armor that they had for the prior trials, Dustafes and Shrigmut both bearing shields in addition to their swords. None of them wore capes except for Basil Dagious, as Uritus had elected to leave his behind with Havian. As with the earlier trials, the competitors were in the dark as to the nature of the challenge they waited to undertake, but it seemed likely that this would be the one that would have them face one another directly.

Uritus looked briefly at the man who stood as he had that morning, hands on hips, directly facing the pair of tall double doors. He did not think there was a world in which the future king actually wished to do anyone harm, but he felt a pit grow in his stomach as he considered that if there was anyone amongst them who might elicit such a desire, it was the fisherman himself. The doors began to open before he had a moment to process this thought.

***

Adiadni moved through the crowded stands, her friends in tow, a string of clasped hands following close behind her. No seats remained as far as they could see, and Adi rejected Jasch's suggestion that she exercise her authority and have a few of the spectators make room for their princess and her consorts. Her father rose from where he sat on his platform and began to speak, and before Adi could tell her friends that they'd be resigned to watching while standing in one of the arena's walkways, a familiar voice called out her name from a few rows down. She turned her head, eagerly scanning the crowd for its owner, and smiled broadly when she saw him.

"Lex!"

The navigator chuckled as he reached her side. "That name sounds good in your mouth, Princess."

She shook her head at him playfully. "I think we're close enough for nicknames by now, yes?"

He nodded affirmatively.

"Then, as your princess, I forbid you from calling me that as though it is my name. Adi will do just fine."

A smile tugged at the corner of his mouth. "Well then... *Adi...*"

She returned his smile.

"We have space for you. All of you. It'll be tight, so some of us may need to get a little... *comfortable...* with one another." He leaned around the princess to offer a sly smile to the row of girls who stood behind her.

Friya blushed furiously as Jasch dragged her away with Kristefani when she spotted Havian next to Uriah's pointed hat.

"That's kind of you," Adi thanked him as they turned to descend the steps.

"Think nothing of it. It's been a joy to have the lot of you join us today. The expressiveness of your friends in particular is..." He thought for a moment and chuckled. "Riveting."

She laughed understandingly. "Well, as I was telling Uritus earlier, your group is far and away one of the easiest to get along with that I've had the pleasure of getting to know..."

"You saw him today?"

Adiadni paused her walk. "I did..."

A knowing look moved across the navigator's face. "When was this?"

She bit her lip and then continued walking. "This morning, by accident... due to my friends', um, *riveting expressiveness...*"

Perplexus laughed.

"...And I may have made an intentional trip to the stables before the race to..." she trailed off.

"Wish him luck?"

She shrugged. "Something like that. Though he doesn't seem to need it."

"Certainly not." They came to a stop in front of their row and Perplexus caught Adi's arm before she could make her way to her seat. "Well, this will be less of a surprise than I had hoped it would be then..." He searched for a moment through his bag before finding what he sought and holding it out to her with an open palm.

She let out a small gasp upon seeing it: a small white stone talisman, not unlike the one the fisherman wore, hanging on a leather cord and featuring the image of a bird in flight.

"Uritus's symbolic figure was far easier to discern than your own, but I did have a dream a few nights ago which led to my choosing this one. May I?"

She nodded and he lifted it over her head so the ornament came to rest against her chest. She held it between two fingers, admiring it. "It's lovely. Thank you."

"You're quite welcome." The navigator moved a pair of fingers beneath the princess's chin and lifted her head to meet his eyes. "I believe in you just as I do in him."

She smiled up at him and opened her mouth to speak, but at that moment, the king concluded his speech, and the cheers of the crowd rang out in the arena as the doors began to open. The two hurried down their row to their seats, where Adi promptly moved Friya out of her own and plopped her into the navigator's lap to *make space*.

They did not remain seated for long, however, as the entire crowd excitedly brought themselves to their feet to catch a glimpse of the competitors, cheering and waving their flags. The warm afternoon sun lit each of the prospective heroes as they exited the holding area, all but Iladder waving to the onlookers.

Adiadni let out a small breath upon seeing Uritus—one that did not go unnoticed by her friends, who shared glances as her eyes remained fixed on the fisherman.

He appeared... taller, and slightly larger in the smooth brown armor that plated his body. He held a single hand confidently out to the crowd in greeting, his other resting on his sword.

When his eyes lit on his party, first Uriah, and then Perplexus and Adiadni, his open hand clenched into a strong fist, and the crowd went mad in response. The smattering of blue flags that dotted the stands that morning had grown into a thick ocean of blue, punctuated by a few pockets of differing colors as the citizens of Suscundos steadily grew in their confidence in their favorite. As the hours and events of the day passed, it was becoming clear to everyone: there was a Hero in their midst.

The spectators silenced and returned to their seats as Agamemnon held out a hand to them. "Welcome, brave competitors," his steady voice boomed, "...to your final trial of the day: the Trial of the Blade. Before we begin, I wish to thank each of you for the work you have put in today. The search for the Adalos is no small feat, and your gracious cooperation has allowed us to grow ever closer to identifying him. Now, as you may have discerned, this final trial will be a tournament-style assessment of your proficiency with your swords—your defensive and offensive capabilities, your footwork, and your ability to best another in close combat. This will, of course, not be a trial to the death. Rather, to become victorious, you must get your opponent defenseless, disarmed, and on the ground. Now, as we have an uneven number of competitors—"

"Pardon me, your highness."

The crowd murmured curiously as Iladder stepped out of the line.

"Yes, Iladder?"

"I wish to withdraw my name from the running."

The murmurs grew louder. Uritus furrowed his brow in surprise. It seemed strange to wait until now to make such an announcement.

Agamemnon held out a hand to quiet the intrigued audience. "I see. Do you feel endangered by the events as they will proceed?"

"I do not. But if I may speak my truth, I am not the one you seek. I am certain of it. I have seen it."

The murmurs grew again.

Agamemnon nodded pensively. "What have you to say of your Keeper's dream?" he finally asked. "Of her assurance that it is you we seek?"

"I believe her dream was true," Iladder replied. "But I also believe that she and the other Prophets were misguided in presuming me to be its subject."

The king folded his hands together contemplatively. "You, of course, are welcome to step away from this trial if you choose…" He hesitated. "But I wish for you to be most certain that your decision is not being driven by fear."

Iladder shook his head confidently. "I am not, your highness. I remain grateful to you and to Meladashing for your dedication to your search. As it is, I do believe the Adalos is here. I believe him to be right beside me." Iladder turned to his left and raised his sword-bearing hand to point to the fisherman, whose mouth opened in surprise.

The chattering of the audience rose again. Adiadni and Perplexus looked at one another, expressions of excited shock tracing their faces.

Uritus looked from Iladder to the audience, now suffocatingly aware that their eyes fixed solely on him. This concentrated attention caused his heart to race. The young Prophet spoke with unshakable confidence. The path that lay ahead was becoming increasingly harder to ignore.

Iladder looked again to the king, "This man does not seek recognition for his good deeds. Though not all would have witnessed it, he nearly abandoned today's race to see to it that I was well when I was thrown from my horse in her surprise. As far as my Keeper's vision goes, Uritus is a holder of viraglas. It can be seen in his eyes as we speak."

The volume of the crowd rose again and Agamemnon once more raised a hand to quiet them. He looked briefly from Iladder to Uritus and then back, giving a singular nod. "Very well. We will take your words into consideration and free you from the burden of such. Thank you for your candor. May you find a steady path as you make your way home."

"Thank you, your highness."

The wooden doors began to open and Iladder looked once more to Uritus as he sheathed his sword. The fisherman moved his right hand across his chest, tipping his head in thanks. Iladder nodded to him and turned, leaving the arena behind.

Agamemnon moved his eyes across the remaining competitors. "Does anyone else wish to bow out?"

They shook their heads. The doors creaked as they shut.

"Very well," said the king. "We shall prepare for our first round: Uritus versus Shrigmut."

The crowd roared. A pair of guards appeared to lead Basil and Dustafes up a narrow flight of steps to await the second round. Another moved between Uritus and Shrigmut, aligning them to face off and then stepping back to await the tournament's start. The opponents drew their swords.

"For what it's worth…" Shrigmut spoke in a low voice, "I am rooting for you as well. But don't think that means I plan to take it easy on you."

"Hah," Uritus chuckled. "As you shouldn't. I love a good challenge."

The two shared a smile. Agamemnon raised a hand above his head. "Let the Trial of the Blade begin!"

He let his hand fall as a horn sounded and the crowd roared, waving their flags and shouting encouragingly to their picks. Uritus and Shrigmut both began to turn, still facing one another, in a clockwise circle. Uritus moved his sword in front of himself with a flourish that roused his fans.

"You're going to have to come at me, Chap," Shrigmut informed him. "I'm not a fan of charging, myself."

"Nor am I," countered the fisherman.

"Count of three then?"

Uritus nodded.

"All right then… One…" Shrigmut lowered his head to bring it closer to his shield.

"Two…"

"Three!"

Both men sprang forward, swords colliding with a loud crash.

Uritus was driven back almost immediately as Shrigmut parried and shoved him.

The fisherman swung his sword low. His opponent was surprisingly quick, knocking it away with his shield and taking a broad swing that forced Uritus back several paces.

The heaviness of the larger man's sword made Uritus's feel almost flimsy in his hand. He relied on his ability to duck and dodge rather than parrying as Shrigmut continued forward with aggressive swings. He had a far reach due to his long arms, and Uritus considered how he might get in closer to disarm him. He discerned before long that his opponent's exaggerated swings left him vulnerable to attack as he recalibrated.

Uritus waited a moment before rushing in to Shrigmut's left side. But before the flat of his blade could make contact with armor, Shrigmut's shield came rushing toward his face, making contact with his nose and driving him back. Adiadni gasped and clutched her friends' hands.

It was a gentle tap relative to the feat of strength Shrigmut was surely capable of. Uritus lifted his fingers to his nose, feeling no blood.

"You all right?"

Uritus nodded, springing back as Shrigmut swung once more.

The fisherman took a quick breath and rushed forward, sliding across the dirt on one hip to avoid the next swing. He came to a stop behind Shrigmut and swung his sword low as he sprang to his feet.

Shrigmut stuck out his shield and successfully blocked the blow. Uritus was swift to grip the edge of the shield as it came his way.

In one brisk motion, he rotated it, forcing Shrigmut's arm behind his back. The large man cried out in pain and released his sword from his hand. He dropped to his knees and Uritus released the shield, causing him to tumble forward.

The crowd went wild. Uritus heard the voice of the king proclaim him to be the winner as he crouched down to help his opponent to his feet.

"I didn't hurt you too bad, did I?"

Shrigmut chuckled and released the fisherman's hand, finding his feet beneath him. "Seems an even trade-off to me. Well done."

A pair of guards and a physician appeared beside them, questioning the contenders to ensure that they didn't require any aid. One guard took Uritus's arm and raised it in the air.

Thousands of approving cries and vigorously waving blue flags arose in response. The two men were led up into the stands as Basil and Dustafes took their places for the tournament's second round.

Arriving at his place, Uritus's ear caught the sounds of his party's voices. He turned his head, waving to them when he spotted them a few rows up. He smiled to himself as he turned his attention back to the arena's floor, pleased to again see Adiadni again at home amongst his family.

The horn sounded as Agamemnon announced the beginning of the second round.

Both competitors sprang to action. Their blades crashed against one another loudly, repeatedly, sending streaks of reflected sunlight across the arena's floor and walls. The two were of similar height and build, and neither appeared to immediately have the upper hand. Basil was incredibly skilled with his longsword, and his many years of training under expert tutors was apparent. But Dustafes's efficient use of both sword and shield kept the two on an even playing field for some time.

Neither hesitated to swing upon spotting an open window, and both were quick to block or sidestep when the need arose. Flags waved frantically in the stands, the purple only slightly outnumbering the red.

Before long, Basil discerned that his opponent's shield was a clear nuisance. When Dustafes thrust it toward him in an offensive motion, Basil grabbed hold of the shield with both hands, tucked its edge into the crook of one elbow, and rotated his body, yanking it away with force.

Dustafes cried out as his shoulder seared with pain and released its grip.

Basil tossed the shield behind him and promptly swung his sword at his opponent. Dustafes, in his disorientation, stumbled back to escape Basil's long blade. But as it soared toward him again, Dustafes's heel caught on a rock, and he was sent tumbling to the earth.

Basil approached Dustafes where he lay and pointed his blade directly at his opponent's throat. He brought a foot down upon Dustafes's wrist, causing him to cry out again and release his sword from his hand. The horn sounded to announce the conclusion of the round, Basil declared the victor.

The crowd applauded, a sound notably less joyous than that made upon the first round's victory. Uritus closed his eyes against the dull ache in his head. *One more round...*

A guard led Dustafes up into the stands and called to Uritus to follow him down. The fisherman looked over his shoulder as he departed, taking in the encouraging expressions of his party and locking eyes with Adiadni. The princess smiled and casually lifted one arm above her head as though she was stretching, allowing her sleeve to drift in the breeze. He returned this smile, nodding his understanding of her sneaky show of favoritism, and descended the steps to begin the tournament's final match.

Basil paced a short course back and forth as he waited for the fisherman to arrive. He shook his head curtly when asked if he would care for a short respite before the final round commenced. Uritus drew his sword.

There passed then a brief eternity, both contenders in battle-ready positions, eyes fixed on one another. The twisted smirk Uritus recognized from the first trial of the day grew on Basil's face. The fisherman took a slow breath, tuning out the cheers of the excited onlookers and focusing on the steady beating of his heart.

The horn sounded, freeing them to begin their duel. Both leapt forward immediately. Their swords collided, remaining firmly pressed until the competitors shoved each other away.

Basil took a series of aggressive swings, forcing Uritus back as he parried.

The fisherman was quick on the defensive. He recognized before long that his opponent relied heavily on his speedy attacks, far favoring them over defending.

He bided his time, bringing his sword up to block one swing and leaning back to avoid another. In the second before Basil could recalculate and launch another attack, Uritus charged, ducked his head low, and grabbed him by the waist.

Basil was forced back several steps by the impact of Uritus's shoulder slamming into his body. He righted himself before the fisherman's attempt could send him to the ground. He moved to the side, forcing Uritus to release and find his feet.

The audience roared at this bout of action. The competitors again brought their swords to clash, holding them in a fight of strength. Several seconds passed with neither swordsman budging. Basil brought his fist between the crossed blades and punched Uritus square in the face.

The crowd gasped as the fisherman stumbled back. Adiadni clutched one hand to the piece of white stone hanging from her neck and the other to Perplexus's arm.

Uritus spat, tasting blood. His head ached and he heard his blood rush through his ears as Basil chuckled menacingly. The fisherman shook his head, again bringing his sword to position, moving sideways in a slow circle. His opponent did the same.

"You're more than welcome to bow out, *fisherman*, if the pain is too much to bear," taunted the man from Vindellaria.

Uritus laughed. "I'm just fine, but I thank you for your concern nonetheless."

Something about the fisherman's casual laugh and words of gratitude infuriated Basil. He allowed this fury to overtake him, rushing at Uritus and swinging his longsword with force.

Uritus parried.

Basil attacked.

And the fisherman once again found himself in a mostly defensive dance, taking occasional swings at his opponent but primarily blocking and ducking. Basil was quick to attack, but Uritus was just as quick to defend, and in the ever-increasing frustration of the more aggressive of the two, Uritus recognized this to be Basil's primary weakness.

Their swords collided and pressed against one another once more. Basil quickly grew agitated and shoved his opponent away. Uritus found his feet beneath him and raised his sword, ready to counter an attack.

Basil positioned his blade at his hip and charged. The fisherman sidestepped, forcing Basil to run past him, and then brought his foot down upon the crimson edge of his cape. Basil was yanked back, promptly crashing to the ground. Bewildered, he held his sword up, swinging blindly to block an attack that did not come.

Uritus waited until the end of one of these defensive attempts to send his blade colliding into Basil's, forcing it from its owner's hands. He moved his blade briefly to Basil's chest and just as quickly sheathed it and the horn sounded a final time.

The crowd went mad. Uritus offered Basil a hand, met with only a hot glare as his opponent brought himself to his feet. The guards and physician arrived. Basil shoved past them, making his way to the arena's doors, his sword still lying in the dirt several feet away.

"And the winner of our final trial is, once again, Uritus Subian of Tosh!"

Uritus raised his fist unprompted this time. The onlookers cried out their approval and praise as the thick sea of blue flags drowned out all other colors

The fisherman brought his hand to his chest, his emotion spilling over into his eyes. He looked to the sky, overwhelmed by his gratitude, "Thank you for getting me here."

The warm Voice that greeted him in return soothed his aching body.

"I never doubted you for a moment."

***

Uritus stood with Perplexus by his side in front of Moonracer's stall. The rest of their party—and much of the city—had departed to prepare for the celebratory feast that would take place in the palace's grand ballroom. But before washing up or doing anything else, Uritus wished to offer his thanks to his horse, without whom he would never have reigned victorious.

"I hoped I would find you here."

Both men turned as Moonracer whinnied a greeting to the princess, beautifully backlit in the stable's doorway.

She rushed forward and flung her arms around the fisherman's neck. "I am so proud of you!"

Uritus returned her embrace, holding her gently, closing his eyes, trying not to drown in her sweet fragrance. He waited to pull back until she did first, but their arms remained around one another even as she did. Perplexus grinned as he watched them.

"I couldn't have won without you," Uritus finally said, his eyes intently tracing the features of her face. He turned to look at Perplexus, "Or you."

Moonracer whinnied loudly and the trio of friends laughed.

"And certainly not without you, Boy."

Adi reached out a hand to scratch the horse's chin and kissed him on the nose when he extended his face to her. She looked back to Uritus, a concerned expression tracing her face. Her hand raised to rest beside the cut on his lip, the sole injury he had sustained that day. "Does this hurt terribly?"

He shook his head. "I was given an elixir for the swelling and the pain. It's but a scratch, really."

She nodded but left her hand still for a moment on his face, her thumb just beneath his lower lip.

"Hey!"

The harsh cry cut through the peace of the stable. The princess and fisherman stepped apart from one another immediately upon seeing Basil enter the stable from the far door.

"You get away from her!"

Perplexus stepped forward, fists clenched.

Uritus set a hand on his shoulder, "We don't need a fight, Lex. But we may need help."

The two shared a brief moment of eye contact and then Perplexus nodded, turned on his heel, and exited the stable.

Uritus turned back to Basil and moved toward him, hands up to indicate that he wished for peace. But Basil did not stop and instead leaned down and rushed forward, grabbing Uritus by the waist and shoving him with force against Moonracer's stall.

Moonracer reared, shrieking loudly.

Adiadni screamed.

The two men scuffled in the dirt of the center aisle. Uritus did his best to restrain Basil but received a quick knee in his stomach. He felt the air knocked out of his lungs and then found himself on his back before he had a moment to react.

"Basil!" Adi's terrified voice ripped through the stable.

Basil's gauntleted hand came crashing into Uritus's nose. Adiadni rushed forward in desperation, taking Basil's right arm in her hands and pulling against him with all her might. He shook her off, causing her to tumble backward, and moved both hands to grip the fisherman's throat.

Adi scrambled to her feet, looking to the stable's doors for a sign of Perplexus or anyone else, hearing voices approach quickly but not quickly enough. She turned back to Basil, screamed his name. He ignored her.

Her heart pounded in her head as she looked at Uritus's face, gasping and turning red. She wasn't strong enough to help him, but she knew if she didn't intervene, he would certainly die at the hand of her betrothed. She felt every ounce of fear and anger she held within her body bubble up in her chest, and as the pressure became too great to bear, she opened her throat and screamed.

"Stop!"

Her voice reverberated through the air, causing the birds in the trees outside the stable to take flight. An invisible force crashed into Basil's chest, driving him back and sending him colliding into the door of the stall across from Moonracer's.

Perplexus arrived then at the stable door, followed by Pressio and a pair of guards. The navigator dropped to his knees at his friend's side, questioning him to make sure he was all right as Uritus gasped for air. The pair of guards dragged Basil to his feet.

"What in Shadow is going on?" Pressio cried, looking first to Basil, then to Uritus where he lay, then to Adiadni.

Tears pooled in the princess's eyes, and though she tried, she could not bring herself to form words. She nodded her head instead toward Basil to indicate to her cousin that he was the one at fault. Pressio turned to face him.

"Couldn't take a loss with grace, I see. Gents, see lord Dagious to his room please."

Basil breathed heavily, one hand clutching his sternum, and attempted to straighten himself. "I can assure you, that won't be necessary."

Pressio chuckled and shook his head, hands resting on his hips. "Oh, I can assure you that it is."

"Come on now…" Basil struggled as the guards moved to each take one of his arms. "This is ridiculous!" He looked frantically to Adiadni, "Tell them this is all just a big misunderstanding."

Adi said nothing, turning her head to look away.

Pressio nodded to the guards and they moved to lead Basil, still struggling, out of the stable. Perplexus helped Uritus to his feet and Pressio moved to his side to check in with him and see if a Healer was needed. Uritus held a piece of cloth to his nose to stop its bleeding as a ring of bruises began to form around his neck.

Basil jerked sideways once more, turning his head and making eye contact with the fisherman, "You will not take her away from me!"

The harsh rasp of his voice sent a chill up Adi's spine as the guards dragged him away. She shook it off and hurried to Uritus's side once her betrothed was out of sight.

"Fuck, you're hurt." She lifted her hand to hover above a cut on his cheek and then quickly dropped it. "Shit. This is my fault." She took a couple of steps back. "I'm sorry."

"Adiadni—" The fisherman moved forward to assure her that she had done no wrong, but she stepped away from him.

"I'm so sorry."

She hurried to the stable's doors and vanished through them, tears spilling onto her cheeks. She hastened to the palace and locked herself away in her room. Though she did ultimately decide to join her parents at their table for the feast, she did not seek out the fisherman for the remainder of the night.

Chapter Ten

"The Burden of Truth"

Uritus's wounds were seen to by a Healer who gave him an elixir for his swelling and his pain as well as to stop his bleeding, though little could be done to eliminate the growing bruises on his face and neck. He washed up and donned himself again in his armor at Uriah's suggestion, this time with the blue cape on his back.

The Wizard was caught up on the incident in the stable and he regarded Uritus compassionately and informed him that if he needed to sit out the feast and rest instead, he was more than welcome to. Uritus was firm in his resolve to attend at least for a bit, thinking his presence as the day's victor was important for the people's sake. Uriah and Perplexus chuckled at this, remarking on how fully and willingly Uritus seemed to be stepping into his role as the Adalos. Uritus reminded them that there was still one final trial to be completed before that was sure. Uriah and Perplexus reminded him that they were sure all the same.

Pressio sought out the king and queen immediately upon leaving the stable to inform them what had happened. Queen Betina hurried then to her daughter's room, taking her up in her arms as the princess sobbed and questioning her to make sure she was not hurt. She asked little about the altercation, seeing that her daughter was fragile and not wishing to press on her wound. Adiadni insisted that she was fine, feeling better after allowing her body and brain to regulate themselves. She assured her mother that she was well enough to attend the feast and quickly washed up and made her way down to the ballroom.

At the same time, Agamemnon made his way to Uritus's room, finding him there with his friend and his Keeper.

"I wish to apologize," spoke the king, pulling the door closed. "I make no excuse for lord Dagious's actions, and I am deeply remorseful that such an occurrence has soured an otherwise spectacular day. I beg your forgiveness."

Uritus nodded graciously. "It is yours."

"Are you hurt?"

The fisherman shook his head. "Not seriously. The injuries I sustained should have no bearing on whether I am able to complete the duties required of me on the journey."

Perplexus snuck a glance at Uriah.

"I am glad to hear it. You must know that I take such crimes very seriously, and I vow to seek justice on your behalf. Such a thing will not stand as long as I watch over the Free World."

"I thank you." Uritus deliberated a moment before going on, "I… don't know what exactly you were told about the incident in the stable…"

"Only that Basil attacked you and that my daughter witnessed it happen."

"How is she?"

The Wizard and navigator met eyes again.

The king responded, "Adiadni is naturally shaken up, but she is also resilient. I am sure it will do her good to hear that you are well."

Uritus nodded, relieved.

"But of the incident?"

He hesitated again. "I only mean to say that, while I had no inappropriate intention when I returned Adiadni's congratulatory embrace, I can understand how, to a man as passionate as Basil, it may have appeared questionable nonetheless. While I cannot relate to the instinct to react violently to a perceived wrongdoing, I also do not feel that it is my right to claim that his instincts are baser than my own."

Agamemnon considered this thoughtfully. "There is a certain protocol to resolving issues of this nature…"

"I understand. You must do what you deem fair."

"It is typical for the political head of a given region to serve as judge when the wronged bring their case before the court."

Uritus grew immediately anxious as he tried to imagine settling this dispute on a grand stage before Suscundos's people.

"He is owed justice."

The king nodded to the navigator, "Unquestionably. The hearing will need to be scheduled but it should proceed swiftly. With a witness to corroborate Uritus's version of events, the scale is already tipped in his favor."

"That is not what I would wish."

Perplexus frowned. "Do you not think he deserves to face consequences for how he has caused you harm?"

Uritus considered again what it would mean to take action in this way. Were he to go to trial, win, and see Basil's judgment played out in full, it still would not feel right to disrupt the search in this way, especially since choosing this path would bring a great deal of further stress upon Adiadni.

"I do not think it is my place to say." He turned from his friend to the king, "I know that there are predetermined ways to go about these things, but if I am honest, I have no desire to participate. I trust your judgment as guardian and believe that you will arrive at an appropriate conclusion, but I do not wish to be a part of it."

Agamemnon appeared hesitant. "Are you certain?"

Uritus nodded confidently. "There are greater things at stake than the bruises that bloom on my skin."

The king was impressed by this. He lowered his head humbly. "Very well. I will see to it that this matter is settled with efficacy and discretion. I thank you for your time." He made his way for the door and then briefly turned back when he reached it, "You should also know that I have confined the lords Dagious to their rooms for the remainder of the evening. Should you choose to attend the feast, rest assured that they will not serve as a nuisance."

Uritus touched a hand to his chest. "Thank you. I look forward to it."

Agamemnon nodded, satisfied, and made his departure.

Perplexus turned immediately to Uritus when the latch of the door clicked back into place, "Are you mad?"

The fisherman and Wizard shared a laugh.

"You would deny the most powerful hand in the Free World the opportunity to serve your aggressor his due? The man has made it abundantly clear that he wants you dead!"

"And if time should prove me to be the Adalos, he will surely only be one of many," Uritus spoke calmly. "Basil does not frighten me."

Uriah nodded approvingly. "The tempest on our horizon will necessitate a wise and collected captain to see us through. Our Adalos proves himself so at every opportunity."

Perplexus nodded and shrugged. "You aren't wrong about that." His eyes traced the purple ring around his friend's collar and his heart blazed with anger. "But if that fish-lipped, beslubbering imbecile looks at you with even a glint of malice in his eye ever again, I'll cut off his hands, stuff one up each end, and toss him in the river to meet his fate on the rocks below."

"See, Lex," Uritus brought his hand up to grip the navigator's shoulder. "I have you. What could I possibly have to be afraid of?"

***

The rest of the family noticed the marks on Uritus's beaten body immediately upon his arrival in the ballroom. They quickly roused, demanding to know who had caused their youngest family member harm so they could seek him out. Uritus calmed them, backed by Uriah and Perplexus as well as the king's promise that the Dagiouses would be dealt with in due time. As for tonight, he told them, they should make merry that their collective efforts netted him three wins that day, and they happily agreed to this as their mugs were filled with ale.

Uritus didn't spend much time at all with his friends that night, bombarded at every turn by strangers who wished him their warm congratulations, some of whom still had little blue flags tucked into their waistbands or shirt pockets. The fashionable bits of fabric appeared to be popular amongst the children of the city in particular, a trend that Fennispar enthusiastically insisted he had started by himself that morning. Shrigmut, Iladder, and Dustafes also found Uritus and praised him for his well-fought day. Uritus moved throughout the ballroom repeating his thanks for as long as he could. Still, he retired to his chamber earlier than he would have liked due to his exhaustion and a bit of dizziness from the ale and elixirs he had consumed that day.

Adiadni also spent little time with her friends, keeping herself chained to the elevated head table in her seat to the right of her father's. The three colorful elvish women gathered at her side for a time, excitedly chattering about the results of the trials, but they soon noticed that the princess's spirits seemed to be down. She shared with them a brief overview of the afternoon's events, telling them firmly that they could not share this with anyone. They swore that they wouldn't and tried in vain to tempt her to the dance floor or at least to share a drink with them. Eventually, they left, as she made it clear that she was tired and not particularly in the mood for a party.

She toyed with her hands and absentmindedly gazed over the crowd, fearing the moment that she would be approached again. But much to her surprise, that moment never came, as everyone's attention was instead fixed on their victor. Adiadni looked at him, noting how he smiled broadly and captivated each individual he spoke to with his humility and his charm. She wished more than anything to be by his side, celebrating his victory along with him, but feared that her closeness to him could be easily misread—or perhaps accurately determined —to be inappropriate now that her betrothal had become an engagement. She felt a sting in her chest as she watched him depart from the ballroom, soft blue cape moving like a wave against his back.

***

The next morning, the princess paced back and forth in front of her father's desk. Her parents stood off to the side, arms around each other as they worriedly regarded their daughter. Both the younger Dagious and his father would be shortly appearing before the royal family to discuss Basil's assault on Uritus and hear the king's verdict.

Adi anxiously tugged on her lower lip with her thumb as she walked. Betina had asked her to confirm that this had not been the first time this week that Basil had threatened one of their visitors, and she had nodded and recalled the story of the happenings at The Gilded Rose.

"Does he seem to have a problem with Uritus specifically?" asked the king.

Adiadni shrugged. "I think… it was many factors. We know Basil to be… easily agitated. I believe he has felt increasingly more possessive, or… *protective* of me since he proposed. I also know he hates to lose, and two Kepu losses followed by three defeats yesterday…" she trailed off.

Agamemnon nodded slowly. "And you say… that Uritus attempted to defend himself but did not do any real harm to Basil, is that correct?"

Adi nodded.

"I see." The king and queen shared a glance and Agamemnon returned his gaze to his daughter, "Now, Basil did sustain a single large bruise on the center of his torso. And when Pressio shared with us his version of events, he said by the time he arrived, Basil and Uritus lay on opposite sides of the aisle…"

Adiadni paused her walk. She wondered if her father was accusing her of not being truthful. She lowered her hand from her face to cross both arms over her chest and lifted her head to meet his eyes, "In my fear, I... called to Basil to stop. And as I did... something cast him back, away from Uritus."

Agamemnon and Betina again turned to look at one another. "Something?" questioned the queen.

Adi nodded, unsure how to fully explain what it was. "It came from... within *me*, I think."

"I see." The king moved his head up and down slowly. Long had he and Betina awaited this day. "Adiadni, we have known you to be in tune with the Divine for some time..."

She nodded again. "I know."

Neither Agamemnon nor his wife had any experience with this way of being, so they were often at a loss when trying to discuss with their daughter the significance of her position. "I am sure I do not need to tell you to be mindful that it does not cause anyone harm..."

The princess nodded once more. "I know."

Silence took the room as each member of the royal family quietly contemplated what should be done next.

Finally, Adiadni spoke, "I have not brought myself to say this before... but I do believe Uritus to be the Adalos. I believe it with my whole heart."

Betina looked to her husband and then to her daughter, "Have you felt this for long?"

Adi shrugged. "I have felt it for some time, though I perhaps did not identify it. And I know there remains one test still to be seen, but I am confident in my belief even so. I feel safe with him. I always have."

"We have also seen promise in him," replied the king, "...especially after all we witnessed yesterday."

"I do wish you had told us this sooner, Love..."

Adiadni nodded, somewhat regretful. "I do too." She straightened herself. "But I am telling you now. I am fully confident that the results of today's Magical trial will prove me to be correct. And so as it is... the facts are that Basil assaulted the Adalos. Regardless of our family's connection to his... I do not think it wise to continue to entertain him as our guest at this time."

Her parents nodded in agreement and then looked at one another, silently communicating. They knew the pressure of her unique identity and feared that the princess was in danger of losing herself in her pursuit to be a worthy leader.

Betina turned again to her daughter, "Love, I hope you know that if you do not wish to go through with your engagement, you do not have to. Your father and I will support you no matter what."

Adi took in a quick breath and lifted her eyes to the ceiling. She did not wish to marry Basil, that was made clear to her this week and reaffirmed at every turn. But she remembered the conversation they had had when last the three of them had gathered here, about the potential risk of severing their connection with the Dagious house. A myriad of potential futures swirled through her mind and she nearly became dizzy considering what might be best for herself, for her family, for her people, for… Uritus.

"Love?"

Adiadni looked once more to her mother and shook her head. "I do not believe that would be best. I just wish for this all to end as quickly as it can. And I wish to cause as little upset as possible."

The king and queen again shared a glance, uncertain looks tracing their faces, and then Agamemnon nodded firmly. "Very well. We will call for Basil and Suprafalo and get this matter over with."

Adiadni folded her hands together as they turned to face the doors. Eventually, they opened, and through them marched Adi's intended and his father, escorted by a pair of guards who remained on either side of the study's large doorway. Basil and Suprafalo came to a stop in the middle of the room. The doors shut behind them. Both men tipped their heads to the royal family.

Agamemnon gave them a sharp nod. "It is the wish of all parties involved in this incident that a judgment be reached as swiftly and peaceably as possible. Uritus Subian has elected not to take part in determining a verdict and I have promised him that I will do what I must as his guardian to protect him."

Adiadni looked briefly at her father. She hadn't realized that he had spoken to the fisherman.

The king went on, "Suprafalo, I have known you for some time and I hope to know you for much more, but your son has caused harm to one of my guests, and that is something I cannot overlook." He turned to Basil, "Have you anything to say for yourself?"

Basil stood tall, his hands held behind his back. "I wish to apologize, king Agamemnon, for having disgraced your house. I happened upon your daughter —my betrothed—in the stable with the fisherman, and I became concerned, for I saw him hold her against himself. His friend did nothing to stop it."

"It was *I* who greeted *him* with an embrace," said Adiadni, and all eyes in the room turned to her. "*I* sought *him* out to congratulate him for his victory, something I would have done for any of you had the trials concluded differently. Something you would have known had you bothered to stop for a moment before charging at him."

Basil nodded slowly. "Perhaps you are right, my dear. My passion is my greatest strength, but alas, also my greatest weakness."

A shocked laugh escaped the mouth of the princess, an exaggerated snort that caused Basil to furrow his brow. She made eye contact with her father and said nothing, instead crossing her arms tightly over her chest again.

"But it remains so…" Basil went on, "…that such actions are deeply inappropriate when committed by one who is tied to another. I find such behavior rather detestable."

Adiadni felt her ears grow hot in her anger. The words that bubbled up inside her chest demanded to be heard.

"So detestable that it is worth spilling blood?" She looked at Basil, fire in her eyes, and he did not respond. She took a step forward. "I hardly consider your blatant lack of self-control to be a *strength*. You arrived here, to our search for the Adalos—a sacred task the line of Vindella has awaited for centuries—with no Keeper to vouch for you, not a hint of gentleness nor humility in your heart, and you believe your attack on one you felt threatened by to be justified by... what, exactly? My show of affection toward him? Are you to monitor the decency of every one of my relationships from here on out now that I have promised you my hand? Should I tell Kristefani that she may no longer hold my arm while we walk, lest you spot us and assault her as well?"

"Adiadni..." The soft voice of the queen sought to encourage her daughter to take a breath, but Adiadni continued, her hands forming fists at her sides.

"Regardless of how you may wish to excuse your actions, you deliberately attacked one of the Free People. One of *my* people, whom I and my entire family line are sworn to protect."

"I understand your upset, my dear..." Basil spoke gingerly. "But ultimately, the fisherman sustained merely some scratches and bruises..."

The princess laughed, a sound far louder than she had expected it to be.

"Merely some bruises? Need I remind you where on his body those bruises are the brightest?"

Basil did not respond.

"It is the tradition of this court to allow you the space to defend yourself, but you may not stand there and lie to my face and act as though you intended to let him go after a few moments with your hands around his throat. I witnessed the entire thing, Basil. He would be dead now had I not been there."

"My darling, had you not been there, I likely would have never attacked him in the first place."

"Oh, that's fucking rich—"

"Adiadni."

The princess paused under the weight of her father's warning but lifted her chin and continued clenching her fists. "Your excuses for your behavior are a pathetic attempt to belittle me into submission. Have you forgotten that I will one day be your queen? That your own title will be but an ornament at best? This ring clings to my finger due to the weight of my responsibility alone..." she held up her left hand and then dropped it, "...and I will not hesitate to do away with it *and* with you for good if you dare try to back me into a corner again."

Adiadni allowed silence to fill the room. She looked to her betrothed with a firm, unyielding glare, waiting for him to speak again. He did not.

Instead, Suprafalo stepped forward, one hand on his cane, the other gesturing superfluously through the air. "Might we all just take a breath and reevaluate for a moment..."

Adi turned to him, the heat of her gaze not lessening at all. "Have you anything to say, Suprafalo, for the way your son cast me into the dirt when I attempted to intervene?"

"He did what?"

Goosebumps traversed Adiadni's arms at the tone of her father's voice and she took a step back so she again stood slightly behind him. The air in the room grew thick, the silence heavy. The king was powerful and commanding without almost ever needing to assert himself. The blood of a leader and a protector coursed through his veins, and he was widely respected throughout the land for it. His presence was more than enough to make one wish to be their best self. No one dared breathe a word when it became clear that Agamemnon was angry.

The king looked at his daughter, "Were you hurt?"

The princess shook her head no.

Agamemnon turned to Basil, "Would you care to explain this?"

Basil swallowed, shifting from one foot to the other. His father spoke again, "Come now, Agamemnon, are you truly not going to question your own daughter on the compromising position she was found in with the stranger? Surely, you also would grow heated should you find Betina in the arms of another…"

Agamemnon furrowed his brow. He extended a hand toward Suprafalo Dagious, gesturing as he spoke in the manner he always did, his voice low, "Do not use my daughter in an attempt to detract from the heinous actions committed by your son. There are no laws in the Free World that dictate the degree to which she may show affection to her friends. Adiadni says this was an innocent interaction. Uritus says the same, and considering the degree to which your son has attempted to skew my perception of yesterday's happenings, I am inclined to believe them over you, who were not there. The fact that Adiadni has elected to continue with her engagement despite all this is more than necessary proof of her loyalty to your son. Suprafalo, you are my guest, and as such I have taken several measures to ensure your and Basil's continued comfort in my home despite the things he has done. I have allowed the both of you to remain in your chambers in the palace rather than sending you away, have elected to hold this meeting here, in my personal study, rather than in the courtroom, and I and my family have done everything in our power to see to it that word of this incident does not get out and spread throughout the city, furthering my citizens' perception that your son may not be fit to one day sit at Adiadni's left hand. You will not disrespect me, and you will not disrespect my daughter."

Adi took several deep breaths, feeling protected and emboldened by her father's firm hand.

The king went on, "From here on out, you are to regard Adiadni as your queen. She is not merely a Vindella, she is the Suvah, the one to whom the whole of the Free World will owe their gratitude for their continued freedom, along with the Adalos. Whether you live long enough to see her take the throne still remains to be seen, but on this day and every day that follows, you will remind yourself that she is my heir, and you will offer her the same degree of respect and submission that you would me. And when the Adalos is discovered —as he will be this afternoon—you will do the same for him."

Basil stepped forward then, extending a hand to the king, "We are grateful, your majesty, for—"

"As for you," Agamemnon turned to face him. Basil took a step back and replaced his hand to clasp his other behind him. "You have threatened not only the safety of the man who may very well be the Adalos, but the safety of the Suvah, my daughter, as well. I can see no other way forward than for you to leave Suscundos immediately and return home to Vindellaria. I am a forgiving man, and I may eventually be willing to look past this whole debacle and welcome you back into the city to celebrate the Suvah's return with the Adalos, as Uritus is willing to do the same. But that will be contingent on my certainty that you will quell this violent behavior of yours so I am positive that this will not happen again. And, of course, if the Suvah is open to this as well." He turned then to look at his daughter, his eyes trustworthy, silently assuring her that he would honor her judgment.

Adiadni looked from her father to her intended and back, contemplating all of this for a moment and then nodding once to the king. "If the one he harmed can be graceful enough to see past all this, I suppose I can as well."

"This is absurd!" Suprafalo exclaimed. "You cannot just send us away like common criminals—"

Basil stepped forward quickly, placing one hand on his father's shoulder and one on his back, "Come now, Father, I believe the royal family has been incredibly gracious."

Suprafalo relaxed with a huff.

Basil moved to face the king, bowing once to him, "Thank you, your grace, you have been exceptionally generous. It seems only fair that I face consequences for my lapse in judgment. I can assure you that this will not happen again." He turned to face Adiadni, "My love…"

Her arms crossed over one another and she regarded him with a flat scowl.

He took a step toward her, one hand extended, "I have let you down, caused you to fear. That is not the man I am nor the man I wish to be. I am sorry. I will do better… be better, from here on out. I wish to be the kind of man you deserve." His eyes pleaded for her forgiveness. "I promise you now that when you return from your journey, I will be waiting, ready, and deserving of your love and continued loyalty."

The princess did not respond but rather nodded briskly to her betrothed. Basil bowed again to the royal family and Suprafalo did the same before they turned and exited the study with the pair of guards. Adiadni breathed a sigh of relief as the doors closed behind them.

***

Uritus awoke the morning after the physical trials with a pounding headache, sore muscles, and stiff joints. He observed upon regarding himself in the looking glass that the bruises on his face and body remained, but the cuts he had sustained the day prior had mostly healed over. He ate a bit at Mikka's insistence and began to feel better after that, but determined he would need to be more cautious in the future when consuming unfamiliar substances. They had done a miraculous amount of help getting him through the grueling physical trials, but their lingering side effects—compounded by his general sense of exhaustion and soreness—left him feeling a bit worse for the wear. He spent the morning stretching, relaxing, and laying out on his small balcony in the sunshine, and found himself feeling significantly better when summoned by a guard for the search's final trial.

Uriah joined him, and they followed the guard to the trial's venue. The day's event was held in the privacy of the palace, the prospective heroes brought one by one before the royal family's council of Keepers for something Uriah described as akin to a character assessment. The mystery that shrouded this particular phase of the search had Uritus feeling somehow more anxious than he had the day before.

The guard led them through the palace, down to the first floor, and then through a door that opened to a wide, winding staircase which descended below ground. Their way was lit by warm yellow torches and the air around them felt cool, the stone insulating them from the hot Summer day. They reached the bottom of the stair and traveled down a hallway where they eventually came upon a single wooden door. Across from the door was a wrought iron bench on which sat Kensus of Mount Venadalis. They waited there in silence until the door opened, and out of the room stepped Dustafes, hair mussed, face slightly haggard. Kensus stood to meet him and the guard led the two of them away back down the hall, Dustafes nodding once to Uritus as he departed. The fisherman took in a few slow breaths as he nervously gazed into the darkness of the chamber beyond the door.

"You may enter," spoke a feminine voice from the room, and when Uritus looked to Uriah for assurance, the Wizard nodded encouragingly and assured the fisherman that there was nothing to fear.

Uritus stepped forward into the room and the door closed behind him. He blinked a few times to allow his eyes to adjust to the dark and then proceeded to a space in the middle of the room which appeared to be somewhat illuminated. The faint beam of light brightened as he stepped into it. He turned to regard the space around him, identifying a wooden table which was also slightly lit from above, behind which sat the three Keepers he had seen before.

"Hello, Uritus," spoke the Healer.

He tipped his head in a greeting, "Hello."

The Healer rose from the table and moved to the fisherman's side. She wore several layered garments colored in shades of magenta, violet, and royal blue. The hems of her skirts tucked into their waistbands to reveal a pair of cinched pantaloons beneath. A thick gold band encircled each of her wrists and ankles, as well as one around her neck and one crowning her head. The vibrant fabric that adorned her illuminated her brown skin, raven-colored hair falling from her head in coarse waves highlighted with streaks of gray. On her feet, she wore a thin pair of blue silk slippers.

Taking his hand in one of her own, she placed into it a small, round vial, stopped with a cork, sealed in golden wax with Suscundos's sacred symbol of the intertwining vines. The liquid inside was dark but shimmered with sparkles of blue.

"Drink," she said, "...and we may begin."

She returned to her seat behind the table and Uritus regarded the vial. "May I ask what it is?"

The Healer brought her arms to rest in front of her. "A creation of my own. Herbs mostly, some algae, water from the falls just outside the city. Consider it to be a truth potion of sorts."

He tilted it in his hand, observing how the waves of glittering blue swam through the vial as he did. "Will it make me feel unwell?"

She shook her head. "It shouldn't. Its primary purpose is to guide you toward the truth. As long as you cooperate willingly, you should feel no unpleasant symptoms."

The fisherman nodded, removed the cork, and consumed the vial's contents.

"Very well, let us begin."

"State your name for us please," spoke the Wizard.

"Uritus Subian."

"Where are you from, Uritus?"

"I was born and raised in Tosh but, more recently, I hail from the White Mountains."

"Welcome, Uritus," the Prophet greeted him. "I am called Olythia, Prophet in service to the Divine as well as our king, Agamemnon. I watch the stars, and have foreseen the coming of the Adalos for some time." Their face was almost fully shaded by the midnight blue hood of their cape. When they moved, the fabric that shrouded them appeared as if to glitter with thousands of tiny, faint pricks of light. Their hands rested on the table in front of them, elegantly folded with one another. Adorning one fair, slender finger was a simple gold ring.

"I am Veldis of Suscundos," declared the Wizard. "Servant of the people of the Free World and Wizard on the council of king Agamemnon." Veldis, a river elf, sat between the Prophet and the Healer. His robe and hat were in the standard style worn by Wizards, navy blue, and in his hand, he held a tarnished silver staff with an ornament appearing as a noble perched eagle. Long, shiny, straight jet-black hair fell down his back, a lock draped across each shoulder, and no beard covered his face.

The Healer who sat to the Wizard's right introduced herself last, "I am Aurena, Suscundos's supreme Healer, hands and feet of the Mother, and trusted confidante of the Free World's present king, Agamemnon Vindella." She regarded the fisherman with intense, dark eyes, peering as if into his heart. "We are honored to have you here."

"As am I to be here." Uritus stood with his hands behind his back, one holding his wrist, the other still clutching the empty vial. He blinked several times as a throbbing grew in his temples.

"Are you feeling unwell?" Aurena tilted her head to one side.

"I am not," the fisherman replied honestly. "It's just... my eyes."

Olythia nodded. "Yes, a symptom of the viraglas. Does it prove to be a distraction in your ordinary life?"

Uritus shook his head. "It does not."

The Keepers nodded to themselves, remaining in silence for a moment until Veldis spoke again, "Now, Uritus, we have a series of questions to ask you, simple ones. You may decline to answer any of them if you would wish, we just ask that if you do choose to answer, you are fully truthful."

Uritus nodded understandingly.

Veldis moved forward slightly in his seat. "Tell us, Uritus, do you believe yourself to be the Adalos?"

Uritus was somewhat taken aback by this question but paused only briefly before answering, "I do."

"Why?" The Prophet's voice was authoritative without being intimidating.

Uritus considered this. "I relied heavily on the assurance of others for a while to serve in place of my own confidence. But over time, on the journey here, after the events of yesterday... I have found myself believing it more and more. Perhaps this is due to the encouragement of others, but my father was firm in his belief that the words we speak over one another and the names we use for each other have deep significance, ultimately molding some of who we become. I've had so many now tell me that they see me as the Adalos, so many who have called me that as though it is my name. I think it would be hard not to believe it."

Olythia nodded, satisfied with this answer, and proceeded with their next question, "Regarding the events of yesterday, you were attacked after the trials by one of your competitors, is that correct?"

Uritus nodded. "It is."

"Do you know why he attacked you?"

Uritus hesitated a moment before responding, "I... believe he saw Adiadni embrace me—her way of celebrating my win—and I believe he deemed this action to be inappropriate."

"You told the king that this interaction was innocent," spoke the Wizard. "Is that true?"

Uritus lifted his eyes to the stone ceiling of the room which he could now more clearly make out. "As far as I am aware, yes. Adiadni and I have become fast friends since I arrived in the city, and she made it known to me that she had hoped I would win. That she believed me to be the Adalos. I think she may have been... concerned that he may react negatively upon discovering that she had chosen another."

"How did that feel," Aurena questioned, "...to hear that the Suvah believed *you* to be the Adalos?"

The fisherman smiled softly, recalling his interaction with the princess in the orchard. "It felt... not at all surprising. As though we met and it was immediately clear to her. She told me when she greeted me upon my arrival in Suscundos that I have trustworthy eyes."

The Healer nodded. "You felt connected immediately?"

Uritus moved his head from side to side. "We felt... at ease with one another immediately. We felt connected... a few days later, but before the initial council."

"And what was it," Aurena continued her series of inquiries, "...that made your connection apparent?"

Uritus thought a moment before answering. "It has never felt unnatural to be vulnerable with Adiadni. I also feel... deeply protective of her. I have since the moment I met her. This I am certain she feels as well," he recalled the way the princess saved him from her betrothed the day before.

The Keepers nodded again.

"On the note of that protective instinct," Veldis addressed the fisherman. "Surely, you are aware that your primary task on the first leg of this journey will be to protect the Suvah."

Uritus nodded. "I am."

The Wizard continued, "And you are aware that once the Sword of Fire is retrieved and you return to Suscundos, that you will be the one we will look to to defend the Free World from whatever comes next, by any means necessary, up to and including leading the Free People into war?"

Uritus blinked twice and swallowed, feeling small beads of sweat begin to form in his palms. Finally he answered, "I am."

"Does that frighten you?"

Uritus shifted where he stood, unnerved by the degree to which Veldis seemed to be able to read his mind. He met the Wizard's gaze, "It does."

"You feel unprepared for such an undertaking?"

The fisherman nodded affirmatively. "I do. To be honest, I cannot imagine ever feeling prepared for so heavy a thing. I have never seen combat..."

"Neither have most who live East of the Looming Mountains."

Uritus nodded again. "I do know that if this is a task entrusted to me, I will not allow my fear to lead my steps, though I know that may not be enough. I know little about war strategy, and the idea of someone losing their life while operating under my authority makes me feel... rather sick."

"I understand," spoke Veldis again. "But imagine now that the war has come. What will you do?"

Uritus felt his face grow hot. He searched his mind for a clear mode of action but none surfaced. He took a breath. "I am but a youth in the eyes of most," he said. "And as much as I wish I could stand before you and tell you I am confident that when the time comes, I will be ready… I cannot. Were I a Wizard who had walked this land for a thousand years, learning every secret and bit of wisdom that it had to offer, I still do not believe I would be ready to take the lives of countless others into my hands. I do not know how one could ever be ready for such a thing…" He paused, looking to his feet and then back up again. "But I also know that sometimes our destinies come for us whether we are ready or not, and as I have stood to face my own before, I will do so again. I am blessed to be surrounded by many with far more wisdom and skill and expertise than I. And should the time come, or I suppose, *when* it does, I shall look to them for their advice and guidance. That is the only way that I can see forward."

The Wizard nodded. "Thank you for your honesty."

Uritus nodded as well.

"Just a bit more and then we'll be finished, all right? I wish to bring our conversation back to the first leg of the journey, to discuss the responsibility of seeing to the wellbeing of the princess."

The fisherman nodded again, grateful for Olythia's communication, feeling soothed by the cool, even tone of their voice.

The Prophet leaned forward, causing their lips and nose to become visible under the hood of their cape. "We believe strongly, as do the king and queen, in your willingness, readiness, and ability to see to Adiadni's safekeeping. Most of this task will concern her physical protection, making certain that she is not harmed by any creatures or enemies you may come across as you make your way West. But what we need to know is… are you prepared to guide her on her journey?"

Uritus blinked. "I'm not sure what you mean. She's studied the map, yes?"

"She has. But guidance in the navigational sense is not the kind to which I am referring."

Uritus waited silently for Olythia to elaborate.

The Prophet cleared their throat. "The king and queen have taken many steps, employed many experts, and sought the wisdom of this council and many more to prepare the Suvah to undertake this journey. She has been readied as best she can, but… it remains true that Adiadni's experience in the real world is limited —something we know you do not share in common with her. And it may be necessary at times to lead her toward certain choices or away from others."

Uritus frowned. "Are you asking if I would be willing to manipulate Adiadni toward certain outcomes? To overlook what she deems best if I do not think she is making the right decision?"

"I am asking… should the time arrive that the princess makes a choice that may ultimately endanger her, are you willing to ignore her orders to keep her safe?"

Uritus felt unwell. He looked across the faces of the Keepers behind the table, each of them with neutral expressions, waiting patiently for his response. "I am afraid I cannot answer."

"Cannot or will not?"

Uritus felt his stomach twist but raised his chin. "I cannot. I do not feel it is my place. Adiadni is not a silly girl nor a naive leader. She has much to learn, yes, as do I. But I believe that there are none who know what is best for her save for herself. I cannot tell you that I would be willing to ignore her wishes, but I also cannot say I would never act instinctually in the heat of a moment and do what was necessary to save her. All I can tell you is that I trust her judgment as much as I know she also trusts mine."

"Very well." Olythia leaned back in their seat again, their face once more becoming shadowed by their hood.

Uritus felt his mouth grow dry. He cleared his throat, unsure if he had given an incorrect answer but knowing none other that he could give.

"Now, Uritus," Aurena spoke then. "You arrived in Suscundos with a party of travelers who will journey West with you, is that correct?"

The fisherman nodded.

"And you are protective of them as well?"

Another nod. "They are my family, to whom I owe my debt of gratitude for much of my education and skill. We care for one another as we would our own blood."

"Of course. This council has communed with your Keeper, Uriah, for some time, and we trust the abilities and character of all of your party members. While we are confident that you will do all that needs to be done to see to the protection of every companion who fights at your side… it remains true that the protection of *one* of those companions must take precedence."

Uritus felt his brow grow sticky with perspiration. "Of course… My main priority will always be to ensure that Adiadni is kept safe…"

"Including," Aurena continued, "…if the one she must be kept safe from is one of your own?"

Uritus frowned. "None of my own would dare raise a finger against her. I'd bet my own life on that."

Aurena nodded. "But should the moment arise that you are forced to choose between the life of the princess and that of one of your party?"

Uritus felt his stomach tie itself in knots. "I do not believe I can answer that question."

"I understand," said the Healer. "Nevertheless, there may come a day when you must. And in the eyes of the king, this council, and the whole of the Free World… there is a correct answer."

Uritus felt his heart rate increase as sweat gathered on his upper lip. He felt dizzy and nauseated, his stomach churning as he tried to envision a moment as devastating as the one Aurena described. He pictured Adiadni and Perplexus on opposite sides of a dark room, a shadowy figure behind each of them gripping a knife to their throats…

"Uritus?"

He blinked against the unsettling vision, turned his eyes back to Aurena, swallowed. "I will do whatever it takes to make certain that the Suvah remains safe."

"Up to and including taking the life of one you love to spare hers?"

Uritus's breaths became quickened and shallow. The dull pain behind his eyes throbbed. He clutched the vial behind his back, knowing that if he loosened his grip at all, it would slip from his hands and shatter on the stone below, but if he held it any tighter, it would certainly crack and cut his hand. He did his best to straighten himself despite feeling as though he may collapse under an invisible pressure, holding his head high as he regarded the Healer.

"Whatever it takes."

The Keepers looked at one another, silently communicating to be sure that each one was satisfied with this line of questioning. They turned again to Uritus.

"Thank you for your integrity," said Aurena. "You are free to go. You will be informed of the results of the search later this afternoon."

Uritus let out a long breath, feeling his body relax. He nodded to the Keepers, "Thank you for your time."

The door swung open and the fisherman exited through it, rejoining Uriah and returning to his room.

***

The navigator launched a thousand questions at his friend before the fisherman could find a seat. Uritus did his best to explain the nature of the Magical trial, leaving out the more unpleasant details of the interrogation.

"Do you think it went well?"

Uritus wasn't sure. "I think it did. It was over quickly."

"Was it worse than you expected?"

"I don't know what I expected." The fisherman brought himself to stand in the balcony's doorway. Outside, Suscundos buzzed on as usual. "Many of the questions they had did not seem to have a clear right answer. Not that I was answering them with that in mind… Like I said, it was quick."

Perplexus shifted his weight from one leg to the other and suddenly noticed a buildup of nervous energy in his limbs. "Care to take a walk through the garden while we wait?"

Uritus looked out over the green and shook his head. "No. I want to be easy to find when they're through deliberating. It's a lovely day, though. I wouldn't be hurt if you wished to go without me."

Perplexus also shook his head. "Nonsense. I'll wait with you."

They did not have to wait long before there sounded a soft knock at the door. It opened before they could answer, and they were surprised when into their room slipped the princess Adiadni, clad in a casual forest-green dress.

156

"Good, you're both here," she said, swiftly crossing the room to stop in front of Uritus.

"Adiadni…" The fisherman's surprise was visible. "Is everything all right?"

"Yes, of course…" A pained look crossed Adi's face as she regarded his battered visage. "I am sorry I did not come to see you yesterday evening. I was… overwhelmed. Are you feeling all right?" She lifted a hand to run it across the scarred tissue on his lower lip but just as quickly dropped it.

"Much better, thank you." Uritus looked across the princess's bare shoulders to the long strips of fabric hanging from her straps to the front and back of her gown, fluttering when she moved as though she had wings.

"What have we to thank for this lovely surprise, Adi?" Perplexus questioned. "I hope you are not here to warn us that Basil comes to finish what he started."

Adi looked to the navigator, "No, he…" She returned her gaze to the fisherman, "He left Suscundos this morning. My family determined that such brutal behavior should not be rewarded with a continued stay in our home or our city." She paused. "I am sorry, truly, for what happened. Had I known he would… That is… I never wished for…"

"I know." Uritus held her eyes for a moment, silently assuring her that he did not blame her for what happened, and feeling the last of his headache dissipate as he did.

Adiadni regarded this change in the fisherman's eyes from sea blue to honey brown and determined that neither shade was preferable to the other. She remembered her purpose and shook her head. "That is not why I am here though." She took a step forward, remaining a few paces away from Uritus but extending her hands to take his. They were warm and rough, as she had remembered them. "I wanted to tell you before anyone else could…"

They stood there for a moment, slow smiles growing across their faces as the weight of this moment became clear.

"It's you." Adi's eyes sparkled. "My parents and the council have determined what we have known for some time to be true. You are the Adalos."

The fisherman released a breath, unsure how to comprehend such a revelation.

"Damn right, he is." Perplexus crossed the room to offer his friend an enthusiastic pat on the shoulder. "How do you feel, Old Boy?"

Uritus considered this. "I imagined I would feel… different. Braver, maybe… stronger, somehow. But at this moment, I feel as if nothing has changed."

"That's because nothing has," the princess said delightedly. "They were astounded by you at every turn. The people love you, I trust you." She looked up at him, beaming with pride. "It could be no one but you."

Uritus found himself lost in the light reflected in the eyes of his counterpart.

"Someone will surely be here soon to tell you the news…"

A knock sounded on the door then, followed by Uriah's inquiry, "Uritus, my boy, are you there?"

"Just a moment!" Perplexus cried.

Adiadni dropped her voice to a whisper, "I was never here." She moved to the open balcony door, one hand still holding Uritus's, and then turned to him once more, "I am so proud of you."

He smiled at her, offering her hand a gentle squeeze, "As am I of you."

She returned his smile and rushed to the balcony as Perplexus moved to open the chamber door. Uriah entered, excitedly embracing the Adalos as the princess reached the trellis and lowered herself to the ground below.

Chapter Eleven

"Dusk"

The 4th of July

Uritus was presented by the king to the city as the Adalos an hour after Adi told him the news, on the steps of the palace with the princess at his side. He appeared in his armor, blue cape draped nobly over his shoulders, and she in a forest green gown of a more formal cut, with sleeves that left her shoulders bare and a fitted brown leather bodice appearing like flexible armor. They extended their hands to the exuberant crowd, feeling notably more at ease in such a visible position when standing there alongside one another.

They moved from their presentation to the celebration in the square which lasted until the sun rose. Neither the fisherman nor the princess remained present for the entirety of the event, feeling physically and mentally exhausted after the happenings of the week prior. Both would ultimately be grateful to have stolen a bit of extra rest, as the week that followed launched them into the final preparations for their journey.

Both were gifted with new saddles, bridles, and blinders for their horses, as well as new bows and quivers, a new sword for Uritus, and a set of armor for Adiadni—all of these fashioned and enchanted specifically for them. The needs of their party were also seen to, each member receiving new clothing, armor, and weapons to replace any they had that were old or worn, though Havian elected to keep his sword, Mikka her armor, and Oripidus his war hammer—heavy-headed with a spike on one end and crafted by his own hands during his time in Quabish. Adiadni in particular was subject to hours more of combative training, and the party members were educated on the path designated by the map and the hazards which may appear on their way. Uriah spent most of his time in the council of the king or his Keepers.

By week's end, the company felt their confidence in their mission strengthened. Adiadni bid farewell to Pressio and he departed East in search of recruits to strengthen the king's forces should the travelers return from beyond the Looming Mountains with a war on their heels. Before they knew it, the time to depart was at their doorstep, and all party members broke from their usual evening festivities early to get a bit of rest before they bid Suscundos farewell the following morning.

All, that is, save for the Adalos himself. Uritus wandered along the winding pathways of the Eastern garden deep in thought. He admired the fireflies that rested in the trees, illuminating their tops and trunks all at once and then fading again, their rhythmic pattern akin to one's breathing. He found the rise and fall of his breath to align with the luminescent tempo. Out here, the anxious musings in his mind quieted, and murmurations of gratitude took their place. He would miss Suscundos, this fantastical, joyful land full of color. But he knew that in the end, he would ultimately return, and it was this small, quiet beacon of hope that he allowed to light his steps as he walked.

He had dreamed for so many years of traveling here and he came to realize that at some point in his later teenage years, he had made peace with the idea that such a dream may well go unfulfilled. But now, here he was, his name cried in the streets by hundreds or even thousands every day, and he struggled to comprehend how *he*, a humble fisherman from a small Western village, could have turned out to be the one whom *Suscundos* had dreamed of for as long as the Free World had even existed. He was not a warrior, nor a sage, nor a particularly compelling spokesman. He was simply *Uritus*. He didn't know if he would ever feel like anything more than that.

"Can't sleep either?"

He looked up the palace wall just behind him to his right and his eyes lit on Adiadni leaning against her balcony's railing. He smiled up at her, a wave crashing in his stomach. She was illuminated by the cool blue light of the moon, hair tumbling across her shoulders as she gazed down at him from the palace's second floor. A tiny breeze stirred the hem of her skirt and the long strips of fabric that hung from her shoulders. The warm golden light emanating from her room behind her adorned the crown of her head with a bright halo, contrasted with the moon's blue highlight across her skin. She was breathtaking.

"I'm afraid not," he finally replied. "Though that's only part of the reason I am out here."

"I understand." Adi tilted her head to one side as it became apparent to her that in the active movement throughout the past week, she had deeply missed the fisherman. The corners of her mouth curled into a smile as she regarded him now, bright-eyed, beaming up at her. She realized that if ever she was feeling lonely, she need only seek him out, as his warm enthusiasm upon being surprised by her presence simply chased away any feeling of it. "Care for some company?"

He smiled at her again, the wave rolling into his chest. "I would."

She nodded her head to her right as she straightened herself, trailing one hand along the balustrade, and Uritus traced his eyes along its edge until they settled on the trellis that led up to it, blooming with soft white flowers. He raised his eyebrows slightly as he returned his gaze to the princess, "Is that… appropriate?"

She shrugged. "Certainly not. But I don't mind if you don't." She turned, clasped both hands behind her, and sauntered through the balcony's doors into her chamber.

Uritus hesitated, turning to look at the garden for a moment, and then finally stepping forward and ascending to the princess's chamber, being mindful not to crush any of the delicate flowers as he climbed.

The room was large and cool despite the warmth of the summer evening, and tiny flames danced on their wicks atop candles mounted on the walls and the sparkling chandelier above. The floor was covered with colorful overlapping rugs of varying shapes and sizes, and the windows, balcony doors, and bedposts sported wispy ivory curtains that swayed in the breeze. The Western wall—opposite the one with the balcony and writing desk—hosted the wooden double doors which led to the corridor. A dressing table and bench stood in the corner to their left, and a wide wardrobe rested on the other side, adjacent to a smaller door on the Northern wall which Uritus guessed opened to a washroom. Against the Southern wall was a tall bookshelf, flanked on either side by large windows, with a burgundy chaise to its right. Across from the bookshelf was the princess's large canopy bed, a chest at the foot of it, a small dresser to either side, and a sizable potted plant beside each. There were several plants in large clay pots decorating the room, many the size of small trees, and climbing the posts of the bed and adorning its canopy were lush green vines of ivy.

His eyes followed Adiadni as she moved about the room, feet bare, not a jewel adorning her body or head, in a casual soft pink gown that highlighted the natural rosiness of her cheeks. She smiled when she saw him.

"What ails you, Adalos…" she asked, tilting her head over one shoulder, "…that you should wander the garden alone at such an hour?"

He smiled, taking a few steps toward her. "The garden is particularly lovely this time of night."

She nodded. "Yes, firefly season is a favorite of mine."

They came to a stop in front of one another, separated by a few paces.

"But surely, their brightness is not the sole thing that keeps you awake?"

Uritus shook his head slowly. Around the neck of the princess was a thin leather cord from which hung a familiar-looking white stone pendant. He smiled when he saw it, reaching up to touch the similar gift that hung around his neck. She did the same, though whether the action had been conscious or not he did not know.

"And you?"

Adiadni sighed and bit her lower lip thoughtfully.

"Would it be helpful to talk about it?"

She shrugged. "Surely, that which burdens me is as easy to ascertain as that which burdens you… I do not wish to place more into your hands while you already have enough to carry on your own."

He regarded her understandingly. "It is not on my own that I carry much of anything. Little would I be without the hands of those who go beside me. I cannot bear your burden, this is true, as you cannot bear mine. But I am willing to hold yours, if only for a moment, if it would feel less heavy for you that way."

The princess released a slow breath as she looked up at the fisherman, contemplating exactly what it was that tied her stomach in knots. As it was, she had all but forgotten the source of her anxieties upon observing Uritus as he moved in the light of the moon below. She understood not how his demeanor remained ever peaceful, as still as the surface of a pool on a windless day even now, on the eve of their departure.

"To put it plainly…" She considered her words carefully for a moment and then gave up, "I do not know what I am doing."

"As the Suvah?"

"As the Suvah, as future queen of the Free World, as…" an image of her betrothed materialized in her mind and she trailed off. "And with each day that passes, I fear that someone will find out."

He furrowed his brow. "Would it be the worst thing if someone did?"

She considered this and shrugged, eyes falling to the floor. "I'm aware that in the grand scheme of things, this is… hardly a worry."

Uritus internally chided himself for not considering how his words would come across. "Forgive me, I did not intend to make light of that which ails you." He swallowed as she again lifted her eyes to meet his. "If it helps at all, I also do not know what I am doing."

Adi laughed. "Do you expect me to believe that?"

He tipped his head to the side. "I'm not sure why I would lie about such a thing…"

She shook her head at him. "Uritus, you are one of the most competent people I have ever known, despite your youth. You have faced every challenge, every trial, every… *altercation* presented to you since arriving here with the utmost grace and capability. Even before that, when you were a boy, you…" She paused, intently searching his face for signs of distress. He nodded to her to go on. She took a breath. "You lost everything. Everyone. And you just… continued on. Had I lost even one member of my family by fourteen, I would have become, and remained until now, a wreck. How?"

The fisherman smiled at her sadly. He had known for some time that this conversation would catch up to them, and he did not wish to shy away from it now. "Well, suffice it to say that I *was* a wreck for some time. For seven years, loss was most of what I knew. Loss and then… the consequential wreckage and then… gathering up the pieces, rebuilding, pressing on. Over and over and over again. By the time I lost my father, I…" He blinked several times, feeling a familiar headache creep across his brow. "I was rather experienced with grief and its aftermath."

Adiadni frowned, feeling tears gather in her eyes. "That's incredibly sad."

He nodded gently, his vision blurring as his eyes became wet. "It is. I would not wish the things I have undergone upon anyone. But if you see me as capable, resourceful, relentless in my pursuit of the Light, then I must tell you that what you see is not some… Magical seed buried in my chest since my birth, nor a talent or a skill I possess that does not come as naturally to anyone else. It is merely because I have known grief, far deeper and more intimately than I believe anyone should. And the steady and fervent pursuit of brighter days that I witnessed in my father during that time…" He paused for a moment, closing his eyes as hot tears carved their tracks down his cheeks, and then opened them and smiled softly as they again met Adiadni's, "I like to think such a spirit lives within me now."

The princess brought her hands to her cheeks to wipe away their wetness, wishing for a moment that she could do the same to his. "I am sorry to have made you speak on something so heavy."

He shook his head. "You needn't be. Stories are meant to be shared. I am sorry to have made you sad."

"No. I have been sheltered my whole life from the world's harshness. Residing inside a pristine, iridescent little bubble. But I am beginning to see…" she cast her eyes off to the side and they darkened, "…that the time will soon come when it will pop."

"That may be true…" Uritus took a small step closer to the princess, eager to alleviate some of her stress. "But I see no reason why that would need to happen tonight."

A smile crept over Adi's face as she turned again to meet his gaze, "I suppose you're right."

He sighed, regarding her for a quiet moment. The fierceness of his adoration of her and his infuriating inability to communicate it properly were an agonizing pair. "Adiadni, I am certain that your confidence in yourself will grow in time, as my own has. You may not feel yourself to be capable, but from my vantage point, you are both the most prepared and most supported person in the whole of the Free World. It is natural—perhaps even wise—to be aware of the ways you do not feel ready. But when the time comes, you'll know what to do. If you don't…" He shrugged. "I'm here to help you. We all are."

Adi looked at him, observing the depth of compassion in his blue eyes, feeling simultaneously seen, warmed, and overwhelmed. And then she watched, wide-mouthed with amusement, as a firefly—having floated in from the open balcony doors—brought itself to a gentle landing on the fisherman's nose and blinked.

Uritus regarded it with crossed eyes and scrunched his nose at the firefly's tickle. The little bug flew away in response, lighting itself several times, and Adiadni began to laugh.

It was a soft titter at first, escaping her lips involuntarily, soon crescendoing into a loud, joyous melody. Uritus watched her with a smile in his eyes, feeling suddenly much lighter as it became apparent that she did and observing how the light of the room appeared to grow just slightly brighter with her every effervescent note.

Eventually, she quieted, bringing her hands to her mouth when she realized just how loud she had become. "Forgive me," she said. "I, um… That was…"

"Adiadni."

The princess brought her eyes again to meet his.

He hesitated, silently deliberating how to most gently tell her that she need never apologize for her joy. His mouth ended up moving before his brain did. "I love your laugh," he told her. "I'd go to the end of the earth to hear it."

"Huh…" She giggled nervously and let out a shaky breath and a breeze moved through the balcony's doors, causing the little flames that adorned the room to quiver. She steeled herself against the tiny prickles that danced across her arms and brought herself to stand a bit straighter, clasping her hands together behind her back. "Well…"

"Well…"

"Well… hopefully, you'll never need to."

Uritus shared this hope. A symphony of cricket chirps had risen to meet the rustling of the leaves within and outside the room. The fisherman turned his head to look out beyond the balcony doors and sighed with an air of melancholy. "I really am going to miss it here."

Adiadni smiled sadly. "As am I. Save for a few voyages to the Holy City, Suscundos is all I've ever known."

He looked back at her in surprise. "You've never traveled?"

She shook her head. "Not really. The purpose of my life up until this point has been to make ready for my… *our* journey. There is no place in the Free World better to do that than here."

"You must be looking forward to getting away then, no?"

She shrugged. "If you had asked me that last Winter, I would have said yes, undoubtedly. There is so much beauty I wish to see in this land. But… I cannot imagine that any of it will stir my heart the way Suscundos does."

She turned her head to look outside, feeling her eyes gloss over. The synchronized brightening and fading of the fireflies lit her delicate features as she bit her lower lip. "I had made it my mission to intentionally enjoy the time I had left in the city before our departure, and I have done so to the best of my ability, but now…" Her lip began to quiver and she attempted to still it. "I just feel that the coming weeks or even months away will have me feeling… not quite myself."

Uritus nodded, watching her as she wrestled with her sadness, and feeling particularly helpless for how he could not take it away. He looked at her lower lashes, heavy with the weight of her tears. He wished to touch her, to hold her, to remind her that her home would always be here to welcome her back, and that even when she was away, nothing could truly separate it from her being.

She looked back at him, blinking and then quickly wiping her eyes, "Forgive me, I know it's silly."

He shook his head fervently. "It isn't. I understand. Suscundos is not even my home and I will hate to be parted from it."

She sniffled, eyes shining up at him with gratitude, "You have an incredible way of making people feel at ease just as they are."

He smiled. "I think unconditional acceptance is something we all deserve."

"I know," she replied. "I do love that about you."

Uritus smiled and took a breath as he stood in silence with his counterpart, the crickets, wind, and gasps let out by tiny flames scoring their undeniable pull toward one another. It was the princess who broke eye contact first, turning her head to again gaze over the garden and sighing sadly.

Uritus kept his eyes fixed on her, feeling her sadness in his own chest, and he contemplated for a moment how he might go about alleviating it before he finally spoke, "I owe my love of this city, my appreciation of its widespread beauty, in large part to you. Viewing it through your eyes has taught me much about why Suscundos is so special, and as tonight is our last here for some time, I would be happy to follow your lead on how we can best appreciate the time we do have."

"Hmm." Adiadni thought for a moment, still absentmindedly scanning the garden. A smile crept across her mouth as her eyes began to light and she turned to the fisherman with a full-fledged idea at the forefront of her mind, "Can I show you something?"

Uritus nodded without hesitation and she grabbed his hand and led him away. They crept out of her chamber and through the halls of the palace, passing the central staircases and making their way to the Western wing. The Adalos followed the Suvah into the library and through a hidden door which she opened by accessing a secret panel in the side of one of the tall bookshelves and pulling on a latch that caused a portion of it to swing open. They entered the darkened space beyond, pulling the door closed behind them, and began to ascend a narrow stone staircase that led them up in a wide spiral. The princess moved a few steps ahead of the fisherman, and he watched as small torches ignited with yellow flames as she passed by, lighting their way as they went. After climbing for several minutes, they came to a stop at the top of the stair before a simple wooden door. It creaked tiredly as Adi lifted the latch and pushed it open and upon following her through, Uritus found himself in a circular room capped by a glass dome.

Wide windows surrounded them, a couple of large metal contraptions set in front of them which appeared to be something like spyglasses. A few small rugs covered the floor, and several cushions as well, with stacks of thick, weathered books leaning here and there against the walls. Filling baskets scattered around the room were dozens of scrolls, the few which lay flat revealing themselves to be maps of the sky's constellations or studies of individual celestial bodies. Several candles stood in candelabras and lanterns, lumpy streaks of melted wax tracing down the metal surfaces, but on this night the room was lit only by the light of the moon and stars.

Uritus's eyes scanned the stratosphere above them, regarding open-mouthed not one, but two falling stars streaking their way across the sky. He broke his eyes from the dome finally upon hearing Adiadni's amused laugh and brought his gaze to meet hers, a playful smile splashed across her face.

"I am happy to see you admire the observatory as much as I do."

He nodded, mouth still open, and again lifted his eyes to the sky. "It's breathtaking."

The princess smiled again and stepped closer to one of the windows, peering out at the land that spread for miles in every direction. "Olythia studies the sky here," she said without turning. "They were kind enough to let me sit and observe as a child while they charted the space above. They taught me about the star clusters, the moon's phases, the way the map moves, changes as the seasons do but always returns to the way it was."

Uritus allowed his eyes to fall from the heavens and land on the princess. He took a few slow steps to bring himself beside her before the window.

Adiadni continued speaking, "They've shown me how the stars themselves foretell my journey... our journey, of its trials and subsequent victory. Veldis taught me how to respond to my Magical instincts, Aurena taught me about the land..." She paused, sighing. "And now, I've found you, and I have everything I could possibly need. To succeed."

Uritus sensed that she spoke these words more to convince herself of her preparedness than him. "Does it tire you," he asked, "...to be seen first as the Suvah rather than just as Adiadni?"

The princess chuckled to herself and released a tired breath. "I suppose it does. Every gown I've ever worn has been tailored to leave my right shoulder bare. My father thinks it important that the people be reminded of who I am so they may be stirred up for the cause. But it *can* be exhausting to be viewed primarily as a symbol." She turned her head from the window to regard the fisherman. "And you?" she asked. "Thrust so suddenly into your own destiny. I'm sure that comes with its own sense of overwhelm."

"Yes..." He nodded. "I keep hoping I might wake up one morning and feel different."

She cocked her head to the side. "Different how?"

He hesitated. "Different than I am. More than I am..."

She frowned, a confused smile on her lips. "What more is there?"

What more is there?

He breathed out a quick laugh. The wave rushed up and over his head and he let it consume him completely. He stammered, "It is just... To be known by merely a few dozen and then suddenly by thousands is a unique transition to make."

"You've handled it rather gracefully."

"Thank you, I have a wise leader who's been a remarkable example."

Adi blushed, gazing outside again. "When you come to understand that your people want what is best for you just as you would wish for them, it makes it easier, I think. All anyone ever truly wants is to be seen."

Uritus nodded slowly, understandingly, keeping his eyes fixed on his counterpart as she looked across her kingdom. "On that note, I must thank you, Adiadni, for the way you have always seen me."

The princess turned to meet his eyes and smiled, "That is a mutual gratitude, to be sure. The way that I feel at ease with you... the way I have never felt the need to don the same mask around you that I do with nearly everyone... it means more than you know." She turned again to regard the land below. "To travel to the edge of this world, beyond its uncharted territory, to go willingly to face that which none before have ever dared to… it feels possible now that I know that you will go beside me."

"I will," the fisherman promised. "And I do. And I will continue for as long as you wish for my company."

Adi smiled. "I know." She turned, bringing her body to face him and extending her hands to take his. "And in spite of my unreadiness… I will make your way. And I will lead you into the dark so that together, we may emerge from it with the Light in hand, so that the Free People need never fear it again."

The corners of his mouth lifted as he witnessed the courage that lit in her eyes. "I know."

They remained that way for a moment or two, feet turned toward one another, hands tied, eyes locked, sparkling with the light of the moon. And as they stood, settling deeper into the assuredness of their respective callings, each felt, ever so softly, their hands begin to warm and their muscles begin to relax. It was Adiadni who first identified the cool spot in the center of her chest and the tiny stone talisman that seemed be the cause. She smiled and raised her right hand to pause beside her face before she broke their silence, "Do you remember what I taught you?"

Uritus smiled and raised his right hand, their left hands making their unconscious way to one another. "I do."

Her grin widened and then she hardened her expression to appear serious and this made Uritus laugh. "Well then," she brought her middle finger to touch her thumb and began to gently rub them together, an action repeated by the fisherman. "May the Divine guide us, may the Source go with us, may the Mother protect us…" She paused, searching for an end to her prayer.

"And may our feet find their way."

The Suvah smiled at the Adalos's offering. They brought their fingers to snap, blue sparks lighting around their fingertips, a tiny flame atop Adiadni's. They laughed in their wonder and surprise.

"You could do that too, if you tried," she said seriously. "Were you to ask the Source for more, I am certain you would receive it."

He considered her words carefully before shaking his head. "I don't want more. I don't need it. I have all I could need now that you're here."

She giggled and blushed and lowered her head. He let out a slow breath and followed her back down to the library.

That night, both the fisherman and the princess slept soundly and awoke in the morn to the radiant color of the Suscundos sunrise.

***

The traveling party gathered in the square the morning of their departure surrounded by citizens eagerly awaiting the chance to see them off. The Adalos and Suvah stood behind the doors of the palace in quiet anticipation of the moment they would be expected to descend the steps and join their companions. With them stood the king and queen and the royal Keepers, who took this time to impart their final blessings and words of encouragement upon the young people as they bid them farewell.

Queen Betina held her daughter tightly in her arms, tears gathering in their eyes as they savored their final moments before they would be parted for the first time. King Agamemnon, too, felt the sting of his sorrow twisting in his chest as he embraced his daughter. He saw before him his child, a precious little bird whom he longed to keep forever in his pocket, sheltered and protected from the harshness of the world around her. But as she stood—head held high, in a white dress that fell to her knees and carved a line across her shoulders, plated in brown leather armor like her counterpart, her hair tied behind her head, and the Sword of Light strapped to her hip—he saw also the heart of the warrior that beat within her chest. Surely she, and he who stood beside her, were the ones who would come to protect them all.

Anxiety pulsed through the veins of the prophesied ones as the king and queen exited through the palace doors and descended the steps below. The trio of Keepers took their leave as the voice of the king could be heard greeting the crowd and remarking on the monumental nature of this occasion. Uritus and Adiadni looked at each other, finding themselves alone in the grand foyer. Neither spoke, listening instead to the vocal enthusiasm of the crowd beyond the doors. The thoughts that traced each of their minds focused primarily on concern for one another, and they shared a small smile before the doors were again opened and they stepped out into a shower of morning light and Suscundos sound.

They paused for a moment at the top of the stairs, each of them holding one hand out proudly as a greeting and a gesture of thanks. Uritus took several long breaths, steeling himself against the sensory overwhelm. Adiadni basked in the noise, allowing the love of her people to wash over her. They descended slowly, joining the king and queen on the final tier of steps as the citizens of Suscundos cast fistfuls of petals into the air. Their party and their horses greeted them when they reached the square, and Adi was quickly wrapped up in the arms of her three friends.

Uritus allowed his eyes to drift, admiring the tangible feeling of love that ricocheted throughout the city. He observed his friends, many of them sharing tearful goodbyes with those they had met and become close to during their time in Suscundos. He caught Uriah's eye as the Wizard beamed with pride at his pupil, and the two shared a smile.

"Tell me, young Adalos, how are you feeling on this fine morning?"

Uritus considered this thoughtfully, looking once more to Adiadni as she crouched down and embraced Fennispar. A smile spread across his lips and he chuckled as he came upon his answer, "Ready."

The Wizard chuckled as well and turned to mount his tall gray horse as Uritus greeted Moonracer and moved to do the same.

"Wait!"

Uritus paused, one foot in his stirrup, and turned to see the dwarf child rushing to his side. He brought himself down upon one knee and Fennispar came to a stop before him. "What can I do for you, Good Sir?"

Fennispar panted tiredly. "You cannot leave without a good luck charm!" He took one of Uritus's hands into his own and deposited into it a small leather pouch, not unlike many the fisherman had seen during his time in Suscundos.

Uritus smiled, opening the pouch and peering inside at the set of green dice. "This is an incredibly generous gift," he said to the boy. "I promise to care for it well."

"It's the only set I've got left..." Fennispar admitted. "But I haven't lost a game since Press gave it to me, so I think it's special."

Uritus was touched by this kindness. He stood, tucking the pouch into his saddlebag and retrieving another before kneeling once again. "Well, it would be a shame to have you fall out of practice in the time that I'm gone. What say you to a trade?"

Fennispar's face lit up as Uritus presented him with the smooth, dark leather bag, and he grinned upon opening it and seeing the deep red dice that lay inside. He flung his arms around his new friend. "I am sorry I cannot go with you," he said regretfully. "But if there is anyone in the Free World who I trust to protect Adi and win the war, it's you."

Uritus returned his embrace. "Thank you, Good Sir. Your vote of confidence means more than you know."

Fennispar departed, excitedly chattering about his new set of dice as he returned to stand with Winchells and Exstarferus. Uritus mounted his horse, noting that his party had already done the same. The king and queen had bidden farewell to their daughter and ascended the steps to stand atop the lowest tier. Agamemnon held out a hand to the excitable crowd and they hushed.

"This is a historic day," spoke the king. "One that will be remembered forever by all who witness it, the beginning of a remarkable story which will be passed down for generations. I am honored, humbled, and proud to know each of you, brave warriors, accomplished craftsmen, noble travelers. Before you lies a tumultuous path, and your willingness to face it head-on will undoubtedly inspire thousands who live today and millions who will in the future.

"To the Suvah, to my daughter, I wish to say how deeply proud I am of you, of the woman you have become. You carry yourself with strength and grace, and your love for your people is strikingly apparent. May our love—that of myself, your mother, and all of your citizens—embolden you as you make your way."

Adiadni smiled, glassy-eyed, pressed her hands to one another gently, and nodded her thanks to her father.

"And to the Adalos, to our long-awaited Hero, my confidence in you is as steadfast as my confidence in Adiadni. You have shown yourself at every turn to be strong-hearted, just, and brave. May the strength of your courage plate your heart as your armor does your body, and may all obstacles which dare stand in your way fall swiftly at your hand."

Uritus touched his right hand to his chest and lowered his head to the king.

"Go forth now, with the wind of the Divine at your back. We eagerly await your return to our fair city. May you find a steady path as you make your way forward."

The citizens of Suscundos sent up their cries, and through the falling petals, Uritus saw the eyes of his party fixed on him. He turned Moonracer around and led them out of the city and to the Clearing beyond.

Book Two:

The Journey

Chapter Twelve

"Fae and Nevyn Alike"

The 5th of July

It was not until they had moved beyond both walls and the doors closed behind them that Adiadni fully processed where they were and where they were going. Uritus called her attention to their path as they left Suscundos behind and she moved Swadalla ahead of the others to ride beside him. From her saddlebag, she retrieved the map, regarding it as they made their slow trek across the Clearing. She knew where they were going and all the places they planned to stop along the way. But she was suddenly struck with the weight of this particular venture, of leading a group with far more life experience than her across a land that she had never before traversed. As she raised her eyes to gaze across the Clearing to the edge of the Forest of Idor, she realized that she had no choice but to find her courage, as she would not be granted a second chance.

"What say you, Adi?" called Uriah from behind her. "Shall we make our way into the forest ahead or find a way around?"

Adiadni looked again at the map and then lifted her eyes to the treeline. The trees were tall, varying in their shapes and species, but all crowned with dark green foliage that danced playfully in the sunlight. They seemed inviting at first glance, but also appeared to serve the same purpose as the walls that surrounded Suscundos—to protect that which lay just inside.

Her eyes traced the edge of the forest to where it met the river to the North. It was via this river that Suscundos received most of their imports, grain mostly, and other crops sent by boat from the Valley of the Sun. But here the river was wide, rushing increasingly faster as the water made its way to the cliffs East of the city. She knew that they were not due for a delivery for some time and that the river would be nearly impossible for them all to cross here on burdened horses without the aid of a boat. She turned her head South, seeing that the edge of the forest stretched for miles in that direction. To divert from the course laid out by the map would delay them by many days.

Still, she hesitated. She trusted the Seven Kings and the things they foresaw, but it remained true that times were different now than when the map was drawn. Whether they deemed themselves to be or not, she regarded the fae as she did all of her citizens—as beings she was sworn to protect. It had been a century-and-a-half since their treaty was passed, and her stomach clenched as she considered that she may be the one to break it. But the pressing matter of their quest remained in her mind of utmost importance and so, uncertain as she was, she knew what must be done.

The sound of her name spoken by Uritus broke her from her contemplative state and she looked at him to see a soft smile of encouragement on his face. Again, she looked ahead.

"We will travel through the forest."

"Very well," spoke the Wizard. "We shall follow the path laid out for us by the Kings. If I may, I strongly recommend that we make our way through Idor with haste."

Adiadni nodded, becoming acutely aware of a queasiness making a home in her stomach.

"What exactly is it we're afraid of beyond these woods?" Oripidus queried. "Do the fae be that vicious?"

"Not vicious, just… tricksy," Punznes offered. "They don't abide by the same rules that we do. They're all Keepers, every one of them, and that means something different to them than it does to us."

"They exist on… a higher plane or something like that?" Havian looked to the woods with intrigue.

"Not quite," spoke the princess. "Rather a plane just a shade above our own. An overlapping one."

The chattering about the mysterious beings continued as Adi began to roll up the map. Her companions shared stories of the history as they understood it, Uriah chiming in from time to time to correct them. Uritus envisioned what the forest may have looked like over a hundred years ago and wondered to himself if it had always been this monumental in size and if it would continue to grow in the future.

He recalled the stories of king Ergo Vindella and the years leading up to when the treaty was signed. Tensions had grown between the Free People and the fae, the Free People wishing for the fae to aid in the Free World's provision of resources and the fae wishing not to be governed. It was solely the fae who dwelt in the Forest of Idor who felt unjustly forced to contribute to a system they had no part in creating, the fae who dwelt elsewhere having cohabitated with the humans, elves, dwarves, and trolls for some time. Ultimately, king Ergo had determined that allowing the fae within the forest to live as they pleased was the most just way that he could see to their wellbeing and thus, the treaty was born.

In the years since, the fae who dwelt within Idor had garnered a reputation of selfishness, untrustworthiness, and, in the minds of some, malice. Uritus didn't think this was fair. He had never considered either of the parties involved in the conflict to be the villain in the story, and he understood the phenomenon of fear tied to a lack of understanding. The longer one group was separated from another, the more space for speculation, rumor, and myth abounded, and it was likely that this would prove to be true on both sides.

Uritus believed the fae within Idor to be as capable of rationale and understanding as he believed the Free People to be. But it remained true that the closer they drew to the trees, the more uneasy he became. He shook this feeling off. The best thing they could do as they entered Idor was keep their heads on their shoulders and be intentional about not making enemies with potential allies. He reminded the group of this and they agreed.

Perplexus made his way up to ride at Adi's right hand as she moved to return the map to her saddlebag. "I'm not sure if we've spoken about it much, but I am something of a navigator myself," he told her. "I navigated for this group as we made our way to Suscundos from the White Mountains, and I'd be happy to offer such services to you."

Uritus affirmed, "He's rather gifted in the field. Never been lost once, not even as a boy. That miner's blood runs through his veins."

Adi smiled at the navigator, "I'm certain I'll rely on your expertise then."

Perplexus gestured to the piece of weathered paper, "I'd be happy to carry that for you as well if you'd like."

The princess hesitated, feeling her fingers tighten their grip around the scroll ever so slightly. She trusted Perplexus, but the idea of passing such a heavy torch of responsibility—*her* responsibility—to someone else so early on in their journey brought on a quiet sense of anxiety.

The navigator sensed her hesitation. "Of course, if you'd feel more comfortable keeping it at your side, I'd understand."

Adiadni breathed a small sigh of relief at this show of empathy. "I would. It's just… the Kings entrusted such a burden to me…"

Perplexus held up a hand. "Say no more. But know that my offer still stands should you change your mind."

Adi nodded and tucked the map safely back into her saddlebag.

Before they knew it, the traveling party had come to a stop before the trees. They gazed up at them, craning their necks to catch a glimpse at their towering crowns and squinting their eyes to see beyond their numerous shadows. The Forest of Idor was daunting and captivating all at once. A cool zephyr brushed past them and into the woods, stirring the grass as it went.

The princess moved her horse ahead of the rest of her party and turned to face them.

"I know little of what we will encounter when we enter the forest," she admitted, a slight tremor in her voice. "Remember that we are the intruders here, and any hostility we may encounter on our way must be met with grace and understanding. This is their home, and they will no doubt wish to protect it as we would our own."

Hearing a hint of a whisper in her right ear, she whipped her head around, scanned the trees behind her, and saw nothing but a silver dragonfly which disappeared as quickly as it arrived. She returned her attention to her companions and Uritus regarded her with concern.

"As Uriah suggested, we will make our way through as quickly as possible. Remain on the paths, avoid the circles. Consume nothing but the rations you carry with you, and keep your wits about you. We'll be all right." She added this last bit mostly as a comfort to herself. She turned Swadalla to face the trees again, gazing up at them and taking in a slow, shaky breath.

Entering the forest, the travelers were immediately taken by the landscape that greeted them. From just outside Idor, the trees appeared daunting, menacing even, their thick trunks and towering faces seeming to say *beware*. But now, as the woods stretched around them, they marveled at the sight.

Sunlight dappled the soft green moss and creeping thyme that carpeted the forest floor, and shadows played here and there as the wind caused the trees to sway. Colorful fruit dotted many of the shrubs that grew around them and hung enticingly from the branches of the trees. Vines of ivy and passionflowers crawled along the ground and snaked their way up the deep reddish wood of the tree trunks. Mushrooms sprouted from the earth and the rot of fallen branches, varied in their shapes and colors but all giving off a sickly-sweet aroma that one noticed when passing them by. Lichens grew across the faces of boulders and bark, and small puffs of cottony seedlings drifted through the breeze. Brightly patterned pollinators drank their fill of the sweet nectar of the flowers, and iridescent beetles meandered from one place to another. The Forest of Idor was a sight to behold.

Adiadni paused and took in a breath as she regarded the glittering forest, allowing Uritus and Moonracer to again arrive at her side.

"Not what you pictured?" the fisherman asked.

"I'm not sure what I pictured," she replied. "But no, I suppose it wasn't this."

The muted clopping of hooves on the forest path and the murmurs of the travelers were the only sounds that met the ears of the Suvah, save for the occasional whispering breeze or rustling brush. Her eyes darted around, searching for movement. Other than the occasional fox, deer, or rabbit, she saw none.

Uritus spoke again, his voice low this time, "Are you feeling uneasy?"

Adiadni nodded, a slight movement perceivable only to him. "Something's watching us. Has been since before we entered."

Uritus turned to look over his shoulder, hearing the snapping of a twig to his left but seeing nothing. "We needn't stay long," he said assuringly, returning his focus to her. "It's, what, not quite two days of riding to the other side? Less even, if we elect not to make a proper camp."

The princess nodded again, only half paying attention to what the fisherman was saying. She strained her ears and squinted at the forest, hearing what she perceived to be faint laughter. Uritus heard this as well and turned to meet the eyes of the Wizard at the back of their train. Uriah nodded to indicate that the fisherman was not alone in what he had observed and a shimmering dragonfly whizzed past as he did.

The paths that crossed and wound their way through Idor were not paved, but rather earth that had been packed down and worn free of vegetation due to centuries of traffic. They moved with the landscape, curving as it did; the largest of them wide enough for two riders on horseback to travel side-by-side, the rest much smaller, some appearing to be difficult for anyone larger than a child to make their way around and below the stooping branches. Glimmering pools of clear water could be seen here and there a ways off from the paths, some of them adorned with lily pads and home to croaking frogs, but most alluring in their stillness with not a ripple dancing upon their surfaces despite the continuous breeze.

The famed circles were not as numerous as they had been rumored to be, but they too could be observed scattered across the forest floor, and the traveling companions pointed them out to one another. Most appeared as expected: rings of mushrooms or flowers with a bare bed of moss in the center, easily identified, easily avoided. Several, however, were a bit trickier to spot. In some cases, the flora at the edges of the rings was sparse, low to the ground, or a shade of green hardly different from the moss within. Others were rather divots in the earth, large stumps broken down by time with just enough space for someone to stand in their centers, or rings of trees one might miss if too focused on the state of the ground before them. The travelers soon determined that looking for the bare centers of the circles was a safer way of being sure they stayed out of any spaces they shouldn't be, and as the rings appeared to overlap the paths only occasionally, they were confident in their ability to avoid them.

The princess's sense of unease continued to grow the deeper they traveled without encountering one of the fabled beings who dwelt within. The sound of laughter—subtly malicious in its tone—continued to echo around them. The rest of the companions began to pick up on it as well, questioning whether it could just be the breeze or perhaps the wildlife.

Adiadni was certain by now that the fae were well aware of the presence of the intruders in the forest. Whether they hid for their own safety or simply to bide their time before they made their attack, she was not sure. She turned her head to look back where they had come from, questioning momentarily if they should turn around. She rejected the idea as she observed that the forest's entrance was nowhere in sight. The only way out was through.

A dragonfly darted past her face and she whipped her head around just in time to catch a flurry of movement behind a tree ahead. She nudged Swadalla's sides, urging her into a trot. "Is someone there?"

The wind surged and the sound of the mysterious snicker grew louder. Uritus called Adiadni by her name.

She did not hear and did not turn and failed to notice that her party had brought themselves to a stop behind her. She continued forward, seeing the figure rush from one tree to another.

"Hello?" she called after them. "We do not wish to hurt you!"

"Adi, slow down."

The navigator's voice drifted over her, no more present in her mind than the whoosh of the wind through the trees. The laughter was clear now, surrounding them on all sides.

Uriah closed his eyes and bowed his head, his voice no more than a whisper, "Come back to us, Adiadni."

"Adiadni stop!" The fear in Uritus's voice ripped through the trees. "The circle!"

The princess was broken from her trance in a manner similar to being jolted from a deep sleep. She gasped as the fisherman's voice sounded in her ears, pulling on her reins and bringing Swadalla to a halt. Blinking, she shook her head and observed the ground before her. The path had grown wide and split off in several directions, each branching off from a large circle framed by skinny white mushrooms—a clearly identifiable faen ring, just in their path. Adiadni and her horse had stopped mere steps before it.

She frowned, chiding herself for missing something so easily spotted, and lifted her eyes to the trees ahead. Whatever creature had been moving about just moments before was now nowhere to be seen. Swadalla whickered, a nervous sound. Adi turned to meet the eyes of the fisherman.

Before she could open her mouth to explain what she had seen, the wind picked up again, whipping strands of loose hair across her face. The forest appeared to darken and the laughter sounded all around them, loud, its many-layered notes sending a chill down Adiadni's spine. The travelers looked up and around. Several reached for their weapons before Uritus called them to stop. Swadalla snorted and stomped, clearly overwhelmed by the ever-increasing unfamiliar stimuli.

"Whoa, girl, you're all right. We're all right."

The sound of the princess's voice did little to calm the distressed horse, and her anxious whinnies, though growing louder, were quickly drowned out by the sounds of the agitated forest.

Uritus felt panic surge through his limbs. He urged Moonracer forward, rushing to Adi's side, Nadarum following close behind.

Adiadni clung to her saddle as Swadalla reared once and then a second time, and the princess was cast to the ground, landing on her back half inside the circle.

Uritus leapt from his horse, not hearing Nadarum as the horseman called after him to be careful. The fisherman brought himself to kneel in the dirt beside the princess, neither aware nor caring that he too had now crossed the edge of the ring.

He gripped her hand with one of his own, the other cradling the back of her head as he anxiously inquired if she had been hurt, breathing a sigh of relief when she shook her head no. Her vision was foggy, her head swimming as the laughter around them deepened, but she felt no pain.

Punznes appeared beside Uritus to assess her for injuries. Qibat soared high into the sky above the forest, and Nadarum struggled to calm the shrieking horse.

The wind whistled in all directions, quickly becoming a rushing whirlwind that spun around the travelers. Several of them dismounted, drawing their weapons as others shielded their eyes from the debris that whipped past.

"Steady, now!" Uriah called over the wind. "We are entering their plane."

Uritus pulled Adiadni toward himself in an attempt to shield her from the wind. She responded in kind, gripping his shirt with all her might and burying her face in his chest. The vortex spun faster and louder as the cries of maniacal laughter rose to meet it. The party felt they were mere seconds from being swept off their feet and then, suddenly…

Silence.

Uritus lifted his head cautiously. The forest looked as it had, vivid, with a peaceful breeze drifting through it. But now there swam around them a thick golden haze, and the seedlings that had previously drifted through the air appeared to be made of twinkling light. Nadarum calmed Swadalla and the rest of the party moved to join their leaders at the edge of the circle, clutching their weapons, eyes darting around the forest. Uritus and Punznes helped Adiadni to her feet. Qibat was still nowhere to be seen.

"Nothing's really changed…" Laivar observed. "Have we truly left our own realm?"

"Not quite."

The unfamiliar voice from within the circle startled the travelers. They abruptly turned their attention to the being who stood there.

They were of average height and build, fair of complexion, pointy-eared like the elves and dwarves, with a silvery-white head of hair partially tied back. They wore a loose white shirt and fitted gray trousers with nothing on their feet, a single obsidian earring dangling from their right lobe. They appeared— surprising to all members of the traveling party—utterly unassuming.

"Long have we awaited the inevitable invasion of the *nevyn*, but I must admit, I expected more of you."

"Nevyn?" Perplexus stood to Adiadni's right, his hand hovering over the knife hanging from his belt.

"The non-fae."

The fantastical stranger chuckled at the explanation offered by the princess. "And who are you, little *nevyna*, so knowledgeable and aware of our ways? I believe I am correct in assuming that you are the one responsible for leading this invasion?"

Adi hesitated, recalling dozens of warnings from elders throughout her life to never give the fae her name. She considered now how she had never been offered a reason why such an action could be dangerous, and as she stood there in Idor, still physically able and not bound despite having crossed the border of the ring, she determined that allowing the fear of the folklore to continue to guide her steps would certainly be of no help now. She turned to meet the eyes of the Wizard and he nodded to assure her that she was safe.

She took a breath and a step forward, now standing fully within the boundary of the circle. "I am Adiadni Vindella, heir to the throne of the Free World, and these are my traveling companions. I ask your forgiveness for the unwelcome intrusion, but I assure you that we do not mean to invade. We wish only to pass through to the other side swiftly and peaceably."

"A Vindella…" The faen stranger regarded her with a note of curiosity shining in their eyes. "Ergo's girl."

"Several generations removed, but yes, he is my ancestor." The princess paused. "And who are you?"

The silver-headed one began to laugh, quietly at first, but then the sound grew, its many notes darkening the forest, crescendoing in a malevolent tone that chilled the blood of the travelers. The light returned as they silenced and their eyes met those of the princess, "I am incomprehensible to you."

Suddenly, the fae disappeared. The traveling companions looked on in amazement as they rematerialized just behind Adiadni and Uritus, "I am a natural wonder…"

Again they vanished, reappearing behind the party and causing everyone to turn their heads to regard them, "An enigma…"

Once more the stranger evanesced, appearing as a row of figures across the far side of the circle, materializing and fading just as quickly until only one solid form remained, "A force eternal and immovable."

Adi swallowed, her stomach churning. She had held a fraction of hope tightly in one palm, praying as they entered Idor that their path through would be smooth and straight, but at this moment, all she saw was gray. She kept her chin lifted so as not to betray the anxious beating of her heart to the stranger or the ones who looked to her for guidance. "I believe that, Friend. But I have given you my name and now, I humbly ask for your own."

The fae's icy-blue eyes narrowed at the confidence of the girl before them. "You've a surprising amount of audacity, little queen, to barge your way into my forest and then demand that I reveal myself to you."

Adiadni shook her head. "I am not a queen. The leader and guardian of the Free World is my father, king Agamemnon Vindella."

The stranger chuckled. "Quite cowardly of your king to send his child to do his dirty work, don't you think?"

Adi felt her blood begin to boil. "Our work is not *dirty*. And this mission is not his but my own. I tell you again, we wish no harm upon you or the forest or any of its residents. We will touch nothing that is not ours—we needn't even make camp if you would prefer it. All we ask is clearance to the other side."

She paused, looking momentarily to Uritus for reassurance. He did not know the right action to take under such a circumstance, but he trusted her judgment and her leadership.

She continued when he nodded, "What I can tell you of my mission is that it does concern you—all of you—who dwell in the Forest of Idor. And should I succeed or should I fail, the force that stands against me will not hesitate at your borders or treat you as a sovereign and independent nation. All fire sees is kindling. You have my sincerest apologies for the upset, frustration, and fear that my and my company's presence in your home has no doubt caused you. But whether you grant my request to pass through or not, you have my word that I will do everything in my power to protect your home just as I will my own when the Shadow reaches our doorstep. All of that said, your patience and cooperation would do much to ensure the efficacy of my mission. So I ask you again, what is your name?"

The silver-headed one regarded the princess curiously, skipping through the fabric of the unfamiliar plane to appear just before her, looking her up and down. "Your ancestors certainly taught you a thing or two about speaking politically," they remarked, circling her for a moment before returning to their place on the far side of the ring.

They let their eyes drift over the other members of the traveling party, fixating briefly on the Wizard and the young man to the princess's left before returning their focus to her, "But I also can be capable of peaceful negotiation, so..." A mischievous smile played at the corners of their mouth. "Let's play a game."

Adiadni shifted nervously. The travelers looked at one another with unsure expressions.

"To show that I am fair and generous, I will allow all of you a chance to guess my riddle. However, I will only accept one answer, and once an answer is given, it cannot be taken back. Should you win, little princess, I will give you my name, and I will clear your path to the other side of the forest."

Adi swallowed. "And should we lose?"

The stranger shrugged dismissively. "Should you lose... you can find your own way out."

Adiadni looked to Uritus. In her silence, she tried to apologize, to communicate that she felt they had no other way forward. She released a long breath as in his gaze she saw nothing but reassurance and understanding. The fisherman knew well the kind of stress his counterpart was under, being forced to make diplomatic decisions on behalf of herself, her party, and the whole of her kingdom mere hours after departing from her home for the first time. He was impressed, as he always was, with the striking amount of grace and dignity she had shown throughout the whole ordeal, despite her obvious fear, and he agreed that to comply with the wishes of the stranger was the best move for all of them.

She turned again to the fae and nodded briskly, "Fine. What are the rules of your game?"

The fantastical one smiled, a look neither specifically sinister nor playful, but perhaps a combination of the two. "It's simple really. I'll tell you a riddle, you give me the correct answer. Does that sound fair?"

Adi considered this. "Certainly. That is... if you can give me your word that there *is* a correct answer."

The fae nodded solemnly, holding their right hand to their chest. "I swear it on the Forest herself."

"All right then."

"Good." They brought their hands to touch one another. "Let us begin. Listen closely."

The travelers leaned forward unconsciously in anticipation.

"I am the light that kisses your eyelids and the dark that tucks you in at night,
The sensation of trying to recall a dream after having awoken—fleeting.

Adiadni's lips parted softly. The only sound that met her ears was the continuous rustling of the wind through the trees as her party also contemplatively paused, replaying the verse in their minds and all arriving at the conclusion that the riddle itself had been meaningless.

After several seconds, the princess began to speak, "I... I am..."

The faen stranger chuckled darkly. "Sorry, little princess. The moment's passed. Best to be a bit quicker on your feet next time."

"You dirty *cheat.*"

The vitriol in Havian's voice rang in Uritus's ears like a threat, and it was quickly followed by the sound of a sword being drawn from its sheath.

"If you think you can get away with that tricksy shit, I'll be happy to show you what happens to those who dare stand in the path of the Suvah."

The fisherman turned, firmly gripping the arm of the swordsman as the silver-headed one began to laugh. "Cool off, Hav. You'll have your share of battles. This is not the one."

Adiadni clenched her hands into fists as the wind again began to race around them, the dark laughter as it rose taking on a new tone of malice.

"Not so peaceful after all, it would seem." The fae remained standing within the edge of the ring, still, not a hair moved out of place by the wind which forced the travelers to brace themselves. "It would appear that the nevyn have not changed and that your selfishness still takes precedence over your promises. I, for one, am not at all surprised. Good luck finding your way out now."

The wind rushed around them, a vortex that came to a head, forcing the companions to cover their eyes to protect them from the dust and debris clawing at their skin as it rushed past. And then, as quickly as it began, the onslaught ceased, and Adiadni lifted her head just in time to see a silver dragonfly dart away into the forest.

Chapter Thirteen

"The Hubris of Havian Elix"

Qibat returned to his post on the physician's shoulder almost immediately upon the ceasing of the second vortex. The travelers were shaken by their interaction with the fae, but they quickly collected themselves and returned to their saddles to make their way out of Idor. Briefly considered and dismissed was the option to turn around and head back in the direction they had come. Instead, the riders pressed on, anxious to find their way to the other side of the forest as the mystical beauty that continued to be revealed around them now appeared hostile rather than enchanting. The golden mist that shrouded them upon entering the plane of the fae had now dissipated, the seedlings again returning to their initial form as fluffy puffs of cloud, and it was these environmental changes—plus the occasional echoing of invisible laughter through the air—that indicated to the companions that they were now shut off from interaction with any faen beings. Adiadni wasn't sure if she should feel defeated or relieved.

They stuck to their plan for some time, no camp, no prolonged stops. But as night fell once and then again and the forest around them remained mostly unchanged, they began to wonder if perhaps the worst of their obstacles had not yet been surpassed. Such fears were confirmed when, two days after their initial departure from Suscundos, they found themselves standing before a familiar circle, its tiny ring of pungent mushrooms all too recognizable to the weary travelers.

The map was of little help to guide them through the forest, its scale too grand to reveal the individual paths that wound their way through. Adiadni found herself consulting it regularly nonetheless, her eyes straining for a potential clue she may have missed. It was clear to both Uritus and Uriah how desperately the princess sought to keep up the morale of her companions despite her ever-growing frustration for how they had somehow become lost. She determined that if they were stuck wandering anyway, they might as well rest when they could, and so they began to camp for short periods in the night, though never building a fire.

Some of them suggested at one point that a pair of them scout ahead and see what they could find. But the idea that the scouts might themselves become lost and unable to find their way back to the group took root in Adi's mind and she refused to let anyone travel too far on their own. Perplexus tracked the sun and the moon to keep them pointed to the West, but somehow they found themselves, again and again, returning before the same faen ring.

Nearly a week passed like this, with days full of slow, steady traveling that had begun to feel less and less like progress, the nights restless and short. Every so often, Punznes sent Qibat up into the sky to confirm that they were headed in the right direction, and the bird always returned with no corrections to report. The travelers had grown weary, the rations they carried with them lessening day by day.

They brought themselves to a stop one afternoon amidst a triad of glittering pools to rest, their prior aim of remaining only ever on the paths abandoned long ago. Uritus and Uriah had stepped away from the rest of their party to convene on their own. Adiadni sought them out, watching the ground carefully as she stepped, the voices of the others fading behind her.

"I just don't know what else to do," spoke the fisherman to the Wizard. He'd spent days thinking through their dilemma and still felt at a loss. "Perhaps we could summon them again, their leader."

"To my understanding, the fae in Idor do not have a leader," Uriah replied. "The one we encountered was playing the role of a spokesperson of sorts. But they cannot be summoned again, not without their name."

"Their name…" Uritus paused where he had been pacing and lifted his eyes to the trees. "That's why they refused to give it to us. Were we to step into a circle again…?"

"That would successfully bring us back to their plane, but we cannot guarantee that anyone will be there to greet us when we arrive. And as it is, the more time we spend in an environment as strange as theirs, the more susceptible our minds will be to trickery and hallucination. It is far safer for all of us to conduct our affairs on the plane where we belong."

"Perhaps we could bargain with them…"

Uritus turned his head at the sound of Adi's gentle voice as she brought herself to stand beside him.

"Surely, my father has no shortage of coin and resources. We could offer them payment in exchange for passage through…"

"A generous offer yes, but the fae have no need for our gold or our coin. They do not barter or make exchanges as we do, at least not here in Idor. They take what they need from the forest and pour their energy back into it. A symbiotic relationship that has existed for centuries."

Adi chewed on her lip anxiously as she considered Uriah's words. "So… are we to just remain lost then?"

"I am sorry that I can not be of more help, my dear. The complex nature of these modern faen customs and culture remain, for the most part, foreign to me."

Uritus looked to his counterpart, feeling an ache in his chest as her sense of defeat showed on her face. He racked his brain for a solution, his mind's eye lighting on only one thing. "Would you be willing, Adiadni, to attempt to return in the direction we came? To travel East and make our way out and around the forest instead of attempting to proceed through? There is much that we do not know about Idor, but it seems likely that *something*—whether that be the fae or the forest itself—is manipulating the landscape, perhaps even toying with our minds to keep us traveling in circles. I cannot say for certain, but I would wager that we may be released from this cycle should we try to go back rather than forward."

Adiadni nodded slowly in agreement. "Yes, I believe you are probably right. It will be unfortunate to have lost so much time, but we run the risk of losing even more should we continue on the path we've been taking. I do fear, though, that even if we do attempt to turn around, we'll just find ourselves arriving before that same damned ring again. Our sense of direction, Lex's skill, and Qibat's eye are all that we have to guide us, and it remains clear that those are of little use to us here."

The Wizard and the fisherman contemplated this. Uritus leaned back and closed his eyes, resting his head against the rough bark of the tree behind him. Still in the air lingered the quiet sound of echoing laughter. He frowned softly as he attempted to tune it out. He knew there was an answer, a simple solution to their predicament that they had somehow missed, and he silently pleaded with the Divine to make such a solution clear. Several moments passed and the Voice did not meet his ear. But there began to arise a familiar sound, one steady and even and subtle, yet undeniable.

He opened his eyes and they locked with Adiadni's, "The river..."

Her lips parted as she too became aware of the distant sound of rushing water. She turned her head in the direction it was coming from. "Of course..."

"Reality is warped here in Idor, but the same cannot be said of the land that surrounds it. Tuvibati is its own entity."

"There are several spots along the river where traversing it will be much easier than it is near Suscundos," spoke the princess.

"Yes, and should crossing still prove to be a challenge, we can simply follow its path. Use it as our guide. The forest may change around us, but the river will always remain where it is."

"Of course. Uritus, you're brilliant."

The fisherman smiled, his hope invigorated once more.

***

Back at their camp, the rest of the companions prepared to return to their journeying. Perplexus, Nadarum, and Punznes moved the few supplies they had unpacked during their stop to their bags as Ilya and Oripidus made certain that their horses were adequately watered and the others savored what remained of their small meal. The ever-present snicker continued to sound all around them.

"I've never before considered the possibility that I might someday go mad, but that fucking chuckle may well be the thing to do it," said Havian as he slowly and meditatively ran a stone along the edge of his sword.

"I don't know why you're bothering with that," Perplexus commented. "It doesn't appear that you'll get the chance to use it anytime soon."

"A blade can go dull from a lack of use," countered the swordsman calmly. "I joined this quest to offer my protective services to the princess. I'll be damned if I'm not prepared to do that when the time comes."

"A bit ironic, considering how Adi would sooner order you not to use it. Your eagerness to wield a blade played a fairly significant role in our becoming stuck here. Or have you already forgotten?"

Havian chuckled. "They were never going to let us out, Lex. Regardless, as long as we're trapped in this loop, I can be certain that I'll have prepared for when the time arises to find a way out. I'd advise you to do the same."

Perplexus shared a glance with Nadarum but did not respond.

Oripidus looked down at the cool water of one of the pools as the horses drank their fill, enraptured by the way the sun rippled across its surface. "I've half a mind to fill our skins from these here ponds before we depart. Do ye think the water tastes as sweet as it looks?"

"Try it and I'll knock you square off your feet," Ilya replied firmly.

"Come now, if the horses may drink and remain perfectly fine then what could it possibly do to us?"

"We don't know. Which is exactly why we must not partake of it."

The dwarf huffed resignedly and shook his head, the thick, coarse braid that fell across his back exaggerating this movement. "We're trapped here either way. Can't imagine it would make much of a difference at this point."

"It appears most everything in Idor was designed to be a trap," Laivar remarked, staring wistfully down into another small pond from its bank where he lounged with Mikka.

"I don't think that's a fair characterization."

The poet chuckled. "What would you call it then, Mik, this intoxicating cycle, this lavish land lush with delicacies which may well kill us if we partake of them?"

The former soldier regarded the glistening surface of the pool thoughtfully. "I think it would be particularly arrogant to assume that any of this place was designed with us in mind at all."

"But why the legend then?" Laivar asked earnestly. "Why the tales stuffed to the brim with intrigue if they're only meant to keep us out?"

"You seem to be forgetting, my friend, who it was that spread such stories, for it was not the fae of Idor, but our parents and their own. Generations of... what do they call us... nevyn? Generations of nevyn who passed down tales to ward their offspring away from land which is not ours to claim. I, for one, am grateful that such stories taught us simply to be wary rather than to fear."

"You've heard the wrong stories then," Havian spoke again, "...if you can truly think of the fae without feeling a hint of terror for the damage they may well cause you."

Mikka kept her attention fixed on the crystal clear water. "On the contrary, Hav. I recognize the power of the fae well, though I do not understand it. I just happen to be of the belief that there is more to them than that, just as there is more to you than that blade of yours."

Havian chuckled. "Fair enough."

The companions continued going about their tasks in silence and Mikka brought her head to rest in her hand as she continued to stare down into the peaceful pond. So cold and refreshing appeared the water, and it brought to mind memories of the icy streams that could be found tracing their way through the White Mountains. It was not large by any means, having space enough for perhaps a half dozen individuals to comfortably rest on its banks—the largest of the three pools the group found themselves amongst on this particular day. It appeared relatively shallow as well, its pebble-covered bottom clearly visible from above the surface. But despite its transparency, Mikka could not help but feel as though it held within it a captivating secret.

She was not foolish enough to dare to take a drink, though her friends around her joked, making lighthearted postulations about what may happen if one did. Instead, she let her eyes move lazily from one end of the pool to the other, allowing it to entrance her as the soft music from Laivar's lute filled the air.

She wondered how much truth there was to the stories about Idor, whether it actually was an intoxicating wasteland stuffed full of temptations that would send one into an eternal sleep should they dare partake of them. It would be only natural if the forest had, over its centuries of evolution, developed some sort of defense mechanism against those who may wish to take advantage of its resources. But having spent days here, harmed by nothing save for the mental fog that kept them traveling in circles, it was becoming clear that the harsh reputation of Idor and its inhabitants may not have been entirely warranted.

It was these thoughts that Mikka mulled over as she gently and absentmindedly brought a hand to touch the surface of the pool and dragged it across the water. A moment or two passed as she admired the pattern of the dancing ripples before she became fully aware that her hand was now wet. She swiftly pulled it away, glancing this way and that to ensure that none of her companions had seen.

Fortunately, the only one who had was Laivar, and he shook his head in a mock chastisement but spoke naught and rather continued strumming on his instrument.

Mikka breathed a sigh of relief and returned her attention to the pond, watching as it again settled.

Then, the water began to move in a way she did not understand—rippling and then parting to make way for something—and her eyes widened as a feminine figure breached the surface.

The human and the unfamiliar being stared at each other in silence for a moment, Mikka's mouth having fallen open with wonder. The watery figure appeared as a woman, with long, smooth hair and delicate hands resting gently upon the bank. But rather than being made up of flesh and bone, her body was as transparent as the water of the pool, possessing a slight blue tint and disappearing where she dipped below the surface. She seemed to be just as captivated by Mikka as the former soldier was by her.

Then, Laivar turned his head, and upon seeing one more being to his left than he had expected, loudly gasped.

His surprise startled the watery creature, alerting the others to her presence. They turned to look for the cause of his reaction, mimicking it when they saw her. A few of them instinctually stepped forward to get a closer look, frightening her and causing her to duck back down into the water.

"No, stop!" Mikka held out a hand to the members of her party and they obeyed, remaining in place and returning to silence. Mikka looked to the water again, deeply disappointed to have frightened the one who dwelt within it. Ever so gently, she touched her hand to the surface of the pool again. "Forgive us, we did not mean to frighten you."

A silent moment passed before the figure timidly reemerged from the pool.

Mikka sighed relievedly. "I am sorry to have disturbed you. My friends and I have been lost here for some time, and we've yet to meet anyone save for the one who greeted us. My name is Mikka Galinzen." Slowly, cautiously, she extended a hand toward the watery being.

She stared at Mikka's hand curiously for a moment but did not take it. "Some call me Avyra," she finally replied, her voice soft and melodic. "I am sorry also to have startled you. We have not seen nevyn in Idor for some time."

The travelers regarded their new acquaintance, unsure what to say.

Eventually, Mikka spoke again, "Are you one of the water folk? My grandmother loved one of you, long ago."

Avyra offered a small smile in response. "I am a naiad, yes, one of many who call Idor's pools home."

Oripidus nervously glanced back at the pool the horses had been drinking from. "I suppose we should apologize for disturbin' yer homes as well..."

The naiad shook her head. "The horses are welcome to the Forest's bounties. She exists for us as much as we do for her. The nevyn may partake as well, we just ask that you take only what you need and give thanks for it when you do."

Laivar blinked in his confusion. "Do you mean to say that none of it will cause us harm? It appears we know even less about Idor than we had previously thought."

Avyra shook her head again. "It shouldn't, though I suppose it might if you took too much. Be wary of the mushrooms though. They can leave the nevyn feeling a bit worse for the wear. But everything else, the water, the fruit, you are welcome to all of it. The Forest is not selfish with her gifts, though there seem to exist many myths that state otherwise."

Oripidus excitedly took his water skin along with Ilya's and plunged them beneath the cold surface of one of the pools. "Thank ye, mighty Forest, for yer many blessin's," he spoke loudly. "May the sweet nectar which springs forth from thine earth fuel our bodies as we continue to make our way."

Avyra laughed and then grew serious, "But you say you've become lost? Syv's handiwork no doubt."

The companions looked to one another.

"Syv? Is that the one who greeted us?" Mikka asked. "Silver-headed with an obsidian earring? Appears sometimes as a dragonfly?"

The naiad nodded affirmatively.

"Are they the one keeping us trapped here?"

The watery being sighed. "That would be my assumption. Word spread throughout the forest after your meeting with them that dangerous beings were making their way through Idor, so we hid. Though, we have been observing you since, and, well, you appear to be quite harmless."

"Does this Syv act on behalf of all of you?" Laivar asked.

Avyra shook her head. "They're one of the oldest who dwells here. They sat on the Court which came to the agreement with king Ergo. We do not have any strict hierarchy of leaders as the nevyn do. But Syv has been here for a long time. They love the Forest and all her inhabitants and wish to protect us at all costs. They offered to address you when it became known that strangers had entered Idor. They seemed almost... enthusiastic to do it. Of course we let them, not sure what to expect from you. But it would seem that they did not give the best impression of us. I am sorry for that."

"You are forgiven. We did not make an entirely positive first impression either," spoke Ilya, shooting Havian a sideways glance. "Might you be able to help free us from this loop? Could we negotiate with them?"

"Hmm," the naiad thought for a moment. "Unfortunately, if Syv has decided that you are a threat, you'll be hard-pressed to change their mind. They are rather fond of games though. If you encounter them again, challenging them to a match of some sort may be your best chance to change their impression of you." She paused and turned her attention again to Mikka, "I do want you to know that though they may be sharp, they do mean well. And they do not speak for all the fae who dwell in Idor. We have heard rumors that traveling with you are the prophesied ones. If that is true, know that you have the support of many, fae and nevyn alike. Your mission will ultimately benefit us all."

"We appreciate that," Mikka replied. "The Suvah and the Adalos have their share of challenges ahead of them. We wish to do all we can to make their journey an easy one. We are sorry, again, for any disturbance we may have caused, but we hope that ultimately it will all turn out for the best."

"As do I. May your endless loop be broken soon. And may the path ahead of you be smooth."

The smile shared by the water nymph and the former soldier lasted for a brief moment and was cut off abruptly as Havian leapt to his feet, startling Avyra and causing her to duck back down below the surface of the pool.

"Finally, a useful clue," he said, gripping his sword firmly. "If it's a challenge the laughing one wants, a challenge they will get."

"Simmer down a minute, Hav," Perplexus urged. "Let's find our leaders and figure out a plan. They may well already have one of their own."

"You're more than welcome to do that if you wish," spoke the swordsman. "I'm ending this."

The members of the party looked at one another with concern as Havian called out the name of the silver-headed one and marched away.

***

"Syv!"

Uritus, Adiadni, and Uriah looked up suddenly at the sound of Havian's voice cutting through the forest like a knife. Wordlessly, the two young people rushed back to their camp, the Wizard following close behind.

"What's happened?" Uritus returned first and did a quick scan of them to see that the swordsman and the physician both appeared to be missing.

Havian called out from a ways away, growing quieter as he sought out the one he blamed for their becoming trapped in Idor. None of the companions noticed that the airy, malevolent laughter had ceased some time before.

"He's got it in his head that he needs to confront Syv to get us out," Perplexus explained.

"Syv is…"

"The one who greeted us…" Adiadni spoke with a note of terror in her voice as her eyes fixed on the pool beside which Mikka still knelt.

Uritus looked at the pool and then back to the navigator, "And Punznes?"

"Gone after him."

"Which way?"

Perplexus pointed Uritus in the right direction and the fisherman took off, calling after Havian as he went, the princess on his heels. Uriah instructed the rest of them to prepare to leave, explaining that they had figured out an exit plan. Mikka hesitated briefly beside the still water before hurrying to mount her horse with the others.

***

Havian continued to march blindly forward, ignoring the words of his friend who hastened after him.

"You're not thinking clearly, Man. Wait a minute," Punznes pleaded. "Let's think this through together."

"We've been thinking for days," replied the swordsman. "The rest of you may be fine with this passive approach, but it has gotten us nowhere."

Punznes sighed frustratedly as Havian again called out the name of the fae he sought. He had known the swordsman for years before either of them came to call the keep their home, and he knew well that when Havian made up his mind, it was a near impossible feat to change it.

Still, he pressed, urging his friend to be rational, "I understand why you are frustrated. We all are. But you need to remain focused on our goal. Provoking confrontation with a being you do not understand will only lead to further delay."

192

"Bad idea," crowed Qibat, who flew alongside them.

To Punznes's surprise, Havian brought himself to a stop as they arrived before the all too familiar faen circle and turned to face him, "I know you mean well, Punzie. And I regret deeply the role I have played in trapping us in this cyclical nightmare. But I also know that the Suvah's goal to remain peaceful and diplomatic, though just, will prove impossible if we wish to make any progress."

"Even so," the physician countered as patiently as he could, "I can guarantee that it would be an unnecessary carelessness to create enemies where there are none."

Havian shook his head. "The fae made themselves our enemies long ago."

Punznes frowned, unsure how to get through to his friend. "That is simply not true. You heard the naiad, there are many even here in Idor who wish only for our success."

Havian sighed sadly and took a step forward, bringing his free hand to rest upon the physician's shoulder. "Things are never as simple as we wish they were. I am sorry for the stress I have caused you. Let me now make it right."

Punznes shook his head slowly, hope draining from his face. "This is not the way."

"I wish there was another. But I swore to protect you. All of you. The time has come for me to do just that."

Havian turned then, and Uritus and Adiadni arrived just in time to watch him step into the circle, their cries after him proving futile. The four travelers paused, looking around and bracing themselves for the rising of the wind. But several moments passed, the rest of their party arriving shortly with their horses, and it became apparent that they remained barred from the faen plane. This angered Havian, and he marched further into the circle, cursing as he went.

"I tried to stop him," spoke Punznes to Uritus, sorrow lacing his voice.

Uritus touched a hand to his shoulder, "You did what you could. Prepare to leave. I'll get him and then we'll make our way out."

Punznes nodded briskly and moved to mount his horse as Uritus followed Havian into the circle, Adiadni lingering at its edge all the while. She felt her heart pound in her chest as she watched her counterpart catch the swordsman by his arm and she contemplated to what degree she should get involved in attempting to rein in the one who had gone rogue. She carried with her an unquestionable authority, the power to spur on or to cease with a single firmly delivered command. But she looked around now at the faces of those who called Havian family, who had known and loved him for years. She considered also the occurrence at The Gilded Rose, the fearful expressions worn by those who witnessed her lash out. If he was unwilling to listen to those he already loved and trusted, surely her voice would be of no use here. The weight of her authority and the fear that her ability to influence existed solely due to her birthright constricted tightly around her throat. She looked on worriedly but said nothing.

"Havian, what are you doing?"

The unbridled anger that shone in the eyes of the swordsman as they met his startled Uritus.

"I am doing what the rest of you haven't the stones to do. I am getting us out."

"But we have a plan! We've figured out a way out already, you're moving in the wrong direction."

Havian shook his head, exhausted. "You need to learn now, Boy, that if you do not rise to face those who stand in your way, you will never make it where you are going." He turned, wrenched his arm out of the fisherman's grasp, and lifted his eyes to the forest.

"Syv! I know you're listening! Show yourself, you fucking coward!"

Uritus turned, distress shining clearly in the blue of his irises as he brought them to rest on Adiadni, Havian ceaselessly turning about the circle and shouting into the trees. The Suvah and Adalos looked at each other hopelessly, unsure what to do short of forcibly removing Havian from Idor on their own.

Uriah spoke then, his volume gentle but tone firm, "Havian Elix, you have lost sight of your header. Return to us at once."

Havian did turn—surprising to everyone—appearing somewhat dazed. He looked to Uriah and opened his mouth as if to speak. He was interrupted before he could by a voice that sounded from behind him.

"Such aggression. Such noise."

All heads turned to regard the faen figure who had seemingly appeared out of thin air.

"You think you can threaten me, shaking your blade and exhausting your voice, and expect me to be willing to respond to such violence? The nevyn remain as demanding as they have always been."

"Spare me your pathetic haughtiness," Havian spat. "You may claim moral superiority for how you would sooner hide than fight. But I know that it is you who have kept us here, walking in circles for days on end, our resources dwindling."

Syv shrugged casually and Havian's blood boiled. "It was not I, nor any of the fae who broke the age-old treaty, but you and your companions. You storm into our home and demand passage through and draw your weapons when your request is not granted, yet you perceive me to be the enemy?"

"You are not our enemy," called Adiadni from the edge of the ring. "And we do not wish to be yours. We are weary, disoriented in our attempt to leave so that you may return peacefully to your way of life. I beg your forgiveness on behalf of my companion, he has grown tired of being tricked, as have we all."

"I can speak for myself, Princess." Havian's tone was harsh.

Syv chuckled, the sound infuriating the swordsman even further. "Had you tried even once to turn back the way you had come, you would have found yourselves free long ago. Your entitlement continues to be your downfall. Your choice to continue pressing on through land that is not yours to traverse—and the consequential effects—are your fault and yours alone. You have no one to blame but yourselves."

"Enough." Havian's voice lowered, his outrage contained but palpable. "You cast your judgment. You look down upon us from that *higher plane* you think grants you superiority, you use the forest as a weapon, and you think because you separate yourselves from us that it will preserve you. I tell you it will not. When the Shadow comes, it will not cease its torment until all the Light within the Free World has been extinguished. That includes the Forest of Idor. Resist all you wish—it will prove futile. And we..." he turned and pointed to the young people behind him, "*They* are the only ones who stand a chance of seeing that such a fate does not befall you. You should drop to your knees and beg their forgiveness for how you have so boldly stood in their way."

Havian spoke this last line in a threatening tone, brandishing his sword. Uritus and Adiadni looked at one another, fear sparkling in their eyes.

"They would not ask it of you," the swordsman continued. "But I have sworn to the king, as have the rest of my companions, that we will do whatever it takes to ensure that they make it to their destination safely *and* swiftly. So as it is, I can see no other option than to challenge you to a duel for our freedom."

"Havian you must stop this at once!" The princess made no attempt to mask the terror in her voice.

The silver-headed one began to laugh as the companions pleaded with the swordsman to withdraw his challenge. He did not turn, rather continuing to stare down the fae, adrenaline pumping through his veins.

After what felt to the travelers like a short lifetime, Syv silenced and returned Havian's glare with an equal intensity. "So be it," they finally spoke. "A duel of swords you will have." They extended their right arm beside them with an open palm and in it materialized a gleaming silver blade.

"All right then," Havian replied. "But I'll have none of that tricksy shit."

Syv chuckled darkly. "Of course. Prepare yourself. We fight to the death."

"No!"

Adiadni's scream slashed through the forest. The party members on horseback looked to each other and then to Uriah, trying amongst themselves to think of how they could undo the dire situation Havian had plunged into, and one by one arriving at the conclusion that the swordsman had chosen his fate.

Uritus looked on anxiously, his temples thrumming with dull pain as Havian turned and approached him. He didn't know how everything had gotten so out of hand.

"What have you done?" the fisherman rasped.

Havian smiled gently, appearing once more as the man Uritus had known since his youth. "I have done what I must."

"But you don't *need* to do this." Uritus felt desperate. "We can turn and leave now," he begged. "We can walk away from all of this."

Havian reached out a hand for Uritus's water skin and the fisherman handed it to him, waiting patiently as the swordsman took a long, cool drink. Across the circle, the fae paced. Havian returned the skin to Uritus's hand and brought his own to rest upon the fisherman's shoulder.

"You may not understand yet, but know that I do what I feel I must for you. I have always known that you have carried within yourself a legacy far greater than all of us, Uritus. Should it take all that I have left to give, I'll be sure you make it to where it is you're going. I swear it." He reached a hand up to his cape and removed from it a small, silver, sword-shaped pin which he placed into the hand of the fisherman.

Uritus shook his head as he stared down at it, at a loss for any words that might reach his friend. A hollow pit of dread made a home in his stomach. There was nothing he could do…

"Hey," the swordsman spoke again, drawing Uritus's eyes back to his. "You needn't worry. I may yet surprise you."

Winking, he moved his hand to his neck and undid the clasp that held his cape in place. He turned again to face Syv, whipped his cape around with a flourish, and wrapped it twice around his left arm.

Uritus retreated from within the circle and brought himself to stand at its edge beside Adiadni. Turning over his shoulder, he locked eyes with Perplexus and gestured for his friend to approach. The navigator urged his horse forward, leaning down to be closer to the fisherman.

"Be ready," Uritus spoke in a hushed tone. "When this all comes to a head, I'll need you to lead them to the river. It's not far from here, just a short trek North…"

Perplexus nodded. "Uriah informed me of your plan. I'll find the way, don't worry." He paused, glancing with a concerned expression at the princess who stood with her arms folded tightly across her chest, her focus fixed on the two who circled one another threateningly within the ring. "And of your better half…"

"I'll get her out. Havian too. I just need you to lead the way."

Perplexus nodded briskly and Uritus returned his attention to the duel.

Surprising to no one, Havian lunged first, unwilling to wait for his opponent to make the first move. Syv sidestepped, swinging their sword in Havian's direction. The swordsman blocked it with the aid of his cape.

The onlookers watched with bated breath as the competitors repeatedly clashed and separated. Syv's fighting style was smooth, appearing to require little effort from them as though they foresaw each of Havian's attacks and parries. They laughed mockingly each time their human opponent lunged and missed. Havian struggled to push down the anger that welled inside him with every chuckle.

But the swordsman considered both his blade and his cape to be extensions of himself, and despite his bubbling rage, he continued to wield each appendage with a stunning amount of poise. This particular style of fighting was uncommon in the modern age, and it was for this very reason that Havian had chosen it as his modus operandi in his youth. There were many ways to wield the cape, both defensive and offensive, and he was an expert at them all.

It was soon clear that Syv preferred to reserve their energy rather than being the one to launch an attack. But every time they did, Havian was quick to respond, using the weight and thickness of the large piece of fabric to his advantage.

Adiadni found herself paralyzed at the edge of the circle, feeling hopeless for how her attempt at peaceful passage through Idor had gone so awry. She felt her fingers twitch reflexively each time the fae lunged toward her companion as though they longed to grasp the hilt of her sword to put an end to this whole confrontation herself. She wouldn't dare, she told herself, for who was to say what could go amiss should she try? But even still, her protective instinct raged inside her chest. Were the moment to arise that she needed to protect him, she knew in her heart that she would not be able to stop herself from trying.

The fight continued, and Havian found his stride. He determined his opponent's attack swings to be weak, almost half-hearted. Each one he blocked with ease.

He swung his sword and then his cape repeatedly, slowly forcing Syv back to the edge of the circle. The piece of fabric was disorienting as it fluttered, somewhat concealing the windup to the sword's next move, and it packed a punch when it struck its target.

He bided his time, jumping back as Syv made a wide swing with their blade. Then, glimpsing his open window, he dove through it.

In one swift motion, he swung his cape around and cast it forward where it landed across the face of his opponent. Gripping his sword in both hands, he positioned it at his right hip and thrust it forward. But to his surprise, he found the piece of fabric dangling from the edge of his blade, the fae nowhere in sight.

He had only a fraction of a second to realize that he had been tricked before the silver-headed one rematerialized behind him and plunged their weapon forcefully into his back.

The world around Uritus went quiet, his heart slamming into his stomach. He turned to see Adi's terror-stricken face and read Havian's name as it left her lips. Looking back to the circle, he watched, body numb, as blood spilled from Havian's mouth.

The swordsman dropped to his knees and collapsed to the ground.

Uritus whipped his head around and locked eyes with Perplexus. "Get out!" he cried. "To the river!"

Perplexus obeyed, turning his horse around and racing away, the party hastening after him.

Adiadni watched, horrified, as dark red blood poured from Havian's body, staining the dirt of the path and leaching into the bright green moss that carpeted the forest floor.

The fae chuckled to themself, raising their sword above their head as if they intended to strike again.

All the rage and fear and frustration and devastation that the princess held within her body bubbled to the surface and she reached an angry hand out in Syv's direction as she cried with all her might, "No!"

An invisible force rushed from her hand across the circle and collided with the fae's shoulder, driving them back several paces.

They looked at her with surprise and then began to laugh, their amusement growing harsher and louder with each multi-layered note. The forest darkened and the wind began to rush around them.

Uritus sprang to action, hurrying to Adi's side as Syv vanished. He brought his hand down upon her arm and she looked at him in bewilderment as though she had forgotten he was even there.

"You need to go now!"

"We can't leave him!"

Her voice was laced with desperation and Uritus returned his gaze to the swordsman's limp body. He whistled for Moonracer, and with Adi's help, lifted the swordsman onto his horse's back. Overwhelmed by the rushing wind and fearful for her life, he ordered her to mount Swadalla and ride to the river. She obeyed, Havian's cape and sword in hand.

Uritus brought Moonracer to keep pace behind her. They plowed ahead through the forest, paying no mind to the flora they trampled in their wake. The threatening laughter continued to spiral all around, debris stirred up by the wind whipping in all directions as the branches of the trees thrashed. Briefly, the fisherman feared that they may still have been stuck in their loop. But no sooner did the thought formulate than he saw, just ahead, the figure of Perplexus on his horse, returned to make sure they got out.

He rode ahead as he saw them, and in a moment, the river came into view, the rest of their companions safe on the other side. Reaching the river's edge, they did not hesitate, feeling as though they broke through a wall of invisible fabric as they leapt across. The laughter and the wind immediately ceased.

Nadarum and Punznes hurried to Moonracer's side, lifted Havian's body from the saddle, and lowered him to the ground where they confirmed what they all knew to be true: his spirit had already departed.

Uritus dismounted and looked around at the faces of those he loved as they clung to one another and wept for the one they had lost. His eyes filled with tears and he met the gaze of the Wizard who held it for a moment before turning his head to the West. Uritus followed his eyes, spotting Swadalla several yards away and, beyond her, the princess, stumbling her way upriver.

"Adiadni!"

Uritus left his party and rushed after her. She did not acknowledge his voice, and when he finally caught up to her, gripped her arm in his hand, and turned her toward him, he saw her face, utterly defeated, wet with grief. He pushed her hair back with his other hand. "Are you all right?"

She laughed through her tears. "I am perfectly fine! It is Havian who—" Her voice was cut off by a powerful sob and she let her eyes fall to the ground, the weight of her counterpart's glassy blue gaze too heavy to bear. She closed her eyes, shaking her head fiercely against the violent images that replayed over and over in her mind.

"I've failed you," she spoke finally, bringing her eyes to meet his once more. "I've failed all of you…"

"Don't say that."

"How could I not? A man is *dead*, Uritus, because I was too foolish, too impatient and naive to just lead us around. I could have gone around! I should have…"

"Adiadni."

She shook her head sadly as she stared up at him, at the tears traveling in hot, fast tracks down his face. "He was your family."

Uritus swallowed hard, but the knot in his throat remained. "He knew what he was doing."

The fisherman meant what he said. Though Havian was rash, he was no stranger to assessing risk. What Uritus had at the time deemed to be the swordsman's attempt at merely calming his friend's nerves, he realized now was his way of saying goodbye.

Still, Adi pushed back, "He should never have had to do any of it! It was my responsibility to make our way, *my* responsibility to lead us safely to the Looming Mountains and through. I told them so many times that I wasn't ready…"

"Adiadni…"

"This task never should have fallen to me, I'm not equipped for it!"

"Stop."

Gently yet firmly, the arms of the Adalos reached out and wrapped around the quivering body of his counterpart, drawing her close to himself. The moment she crashed into his chest, she dissolved into her tears, each violent sob wracking her body. He held her tightly, his grief falling into her soft hair, inhaling deeply her scent of juniper and rosewater as he attempted to regulate them both. They remained that way until their breathing had mostly returned to a normal pattern and the wells of their tears ran dry, then made their way back downriver to rejoin the others.

By the time they returned, Uritus's patchwork family had already begun gathering stones from the river and stacking them around Havian's lifeless body. Adi moved to her saddle and gathered his cape, which she folded as nicely as she could and set atop his body, and his sword, which she laid atop that. The sun had begun to set when the grave was completed. Uriah lit a fire, and the companions gathered their tired bodies around while Laivar sang. From his pocket, Uritus retrieved the sword-shaped pin and offered it to Punznes. Though the physician argued that Havian's gift to Uritus should stay with Uritus, the fisherman insisted, pinning it reverently to his friend's collar.

They remained until the fire burned out of its own volition. They then brought themselves to mount their horses, certain that even if they tried, they would be unable to get any sleep. With Perplexus leading their way, they rode North-and-West for the Valley of the Sun, where they would take time to rest and refuel. The embers of the fire cooled and the smooth stone that made up the grave gleamed ever so slightly in the moonlight as they left it behind.

Chapter Fourteen

"The River Beneath Us, The Willow Above"

The 13th of July

"**W**elcome, your highness! You must forgive us, we were not expecting you…"

Adiadni smiled weakly. "Oh, that's all right…"

The travelers were weary by the time they arrived in the Central District of the Valley of the Sun—the land also known by many of its locals as Ehjonadi, its historic name—and the Wizard and princess sought to procure them rooms at a pair of neighboring inns.

"We will be honored to host you as you make your journey West! How many rooms will you be needing?"

"Um…" Adi turned her head to look out the window. "Just three, I think…"

"Very well, we will have them ready right away. Give me just a moment, I'll fetch someone to deal with your horses—"

"Oh, I think someone already did…"

"Very well, your highness. How has been the journey so far?"

Adiadni craned her neck to see her party outside. They did not appear visibly upset, only tired. Her heart ached for them, and at every quiet moment when her mind was allowed to wander, she was sickened all over again by her first glimpse of death.

"Your highness?"

Her attention snapped back to the innkeep.

"Your journey. Has it been a blessed one?"

The princess cleared her throat and forced a smile.

***

Outside, the companions waited in silence for Adi and Uriah to acquire their rooms. They had ridden through the night, had little appetite for more than water. They agreed before arriving here that they would not speak with anyone they met about the events that took place in Idor. Adiadni in particular thought it especially important that the Free People be given no further reason to be fearful of the fae. So, though the Valley's citizens went about their midday tasks and paid little mind to them, they did not discuss the happening that had burned a scar into their collective mind's eye.

To Uritus, the hours they had spent riding to get here had passed like a strange, unsettling dream. His body was numb, his mind the same. He longed to collapse into the solitude of his room and allow his grief to consume him, but he knew that his heart would not allow him to. He looked from face to face of the family that surrounded him. However he was able, he would find a way to help ease their pain.

A pair of stable girls arrived then to collect their horses and the travelers retreated to their rooms—Adi, Uritus and Perplexus, and Nadarum and Ilya at The Eagle's Bane; and Uriah, Punznes and Oripidus, and Mikka and Laivar at The Bleating Lamb next door. Neither Uritus nor Perplexus knew the right words to say to the other, and so did not speak at all.

When evening came, they gathered in the common room of The Eagle's Bane to dine. Nadarum and Ilya did not join them and—due to the heaviness of the circumstance—the others elected not to seek them out. The tavern's patrons were loud and lively as they dined and drank and sang and played cards, blissfully unaware of the event that left the newcomers shaken. Adiadni found it somewhat jarring to be surrounded by such high levels of mirth when she felt not a drop of it inside her. Nevertheless, she still sought to do right by her companions, and so informed them as they dined that they would remain in the city for an additional day and night to be sure that they were adequately recovered to proceed on their journey.

Uritus found himself, for the first time, disagreeing with a decision made by his counterpart. He knew that she meant well, that she desired only what was best for them. But it remained true that they had already lost quite a bit of time. Of course, they weren't on a strict schedule—there was no designated date by which they should reach their destination or return to Suscundos. As long as they made it beyond the Looming Mountains and back before the snow came, they would be fine. So he said nothing but rather nodded briskly when she looked to him for confirmation. When the group split off from one another after their meal in search of comfort or distractions or something else entirely, he remained by her side.

Perplexus joined them as they wandered about the large smoky room, seeking out something they did not yet know. Shortly, they arrived before a table of locals playing cards and lingered at one end, observing as the game played out before one of the players asked if they'd like to be dealt in.

Uritus was prepared to politely decline, but was surprised as Adi moved to one of the table's benches and plopped herself down between a pair of burly farmers. Perplexus followed suit, taking a seat on the opposite side of the table next to a dwarven woman. Beside her, an old man with a thick white mustache proceeded to deal four cards to each player. These remained in a row, face-down on the table in front of them. The princess caught the eyes of the fisherman briefly, a questioning glance to make sure that he did not wish to participate. He smiled and gestured to ask if she would care for a drink. She nodded, returning his smile, and he departed to fetch one for her.

When he returned, a mug of ale in each hand for his two friends, the game was in full swing. The game, called Frali, was simple and straightforward. Of the four cards they were dealt, each player was allowed to view only their two middle ones as well as the rightmost card of the player on their left, and the leftmost of the player on their right. On their turn, each player would make a claim—based on their knowledge of the cards in their hand—of what they believed the total value of their hand to be. The aim was to get close to their actual total without going over, and each consecutive player after the round's first had to claim a higher sum than the one claimed by the player before them. At any point, any player could challenge another's claim, after which the challenged player's cards would be revealed and a point would be awarded to the player who proved to be correct. A new hand was dealt to the challenged after that and a new round proceeded. Each game lasted until a victor netted three points.

It was easy to learn and easy to play, even when inebriated, which was part of its aim. The people who dwelt in Ehjonadi were, in great majority, farmers and distributors of the city's bounty throughout the neighboring region. They were honest, diligent, salt-of-the-earth people who valued play just as highly as work and sought a healthy balance of both in their everyday lives. The foreigners were amused to learn that it was customary for the victor of a game of Frali to be awarded the honor of buying the next round for the table, and after their third game, when Perplexus reigned victorious, he was delighted to retrieve his prize.

As the mustached man began to deal for a fourth game, Adiadni stepped away from the table and finished what remained of her drink.

She had begun to feel a bit lighter. Being again in a land where the laws of nature were straightforward and the people were friendly and hospitable made her feel sturdier on her feet. Still, her heart ached in the fleeting moments when she looked at Uritus and saw his face tired with grief, or observed how he opted not to play or drink or even really talk with the rest of them. She longed to find a way to make him also feel a bit lighter, even if only for a moment. She searched her brain for a fragment of an idea, kicking herself when she found none. Wordlessly, she moved to stand beside him as they waited for their victor to return and gently brought her head to rest upon his shoulder. And though she did not know it, the fisherman did feel a bit lighter, even if only for a moment.

When Perplexus did return, he brought with him more full-to-sloshing mugs than Adi had ever seen one person carry, and the sight of him caused Uritus to burst into laughter. The navigator held in his own amusement as he clunked most of the mugs onto the table for his competitors and then offered one to each of his friends. Adi graciously accepted, Uritus politely declined, and Perplexus shrugged, finished the extra in three gulps, and set the empty mug on a nearby table.

The two men fell into step behind Adiadni as she returned to slowly meandering around the perimeter of the room, eyes affectionately observing those who gathered and went about their lives there. Lightness and heaviness came in quick waves for the princess as they walked, drinking warmth in from their mugs. Perplexus abandoned his second empty vessel on a table as they passed it and then pulled out his pipe and began filling it with smoke.

Adiadni eventually brought them to a stop before the room's center aisle, long tables with long benches stacked in rows on either side, almost every seat full. Snippets of excited conversations could be heard at every turn, in the common tongue as well as, Uritus speculated, *ingosoni*, the mostly-forgotten language that was once widely spoken in this region, of which Ilya knew some and Nadarum knew very little.

"Hello, old friend! How goes your harvest?"

"Yurdo gumacha suri…"

"What're the odds either of you happens to have a match?"

This last snippet came from Perplexus, as he had come to realize he had none himself.

Adi turned to face him, set her mug in his hand, and then brought one of hers to cup around her other. With a single quick snap, a tiny blue flame formed atop her fingertip, and she brought it to touch the bowl of the navigator's pipe and then extinguished it. He stared at her through the smoke with a bewildered smile on his face. Had his pipe not been held between his teeth, his mouth would have fallen open.

Uritus looked around to assess if anyone present had witnessed this innocent show of power and released a breath when it became clear that none had. The fisherman wasn't sure why he felt anxious at the thought that it might become known that Adi was a casual Keeper.

Lex took a long drag of smoke. "Who taught you that fun little trick?"

"Been working on it for a while."

The navigator nodded, impressed, and across the room spotted Oripidus, Laivar, and Mikka sitting at a table with some new friends. He regarded the two beside him, one looking around with curiosity, the other with a note of uneasiness, and in an attempt to glean an idea of what their next move should be, he asked them, "How are we feeling?"

Uritus looked to Adiadni, Adiadni looked to the floor, absentmindedly chewing on her lip. She'd had two and a half drinks—a degree of inebriation she usually reserved for celebrations—and she observed that this ale seemed to be doing something different than she was used to. She explained this to her friends.

"It feels almost…" the word she sought was on the tip of her tongue.

Perplexus smiled understandingly. "Fuzzy."

Adi turned this word over in her mind and nodded when she determined that it felt right. "But not foggy. Just… warm."

"Do you think you've had too much?"

The princess looked down into her mug, considering genuinely the question posed by her counterpart. This beverage was foreign, unfamiliar, and it was exceedingly likely that it was stronger than the stuff she was used to. Were she to finish what remained in the cup, she would undoubtedly have had *too much*. But even so, she found herself annoyed by how he felt he had the right to ask.

Bringing her mug to her lips, she took two more long gulps before handing it to Perplexus, who finished it off.

"Now I've had too much."

The fisherman nodded briskly, saying nothing. He followed when she turned and made her way to the table where their other friends communed. Laivar strummed along enthusiastically with the trio who sang from the tavern's small stage while Oripidus and Mikka toasted small wooden teacups and downed their contents in a single swallow.

"What have you there?" the princess asked curiously.

"*Eoher*," Mikka replied. "Tea from the root of the ribbon shrub. It's supposed to calm you down, help you sleep, something like that."

"And how do you feel?"

Oripidus reached for a tall clay pitcher and poured three more cups. "No different than before. See for yerself."

Adi and Perplexus took up their cups and Laivar claimed the one Uritus didn't want and they toasted and partook of the tea. It was sour and cold, and it was as Oripidus said—that it appeared to have little effect on one's physical or mental state, at least upon initial consumption. Whether some sort of change would take place over the course of the night still remained to be seen.

Uritus turned to Mikka, "Have the others retired already?"

She shrugged. "I assume so. Though, I've still yet to see the lovebirds."

"Has anyone seen them since we arrived?"

Those at the table shook their heads.

"I feel like someone should go look for them. Make sure they're all right."

"I'm sure they're perfectly fine," spoke Laivar. "Everyone copes in their own way."

The fisherman returned to silence. Oripidus challenged Mikka to a game of Kepu, wagering two silver coins against her dice, and she enthusiastically accepted, Laivar continuing to strum all the while. Adi gently touched her thumbs to her fingertips, one at a time, as she stood at one end of the table. She watched for a while as the game played out, Mikka reigning victorious in the first round. The princess lifted her head, observing those who socialized and made merry around them. Noticing the change in her focus, Uritus inquired if she was feeling all right.

She nodded slowly and took a step away from the table, prompting the fisherman and the navigator to move with her. "I'm feeling something…" she began tentatively, "…that I can't say I've ever felt before."

Her friends waited patiently for her to elaborate.

Looking around once more, she landed on the word she sought, "Anonymity. I wear my birthmark upon my shoulder, my tiara upon my head, and I am certain that at least *some* here know who I am. Yet, I do not feel as though I am being watched at every turn. It's foreign and it's… quite a relief." She met

Uritus's eyes, "It's something I'm not sure I'll ever get the chance to feel again. And I suppose while it's here, I do not want to miss it."

The fisherman regarded her understandingly, happy to help however he could. "How do you wish to make the most out of such a rare gift?"

She shrugged. "I'm not sure. Though… I do love this song…"

"Say no more." Perplexus extended his hand to her and spun her away down the aisles of the tavern.

There proceeded then a couple of hours where the companions who remained in the common room of The Eagle's Bane were able to lose themselves in the lively energy of the community who hosted them, forgetting that which weighed heavy on their hearts. There was more drink and more song and more games and more dancing, Adi and Perplexus at one point bringing themselves to step in time with a particularly energetic song atop one of the tables.

Uritus watched quietly as the events of the evening proceeded, half with relief —happiness even—for how his friends always managed to find a spot of joy in an otherwise stifling period of sadness. The other half was tired, worn out from bearing the weight of his sorrow as well as that which he held onto for his friends so they needn't for a time.

Everyone copes in their own way.

Laivar was right, this he knew. The fisherman was intimately familiar with loss and grief, due to his personal experience as well as many instances of being a witness to that of others. It was the universal experience of grief that led his second family to one another; the cold, dull ache for rest or relief or answers that led each of them to find themselves wandering through the White Mountains where they were welcomed in by a kind-hearted Wizard with more space than he needed. Uritus felt as though he had grief down to a science. He knew all its steps and the order they often came in, and he had to remind himself that this was not the same for everyone. Many were the methods he had observed in others to process, understand, rationalize, forget. Determining when to allow these processes to play out on their own and when to gently remind those he loved that in order to make your way through grief, you have to allow yourself first to feel it, was a fine line that he wasn't quite sure how to walk.

Evening bled into night and the energy of the room mellowed as though the various inebriants worked in tandem to ensure that everyone would retire in enough time to be well-rested the next day. The companions determined that this was the right move for themselves and began wishing one another goodnight when Adiadni—overcome with a feeling of intense physical warmth—abruptly turned and departed from the room. Uritus watched her leave and turned to Perplexus, the same confused expression on each of their faces. The fisherman hastily bade farewell to his family and hurried after her.

He found her outside the inn, just around the left corner of the building, standing in the dirt road there and looking out over the wide fields beyond. The Valley of the Sun was divided into four triangle-shaped quarters, the majority of which was made up of farmland. In the middle of the city was a centralized district where craftspeople and establishments like taverns and markets thrived.

This center piece of land, comprised of the tips of the four triangles, was known affectionately as *the Fifth* amongst those who dwelt there and around.

The princess and the fisherman stood now at the edge of this Fifth, farmland stretching for miles in front of them. The night was clear and the air was as warm and sticky as could be expected of a mid-Summer evening and the moon shone bright above them. Frogs croaked and crickets chirped and cicadas sang in a multi-layered chorus. Fireflies blinked here and there as they lazily floated over stalks of barley, not nearly as numerous as in Suscundos but beautiful nonetheless. Uritus wordlessly brought himself to lean against the wall of the inn as he waited to see if Adiadni cared to speak about that which was obviously weighing heavy on her mind.

Several quiet moments passed before she finally elected to speak, "You didn't need to follow me, you know." She looked half-heartedly over her shoulder. "Certainly there is nothing that may threaten my safety out here."

"You're probably right," he replied. "But surely you do not think that your safety is the only reason I might seek you out."

The princess softened, uncrossing her arms and bringing her hands to toy with one another. "I'm sorry if I've been cold. I've just felt particularly overwhelmed and I'm not quite sure what to do about that."

"I understand."

She knew he did. Of course he did. He had been with her through the whole traumatic ordeal, seen the same blood-curdling things she had. No doubt he was feeling everything that she was and to a greater degree. She turned to face him, "I know you will not allow me to, but I do wish again to express how sorry I am for—"

"You're right," he interrupted her. "I will not allow you to."

"Yes, but if I had only known…"

"You couldn't have known."

He was right. But still, it did little to ease the burden of her guilt. She cast her eyes to the ground, unsure of what to say.

Eventually, he spoke again, genuine care frosting each of his words, "How do you feel?"

Adi mulled over this question for a while. She felt warm still and *fuzzy* as she had before, but also tired, restless, vaguely dizzy, overwhelmingly guilty, and deeply sad. "Too much to say," she ultimately replied.

He nodded, intimately familiar with such a feeling. "Can I help?"

She lifted her eyes to the fisherman's face then and released a long, slow breath and felt for the first time in many days as though her heart was perfectly still—not fluttering anxiously in the way she had grown accustomed to. The warm brown of his eyes covered her, saw directly through her to her core in such a way that made her feel recognized and decidedly less alone. Her prior desire to lose herself in the lushness of her newfound anonymity had all but vanished. She wished now only to bury herself into his chest, to let the whole world fall away around them until the weight of her sorrow was alleviated. But knowing not how to express such a want, she answered simply, "I don't know."

Uritus could not help but feel that this was not entirely true. "You do not know what you need or you do not think I can provide it?"

"A bit of both, I suppose."

He regarded her compassionately. She appeared before him so tired and so frail, burdened by the weight of sorrow and regret. Her dress—pale blue, more casual than those she had worn in Suscundos—fell to her knees and fluttered when she walked or danced. But now, she stood perfectly still under a clear sky on a windless night and the piece of fabric hung loosely from her body. And this, paired with the cold light cast upon her shoulders by the moon and the way she tugged at one hand with the other—the way he observed she always did when she felt nervous or unsettled—had him feeling desperate to alleviate some of the pain she felt, even if just a fragment of it.

Slowly, he took a step forward. She responded in kind, bringing herself to him as though she had just been granted permission, and allowed him to wrap his arms around her, sturdy, stable. He smelled of earth, the way it did when it was damp after rain, and of salt, like the air that kissed her face on the cliffs of the Holy City. The warmth of his breath in her hair felt entirely familiar, it felt like…

Home?

But not like one she'd ever known. Rather, like one she always knew she was somehow bound to crash into. She took a small step back so she could look up into his face, loosening her grip where it had been clasped around his back. He returned her gaze, a soft smile moving across his face as he observed that the worried look that had just adorned hers had since vanished. And then, delicately at first and gradually growing in confidence, she lifted her face to his, pausing as their foreheads touched.

Uritus tensed against the mounting pressure in his brow. "Adiadni…"

"You ask if you can help," she spoke softly, "…and I do not know how, but I am certain that you can. I just want…" She withdrew her face from his slightly. "I need to just… not… *feel* this anymore."

"Not feel what?"

She shook her head, a look of bewilderment on her face. "Any of it."

He smiled at her sadly and lifted a hand to move a mass of dark curls away from her face. As softly as he could, he ran his thumb along the length of her eyebrow, feeling the smoothness of her skin beneath his fingertip. *She is not yours to hold.* "I do not wish to be the one who has to tell you this, but you *must* feel it—all of it—if you wish to ever be free of it."

"No…" She stepped away from him abruptly, turning again to face the fields and pressing the heels of her palms into her temples. "Just…" She completed the full circle, turning to stand close to him yet again. "Just… just… just…"

Gripping the fabric of his shirt in her hands, she stared up into his eyes for a moment and saw that his gaze did not waver. Without hesitation, she stretched her neck to bring her face back up to his, this time with no intention of pausing.

"Adiadni..." Uritus's voice was hardly above a whisper. *She is not yours to hold.* He steadied himself against the quickening of his pulse.

She dropped her head to crash into his chest, groaned frustratedly, and lifted it to look at him once more, "You speak my name like it is the air you breathe. You cannot tell me you do not wish for the same things I do."

She is not yours...

"Not everything that I would wish is mine to have."

She blinked at his resolve, nearly missing his confirmation of her suspicion. "But if there was one who could grant it for you?"

"Adiadni..."

"Uritus."

His eyes traced across all the exhaustion and frustration and desperation she wore on her face. She was offering him what he wanted, the chance to free her from the weight of the burden she bore, begging him to take it. But as sure as his heart beat in his chest, he knew that nothing he had to offer her would truly make a difference were she not willing to look her grief in the eye just as she looked in his now: with uncertainty, but with boldness. Though he did not want to, he broke his gaze from hers as he gently moved his hands to take her own, and she released her hold on his shirt.

He ran his thumb across the smooth round stone crowned by the silver ring on her left hand's middle finger. "There is someone who waits for you."

She shook her head. "I desperately wish he wouldn't."

"Even so... I believe we would both be regretful were I not to encourage you to remain faithful to your prior commitments."

"Fuck my prior commitments. I just... want to get lost for a minute..."

She is not yours...

He looked at her sadly, still cradling her hands. "I think you are overwhelmed and tired and almost certainly traumatized. And I believe that if you allow yourself to get lost at this stage, you will have a hard time finding your way back."

She ripped her hands away from his abruptly and took a step back. "Don't patronize me."

"Forgive me, that was not my intention..."

"You don't know me and you certainly don't know what I need."

"Perhaps not."

Adiadni blinked, suddenly aware of where she was and what she had been asking of him, having been entirely willing to forget about the one to whom she was still betrothed. She shook her head almost as if to wake herself up the rest of the way.

"I am so sorry." She looked at him with regret and then with shame, "I don't know what came over me, I… Forgive me."

She rushed back around the corner of the tavern and inside. Uritus sighed and brought himself again to lean against the tavern's wall. He remained for several minutes, watching as the last of the fireflies blinked, and allowed himself to succumb to the pain that made its way behind his eyes.

She is not…

***

When Uritus eventually retired to his chamber and upon his rising with the sun the following morning, Perplexus was missing from his bed on the other side of the room. Uritus didn't have the energy or sense to be worried about him. He knew that should the navigator find himself in a scrap, he was more than capable of figuring his way out. Arriving to break his fast in the common room of The Bleating Lamb, he noted that Perplexus, Ilya, and Nadarum were all still missing. Uriah told him not to worry and promised that if the absent three had still not been heard from by the evening, the others would go out in search of them. This did little to bring the fisherman peace. Punznes offered to send Qibat out to see if maybe the bird might have a chance of spotting them from the sky. Uritus nodded briskly and thanked him for the offer and then sat in mostly silence for the duration of their meal.

The others spoke matter-of-factly to one another, sharing their plans for the day and agreeing to meet again at the tavern next door to sup when evening came. Uritus found his attention repeatedly returning to Adiadni who sat quietly, shoulders hunched at one end of the table. Occasionally, their eyes would find their way to one another, but she was always first to break contact.

She kept to herself mostly as they ate, once proposing the idea of remaining an additional day and night in the city should they need it, particularly if the absent ones still had not been located by nightfall. Uritus found himself clenching his jaw at this suggestion and chastised himself for his impatience. She was only trying to help.

The meal ended and the companions separated. Adi caught Uritus by the arm just outside the door of the inn. He turned to face her.

"I wish to apologize… About last night…"

"Think nothing of it."

"I wasn't feeling like myself. I don't know why. Or, I suppose, I have a guess as to why. But either way I… said some things that I regret, and I'm sorry. I hope you can forgive me."

"Already done."

She smiled gently, a bit of life returning to her face.

"Hey, would you look at that? My two favorite people!"

Lex. Uritus and Adiadni turned to see the navigator strolling lightheartedly down the street toward them, the strap of his bag slung across his chest, a mostly eaten pear in his right hand.

Uritus shook his head relievedly as he looked him up and down. "Where in Shadow have you been?"

Perplexus smiled and shrugged as he came to stand beside them. "Oh, you know. Exploring."

"Did you sleep at all?"

Lex did not respond with words but rather shot his friend an amused glance and Uritus elected to drop it. The navigator tossed the core of his pear into a patch of nearby grass and took to rifling through his bag.

"I was almost worried about you."

Perplexus chuckled. "Well, I can assure you that I was perfectly safe. The two of you will never guess what I stumbled upon." His fingers wrapped around what they had been looking for and produced it, holding it out in an open palm with pride to his friends.

"What is it?"

Curiously, the princess reached out and took the object into her hands. It was delicate and papery and lightweight, wrapped in a piece of cloth and tied with a string of cord. She unwrapped it carefully, unfurling the cloth in her hand to reveal three dried flowers. She picked one up and held it to the light, twirling its stem slowly between her thumb and forefinger as she tried to identify why it seemed so familiar to her. She gasped gently when it clicked in her mind.

"*Kuffa* flowers!"

The navigator grinned. "They're called *yuzh* when they're dried."

Adiadni nodded. "Aurena keeps a kuffa tree in the Eastern garden and Press says they're plentiful in the Eldest Forest. I've always found them to be beautiful but I've never seen them like this."

The flowers in their natural state were trumpet-shaped, cream-colored at the bases of their petals and gradually becoming a dark shade of magenta at their tips. They appeared as the shape of a star when observed head-on, and thus were also known by some as *cosmos drops*. Now, in their dried form, the petals had folded in on each other, forming crunchy, two-inch-long bundles of powerfully sweet perfume that reminded Adi of magnolias.

Uritus looked from the flowers to each of his friends who regarded them with wonder, "Would it be especially embarrassing if I admitted I know not what makes this yuzh so special?"

"No, not *especially*," Perplexus winked.

Adi held one of the flowers out to Uritus and he took it. "They're Catalysts," she explained. "Much like the stone that makes up the palace. The Healers keep them for many purposes, to aid in the curing of both physical and mental ailments."

"When consumed by a healthy person though, they're said to bring clarity and peace," Lex chimed in. "After the hallucinations settle, that is."

"I see." Uritus looked down at the fragile treasure in his hand. "I take it this is what you have planned for your day then?"

Perplexus shrugged, taking the flower from Uritus, placing it back beside the others, and gently wrapping them again in their cloth. "I've looked for them in this form for years. They're hard to obtain, especially the further North you get." He secured the bundle with the piece of cord and tucked it safely back into his bag. "I certainly won't be turning down the opportunity now, but I thought I'd see if you two wanted to join me."

The princess and the fisherman looked at one another, she with an expression of intrigue, he with one of hesitation.

Lex observed this. "It's perfectly safe," he clarified. "The heavier effects last no more than twenty minutes, so I figured we can take turns."

Adiadni searched her body for signs of uncertainty. Finding none, she confidently proclaimed, "I'm in!"

…just as Uritus said, "I don't think I will."

His companions looked at him, the question *are you sure?* hanging from their lips.

"I'm sure," he told them. "I don't particularly wish to feel altered at this time. But I will sit with you while you do, make sure you're all right."

Perplexus chuckled, affectionately bringing a hand to clap on his friend's shoulder, "Always the nanny, never the child."

"How shall we consume them? As a tea?"

The navigator shook his head, tapping twice on the pipe tucked into his belt. "Smoke is best. I got my hands on more matches so we're ready to go. Though… I suppose we could see about making a tea if you think the smoke might be too harsh for you."

Adiadni shook her head. "I'll be fine."

"All right then. I know just the spot. Follow me."

Perplexus turned and led his friends away down the dusty street and beyond the edge of the Fifth, headed South-and-West, nodding *ezo* to the locals who greeted them cheerfully as they passed. They followed the dirt paths that sliced between sprawling fields thick with agriculture in varying stages of growth. Fair green wheat swayed in the gentle breeze and towering stalks of corn offered a bit of shade from the scorching sun. Insects hopped and buzzed around them, their humming adding to the symphony of the hot Summer day, and the sky stretched above them, azure and cloudless.

Nearing their destination, Perplexus led them to cut through a corner of one of the cornfields. Uritus was especially careful not to trample any of the growing things even though he made up the tail of their traveling party. The leader and second-in-line were not intentionally destructive or careless, but their excitement had them focused on their end goal, their destination, rather than the path they were taking to get there. The fisherman kept his eyes peeled and ears open for others who may have been going about their lives nearby but observed none as they moved further away from the city.

Before long, they approached the place they sought. Perplexus moved his hands in front of him and parted the last of the corn and Adiadni took in a breath as she observed the space beyond.

Several yards beyond the edge of the cornfield was a grove of lush trees, flourishing on the bank of the river Tuvibati. The spot picked out by the navigator was easily identifiable. They made their way to it—a patch of soft green grass encircled by the wispy fronds of a large willow. The ground sloped down just beside the tree, making way for the cold water that babbled as it rushed by. Idor could be seen on the other side of the river, and Adiadni was grateful for the thick growth of the willow which mostly shielded it from view. She positioned herself with her back to the forest and awaited instruction from the navigator.

He encouraged his friends to get comfortable and they brought themselves down to sit, finding the grass just as soft as it appeared from afar. Perplexus pulled out his pipe and the kuffa flowers and settled in against the trunk of the tree, thick roots twisting into the earth to his left and right as though to create a seat designed by the tree herself. He got to work preparing the yuzh, slowly and meditatively unfolding the cloth, crushing one of the flowers in his hand, and packing the petal fragments into the bowl of his pipe. The gentle breeze that wafted around them caused the wispy walls of their makeshift sanctuary to sway back and forth.

"There's no telling what it is we'll see," Perplexus addressed the princess. "Though there is a high likelihood that we may forget our visions are not reality. The sedative effects will keep us here, resting, dreaming, until the visions have run their course and then we will wake, possibly feeling drowsy for a time afterward but otherwise returning to normal."

Adi began to feel nervous as the weight of the choice she was making set in. "And in the long term?"

The navigator shrugged casually. "Some say the world is more colorful, some notice no change at all. Such variance from one individual to another leaves the mystery mostly hidden."

"Can I ask why, then, you've sought it for so long? What is it you hope to attain?"

He smiled down at his pipe. "The chance to say that I've embarked on such a rare adventure. My palms are open to all else that may come my way, but should I leave empty-handed, I still will have been blessed with far more than many and that is enough for me."

Adiadni nodded in quiet admiration of this response.

"And you?"

The princess hesitated as she contemplated this and then answered honestly, "I haven't thought about it. Should I have?"

Perplexus shrugged again. "I suppose to some it is a grand pilgrimage of sorts but it makes no difference to me."

Uritus observed Adiadni for a few quiet moments as she chewed on her lip. She was unsure, that was clear, but he was hesitant to say anything after his attempt to do so the night before. He wished only to remind her that she could step back from this choice if she wished, that neither he nor Perplexus would hold her to it if she were to decide that she didn't want to. But in her grief, she had grown a bit reckless, stretching out her fingers to grasp at any distraction or numbing agent that she could get her hands on. Knowing that she had before and likely would again plunge headfirst into a rushing river of carelessness should he dare imply that she wasn't a strong enough swimmer, he elected to keep quiet.

Perplexus replaced the remaining flowers in his bag and turned to the princess, "Since our friend is kind enough to serve as our anchor, we can go up at the same time if that sounds all right to you."

She offered him a short nod.

"You all right smoking first?"

She blinked twice. "First?"

"In an ordinary situation, I'd get it started for you, but I'm not sure how quickly the effects will take hold and since Uritus doesn't smoke, I want to make sure I'm conscious to help you." He reached into his bag, looting through it for his box of matches.

The princess swallowed, clutching her hands together and bringing herself to sit a bit straighter.

"Are you comfortable?"

She nodded.

"You'll want to be somewhere you can be prepared to lie down, your head will be too close to the slope there. You can turn the other way, or—"

Adiadni quickly brought herself to her knees and crawled several paces forward, gathering the layers of her gray-green skirt so as not to trip on it. She brought herself to recline on her elbows in the wispy grass and calmed ever so slightly as she gazed up at the twisting branches of the willow tree above her. Perplexus found his box of matches and brought himself to a knee beside her. Uritus watched his friends settle into position and drew in and released a long breath.

"Don't take too much. Hold it in your lungs if you can before you release." Retrieving a match from its box, the navigator brought it to strike against the sole of his boot, eliciting a small smile from the princess.

"Where'd you learn that fun little trick?"

Perplexus chuckled and brought the pipe to her mouth. "Inhale as I light."

Adi followed his instruction and her lungs filled with smoke, bitter and floral and charred. Her throat burned and tears gathered in her eyes and she managed to hold the smoke inside her for about a second and a half before she was reduced to a coughing fit.

"Are you all right?" Uritus looked on from where he sat a few feet away.

She nodded between coughs.

"Have you had enough or do you need a bit more?"

Adi looked briefly from Perplexus to his pipe and then took its stem between her lips again, inhaling and being taken by the coughing almost immediately. Perplexus had just enough time to offer her a sip from his water skin before she leaned back and collapsed into the grass, appearing to her two friends as though she had fallen into a deep sleep.

***

When she again opened her eyes, she found herself lying still in the grass beside the willow. Between its fronds, she could see the sky turning golden overhead with the setting of the sun. She sat up and looked around, spotting Uritus sitting on the bank with his feet in the river, his back to her.

"Have I been gone long?"

The fisherman responded but did not turn, "You could say that."

"I didn't realize." Adi hurriedly rose to her feet. "I'm sorry to have kept you waiting, I thought I'd be no more than twenty minutes. I probably wouldn't have done it had I known it'd be too long."

"Any length of time spent without you is too long, Adiadni."

She looked at him curiously and a soft breeze moved across her shoulders, causing her to shiver.

"But had it been longer, I'd have waited for you still."

A sense of guilt began rustling around her stomach. "Well, I'm here now."

"Are you?"

She blinked in confusion and furrowed her brow. "We are speaking, are we not?"

Uritus did not reply.

She went on, "Listen, I am sure that dealing with me over the past several days has required a great deal of patience on your part, and for that I am grateful. I have not been fair to you and I still feel bad for that, but I wish we could just leave this all behind."

"As do I."

Adiadni turned to regard the space that surrounded them, recognizing for the first time that the navigator was nowhere to be seen. She looked again to the fisherman, his back still facing her, his attention fixed straight ahead. "Where's Lex?"

"Gone."

"Gone where?"

"Forward."

The princess frowned, not understanding. "And the others?"

"Gone too."

215

She blinked. "But you stayed?"

"Yes."

"Why?"

"You know why."

"Tell me anyway."

The fisherman paused and she heard him take a long breath before he spoke again, "It is you who goes before me, Adiadni. If you do not light the way, then I cannot follow. You are the Way-Maker."

Adi knew this was true but was unsatisfied with this answer. "Is that all?"

Uritus did not respond.

The princess looked at her feet. "I do not see how I can light the way if I don't know where I am going."

"You do know."

"Well, maybe I do not wish to."

"Would you rather go back?"

She frowned at this query. "Of course not. I told you last night, I just… want to pause for a minute."

"It's been more than a minute."

He was right and she knew it. She sighed sadly. "Are you upset with me?"

"No."

Still, he did not turn, and this frustrated her. She moved to his side, bringing herself down to sit upon the bank to his right. "Then why won't you look at me?"

He turned his head in her direction and she felt chills move across her arms as his eyes traced the features of her face. Gently, he reached out a hand to tuck a rogue lock of dark hair behind her ear. He kept his palm there against her cheek and she relaxed into it, his eyes honey, his hand stone. He spoke then, voice merely a whisper, "I wish that I could do more to help you find your footing again. But I am certain that you will in time. Until then, I'll wait here as long as you need me to."

To her dismay, he pulled his hand away from her face and brought it to rest on the bank as he turned his head to gaze once more across the river. She looked down at his fingers nestled in the soft grass and brought her hand down to rest atop them.

The second her skin made contact with his, she was violently sucked away. She gasped as a dark swirling tunnel formed around her. Before her eyes flashed a series of images, most only lasting a fraction of a second, but each feeling as real as the next. She saw streaks of lightning and flames licking at dark stone; Uritus taking her face in his hands and pulling her toward him; Uritus tightly gripping a sword in his hand with an endless sky above him; Uritus standing at the edge of a pale, cracked expanse of desert; Uritus held in her arms, his skin pale and cold, his shirt drenched with blood.

She gasped for air and opened her eyes and the next thing she knew, she was back under the willow, the sun high in the sky as though she had never left. She heard voices and turned her head to see her friends, Uritus resting his arms on his knees, Perplexus lounging on his side next to him.

"...A sprawling sea, bluer than anything I've ever seen, it was impossible to tell where it touched the sky. Had the ship not been below me, I'd have had no idea that was what it was."

The princess shook her head and sat up, bringing her hands to rub the sleep out of her eyes.

"There she is!"

She could hear the smile in Lex's voice.

"You were out for a long time."

Uritus regarded her with relief and concern, "Are you feeling all right?"

The princess briefly brought her eyes to meet the fisherman's and nodded.

"What did you see?" The navigator sat up excitedly. "I was just telling Uritus how I fully believed myself to be a sailor until I awoke."

Adiadni's lips parted and she looked from Perplexus to Uritus and felt a sick, twisting feeling in her stomach as she recalled the images which were still all too vivid in her mind's eye. Once more, she turned her attention to the navigator, shrugging halfheartedly, "Nothing of import really."

"That's too bad."

It was clear to Uritus that this was not true, but he felt it was not his place to address it. Perplexus went on, detailing his mystical excursion, and he and Adiadni listened until she remarked that she was feeling warm. Perplexus sprang to his feet and helped Adi to hers, declaring that he knew just the solution, and then led them away, the boughs of the willow continuing to sway softly in the breeze as they departed.

***

Before long, the three friends found themselves at the door of a long glass building, greenery growing across its walls and roof as though it had been abandoned for years. Perplexus explained that he had passed it by on his adventures the night prior and how he was glad now to have the chance to explore it further. He cleared the brush from the door and pried it open and they stepped inside. Both the fisherman and princess were taken by the sight that greeted them: a long clear pool beneath a domed glass ceiling. Vines grew freely around the outside of the building and forced their way in through the cracks in the roof, thick enough to make the space feel deeply private but not so much as to fully block out the warmth of the sun.

Though she still felt haunted by the visions brought to her by the yuzh, Adi was overjoyed at this discovery, and she told her friends so. Her head ached and she had begun to feel hungry, but the water looked cold and fresh despite how long it had likely been here undisturbed, and in this moment, it was the only thing she craved.

Perplexus set his bag on a stone chair, kicked off his boots, and pulled his shirt over his head as he asked her if she cared for a swim, and she nodded enthusiastically. Slipping out of her dress to reveal the sunflower golden stays and emerald-colored bloomers she wore beneath it, she tossed it on the chair along with her boots and dove headfirst into the pool after him. She gasped as she surfaced, the frigid water having knocked the air from her lungs. She felt refreshed and intoxicated and *alive* as she swam beside the navigator, and she allowed herself to become lost in this feeling.

Uritus declined when she asked him to join them. This rejection stung her, but she did not allow it to retain her attention. The fisherman carefully removed his boots and set them to the side as he lowered himself to the pool's edge and sank his feet into its clear water. He breathed in deeply the scent of the Summer day and watched his friends admiringly as they splashed about and reveled in the treasure they had stumbled upon. They appeared so carefree, laughing, racing one another from one end of the pool to the other. He did not mind when their playfulness caused the water to splash onto his trousers and he found himself wishing that he could set aside this grief and become swept up in joy the way they did. He was tired still, and deeply sad, and this sadness pricked his heart with memories of the friend he had lost every time he tried to focus on something else.

Perplexus needed joy to process his grief, just as Uritus needed to allow his own to wash over him. But Adiadni—never before having witnessed tragedy to this degree—knew not what she needed, and the fisherman saw this. She was eager to cling to anything at all other than the heaviness of her sorrow, and it had grown tiresome to walk the line between allowing her natural processes to run their course and pointing her in the right direction. She looked at him every so often as she played, observing each time how he watched his feet move slowly back and forth in the water.

And then, all at once, a tidal wave of compassion for him crashed into her chest. He had been so gentle and patient over the past couple of days as she pranced around Ehjonadi with Perplexus. While she knew he would almost certainly shut down any attempt she made at apologizing, she felt it of great importance that she try anyway. When the time finally came that they decided they'd had their fill of the pool, she quietly asked the navigator if she might have a moment alone with the fisherman. He agreed without a word, left her with his shirt to wear while she dried off, and departed, telling Uritus that he was off in search of food and that he would catch up with them later.

Uritus stood, shaking his feet dry. Adi stood at the edge of the pool, wringing excess water from her hair which grazed the tops of her hip bones when wet. Sunlight streamed lazily between the lush vines, casting golden rays across the water and warming the princess's shoulders and face. Worn out though he was, Uritus found himself struck by the undeniable beauty that crowned his counterpart. The sleeves of Perplexus's shirt were too long and the piece of white fabric hung loosely from her shoulders, making her appear as she had the night before—tired, sad, uncertain. Still, her kindheartedness, noble grace, and strength showed plainly on her face, and as he looked at her, he felt nothing but quiet admiration for everything that she was.

Eventually, once she had squeezed every last drop of water from her hair that she could, she brought herself to face the fisherman, arms crossed tightly over her chest. "I wish to tell you that I am sorry," she said.

He tilted his head. "I have forgiven you already for anything you could possibly feel sorry for."

"Yes, I know. But I feel sorry anyway."

"For what?"

Adi looked at her feet, shuffling from one to the other. "I don't know." She paused for a couple of seconds and then lifted her eyes to look at him once more, "I just cannot ignore the space that exists between us now and I cannot help but believe that its existence is my fault."

This made Uritus's heart ache. "It isn't your fault."

"Then why do you look at me differently than you used to?"

The fisherman's lips parted.

"Do you pity me?"

"No."

"Then why?"

Uritus clasped his hands behind his back, mulling over his words. "I… do not feel it is my place to say."

Adiadni's sorrow showed clearly on her face. "Have we truly fallen so far that you feel you must ask for my permission to speak your mind?"

The fisherman sighed sadly. "Adiadni, you are my queen. I will always default to your leadership and I will always follow where you lead…"

"But is that all?"

"All?"

"Is that all I am? To you…?"

"Of course not."

Silence fell between them, both wishing to offer assurance to the other but neither knowing the proper way to do it.

Finally, she spoke, "I cannot do this without you, you know."

He nodded gently. "I know. Neither can I without you."

"And the only way we can make this work is if we trust each other and learn to communicate."

"You are right."

"Well then?"

The fisherman sighed and took a few slow steps toward her, gingerly taking her hands in his own. "As much as you are my queen," he began, "…you are also my friend. And as yours, I believe I should let you know that I fear you have not been allowing yourself to feel your grief."

Adi made a sound—half bemused laugh, half frustrated sigh—and stepped back, pressing her hands to her temples. "I have done nothing *but* feel it."

Empathy squeezed his chest.

"I know I have done far too much to turn my attention elsewhere, I know that. But if I think of him... of Havian, I see... blood spilling from his mouth and coating the forest floor, and I think only of how utterly I failed him. A hundred times I could have turned us around, made a different decision. And had I, he likely would still be here with us."

"Just as you could have chosen differently, so he could have."

"But it never should have been his responsibility to choose."

"And it never was."

Adi took in a shaky breath and allowed her tears to fall freely.

"He did what he felt he needed to, just as you did," Uritus went on. "Any one of us could have done any number of things differently, but the outcomes that would have ensued will forever remain a mystery."

She nodded hesitantly. "Even so, I cannot see how I could ever forgive myself."

Uritus sighed and slowly moved a hand to hold her face.

She relaxed her head into it.

"I wish that I could take your pain from you. I wish that I could hurry your process of healing along, but it is not in my power to do so. All I can do is assure you that I will remain here for as long as it takes for this heaviness to pass. Longer still, if you would have me."

Adiadni closed her eyes and released a slow breath. "I know."

She opened them again and they locked with his once more, and immediately her attention became fixed on the state of his own heart. For all the devastation and remorse and weariness that left a cold and hollow pit deep in her stomach, how much more must it have been for he who had known the swordsman and loved him like a brother? Gently, she took his hand from where it still rested against her face and brought it to her heart, clutching it. "I'd do the same for you if you'd let me..."

Uritus let out a long breath through pursed lips and relaxed his body where he realized he had been tensing it, and all at once, his sorrow flowed out of him, traveling down his face in rivers of hot tears. Adi saw his eyes shift to their brilliant blue just before he shut them tightly, realizing for the first time that his healing process had been stalled due to her unwillingness to begin her own. She fought against her natural instinct to succumb to her feeling of guilt and instead brought her other hand to cup around the back of his neck, brought his face down to her level, and touched her lips to his forehead, his skin warm and smooth beneath them. They stayed there until he calmed and his breathing returned to normal.

He lifted his head and she ran her sleeve along his cheek to dry it. He loosened his hold on her where his arm had been looped around her waist, but their left hands remained tied to one another against her chest.

She lowered her right from his face and brought it to touch first the amonii tied around his neck, then the small piece of white stone. "Do you think Lex is all right?"

"I do."

"I fear I may not have been the best influence over the past couple of days."

Uritus breathed out a tiny laugh. "Even so, I do think he is fine. This is how he grieves. It's different from the way I do, but he knows his way around grief and through it. Honestly, I think it's been helpful for him to have you along. My method of grieving is far more gray than his own."

Adi nodded, glad to hear this, but then again became sad. "And the others…"

Uritus lifted his eyes to the cracked glass dome and the greenery that grew upon it. "Sadly, grief is the string that has tied us all together from the start. A tangled web in each of our hands, sat up around the fire, sorting through our mess together." He breathed out another laugh, eyes shining with grateful tears. "Isn't that just the thing that makes it so sacred?"

Adiadni's lips parted and she gazed at the fisherman with a sense of pure adoration. So warm was his outlook, always, and the way he kept his face turned toward the sky even when he felt defeated reminded her of the Light that always follows the dark. He looked at her and smiled brightly. She did as well, admiring how a bit of life and color had returned to his countenance.

He moved his gaze reverently across her face. The sun had just begun its downward arc into the Western sky and it shone as a golden crown upon her head and caramel highlights in her deep brown eyes. Her skin creased at the corners of her mouth, exaggerating her smile, and her lips were soft, colored like rose, rose like the gentle scent that wafted from her skin. She was incomprehensibly beautiful, and though he had known this since the moment he first laid eyes on her, it still happened, every so often, that the sight of her made him forget to breathe.

She is…

Slowly, barely moving, he felt himself beginning to pull toward her—not with any specific intention, but like a honeybee to a flower, like instinct, like gravity. And then, before he could consider what he was doing, she brought herself to stand a bit taller and began to speak. He blinked, again becoming aware of his feet beneath him.

"I may be just beginning to learn how to navigate my way through grief, and I may not be any good at it, but I think I know something that might help."

She smiled up at him hopefully. He nodded, glad at her excitement, and she hurried to gather her things. Uritus found and pulled on his boots and followed Adiadni out of the pool house and back to the Fifth to find the others.

Chapter Fifteen

"The Rescue Mission" or "The First Battle"

The 14th of July

Ilya's dark eyes fluttered open and squinted in the bright light of the afternoon sun. Her mouth was dry and her head seared with pain and she felt the scratching of the rough bark of the tree where her arms were bound behind her back.

Bound.

She moved her eyes this way and that, stiffening slightly as she heard movement, and spied a half-dozen humanoid figures hobbling about not far away. She blinked several times to get her vision to focus. To her left was the river lazily winding its way through a canyon, its tall red walls staring down at her as she craned her neck upwards. Several yards ahead—North, she guessed, due to the placement of the sun—were her and Nadarum's horses, nickering nervously, resisting whenever one of their captors tried to lead them to the water to drink. Dotting the bank leading up to them were a handful of crudely assembled tents. And closer still—a few feet away and bound to a short coniferous tree—was her husband, head slumped over one shoulder, blood leaking down his left temple.

She startled as a pair of their captors began to speak to one another in a harsh tongue she did not understand. Nadarum groaned in his sleep and she looked at him with concern as the gritty bites of language continued scratching at her ears. *Gish?* The archer had never before heard the tongue spoken by the goblins. She had traveled this land from one end of the map to the other, met many of its peoples and engaged in their customs. These creatures were shorter than the average human or elvish man, with thin, oily hair and gray-toned complexions, unlike any she had met before and bearing an uncanny resemblance to the images she had seen in books of the Nameless Sorcerer's half-alive servants. Where they could have come from, she didn't know, but it was clear that the energy of this land had been shifting for some time. If the goblins had begun their invasion already, the new war would not be far behind.

They couldn't have been there long. The last thing she remembered was the ambush as she and Nadarum made their way back from his family farm, having been turned away by one of the laborers before even reaching the farmhouse. The altercation had happened that morning, which meant it wouldn't be long before their companions came looking for them.

"Nadarum…"

He stirred at the raspy whisper of her voice but did not wake. She could not physically touch him, even with her boot stretched out as far as she could reach it, and she spied nothing nearby that would prove of any use to help break free. She identified their weapons and bags in a pile near where their horses were tied and sighed frustratedly as she began to recognize that their best chance to escape was likely to sit patiently and await their rescue.

No sooner did she have this thought than a rustling sounded in the tree above her along with a familiar caw, and she looked up to see Qibat resting on a branch.

"Oh, thank the Mother you're here. However did you find us?"

"Looked for you," the bird crowed softly. "Followed."

Ilya nodded, eyes darting back and forth to make sure none had heard them converse. "Well, we've found ourselves in a bit of a tangled stitch so I'll need you to fetch the others. Tell them we're being held by goblins. Quickly," she paused as a chorus of agitated voices arose from several feet away, an altercation that seemed heated. "And quietly."

Qibat cawed once to indicate that he understood and took flight up and out of the canyon. Nadarum groaned again in his sleep. Ilya feared for his well-being.

"It won't be long now, Darling," she whispered. "Help is on the way."

***

Adiadni stood at one end of Uriah's room in The Bleating Lamb; across from her, five of her traveling companions conversed, having been gathered there by Uritus and Perplexus before their original planned meeting time. Uritus stood to her left, Uriah to her right, and at the far end of the room stood two empty chairs, reserved for the couple native to this city whom they'd hoped by now would have returned. The princess briefly questioned if she wished to proceed with her planned address, feeling it not quite right without Nadarum and Ilya present. Her advisors beside her urged her gently on, the Wizard with a soft pat on the shoulder, the fisherman with a soothing smile. She looked ahead and cleared her throat and the others came to attention.

"I wish first to say how truly sorry I am for the loss of one whom I know you all dearly loved. And I am sorry for waiting to address it until now. I am sure by this point, it is clear that I do not know what I am doing... as the Suvah or as, simply, a woman in grief. Over the past few days, I have allowed mine to get the better of me. Forgive me as I sort my way through it."

Her companions regarded her solemnly, a peaceful breeze wafting in from the open window.

"All of that said, I did not gather you all here to speak of myself and my own sorrow. I suppose I am just wondering... how you all are doing."

They paused, looking at one another until Mikka responded, "I believe I speak on behalf of all of us when I say that we are tired."

The others nodded in confirmation of this.

"Havian was a damn fool, but... he was our brother. His loss has been difficult to bear," Oripidus spoke, clearing his throat.

Adiadni nodded, listening intently.

223

"It's probably been hardest on you huh, Punzie?" Perplexus brought a firm and caring hand to the shoulder of the physician who sat in a worn velvet armchair.

Punznes sighed heavily and rested his hand atop the navigator's but did not speak.

Adi continued hesitantly, "I, um… do not wish to ask anyone to speak on more than they are willing. I know loss can be a sensitive topic…"

Punznes smiled amusedly. "Not for us, it's not."

The others chuckled and the princess relaxed but still paused before speaking again. "I just… there are images in my mind… of Havian's last moments and… I suppose I wish to replace those images with less gruesome ones. I wish to, retroactively, know and love Havian as you all do, to solidify my memorialization of him with a clearer picture of who he was."

Laivar chuckled. "Havian was a complex man—as are we all—but he was also entirely himself, all of the time."

"He taught me how to smoke," Perplexus said through a laugh. "When Ilya found out shortly after she moved in, she looked like she wanted to smack him upside the head. By week's end, he had hunted down a box of the pinkberry truffles that you can only get here and she dropped it. She didn't stop being annoyed, but she was grateful for the little bit of her home he had given her as a peace offering, and their alliance was forged ever since."

Adiadni nodded slowly. "I do feel bad to not have her and Nadarum here for this…"

"They're more than likely visiting old haunts," Mikka inferred.

"They're generally private with their grief," said Laivar. "I, however, am rather loud, and you all will be hearing the ballad I am writing for our fallen friend as soon as it is completed, I assure you."

"Has it a title?" Oripidus asked.

"Not yet, though I am open to suggestions."

"Call it *The Hubris of Havian Elix*."

The others devolved into laughter at the bluntness of Mikka's suggestion.

Perplexus smiled fondly up at the ceiling. "The audacity of that man was truly something to marvel at."

"It was such outlandish audacity that netted him most of the things in life that he wanted," Punznes shared. "We grew up together in Lorethh, and the moment that boy got his hands on a sword, he understood clearly who he was. We found it amusing, our companionship, with his natural proclivity to fight and mine to heal. The cuts and scrapes on his body that I mended over the years were too plentiful to count."

The companions regarded the physician silently as he spoke.

"There came a period, years ago, when both of us found ourselves stumbling through grief at the same time. The woman he had called love since he was twenty-one had left him—nearly seven years of partnership ripped from his fingers without an explanation. And my sister… had finally succumbed to the illness that had plagued her since her youth. We lost ourselves in our drink. It was helpful, as it usually is, to have someone you love nearby who can understand your pain and commiserate with it. Truthfully though, we were not good for each other back then.

"But eventually, he had enough. He knew—he was fully confident—that this bleak place he had come to was not his destiny. So he chose to leave. He had heard about the soul-healing often found by those who sought out the White Mountains. He asked me to come with him but I… I was still stuck. So he left without me."

Uritus looked at his friend compassionately. He had heard this story many times, but under the present circumstances found it markedly more moving than ever before.

"And though he knew not exactly what he sought, he found it. Shortly after journeying into the mountains, he settled into a home with an old man and a pair of teenage boys."

Oripidus interrupted, "Were Nadarum here, he'd tell ye to treat yer elders with respect." Uriah chuckled.

Punznes looked from Uritus to Perplexus, "In truth, I think you two did a marvelous bit of work helping him feel like himself again. He'd always had a youthful spirit, and he was grateful to have the opportunity to utilize his skills again, to share his knowledge with you both."

"It didn't take him long to become one of us," Perplexus remarked. "I remember those early days fondly."

"But even amidst his newfound contentment… he never forgot about me."

A lump rose in Adi's throat as she witnessed a tear slip from the physician's blue-gray eyes.

"He wrote to me, told me what he'd found, informed me there was space for both myself and Qibat should I want it. It took me a bit of time still to snap out of my haze, but he did not relent and eventually returned to drag me out himself. I was irritated at the time and not willing to yield to change. But he was—and remained up to his end—as stubborn as an ass, and he would not allow me to lose myself despite how I longed to. Becoming a part of a new family healed me in innumerable ways and I longed to find a way to thank him for never leaving me behind, but… he insisted that this was his contribution to mending my own scrapes and bruises as I always had his."

Mikka sighed, a mixture of sadness and fond memory. "That man prided himself on his ability to fight but his ability to love was just as fierce, and… I'll always remember him for that."

Punznes nodded. "We all will. And it does bring a bit of peace to know that he went out exactly as he always wished."

Laivar laughed, "A sword in his hand, a fire in his eyes, an unobtainable wish in his heart."

"He lived and died by the sword and he wouldn't have had it any other way."
The physician leaned back in his chair and stared up at the ceiling. "I'm still
mad at you, you bastard, for leaving us so young. Rest assured that when my
time comes and I find you out there, I'll punch you square in the mouth for the
sorrow you've caused us, but not before I smother you with an embrace big
enough to make up for the years lost." He lowered his head, meeting eyes again
with the princess, "What you need to know about mourning, Adiadni, is that it is
a continuous process which in some cases never fully ends. You begin to feel as
though perhaps you have made peace with your loss and then it hits you square
in the chest when you least expect it. But to quote our fallen one, *to have
mourned to an unbearable degree means that one has loved to his greatest
capability, and that is always something to be grateful for.*"

Adi nodded solemnly. "Thank you for that. Thank you all, really, for sharing.
I am learning over and over again that this is a mission that I certainly cannot
accomplish on my own. I need you, all of you—your wisdom, your skills, your
experience—to make it to where we are going."

"All we have is yours, princess," Mikka declared.

"Aye," added Oripidus, "Yer one of us now whether ye like it or not."

The room laughed and Adiadni sighed, feeling as though a burden had been
lifted from her shoulders. Then, just as the companions had begun to chat
lightheartedly about their plans for the remainder of the evening, in from the
open window floated the raven.

He cawed as he landed on Punznes's chair, and the physician greeted him and
fetched a walnut from a pouch on his belt for him. "Welcome back, my friend.
Did you have any luck in your search for the missing ones?"

"Found them."

The room came to attention.

"That's good news," Punznes remarked. "Are they far?"

"West," crowed Qibat. "Bound."

"Did he say bound?" asked Adi. "Where are they going?"

"Bound," replied the bird promptly, "Wrists."

The energy in the room shifted to urgency. Uritus felt his heart begin to pick
up its pace. "Are they being held captive? By whom?"

Qibat responded again, and those in the room looked at one another with
worry and surprise when they heard him say, "Goblins."

"In the Free World?" Mikka voiced the query on everyone's minds.

"Not far."

"Shit."

"Come," spoke Uriah urgently. "Gather your belongings, we ride after them.
Are they camped, Qibat, or moving?"

"Still. By the rocks."

"Can you show us the way?"

The raven cawed affirmatively and hopped to the windowsill.

"I'll settle our debts with the innkeeps," spoke the Wizard. "Prepare for what may well be a violent confrontation. We leave immediately." Swiftly, he departed, and the others hurried to make ready to leave.

****

Uritus gripped Moonracer's reins, scanning the street for Uriah as well as Mikka and Laivar who were making certain that the group was adequately stocked with supplies and rations. Qibat perched on Punznes's shoulder, ready to show them the way.

Adiadni moved to her saddlebag and called Perplexus to her side. From it, she produced the map, turned, and thrust it into his hands. "I am the one who makes the way but you are the one who finds it," she said.

The navigator smiled. "I'll guard it with my life. I'll get you where you're going."

She nodded. "I know."

Shortly, the others arrived, and they mounted their horses and rode off after the raven, headed West. The sun had sunk low in the sky by the time they neared the place where Qibat had spotted the missing ones, and they brought themselves to a stop while Mikka and Perplexus went ahead to scout out the camp. The bird's wording of *by the rocks* was an accurate descriptor of this place. The grassland they traversed to get here became dotted by rock formations, sandy in color and then becoming a deep shade of brick-red as they approached the canyon. About a half-mile North of where they sheltered between a few of these formations was Cevyna, the wide stone bridge they would need to cross to continue their journey. They dismounted and donned their weapons, speculating about what may have happened as they awaited the scouts' return.

Adi felt sick. The weight of the sword on her hip seemed heavier than usual. How had it come to this already, a hostage situation mere miles from her home, just a few days after a violent clash that had resulted in the death of one of her party members? When they left Suscundos, she expected that their journey would become difficult only upon their arrival in the Looming Mountains, but now, they were fighting to even make it there. She identified the feeling of guilt that began to grow within her body for how she had misled them thus far and shoved it down. It would be of no use to her here.

"I just find it incredible that of all of us, those two were the ones who got themselves captured," Laivar remarked, stringing his bow. "No offense to the lot of you, you're exceptionally skilled, but they're far and away the most capable out of all of us. Makes you wonder what this generation of goblins is like."

"They were surely outnumbered," Oripidus theorized. "There be no version of those dead-eyed halfwits that could do any lastin' damage to one of our own without a whole squadron behind him."

Uritus remained quiet, his mind all too loud, myriad questions elbowing one another for a chance to stand at the forefront. *Were these truly goblins or something else entirely? Had they come from beyond the Looming Mountains? Who had sent them? Were they here by happenstance or was the traveling party being hunted?* And, most troublesome of all, *if they were here now... how many more must there be already scattered throughout the Free World?* He shook the thought away. This was hardly the time to fixate on what they presently had no power to control.

Shortly, the scouts returned with the raven, and the others gathered around to learn what they had seen.

"They're goblins all right," Perplexus confirmed. "About a dozen of them, from the looks of it."

"Cake," said Mikka. "We could take them in our sleep."

"They're bound to a pair of trees at one end of the camp on the bank of the river. There's a path of sorts that leads down into the canyon, but there is little cover on the way. We'd almost certainly be spotted before we reached the bottom."

"It will be best to wait for the cover of night before we attempt our rescue," Uriah stated.

"Fuck that," spat Oripidus, brandishing his war hammer in his anger. "Ye heard Mik, we can take 'em. Show 'em what happens to those who deign to stand against the Free People."

Punznes was hesitant, "There's no saying what they might do to Nadarum and Ilya during the clash. Sure we *could* theoretically win a confrontation, but at what cost?"

"Punznes is right," Uritus spoke. "Such confidence is a necessity to the victor, yes, but also a crutch for the fool. Should we not take a lesson from our fallen brother?"

"It isn't just about him anymore," Perplexus remarked gravely. "It isn't about any of us."

"What do you mean by that?"

"I mean that if the goblins are here now, sent by who in Shadow knows in search of us, how many more crawl their way across the Free World already? If they are here now then the war has already begun."

Uritus felt his muscles tense at this suggestion. "We do not know that they came here in search of us."

"Even so, they are here for a purpose. They did not crawl up out of the earth and resurrect themselves. Someone created them and someone sent them here. Whether it's for Adi or you or intel or to terrorize the Free People, we would be doing them a disservice if we did not cut out the rot where we find it."

"Lex, I do not wish to spill more blood than is absolutely necessary..."

"So, what? We quietly recover Nadarum and Ilya and ride ahead without a word? If we leave this scum behind alive then we condemn our people to death."

"You don't know that..."

"I won't risk that!"

"Stop," the princess's voice was quiet and soft but even so, it cooled the passionate energy that had begun to boil over amongst the party members. She took a breath. "I do not wish to step on anyone's suggestions, but I do wish to be rational with our decision-making. Punznes makes an important point—should we charge headfirst into a clash of swords, we very well could lose the very souls we came here to save. What may play out after this remains to be seen, but right now, I will do all that I can to ensure that those two lives—the two we have the present capability to protect—make it out of here safely. I haven't the energy to care about what may come next." She was tired, as were the rest of them, and they absorbed her words in silence.

"Adiadni is right," Uriah declared. "If the war *is* truly here as you believe, Perplexus, then we must be thoughtful and wise with all our steps as we proceed. There is little room in deadly conflicts for ill-conceived plans."

Uritus swallowed at the heaviness of such a notion but nodded firmly all the same. "We are all physically capable, yes, but we are also smart, and I believe with our respective skills that we can accomplish this swiftly and cleanly. We owe it to them at least to try."

Mikka nodded, accepting this decision. "Our friends are relying on us."

Laivar set a comforting hand on her shoulder, "I'm sure they're holding up, Mik. Those two are resilient and scrappy."

"That they are..." Uritus turned his head to the canyon. "Perhaps we may rely on them as well."

***

Ilya awoke with a jolt and a gasp and saw that it was now night. Several yards to her left burned a fire around which sat most of the goblins, one of whom stirred when he heard her wake. He stood, picked up a small wooden bowl, and from a skin, poured a dark liquid into it as he approached her. Arriving just before the archer, he thrust the bowl in her direction, saying something to her in gish.

The liquid stank like vinegar. Ilya jerked her head away.

Angrily, the goblin grabbed her face, squeezed her cheeks to force her mouth open, and shoved the bowl up to it.

The taste and smell of it stung her eyes. She looked the goblin straight in the face as he released her and spat it back at him.

He took a half step back, wiping his face with his sleeve. He righted himself and glared at her for a moment before raising the bowl in his hand and dashing it with force against her cheek.

This act of violence elicited a round of cheers from the others around the fire. Ilya's face stung and she felt a warm trail of blood trickle down her cheek and drip onto her collarbone. Even so, she turned to face him again as began to make his way back to the fire and shouted after him, "The Free People buried you once and we'll do it again!"

The goblin stopped in his tracks, turned again to face her. She knew defiance would result in further abuse, but she did not squirm, continuing to glare furiously into his face as he approached her.

Coming to her side once more, he crouched down and brought his face close to her own. She held her breath to avoid inhaling the stench of him.

Her stomach dropped as he began to speak, "That was a different world, Sweetheart. Best make way for the new." He stood and walked away and she released her breath, shivering as he rejoined the others.

His accent was unusual but his words were clear and what's more, he had understood her own. She didn't have the time to consider the ramifications of this before Nadarum groaned and blinked and lifted his head from where it had been slumped.

Ilya breathed a sigh of relief. "It's about time you woke up!"

The horseman smiled dizzily and then regarded his wife with concern. "You're bleeding…"

"*You're* bleeding!"

"It's just a scratch…" he mumbled, again beginning to doze off.

"Look at me!"

He blinked several times, his head wobbling from side to side. "Hmm?"

"I'm going to get you out of here."

He chuckled, a quiet hum. "Of course you are, Plum."

She didn't have the mental space to be amused by his lightheartedness. A rustling sounded in the tree above.

"Damn, it's good to see you." She heard a gentle thud on the ground to her right as she greeted the bird. She looked down. Lying there in the dirt was a small knife, a curved, single-edged blade sprouting from a smooth, bone-white handle, the smaller of the two Perplexus carried always on his person. She curled one leg around to kick it closer and took it in her hand.

"Quiet," spoke Qibat softly. "Won't be long now."

"Thank you, Friend," Ilya whispered. The raven took flight.

***

Atop the canyon's rim, Adiadni, Uriah, Laivar, and Punznes were poised between jutting rock formations, arrows at the ready in the hands of the two elves, the physician positioned as a lookout several feet away with his bow drawn. Below, they could see the goblins gathered around their fire, the few who meandered further upriver by their supplies and the two horses, as well as the trees to which their captive party members were tied. The narrow, rocky path that carved its way down the canyon wall stopped just a few feet South of where the horses were tied, and the four remaining party members silently crept their way down it.

Uritus turned to those still on the rim and signaled to them. Uriah stepped fully into the shade of the rock nearest him and produced a warm yellow flame in the palm of his hand. Adi and Laivar waited for the second signal, upon which they would set their arrows alight, readying the distraction.

Perplexus had grown irritated during their planning phase when Uriah refused his suggestion that the Wizard send down the fire on his own. He thought it would be more efficient as all the archers could then devote their focus to keeping watch. Uriah had reminded him that it was a qualifier of his ongoing partnership with the Source that he not use his gifts to needlessly bring harm upon the earth. Though Perplexus felt that in these circumstances, such actions were certainly not *needless*, he did not push back.

Uritus raised a hand as they approached the canyon floor—the second signal —and Adiadni and Laivar responded by promptly lighting their arrows and firing them down into the brush just North of where the horses were being kept. The flora caught fire as well as the attention of the few goblins who lingered there. Mikka and Perplexus hurried toward them as their backs were turned, bringing their knives to their throats and draining the life from their bodies as Oripidus hastened to locate Nadarum and Ilya's things.

Uritus moved stealthily in the opposite direction, utilizing the cover of the brush as he brought himself behind the tree to which the horseman was bound. Ilya spotted him as he approached. He nodded to her, relieved to see that she appeared in good health. In her hand she clutched the small knife, having already cut through her bonds.

"Mmm?" Nadarum groaned tiredly as he heard Uritus arrive behind him. The fisherman and archer were grateful that this sound was not loud enough to pull the attention of the goblins away from their rowdy conversing.

"Hello there, Friend," Uritus whispered, pulling his dagger from his belt. "Fear not, your rescue has come."

He sawed through the rope which kept the horseman's hands tied to one another. Once Nadarum was free, he began to tip over slowly to one side, forcing Uritus to catch him and set him upright again.

"Shit, you're in bad shape." He looked across to Ilya, "Can he stand?"

"I don't know," she admitted. "He's been going in and out all day. It'll be hard to carry him..."

"We've thought of everything," the fisherman assured her.

"Have you any water?"

He nodded, loosening the skin from where it had been slung across his chest. He brought it to the lips of the horseman. Nadarum took in a small bit but was not conscious enough to lift his head for a full drink. Uritus stood and took a slow couple of steps toward Ilya before a twig snapped somewhere just behind her.

He darted back behind the tree as the goblins turned their heads, staying there until they resumed going about their evening activities.

"Forget it," said Ilya.

The fisherman understood. "I'll be back for you in a moment."

Ilya nodded and Uritus vanished to ensure that the tasks of the others were moving along swiftly.

Adiadni's heart pounded as she watched the events of the rescue unfold. The plan was proceeding smoothly, and only a few more stages remained until their mission was complete. But still, she could not ignore the incessant ringing in her ears that something was bound to go wrong.

Uritus returned to where the others had freed the horses and collected the effects of the captives. He gestured again to the ones atop the canyon wall.

Once more, Adi and Laivar touched their arrows to the flame in the palm of the Wizard and then released them, this time aiming at the brush on the far side of the river. The dry shrubs went up in flame and the goblins who still sat around their own contained fire looked over in bewilderment and began to stir, rising and hurrying to the edge of the river to see what might have been the cause.

Uritus gripped the reins of Nadarum's horse and turned over his shoulder to address his friends, "Keep an eye out. I'll get them and then we'll be out as soon as we came in."

They nodded, securing Ilya's horse's saddle. Uritus turned, swiftly and silently leading the stallion back to where the captives still waited. He made it only a few steps before, out of one of the small, shoddy tents crawled a goblin who came face-to-face with the fisherman when it brought itself to its feet.

Uritus was frozen where he stood. The goblin also seemed baffled by this interaction.

The two stared at one another for what felt like an age before the goblin was suddenly struck by two separate flying projectiles. The first, an arrow to the head, let loose by their lookout on the ridge above. The second, a dagger buried deep in its gut, its elegantly carved alabaster handle the undeniable handiwork of the navigator.

The creature took in a sharp breath as its life was extinguished. It remained on its feet for a full second before it collapsed into the river with a splash.

Uritus's heart stopped as the heads of the goblins turned abruptly at the sound. All at once, they erupted into action, taking up their weapons and rushing upriver toward the invaders. Perplexus raced forward and retrieved his dagger, Mikka and Oripidus on his heels.

"We'll cover you!" he shouted to Uritus. "Get them out of here!"

"Lex!" Uritus screamed his name but the navigator did not listen and the three charged headfirst into combat.

Ilya's horse shrieked at the sudden chaos and barreled up the canyon path. Uritus held tightly to the stallion's reins and hurried to where the captives were still waiting.

The realization of her greatest fear ripped through Adiadni's body as she watched the clash break out below. Punznes and Laivar reacted quickly, firing down upon their enemies to thin their numbers for their friends on the ground.

The princess remained frozen by her terror for all of two seconds before she turned suddenly and raced to the canyon path.

"Adiadni, no!" Uriah caught her by the arm before she could begin her descent and gripped it tightly, spinning her to face him. "You cannot go down there, I forbid you!"

"Uriah, they're going to die!" She looked up at him with wide, terrified eyes, trying to free herself from his grasp.

"You cannot—"

"I exist for no purpose other than this!"

He regarded her fearfully, the determination on her face, the fire in her heart, and with a sad sigh, he released her. "Go."

She turned urgently and raced into the canyon.

Ilya stood and rushed to her husband's side immediately as the fight broke out. "Nadarum, you need to wake up."

She shook him desperately, repeatedly patting one of his cheeks to bring him back to full consciousness. He stirred, just beginning to wake when she was forcefully grabbed from behind and ripped away from him.

She fought back against the powerful pair of arms that lifted her off the ground, but with every movement, they gripped her tighter. In desperation, she slammed her head back into her captor's chin. He released her, reeling and spitting blood.

She pulled Perplexus's knife from her boot as she landed and turned, making a swift cut in the back of his leg. He shrieked, swinging one fist toward her where it collided with the side of her face and sent her flailing.

She flipped herself over and scrambled backward as he righted himself and lumbered toward her. Her hands slipped into the cold water of the river as she clambered to its edge, and just as her captor raised his jagged knife above his head, he was struck by something from behind.

He crashed to the ground with a thud, revealing behind him, Nadarum, a bloodied rock in his right hand.

"About time you woke up."

He smiled down at his wife, a straight row of bright white teeth, and extended a hand to help her up. She righted herself and he immediately began to stumble but was caught by the fisherman before he could fall.

"Come on, Big Boy, time to go." With Ilya's help, Uritus got Nadarum situated in his saddle. "You next."

Ilya didn't have time to respond. She spied a cluster of bodies hurrying at them from downriver, at least twenty, maybe more. She whipped her head around and saw the enemies still closing in on her friends.

"Ilya—"

She slapped her hand against the thigh of her husband's horse, ripping Nadarum's bow and quiver from the saddlebag as he galloped away.

"You'll need my help to get them," she addressed Uritus before he could question her. "Hurry!" She slung the quiver across her back and strung the bow as she rushed upriver to the others. Uritus followed.

Oripidus, Mikka, and Perplexus were spurred on by each other's war cries as they made quick work of the goblins who advanced upon them.

"Give us what ye've got, ye rancid bastards!" Oripidus's hammer crushed the bones of all who got in its way.

The bruises and cuts that peppered their skin were not felt by them. Their minds remained solely on their fight. As the numbers of the goblins who attacked them from all sides began to dwindle, they spotted Uritus racing toward them and Ilya, several feet behind him, rapidly firing arrows into a new wave of enemies.

All of them turned at the sound of the princess's voice from the bottom of the canyon trail, "Everyone fall back, now!"

Uritus diverted his course. Ilya did the same, slowing, taking down the last of the enemies who surrounded her friends.

Perplexus looked beyond the archer at the two dozen goblins who advanced, many of them larger and taller than himself. As the others turned to retreat, his desperation to bring an end to this madness here and now burned hot inside him.

"Mik..."

The former soldier stopped in her tracks, looked back at Perplexus, traced his gaze downriver. She met his eye, "Okay."

"Okay."

"Okay?" Oripidus turned to watch the other two rush toward the oncoming enemies and immediately diverted course and hurried after them. By this point, the other three had caught on to what was happening.

"Damn it, Lex!" Ilya cried, snatching arrows from fallen bodies and racing downriver.

Uritus looked to Adiadni, an expression of panic on his face, "I can't leave them."

"*We* can't."

"Don't—"

"They need us!"

"Adiadni!"

The princess tore after their friends, pulling her sword from its sheath. She did not allow herself to think as she approached the fight, slashing her sword into the back of the first goblin she came near, allowing Oripidus to slam his hammer into the creature's face.

Adiadni felt her body physically react to the shock of the violence that splattered around her, but she didn't have a moment to acknowledge it. At every turn was a new enemy encroaching on one of her companions, her friends, her *people*. All she could do was respond to everything as she saw it, slashing her sword frantically, partnering with those who fought beside her to offer them the brief respite they needed in order to finish the job that she, even now, could not fathom.

Uritus plunged his sword through the back of a goblin before it could swing its blade at Perplexus and the creature squealed as it died.

The navigator nodded to the fisherman as he pulled his blade back out of its body. "Good to have you here, Old Boy," he said with a smirk before charging another.

Uritus continued cutting his way through the fight, guided by his instinct. The initial shock of taking a life wore off quickly, a necessity for survival. The armor crafted for him by Zaphron was sturdy while still allowing him the freedom to move quickly and efficiently. It did not take long for the motions of war to feel natural in his body, and such a realization startled him. He kept his head down, focus forward. He would get them all out. He had to.

The arrows that rained down from their allies above and those fired by the archer on the ground were less useful in taking down the goblins of larger stature, and the group quickly learned that they were resilient in many areas.

Even so, the ranks of their enemies had begun to thin. Those who remained were the strongest of them all. Spread sparsely along the riverbank, the companions pushed on.

Adiadni felt her strength waning with each slash of her blade. All she knew to do was react; her mind wasn't clear enough to recall the specific details of her training. She would wound an enemy, watch as they were cut down, turn, and repeat this process, over and over until it began to seem that her blade was less effective against the last of the sizable goblins.

Hearing a grunt behind her, she turned, bringing her sword above her just in time to block an attack.

The goblin swung again.

She parried once more. She thrust her blade toward her opponent, gasping as he stepped aside and caught it in his hand.

He gripped it tightly, dark, viscous blood flowing from his fingers. The princess watched in shock and horror as he tightened his hold around the sword and ripped it out of her hands, sending it flying behind him. Adi reached behind her for her bow only to be struck with the realization that she had left it atop the ridge.

"Shit."

Defenseless, she stumbled back and away from her rapidly approaching enemy. He raised his hand, striking her with force across her face and sending her collapsing upon the riverbank.

The dark red clay was slick under her hands. She spun around to watch her attacker raise his sword in his non-bloodied hand, howling a horrible sound.

The princess squeezed her eyes shut, bringing a hand reflexively up to cover her face. She took in a sharp breath and held it, hearing suddenly a loud crunching sound followed by a splash.

She kept her eyes shut fast, daring not to move or even breathe and awaiting still the blow that would take her life.

One second passed.

Another, before she fearfully opened one eye and then both, seeing above her, Uriah, the head of his staff covered with the rancid black sludge that leaked from the bodies of the dead goblins.

Around them, the battle had reached its end, each of the companions panting amidst the carnage. The Wizard sighed heavily as the princess scrambled to her feet and brought himself to stand beside the water's edge. He lowered his staff and dipped it beneath the surface, watching as the river washed it clean.

Uritus looked around as the sounds of war silenced, dazed, body vibrating. He frantically looked around to make sure his companions in the canyon were not badly hurt. Mikka had sustained a gash in her leg. Oripidus helped tear off her shirt sleeve to tie it around her thigh. The others, though battered, appeared to be fine. Ilya moved from one fallen corpse to another, gathering arrows as she went. The riverbank was covered in butchery.

Uritus looked down at his sword, slick with dark blood, and saw that his clothing and armor were the same. He felt heavy and deeply tired. He wiped his sword clean and sheathed it.

Perplexus knelt beside one of the bodies, pulling his knife from its back. Uritus was all but overwhelmed by the myriad emotions that swam through his head. He felt frustration and anger take the forefront. He marched toward the navigator.

"What the fuck were you thinking?" He shouted louder than he had intended to.

Perplexus stood, pulling a cloth from his pocket. "I told you. We would have been endangering who knows how many lives if we allowed the horde to go about their business."

"So you risked our lives in pursuit of your own goal?"

The navigator frowned, wiping his knife clean and tucking it back into its sheath. "I never asked you to come with me."

"It isn't about me!"

"You need to relax, Old Boy, we all made it out alive."

The fisherman felt his face grow hot. "For fuck's sake, look around you! Can you not conceptualize how bloody lucky we are to be able to say that? Mikka is hurt, any one of us could have died, all because you are too rash and hot-headed to consider how your actions may affect those around you."

Perplexus became serious, never before having witnessed his friend lash out in anger. "I understand why you are upset, of course, but we're all right, Mik is going to be fine, we made the right choice."

Uritus stared at him in bewilderment. He felt mad with worry and sick to his stomach. "So even now, you stand by your actions."

The navigator straightened himself and spoke firmly, "I do. Were I to be offered the choice again, I'd make the same one."

Uritus shook his head. "Damn it, Lex, it was never your choice to make!"

"I gave no order," Perplexus doubled down. "You followed after me of your own volition."

The fisherman laughed an incredulous laugh. "Do you truly think there exists a world in which any one of us does not?"

Perplexus fell silent.

Uritus stepped toward him, lowering his voice a touch, "What you must learn now is that your actions have consequences. Not just for you, for every single member of this party, for the whole of the Free World. You pledged your sword to me, to Adiadni, *and* to this mission, and we cannot afford to take unnecessary risks based on principle. Have you already forgotten Havian?"

The fisherman's voice broke on this last sentence. Perplexus sighed sadly.

Uritus took a breath before he went on, "I do not know how to reach you. That terrifies me. Before anything else, you are my friend, and I will always seek to protect you. I need to know that you will learn from this instance and act with more rationale in the future."

The navigator hesitated, shifting his weight. "I do hear you. And I promise you that I will try. But if you are asking me to set aside my protective instinct for the sake of your own, then I tell you now, I will not."

Uritus furrowed his brow, pain thrumming in his temples as it had been all night. Before his upset could again begin to boil, he felt a light touch on his arm. He turned to see Adiadni, blood-soaked and battered.

Ilya's voice called out from behind him, "Uritus, Mik can't carry herself out, she's losing blood."

The fisherman turned and hastened to her side, applying pressure to Mikka's wound as he sent the archer to fetch a horse. Adiadni took several steps closer to Perplexus and he turned his attention to her, guilt churning in his stomach as the consequences of his actions began to set into his mind.

"You are an important member of this party," she said. "You play a vital role in this mission. You are passionate and bold and fearless, and those traits are precious and invaluable."

He lowered his head to her slightly, "Thank you."

"But you are out of your depth if you think that your actions will always be acceptable or justified in pursuit of the greater good. I value you, trust you, and *need* you here with me. We all do. But I tell you now and I tell you only once: if I ever give you an order again and you elect not to take it, I will not hesitate to send you home. Do you understand?"

He nodded once in a show of respect. "Heard."

Adi turned and marched away, taking up her sword from the riverbank and traveling up the canyon path to make sure that Nadarum had made it safely to the care of their allies above. Shortly, Ilya rode down with her horse as well as Mikka's, and the companions hurried to help the injured one up.

"Can you ride?" Perplexus questioned her.

"For a while at least."

"We need to get you to a city. Nadarum too," said Ilya, worry in her voice. "We're not far from Ehjonadi."

"No."

They all turned to look at Uritus.

"We cannot go back."

"I'll be fine," Mikka insisted. "Punzie will have us stitched up in no time."

Ilya shook her head. "Nadarum is in bad shape. He needs to rest."

"Ilya, Lex was right. The war is here now. We know not who sent these goblins but we cannot merely hope that this is the last of them. We have to keep going." Uritus did not say it, but he feared that a confrontation as violent as this was surely only the first of many.

"Uritus is right, we must continue," spoke Uriah. "The Lake Provinces are not far. We will stop and rest there, but we no longer have the time to delay. The enemy is on our heels."

The group knew by this point that they would always default to Uriah's word. If he was speaking up now, there likely *was* a correct answer, and they were wise enough to follow his direction. He held back his opinions in almost every case, wishing to grant those around him the freedom to make their own decisions. But never would he allow them to walk blindly into the fire without first warning them that it was there. His present sense of urgency was clear to them all, and the seriousness of their situation began to set in. The path ahead of them would be riddled with far more obstacles than they had previously thought.

Ilya and Mikka made their way back up and out of the canyon. Shortly, Adiadni returned to the bottom on her horse, leading Oripidus and Uriah's.

She came to a stop before the four men still there. "What are we to do about the bodies?"

They looked around, dozens of corpses on all sides.

"We cannot just leave them here."

Uritus sighed tiredly. "I suppose we could burn them, but we do need to move on. At the very least, the injured ones need to."

"Perhaps we could send a group ahead while the rest of us see to the wreckage," suggested Oripidus.

Perplexus shook his head. "I see now that it would be foolish to split up. We're far safer as a full group."

Adiadni hesitated before turning to Uriah, "The bodies themselves are not our only concern. We must get word to my father about what we have seen."

The Wizard nodded solemnly. "You are correct."

"But we cannot go back," she continued. "And I do not wish to wait until we are able to procure a raven at our next destination."

"Might we just send Qibat?" Perplexus offered.

"I considered this, but he has proven too valuable to us. Were it not for him, who knows what wretched fate may have befallen Ilya and Nadarum?"

The companions considered all of this in silence before Uritus spoke again, "Adiadni, I understand the urgency of the matter, but I do not see how we will be able to send word until we reach our next destination. We'll find a swift rider, they'll reach Suscundos in a matter of days."

The princess chewed on her lip and sighed. "My father is preparing for an invasion which he believes is still yet to come, gathering troops for the war that we are presently riding into. Tuvibati Canyon is not in the Western Provinces, it is deep into the Free World, and the fact that the goblins have managed to make it here undetected..." she trailed off. "I will have to send someone back to the Valley to find a raven, there is no other way."

The group pondered this in silence.

"Perhaps instead we might slay two goblins with one arrow and toss the bodies into the river."

The companions turned to look at Oripidus.

Perplexus spoke, "Wouldn't that pollute the water?"

"Aye, to some degree," the dwarf replied. "But they'll have reached Ehjonadi by tomorrow, Suscundos not long after that."

Adiadni nodded with growing assurance. "Someone will see them, identify them, and send word to my father on their own. The farmers rely on the river, there is no way they will miss them."

"They'll get word to the king far quicker than any of us could." Uritus brought a hand to clap on the blacksmith's shoulder. "Well done, Rip."

Oripidus dipped forward in an exaggerated bow. "Thank ye very much, I know."

The companions hurried to complete their task, electing to leave two goblins of different sizes behind on the bank in case someone from the city tried to trace them to their origin. On several of the bodies, they tucked small notes, inquiring of the finder to send word to the king of their presence in the Free World. The corpses, unburdened by their weaponry and heavier armor, drifted slowly downriver, coloring the water as they went.

The group then mounted their horses, crossed the bridge, and made their way West, bound for Tosh.

Chapter Sixteen

"The Ghost of a Home Long Gone"

The 15th of July

The sky was gray and thick with clouds as the traveling party approached the town that the Adalos had once called home, and the sight of it struck him with a profound familiarity. He had not set foot in Tosh since he had left nearly ten years prior, and as his eyes moved across the aged wood of the town as it appeared before them, he struggled to identify exactly how he felt about being back.

His friends stole glances at him from time to time, attempting to gauge the state of his heart. The heaviness of such a return was not lost on any of them.

Shortly, they arrived in the town's square, the market silent and empty. Several of the companions hurried off in different directions in search of anyone who could offer them supplies or aid.

Uritus hesitated, overcome by a ghostlike sensation. He met the eye of his mentor, "Uriah, I think I need to…"

The fisherman trailed off and the Wizard lowered his head. "Say no more. We will find you later."

Uritus nodded briskly and rode away. Adiadni watched him leave, turned to look at the physician who tended to the wounds of the injured, and then to Uriah. She opened her mouth as if to speak but just as quickly shut it again.

Uriah read her mind, "If you wish to go after him, I am sure he will not fault you for it."

"I'm sure you're right…" She paused. "I suppose I just do not wish to intrude. That is… if he is the type who prefers to work through his grief on his own."

The Wizard sighed sadly. "He is undoubtedly capable of it, if only because he once was backed into a corner with no other choice. But even the strong can benefit from a sturdy shoulder. I am certain that if you offer him your own, he will be grateful."

She nodded and, without another word, rode off after the fisherman.

She passed by worn, sleepy structures as she went, and found herself leaving behind the main fixtures of the town and heading toward a strip of cottages, presumably on the edge of the lake. The further she went North-and-West, the clearer the peaks of the White Mountains, and she drew in a sharp breath as she beheld their majesty. Nothing she had seen in books or works of art had captured anything more than a fragment of their beauty.

Shortly, she spotted Moonracer grazing on sparse grasses near a rickety old barn, and she brought Swadalla to a stop beside him. Rounding the building's corner, she saw the fisherman, and she halted abruptly and gasped as she regarded the scene before her.

Uritus stood at the edge where the ground stooped down. Beyond him, as far as the eye could see, stretched miles of cracked white earth. The Plentiful Lake was gone, and in its place, the desert Uritus had stood before in the vision she had seen mere days prior.

He heard her approach and turned briefly to look over his shoulder before returning his attention straight ahead. "It was still here when I left," he said. "Came right up to the shoreline. There was even rain then. Granted, it was the first we'd had in some time, and it only lasted about half a day, but…" he trailed off. "It's hard to comprehend how it got so bad so quickly."

Adiadni took several hesitant steps until she came to stand beside him but did not speak.

"This is foolish," he said with a half laugh, "But I cannot help but wonder if things might be different here had I stayed."

The princess felt the sting of gathering tears as she listened.

"Of course, I cannot control the weather," he continued. "In truth, I couldn't have done much of anything. I was only a boy. My father told me and thus I've believed my whole life that there is a hand of favor upon it, upon… *me*. Perhaps if I had attempted to make a life for myself here after he died, such favor could have extended to the rest of Tosh as well."

"The whole of the Free World would be different had you stayed."

"I suppose."

They were interrupted by the sudden sound of approaching hooves and both turned to see Perplexus round the corner of the barn on his horse.

"Uritus, there's no one here." The navigator looked from his friends to the space that lay before them and back, "We've searched the whole square, knocked on every door. The town was abandoned some time ago."

Uritus sighed sadly, turning back to where the lake should have been as he absorbed the information he already knew to be true.

Perplexus and Adiadni regarded him sorrowfully as the navigator continued, "We've sent the injured ahead into the mountains with Punznes and Ilya. Qibat's on the way to alert Zaphron and Robalto that we're making our way home and will require aid. They sent me to fetch you…"

Uritus did not respond and Adi looked back and forth between the two men apprehensively before she addressed the one on the horse, "Go on ahead. We won't be long here."

"Are you sure?"

The princess nodded and the navigator departed without another word.

Silence hung in the air between the two who remained. Uritus kept his attention fixed on the empty basin, Adiadni's on Uritus. She was at a loss for how she might bring him any source of comfort, so she remained by his side in silence until he elected to speak again.

"I wasn't sure what to expect when it became clear that I would return here. I suppose, after so many years, I thought it might feel somewhat foreign to me, and it does, but… I stand here now, yards away from the place I was born and… I feel as though I am fourteen again."

Adiadni turned her head to regard the cottage North of the barn and then looked at him again. "I'm sorry. I wish I had more words than that."

Uritus shook his head. "You needn't be."

"But I am. My family knew not of the plague nor the drought. Perhaps if we'd known, we could've…"

"You were a child, as was I. Nothing I could have done would have made any difference and the same is true of you."

"No. We could have divined the cause, a solution, the outcome. At the very least, we could have helped the village residents relocate when the time came."

"But as you said, you did not know. That is no fault of your own."

The princess sighed and gazed across the cracked landscape. "The fact that those in the Lake Provinces did not know that they could request aid is a direct failure of the crown."

Uritus turned to look at his counterpart.

"We have been blessed with peace for centuries and therefore have not needed to expend our resources to protect our people as we would during wartime. I've lived my whole life believing that our energy was being spent elsewhere, particularly to provide during times of need such as this. That a change to our landscape this significant and devastating could happen in a matter of years without our knowledge is proof that we haven't been doing our job." Frustratedly, she snatched her golden tiara from her head and frowned down at it in her hands. "What purpose does this even serve beyond symbolism?"

Silence hung in the air for a moment. Uritus took a step closer to Adiadni and set a hand on her shoulder.

She looked up at him suddenly, "I'm supposed to be the one comforting you."

He smiled, a look of both amusement and genuine gratitude. "I assure you, I need no comforting."

"No one would blame you if you did." She reached a hand up to take his where it rested.

He nodded, knowing she was right. He turned his focus inward and searched his heart for what presently dwelt there. He found no anger, no hopelessness, no true regret. Merely a dull ache, and he voiced this to the princess.

"It is as Punznes said, that grief remains long after the initial wound has healed. Like a scar. My own has been cut open and healed many times over. A burden I learned how to bear long ago. You needn't worry about me." He paused, offering her a grateful smile. "Though, it does make me feel profoundly better knowing that you do."

She nodded. She wished that he would allow himself to be vulnerable, but still, she understood. She released his hand, still clutching her tiara in her other, and they turned again to the expanse of dry earth.

Adiadni's stomach twisted as she recalled again the images from her vision. She had thought them to be mere hallucinations, her mind's way of making sense of the yuzh as it burned its way through her bloodstream. The realization that this may not be the case had slowly set in since the moment she rounded the corner of the barn and was confronted by one of the images she had seen, as clear and vivid as it had been beneath the willow. She felt herself begin to spiral as she considered what this could mean.

Uritus spoke, breaking her from her trance, "There's light still, Adiadni, even here."

She blinked several times and traced the length of his outstretched arm and saw, through the fog, the unmistakable glimmer of sunlight dancing upon water.

"I suppose it could just be a mirage," he said, lowering his arm once more.

She shook her head. "Even if it is… there is Light wherever we choose to find it."

He chuckled softly and then turned his head in the direction of the old cottage. The princess followed his gaze.

"You do not need to come with me," he said. "But I am certain that I would regret it were I to come all this way just to leave without visiting the house."

"I would like to come with you," she replied. "Unless, of course, you would prefer to be alone."

He shook his head. "I'd always prefer to have you along, Adiadni. Even to such a place as this."

She nodded, feeling a slight warmth grow in her chest, and followed him as he made his way up the hill to the cottage. He hesitated momentarily before reaching the door, his eyes tracing the facade of the place he had once called home. The patch of dirt where the garden had once grown was dry and dusty. The thatch that covered the roof was thin and sagging and the wood of the walls appeared as though it would collapse if struck too hard. Uritus approached the door and gently pushed it open.

He was struck with a heavy sensation of melancholy upon stepping inside. The interior of the house appeared just as the exterior—as a skeleton, a shade of what it had been, the weary bones of a home that had once been brimming with life. It was dusty and dim, the windows framed by tattered curtains and coated in layers of built-up grime. He wandered through the main room, observing the rickety wooden furniture that still stood there, and then proceeded through the door of the room to the right. Adiadni followed him, arms folded tightly together as she looked into the room and spotted three dilapidated bunk beds, one against each wall, a window behind and a small wooden chest to the right and left of each.

Uritus turned to meet the eye of the princess before gesturing to the top bunk against the wall opposite them. "That was mine," he told her. "My older brother,

Erclidus, slept below. Vexol there, the third-born," he pointed to the leftmost bunks, "...and Donlimites beneath her. She was the first born of the triplets." He turned to the bunks on the right, "And then Perien and Tevel there, the youngest boys."

Adi nodded, looking from one bunk to the next. She tried to comprehend what it would be like to suddenly lose Fenn. The thought brought tears to her eyes. Uritus left the bedroom and paused, looking from the empty dining table to the cold hearth to the stool beside the dusty bookshelf. It was mostly bare, and the few remaining books were brittle and overgrown with cobwebs.

"It pained me to leave these," he said, crossing to the bookshelf, taking one of the books in his hands, and gingerly thumbing through its pages. "I took all that I could. These are mostly historical accounts and such, all things I knew I could find elsewhere."

"And did you?"

The fisherman smiled as he shelved the book once more. "Indeed. Uriah's library far rivals this one. But still, I do hate to see a book fall to a state like these have."

"Perhaps we could have someone fetch them and bring them to the keep? And anything else here you might wish to have..."

He shook his head. "That won't be necessary. There is nothing here that I will glean more from than that which I already have."

The princess responded with a silent nod.

Uritus turned toward the closed door of the room to the left and stared at it for a quiet moment before approaching it with a deep breath. He gripped the handle and pushed the door open, revealing the room where he had spent his last moments before deciding to leave Tosh behind. He brought himself to lean against one side of the doorframe to allow Adi to see beyond him.

The room was as he remembered it. On one end, a wardrobe, one door ajar, revealing a few threadbare articles of cloth within. Across from it, a pair of armchairs, appearing as though they would collapse if pushed to hold up more than their own weight. And on the other end of the room, tucked into the corner, a bed, neatly made with tattered sheets, and a heavy chest at its foot. All around the room, through the cracked windows and peeking around thin curtains shone dusty beams of dim sunlight.

"I was born in that bed," Uritus spoke, gesturing toward it. "Me and all my siblings." He hesitated for a moment, lowering his hand before saying finally, "My mother died there."

Adiadni's mouth fell open. She looked from the bed to her counterpart, tears tracing gentle tracks down her face.

"My father too. Nearly seven years later, on my fourteenth birthday." He drew in and released a long breath. "It rained that day. First time in what felt like an age. That's the only time in my life I can say I ever felt... truly lost."

He felt his heart squeeze—his grief making itself known. He returned his focus to her and continued, "They said things to me, both of them, before they died which I still hold close to my chest today. They remained so... *bright*. So hopeful, even in what they knew to be their last moments. They used the last of their Light to bring me some semblance of comfort when I felt my world was crumbling. Everything I now am I owe to them. The hope that I feel now, which initially prompted me to leave... It was their final gift to me. That and... this." He hooked a finger under the leather cord which held the amonii against his chest and released it.

Adiadni looked at the partial piece of shell faintly glimmering in the light and then again at Uritus's face, his eyes brilliant blue, "I know you do not wish to hear me tell you that I am sorry... and I do not tell you as a means of communicating any pity I may feel for you, but I wish..." She paused abruptly as her body was taken by a weighty sob. "I desperately wish that I could have been here. Sat with you, mourned with you. Told you that it would be fine. I cannot fathom living those years and coming out of them alone. No one should ever have to, *you* should have never..."

Uritus stepped toward her without a word, brought one arm around her, and the other hand to cup her face and draw it into his chest, holding her while her tears fell. He rested his chin in her hair, breathing in the scent of her until her sobs lessened, and then lifted her face to look up into his.

"I hear your heart," he told her. "And it means more than I know how to say. But I promise you, I am all right. The place I now call home, the people I now call family... the grand destiny that I am still struggling to comprehend... I would have attained none of it had I not left. I know that you wish you could change things and I believe that to be a reflection of the goodness in your heart. But there is nothing left for me here. That was clear to me long ago."

The princess nodded understandingly.

"And destiny aside..." he continued softly, "I am glad that the path I have trod has led me to you." He looked down into her sparkling eyes, felt the coolness of her face in his hand. "I have not known you for long, but I can say assuredly that you are one of the dearest friends I've ever had."

She smiled up at him, her gaze tracing the length of his nose and the curve of his lips before again returning to his eyes, "I'll be sure to rub that in Lex's face when next we see him."

Uritus burst into laughter and Adiadni joined him, relieved to see his countenance brighten again.

"We really should make our way to them," he spoke when they settled. "If we're quick, we should be able to make it to the keep before dark."

She agreed and they departed, the fisherman carefully closing the door behind him. He turned back to the cottage once they were several paces away, brought his right hand to touch his chest, and lowered his head solemnly. "I am sorry to leave again," he spoke softly. "But there is more that I must do elsewhere."

A gentle breeze floated past his face, catching the attention of the princess who stopped and turned.

"We go with you still."

A smile crept across the fisherman's face, and he raised his head and turned to follow Adiadni back to their horses.

***

They arrived at the Alabaster Keep in a matter of hours. Adiadni noticed as they rode through the White Mountains that the peaks appeared to be making way for them, parting and slipping by like icebergs being passed by a ship. Uritus explained that he and the others had also observed this sensation, that the more urgent their mission, the quicker they arrived at their destination within the range. The princess was amazed by this and continuously baffled by the size and sheen of the mountains' glistening faces. She felt at peace here, courageous, and profoundly hopeful. There was Magic in this earth and it reminded her of home.

Zaphron Hammitt greeted Uritus and Adi with a warm and excited embrace upon their arrival. She poured affirmations over the Adalos, gushing with pride for the great tales of his success their companions had regaled her with. The leatherworker was tall, with broad shoulders and strong, rough hands, and the brightness in her smile communicated how thrilled she was to finally be meeting the princess whom the others spoke so highly of. Her twin, Robalto—of striking physical similarity to his sister but considerably more reserved—offered the Suvah a firm handshake and thanked her for the role she was playing in their salvation.

Such praise struck Adiadni with a profound sense of duty, but not one that frightened her. Rather, it made her feel honored for the opportunity to give what she had for this land and people, and deeply conscious of the seriousness of such a responsibility. It was simply not an option for her to fail.

The princess went away with the others to tour their home and check on the wounded. In the hubbub, Uritus slipped away in search of Uriah. He was invited into the Wizard's chamber upon knocking on the door and slipped in without a word. He spotted his mentor on the far side of the room, standing in the open doorway of his balcony, looking over the mountains. The fisherman crossed the room to stand beside him. They remained next to one another silently for a few moments while Uriah puffed on his pipe.

This time, it was the Wizard who spoke first, voicing a simple, "How are you feeling, my boy?"

Uritus chuckled at the simultaneous simplicity and complexity of such a question. "I believe I can still say that I am well, mostly. The past weeks have been a lot to wrap my head around. Just when I think I've grasped one thing, I am struck by another."

"Mmm."

Uritus looked up at his mentor. Uriah had always an appearance of stoicism on his face. He was not outwardly expressive with his emotions and this, paired with the knowledge that he had lived a life far longer than most could comprehend, had most who knew the Wizard under the impression that he always had everything under control. It was why they felt safe with him, why they trusted him though they knew only fragments of his full story. But Uritus

246

looked at him now, at the far-away look in his eyes, and could not help but feel that something was weighing heavy on his mind.

"And you?"

The Wizard sighed, chuckling softly. "As you have said, the days and weeks we have witnessed have left much to be considered."

The fisherman nodded, looking out over the mountains which blushed in the light of the setting sun, a knot in his chest that needed to be worked out. "I am different now than I was when first we left here," he spoke suddenly.

Uriah turned to look at him. "How is that?"

Uritus rested his hands on the balustrade, shifting his weight from one foot to the other with a heavy sigh. "I have taken life," he finally said, a note of unsettledness in his voice.

The Wizard regarded his pupil with compassion, "How does such a thing make you feel?"

Uritus shook his head, uncomfortable with the truth. "To be honest, I do not feel as bad about it as I believe I should. Should that frighten me?"

"No. You did what you felt you must."

The fisherman shook his head again, firmly this time. "Everyone keeps saying that. Havian, Lex… I know that the goblins would have killed *us*, that they wouldn't have stopped with us. I just…" He paused with a frustrated sigh. "How can any of us ever truly know that we've done what is right?"

The Wizard chuckled softly. "We cannot."

This was becoming clearer by the day. "I understand more, the older I get, how many things are gray."

"Mmm." Uriah puffed thoughtfully on his pipe.

The Adalos paused for a moment, looking up at his teacher. "Have you… taken life… since the war?"

Uriah shook his head. "I have not."

"And… how are you handling that?"

The Wizard sighed. "This last time was as bleak and harrowing as the first and all those in between. I wished to lay down my sword for good once the Hope War had reached its end. But I knew if I lived long enough to see the next, I would not be granted such a luxury. As it is, I am grateful that I have been able to remain peaceful until now. To kill is an action that never becomes easier, and I believe it shouldn't. Nonetheless, were I presented with this choice again—to allow someone I love to fall at the hand of another or intervene—I would remain true to my prior instinct. Such times do not grant us the luxury of passivity. At least, that is my personal compass."

Uritus nodded, looking again over the cold stone that darkened with the coming of night. He recalled the events of their battle in the canyon, trying to remember the emotions he had felt in those moments. "When Lex ran into the charge, and then the others, and Adiadni… I didn't have a moment to think. It was as if my feet moved for me. I didn't have the chance to consider what I was about to do before I did it."

"That is your instinct. You were right to listen to it. You will need to become intimately familiar with its voice in the coming days."

The fisherman nodded and a rapping sounded at the chamber door behind them. They turned as the door was pushed open to see the navigator's head peer around it.

"I don't mean to interrupt, I just wanted to let you know we'll be preparing to dine before too long."

Both men nodded and Uritus spoke, "We'll be down in a short while, thank you."

Perplexus watched the Adalos and the Wizard turn again to gaze over the mountains in silence. He quietly stepped back from the chamber door and pulled it shut. His hand lingered on the latch for another moment before he turned, catching the eye of the princess who made her way down to the ground floor. She tipped her head over her shoulder gently, observing that something about his demeanor seemed unusual.

He released the latch, sighed, and offered her a half-hearted smile. "I fear he may still be upset with me."

"Why would he be upset with you?"

Perplexus raised an eyebrow, an amused expression on his face.

"Right." The princess felt silly for having forgotten such a serious event. She toyed with her hands, looking at the closed door and then again at the man beside it. "I don't think it's you," she finally said. "Our Hero has a lot on his mind at the moment."

Perplexus nodded slowly, turned as Adi arrived beside him, and began walking with her down the hall. "Yes, of course he does."

Adiadni looked up at her friend's face, a heaviness on it that she had never seen before.

The navigator hesitated for a moment at the top of the single curved staircase and then spoke as they descended to the main entryway below, "He used to… talk to me about things."

Adi's lips parted as sympathy squeezed her heart.

Perplexus went on, "I don't blame him for doing so less as of late… and that isn't meant as a slight to myself. Rather I… I know that he has undergone a rather jarring shift when it comes to his understanding of himself, and then been suddenly shoved onto a path to blindly race toward a weighty destiny that he is still just beginning to realize. All of this is true of you too, of course."

The princess shook her head. "I've always known who I am, for the most part. I struggle to grasp what it must be like to wear his boots."

Reaching the bottom of the stairs, they could hear the music of laughter singing from the dining hall. Perplexus halted his walk and he and Adi turned to face one another.

"It's hardly something to complain about," he went on. "Old Boy's got the weight of the world slung across his back. I'm happy to offer him anything and everything that I have to give, even if that is merely... my absence. I'm just grateful to be along for the ride, but..." He paused, sighing heavily. "We grew up together. And now, it's hard not to feel a bit... lost, at times."

Adiadni's heart hurt for him. She knew how intimately he and the fisherman knew and loved each other but also understood how displaced the navigator must be feeling. She took a step toward him and brought a caring hand to rest on his shoulder, "He admires you so deeply. He talks about you all the time." She smiled. "I cannot speak to the complexities of a relationship as sacred as yours, but... I can tell you assuredly that he needs you more than you know. You still have much to learn from one another."

Perplexus smiled and lowered his head to her graciously, and then atop the stair appeared the fisherman. He grinned upon seeing the two who stood below, and they at him, and he descended with a lightness in his step.

Reaching the bottom, he brought his hand to rest upon Perplexus's shoulder. "I meant to thank you for allowing Adiadni and me a bit of time back in Tosh. I think it was good for me..."

Perplexus also lifted his hand to his friend's shoulder. "I understand. I'm glad to help in any way I can."

***

In the dining hall, the table was laid. The meal was neither showy nor elaborate, as those in the White Mountains had access to far fewer varieties of produce than those further South. Nevertheless, the Hammitt twins had caringly labored in the kitchen when they learned that the family would be joining them. They thought such an occasion—the return of their loved ones, the welcoming of a member of the royal family to their table, the celebration of the journey of the prophesied two; as well as, they learned upon the party's arrival, the remembrance of the fallen one—was deserving of as noble of a meal as they could muster. Set out on various boards and platters were an assortment of cured meats and fish, bread and butter, hard cheese, cabbage, potatoes, a few jars of pickled vegetables and honey and fruit preserves. Adorning the walls of the room, the chandeliers above the table, and dotted between the dishes and platters were dozens of ivory candles, their cold yellow flames reminding the princess of those in her own home.

The trio of young people found their seats as the others continued to chat. Nadarum moved around the table with a pitcher of dark wine, filling glasses as he went, and Uritus greeted him, saying that it was good to see the horseman clear-headed and on his feet.

"You know, the two of you never did tell us how you wound up in that scrap in the first place," Laivar remarked to the ones they had rescued. "You left The Lamb initially of your own volition, yes?"

"We did," Nadarum replied. "We discussed it, and as it had been nearly twenty-five years since we left our homes in the Northern District, we determined that it was as good a time as any to attempt a visit."

249

"How did it go?" asked Mikka. "You didn't part on particularly amicable terms. Were you nervous?"

Both horseman and archer shook their heads. Nadarum answered, "How they have chosen to feel about us and our love is their trouble, not ours."

"We weren't even certain we'd find them there after so long," Ilya added.

"And were they?" Zaphron questioned.

"Yes and no. We traveled first to my family farm where we were greeted by my sister and she informed me that our parents are dead."

A solemn silence fell upon the room.

"Apparently, they passed not long after I left with Nadarum. I admit that hearing the news did for a moment make me wonder if perhaps leaving was not the best decision, but… the truth is that they abandoned me long before I did them. The only true regret I have carried throughout the years is that I could not bring Maium with me. But it was good to see her. She has done well managing the farm on her own. We spent that night at the farmhouse, though truthfully, she and I did not get a wink of sleep."

"I'm glad you were able to reconnect with her," spoke the leatherworker. "Surely, such a thing was able to brighten such heavy news."

"Indeed."

"And what of your family, Nadarum?" queried the bard.

The horseman chuckled, a sound of amusement with an undertone of heaviness. "We did make our way to my family farm the morning after we spent the night at Ilya's. But whoever dwelt there, be it my father or just my brothers, had us sent away when they saw us approach."

"That's quite harsh," Oripidus remarked. "Did it upset ye?"

Nadarum paused before filling his own cup and taking a seat at the table. "It did not. I was willing to reconcile, but in truth, I was not looking forward to it. Keeping the door shut was their choice. I remain responsible for only my own."

The Wizard entered the hall and took his seat and the others proceeded to gather food onto their plates.

"It was when we had just begun to make our way back to the Fifth that we were ambushed. Nadarum, I'm not sure how well you remember this part…"

"I've a foggy recollection of being hit on the side of the head, but the rest till the battle is all but black."

Ilya went on, "I saw a few figures step out of the fields when I heard you get hit. I was struck moments later. By the time I awoke, we had already been moved to the canyon."

"And they were goblins? All of them?" Robalto inquired.

"Well…" Nadarum paused. "They all appeared to be. But several were of greater stature than one would expect goblins to be. Otherwise, they all shared the same characteristics, the same rotten blood."

"How great of stature? Greater than even you?"

The horseman looked to his wife for confirmation and she nodded. "The one you killed upon waking was taller than you, certainly. The rest weren't quite so, but imposing all the same."

"I was in a combative position but I do recall looking up when we crossed blades," Perplexus shared.

Laivar asked, "Have you seen such creatures before, Uriah?" and the rest of the table turned to regard the Wizard in anticipation of his answer.

He shook his head slowly. "Never. Though, I suspect they share the same neural connection as the goblins of standard size. It seems natural that the conjurings of the Sorcerers would have grown stronger in the past centuries."

"Stronger they may be, but still no match for our own," sang Zaphron.

"There is something about this new generation of half-living that I believe we must take into account."

The heads at the table swiveled at Ilya's statement.

The archer took a sip of her wine, replaced her cup on the table, and leaned forward to regard her friends. "Perhaps not all of them do, but at least one goblin spoke in the common tongue."

The companions began murmuring about this.

"I searched this afternoon through the library, and nowhere in the historical accounts is any mention of a goblin speaking anything but gish."

"Are you most certain?" The seriousness in Uriah's voice brought the murmurs to a halt.

"I am. I thought I was merely dazed at first, and he was admittedly difficult to understand, but I am sure he spoke to me in the common tongue. He responded to something I said that he understood."

"What did you say?"

The archer paused as she tried to recall. "I threatened him. Told him we rid our land of them before and that we would again."

"Atta girl," said Oripidus.

Uriah nodded slowly, sitting back in his chair as he pondered this before turning to the carpenter, "Robalto, how soon would you be able to procure a raven and send a message to the king?"

"I can leave for Akmen first thing in the morning."

"Good. Whether it is only some of them who speak our tongue or all, this development in their evolution is a critical piece of information. Their ability to understand us means they may glean information from our people through subterfuge or tactics of a more brutal nature. And their ability to speak it…"

"Means they may more easily relay such information to someone else," Uritus finished the Wizard's thought with a growing feeling of unease. "Whoever sent the goblins has been planning their invasion for some time."

Uriah nodded seriously. "I believe you will agree with me, Adiadni, that sending word to your father is the best course of action?"

All heads turned to the end of the table opposite Uriah where the princess realized that the Wizard was prompting her to be the one to make the decision. She nodded. "Certainly. By now I would hope that someone from the Valley has already sent word to him about the bodies they discovered, but this will ensure that word reaches him. It is best that he knows all he can."

"Of course." Uriah turned once more to Robalto, "I'll have the letter to you before the night's end." With that, he rose from the table and swiftly departed, pausing to encourage the others to finish their meal, as it would be the last one of any note until they returned here, back from beyond the Looming Mountains.

For the most part, they succeeded at this, each of them voicing abundant gratitude for the two who had prepared the meal for them. Laivar was quick to entertain them with story and song, many of his tales recollections of the events of their journey thus far. Uritus found it surreal to be the subject of so many artfully told stories. Laivar did embellish to some degree—as was consistent with his fantastical nature—but every tale he ever told was shared exactly as he had observed it: as wild and daring and colorful and bright. The family retired to their chambers with full bellies and full hearts.

But Adiadni lay awake for most of the night, gazing at the cold patch of moonlight cast on her floor from her window. The Looming Mountains were not far, and neither was Dagamor.

Chapter Seventeen

"A Crooked Path and a Shifty Guide"

The 16th of July

The Adalos arose before the sun the following morning, as he often did. His initial plan had been to lounge in his room until the group collectively broke their fast before setting out again. But the sky outside the keep turned from black to gray and he suddenly found himself feeling undoubtedly awake. He dressed and proceeded to make his way outside. He wasn't sure where he was going, perhaps to sit beside one of the streams while the sun came up, perhaps just to wander for a time alone with his thoughts. All he knew was that he had been struck with a longing for the taste of the brisk mountain air, and he honored it.

The air did have a chill to it, familiar, despite the Summer season. The sky was wide and cloudless and he could still make out the faint impressions of the brightest stars which had yet to be tucked away by the day. He moved out of sight of the keep, headed West, when all at once, he felt that unmistakable pressure grow behind his eyes.

A wind rushed all around him. He heard a sound—a prolonged, repetitive whooshing—and the corners of his mouth lifted into a smile as the whooshing ceased and he turned to regard its source behind him.

There, in the pale morning light, stood Milion.

The dragon was ethereal and majestic. Uritus was astounded by his beauty all over again every time they met. His scales shone in shades of sapphire and obsidian, his belly silver. It seemed to the fisherman that he had grown somewhat in the time since last they had seen each other. Milion folded his wide wings across his back and lowered his head as Uritus approached. Many times before had the man called to the beast, but this was the first instance that the beast had come to the man without first being summoned. Uritus brought a gentle hand to stroke the dragon's large face.

"Hello, Friend." Uritus brought up a hand to rest on his face. "It's wonderful to see you again. I know it's been only a few weeks since I departed, but I hope you've been holding up fine without me."

From the dragon's belly rose a low rumbling, a sound the fisherman had come to know as an affirmative one. Uritus suddenly remembered the conversation he had had with Nadarum just before the Trial of the Saddle. He furrowed his brow into a curious expression. "Did you… summon me?"

Milion rumbled again and the sound reverberated through the fisherman's body.

Uritus chuckled, struck by the wonder of his connection with this creature. "I'm sad to say I'll be departing again today. But I'm glad to see you before I do. Your presence is remarkably inspiring."

The dragon snorted as if to say he knew.

***

The Suvah rose from her bed with a heavy sigh as the morning's first rays of light streamed through her windows. She crossed the room and brought herself to stand before the looking glass. She was physically and mentally exhausted and it showed in her eyes. Adiadni had not slept a full night since she'd left her home, and she was frustrated by how she had been unable to take advantage of the opportunity to do so the night prior. She'd tossed and turned for hours, trying desperately to find a comfortable position, but every time she closed her eyes, her mind swam with the images she had seen in her vision. The haunting shape of Uritus's body, lifeless—or at least near it—in her arms, left her stricken with fear and covered in cold sweat until she eventually decided to give up on sleep entirely.

She laid up for hours, snapping her fingers to light a flame and then seeing how long she could hold it. It always choked out with a tiny puff of smoke before a minute had lapsed and she would sigh frustratedly and try again. Eventually, her exhaustion won out, sucking her into a deep rest for a couple of hours until the light of the morning sun snapped her awake. She pressed palms full of cold water to her eyes to quench their burning and then braided her hair, dressed, and departed from her room.

It had been decided long ago that once the travelers reached this phase of their journey, they would proceed West on foot. The Swamp of Sigmount was too treacherous and unpredictable for horses to be anything more than a burden there, so Adiadni made her way to the stable to bid farewell to Swadalla. She ended up making her way around to every stall, thanking the horses for carrying them thus far and making acquaintance with Zaphron and Robalto's. She lingered a while longer with Havian's mare, where she stroked her chestnut coat and told the animal that she was sorry for the loss of her rider.

Suddenly, the princess heard a sound emanating from beyond the doors on the far side of the stable. She turned her head, observing that the horses did not seem to be agitated by its presence. Tentatively, she made her way to the doors, gasping and leaping back when she heard the sound again. Reaching them, she gripped their handles, took a deep breath, and flung them open. The sight that greeted her knocked the air out of her lungs.

She saw Uritus, sharp white peaks beyond him, and before him, an enormous dark blue dragon. Both man and beast turned their heads when they saw her. The dragon abruptly spread his wings and soared away into the sky.

The wind stirred up by his flight hit Adiadni with force and her mouth fell open as she watched him disappear beyond the mountains.

The sudden arrival of the princess and subsequent departure of Milion surprised Uritus, and for a second, he considered asking the dragon to return. He quickly rejected the idea, deciding it would be better for Milion to allow him his

254

space. Instead, he watched him proudly as he faded into the sky. The fisherman turned back to regard Adiadni, her eyes wide, mouth still agape. Her hair hung over her shoulder in a long curly braid, and no tiara crowned her head. She was clad in a white shirt and dark brown trousers which were a bit too long—Ilya's, he guessed—her boots on her feet, and her little stone depiction of a bird around her neck. She looked like a true adventurer, and he regarded her with a smile as she kept her eyes fixed on the ether above them.

"That's... it's..." The princess found herself at a loss for words.

Uritus chuckled as he approached her. "Milion is his name."

"Milion..." she breathed the name of the noble creature with reverence and finally allowed her gaze to drop to her counterpart, "He's beautiful."

The fisherman nodded, refraining from saying what he wished to.

"I've seen depictions of dragons in books but... none of them..."

"I know. It's something entirely different to behold one in person."

"And you've known him since...?"

"Since I came to the White Mountains. I found his egg the day I met Uriah."

Adiadni nodded slowly, looking once more to the sky and then back to the man before her. "I continue to be reminded of how abundantly clear it is that you are the one. And also amazed at how... the timing of everything lined up so perfectly."

"It is true. I do not believe that bad things *must* happen to make way for the good, but I do remain baffled by how both Uriah and I felt called here at the same time. Had my father's death come any sooner or any later, I cannot say for sure that I would have ended up in the same place. The moment of our meeting was not mere happenstance, it was..."

"Destiny."

Uritus smiled down at the sweet face of the princess. "Yes, I suppose it was."

Adiadni brought her lower lip between her teeth and dropped her eyes to regard the pair of cords around the fisherman's neck. "My own is... just a short trek ahead."

"That it is."

She took in a shaky breath and released it. "I just keep trying to remind myself that I have all I need to reign victorious."

"You do," he spoke softly, taking a small step toward her. "There exist none on this earth who can accomplish what you are going to. And I'll be beside you the whole time. We all will."

She nodded hesitantly and allowed herself to melt into his embrace, but a subtle note of anxiety continued to itch at the back of her mind all the same.

***

The mountains made way for the travelers as they departed and they found themselves standing at the edge of the Swamp of Sigmount before midday. The wetland stretched out in front of them in dull shades of brown and green, fog clinging thickly to the tops of the skinny trees that dotted the landscape. Behind Sigmount, through the clouds, the companions could make out the dark, Shadowy silhouettes of the Looming Mountains. They regarded the land in silence, tangibly aware of the dangerous path that lay ahead. One by one, each of them turned to regard Adiadni, awaiting her word.

She remained where she stood, eyes fixed straight ahead as she addressed them, "As it was in Idor, we have been given no direct path to make it through to the other side of the swamp. The earth is soft and the mud is sticky, so we will be forced to proceed carefully and be mindful of each one of our steps. There is also, of course… the matter of the creatures who…"

A sharp, raspy shriek sounded from somewhere within the swamp. The companions startled, several hands instinctively jerking to their weapons.

The princess swallowed to steel her nerves. "I remain steadfast in my desire to carry on as peaceably as we may, but… I also understand that this will not always be an option. Stay always with the group, or go in pairs if you must separate. We will be safer together."

The others nodded, remaining where they stood, and Adi realized that they awaited her first step. She took a series of breaths… one… two… three… and made her way into the fog, her party following after her.

Surprising to no one, the trek through Sigmount was slow. The group discovered that the ground was deceiving in its level of firmness, and before an hour had lapsed, nearly all of them had mistakenly taken a step only to find their boot sunken amongst the reeds. Adiadni found herself exceedingly glad that she had abandoned her traveler's gowns in favor of Ilya's trousers. The fog continued to swirl around them and the clouds remained resolute in their hiding of the sun. The mist stirred up by the heat of the day occasionally grew thick enough to block their view of the Looming Mountains entirely, and Qibat did his part to make sure they continued to some degree in the right direction. There was no *straight West* in this case, as the party was at the mercy of the landscape. The path they carved through the wetland was exhausting, tedious, and disorienting.

The only wildlife they observed for some time were the mosquitos who greedily fixed themselves to any bare patch of skin they could find. Punznes passed around a small bottle of fragrant oil, encouraging the others to apply a bit to their pulse points to ward off the thirsty scavengers. It did help to some degree, but still, every few minutes, a slapping sound echoed through the swamp as the travelers continued their war against their present adversaries. The croaking of frogs and calls of birds met their ears from time to time, as well as the occasional bone-chilling shriek of the unknown. It was hard to discern exactly how far away the unfamiliar creatures were or whether they seemed to be approaching or moving further away. No flurries of movement met their eyes, no rustling in the shrubbery or sounds of scurrying. So they continued despite their unease, always with pairs of eyes peeled in every direction.

"On the bright side," spoke Nadarum as he freed his foot from a particularly viscous puddle of muck, "If we are struggling this much to make it through the swamp, we likely do not need to worry about encountering any goblins on our way."

"Damn you, Man, I hadn't even thought of goblins all day," Laivar cursed.

"Oh how lovely it must be," teased Mikka, "To have the ability to detach from one's brain."

Laivar nodded seriously. "It is a skill not granted to many, thus I practice it as often as I can."

"Our horseman speaks the truth though," Uriah stated. "Our enemy is not a fool, and it would be unnecessarily foolish to send troops blindly into a landscape as hostile as this."

"Perhaps that's why the Kings ordained such an unusual path," Adi theorized, still trying to make sense of their motivations. "So we may be somewhat protected on the last leg of our journey."

"Indeed. Though, of course, we must keep our guard up all the same. The Kings knew not of the existence of the entroleps when the map was drawn."

"Do we know that they truly exist?" Oripidus asked, smacking his hand against his neck. "Could it be that some sorry bloke heard an unidentified bird and invented the creatures based on how frightened he was?"

The Wizard thought for a moment before he replied, "Over the years, there have been scant few observations of those who are rumored to dwell here; however, the accounts of those observers have been consistent with each other. They all claim to have spotted a figure through the fog, humanoid and hunched with an engorged cranium. Many have tried to discount such tales with theories that perhaps the air in and around the swamp toys with one's mind. That may well be true, but there remains no explanation as to why the accounts are so similar to one another though the instances of the sightings were, in many cases, separated by over a hundred years."

Laivar chuckled. "So we know not where we are going nor who lies in waiting to greet us nor whether they even exist at all. Perhaps we are the fools, waltzing willingly into the open jaws of a trap."

"Thus is the nature of adventure," replied Perplexus, and the others hummed in agreement.

They continued speculating about the nature of the swamp creatures as they made their way, and Uritus kept his attention focused on the land around them. His ears were especially sensitive to each howl, each twig that snapped, each splash of a toad flopping into the water. He kept one hand always on the hilt of his sword, the other available to offer to Adiadni if ever she tripped or got stuck. His feeling of quiet anxiety remained consistent, like a slow burning fire, and the adrenaline that flowed through his veins as a result kept his mind alert and his eyes blue. He did not wish to say so out loud, but he was quite certain that they would not make it to the other side of Sigmount as uneventfully as they hoped.

A full minute had not yet lapsed since he had this thought before the fisherman came to an abrupt stop, holding a hand up to signal to the others to do the same. They responded by halting and falling silent, the archer nocking an arrow and drawing her bow. Perplexus and Punznes turned to keep watch on the land behind them. The others squinted their eyes and peered into the brush to see what the Adalos had seen.

Uritus crouched down, his attention fixed on the shrubs surrounding a tree several paces ahead. He rubbed his eyes and blinked as he attempted to focus, wondering for a moment if he had truly seen movement or if the swamp was deceptive like the Forest of Idor. He took a few cautious steps forward, knowing they needed to be certain they were safe before proceeding.

There was a rustling and a flurry of sudden movement, and Ilya nearly released her arrow before it became clear to all watching that the creature that had emerged from the brush was merely a bird.

The companions breathed a collective sigh of relief.

Uritus relaxed his body, straightened himself, and turned to face his group, "I'm glad to have been wrong this time. But even still, I think we—"

He was cut off abruptly as something collided with his back, sending him tumbling to the ground.

He heard a scream, and several of his friends shouted to one another as he fought against whatever it was that clawed at the armor on his back and arms. It took only a few seconds for the creature to be lifted off of him, crying a harrowing, guttural sound, and the fisherman flipped himself onto his back to behold it.

Struggling to free its arms from Nadarum's firm grasp was an entrolep, strikingly more similar to his imaginings of the creatures than he would have expected it to be. Mikka stood in front of it, a knife poised to kill in her hand, and in the shouting of his companions and the shrieking of the beast, Uritus heard two clear words:

"Wait!"

…and…

"Stop!"

He leapt to his feet and caught Mikka's arm before she could bring it down. "No, wait!"

The group silenced, several of them still looking around to ensure that this creature was not accompanied by more. The entrolep thrashed, snarling and kicking up the muck of the swamp.

"Let us be done with this, Uritus," said Nadarum.

"No, just… wait a minute."

Mikka stepped back and Uritus lowered himself to look the creature in its face. After a few moments of struggling, it had grown clearly tired, realizing that its attempts to escape were futile. It was gaunt, skin clinging to bone with no flesh between, and its slick skin was pale green, fading to a muddy beige on its hands and feet and the enlarged part of its skull. Uritus was grateful for his sturdily crafted armor as he looked at the sharp black claws that slashed as it kicked. The fisherman continued to wait until the entrolep had all but ceased moving.

It began to tremble as it beheld the fisherman with bright green catlike eyes. Its nose was flat, resembling that of a pig, and it had a small thin mouth lined with short sharp teeth. It howled once more at Uritus in a final attempt at intimidation before going limp in Nadarum's grasp.

He observed it for a moment in silence before addressing it directly, "Speak."

The creature did not respond beyond a weak attempt to wriggle out of Nadarum's strong hands.

"Uritus, this seems unnecessary…" said Ilya tentatively, her arrow still poised at her mouth.

Oripidus grew frustrated, "Just kill it so we may be on our way."

"Let him continue."

Adi's voice brought the rest of the group to silence once more.

Uritus nodded to his counterpart and she to him. He returned his focus to the creature, "I ask you again, speak. I know you can, I heard you before. It'll be better for you if you do."

The man and the entrolep stared at each other, the fisherman soft yet unyielding. He squinted ever so slightly as he saw a flash of what appeared to be suspicion in the creature's eyes. They remained there for several moments and the others grew impatient. Uritus addressed the beast once more, "If you wish to be let go… I need you to speak."

The entrolep grumbled as if annoyed, and then raised itself on its haunches and howled with all its might in Uritus's face. The fisherman remained steadfast where he knelt. The rest of the party gripped their swords and drew their bows, looking around to ensure that the beast wasn't calling to more of its kind. Then, surprising to all but the Adalos and his counterpart, it spoke.

"Kill me later, kill me first. Why should I give ye my words?"

"Huh," Nadarum chuckled, astounded.

Uritus met his eye with a slight smile and looked again at the creature, "I do not want to kill you. But need I remind you that you ended up here because you first tried to kill me?"

"Skin too tough for the sharpest hands, what kind of beast are ye?"

Uritus tilted his head as he regarded the creature, clearly of greater intelligence than any of them had anticipated. "I am a man," he replied. "A human named Uritus…" He hesitated before asking, "Who are you?"

"My name is my name is my name."

"But you do have a name?"

"My name is my name is my name."

"All right."

Uritus turned, met Adiadni's eye and then Uriah's, silently communicating that he did not know what to do. In unison, both the Wizard and the Suvah nodded gently to encourage him to continue. The others looked back and forth between the conversation and their surroundings, feeling increasingly more confident that there would be no rapid approach of violent enemies.

The fisherman turned again to face the creature, "We call your kind *entroleps*. What do you call yourselves?"

"We are the swamp and the swamp is we."

"I see. Have you ever met a human before? Or perhaps a dwarf or an elf?"

"No one comes here. No one likes it. We don't even like it."

"Then why do you stay?"

"We are the swamp and the swamp is we."

"Right." He pondered his next question. "How many of you exist here?"

"As many as there are."

"Fine." He paused again, observing that the creature had ceased its struggling. "Why did you try to kill me?"

For the first time since the conversation began, the entrolep hesitated. "No one comes here. Forbidden to come, forbidden to leave."

"By whom is it forbidden?"

"The man in the black cape."

The energy in the air changed at this revelation and everyone present felt it.

A shiver ran down Adi's spine and her mind suddenly swam with images of a long-forgotten memory. "Uritus…"

He turned to her and nodded to communicate that he was almost done. "Who is the man in the black cape?"

"He is the only one who may come and the only one who may go."

"I see…" The fisherman took a frustrated breath and then made a final attempt, "I ask you again, can you tell me your name?"

"My name is my name is my name."

Uritus sighed and stood to his feet, looking down at the creature for another moment before addressing the group, "I think we should let him go."

"Uritus, I respect your leadership, but that is a stupid fucking idea."

Oripidus snorted at Ilya's bluntness and Uritus turned to regard them, "I don't see what other choice we have. We cannot tie him up and bring him along with us."

"If we let him go, we cannot guarantee that he won't return in the night to slit our throats."

Uritus frowned at the navigator. "Then what do you propose we do?"

Silence fell upon the group. The companions looked around at each other.

Finally, Perplexus spoke, "No one else wants to say it, but he already did himself. Either we kill him now or we release him, wait for him to return, and kill him then."

"We cannot do that, he's done no real harm…"

"But he will."

"You can't say that…"

"And you can't say that he won't."

Uritus sighed with frustration and crouched down before the creature once more. "Can you promise that if we set you free, you will do us no harm?"

"Forbidden to come, forbidden to leave."

"Uritus…"

The fisherman ignored Adi's voice. "We have a bit of food. Clean water. Perhaps we can offer you this, strike a bargain."

"We do not eat, we do not drink, we do not sleep."

Uritus sighed again.

"All right, fuck this."

Uritus turned to see Perplexus approach, pulling his knife from his belt and spinning it in his hand with a flourish. The group erupted into cries of argumentative noise and the creature began to writhe and shriek as it realized what was happening.

"Wait! No!"

Uritus stepped toward Perplexus and gripped the upper edge of his breastplate.

"I can show ye the way!"

The two men immediately forgot their standoff and regarded the struggling entrolep.

"What do you mean, *the way*?" questioned Uritus.

"The way out!" the creature cried, calming a bit. "The swamp is a maze, see? Designed to dizzy. Ye'll get lost on yer own, but I know the way. I'll show ye! My knowledge for my life!"

Uritus, Perplexus, and the rest of the party felt a sting of compassion for the creature. Not even the navigator wished to kill him, but still, he clutched tightly to his dagger, keeping a watchful eye on the strange being always.

Uritus turned back to regard the Wizard and the princess, "I think we need to convene."

Both nodded. Uriah turned and headed back the way they had come and Adiadni followed him.

"What am I to do with him?" asked Nadarum, his hands still clamped around the entrolep's wrists.

"Tie him up for now, make sure he can't hurt anyone. The rest of you, keep a lookout for more of them. We'll be back shortly." The fisherman turned to follow the path carved by the Wizard, pausing for a moment. "Lex."

The navigator swiveled his head to regard his friend.

"You too."

Perplexus smiled, turned, and followed him into the mist.

They could still make out the shapes of the others from the place they came to a stop beside a tree. The fog had grown thick and Adiadni positioned herself facing the group so she could ensure that they remained in plain sight.

Uritus turned to her first, "You had something you meant to say. When I was talking to the entrolep…"

"Right…" The princess folded her arms across herself as a cold breeze floated by them, a sign of the coming of night. "He… spoke of a man in a black cape…"

"Yes," affirmed Uriah. "A potential clue as to our primary adversary."

"He could be speaking nonsense," Perplexus reminded them.

"Yes, but… I don't think he is."

"Why not?" Uritus waited patiently for the princess to explain. She kept her eyes fixed on their party members several yards off.

"I believe I…" She hesitated, unsure how exactly to voice her instinct. "I believe I have seen him before. The man in the black cape."

The three men looked at her with confusion and intrigue.

"I, um…" Adi turned to look up at Uriah, "I have dreams sometimes."

The Wizard nodded to communicate that he knew.

"I am not saying that I am a Prophet, but… I've told Olythia what I have seen and they believe that I receive… glimpses."

"Glimpses?"

"Yes," the Suvah paused as she met her counterpart's eye. "Not full visions as they and the Prophets do, but… little fragments of the same nature."

"Always of things to come?"

Adiadni looked at Perplexus and then beyond him at the others standing in the mist. "Perhaps. Even for the Prophets, the visions they receive are not necessarily guaranteed. They're more like… potentials. Outcomes which may come to pass if the path is not…" she paused as she met Uritus's eye, "…changed."

"Do you mean to say you've glimpsed the man in the black cape?"

Adi snapped back to attention and answered Uriah, "I think so. I had completely forgotten about it until the entrolep mentioned him. I was young and prone to what, at the time, we thought to be recurring nightmares." She looked again past Perplexus to the others. "I have forgotten many of them, but the ones Olythia thought to be of note all featured the same man."

"What did he look like?" asked the fisherman.

"I did not ever see his face," she replied. "Or rather, it did not leave any notable impression. He was tall, broad-shouldered, and he wore always a heavy dark cape with a hood he never used."

"An old man or a young one?" questioned the Wizard.

Adiadni tried to recall. "I… don't really know. I do not remember him looking especially old, and he carried himself like a man in good health. But… to me, he always felt…" She paused, shivered. "Incomprehensibly ancient."

"Hmm," Uriah pondered this. "Do you remember anything else of note from your visions?"

The princess searched her memory again, eyes lifted to the sky. "He was always walking ahead of me, toward the setting sun. We'd be out in a clearing of some sort. The wind would catch my skirt, tug me forward toward his hand, held out as he turned to regard me. I would look around, back the way I had come, and there was no city, nowhere else to go. I remember feeling… all but helpless. Like if I wanted to return to civilization, I had no choice but to go with him." She looked to Uritus, "That was always when I woke. Before I was able to choose."

"Did he ever speak to you?"

Adi turned to Uriah with a shake of her head. "Not that I can remember. I do think though that the entrolep's mention of him is no mere coincidence. It had been years since I thought of the dreams."

"When last did you see him?" the Wizard asked.

"My last dream would have been…" She blinked, staring at the figures in the fog. "The last night you came to visit me, my thirteenth birthday."

Uriah nodded pensively but did not speak.

"I believe this to be enough motivation to keep the entrolep near us."

"Suppose he does not truly know the way," Perplexus countered. "What if he is just biding his time until the opportunity arrives to strike?"

"He has no motivation to want to hurt us," said Uritus. "He knows that there are many of us and that we can easily overpower him. *And* he believes that our *skin*," he knocked a fist against the armor covering his chest, "…is too strong to be penetrated by his claws. At this point, we can also assume that his kind does not operate in packs. We'll continue to utilize both you and Qibat to ensure that we remain traveling mostly West."

"And the longer we keep him with us, the more likely we are to glean information from him about who our enemy may be," Adi added. "It makes far more sense to keep him alive."

Perplexus sighed and looked at his boots before raising his eyes again to regard the princess, "I will default to your leadership, of course. All of you seem to be in agreement. I only wish to reiterate that I do not trust him."

"Why not?" asked Uritus, and the navigator met his eye. "If we think of him as merely a frightened creature, his attack on me is fully warranted."

Perplexus sighed again. "I know that I have garnered somewhat of a reputation for myself as one who is fine spilling blood. Perhaps even as one who seeks such opportunities out. But that is not the case. I do not wish for such a thing any more than you do, it is just..." He paused, took a breath. "I witnessed the landslide that killed my parents. It took others too, not just them. I have seen with my own eyes violent death on a large scale and... due to that, I believe I have more of a stomach for it than most of you. If I may commit the act and spare you the need to... I will. Every time."

He looked across the faces of those in the circle. "I have been appointed a task by the Free World's king to ensure that the two of you make it beyond the Looming Mountains and back, alive. This is not a task that I take lightly. At every turn, when presented with any decision, I will make the choice that I believe necessary to keep you safe. That is my sole focus. And if we suspect that this creature has some sort of connection to our enemy, I believe that makes him all the more a threat. Again, I will respect the decision that you make, but if we choose to free him or keep him with us, I will continue keeping a watchful eye out until we are free of this place."

They all nodded understandingly and Uritus asked, "Is there anything we might do to make you feel better about utilizing him as our guide?"

The navigator pondered this. "Not to any significant degree. But I suppose if you were able to get him to budge a bit, coerce him to offer a mite of information, that may help."

Uritus thought for a moment and then turned and made his way back to the group. The others followed. As he approached, he saw Nadarum and Mikka each holding firmly to the end of a rope, both ropes tied around the neck of the entrolep who stirred upon seeing the fisherman appear through the mist.

Uritus walked directly to the creature and crouched down to meet his eye. "We wish to keep you alive and to utilize your knowledge of the swamp to lead us to the Western side. Can you do that?"

"I can, I can, I can! Release me and I'll show ye!"

"I intend to," spoke the Adalos. "But before I can, I need to be sure that I can trust you. I will promise that we will not hurt you if you can promise that you will not hurt us—"

The creature began to move with some excitement, straining against the ropes that bound him. "Yes, a fair trade it will be!"

"...And," the fisherman continued, "If you can give me your name."

The entrolep hesitated, narrowing his eyes to thin slits. "My name is my name is my name..."

"I understand that," Uritus replied. "But that will not be good enough, I'm afraid."

The beast hesitated still, looking beyond the man to those who stood behind him.

"We won't hurt you, you won't hurt us, you will guide us out of the swamp, and we will part ways peaceably there, yes?"

The creature returned his gaze to Uritus.

"Your name. Please."

The entrolep let out a prolonged groan and then spoke, "I am… Yider."

"Thank you." Uritus lowered his head to Yider then turned over his shoulder to regard Perplexus, "Good enough?"

The navigator paused for a moment and then nodded once.

"All right," said the fisherman, turning once more to the entrolep, "I'm going to let you free now."

Yider panted excitedly as Uritus reached to loosen the ropes around his neck, dipping his head so the man could easily lift them over it one at a time. Uritus stepped back as the creature was released, as did Nadarum and Mikka, each keeping their eyes fixed on him while winding up the ropes. Yider looked at Uritus and then the others, visibly nervous, and then turned to face the same direction as the fisherman.

"This way."

Uritus followed the entrolep and the others fell into step behind them.

***

They did not make it far before the sun descended in the sky, revealing the towering outline of the Looming Mountains as it sank. They found a place to set up camp, confident after sending the raven into the sky that they had made a bit of progress in the right direction that day. A small scrap of paper passed from one pair of hands to another, the Wizard's hasty scrawl reminding them to not discuss anything regarding their mission while in the presence of their new guide.

The Suvah and the Adalos were encouraged to get as much sleep as they could and the others remained awake in shifts. Throughout the night, Yider wandered from place to place, finding a spot to rest for a time under a tree or beside a bush and then moving somewhere else. One of the two who remained awake kept their eye always on him, the other on the space around them. Less frequent at night were the ghostly howls that echoed through the swamp, but now and again one would cut through the dark, sending chills through the bones of those who heard them.

That night, the princess slept precious little, but when she did, she dreamed again of the man in the black cape. This time, she did not stop to look around but rather took a step toward him and tried with all her might to focus on the features of his face. She found herself stricken with terror as she gazed into his eyes, and when she again awoke, she found that she remembered nothing of what he looked like. She remained where she lay, staring up through the mist at the Shadowy peaks until the others awoke and they again set out after the entrolep.

The path they took remained winding and slow but noticeably easier to trek, and the travelers found themselves stepping far less often in places they shouldn't. Occasionally, one of them (usually Uritus) would attempt to make conversation with the entrolep. He remained mostly unhelpful, unwilling to offer any more information about the man in the black cape and occasionally ignoring questions entirely. By the end of their second day trudging through Sigmount, Qibat confirmed that they were pointed West. But Perplexus began to suspect that they had made little progress, the mountains appearing as far away as they had the night before. Not wishing to sow division amongst the group, he kept this observation to himself.

Two more days and nights elapsed, following the same pattern, and finally, the navigator brought himself to rest beside his friend before they turned in for the night and expressed his concern.

"I too have begun to wonder this," affirmed the fisherman with a low voice. "But it remains true that he has made no further attempt to harm us. Can you articulate the heart of your concern?"

Perplexus studied the creature as he dug through the muck several yards away from where the party rested, He took a long draw from his pipe. "I admit, I do feel compassion for him, as I know the rest of you do. There seems to be no pleasure or joy in his life. I cannot imagine the heavy emptiness of such an existence. But his connection to the one we believe to be our enemy has itched at my mind these past days. I fear he may be leading us in circles in an attempt to wear us out or thin our rations… Or perhaps that he intends to keep us here until the one he serves may arrive."

The head of the entrolep abruptly shot up and stared perfectly still into the distance for several moments before he resumed his digging.

The fisherman considered the words of his friend as he regarded the creature, empathy in his heart for both of them. "We'll give it one more day," he said. "If by tomorrow night we still feel no closer to the Looming Mountains, we will release him and proceed on our own."

Perplexus nodded, satisfied with this, and the two men settled in for the night. The navigator remained awake along with the others who took their shifts until the early hours of the morning when exhaustion finally laid its claim on him.

***

In the night, as she had each night since their first in Sigmount, Adiadni was visited by the haunting Shadowy figure. They stood in the field as they always did, but this time, she looked beyond him and was able to make out the vague shape of the Looming Mountain range in the distance. She looked at his face to see that he also looked straight ahead, but his hand remained open, outstretched in her direction.

Without thinking, she opened her mouth and spoke, "Tell me your name."

He immediately turned his head to face her. His piercing gaze kept her frozen where she stood. He moved to stand in front of her, raising the hand he had originally held open to brush lightly against her cheek, and the princess struggled to regulate her breathing. He leaned down slowly, bringing his mouth right up against her ear, lingering a moment as if he could sense her fear.

"You will know my name soon, Adiadni."

266

Adi opened her eyes with a gasp and sat up to find herself back in the swamp at the break of day. She looked around at her companions, finding them all to be resting save for Punznes and Oripidus who sat up on the night's final watch. But then she noticed the place where the Adalos had laid to rest to be empty, and she spun her head around, spotting his figure through the fog before she had the chance to panic. She looked to Oripidus who met her eye and nodded when it became clear that she intended to go after him. The princess rose and departed into the mist as the sleeping ones began to stir.

Uritus turned his head as she approached and smiled, noticing how her recently adopted traveling uniform closely resembled his own. He returned his focus to the swamp and they regarded it silently until he spoke, peace in his voice, "There is Light wherever we choose to find it."

She laughed softly, her attention still on the scene spread out before them. They stood at the edge of one of the larger ponds, illuminated by the soft peachy-pink light of morning. Rays of sun rippled lazily across the water's surface, long shadows cast by the trees and reeds. A pair of birds bathed at the edge of the pool opposite them, and Adiadni found herself growing emotional at the sight. Uritus brought an arm around her and pulled her close when he noticed.

"There is so much beauty in this land," she said, sniffling. "It's nice to be reminded of that."

He looked down at her with a warm gaze. "It is."

She turned her head to look beyond him, hearing the sounds of the others rising and making ready for the day behind her. He looked where she did and then down at her again, a question in his eyes. She did not answer it with words but instead began to walk forward. The fisherman without hesitation followed her into the fog.

They could still hear the faint voices of the others as they came to a stop, and both of them stared in silent awe up at the dark faces of the Looming Mountains, seen clearly from beyond the edge of the swamp.

Above their towering peaks swirled thick, dark clouds, and lightning periodically lit up one mountain and then another. They were striking and massive and Adiadni found herself thinking that to some, they might even be beautiful.

But before she could consider the things that lay beyond, Uritus spoke, "Why would he lead us all the way here only to stop just before we reached Sigmount's edge?"

The princess frowned and looked up at her counterpart.

"Come quickly, we must inform the others."

They turned to make their way back but stopped abruptly as Yider appeared in their path.

"Where goes ye?"

The young people met eyes and then returned their attention to the entrolep.

"We saw that you've brought us to our destination," Uritus answered honestly. "We thank you for your aid. We will remember you as we make our way forward."

"No one comes here. No one leaves."

"Well… it's time for us to—"

"No one leaves!"

Before they had a moment to react, Yider lunged for them.

Adiadni screamed.

The fisherman jumped forward to meet the creature and was tackled to the ground. He fought against the violent, slashing claws and the princess looked on in wide-eyed fear. Their armor and weapons were left back at the camp. She had to do something.

She submerged her hand in the water, retrieved a heavy stone, and then rushed forward and swung it at the beast.

It crashed into the back of his head, sending him flailing into the mud. He shook his head and attempted to right himself. Yider turned to look at the princess, howled a terrifying sound, and dove toward her.

Adiadni swung her rock again and felt the crunching of bone as it struck once more the entrolep's head. Yider collapsed into a pond, still, lifeless, and dark blood colored the water.

"What's happened?"

The princess released the stone from her hand and it tumbled to the ground as the first of their companions arrived at the scene. They saw the blood on her shirt, the rock, the body, and then the collective heartbeat of the party came to a halt as they heard Uritus gasp.

Adiadni screamed and flew to his side, arriving there just as Punznes did. The fisherman's shirt was torn to shreds, deep, bleeding gashes in his arms and chest. Uriah immediately began to give orders, commanding the others to build a shelter and a pit for a fire to boil water for bandages. Perplexus joined the two beside the body of the injured, removed his cape, and pressed it firmly against the fisherman's chest. The princess held Uritus's face in her hands, her breaths sharp, her tears many.

"Can you stitch him up?" Lex anxiously questioned the physician.

"I can, but only once he's stopped bleeding."

"No no no no no…" Adiadni pleaded with him as he began to fade in and out of consciousness. "You can't go, you can't go, we need you, *I* need you!"

Then, before hopelessness could set in, the princess's head was thrown back and the world went quiet around her. Before her eyes flashed a series of images —botanicals she had seen before. When she snapped back to awareness, she knew clearly what she had to do.

"Laivar!" she cried. "Do you know the glassleaf plant?"

"I do."

"I need it. The roots, not the leaves, and ghostberries. They're shiny and white and grow in clumps. Both of those mashed into a paste for the wounds. Quickly!"

The poet hurried off into the swamp with Mikka and Qibat in search of the ingredients.

"Anything else?"

Adi lifted her eyes to the navigator, "The kuffa, ground with water. We'll need to make him drink."

Perplexus ran to locate his bag and the flowers within. Punznes and Adiadni continued pressing on Uritus's wounds.

"I trust that you know what you are doing, but kuffa will slow his heart," the physician warned. "It's slowing too much already. If we give him that, we run the risk that it will stop entirely."

"The bleeding won't stop unless his heart does. It's temporary. He will come back."

"Are you sure that will work?"

"It has to."

Shortly, the others returned with the paste and the flowers. Punznes began applying the mash to Uritus's deepest cuts. Perplexus held the fisherman's mouth open while Adi poured the flower mixture into it. He sputtered as it went down but swallowed it all.

When this was done, Nadarum helped Perplexus and Punznes move the Adalos into the shelter fashioned from their capes and some rope and the branch of one of the larger trees. The Wizard, having lit the fire through which Ilya ran each of the physician's needles, brought himself to a seat directly across from the shelter and rested his staff across his lap. He removed his hat and set it to the side, brought one hand to rest against his chest, the other to his belly, and lowered his head, muttering continuously under his breath all the while.

Ilya rushed the needles to the shelter and Nadarum and Perplexus exited and the companions brought themselves to settle to the ground nearby, bleak expressions worn on their faces.

The princess moved into the navigator's open arms where she collapsed and allowed her sobs to overtake her.

Chapter Eighteen

"A Layer Deeper"

The 20th of July

Adiadni was difficult to console. Perplexus brought them to the ground, backs to a boulder, holding her tightly and rocking from side to side while the others retrieved the rest of their belongings from last night's camp. Mikka and Oripidus had offered to keep watch over the place they now rested. They paced back and forth, sword and hammer in hand, staring off into the misty swamp.

Ilya helped Nadarum move the body of the dead entrolep somewhere further away, not knowing how long they would need to wait here. Laivar moved back and forth between the fire and the tent, aiding the physician with anything he needed. Uriah remained, legs crossed, in a prayer position.

The navigator kept his arms around the princess, noticing how, slowly, her sobs began to lessen before she abruptly sat upright. She stared into the fire, shaking her head back and forth and then finally saying, "This is all my fault. I should have listened to you…"

Perplexus shook his head. "Don't do that. It isn't helpful."

"But it is true." She looked at him with an expression of deep regret. "You knew that Yider wasn't to be trusted. You were so sure of it…"

He shook his head again. "You did the best you could. You had as much information as I did—"

"No."

He regarded her with confusion.

"I knew…" Adiadni felt her breath begin to again grow rapid and uneven. "I knew we would end up here. I saw it. I saw him in my arms and the blood and…" Tears spilled onto her cheeks.

"When did you…"

"In the Valley. Under the willow."

The navigator's lips parted as he suddenly understood why she had not wanted to talk about her experience after smoking the yuzh.

"I thought it was just a nightmare, but there were… other images too. And one thing that I saw came to pass in real life but I didn't know what to do and I… I could have stopped it. Lex, if he dies it'll be because of me." She lowered her head and sobbed, her tired body shaking under the weight of her grief.

"Hey, look at me..." Perplexus took her face in his hands and lifted it to his, "*Look* at me."

She did, blinking up at him through her tears.

"If he *lives* it will be because of you." He released her face and she sat upright again. "What was that?"

The princess wasn't sure how to answer.

"How did you know what he needed? From my perspective, it looked as though for a few moments you... went into a trance."

Adiadni recalled the incident. "I suppose I did."

"What did you see?"

She lifted her eyes to the sky as she recalled the details of her vision. "I was in a room not unlike Aurena's greenhouse. I saw a wooden table and a pair of wizened hands that picked up ingredients and dropped them into a mortar to be ground."

"Did she train you to become a Healer?"

The princess shook her head. "She showed me her practices, taught me some of the basics of herbology and naturalism, but... I was not in the moment searching my memory for knowledge I knew I had. Rather... I feel like the Mother knew that I needed it and so... she gave it to me."

"So, you heal and you receive glimpses and you produce fire. You're a multi-practice Magic Keeper."

"I appreciate the flattery though I do not believe it to be entirely accurate."

"Why not?"

Adiadni leaned her head back to rest upon the rock. "I don't know. I am not well practiced at any of those things."

"Perhaps not, but mastery of skill takes time. The regular Wizard apprenticeship can last for fifty years. You are young still."

She nodded silently and he, sensing that her worry still constricted tightly her mind and heart, wordlessly brought an arm around her. She lowered her head to rest upon his shoulder and they remained that way for some time, the crackling of the fire and odd shriek from the swamp the only things which broke through the silence. The others remained solemn as well.

After a time, Nadarum and Ilya alleviated the watchers of their shift, and not long after that, the physician emerged from the tent. The companions perked up at his arrival, eagerly awaiting any news. He told them that he had been successful in stopping the Adalos's bleeding and stitching up his wounds, but all they could do now was wait for him to wake. He noticed the dejected look on the Suvah's face and tried to encourage her, praising her for her quick thinking. She offered him a weak smile but did not respond otherwise.

The day waned on and night drew near and the clouds which continued to churn above the mountains did not help to alleviate the ominous energy that choked out the air around them. Periodically, Punznes would return to the tent to check on the sleeping one, always rejoining the others with nothing new to report. As the sun began to set, the lookouts rejoined them, and the tired travelers began to pass around their evening rations. Uriah remained where he sat.

The only noise that sounded from the camp at the swamp's edge was the popping of the wood in the fire. Laivar's desire to pull his friends away from their thoughts of doom pressed insistently at his chest.

"I suppose it may not be the kind of thing you may wish to hear at the moment, but I believe I've finished Havian's ballad."

The others shifted their attention at the sound of the bard's voice. "Play it then," Ilya encouraged him. "Your songs are always welcome, both in the light and in the dark."

Laivar smiled, reached for his lute, and settled it into his lap. And as he played for them and sang of Havian's bravery and shortcomings, his triumphs and his end, smiles grew across the faces of his friends, and each one began to feel profoundly more at peace.

"There once was a boy
Fixed his hand to a blade
Swore he'd be the best warrior that ever was made
He was right, he was wrong
And he fought till his end
Let me tell you the story of Havian again

He'd spar with a passion
Besting all who he faced
He did it all somehow with charm and with grace
A cape in his left hand
For attack and defense
Of those who stood to face him, not one stood a chance

And then he met a girl
As many young men do
He told her he loved her and she loved him too
But she left him one night
In the blink of an eye
He felt his world darken like clouds in the sky

That's when our warrior
Lost himself to the drink
He wished not to feel nor to love nor to think
But his tale was not over
Of this he was certain
So he left home before his condition could worsen

Havian traveled far
From all that he had known
To seek hope in the mountains where brightest stars shone

He found there a keep
And a small patchwork family
And when asked to stay, he said he would gladly

He shared all his knowledge
And learned much from them
Returned once to rescue a still grieving friend
He found a new purpose
Up there in the mountains
And blessing that flowed from the earth like a fountain

And then he caught word
Of a dangerous quest
That the Suvah would take with the Adalos out West
He knew he'd been training
For this very mission
Offered up his sword and traveled along with them

But not far on their journey
They encountered a foe
Far stronger and stranger than any he'd known
He knew he could beat them
Knew he had to try
He'd free them from their circles if it meant he would die

And so we have reached it
Our warrior's great folly
Never had he lost, so he thought he'd win always
But were you as gifted
As he was with a blade
Perhaps no different of a choice you'd have made

He said to his foe
'Be you fae or nevyn
You've stood in our way long enough, and I'll end it'
The enemy was far
Too keen for a fight
Still Havian resolved to use the last of his light

He fought well and fairly
Gave all that he had
When he died, his companions were utterly sad
He felt it his duty
His alone to free us
And that'd be The Hubris of Havian Elix"

These last lyrics reminded Adiadni of the importance of the community gathered around her now. She felt she had been learning time and again how impossible this task would be without the aid of others, and she found herself profoundly grateful for the ones who journeyed alongside her. "Have you always had a proclivity for music, Laivar, or did you find it later in life?"

The bard chuckled. "I have sung since my mouth learned how to form words." He leaned back against the log that supported him. "My first instrument was a flute I stole from a booth in one of Myrell's markets. I taught myself to play it mostly in secret. My father could not stand the sound."

The princess tilted her head over one shoulder. "Is he… not fond of music?"

Laivar chuckled again. "My father is… an academic, as he trained my brothers to be. He believes the pursuit of things other than knowledge to be rather silly and frivolous."

"Even music?" Adiadni grew sad. "Knowledge is one of the most valuable things we have, but only one. A life without music sounds like one quite shallow and dull." She paused as the others laughed lightly. "Forgive me, I do not wish to speak ill of him…"

"Not at all, you'd be correct. In my eyes, his life is the purest shade of beige that exists."

"Laivar and I first bonded over our fathers' lack of approval," shared Nadarum. "When my mother passed, I believe my father's concept of love was fractured, and so when I told him that I would marry Ilya, he could not comprehend why I wished to *give up* my youth. As though I have done anything but gain from her presence in my life."

Ilya smiled at her husband and leaned into him, sticking one boot out to touch Laivar's as he spoke again.

"Indeed, your father could not comprehend love, and for mine… it was joy. Specifically, the joy that comes from creating and observing art. I studied history at his request and I am glad to have done it. What is the past but a long string of connected stories? But it would never be enough for him. My mother passed when she gave birth to me and, though he denied it, I believe he always resented me for that."

Adi's eyes grew misty. "I am sorry to hear that."

The bard shrugged. "I suppose I once was, but in the end, it was his relentless dissatisfaction with me and my chosen path that ultimately led to my leaving Myrell and finding the support of the family I have now. In retrospect, I am grateful for some of the ways he pushed me. I am proud to be a history keeper and to do so on my own terms, lute in hand. An opportunity I must thank you for as well, Adiadni."

The princess nodded seriously. "I am glad to have you with us. Your contributions to our quest are both meaningful and necessary. And I speak not only of your record-keeping, but your art as well. How much more hopeless we would be without it."

"See, Laiv, there's room amongst the warriors for even a silly man such as yerself," joked the dwarf, and the others laughed.

"You hail from Quabish, right, Oripidus?"

He nodded, impressed at her memory of the fleeting detail he had mentioned upon their introduction. "Aye, I worked much of my life in the jewel mines there before devotin' myself to blacksmithin'."

"What prompted you to leave?"

The dwarf hesitated.

"Of course, you do not *need* to tell me…"

"Nay, I am more than willin' to tell my tale but… ye may not like it."

The princess frowned curiously and waited for him to continue.

"I began workin' at twelve years old alongside my uncle and the cousins he raised me with. The work was hard, but we dwarves love a challenge. We were entitled to the fruits of our labor, so I sold mine and saved the profits. I hoped that I might one day build a home for myself and my family. But after a time, the mine was acquired by the Dagious house…"

Adiadni nodded slowly, beginning to understand Oripidus's hesitation to share.

"There were policy changes made. None of the miners ever met the one who was now our boss. His orders were passed on by those he appointed to oversee the mine's goin's-on. No longer were we permitted to keep what we found, instead bein' required to turn in all we harvested every day at its end. We were compensated with a meager wage and told that the majority of the profits we produced would be used to upkeep the infrastructure of the mine. Though I was encouraged to remain in my position, in truth, I was rather annoyed by all of this. So I left and began my apprenticeship as a blacksmith."

Oripidus paused and Mikka stretched out a hand to rest on his shoulder. He continued, "It was not a full year since my departure from the mine when there was a cave-in. The damage took the lives of many—includin' two of my cousins —and injured several more. I would end up spendin' all that I had saved to help provide some aid to the injured ones, my uncle among their ranks. But his injuries ultimately took his life and I found myself quite angry at the negligence of his overseers."

Adiadni shook her head with a frown. "A warranted emotion. I am sorry. There is no room in the Free World for such selfishness."

"Unfortunately, such selfishness reigns on even so, in Quabish as well as the Vindellarian mines. I do not fault ye, princess, for yer connection to the Dagious house. I understand that the nature of politics is complicated and I am sure that it is especially true for ye. But ye asked for my tale, so there ye have it."

"I do thank you for sharing," she replied. "I do not take such a thing lightly. I am not sure yet what power I have to change things but I *will* seek justice on your behalf."

Oripidus chuckled. "I am sure ye will. But rest assured that I am happy now. I was able to commiserate with a boy who also lost his family to the dangers of minin', and such a bond brought each of us a bit of peace, I think."

Perplexus nodded with a smile. "Happy to have you as part of the family, old man."

"Come now, Lex. Show a bit of respect for those who have gone before you," said Nadarum, and the others laughed.

"I think that just leaves you, Mikka," said Adi, all eyes turning to the former soldier. "I've been granted the privilege of hearing everyone else's story, and I'd be honored to hold yours as well if you'd care to share it."

"I would, of course," Mikka replied. "But I suppose I must give a bit of a disclaimer before I begin mine, as Rip did. It's hardly a fun tale to hear."

Adiadni nodded encouragingly and Mikka took a breath before she began.

"As you know, I enlisted in your father's army when I was young, newly seventeen. Both of my parents had offered their service to the crown in their youth. They met on assignment accompanying a trader's caravan and later settled in Vindellaria. Oh, how I pestered them to tell me their stories again and again of the times they clashed with bandits. Such altercations happened only a handful of times over their combined few decades of service, but all the same, I was eager to enlist, to offer my strength and my skill to help and protect others as they had. I would have enlisted even younger than I did, but they encouraged me to savor my youth and devote myself to my studies, and I am grateful to them for that.

"But anyway, I did eventually enlist, and though my service was entirely peaceful and my sword remained untouched, I found still a meaningful purpose in the king's army. Stories were shared amongst the troops about the heir with the birthmark born to Agamemnon and Betina, and I eagerly anticipated the day that I might take up my sword to fight the Shadow along with my fellow soldiers. I became fast friends with many in my squadron, and these relationships eased the burden of missing my parents. But as you have no doubt observed, not one of us who dwell together now in the White Mountains arrived there without a series of sour circumstances that drove us to leave what we knew behind in the first place. For me... such circumstances began when I fell in love."

Adiadni's lips parted. She felt a stinging in her chest, but remained silent as she waited for the former soldier to continue.

"Love wasn't something I ever sought for myself. I was quite content in my early life and did not feel I was missing anything. But as it happens for many people, love found *me* when I least expected it and knocked me flat on my ass.

"Her name was Seryc and she was the most beautiful thing I had ever seen. She had been transferred to my squadron from one in Cropidea after finding that she disagreed with the severe heat of the South. We fell into step immediately. We shared the same sense of humor, the same devotion to our work. It took me some time to realize that what I felt was love—the romantic kind rather than that I had for all my friends. But when I realized, I had no thought in my mind other than how I needed to let her know.

"So I did one night before we retired to bed, and, to my delight, she told me that she felt the same for me. She kissed me and I felt like I was drifting amongst the stars. But shortly, another member of our squadron happened upon us. It was a bit awkward, but we hadn't done anything wrong. There exist no laws that would forbid soldiers from entering into relationship with one another, and of course, such a match worked out for my parents. But Seryc panicked and… in her panic… she told him that I had forced myself on her."

Adiadni frowned, her eyes brimming with tears again. Laivar brought himself to sit a bit closer to Mikka and rested his head on her shoulder.

She smiled softly, sadly, and then continued, "I didn't actively object with much fervor right away—something that I now realize was a mistake—but at the time, I was mostly confused. For half a second, I thought she was playing at some sort of bad joke, but she did not take it back, she…" Mikka paused, swallowed. "She doubled down. Told the whole squadron. And because I was bigger than her and had a reputation for being quite passionate and aggressive and… rather than utilize that passion and aggression to fight back… All I wished to do was try to talk to her, to understand where I had gone wrong. Of course, now I am both older and wiser and I know that I was not to blame. But the damage was done. I had not a friend remaining amongst those I traveled with. So I left. Tried to get as far away as I could from the place that had hurt me. And, well, you know the rest."

Around the fire passed a flask of strong liquor and all but Adiadni took a sip. She met Mikka's eye through her tears, "I hate that that happened to you. I am of the belief that love is the thing to hope for and the thing to hold onto. Betrayal such as that is of the most jagged of wounds." She sniffled and wiped her face with her sleeves and Perplexus wrapped a caring arm around her once more. "As is true when I hear all of your stories, I am deeply sorry, and it wracks my entire body and mind to know that there is nothing I can do… nothing I could have done to shield you from the cruelty of life."

Mikka smiled warmly. "The seal of the protector is worn clearly and beautifully around your neck."

Adiadni touched her hand to her chest and felt the cold piece of stone there. "I just… I continue to be amazed by you. All of you. Each of you all but on your own, you trusted your instincts, and in so doing, found one of the most precious things that anyone can have: a community who sees you just as you are."

"And who loves us for all of it," Ilya added, her voice like warm honey in the brisk night.

"And, Mikka, I know this won't count for much, but I meant it when we met and I said that Crystella had only the best to say about you. The same was true of her troops. She was truly saddened when she heard that you had resigned. I know it did not matter at the time, but you *did* have at least one friend still in the East when you left."

Mikka smiled and touched a hand to her chest. "Thank you, Adi, that means more than you know."

"I hope you do know, Adiadni, that such a community is yours as well," said Laivar, and the others nodded in agreement. "I am sure that you have no shortage of people at home who love you, and your friends in Suscundos do seem quite lovely, but you must not think that you can spend any length of time with us and not be subject to our unending devotion to one another. Each one of us would willingly fight and die for you, and not merely out of obligation."

"Well, I hold hope that it will not come to that, but I thank you all the same."

"We were quite taken with you from the beginning, Adi," said Ilya. "It was clear that you were the perfect addition to our little team."

"You've filled a crack that we did not realize was there," Nadarum added.

"Like a patch on a well-worn quilt," Laivar chimed in.

"A part of us we would surely be lost without."

All heads around the fire turned and the party collectively gasped as they beheld their Adalos awake and on his feet.

In an instant, the princess was off the ground and in his arms, and the others excitedly rose and gathered around to greet him. Uriah raised his head with a small smile, replaced his hat upon it, and moved to join the others.

Adiadni pulled back a bit, realizing she had been squeezing rather tightly around Uritus's bandaged torso. "Are you in pain?"

He shook his head. "Not a bit."

Punznes approached with an air of curiosity and tenderly lifted the edge of the bandage on one of the fisherman's arms. Frowning, he unraveled it with increasing speed, and when it was fully removed, found that there was not a scrape or scab in sight. The wounds that had nearly claimed Uritus's life had all but vanished. All that remained were thick, shiny scars, an eternal reminder of the entrolep from Sigmount.

"It's a miracle…" the physician marveled as he removed what remained of the bandages. He lifted his eyes to regard the princess, "You are…"

Adiadni clucked her tongue at him with a shake of her head, but Uriah spoke before she got the chance, "Denial of your gifts will serve neither yourself nor the rest of us."

The princess nodded understandingly and Perplexus found Uritus a shirt and the party moved again to gather around the fire. Punznes dipped briefly back into the tent and returned bearing both the amonii and small piece of carved stone which he returned to the fisherman. Adiadni stuck herself to Uritus's side and he kept his arm wrapped around her as they settled down against the boulder.

"Do you remember any of what happened?" the horseman questioned the Adalos.

Uritus leaned his head back as he tried to recall. "I remember wrestling with Yider, of course. And then I remember him being thrown from atop me, and the face of the saint who appeared in his stead… Is he…"

"Dead," spoke Oripidus matter-of-factly. "The Suvah saw to that."

"Right." Uritus looked at Adiadni huddled at his side. "Thank you. I believe your courage saved my life."

"She *did* save your life," Punznes affirmed. "I did my part to stitch you up, but had Adiadni not been so swift to act—in facing the entrolep and seeing to your wounds—nothing I could have done would have made any difference. I was not being hyperbolic when called your healing a miracle."

"Adiadni has done a greater thing than most Healers ever get the chance to," said Uriah.

Adi felt uncomfortable to be subject to so much direct praise, but still, she knew they spoke the truth. Whatever ancient spirit had possessed her in those moments had placed her directly between Uritus and the Great Beyond. There was more still for him to do here before he departed.

"I do remember hearing your voice," the fisherman said to her. "Many voices, panicked ones. Yours was at first, but then it wasn't. It was sure. By that point, I couldn't focus on anything. My vision had begun to blur and I felt warm and, all of a sudden, very cold. One of you had me drink something…"

Perplexus offered an explanation, "Kuffa flowers ground with water."

"Huh." The fisherman leaned his head back against the boulder as the pieces of revelation slid into place. "That would explain where I ended up then."

"You fell asleep just after you drank," said Adiadni. "Did you dream?"

"Something like that," Uritus paused. "I believe I saw my father."

***

When the fisherman opened his eyes, he found himself still at the edge of the swamp, the Looming Mountains towering ominously overhead. He sat up and looked around. There was no person present, nor creature, nor sound. Bringing himself to his feet, he turned to face the mountains.

They were dark and tall, with sheer, pointed peaks that scratched the belly of the sky. Distant roars of thunder rolled down the front to meet his ears and he shivered, reaching toward his sword reflexively and realizing that it was not there.

With Dagamor as the focus of Adiadni's half of the prophecy, Uritus realized he had not tried to comprehend the terror that was reasonably tied to such a task. The mountains themselves seemed enough like the barrier they would need to face on their journey. The idea that beyond them—within them—dwelt a creature all the more fearsome and mighty left him feeling grateful for how the things he would face on his own, for the most part, still remained unseen. Adiadni's willingness to come here, knowing exactly what she was up against, was a true testament to her courage.

"You shall learn from her example, as she has learned from yours."

Uritus spun around at the sound of the familiar voice, his sense of surprise only growing when he beheld its owner.

"…Father?"

Standing there, the landscape of Sigmount stretching all around him, was Odipar, as sturdy and solid as Uritus had known him to be. The young fisherman rushed forward with urgency, crashing into the solid, warm embrace of his father where he was immediately taken by his tears.

"I cannot believe this…" he said, pulling back. He frowned, his gaze as blue as the one he stared into. His father looked as he remembered him, skin tanned and rough, hair black as night, smile bright as day. "But if you're here… if *I'm* here… am I…"

Odipar looked at his son patiently but did not speak.

Uritus paused, looked over his shoulder at the mountains, and then back at his father, "Am I… dead?"

Odipar chuckled and shook his head and Uritus released a breath as he realized he felt relieved. "If you were, I would have come to send you back. Your destiny is far from complete."

Uritus knew this to be true.

"How has been your journey, my son?"

Uritus sighed and then chuckled as he tried to think of a succinct way to sum it up. "It has certainly been an adventure. I've found myself falling back and forth between joy and grief over and over."

Odipar nodded understandingly.

"If I'm not dead, then…" The young man hesitated. "I can only assume that I will wake before too long."

"And what is it you hope to gain from the time you have here?"

Uritus released a breath, a sad laugh. "More of it."

His father smiled compassionately.

"I want to tell you things," Uritus went on. "I assume you know them already, but I find myself overcome with the desire to regale you with tales of what has happened since… even just since this Spring."

"I will gladly listen to all you have to share, my son."

"But…" the Adalos paused, looking around again and then back to his father, "If our time is limited, I suppose it would be wise to put aside such a desire and instead glean what I can from it. Does that make me selfish?"

"Not at all." Odipar took a small step forward and set his hand against his son's face, "Anything you would ask of me, I will gladly give you, in death just as in life."

Uritus sighed peacefully. His father—or this *shade* of his father he was meeting here on this plane—remained as gentle and steadfast as he had always known him. The young fisherman considered now how natural it was that he turned to the White Mountains in his time of near-hopelessness. Their energy was the same as Odipar's, the same as Maja's, the same as Uriah's, and the family he had now. Such groundedness inspired him and propelled him forward, even if he didn't always understand why.

The Adalos considered the time he had left and wondered if he would simply wake as if from a dream or be torn violently from this place. He mulled over the questions he longed to ask his father, multitudes more sprouting in all the corners of his mind until he was nearly overwhelmed by them. If he tried, he would not be able to name all the things he learned from his father, all the wisdom he had gleaned from watching his life. How could he possibly choose now a sole, and perhaps, *final* thing to seek his guidance on? The fisherman contemplated all of this for several seconds until suddenly, his mind quieted, and the question was there, as clear as his father before him now.

"How did you know that you loved my mother?"

Odipar smiled. "As you know, she and I grew up alongside one another. We were friends from the beginning and I loved her since then. But it was not until our teenage years that I began to feel differently toward her. I was fourteen when I got my boat, and with it came a new load of responsibility. My working days were long and hard, so I began to see her less often. It was during this period that I came to see how severely I missed her. We'd spent most every day together as children, but now we were getting older and things had begun to change. We still saw each other often, multiple days a week when I would go to the market. While our friendship was still strong, its changes were evident. So I became more active in seeking her out. I'd find any excuse I could to go to the market. Every day I spent away from my boat, I'd find her and help her with her tasks, do anything at all just to be near her. Ultimately, it was my mother who made me aware of the severity of my feelings for the girl who would one day be yours."

Uritus had only the faintest memories of his paternal grandmother as she had passed when he was very young. "What did she say?"

Odipar smiled again. "She told me that friendship is beautiful and powerful, one of the purest and most solid things we can hold on this earth. But she added that sometimes, within those friendships, one uncovers something different—a rarer form of relationship that not all are blessed to find and even fewer are blessed to keep throughout all of life's seasons. A layer deeper, just as every other phase of our friendship had been up to that point. She told me that my relationship with Maja was sacred and would continue to be no matter how we chose to frame our love for one another. But she believed us to be standing on the precipice of a choice.

"I was seventeen and I denied her assumptions, but the more I thought about it, the clearer it became that she was right, as she usually was. In every moment, whether joyous or devastating or simply mundane, I thought first of Maja and how I longed to share it with her. In her grief, I was happy just to sit beside her, to hold her or listen to her or wait with her until she felt less heavy again. I began to realize then how truly and remarkably beautiful she was, and I felt quite silly for having never noticed it before. She was brave and passionate and wise beyond her years. I was lucky to have her already in the capacity that I did. But slowly after my mother shared her observations and then all at once, I needed Maja to know what I felt, even if only for integrity's sake."

Uritus knew the rest of this story well. His father had gone to his mother's house in the middle of the night—a ritual not out of the ordinary for them—and when she came outside, he saw her in the light of the moon and plainly stated that he loved her. She had laughed at him, not for very long, but for long enough to make him feel nervous. And then, to his relief and hers, she told him that she loved him as well and that she had for some time. She'd spent the past several years patiently waiting for the day that he would inevitably realize the same for himself. He expressed that he felt regretful for the time they had *lost* up to that point, but she quieted his heart and returned this focus to the time they had *now*. They were wed not long after they turned eighteen.

"So, to answer your question, there was no singular moment when the realization that I loved your mother dawned on me. It came on quietly, like the first rays of sunlight in the morning, gently warming my face until suddenly, my eyes were opened and the day shone brightly before me, as radiant as the sun and the moon and all of her stars. The moment you know is beautiful, yes, and it can feel exhilarating and freeing to be lucky enough to catch it when it happens. But the moment that truly matters is the one when you choose to transform that love from merely a feeling into an action, and all the moments that will follow when you make the same choice again."

Uritus nodded slowly, letting out a long breath.

"There is one you believe you may love."

It was not a question.

"Yes. But I don't know how to be sure that the closeness we share is truly that which makes way for such a love, or rather just... a byproduct of our entwined destinies. We *need* each other on some level that is apparent to us and everyone around us. Two people could not help but bond under such unique circumstances. But I just feel... differently about her than I do about anyone else I have ever loved. And of course I do, but... I don't know what that means." He paused, sighed. "There is also the added layer of how she presently wears another man's ring..."

Odipar smiled at his son, moving his hand to the side of his face again. "I am sorry that I cannot guide you further. Such choices belong to you and you alone."

Uritus turned suddenly to look over his shoulder as he heard the faint echo of a familiar voice calling his name, a tone of distress sounding from the mountains.

She is...

He returned his gaze to his father, "I understand. I still wish that I had more time than I do..." He paused and then proceeded assuredly, "I think I need to leave this place of my own accord."

Odipar nodded. "I am proud of you, my son."

"I know." Tears welled in Uritus's eyes. "Thank you. I wish I had more than that."

His father shook his head. "You have all that you need."

The Adalos embraced his father and then turned and began to walk urgently toward the Looming Mountains. The thunder rolled on and the voice cried out to him again and he broke into a run. Then, all of a sudden, he found himself blinking up at the roof of the tent, and that same familiar voice—a peaceful tone this time—drifted on the breeze to meet his ears.

* * *

Uritus left out the details of his conversation with his father when he recalled the story for his friends around the fire. The shape of the princess warmed his right side, and though he spoke to all members of their party about how real his vision felt, he thought only of her.

"Well, I would say I am sorry to have pulled you away from your time with him, but in truth, I am not. If it makes me selfish, then I wear such a title proudly. I am very glad to have you back with us again," said Perplexus with a smile, and the others agreed in a chorus.

In due time, the party determined that it was time to rest before they embarked into the range the next day. Uritus and Adiadni remained where they sat as the others turned in for the night, listening to the crackling of the fire and occasional sounds of thunder from behind them.

The princess rested her head on the fisherman's shoulder, tracing with one finger the scars that decorated his skin. "*Upon his chest will be his calling...*" she spoke under her breath.

"We match now," he said, stretching out one arm and holding it beside her right shoulder.

She tugged on her neckline to lay bare the bit of skin and saw that the long, curved tracks left in his by his assailant did, in a funny way, vaguely resemble the swirls of her birthmark. She lifted her face to meet his gaze and his breath caught in his throat for a moment as he beheld her brown eyes in the light of the moon.

"I don't have words to say how grateful I am that you found your way back to us," she whispered. "To be honest, I..." She paused and blinked, trying to recall if the fisherman's eyes had been blue since he awoke. "I would have been quite lost had you departed for good."

"I know," he said. "I am sorry to have given you a fright. I suppose I will have to get used to wearing my armor all the time." He paused, traced his eyes across her face. "I want you to know that I will continue to find my way back to you, as many times as I need to. I would never let you face such a journey alone."

The princess smiled, breathing deeply his familiar scent that made her think of rainwater and sweetgrass. "I know."

That night, both slept soundly side-by-side and neither of them dreamt.

* * *

The following day, the travelers had come to stand at the base of the Looming Mountains, and they waited in solemn silence for Adiadni to lead them forward. The front met the swamp in a harsh black line. The rubble from the mountains, brittle and sharp, made a crunching sound beneath one's boots. The range sloped upward, gently enough that one did not initially realize they had embarked up an incline until they turned to behold the swamp below. The mountains themselves

283

were sharp and jagged, similar to the White Mountains in only their steepness and insurmountable peaks. The party could see the space between where the base of one mountain met another, a winding path that made it difficult to tell what may be around the next bend. Above, the dark clouds rumbled, choking out the light and setting an ominous tone for the next leg of their journey. A deep, chilling roar sounded from somewhere within the range.

When the princess finally spoke, her tone was flat, "I know I do not need to speak on what lies beyond. I am hopeful that we will not need to search long before we find the enemy within. And though I am sure I needn't, I remind all of you that slaying Dagamor is my task and mine alone." She paused and swallowed the tremor which had begun to grow in her voice. "I'll get you through to the other side. I promise."

Uritus looked at her with an encouraging smile but she did not turn to regard him. Instead, she took a deep breath, steeling herself against the steady increase of her heartbeat. She lifted her eyes to the peaks and frowned at the clouds, not sure if they were truly creeping slowly East or if they merely appeared to be. For the briefest of moments, she almost wished to turn back and sprint in the opposite direction, to find a place to hide from the storm as it continued to grow. But then she heard a faint little sound, one which seemed out of place in this landscape, and she lowered her eyes to regard where it came from.

Several feet before her, singing its cheerful song, was a little brown sparrow. She looked at it and felt as though it saw her too. It chirped twice, spread its wings, and flew away into and beyond the mountains.

Adiadni nodded to herself, took one more deep breath, and stepped forward into the range. Another rumbling growl met their ears, but she did not flinch, instead keeping her gaze fixed solidly forward as she led the others into the darkness.

Chapter Nineteen

"Suvah"

The 21st of July

The range was winding and hostile and cold. The mountains were consistently massive and intimidating and the spaces between them sometimes opened up to wide, stark stretches of land with no plant or animal life in sight. They were struck from time to time by gusts of frigid wind, and though the clouds continued to churn above them, they never felt as though they were at risk of being caught in the rain. They had entered the range at its Northern end and with Perplexus's help, they proceeded slowly South, the roars of the unseen enemy occasionally reaching their ears.

Uritus observed how the landscape seemed to remain unchanging as they moved, but in a manner not at all similar to that of the range they called home. The White Mountains were consistent in how they made one feel supernaturally at peace. It didn't matter where you were within them, when you were there, you could not help but trust that they were there to protect you. The Looming Mountains, on the other hand, looked and felt like a hostile barrier, and the sameness of the landscape as they continued to wind their way through it left them in a constant state of unease. It seemed as though all it would take was one wrong step to become trapped in an eternal loop of anxious wandering. The fisherman moved his hand to touch the piece of shell that hung from his neck.

Adiadni abruptly stopped in her tracks and held out a hand to tell the others to do the same. She hadn't seen or heard anything out of the ordinary. but rather felt her stomach drop as it did when she miscounted the downward steps on a staircase. She waited several moments in silence, eyes darting back and forth, and was all but prepared to lead them on again when a sound reached out to them from the darkness.

The princess and the fisherman looked at one another to determine if they'd heard the same thing. The sound was faint enough to be written off as an auditory hallucination, but as Adi looked around at the other members of her party and saw the same look of confusion on each of their faces, she was certain this could not be the case.

She took a single step forward. Suddenly, a figure appeared from around a curve up ahead, and the princess drew her sword. "Who goes there?"

The figure was hobbling and hunched, moving slowly like an old man but seeming to have the appearance of a younger one as he approached them. He walked with a limp, and wrapped tightly around his body was a dark tattered cape.

"Who are you and where are you from?"

The man lifted his eyes to them and, seeing how tired and frightened they looked, Adiadni felt a sting of compassion for him.

"Please..." he spoke, his voice hollow and raspy. "I need water..."

"Adi?"

The princess turned at the physician's questioning voice and shook her head before looking once more at the one who still staggered forward. She asked again, "Who are you and where are you from?"

"From the... other side." He stopped his walk and raised himself up. It appeared to take all of his strength to do so. "I've been wandering for days... Please... water..."

"What is your name?"

The man stumbled, his body swaying back and forth, and as he tried again to take a step, he collapsed to the ground. Adi turned to Uritus with a look of uncertainty, sheathed her sword, and hurried forward with Punznes to offer the man their aid.

***

"I don't know what to do."

Adiadni paced back and forth several yards away from the fire around which the party tended to the delirious man they had just managed to revive.

"I feel I've said that a hundred times in the past weeks, but I mean it this time. I do not know what to do about him, and the more I think about it, the more it feels like we haven't a choice at all."

Uritus, Perplexus, and Uriah regarded the princess in understanding silence.

"We cannot just set him wandering again," she went on, shaking her head. "Whether he is from East or West of here, he is still a *man*. It would be senselessly cruel to abandon him, especially in this state."

"Is there any part of you that suspects he might be the man in the black cape?"

Adiadni paused as she considered Uritus's question. "I do not think so. I haven't been able to retain a clear picture of his face, but... his cape is not tattered like the stranger's is. And there is a distinct feeling in my stomach when I am around him and... I do not feel that here."

The others nodded, confident in her judgment.

"I do find it suspicious that he did not tell you directly whether he was from our side of the range or the other," noted Perplexus.

"He knew not from whence we came and yet assumed it was not the place that he did..." Uritus frowned.

"He is clearly confused... but yes. If he is from the West, he may well be tied to our enemy. Were he from the East... I cannot imagine why he would have come here." Adiadni paused her walk and turned her head to regard the man as he clumsily attempted to drink from a water skin.

"None in the West would know of the prophecy. Uriah is obviously a Wizard, but there is no reason this stranger should know who we are unless we tell him," said Uritus with a note of hopefulness.

Adiadni nodded slowly. She hadn't worn a crown in days, and the shirts she had adopted in place of her traveler's dresses kept her birthmark always hidden. If the man came from the West—provided he was not a Seer—their mission should remain cloaked by secrecy.

"Well, we obviously cannot be certain who he is, even if we do get answers out of him. And other than sending a pair to escort him to Judii, as much as I hate to say it, I think keeping him with us is the only answer." The others nodded slowly and Adi searched their faces for some sort of solid affirmation or hesitation. "Is no one going to object?"

The silent three looked at one another and Uritus spoke, "From all angles, it does appear to be the wisest decision."

"Of course, I do not feel good about keeping another potential enemy close, but it makes far more sense to do that than to run the risk that he may relay information to an even greater one. We act not only for our own wellbeing but for that of all the land as well," Perplexus added.

The princess looked to the Wizard, "Uriah?"

He nodded seriously. "We will be sure to keep a watchful eye on him."

"Okay."

Again she turned to face their party, hands forming tight fists at her sides, and led the council back to rejoin the others. "It'll be as before," she addressed them as she arrived beside the fire, and they quietly nodded to themselves.

"Before?" The strange man appeared to be clearer-headed now that he'd had a bit to eat and drink.

Adi ignored his query, bringing herself down to a seat between him and Punznes. "Feeling better?"

"Indeed. Your company has been quite hospitable."

"I'm glad to hear it. You were rather disoriented when we happened upon you…" Adiadni paused, tilting her head as she studied his face. "Tell me again how it is you ended up here?"

The man hesitated, his eyes darting to the sword that hung from her belt.

"You are safe with us as long as we are safe with you," she assured him.

He nodded apprehensively. "Of course." Looking around at the companions who kept a close eye on him, he returned his gaze to his questioner and continued, "I am trying to find my way East of here."

The travelers did not let their interest in this admission show on their faces.

"Anywhere in particular?"

He blinked. "No, I…" He looked around, leaning a bit closer to her as he lowered his voice, "I had to get out of that place."

The princess frowned slightly. "Out of what place?"

"That endless wasteland…"

"West of the mountains?"

"Well yes, I…" He paused, eyes moving across the party members again. "You are f- from the East, yes? You… you will not send me back?"

Adi frowned again. "Are there people there who wish to hurt you?"

"There is *nothing*," he said with a chill. "No civilization and no sound."

"And how is it that *you* ended up there?"

"I…" he blinked. "I suppose I… don't really know…"

"I see." Adiadni rose to her feet. "And I take it you have no name as well?"

"I do not know…" He looked around nervously. "Forgive me, please, I've been wandering for so long…"

"We aren't going to hurt you," the princess responded, her voice flat. "But surely, you understand that we will need to keep you with us."

"Of course, of course. Can you get me out of here?"

Adi sighed, feeling suddenly sad as she beheld the hope on his face. "We will try."

***

The travelers gathered their things and continued to make their slow trek South until nightfall, the stranger moving with them, bound by his wrists. They stayed up in shifts again that night and the man slept soundly, though eyes remained fixed on him the whole time. The Shadow that blanketed the night choked out all light save for that radiating from their steady-burning fire. Even when day broke, the Shadow let little light through to shine upon them, so groggily they rose and proceeded on again.

The party was grateful to have had a fair bit of experience up to this point wandering through uniform landscapes which seemed as though they would never release them. The maddening nature of the sameness of everything here was alleviated somewhat by the knowledge that they were approaching the end of their quest. Occasionally, the mountains would roar, and Adiadni would lift her eyes to the peaks to see if she could catch a glimpse of the sound's source, but never did it seem that they were any closer to finding the beast than before.

In truth, she didn't know what signs to be looking for. There were no tracks or visual indications of movement, and the roars seemed to be coming from all around them rather than sounding from a singular location. In all of her training to come here, she had not been given a single clue as to how she might find the Dagamor, and while she did not fault her teachers for this—as they no doubt had told her all they knew—she found herself exceedingly aggravated for how she was simply expected to figure it out on her own. It was easy for those in her life to encourage her toward this ominous task with hopeful smiles, confident that she would reign victorious. All they needed to do was trust in the ability of someone other than themselves and the word of several who were long dead. The Suvah had grown tired of being told that all she needed was to hold onto hope, that she would be fine if she had faith in herself and those who came

288

before her. Because now, she stood at the doorway of that very fate, and she felt no more assurance in herself than she had before. If the success of her mission truly hinged on faith alone, then that did not bode well for the approaching battle.

She expressed none of this to her companions. She couldn't have, even if she had wanted to, due to the continuous presence of the stranger who now journeyed with them. But she knew that even with friends as loving and gentle and patient, hopeful and encouraging and understanding as they, were she to share her fears with them, they could still offer nothing more than her parents or the Keepers who trained her or her companions back in Suscundos. Though she was sure of their love and support, the reality was setting in all the more that this task truly *was* hers alone. As her eyes continued to anxiously search the range for a glimpse of her opponent, she began to slowly succumb to that familiar feeling of sad loneliness that she had almost entirely forgotten.

Eventually, the world around them began to darken, and though they could not see the sun, they concluded that night was drawing near. When they had built their camp and portioned out their meal, Adi asked Mikka to spar with her, thinking that being reminded of the most efficient combative techniques would ease her anxieties. The former soldier was happy to oblige, and as she and the princess found a spot several feet away from the fire to engage in their mock combat, Uriah and Uritus came to rest out of earshot of the others.

Quietly, they watched the sparring take place, the sounds of clashing swords traveling through the air to meet their ears. Uritus noted considerable growth in Adiadni's ability since their clash in Tuvibati Canyon. She was more controlled with her movements, more calculating. Her determination was displayed plainly on her face. Every time Mikka bested her, she'd right herself or grip her sword tighter and insist they go again. The fisherman struggled to understand how she could be unsure of her gifts when they were so plainly seen by everyone around her.

"She is just as I imagined she would be," spoke Uriah with pride in his voice.

"How's that?"

"Bold, despite her fear. And gentle despite said boldness. Both sides of the coin are necessary for a competent leader and warrior alike."

The Wizard spoke the truth. King Agamemnon was a wise and just leader, but the fisherman imagined the world that would come to bloom under Adiadni's reign and felt his heart swell with excitement for it. Her love and adoration for this land and its people was evident in her life. She had a heart that burned for justice and freedom and the drive to fight for those things. Uritus believed wholeheartedly that the Free World would flourish in ways it had yet to when she took the throne.

"The fulfillment of her destiny draws near," Uriah spoke again, his tone serious. "She will do something that no one else can. And then your own destiny will be hot on your heels."

The Adalos nodded solemnly. "I understand."

"I am sure you also understand that… just as I am forbidden from intervening in her battle, so are you?"

Uritus furrowed his brow. "Of course…"

"No doubt, it will require a substantial amount of strength to resist your protective instincts when the time comes," Uriah went on. "But I must reiterate how important it is that you do."

Uritus frowned and turned to regard the Wizard, who paused for a prolonged moment before elaborating.

"I cannot say for certain what may come to pass were you to attempt to aid her. But I do know without a doubt that there is only one who may fell the Dagamor, just as there is only one who may bear the Sword of Fire. You will not have the same hand of protection over you during her battle that she will, so as difficult as it will be, you *must* refrain from intervening. Even if she asks for your help."

The fisherman nodded briskly and returned his attention to where Adi and Mikka sparred. *Even if she asks for your help.* Uritus felt that he couldn't deny her if he tried. To do so in this case would be for the greater good, he understood that. He could not truly protect her or conquer the Shadow if he was killed in an attempt to rescue her from something she didn't need to be rescued from. He took several deep breaths in an attempt to still his mind. She was not a fragile thing. She was a warrior and she would be just fine.

The unwavering fire of their camp crackled and popped between the sounds of the clashing blades. The party partook of their evening rations in silence, sharing with the stranger whose wrists they had temporarily freed from their bindings. Perplexus observed the man intently, watching him as he ate, his gaze fixed on the dueling two.

"Are they training for anything in particular?" asked the man of the companions who responded with continued silence. "They're quite good. Whoever you are hunting had better watch their back."

"No one said we were hunting someone," replied Perplexus with narrowed eyes.

"Right, of course," the man paused, looking around. "Might it be the case that someone is hunting *you*?"

Nadarum and Ilya shared a suspicious glance across the fire.

"I do hope you would tell me if my life may be in danger." The stranger lowered his voice, leaning a bit closer to Perplexus as he spoke, "There are legends about… the being that dwells here. It is said to be fearsome and undefeatable, made of the mountains themselves," he paused. "I know I am hardly in the position to make suggestions, but I must implore you to find a way out of here as quickly as you can."

Before the navigator could respond, Mikka approached the fire, armor clattering, and addressed Nadarum, "Take my place, won't you? She's kicking my ass. Too much youthful energy, that one."

The horseman chuckled. "You're in far better shape than I am, Mik, but yes, I'll sub in for you." He picked up his sword and moved to meet the princess on her makeshift battleground and Mikka plopped herself down to a seat beside Oripidus.

Finally, Perplexus addressed the stranger, "I understand that this place frightens you, but we remain resolute in keeping the details of our journeying to ourselves."

"I am curious who shared such legends with you," Punznes added, suspicion in his voice. "You cannot remember your name nor how or where you existed West of here, yet stories of what dwells in the mountains remain fresh in your mind. Curious."

The man chewed the last of his food slowly. Mikka's eyes found Laivar's and she frowned, curious what she missed. Finally, the stranger swallowed and spoke, "I apologize, my memory is still spotty, yes…"

"You won't benefit from lying to us," Ilya cut him off. "You have your reasons to retain your right to privacy, that we understand. But if you refuse to tell us anything about who you truly are, then you certainly may not snoop around in our private business. Is that clear?"

"Quite."

Perplexus was quick to bind the man's hands again, and the princess returned to the fire with the horseman, the fisherman and Wizard arriving shortly thereafter. Adiadni sheathed her sword and fixed her gaze on the stranger. The group came to attention, sensing the serious energy she carried with her.

"My company informs me you have many questions about where we are going and what we seek."

The man regarded her silently.

"Of course, I understand your concerns. Were our relationship to take a hostile turn, it is you who would be in danger. Your instincts of self-preservation are natural and understandable."

Uritus furrowed his brow, unsure of Adiadni's aim in this confrontation.

"I am sure as well that *you* can understand that we share such instincts, you and I. And also that I will do whatever it takes to see to the well-being of my companions. I do not wish to use my hospitality as a weapon, but I remind you that we have been exceedingly patient and generous since you have been in our care. I intend to continue along this path, as I value humanity above all else, but I wonder if we may reach an agreement that might serve us both."

The stranger nodded slowly.

Adiadni took a breath. "My proposition is that we exchange information."

The others around the fire shared uncertain glances.

The princess continued, "I remain resolved that I cannot tell you where we are going, nor the purpose of our mission. And anything one of us asks of the other, we must ourselves be willing to answer. Does that sound fair?"

The man nodded again. "I believe so."

"Very well." Adi paused, remaining where she stood on the opposite side of the fire. "As I am the one who proposed this exchange, I will allow you the first question."

"Thank you, that is a generous offer." His eyes moved nervously from one face to another which watched him in anticipation. Eventually, he returned his attention to the princess and spoke tentatively, "If you… do not receive the information you are seeking from me… do you intend to kill me?"

Adiadni's face—which had maintained a neutral expression up to this point—shifted to one of compassion. She shook her head. "I do not. I will stay my blade as long as you remain peaceful and will ask my companions to do the same. In truth, I would much prefer it that way."

The stranger nodded, satisfied.

The princess proceeded with her first question, "Does your urgency to leave this place stem from the fact that you are being sought after?"

He hesitated a moment before answering, "Yes."

Adiadni did not allow the surprise of this response to show on her face, though she noticed the others in the camp exchange interested glances.

The man spoke with less pause this time, "How is it that someone as young as yourself came to be the leader of such a group?"

"A valid question. Without going into too much detail, I can tell you that I was appointed a mission and these noble souls offered me their swords and their companionship." Adi paused, mulling over her next query. "What is it you plan to do once you've made your way East of here?"

The stranger blinked. "I suppose… I haven't thought about it. I don't know what exists there, but… if I could choose, I would find a peaceful place to live out my days, far away from here."

"A noble aim. Would you say your fears of your pursuer would be alleviated were you free of this place?"

"I… do believe it is my turn to pose a question."

Adi nodded briskly. "Right. Go on then."

The man considered his wording for a moment and then asked, "Who was it that ordained your mission?"

The Suvah paused, becoming acutely aware of her heartbeat. Her eyes flicked to Uritus and he shook his head, a subtle, hardly noticeable movement. She returned her gaze to the stranger, pressing on despite the anxiety that grew in the pit of her stomach. "I will answer that… but only if you can give me your name."

The party turned to regard the man with bated breath. He shifted nervously where he sat. "I am sorry… I do not know…" He frowned. "Surely a name cannot be that important…"

"But it is, I'm afraid."

Adiadni lowered herself to a squat, staring intently into the yellow fire that warmed her face. She considered their journey up to this point, its twists and turns, their victories and missteps. The stakes of their mission grew with each mile they traveled, with each cycle of the sun. For every single thing she said and did, she had to consider its impact on a grand scale, turning it over in her hands until she had observed its every facet, contemplated each possible outcome. Long gone were the days when she had room to hesitate, to be uncertain, to fear. Countless were those who relied on her to assure the safekeeping of their fates. She raised herself with a sigh once again and lifted her eyes to Oripidus, "Bring him to me."

The dwarf rose without a word and nudged the butt of his hammer into the stranger's back. The bound man's countenance shifted to one of trepidation as Perplexus helped him to his feet. Silently, Oripidus led him around the fire and brought him to stand before the princess, Nadarum stepping forward to keep a strong hand on one of his shoulders.

The man began to anxiously stammer, "Wait... please, I... I am sorry. Perhaps I can remember something else that may be of use to you—"

"I am not going to hurt you," Adiadni spoke calmly and the man quieted. "I am sorry to have kept you as our prisoner. I wish only to protect my company. It is clear that we have little to offer each other at this point save for prolonged anxieties. So I am setting you free." Swiftly, she drew her sword and cut his bindings, and he looked at her with confusion.

"I'm not quite sure what you mean by—"

"Lex," Adi cut him off. "Point him East."

Perplexus hesitated only a moment before moving toward them and following her order.

Uritus approached the princess as well, stopping at her side as the navigator oriented the stranger. He spoke under his breath, "Are you quite certain?"

She briskly replied, "I am," and offered no further explanation. The fisherman found his hands behind his back and remained silently by her side as Perplexus returned to stand beside the fire.

The man stared off into the distance for several seconds and then began shaking his head back and forth. He turned again to regard her, eyes wrought with worry, "Please do not send me away. I will become lost again, I am sure of it!"

"I did not wish for things to go this way," the princess replied earnestly. "But I cannot trust you if I do not know who you are, and you will not be able to find peace until you are released from this place. May you find a steady path as you make your way forward." With that, she turned and began to make her way back to the camp, Nadarum and Uritus following after her.

"No! Wait! I will not pry any longer, I am sorry!"

The desperation in the man's voice pained the fisherman to hear, but he kept his attention fixed on the fire, not wishing to undermine or question Adi's leadership.

"We can reach some sort of agreement, I am sure of it! Please, Adiadni, I beg you to reconsider!"

The Suvah stopped in her tracks, turned again to face him. "How do you know my name?"

He blinked. The companions looked at one another, confused, suspicious, and on edge.

Adi pressed the issue again, "I've been especially mindful not to give it to you."

The man stammered, "I... I don't know. I am sure I just overheard someone call after you..."

"No," Adiadni shook her head. "You heard our physician call me Adi when we first found you, but no one has addressed me by name since."

The stranger shifted his weight and did not respond. The princess frowned as she studied his face. Every one of her nervous system's alarm bells was ringing frantically in her ears. Her body was screaming at her that he was not safe, he was not right, he wasn't who he said he was. The tips of her fingers buzzed with anxious energy and every hair on her arms and the back of her neck stood on end. He obviously couldn't be trusted, but was such a thing enough to warrant aggressive action on her part? At that moment, a bright flash of lightning lit up the sky, and as the thunder cracked, Adiadni watched a hint of a shadow move across the man's face, a flicker in his eyes.

Flames licking at dark stone...

The Suvah drew her sword.

"Adiadni..."

"Get behind me."

Her tone was aggressive but still, Uritus hesitated. Nadarum set a hand on the fisherman's shoulder. The two shared a silent glance and Uritus relented, moving to join the others by the fire, several of them with weapons in hand.

"I must admit, I am impressed," spoke Adi to the stranger. "Preying on my compassion, trying to convince *me* to lead *you* out of here. Your ruse nearly had me fooled."

The man's eyes darted to the shining blade clutched in her hand. "You promised to remain peaceful..."

"And you swore you couldn't recall your name, but that's not true, is it?"

Silence met her again.

"I came here searching for something," she went on. "I had an image in mind of what that thing might look like. I thought it would be larger, louder, fiercely aggressive, undeniably clear. And what's more, I thought I would have to walk for days or even weeks to find it. But instead, you found me and almost slipped right under my nose. Isn't that right, Dagamor?"

She could hear the muted gasps of her companions as she made this accusation. Again, the man did not respond right away, and she felt her heart pound in her chest as she waited. She kept her feet firmly planted, head high, fingers gripping the hilt of her sword despite how her palms had begun to sweat. She stared at him with relentless heat and then, to her surprise, he began to laugh.

The sound sent a shiver through her bones and reminded her of what it felt like to be trapped wandering in the Forest of Idor. What began as the chuckle of an ordinary man shifted its tone and darkened to something menacing. Thunder clapped overhead and the distant roars of the mountains sounded all around them, merging with the laughter of the stranger. He snapped his head forward suddenly, causing the princess to jolt, and his eyes—now blood red—locked with hers as her breath caught in her throat.

"Clever girl."

She swallowed, her mouth dry.

"You do know that old phrase, *'When two be joined by the hand of Fate...'*"

"*'...Neither space nor time can divide them...'*" Adi finished softly.

Dagamor chuckled. "I have been waiting for you for a long time."

The Suvah frowned and shook her head. "Why the act? Why disguise yourself? Why try to pass for one who is fearful and helpless?"

"Were your own life the one hanging in the balance, would you not do whatever you could to save it?"

Adiadni did not respond.

"You see, little princess, you and I are not so different. Each of us created, ordained, predestined for violence. Bound to collide, regardless of our feelings on the matter. I pity you just as you pitied me when first we met. Your blind trust of those who guide you will result in more deaths than you could ever be capable of saving."

Adiadni shook her head again. "But had you taken my offer and left when I freed you then surely you would have been spared. Why stand to face me at all?"

"Why leave the safety of your home to seek me out? My purpose, at the end of all things, is to guard the West against those who would seek to invade, just as yours is to find and destroy me."

"We do not mean to invade, we..." Adi cut herself off before she could mistakenly reveal the intimate details of their mission. Her stomach tied itself in knots.

Was he right? All her life she had been led to believe that Dagamor was a mindless beast, rock and magma, terror and fury, nothing more. At this moment, she desperately wished that was the case. Far easier would it have been to harness her courage and wield her sword than to stand here and consider each thing her adversary said in an attempt to determine whether he was trying to manipulate her or if she had, as he suggested, been manipulated her whole life by those she trusted. She felt the cool hilt of her sword in her hand, contemplated its weight, its form, its predestination. To the surprise of all who looked on, she returned the blade to its home at her hip.

"Regardless of what you may think… I never wished for any of this." She spoke with confidence despite her lack of assurance. "I never wished to leave Suscundos, I never wished to come here. I never wished to spill blood and I would very much prefer it if I never had to again. I do not know who or what you are, if you bleed, if you dream, if you love, if you wish you could. But I do know that while our destinies do always find us, sometimes we are offered moments when we may choose our paths. I believe this to be one of them."

The companions exchanged unsure glances again and Uritus kept his eyes fixed on his counterpart, blinking against the mounting pressure in his temples. He feared for her well-being and knew not her aim in this confrontation, but trusted that she knew what she was doing. He lifted his hand to his chest and lightly touched the little white stone which rested against it. As he did, the princess felt a distinct cooling sensation grow from the place where her own talisman lay.

She raised her head and finished her speech, "I promised to remain peaceful as long as you did and I will stand by that promise. I do not need to kill you to continue on my way. Leave us in peace and we may be done with this." She turned, locking eyes with the Adalos, and made her way back to rejoin her company.

"I'm afraid I can't do that."

As he spoke, the Dagamor's voice became deeper, harsher, sending a chill through the body of the princess as she spun to face him. He crouched down and touched his hand to the earth. From it, he produced a jagged, hulking club made of sharp black rock. The Suvah drew her sword once more. Dagamor chuckled —a sound like stones being ground against one another—and began to slowly pace like a predator caged and left to starve.

Adiadni took several steps toward him and halted, rooting her feet firmly into the ground beneath her.

"Your commanders have a foolish amount of faith in you to send you here to face me so young and inexperienced," goaded the enemy with a sneer, his tattered cape swishing behind him as he walked.

"That they do. I intend to make certain that such faith is not misplaced."

"We'll see about that."

A vast network of lightning lit up the sky and the princess startled as thunder cracked and roared. She barely had time to again lower her eyes to her opponent before he rushed at her, swinging his club with force.

She leaned back just in time, feeling the rush of air stirred up by the brutal weapon move over her body. She righted herself, gripped her sword with both hands, and slashed it fiercely at her attacker.

He took a step back and she missed. Over his head, he swung his club again, allowing Adi only a fraction of a second to jump out of the way before it came crashing down. Chunks of brittle rock spiraled in all directions. The princess found her feet again.

Uritus's heart became lodged in his throat as he watched in terror the battle play out. Adi was quick on her feet but clearly disoriented, swinging her blade blindly whenever she got the chance but mostly just trying to stay alive. Nadarum kept a strong hand on the fisherman's shoulder, an act intended to provide comfort as well as serve as a safeguard against the younger man's urges to get involved. Uritus ground his feet into the earth and formed his hands into fists. He would not ruin this for her, would not needlessly risk his own life or anyone else's.

But he longed now, more than he ever had, to *run* to her, to fight at her side, to fight so she didn't have to. As he had since they first spoke of her burden in the orchard, he longed to take it away from her so she need never feel its heaviness again. He shoved these thoughts aside, tightly gripping both neck ornaments. Her fate lay now in her hands alone. Wordlessly, he pleaded with the Divine to give her strength.

Adiadni grew aggravated with her inability to land a hit on her attacker but reminded herself that just as he had evaded her, so had she evaded him. Dagamor put a devastating amount of force into each of his swings, and the princess knew she could not allow him to get a direct hit. Her armor, though tough, would do little to defend against so crushing a blow.

She leapt away from him, forcing him to approach as he wound up for another swing. But this time, she rooted her feet, raised her sword, and when his jagged club came crashing down, she swung her blade to meet it.

The weapons collided and the club shattered, splintering pieces of rock sent flying in every direction.

Adi jumped back and raised an arm to shield her face. She felt the rubble collide with her gauntlet and breastplate, heard the pattering of thousands of tiny fragments against her body and across the ground.

She lowered her arm and raised her sword, prepared to attack, when suddenly before her eyes, the club began to reform in Dagamor's hand, chunks of rock rising from the earth to take the form of the weapon yet again. In her astonishment, she missed her window to attack.

The deadly dance began again and Adiadni soon realized that her body was exhausted. No amount of training or preparation could have possibly readied her for the real thing. War—even just the limited taste of it she had gotten so far— was brutal and merciless. She managed to slash her sword at her enemy quickly enough to make a small cut on his hip, but he fought on unfazed.

He swung his club one way, recalibrated, swung it back in the other direction. Adiadni, mistakenly believing that it was her turn to launch an attack, failed to move out of the way.

The club collided with her body and she was sent flailing, doing a half-turn in the air before coming to land face down. Her chin and hands felt the stinging scrape of rocky earth as she slid to stillness. *Hands*. Both of them. She lifted her head and spied Emipera lying several feet out of reach.

"Adiadni!"

The Suvah scrambled to flip herself onto her back, the voice of the Adalos moving through her ears but not registering in her brain.

The Dagamor approached, club rising overhead.

Nadarum moved his second hand across Uritus's body as the fisherman instinctively lurched forward. Uriah lowered his head and touched his hand to his chest. Uritus screamed her name again, internally begging anything that could hear to intervene.

An instant before Dagamor's club could begin its downward swing, an arrow whizzed through the air and glanced off his right shoulder blade.

Ilya.

Dagamor cried out in pain, the roars of the mountains sounding from every direction. Adiadni looked to the archer, as did the other party members, and Dagamor turned around.

"No!"

Adi screamed as her enemy stepped toward her companions. They clutched their weapons, remaining in place, but prepared to fight back. Nadarum abandoned his hold on Uritus, drawing his sword and planting himself in front of his wife.

The Suvah leapt to her feet, rushed to grab her weapon, and then turned and sprinted toward Dagamor. She had no strategy, no plan of attack. Only an aim, an instinct that had burned hot in her chest since the day she was born. She could not protect everyone, but right now, she *would* protect them.

She slid on her knees toward her enemy, swung her sword with all her might. She felt it vibrate in her hands as it tore into his cape, his shirt, and finally, the flesh of his back.

Hot blood splattered across her face. Dagamor threw his head back and roared. The sound shook the earth. He released the club from his hand in his agony and it shattered into a pile of rubble as it hit the ground. The dark clouds above swirled with increasing speed and bitter-cold wind rushed all around, forcing the fire of the camp to shrink as it clung to life. Before the Suvah had the chance to consider making another attack, her foe began to change his form.

Dagamor writhed as his skin swelled and hardened, splitting through his clothes which charred and turned to ash before they could hit the ground. The enemy began to grow, his cape growing with him, and he peaked at a height of over ten feet. The shell that now plated him darkened and cracked, splitting apart to reveal channels of flowing lava beneath. Two pairs of short, curved horns sprouted from his skull, crowning his head as his mouth split open and roared once again.

The reverberations of the sound shook the mountains and Adiadni stumbled while attempting to remain on her feet. Her mouth fell open, a single tear slipping down her cheek as she gazed fearfully into the face of her destiny.

She felt her feet frozen in place as Dagamor turned and took several booming steps toward one of the peaks behind him. He thrust his hand into its side as thunder roared, and when he moved to face the princess once more, a new club

—twice the size of the last—was clutched in his hand. Adi gripped her sword, shoving aside the thoughts that it would do nothing to defend her now.

With a resonant roar, the monster from the mountains brought his club hurtling toward the Suvah.

She dove out of the way. She heard the crunching noise it made when it collided with the earth and knew that a single hit from this weapon would claim her life. With Dagamor grown to his true form, his strength had increased tenfold. He was slower moving now, but even so, he managed to launch several swings at Adiadni before she had the chance to attack.

All of her energy was quickly spent dashing to escape the claws of death and then attempting to reorient herself before they reached for her again. In the moments when she did glimpse a narrow window to attack, she hesitated just long enough that she missed it. She pushed herself, knowing she had to take a chance.

When Dagamor raised his weapon again, she dashed between his legs. She sliced her sword this way and that, metal crashing against rock, lava spraying from the cuts and quickly hardening into black stone.

Dagamor roared and turned to face her. Adiadni watched in devastation as the beast's shell regrew in the places she had cut, and dove out of the way of yet another near-hit.

It could not go on like this. She could not allow him to wear her out. The next time Dagamor calibrated his swing, she stood her ground to face him. Down came the club, whooshing through the air as it approached her. Uritus called her name again, taking a pair of steps forward without intending to. Perplexus locked his arms around the fisherman's chest, watching fearfully as the Suvah raised her free hand.

The club crashed down to meet her, and Adiadni, face and hand still raised to the sky, watch the rock shatter, falling all around but never touching her.

Those who witnessed this would have observed the nearly invisible curve of an iridescent blue shield and the fragments of stone sliding off its surface. A proud smile moved across the Wizard's face.

The Dagamor staggered back in shock as his mighty weapon crumbled. He roared up into the swirling Shadow and the rubble below his hand began to take on the form of a new weapon. The jagged rock gathered and compiled itself into a massive flail in his hand. The rock cracked and ground as the links of the chain moved against one another, the head of the mace adorned with sharp spikes that would easily pierce the body of any it collided with.

The princess let out an exasperated sound, part groan, part whimper, part laugh at the growing absurdity of the situation. She allowed her sword to dip toward the ground. It felt like a meager plaything in her hand.

But she was not done. Following in the footsteps of a man she had hardly known, she was resolved to end this here and now. Even if it took all she had left to give. Even if it claimed her life.

She looked down at her left hand, palm open, fingers spread wide. She raised her eyes to the Dagamor, to the heat emanating from his mouth as his roar split the sky. And then, she dropped her gaze and it met the brilliant blue eyes of the Adalos, and she knew the time had come to fulfill the promise she had made him before they left Suscundos.

"...And in spite of my unreadiness... I will make your way."

The Suvah raised her left hand and screamed.

The frigid wind, once wild and unpredictable, began to spin under her command, spiraling with increasing speed around the monster, whipping rock and ash around him until he was forced to cover his face.

Adiadni released her hold on the vortex, observing for a moment as it sustained itself. She looked down at Emipera, at her gleaming silver face, gripped her hilt with the last of her strength, and plunged it into the air with a gritty cry to the heavens.

The sky split open, a bolt of white lightning shooting down and connecting with the blade. The Suvah felt her entire body charged with power, heating, sparking, ready to alight. She spun her sword around, gripped its hilt like a spear, and with all she had left within her, launched it through the air at her enemy.

A second bolt of lightning traveled down from the sky to meet the Sword of Light in mid-air, and together, they crashed into the chest of the Dagamor.

Instantaneously, the rocky shell that plated him burst.

Adi and the others on the ground raised their arms above their heads and turned to shield themselves from the flying shrapnel. An ear-splitting roar shook the heavens and the earth. The fiery core of the beast that remained began to twist and writhe. The onlookers watched as it shriveled to the ground, burning to ash until all that remained was the tattered fabric of the cape and the silver sword that lay atop it.

The family by the camp erupted into elated cheers, embracing each other and weeping with pride and relief.

Uritus looked to where Adiadni still stood with a shocked look on her face. He called out to her, taking several urgent steps in her direction. Hazily, she turned her head to look at him. And then the Suvah, all her body's resources spent, dropped to her knees and collapsed upon the rubble of the mountains.

Chapter Twenty

"Invaders in Vegard"

The 22nd of July

Uritus gazed across the fire at Adiadni with admiration and attentiveness. She sat between Mikka and Ilya, head resting on the archer's shoulder, eyes fixed on the dancing flames just before her, her mind clearly miles away. The party had been moved to urgent concern when they saw her body drop to the ground, but she had quickly revived, and once Punznes had offered her a tea for her pain and a salve for her scrapes, they were inclined to believe her when she told them that she was feeling much better. They marveled at the feat she had accomplished, remarking on the miracle they had witnessed at her hand. But she had little to say in response, so they shifted their energy to curate an environment of rest. Perplexus retrieved the Sword of Light and the cloth it lay upon.

Now the sword, safely tucked back into its sheath, rested off to the side with the princess's armor. The cape joined the rest of the monster, burning to ash in the fire. For one who ended the day with a miraculous victory in hand, Adiadni appeared, from the fisherman's vantage point, as one who felt utterly defeated. Her shoulders slumped and her eyes glazed over and every breath she took appeared to require a considerable amount of effort.

Uritus could not help but note how significantly she had changed in the weeks since they departed. She was less emotionally guarded than she had been, having come to love and trust the people who journeyed with her. She was bolder now, and whether or not she felt more confident in herself, she moved with unquestionable authority, charging straight ahead into the unknown, all the while being mindful not to trample any who lay in her path. Though honest about her fears, she was unbridled by them. Her convictions kept them safe, focused, pointed straight ahead. Uritus felt as if his heart would split at its seams for how proud he was of her.

"Our Suvah is not the only one who has done a bold thing tonight," spoke Nadarum, shifting his eyes from Adi to Ilya. "That was a risky move, Plum."

Ilya laughed. "Are you trying to scold me?"

"He wouldn't dare."

The horseman chuckled. "Mik's right, I would never. I understand the impulse completely. I am just more prone to rule-following than you are, and I thought we were all in silent agreement about the same thing."

"We were. I held that arrow for a long time, and my releasing it was not for a lack of strength."

"Nay, it was the evidence of it."

The archer smiled at her husband's affirmation. "It *was* undoubtedly foolish, and I was aware of its foolishness when I did it. But my values simply would not allow me to do nothing."

Uriah cleared his throat and their heads swiveled in his direction. "I should chide you, Ilya, for your blatant disregard for the instruction you were given, but I know also that sometimes, such circumstances require that we follow our instincts rather than our orders. I certainly do not encourage any of the rest of you to follow her example; however, at the end of all things, I am grateful that our archer had the boldness to do what the rest of us did not."

One by one, the companions began to succumb to the allure of sleep. The night had grown still and quiet, interrupted by neither wind nor thunder despite the incessantly swirling clouds. Adi groggily lifted her head, offering Ilya a small smile when she made her way to fall asleep beside her husband. The princess's tired eyes drifted across the party members and landed on the fisherman. He smiled at her, setting a gentle hand on the ground beside him. Adiadni stood and moved around the fire to sit at his side.

She brought herself to rest in the crook of his arm and they sat together silently as the others dozed off. Even now, after traveling on foot for days, sleeping on the ground every night, and pushing herself to the brink of death, Uritus noticed how the sweet and vibrant scent of the princess still clung to her skin. It had become clear to him that no circumstances they encountered had been at all capable of dulling her radiant beauty. No matter how she looked, what she wore, how she felt, what she did, he remained utterly captivated by everything that she was. She shifted at his side, turning her body to lean further into him. He lifted his eyes to the clouds and released a long breath.

Lowering his head again, he brought his chin to rest atop her dark curls. "Do you want to talk about it?"

He felt her body rise and fall as she sighed. "Even if I did... I'm not sure what I'd say."

Uritus thought this to be a perfectly acceptable answer and did not press the issue further.

The sound of the crackling fire was met only by the steady breathing of the sleeping ones until the princess spoke again, "I just fear that perhaps we have less say in what happens to us than I had thought."

Uritus sat up a bit, lifting his head so he could look down at her. "What do you mean by that?"

"I don't know." Adi raised herself to sit upright, staring still into the fire. "I did try to walk away. I thought it might be the answer. Thought I could find a loophole in the prophecy, vanquish Dagamor with grace rather than..." she trailed off, shook her head.

"Do you regret what you had to do?"

She shook her head again. "Not at all. It needed to be done, I see that now. I'd do it again if necessary. But ultimately, what happened with Dagamor is the same thing that has happened my whole life. Someone *else* decided what I needed to do. What I wanted didn't end up mattering."

Uritus nodded empathetically.

"For as long as I have existed, one wrist has been bound to that blade. The other..." She pointed to Emipera and then formed her left hand into a fist, feeling the cold hunk of metal encircling her middle finger. She trailed off again. "I just felt so strongly that the moment had come to carve my own path, away from what others believe I will do or be. But I was wrong."

The fisherman's heart hurt for her. He remained bound by the inability to find the right words to help.

Adiadni sighed frustratedly. "I feel so fucking selfish talking about this. I know what I have, I know it is far more than most could even imagine. I am sheltered and protected and fed and clothed and *adored*. What more could anyone possibly want? I haven't the right to feel like this..."

"Like what?"

A breath caught in Adi's throat and her eyes brimmed with tears. She frowned and forced them closed, shaking her head against the discomfort that tied itself to vulnerability. When she opened them again and they locked with the fisherman's, she saw plainly the care displayed in his own and brought herself to take a deep breath.

"Deeply sad. And terribly alone."

Wordlessly, he pulled her into his chest as she cried.

"I'm fully aware that I'm not," she spoke through her tears. "I have family and friends and you lot... It isn't rational."

"Unfortunately, our fears don't give a damn about rationality."

Adi laughed tiredly and the sound lightened Uritus's heart. She lifted herself again and dried her eyes and he moved a gentle hand to hold the side of her face.

"As someone who has an unquestionable *right to sadness*, I can tell you that it comes for us all, sometimes for no rhyme or reason. I am sorry I cannot help more than that. While I will always affirm your feelings... your life and the nature of your duties and relationships remain incomprehensible to me. I am sure that has contributed to your feeling lonely over the years. Though there are countless people who love you, and many who can empathize and understand to varying degrees, none can fully relate. There is only one Suvah. Of course such a thing would make you feel isolated."

Adiadni released a breath through pursed lips and smiled up at the man who always made her feel heard, who always seemed to understand despite his insistence that he couldn't.

"I wish I could tell you that someday you won't feel this way anymore, but alas, I am not a Prophet. I *can* tell you, however, most assuredly, that I am here and that I will continue to be. It just so happens that I am also the only one of my kind. Of course, I am still figuring out what that means. But I am lucky to have someone I can look to whom I trust, whose example I may follow when the time comes that I must lead." He paused as he looked down at her, feeling nearly overwhelmed by his adoration for the person she was. "You have done incredible things since you left home. I hope one day you can appreciate yourself for them. Until then, I am happy to do so in your stead."

Adi dipped her head forward and fell into his chest, where she remained until morning.

***

"Damn it all. The monster was right."

As the companions stepped beyond the confines of the Looming Mountains, they gazed down at the valley that rolled out beneath them to find that it was, by all appearances, a barren wasteland. Mikka was the only one who spoke, voicing the thought on everyone's minds as they stared in silent bewilderment at the scene before them.

Everything was gray. In truth, *everything* was a generous word to describe that which lay immediately West of the Looming Mountains. The earth was flat, cracked, and barren of life. Here and there from the ground sprouted the crooked husk of a long-dead tree. But that was all. No civilization and no sound greeted them as they proceeded into the wastes. The sky above was cloudy but not at all textured, just a single endless expanse of monotony. Most surprising of all was the way the Shadow, endlessly churning, did not extend beyond the mountains over the land claimed by their adversaries.

Perplexus retrieved the map from his bag when they reached the bottom of the slope into the valley and handed it to Adiadni. She unrolled it, stared down at it silently for a few moments, and rolled it up again.

"It cannot offer me more information than I already know," she said. "We are given only the approximate location of the marker, about three miles in from the edge of the range. It is, however, difficult to tell our exact location as this side of the mountains is uncharted."

"We're just shy of thirty miles South from our starting point if my estimations are correct," Perplexus offered. "We shouldn't be far."

"The location of the Sword of Fire is said to be cloaked though, yes? Will we be able to easily find it?" questioned Laivar.

"We will," Uriah assured them. "When we are close, the place will make itself known to us."

"The image of the marker on the map appears to be a pair of tall trees intertwining with one another," Adi shared. "I suppose we will just... make our way inland."

"Faith has carried us thus far," spoke Nadarum with a shrug. "What's three more miles?"

"We must still be wary as we move," the princess reminded them. "We are in enemy territory now, and we know not what lies in waiting here."

The companions nodded with an air of somberness and fell into step behind Adiadni as she led them on.

The land beyond the Looming Mountains remained ominously, eerily quiet as they proceeded. The sounds of their boots even as they made contact with the earth were but a whispering crunch. The silence of this place and the stillness of the land around them had the party members on edge in a way they had yet to feel since setting out. When the Free People shared stories and legends of the West, they spoke always in hushed tones as if the unknown enemy might overhear. Such cautious unsettledness felt appropriate now that the travelers were here. Flat land stretching all around them would ordinarily lend them a sense of security for how they would be able to see if they were being approached. But something about this place left each individual fearing that if they were found here, they would be at the mercy of their captors.

An hour had not yet lapsed when Punznes noted the light that appeared to be emanating from Adiadni's sheath. She drew her sword and the party regarded in wonder Emipera's pale, shimmering glow.

"We are not far," the Wizard informed them.

Adi kept Emipera ahead of her as she walked. Subtly, slowly, and then with increasing brilliance, the blade brightened to the point that Uritus grew concerned it would serve as a beacon, alerting their enemies of their presence in the unfriendly territory. As it brightened, the princess's steps became quicker, bolder, and more excited, eventually breaking into a pace that had Oripidus cursing under his breath as he struggled to keep up with the longer strides of his companions.

Before Adiadni had the chance to break into a run, Emipera collided with something solid and invisible, and the princess skidded to a stop.

She raised the blade once, twice, to tap on the tall object that stood in their way, and then lowered it. Stepping forward, she stretched out her hand until it made contact with the object's surface, rough in a way that was intimately familiar to her. She turned her head to look over her shoulder, "Uriah…"

The Wizard had already begun to make his way to her side. He took his staff in both hands and raised it in the air. Adi took several steps back. Briefly, Uriah lowered his head, muttered an incantation under his breath, and then lifted it again. He brought the head of his staff to touch the object, and a rippling effect began from that spot outward, bringing into the light and revealing the pair of twisted old trees shown on the map. The trees—healthy and alive, lush and green—appeared strikingly out of place here. Their boughs swayed and their leaves ruffled despite the lack of a breeze, and the companions found themselves feeling profoundly emotional to see their first glimpse of natural life in days. The depth of this moment and what it represented was not lost on any of them.

The trunks of the trees entwined and grew into one at their midpoints, the branches that crowned them stretching out as a singular canopy. The space beneath where they joined opened just enough for one person to walk underneath. As the wonder of their initial reveal wore off, the companions took note of the way the earth sloped up just behind the trees, creating what they presumed to be a cave just beyond the darkened doorway of the wide trunks.

Adiadni sheathed her sword. With slow reverence, she approached the opening, only to be stopped before she could move beyond the doorway. She frowned and stretched out a palm which met an invisible wall, sending faint blue ripples out from the place her hand touched.

"Uritus."

The party regarded the Adalos as he stepped forward to join his counterpart before the trees.

She looked at him as he arrived at her side, "I believe this is the place where I must pass the burden of leadership to you."

He nodded solemnly, gazing up at the crowns of the trees in humble admiration of their symbolism, feeling as though they were whispering to him. He lowered his gaze, stretched out a hand, and found that it moved through the barrier with ease. "I don't suppose we have the means to make a torch…"

Adi shook her head. "Do you think you could hold a flame if Uriah produced it for you?"

Uritus chuckled softly. "I appreciate your faith in me, but such a skill is yours, not mine."

The Suvah chewed on her lip, and her eyes lit up when a solution became clear in her mind. She reached a hand to her belt, produced the Sword of Light, and held it to the Adalos with open palms.

He gazed down at it in silence, eyes tracing the engraved elvish text that ran down its fuller. Her half of the prophecy. "I know it isn't, but… it feels almost irreverent to take it from you."

She laughed at his seriousness. "Think of it as a loan. You'll have it back to me before you know it."

He nodded once and gripped Emipera's hilt in his left hand. He was surprised upon raising the sword in the air to feel how light it was, this razor-thin wisp of a blade that had slain the most imposing enemy they had come across thus far. He positioned it before him and stepped beyond the doorway of the cave.

He had to crouch a bit as he took the first several steps down into the darkness. Reaching the place where the ground was level again, he moved the Sword of Light from one side of his body to the other, finding the cave to be small and shallow. He ran his eyes along its walls, earth and rock and the occasional root but nothing more. The ceiling was the same. The floor was uniform except for a partially disturbed mound next to the wall opposite him. He approached it slowly and brought himself to crouch down. From outside, he heard the faint caw of a raven.

He reached his hand out and brushed away some of the dry dirt, finding the edge of a piece of cloth just below the surface. It did not take much effort on his part to uncover the object fully, over three feet long and bound in aged fabric. Carefully, the fisherman lifted the parcel from the ground. He turned, hearing the caw a second time, and departed from the cave.

The white light on the other side of the doorway stung his eyes. He found his party there as he had remembered them, their faces brightening when they saw him return. He lowered the Sword of Light and returned it to his counterpart.

"Is that it?"

He dropped his eyes to the bundle in his right hand. "I believe so. There was nothing else there of any—"

A series of loud caws cut Uritus off.

"What's up with him?"

"I don't know," Punznes admitted, stroking the feathers on the bird's chest with one finger. "Qibat, what's the matter? Do you feel unsafe?"

"Not alone."

A sudden heaviness dropped upon them. Each of the travelers felt the air grow noticeably still, thickening as though it wished to choke out the breath from their lungs. Every hair on the back of Adiadni's neck stood on end and the silent moment that lapsed then seemed to linger for an age.

"You should heed his warning. He knows what he's talking about."

The companions whipped around, drawing their weapons at the sound of the voice to find a dark-haired man mounted on a tall black horse. Adiadni sucked in a sharp breath and felt her stomach drop.

"You won't be needing those."

With a casual flick of his wrist, he sent their weapons flying to the left, crashing to the ground with the loudest noise they had heard all day. Uriah retained his hold on his staff, gripping it in his left hand and holding his right out, poised to cast if need required. The clothbound object remained clutched in the hand of the Adalos, paralyzed where he stood at the appearance of this new adversary.

"In truth, I expected a far more fearsome-looking bunch when it came to my attention that there were invaders in Vegard." Cold blue eyes scanned the group and landed on the princess, "You, however, are just as I thought you'd be. Lovely to finally meet you in person, Adiadni."

Adi was hyper-aware of her heartbeat as it raced. This man in his black studded armor, no more than ten years her senior, was far more powerful and intimidating than she had expected him to be. The heavy velvet cape that fell from his back was a clear indicator to the others as to his identity. She clenched the tip of her tongue between her teeth to remind herself that it was wisest not to speak to him at all.

"You, however, are a surprise to me," the man spoke again, shifting his attention to the Adalos. "I have seen much that will come to pass in the approaching days, yet, somehow, you managed to evade my eye. Curious. Even so, it *is* good to see you again, little brother."

"Little br—" Adiadni looked to Uritus as the pieces of the puzzle slid into place, his eyes and mouth wide, his face pale as the dead.

"Did he not tell you about me? Shame. I would've thought my leaving would have left a more searing scar."

The princess frowned as she returned her attention to the man on the horse. "You're Erclidus…"

"Ah, so he did after all. That makes me feel better."

"What do you want?"

Erclidus chuckled at the harshness in Adiadni's voice. "Patience, little bird. We've only just become acquainted with one another."

"Do not prolong our interaction in a feeble attempt to exercise power," the Wizard warned. "We have traveled long and conquered many adversaries to get here."

"So I have heard. And now your aim is… what exactly? Surely, you did not presume you could storm our borders, steal from our land, and return home untouched."

Uriah sighed, his frustration evident. "Erclidus, tell us why you have come."

The man in the black cape sat back a bit and the horse shuffled his hooves. He stared at Uriah for a prolonged moment, eyes narrowing just a touch. "Very well. I have come to relay a message from my mentor, the High Sorcerer Velup, commander of Vegard's armies and… I believe, *your* elder brother, is that correct?"

This piece of new information which shocked the companions nearly drifted right over the fisherman, who at this moment was still feeling dazed and in disbelief. What Uritus had thought at first to be a vision of a ghost was truly his flesh and blood, as real as the last day he'd seen him. This brick in the chest was immediately followed by a second one: the evident truth that this very flesh and this very blood was *here* in the West, the very enemy they had feared all this time. And finally, the third brick—the understanding that the fisherman's mentor was of the same flesh and blood as the man who had lured his brother away from home in the first place. He received this information, compartmentalized it, and shoved it in a crumpled mess to the back of his brain.

"The message?"

"Well, I suppose more of an invitation than a message. I'm to bring you to the Ashen Keep. He wishes to speak with you in person. It's quite generous actually, he's arranged a feast to welcome you to Vegard."

"Hmm," the Wizard grumbled with indignation. "Would I be right to assume that such an invitation does not allow us the freedom to decline?"

Erclidus chuckled. "You would. But come now, you needn't look so glum about it. Surely, it'll be nice to be sheltered from the elements after so long a voyage."

The eyes of several of the travelers darted to the place where their weapons still lay.

"You are welcome to bring those with you, but I would think twice before attempting to wield them."

Perplexus approached the pile first and the others followed suit, each debating with themselves if they felt it worth the personal risk to attempt to fight against this new enemy. To the relief of both the Wizard and the princess, none took the chance.

"Wise," spoke the man in the black cape. "Follow me."

***

The party traveled in a silent row as they allowed Erclidus to lead them to the Ashen Keep. Uriah walked ahead of the others, behind the horse, and Nadarum remained at the end of their line, keeping an eye out as they moved North-and-East. The land around them remained flat, gray, and uninteresting, and when they arrived at their destination, it was immediately clear how it came by its name.

The keep was utterly imposing, surrounded by thick stone walls, gray as fire's footprints. There was only one entrance to the South, a tall iron door that lowered slowly on thick black chains. Beyond the door was a short bridge, beneath the bridge, a deep cavern appeared to carve into the earth for miles. But upon closer observation, the companions came to realize that it was filled with a thick, dark liquid that bubbled and steamed. The other side of the bridge opened up to ground carpeted by familiar dark gravel, and the keep's main structure—a wide square building with a singular tower jutting up from its center—was built of the same ashen stone as the walls.

The building's two front doors, positioned at the top of a wide staircase, towered over them as they approached. The doorframe was tall, curving into a sharp arch like the yawning maw of a sleepy predator. The doors began to open outward as Erclidus stepped down from his saddle. A man in a simple gray uniform took the reins from him and led the horse away around the left corner of the fortress. The companions were unable to catch a glimpse of what lay just behind the massive building, but they heard the distant sounds of what they presumed to be blacksmithing and carpentry tools before the loud and sudden creaking of the gate as it closed behind them.

Erclidus proceeded up the steps, cape shifting behind him as he walked, the spurs of his boots clicking haughtily as he mounted each stair. The group followed him, first Uriah, then Adiadni, the rest moving in a mass together with Uritus at its heart. The interior of the building was predictably dark, a damp chill in the air. They squinted as their eyes adjusted, taking in what little light they could from the dim torches that lined the walls. The entryway where they stood was large and relatively void of decoration. Two hallways opened to the right and left, and at the back of the room was a pair of staircases, one on either side. They abruptly turned toward one another at their midpoints, climbing until they met a landing that overlooked the first floor.

Standing atop the landing was a tall, thin man they presumed to be Velup. He did not look much at all like Uriah despite their relation, save for his height and head of close-cropped white hair. The beard on his face was short and neatly trimmed, and his skin, though brown and weathered like his brother's, appeared far thinner and of a distinctly ashen tone, as though his blood had departed from

309

its surface to feed his body's most vital systems. The robe that cloaked him was also an ashy-gray, of a smoother and finer fabric than the Wizard's, with a hood that draped airily over his head. He did not speak as the newcomers entered and the doors closed behind them.

"Welcome to the Ashen Keep," boomed the voice of the man in the black cape. "I trust you will find your quarters to be adequately prepared in anticipation of your arrival. Before we show you to them, though, there is one pressing matter we must first see to." He turned and his eyes locked with Uritus's as he began to remove his gloves, "I'll take that off your hands if you please."

The companions turned to regard the Adalos and he swallowed, remaining in place. He felt the weight of the bundle in his hand and tightened his hold around it, this thing they had journeyed so far and sacrificed so much to retrieve. Was this it? Had their mission failed? Did he have any choice other than to simply hand it over? They were not in the position to start a fight, and in truth, the fisherman had no desire to. Reluctantly, he stepped forward and set the parcel into his brother's open hands.

"Good choice."

A pair of attendants entered from the darkened hallway on the right, bearing a wooden table which they set in the middle of the room just behind Erclidus. He turned and approached it, gently setting the object down on its surface, and spoke again as he began to free it from its cloth bindings, "I am appreciative that meekness and peacekeeping are amongst the most prized traits of you Easterners. Makes you all the more primed for defeats both great and small."

The last of the cloth fell away to reveal a gorgeous piece of craftsmanship: the Sword of Fire, soft golden light emanating from within its sheath. The Sorcerer's apprentice took it in his hands, feeling its weight, admiring its sheen. He turned, allowing the companions their first glimpse at the treasured weapon. Its sheath was crafted of matte brown leather with gold trim, and its hilt gleamed like sunlight.

"You are even more remarkable than I imagined you," crooned the man to the blade, running a single hand affectionately up the sheath to tighten around its grip. "The world will look fine beneath our boots."

Erclidus drew the sword. Those in the room squinted at its brilliant glow, magnified by the darkness of this place. The stunned silence that captured them lasted for only a moment, interrupted by a sudden cry of pain.

The Sword of Fire crashed to the ground, its sheath along with it, and Erclidus cursed as his right hand flew to grip his left. A bright redness showed clearly on his palm, evidence of his pain, and those closest to him observed what appeared to be smoke emanating from the wound.

"It fucking burns…"

"Only one may bear the Sword of Fire," spoke Laivar, a note of smugness in his voice. "Do you not know your history?"

Frowning, Erclidus brought himself to stand taller, eyes moving from the bard to the Adalos. "Pick it up."

Uritus hesitated for only a moment before stepping forward.

"*Don't* try anything."

Uritus sighed, stooped down to retrieve both the sword and its sheath, and raised himself again. "I have no desire to fight you," he spoke in a calm tone before replacing the weapon in its home.

Erclidus narrowed his eyes at his brother and swiped the sword from his hands. "You will now be shown to your rooms. Feel free to partake of the amenities provided for you, we will summon you in time for the feast."

With that, the man in the black cape turned on his heel and disappeared down one of the darkened halls.

***

Attendants clad in gray uniforms led the companions to their rooms, not even Nadarum and Ilya being permitted to share a chamber.

Uritus paid little mind to the maze of halls he wound through before coming upon his quarters, his mind still buzzing. He retreated into the sanctuary of solitude and shut the door behind him, succumbing to his stomach's sickness shortly thereafter. His temples throbbed and his heart ached. Erclidus was alive, Erclidus was their enemy. He had hardly a moment to attempt to process what he now knew before he was interrupted by a rapping on the door.

It creaked, pushing open without invitation. "Your presence is requested in the master's chambers."

Uritus sighed and followed the gray figure which led him once more through the maze. He did not consider until after he had been ushered into the new room exactly which *master* had summoned him here. He didn't know which of the two adversaries he would prefer to see at the moment. The list of questions he wished to confront his brother with was a mile long and ever-growing. But every answer he received would surely lead him only further to the realization that Erclidus was not the person he once knew. The fisherman clenched his hands into fists and looked around the room.

It was actually a series of connected ones, dark and cold but otherwise entirely different from the rest of the keep they had seen thus far. Layers of carpets and draperies in dark, muted shades of green, burgundy, and violet lent an air of originality to the space. The chamber he stood in appeared to be a lounge of sorts, separated from a study area by a single step that elevated the desk and bookshelves. Through the open door at the study's far end, Uritus spied the foot of a bed, and to the left was another door, fully closed. Torches lent light to the room as they did elsewhere in the house, and in every corner were stacks of books and piles of scrolls which made the space appear elegantly cluttered.

Uritus noticed movement just beyond the study door and his expression turned stern as his brother emerged from it. "Why?"

Erclidus halted, clearly taken aback by Uritus's direct tone. "Why…?"

"Why any of this?" the younger man questioned angrily. "Why all of it?"

"Let's settle in for a moment before we start clawing for answers, yes?" Erclidus strolled to a table in the lounge portion of the room and gestured to a tray atop it. "Tea?"

"I'll refrain."

"Suit yourself."

The dark-haired one took his time preparing himself a cup and Uritus regarded him with what he realized to be a growing rage. He didn't know this version of his brother at all. He walked with pride, moved with arrogance, spoke with a sickening self-assurance that made clear his opinion that he was far above all those he addressed. Uritus resented him for the way he looked like a twisted shade of their father.

"Now," spoke Erclidus as he settled down on a sofa. He propped his boots on a pair of thick cushions, sharp spurs hanging over their edge. "It's been, what? Nearly ten years?"

"Twelve."

"Right, of course." The man in the black cape lifted his cup to his lips with painstaking composure and took a drink. "How have you been, little brother?"

Uritus released a burst of incredulous laughter. "How have I been? I thought you were dead!"

"Whyever would you think that?" The older man did not move from his reclined position. "You saw me leave with your own eyes, in good health, of my own accord."

Uritus blinked in astonishment at his brother's relaxed manner. "You left home," he spoke slowly to ensure his message was clear, "...as a teenager, with a man who had successfully manipulated you. As far as Father and I knew, he was a trickster and a fraud. We thought for sure he'd sell you to bandits... That that would have been the kindest of fates for you."

Erclidus breathed out through his nose—an almost laugh—and leaned forward, setting his cup on the table beside him. He brought his feet to the floor, arms to rest on his knees, fingertips to touch one another. "So... you are telling me that over a decade has passed since I departed with Velup, and never once did you consider that I was telling the truth about who he was?"

The Adalos paused, sorrow stinging his chest. "Had he been who he said he was... I could have never comprehended a world in which the boy I knew would have desired to go with him."

The elder Subian frowned. "I am not the boy you knew."

"Oh, that is abundantly clear." Uritus clenched his fists and released them with a sigh. "I just want to know why you left. What did he say to you that was so convincing that you would abandon your family to follow him?"

"Is that truly such a mystery to you?" Erclidus paused. "You lived through the same years as I. You saw the lack, you learned the smell of death. You became proficient in building fire by assembling the pyres of your dead siblings. You knew the same horror, felt the same grief. He didn't need to say anything. He didn't need to manipulate me. He offered me a way out. I took it. Plain as that."

Tears gathered in the eyes of the younger man. His brother was right, they *had* felt the same pain, and Erclidus's admission that he was well aware of that fact and yet had abandoned them anyway stung the fisherman all the more.

"I waited for you, you know. Every night, Divine be damned, when the sun started to go down, I turned my gaze South and I *looked* for you."

"Waited?" Erclidus let the word hang in the air. "Why'd you stop?"

Uritus frowned and then his expression softened. "You don't know, do you?"

The man in the black cape did not respond, but a glimmer of emotion showed on his face even so.

"Father died," Uritus said plainly, resentment burning a hole in his chest. "Two years after you left. His heart grew tired."

Still, his brother said nothing.

"I left after that."

Erclidus paused, blinked, cleared his throat, and then straightened himself where he sat. "It was only a matter of time," he said. "That was always the problem. We had no control over anything there. We were boys, watching the sand of our lives slip away through our fingertips. I don't have to be afraid of loss anymore. I built something better for myself."

"*You* built it?"

The man in black ignored this question. "If you are honest with yourself, you will no doubt admit that you would also not return to the life you once lived. Why would you trade the freedoms you have now for squalor?"

"I did go back," the fisherman replied flatly. "About a week ago. There's nothing left."

"Of course not. The drought would have seen to that by now."

Uritus frowned, bothered by the manner in which his brother said this. "Did… Velup have anything to do with the drought?"

"Suppose he did. Does it matter at this point?"

The Adalos frowned again, more confused than he had been before. "Did you know that when you went with him?"

"Of course not. I wouldn't have understood."

"*I* don't understand…"

Erclidus shook his head, rose, retrieved his cup from the table, and began to pace the length of the room. "Just as the Easterners have known for centuries that there would one day come another war, so have those in Vegard. We have access to the same *source*, as you call it. We can divine things just the same." With one hand, he loudly snapped, a bright orange flame springing to attention on his index finger. He touched it to the bottom of his cup, holding it there as he paced. "The man who works the land looks to the coming seasons to determine his steps. What does a diligent farmer do to make ready for the harvest?"

Erclidus paused, extinguishing the light on his finger as his cup had begun to steam. It took Uritus several seconds of silence to realize that his brother expected him to answer. He refrained from rolling his eyes as he indulged him, shrugging, "He… sows his seeds?"

"A critical step, yes, but first he must *till the land*. Prime his enemies, weaken them so they more readily accept their defeat. The drought was only part of the plan, our family members merely casualties."

Uritus felt a breath catch in his throat, fighting against asking what he knew he must. "The plague too?"

Erclidus gave a single nod and Uritus broke down in tears. The older man regarded his brother, silently sipping his tea.

Uritus looked at him with bleary eyes, "Is that all it is then? Power of control over your own life and… the destruction of others?"

The man in the cape shook his head. "On the contrary. Not merely destruction of life… *Creation* of it."

The fisherman blinked. "The Dagamor was birthed centuries before you were. You had nothing to do with—"

"No, that one I owe to my predecessors, of course. My creations walk amongst my armies as we speak."

Uritus laughed. "You expect me to believe the ancient Sorcerers charged *you* with creating their hordes of goblins?"

"Not at first, of course. It took time to hone my skills. Life is a delicate balance. I had to prove I was capable of creating the right one."

The younger man frowned, still not understanding. "So… your initial half-life creations are… lying dead in a pit somewhere? Wandering this wasteland with no purpose or aim?"

Erclidus chuckled and the room darkened for a moment. "No. They're a bit closer to home than that."

Uritus felt his heart pick up its pace as the final pieces clicked together in his mind. "The entroleps…"

"If that's what you call the swamp beasts, then yes. Though, not all of them. The first few were Velup's."

The Adalos swallowed, his mouth dry, his head dizzy. "And Yider…"

Erclidus lifted his eyes to the ceiling as though he was trying to recall. "Yes, I think that sounds right."

Uritus sighed, exhausted, and then pulled open the collar of his shirt to reveal the scars on his chest. "He nearly killed me."

For once, the older man did seem taken aback. But as his eyes moved across the curved markings on his brother's skin, they landed on the shining thing that hung around his neck. "Huh. So he did end up giving that to you. You were always his favorite, I guess. Explains why I couldn't see you though."

Uritus looked down and gripped the amonii in his hand. "What do you—"

"That's enough questions for now, I think, yes?" Erclidus turned and waved his free hand vaguely in the direction of the door, prompting it to open. He ascended the step to the study level and turned once more to look his brother in the eye. "I'll see you at dinner."

Uritus hesitated, half of him wishing to storm off, the other, to run to his brother and shake him awake. "It doesn't have to be like this..." he spoke, taking a gentle step forward.

The man in the cape shook his head. "It's too late for that now."

That wasn't true. Uritus couldn't allow it to be true. Nevertheless, he turned, sorrowfully departing from the room, not turning around as he heard the door close behind him.

Chapter Twenty-One

"Reconnaissance"

The 23rd of July

Laivar sprang to his feet immediately upon hearing three urgent knocks from the other side of his chamber door. His eyes moved around the room, spotting his bow and knife which he had left beside the doorframe. He cursed at himself for having set them in such an inconvenient spot. At the foot of the bed was his lute, and he snatched it up without thinking as the door pushed open. His entire body tensed. He gripped the instrument's neck and raised it over his head, poised to strike, when around the edge of the door poked a familiar head of short blonde hair.

"Blessed Source, Mik, I thought I was meeting my end."

"What the shit were you planning to do with that?"

The bard felt suddenly silly as he lowered the lute to his bed. "One of these days, my quick thinking is going to get you out of a scrap and when it does, you'll rue the day you mocked me for it."

"You were actually prepared to sacrifice Melodia to save your ass. Your lover for your life!"

Laivar straightened himself, tugging on the bottom edge of his vest to smooth it out and then brushing imaginary dust from his sleeves. "Fate willing, I'll be granted far more lovers before my time is up. If Fate feels so inclined, each of them broader-shouldered and more virile than the next. But until I have a devoted collection of burly men to do my bidding, the charge of my protection is in my own hands, and, at least for now, I only get one life. Besides, she'd sacrifice me too, were she sentient."

The raspy whisper of the dwarf met the poet's ears from beyond the door, "All right now, Mik, that's enough of the jibber-jabber."

"Right." Mikka looked again at Laivar and nodded her head toward the hall. "Come on then. We're going searching."

"For what, exactly?"

The former soldier shrugged. "The sword, enemy secrets, military information, anything we can find. Our leaders will understandably be occupied with their own personal affairs, but while we're in the belly of the beast, we must use our time. You in or out?"

"The others?"

"Splitting off separately. We'll cover more ground that way. Come on!"

Without another word, Laivar hastened to join them, pausing briefly at the door and snatching up his knife before they carried on their way.

***

It had been nearly a week since the princess had had the luxury of a bath but she was unable to lose herself in the ritual the way she ordinarily would. The knowledge that two of the people she trusted most had—each of them—a secret, powerful brother with unclear yet undoubtedly twisted motivations made her dizzy if she tried to comprehend it. She could understand, to some degree, Uriah's reasoning for withholding such information. He had built a reputation for himself over hundreds of years as one who was private with his personal life and who refrained from sharing his multitudinous library of knowledge unless it was explicitly relevant.

Uritus, on the other hand, had been intimately honest with her about the events of his past, or at least, so she had thought. He had led her to believe that his entire family had died, that he was the last that remained of the Subian line. Of course, he hadn't said that to her specifically, but it had certainly been implied. She shook her head. She didn't want to be angry with him. In truth, the only thing she did want at this moment was to *be with* him, to figure their way out of this situation together. She finished combing out her hair and moved to the bed.

Elegantly draped upon it was an exquisite maroon gown. A gift from her hosts, she could only assume. She had no desire to indulge them. If anything, she wished to rebel against their facade of welcoming to make it abundantly clear how she felt about being kept here. But even so, now freshly clean, she looked over at her traveler's uniform, stained with dirt and blood, at the trousers which didn't even fit her properly, and, with a tired sigh, moved to don the gown.

Its fabric, though lovely, shimmering as it moved in the dim light, irritated her skin. She regarded herself in the looking glass and was startled to realize that she did not recognize the woman who returned her gaze. It wasn't that she looked all that different, though the scrapes and bruises dappled across her skin did provide her an air of ruggedness that she found herself to be quite fond of. This gown was not tailored in the same manner as those she sported in Suscundos. The skirt was fuller, the embroidery intricate and flashy, and—the most notable difference of all—both sleeves traveled all the way up from her wrists to cover her shoulders. Her birthmark peeked out still from the edge of the square neckline, but she determined it was not its hiddenness that was making her feel not quite like herself.

Her curls slowly tightened as her hair began to dry, and had she brought her tiara along after they had departed from the White Mountains, she would have retrieved it and set it upon her head to determine if that was the thing that was missing, though she still did not suspect that to be the case. She frowned at herself, and then all at once determined the dress itself to be the problem. There was no issue with the way it looked—it was undoubtedly a masterfully crafted garment. But the longer it clung to her body, the more she realized how truly

317

heavy it was, as though it had been fashioned specifically to bind her, to make it difficult for her to run away.

Adiadni suddenly felt herself growing very hot, and she hastened to the dressing screen, desperate to peel the fabric off her skin, but was interrupted before she could make it there. She froze at the sound of the knocking, watching fearfully as the door pushed open, and then letting out a tiny sigh as the attendant just behind it revealed themself.

"Your presence is requested in the library."

"Of course it is," the princess muttered under her breath.

"Pardon?"

"Oh, um… might I know who it is that wishes to see me there?"

"The master."

"Right." Adi hesitated, one hand tugging at the other. "I don't suppose I might be allowed a moment to change first?"

"There's no need. You look lovely."

She nodded, forcing a grateful smile, and then reluctantly gathered her skirts and followed them into the darkened hall.

***

"I swear on all I hold dear, Lad, let out one more nervous yelp and I'll silence ye myself."

Laivar had startled at the sound of a pair of heavy books being knocked from their shelf and thudding to the floor. "This place makes my bones want to clamber out of my skin," spoke the bard with a shudder.

"Mik, nearly all of these cabinets are locked, I don't think we're goin' to find much of any value here."

Mikka sighed frustratedly down at a useless stack of papers, her hands resting on the edge of a large desk. "We keep looking then. We didn't come all this way to—"

She stopped speaking abruptly. All three spies froze as the door to the study they rifled through suddenly opened.

An attendant stepped into the room, a woman with long dark hair and tired brown eyes who also came to a sudden, surprised halt. "I… do not think you are supposed to be here…"

"Oh! Um…" Mikka recognized this attendant. She had led half of the companions away to their chambers, winding down halls and dropping them off one by one. It had been dark, but she was certain this was her. The former soldier knew at this moment that their lives were at risk just as much as their mission was and so, quick on her feet as always, she slid around the desk and started to talk, "Sorry, we seem to have misplaced something of ours. We were just trying to find it again."

318

The woman in the doorway narrowed her eyes slightly. "Find... what exactly?"

Mikka chewed on her cheek, her mind running nearly too fast for her to keep up. "You... showed us to our rooms earlier, right? You look familiar to me." She took a quick step toward the attendant and extended her hand in a greeting, withdrawing slightly upon seeing her start. She softened her demeanor, setting her hand gently against her sternum. "My name is Mikka Galinzen. What's yours?"

The woman looked her up and down, clearly attempting to determine whether she might be dangerous. "I am called Alidistris," she finally said, and Mikka responded with a nod and a warm smile. Alidistris's dark eyes shifted to the elf and the dwarf, still standing awkwardly on one side of the room.

"Uh, I'm... Laivar Lethiel," the poet offered nervously.

The blacksmith sighed. "And *I* am Oripidus Vengar."

Alidistris nodded, clearly feeling more at ease though she kept her hand still on the partially closed door. "We've never had Easterners here before..." she said tentatively.

"We are honored to be the first then."

A silence hung in the air between them and Alidistris turned her head to gaze nervously down the hall. "I do mean it when I say you shouldn't be in here. I could get in trouble if I don't ask you to leave..."

Mikka furrowed her brow. "Will they hurt you?"

The attendant met her eyes, a pained expression on her face, but said nothing.

"We wouldn't want that to happen," Mikka said, watching Alidistris noticeably relax. "We have no quarrel with you. In truth, we believe your superiors are hatching a plan to wreak destruction upon our people and our land."

"Mik..."

She went on despite Oripidus's warning, "I'd be willing to wager that they have already been unkind to their own..."

Alidistris drew in a tired breath and nodded ever so slightly.

Mikka paused as she considered how to proceed. "We believe that we and our leaders, with the support of our people, might be able to stop them. At the very least, we will try. If we succeed, we will ensure the continued freedom of said people, and perhaps... of yours as well."

The former soldier's companions looked at her with bated breath.

"What I am trying to say is... we fight not only for our own gain but for yours as well. I do not wish to be the reason that you get in trouble, so whatever you choose to do next, I will understand. But know that if you would ask it, neither myself nor my company would deny you our protection. Freedom is not freedom if it is enjoyed only by the victors."

The time of silence that passed then as Alidistris considered Mikka's words held the breath of the three spies for ransom. The attendant looked again down the hall, and before the companions could consider what was happening, she stepped fully into the room and shut the door behind her.

"If you *can* end Velup's reign… it will be for the better. I have duties I must attend to… but as far as I am concerned, I did not find you here."

The trio collapsed into the arms of their relief.

"But you won't find anything of value in here," she continued, and Oripidus huffed proudly to find that he had been right about that. "You'll have more luck in Octrusial's quarters, just through there." She nodded her head to her left, a wall with a pair of bookshelves framing a large, eerie painting—a detailed, close-up image of a human eye.

Laivar approached the wall and found that the panel sporting the eye was easily pushed open to reveal a hidden chamber. Oripidus hastened after him.

Mikka looked to Alidistris with grateful eyes, "Thank you. Truly. We will not forget you."

Alidistris responded with a smile and a nod and the companions disappeared into the new room.

***

Adiadni did not hear her summoner enter the library. She had not been waiting there for very long, but it had been long enough that, in her state of heightened anxiousness, she had begun to wonder if perhaps she was there by mistake. Tired of pacing this same short path across the thin rug, she had taken to scanning the perimeter of the room, her eyes running over the myriad volumes stacked high on the shelves.

There were thousands of them, towering so far above her that she was baffled by how they were reached until she remembered that in this place dwelt at least two who were capable of manipulating objects. She craned her neck, feeling lightheaded as she tried to see the place where the shelves met the ceiling. She found it impossible under the weight of the Shadow that pressed down upon her.

"That color suits you."

Adi spun around, startled by the voice, bumping the edge of a table as she turned and momentarily losing her balance.

"Forgive me, I didn't mean to frighten you."

The princess narrowed her eyes at the man in black, caught off guard by how he appeared before her sans cape. His armor, too, was gone. Plating his body now was a simpler ensemble, black trousers and shirt with an embroidered black coat atop it, its patterning only visible when the dark, silken thread caught the dim light. She had to lift her head to look at him as he stood above the sunken space in the center of the room where she had awaited his arrival. Gently, she formed her hands into fists, realizing she felt suddenly vulnerable.

"I mean it though," he went on. "The red is incredibly flattering. It makes you look powerful."

320

"I don't really care for it."

"The color? Or the gown itself?"

"Does it matter?"

Erclidus chuckled. She was clearly irritated and at this moment did not care for the rigidity of niceties. "I suppose not. Looking at you now though, I must say, I do wish I had thought to provide you with a crown as well. I'll remember that for next time."

Next time...

"This will help for now."

Gently, he lifted his right hand and twirled it in the air, an elegant, lazy motion. Adiadni stiffened, bracing herself for some sort of strike. None came.

Instead, the princess noticed herself begin to feel suddenly... *different.* Lighter, warmer. It took only a moment for her to discern that her hair was now fully dry, and she ran a hand through it to confirm that it was so. One corner of her summoner's mouth lifted slightly, clearly pleased to have surprised her. She lowered her hand again and narrowed her eyes at him.

"Why did you call me here, Erclidus?"

He lingered where he stood beside the library's closed doors, one hand holding his other comfortably behind his back. Slowly, he began to walk forward, heavy heels and clicking spurs echoing up into the cold air. He descended one cool step at a time into the sunken area. To her relief, he did not approach her, instead lingering beside a table on the opposite end of the space from where she stood and setting his right hand calmly upon it. Dim light danced over the surface of a silver ring that encircled his index finger—it and the spurs the sole details of his ensemble that were not black.

"I can only assume that you have many questions. I would like to offer you the opportunity to pose them."

Adi frowned, unsure of his motivations. She wished to observe this trap, circle it, understand it before she attempted to dismantle it. But all the while, her curiosity tugged gently at her wrist, urging her to move in just a little closer to get a better look.

"How did you know we were coming?"

He smiled slightly and it startled her then just how much he looked like his brother. "All right, straight to the point." He did not turn to face her, rather keeping himself oriented toward the wall opposite the doors. "We've kept an eye on you over the years. Checked in on your progress, saw you ready yourself for your journey. When you slayed our watchdog, we knew the time had finally come."

Adiadni maintained her composure despite feeling physically sick. "We?"

Erclidus looked over his left shoulder to regard her, "Myself, and my comrades."

The princess shook her head, trying to sort her thoughts. "Are you a Seer?"

"That is not my specialty, no. That would be Octrusial." He tapped his fingers on the table and then moved his body to face her, bringing himself to rest against the back of the sofa beside it. "My turn." He paused for an uncomfortable length of time, studying her. "Have you dreamt of me as I have of you?"

Adi dipped her head over one shoulder with a slight frown. She had assumed up until this point that he had been the one who had sent the dreams. "How is it that you have dreamt of me?"

Erclidus chuckled. "Vaguely but nightly for many years."

"Did you know who I was?"

"Not at first. Eventually, I would come to recognize that pretty little marking on your arm and deduce your identity from that."

"When was that?"

"Seven years ago. But you're attempting to skirt my question."

She wasn't. But her search for information urged her onward still. "I have dreamt of you, yes."

That haunting smile moved across his face again. He made no attempt to stifle it. "What happened in your dreams?"

She shuddered internally as she remembered the way they made her feel. "Nothing of import."

He nodded, clearly not believing this but electing not to question her further. The ease with which he allowed silence to claim the space between them had Adiadni constantly reminding herself not to squirm in her discomfort.

"Have you any other questions?"

She felt she had a thousand. "You obviously have some sort of intention in bringing me here beyond just sating my curiosity, so what say we put this little game to bed and get to that, yes?"

His head lolled to the side and his cold, persistent gaze made her shiver. "Is it so unbelievable that I might just want to talk to you?"

"Do you spend time socializing with all those you keep captive?"

"You are not my captive." He stood up straight, shaking his head seriously. "None of you are. You are free to leave whenever you please."

"So if I left out that door right now, you would let me go?"

"I would."

"But…?"

He exhaled an amused laugh and shrugged. "But… I'd rather you didn't."

"Why?"

He stared at her intently with a sigh and a smile and a small shake of his head. "I am someone who values looking to the future. You are the beacon of it back in the place you call home. The sacred symbol, the shining star of freedom and hope… Is that correct?"

The princess did not respond.

He lingered in the pause for a moment. Then, setting his hands behind his back again, he began to cross the length of the sunken space. "When I first came here, I wasn't sure what to expect. Beyond gaining control over my fate, I did not have many ambitions. I wished only to learn as much as I could from the man who had offered me refuge from the place I had grown up. But the more I learned..."

A snap and then a flash of hot flame.

"...The more I realized that sorcery came quite naturally to me. My talent grew, as did my predecessor's trust in me. He had given me the most valuable of gifts: power over my destiny... and so much more." Gently, he touched his index finger to his middle, his middle to his fourth, passing the flame from one fingertip to another down his hand and back again. "I can be whoever I wish to, do whatever I choose, and once the land East of the mountains is ours again, I intend to."

Adiadni swallowed as he paused his stroll just before her, holding out his right hand and moving the flame to burn hot in his palm.

"But before that day comes... there is more work to be done." He closed his hand into a fist and the flame extinguished. "There will be waste and want and great sacrifice. I am most sure that such grueling times will ultimately be well worth it; nevertheless, I seek always to carve the most efficient path forward that I can. And as I have continued on my way, I have found you in the middle of it."

He paused, allowing the Suvah the opportunity to speak if she wished. She did not.

He continued, "You have turned out to be exactly who your people believe you to be. Powerful. Bright. Successful... for the most part. I would certainly have regretted it if I allowed you to pass through my land without at least stealing a conversation with you. We might be able to help each other, you and I."

Adiadni let out a sound, a surprised laugh of sorts. "Do you mean to propose an allyship?"

"Think of it more as... a partnership."

His eyes moved over her leisurely and she clenched her jaw. Their blue was intimately familiar to her, but at this moment, the deep, inky shade made her feel cold, bare, utterly exposed. *Seen* in a way almost no one had seen her, in a way that made her feel defenseless, made her feel sick. She shook her head. "Why me? Why not anyone else... Why not Uritus?"

He sighed and made his way to an armchair situated to her right. "My brother is... deeply principled in a way that can be blinding."

"You do not think me principled?"

"I think you are smart." He reached the armchair and turned again to face her, resting his left hand on its back. "And what's more, I think you will do whatever it takes to save the lives of your people."

She paused, fully aware now that the trap had ensnared her. "What would you ask of me?"

He regarded her silently for several moments. "Fate has bound us to one another, Adiadni. Whether we understand it or not, for some purpose, we have found ourselves here, powerful forces beyond comprehension. Now, we have the option to choose: will our collision be one of destruction or will it be one of rebirth?"

The princess narrowed her eyes at him. "Even if there existed a world in which I would ever consider tying myself to you, I cannot imagine why I would ever trust you. You clearly make your decisions based upon what will yield the greatest outcome for yourself."

"On the contrary. This is about you just as much as it is about me." He softened his gaze and took several slow steps toward her. "I am merely trying to offer you the same thing Velup gave me—a way out."

Adi crossed her arms tightly over her chest as he arrived before her. She studied his face, the warmth he wore on it, her instincts of self-preservation making her incapable of believing that he might be genuine. She raised her head proudly, "I will fight, I will bleed, and I will die for and alongside the Free People. There is nothing you could offer me that could cause me to waver on that position. *That* is the destiny that *I* will control."

Erclidus nodded. "You say that now. But watch—the coming days will not be kind to your citizens or your land. We have the sword now, thanks to your excellent tracking—"

"The sword that you cannot wield?"

He narrowed his eyes slightly and brought himself to stand a bit taller. "Whether by your willing surrender to me or by force, I *will* have what is rightfully mine."

Adiadni laughed and clapped at him mockingly. "A stunning proposal. And an exquisite show of character. Were you truly trying to win my affection, you would call your armies to refrain from storming my borders."

"Were I truly trying to win your affection, I would have brought you a ring. But it would appear that someone has already done that." He took her left hand forcefully in his and pulled it closer to regard the symbol of her engagement. "Your beloved has garish taste."

She ripped her hand away from him, insulted despite how she hated the ring herself.

"I expected you to react this way," he spoke casually of her defiance. "Why wouldn't you? You have been made to believe your whole life that we are the villains. Were you to accept my hand right away, I would question your loyalty. I encourage you to take some time to consider it. I think you will find entering into this partnership and ultimately ruling this land together to be the best option for all parties involved."

He took a step closer to her, towering over her. She stood her ground, shaking her head at him once more. "Is that a threat?"

"Rather… a push in the right direction."

The cool arrogance that cloaked him made the Suvah's blood boil. "You say that you wish to offer me a choice, yet if I do not choose as you would wish, you will murder my citizens and burn my land. That is no bargain. You mean to back me into a corner because I have something you need."

Adi saw the muscles in his jaw clench as he attempted to quell his irritation with her. "Well, as I said before, you are in my way."

"What then could *I* possibly have to gain from submitting to your will?"

"The knowledge that you did everything in your power to save the people you love, of course."

The princess frowned but did not respond.

"You see Adiadni, you and I are not so different. Both of us look at the land to the East and see the brimming potential, the radiant future that could blossom there under the right guidance. You are beloved by your citizens. You have influence and knowledge of the avenues that you must take to maintain said influence. But you do not truly have control over the gifts that you have been given. No one has shown you how to access the depths of your power. That is a well that runs deeper than you can imagine. But the same is not true of me. I can help you. With my strength and your authority, we can usher in a new age unlike any this world has ever seen. You need me just as I need you. After all, what purpose does the Light even have without darkness to magnify it?"

Every pulse of Adiadni's heart beat violently against her ribcage as if it wished to be freed. The icy gaze of the man in black was firm and not actively threatening, yet the princess arrived at the sudden realization that if in the next moment, he *lost* that control over his power that he so prided himself on, no one would be the wiser. She knew she had to tread carefully as she proceeded onward.

She spoke slowly, "You and your superiors—"

"My *peers*."

She paused, evidently having struck a nerve. "You… wish to bring an age of Shadow into the Free World. Why would the Shadow ever wish to meet the Light?"

For the first time in a long time, Erclidus moved his eyes away from her. They traveled slowly up the length of the wall behind her and the princess felt a shiver run up her spine. The air grew deafeningly quiet, eerily still, just as it had when the man in the black cape had first come upon them. She looked around his shoulder to the torch on the wall behind him and sucked in a quiet breath as she realized its flame was shrinking. She turned to one side, then the other, seeing that all the torches were doing the same, and then she looked up. And as the air around her grew ever colder, the darkness began to descend.

Adiadni's breath became shallow and uneven. The torches extinguished fully and the princess felt she would grow mad in the darkness and silence that followed. It lingered for so long that she wished to cry out to him, to beg him to free her from this torment, but in her fear, she remained paralyzed.

A hot orange flame suddenly sprang to life in the palm of the man before her. She released her breath in her relief for the light and the warmth.

"In the dark... beneath the Shadow... *everyone* looks to the one who holds the Light."

Adiadni's lips parted as a single tear slipped down her cheek. Her feeling of fear rapidly turned to rage. Her jaw clenched, her expression hardened, her hands formed into fists. With a burst of vibrant energy, she opened her hands and moved them out to her sides and the torches became engulfed in bright white light.

"Huh." Erclidus looked around them with a surprised smile and allowed the flame in his palm to die out. "That's quite good." He looked at her then and his expression turned sinister as he shook his head calmly back and forth. "Perhaps your anger is the key to unlocking your potential."

Adiadni let out a strained noise and then the white fires choked out and she was plunged again into darkness.

To her relief, Erclidus did not make her linger in it any longer and raised his right hand so the dim flames grew once more upon the torches, silently shaking his head at her. "There is so much that I could teach you."

The princess frowned as she stared up at him. "Do you want to know what I think of you, Erclidus?" He did not answer, but she was certain all the same that he did. "I think that you are ambitious. And calculating. And I believe you to be someone who is ruthless in pursuit of your aims. That is a trait that I will admit we do share—our devotion to our chosen paths. But that is the place where our similarities end. And while you are undoubtedly clever, you are a *fucking fool* if you think that you may come before me, threaten me, threaten my people and the place I call home, and suggest that I submit to your will so that those people might maintain some hollow semblance of their freedom."

Erclidus hardened his expression and brought himself to stand taller.

"I've dealt with men like you before. Divine willing, once this is all over, I'll never have to again. But hear me clearly when I say that I would sooner *die*, right here and now in this library at your hand, than ever sacrifice the freedoms of those I love so that I might be spared."

His expression turned to one of rage. "I will have what is mine, Adiadni. Whether you give it to me, or whether I have to burn our homeland to the ground, I will *take* what is mine."

He reached his left hand out abruptly and grabbed her arm.

She let out a shriek, alarmed by the pain of his grip. Instantaneously, bright white sparks flashed around the place he had grabbed her, and he released her with a pained gasp.

He looked down at his hand, a red mark still streaking its way across his palm. "I don't think I've ever seen that before."

He looked at her with an intent that made her feel internally cold all over again. With force, he reached out his hand and gripped the lower half of her face. "Do it again."

Adiadni froze in her fear, but before she could react, one of the library's doors abruptly pushed open. Erclidus released her and turned and the princess's body relaxed upon seeing Perplexus and Punznes enter the room, Qibat with them.

The man in black was visibly irritated. "I don't recall hearing a knock."

"I *do* recall hearing a scream," responded the navigator, turning his eyes to Adiadni. "Are you all right?"

Adi did not respond with words but rather gathered her skirts and hurried up the steps of the sunken area and out of the library.

Perplexus returned his gaze to Erclidus and narrowed his eyes, "I would think twice before laying a hand on her again."

The blue-eyed man chuckled. "The whining of the dog means nothing to the boot."

The navigator felt a wave of heat move over his body. "The boot underestimates the pack."

"You've a quick tongue for a man with no more than a knife and a temper."

"You've got a hot head for someone who's no more than a Sorcerer's apprentice."

"Lex, rein it in."

"Rein it in."

The subtle note of distress in the physician's voice, echoed by the raven, was enough to cause Perplexus to take a breath and step back toward the door.

"And so cowers the dog."

Perplexus turned and departed from the library with Punznes.

***

In a windowless tower high above the Ashen Keep, Uriah stood in silence on a bare stone floor across from his brother. Velup's countenance, pallid and stern, remained unchanging as he looked the Wizard over from head to toe. Uriah maintained his silence in his anticipation for the Sorcerer to speak.

After several minutes, he finally did, "I suppose this would ordinarily be the moment that I welcome you to Vegard, but it would be dishonest of me to lead you to believe that you are welcome here."

"I am pleased that you have found the value in integrity since last we met."

Velup narrowed his eyes and shook his head, chuckling darkly. "There are many things about me that have changed since then."

This was true to some degree. The years that had lapsed following the final clash of the two brothers had clearly worn the older man down. Velup kept himself standing tall and proud despite his spine's natural proclivity to hunch. His hands were bony and claw-like, jagged yellow fingernails sprouting from the end of each finger, a thin silver band encircling one of them. The cloak that hung from his thin frame glistened in the rare moments that it caught the dim torchlight. Uriah suspected that its looseness had little to do with a preference of personal style.

"It would appear as well that just as many things have, unfortunately, remained the same."

The Sorcerer cleared his throat. "It has come to my attention that king Agamemnon wishes to declare war on Vegard."

Uriah frowned. "The king wishes no such thing. There are none in the Free World who would desire to return to the violence of the ages past."

"That is interesting to hear. One would think his actions would align with so serious a stance. To send a troop of soldiers led by his heir to invade our borders would certainly imply aggressive intent."

"Do not attempt to rewrite the events as they have occurred, Brother. The goblins we clashed with in Tuvibati Canyon did not wander there of their own accord."

"That is fair enough. Though in my defense, I did not send them there to attack you."

"Merely to kidnap our party members so that you might torture them for information?"

"Yes. Merely that."

The Wizard sighed. The past five-hundred-some years of peace had allowed him to shut the memory of Velup away as if into a locked cupboard. The war had played out and reached its end, and the scant few of Arkenn's enemies who remained had retreated beyond the safety of the Looming Mountains. In the chaos and subsequent celebration, the rebuilding of the land now called the Free World, and the forging of the sacred weapons and the prophecy, Uriah had no way to be certain if his brother was dead or alive. Even so, from the dusty cupboard would occasionally echo the faintest of persistent tapping. When Erclidus had stated the name of the ghost he had once known, the Wizard found that he was not, after all, wracked with any truly crippling sense of surprise.

"I understand that you are privy to biding your time, but at this moment, I have precious little. Why have you sent for me?"

Velup chuckled again before falling into a brief fit of laborious coughing. He tucked a kerchief into his sleeve and brought himself again to stand at his full height. "In truth, I was pleased to learn that it was you who was accompanying the girl here. I would have found and taken the sword anyway, but with you here, I may more efficiently deliver a message, both to you and the king."

"What is your message?"

Velup cleared his throat again. "Surrender."

"Hah!"

The loud burst of laughter emitted by the Wizard took the Sorcerer by surprise. He furrowed his brow. "I am quite serious."

"The audacity of the self-obsessed will never cease to astonish me."

"*You* are but a—" Velup's sudden fit of rage was forced to submit to the hacking of his lungs a second time. Uriah's eyes narrowed at him as he straightened once more, pausing before he spoke again, "Of those who live in the East, you are one of the only ones remaining who knows the horrors of war."

Uriah frowned, his fingers tightening their grip on his staff ever so slightly.

"I remember what it did to you. You were wrought with your grief. Your people suffered needlessly—"

"The people's pursuit of freedom from the oppressor is *never* needless."

Velup hardened his expression. "Nevertheless, the land which was stolen from my predecessor will again bend to the will of the West. I and my allies have had centuries to build our strength, to grow our numbers and our power. Your feeble minds cannot even comprehend the weight of that which is coming. Of course, you will not go willingly. You will rouse your masses and fortify your cities and face us with hope and nobility in your hearts, but it will all be for naught. Your people will suffer—again—and this entire land from Vegard to the Emerald Sea will be wrought in Shadow once more."

Uriah remained calm in the silent moment that lapsed then, and Velup stifled a small cough as the Wizard looked him over. Uriah felt sad for his brother. All the years he had spent here stewing in his anger had turned him into a hollow wisp of a man, no joy in his life, no feeling in his heart. Like a parasite, leeching off Source energy for centuries until the only thing keeping his rotting corpse alive was his will to conquer others beneath his boot.

The Wizard raised his head. "Perhaps. Or perhaps you have underestimated what you are up against."

Velup laughed. "A pair of youths do not frighten me."

Uriah regarded his brother for a moment before speaking again, "Is that the sole reason you abducted Erclidus from his homeland? To gain knowledge about the nation you intended to lay siege upon?"

"Not just. When we saw that there was something unique about the heir born to the Vindella line, that she was prized in a way others before her had not been, it was clear to me that the time had come to seek out a new generation to pass my skills onto. The boy's knowledge, meager as it was, of the history of the East was a pleasant surprise."

The Wizard shook his head at the Sorcerer. "Poisoning yourself was not enough?"

Velup chuckled. "He is a fool, but he is driven and exceptionally talented. He has accomplished much in his years and he is eager, as we all are, to usher in the new age."

Uriah sighed, feeling pain in his heart for Erclidus.

"I offer you one last chance," said the Sorcerer with a sneer. "Surrender to me now and spare your people of the horrors which haunt your nightmares."

A moment of solemn silence passed between the two brothers, and then Uriah departed from the tower.

"So be it."

***

"Well, this room certainly looks important."

"Fine. Last one. The others may well have found it already."

Ilya and Nadarum snuck quietly into a dimly lit study that appeared to double as a living space. The archer immediately took to opening drawers and cabinets while her husband surveyed the room.

"I do think it would be worth it to look through some of these scrolls," spoke Ilya, pressing on a door that opened to a washroom.

Nadarum completed his initial scan of the place and moved quietly to the final door, this one partially open. It was a bedchamber, presently uninhabited. The horseman's demeanor turned suddenly serious as he spied a familiar piece of cloth draped over a dressing screen. "Plum, I think it would be wise to begin bringing our investigation to a close."

"Why, Darling, what's the matter?" Ilya hurried to her husband's side and drew in a breath when she saw the cape which had prompted his concern. "If this is where he sleeps, we've got a real chance to find it!" Rapidly, she crossed the room and pulled open the doors of a wardrobe.

Nadarum kept a hand on his sword as he moved back to the main door and pressed his ear against it, relieved to hear no approaching footsteps.

The archer shut the wardrobe frustratedly and turned to look around the room, spying a large chest at the foot of the bed. She crossed over to kneel before it, took in a deep, hopeful breath, and attempted to raise its lid. To her joy, she found it to be unlocked, and such joy multiplied when she peered inside and saw the beautiful golden blade tucked snugly in its sheath. She retrieved it and raced out of the room to show Nadarum.

He laughed and shook his head in wonder. "You are a limitless force."

They made their way back down the halls to their rooms, looking around every corner in hopes that they might stumble upon one of their friends. They startled and then immediately relaxed as they observed a tall figure with a pointed hat approach them.

"Pack your things," spoke Uriah with urgency. "We are not welcome here. We never were."

Nadarum and Ilya shared a glance and the Wizard's eyes moved to the weapon in the horseman's hand.

"Give it here."

Nadarum obeyed.

"Tell the others, if you happen upon them. We must leave at once."

***

Uritus had to restrain himself from barging into Adiadni's room upon hearing about her interaction with his brother, opting instead to knock worriedly at her

330

door. It made him feel sick all over again to think of her subject to Erclidus's cruel and careless whims. He held his breath as the seconds dragged by before her voice met his ear.

"I do *not* wish to be summoned!"

He was relieved to hear her and then immediately saddened by her tone. She had been crying. He opened the door and stepped inside. She was on her feet and visibly grateful to see him, a pool of shimmering burgundy fabric lying near the dressing screen.

"They told me what happened..." he said, closing the door behind him. "Are you all right?" He took several long strides toward her, halting abruptly as her expression became suddenly stern.

She shook her head back and forth, eyes still wet, arms crossed tightly over her chest. "Brother?"

The fisherman closed his eyes and let out a long sigh.

"You led me to believe that your entire family was *dead...*"

"As far as I knew, they all were."

"But you did not see him die... He was not taken by illness the way the others were."

Uritus sighed again. "No. He left with Velup of his own free will."

"I do not understand..." Adiadni's feeling of betrayal was displayed plainly on her face. "I thought we... told each other things. Why would you keep that from me? I feel like a fool, like I don't even know you at all. Maybe I don't..." She paused. "Did the others know the truth of what happened to him?"

"Uriah did. And Lex. No one else."

She shook her head at him again, tears stinging her vision. "Were you... *ever* going to tell me? Had things not turned out this way?"

Uritus did not respond.

"Fuck, I feel sick." Adi pressed a cool palm to her forehead and took a breath, keeping her eyes closed as she spoke again, "I know I am not entitled to information about your life. We've really only just met. I had just been under the impression that in the same way that I trust you with everything, you trust me as well. That's incredibly unreasonable of me. I just feel stupid." She opened her eyes, tears falling freely as they met his. "Stupid and naive and... overwhelmed. These days continue to be far more than I ever bargained for."

Silence hung in the air and Uritus felt a heavy pain surge in his chest. He had never meant to make her feel this way, never intended for any of this to happen. "You must forgive my lack of words," he spoke finally. "This new information has been difficult to digest."

Immediately, Adiadni softened. She dropped her hands to her sides. "Shit. I'm sorry." She crossed the room and took his hands in hers. "Of course this is worse for you. I'm being selfish. Are you okay?"

He smiled down at her, at the genuine care in her eyes, and shrugged sadly. "I don't know."

"I cannot imagine what a nightmare this has been for you..."

He sighed with a heavy nod. "At this point, I've given up on the hope that I might somehow wake up."

A lump grew in Adi's throat. She felt helpless to offer him any solace, guilty for how she had compounded his grief. Though she reached for them, she found no words that she felt might be of any use. And so, silently, she brought her arms to wrap around him and pulled him tightly into her embrace.

Uritus felt his entire body relax with a sigh and wrapped his arms around her shoulders. She was cold but she warmed him even so, heat moving lovingly from his core out to his limbs. And for the first time in many hours—perhaps even in many days—he forgot all about the road they had taken to get there and the path that lay ahead. He forgot Suscundos and Havian and the blood that had stained his hands and clothes; he forgot the prophecy and the swords; he even forgot Erclidus. All of his sorrow and all of his fears melted away until the only thing that remained in his mind's eye was her—the woman he loved.

He took her face gently in his hand and lifted it to meet his gaze, "It was never my desire to hurt you. I am truly sorry."

She shook her head fiercely. "You do not need to be..."

"I am all the same," he paused. "The reason I did not tell you about him has nothing to do with you. The truth is... I am ashamed to speak of him. I feel sorrow for him, for the way his fear and his grief drove him to forsake what he knew in pursuit of some semblance of power. But mostly... I feel guilt for how I could not reach him in those last days before he left. I know such a feeling is of no true use to me, and that I cannot take responsibility for the actions of another. Even so, I cannot help but feel that... perhaps if I had tried harder, I could have stopped him, and, by extension..." he trailed off. "It doesn't matter. The point is that I never meant to make you feel like I don't trust you. I do, more than most anyone I've ever known."

"I know..." Adi swallowed, attempting to still the tremor in her voice. "I just sometimes feel like..."

Uritus waited patiently for her to find her words.

"I just cannot help but feel like... like I need you more than you need me."

A surprised expression moved across the fisherman's face. "Nothing could be further from the truth."

She nodded slightly but did not look convinced.

"Adiadni, I..." He cleared his throat, took her face in both hands. "It is not an exaggeration to say that I would be dead without you. Everything I have done since arriving in Suscundos, every single thing of note that I have accomplished —the trials, the battle, the journey—all of it is because of how you have spurred me onward. You have placed yourself, on more than one occasion, between me and that which would wish to harm me, and for that, I am forever in your debt. Everything that I will do in the days to come, I will do because you saw me and fought for me. Do not underestimate your place in my life. I feel desperate for how much I need you.”

Adiadni’s lips parted, eyelids fluttering, but another knock followed by the opening of the door prevented her from responding.

“Good, you’re both here.”

Both young people turned their heads to find Perplexus standing in the doorway.

“I’m sorry to interrupt, but it’s time we were on our way.” The navigator was already dressed to leave, Uritus’s bag held in one hand.

He tossed an object to the fisherman who caught it in mid-air. The Sword of Fire. “How did you—”

“We’ll have plenty of time to catch up when we’re free of this place. Can the two of you find your way back to the main entrance on your own?”

Uritus nodded.

“Good.” Perplexus disappeared down the hall and Adi hurried to don her armor and gather her things.

***

The Adalos and the Suvah were the last of the companions to arrive in the entryway. Uriah spotted them as they hastened down the steps to the first floor and he hurried to open the doors.

“Leaving so soon?”

The voice that interrupted them, ordinarily chilling, sent a wave of irritation through the party.

Adiadni turned, spying the man in black as he emerged from the shadows. “You said we were free to go whenever we pleased.”

“I did. And I meant it. But certainly, you are tired from your traveling, and we have already prepared our table. Perhaps you might—”

“Silence, Erclidus. We have indulged you and your master long enough.”

The blue-eyed man’s brow twitched and he raised his head. “Nevertheless, I must insist.”

Uriah ignored him, turned back to the doors, and pulled on them to find that they were locked.

Erclidus chuckled. “You know, it’s quite rude to storm out just before dinner. The feast we have planned will no doubt be beyond your expectations.”

From the darkness behind him appeared a figure that several of the party members had seen before.

The intensity in the Wizard’s voice was unlike any his companions had heard before, “Give us the key.”

“See, I could do that…” The spurs on Erclidus’s boots sang as he took a series of slow steps forward. “…But I can’t figure out why I would. Now, the plan had

333

been to bring you here, try to talk some sense into you, send you on your way when you proved you could not be reasoned with. You are clearly willing to take the most difficult route forward, to face the death and destruction that will come for you with blind courage. But if I *don't* let you out... well, that would make my path all the smoother."

The travelers tensed, each of them readying themselves in their minds for a fight. But the flurry of movement which leapt to life in the next moment took everyone by surprise.

In an impulsive fit of bravery, Alidistris sprang out of the shadows, her hand reaching for the key tucked into Erclidus's waistband.

His reflexes were much too quick for her. He stepped aside, raised his hand, and dashed it across her face.

"Stop!"

He did not turn at the sound of Adiadni's pained scream. "You aren't needed here," he spat dismissively. "Return to the dining room at once."

Alidistris shakily raised herself to her feet, using one arm to sweep the river of shiny black hair away from her face.

"Now."

She turned and dejectedly began to depart from the room.

"Wait!" Mikka took several urgent steps forward.

Alidistris stopped to look at her.

Mikka's heart raced and she took a breath to try and calm it. "Come with us." Erclidus laughed but the former soldier ignored him. "You do not have to live this way. There is a whole world out there, a vibrant one, whose people will welcome you with open arms. Come..." She took another step forward, extending her hand to the woman who had risked her well-being to help them. "Be free of him."

Alidistris hesitated for several moments, hands forming tight fists at her sides, but her dark, glassy eyes never left Mikka's. After what felt like a short lifetime, she stepped forward, reaching out for the open hand of her rescuer.

"Absolutely not."

Erclidus lunged forward before the two women could join hands, grabbed a fistful of the attendant's hair, and yanked her back toward him. Chaos erupted in the moments that followed, a flash of silver, a tearing sound. The bundle of dark tresses clutched in the hand of the man in black fell suddenly limp, cut free by Mikka's blade.

"Go!"

Oripidus bashed his hammer against the door's lock. Two crushing blows caused the metal to warp and then splinter enough for Uriah to force the door open. Qibat soared out first, eager to escape the stale, indoor air.

Erclidus looked on in dumbfounded rage as the companions poured out of the keep. He opened his hand and let Alidistris's hair fall to the floor, and just before he allowed himself to submit to his defeat, a flash of gold caught his eye as it slipped out the door.

The companions raced to the bridge. A hot orange ball of flame burst to life in Uriah's right hand. He hurled it at one of the chains that kept the door of the wall sealed shut. It collided with the chain, sending hot sparks flying in all directions as the metal links melted and broke free of one another.

"Stop them! He has the sword!"

Uritus turned to see his brother race out of the keep just as guards appeared from around either side. A second flame lit in the hand of the Wizard, but it was almost immediately extinguished with a cry of pain as an arrow struck Uriah in the shoulder.

Adiadni began to panic. The companions drew their weapons, those with bows already firing upon the masses who approached. They would not win a fight, and if they did not leave now, they were surely doomed.

She turned her attention to the door's second chain and thrust her hand in its direction. She closed her eyes and focused her energy, bubbling from the depths of her being and then suddenly bursting forth. The princess closed her hand and, with an energetic cry, ripped her arm back toward herself.

Instantaneously, the chain snapped in two, freeing the door from its half-bind. The giant hunk of metal fell to the earth with a crash and the companions rushed out beyond the wall and into the night.

Erclidus threw up his hands in frustration. "Let them go," he ordered his troops, looking neither to the right nor to the left and regarding none of those who were injured. "They will meet their end soon enough."

He turned and marched back into the darkness of the keep, spurs clicking angrily as he went.

Chapter Twenty-Two

"Midnight"

The 25th of July

Safe once more within the shelter of the White Mountains, the companions assembled in their foyer. They had traveled urgently to get there, sending Qibat ahead to inform the Hammit twins that they would soon return and that Uriah was injured. Robalto would hear this word and immediately ride out to meet them where they snaked their way around Sigmount's Northern edge, the Wizard and physician's horses in tow. Now, the others, having just arrived, were pleased to hear that Uriah was in much better shape. Food had been prepared and their table had been laid and a room had been organized for Alidistris. The travelers were weary, though glad to be back, and exceedingly anxious to share what they now knew of their enemy. Zaphron presented Adiadni with a note which had arrived for her by raven that morning and she took it with her as she ascended the stair to her room.

"I'm sure the rest of you have your own interesting discoveries to share, but I think mine and Punzie's takes priority," spoke Perplexus above the chattering voices.

They hushed in anticipation.

"We believe Velup means to attack the Mirrored Cities."

Silence.

Perplexus dropped his bag to the floor and searched through it until he found the folded sheet of parchment he was looking for.

"We found it in a desk," Punznes said. "It was the only thing there of its kind so we cannot say for sure if it is a legitimate plan…"

"There were sketches of Judii and Lorethh scattered throughout Octrusial's quarters," confirmed Laivar, snatching the annotated map out of the navigator's hands.

"Octrusial?"

"The Seer."

All heads pivoted to regard Alidistris.

She looked nervously from one face to another. "I do not know much of anything about their plans, I'm afraid. But I do know a little about the ones Velup trusts."

The companions nodded approvingly.

"We are glad to have you with us, Alidistris," Uriah stated, affirmative sounds from the others echoing this sentiment. "You are a testament to the free will of the people in the West. No doubt by this point, you have surmised that this particular company is and will remain at the heart of this rising conflict. We, of course, will not ask you to devote yourself to this war to the same degree that we will ourselves, and we will find and organize a place of refuge for you no matter what. But the information you have could be vital for our understanding of what we are up against, so if you are willing, I request that you join us when we present our findings to the king."

"Oh, um... I don't know if I..."

"Think about it," the Wizard encouraged her. "We will not press you on the issue tonight, as you are no doubt fatigued. You may dine here and bathe and rest as you need to and explore as you like. If you determine that you would prefer to seek your peace, we will understand. But we depart for the capital in the morning, so I will need your decision by then."

Alidistris nodded politely. "Thank you. I wish I could express my gratitude with more fervor than that."

"There is no need. You owe your freedom to yourself most of all."

***

The companions separated to unburden themselves of their armor before they partook of their meal and Mikka led Alidistris to her new chamber. The woman from the West moved through the room in awed silence, running a hand lightly over the fixtures she found there.

"I've never had a room to myself before," she stated plainly.

The former soldier watched her from where she rested against the doorframe. "I hope it is to your liking."

"Very much, yes."

"It used to belong to a friend..."

"Oh?"

"He, uh," Mikka cleared her throat. "We... lost him on the journey West."

Alidistris turned suddenly, sorrow in her eyes. "I'm sorry to hear that."

The blonde woman wondered if she shouldn't have brought him up.

"What was he like?"

Mikka gave a half-smile, raising her eyes to the ceiling. "Proud. But loving. Willful and strong. He was our swordsman—many who dwell here owe their skills to his teaching."

"How did he die?"

The former soldier paused, lips parted, unsure how to proceed.

"Forgive me, I shouldn't pry."

"No, it's all right..." Mikka sighed. "Truthfully, I am quite angry with him. His death was needless. He unnecessarily confronted an enemy whom he stood

337

no chance to best, and now the rest of us are stuck here, trying to figure out how to make do without him." She laughed, bleary-eyed, and shook her head. "It really is quite like Havian to meet a striking end so that he is on our minds always, even during such unprecedented times. Dramatic bastard."

"Was that his name?"

"Havian, yes. He was our brother, and now his bones claim space in the earth beside the river Tuvibati." She paused before meeting the teary dark eyes that looked to her, "Forgive me, I do not mean to make you feel sad…"

Alidistris shook her head. "I have been sad most of my life. Thanks to you, I can now envision a future where that does not have to be the case."

"What does such a future look like for you?"

The woman from the West crossed the room to regard herself in the looking glass with a sigh. "I haven't the faintest idea."

Mikka looked at her with empathy in her heart. She knew little of the life Alidistris had led up to this point but was confident that it was something that had been endured rather than enjoyed. "I'm sorry about your hair…" she said, chewing her cheek awkwardly. "In the moment, it felt like the right thing to do…"

"You needn't worry about it." Alidistris ran a hand slowly along the few longer locks that remained. "In truth, I am glad to be free of it just as I am glad to be free of that place."

"I can help you fix it later."

Alidistris met Mikka's eyes in the glass and smiled warmly. "Thank you. You've been very kind."

Mikka lowered her head gracefully. "You are welcome to get your rest here if you need it, but we will be reconvening in the dining hall shortly if you wish to join us."

Alidistris smiled again, her eyes brightening. "Thank you, I think I will."

***

The evening waned on, the family partaking of their welcome feast and conversing with energetic voices as Robalto and Zaphron were caught up on the past week's events.

Uritus found himself to be a victim of the fog that plagued his mind. As the others spoke of strategy, their endeavors in espionage, and the most efficient route they might take to return to Suscundos, the Adalos remained in a daze.

The details of his last conversation with his brother played over and over in his mind. He did not notice the sound of his party's laughter or the way the smoke curled up from the candles that lit the table or the taste of the food that passed through his lips. He did not observe when Mikka and Alidistris eventually joined them and did not hear the others sing the praises of the former attendant's cleanly cropped hair. In his haze, he did not even notice that Adiadni made no appearance at the table at all.

338

He felt haunted by Erclidus. It was Laivar who ultimately recognized the glazed-over look in the fisherman's eyes and encouraged him to retire for the evening with a loving pat on the hand. Uritus drifted out of the hall without speaking a word.

The thing that would ultimately snap him out of his vague haze was the gentle creak of wood as his chamber door was pushed open. He turned, his attention immediately focusing as he saw the fair figure standing there.

She shut the door behind herself. "My father is unwell."

Uritus's face dropped.

The princess pushed on, "Apparently, he began feeling ill shortly after we departed but they did not wish to send for me for fear that I would worry. Naturally, now I am incredibly worried..."

It was at this moment that Uritus shook himself free of his shock and truly saw her where she stood. Face distraught, white dress that fell to her knees, boots on her feet, tiara on her head. "You're leaving..."

"Tonight. I've already told Uriah." She cleared her throat and the fisherman felt his head begin to swim. "They're sending someone on a gryphon for me so... it must be fairly serious."

At this moment, when he ordinarily would have hurried to embrace her, he felt stunned by the promise of her absence. "I am so sorry..."

She did not acknowledge this, rather closing her eyes and taking a deep breath as she steeled herself to continue, "Obviously, we are hopeful that this will simply pass over him, but... if it does not..." She opened her eyes finally and they met with his. "If it does not, then I will need to begin my preparations to take the throne."

Uritus considered the implications of this. "Does that mean..."

"I will be wed."

The stillness in the next moments suffocated both of them.

He broke free of it first, voice wavering, "Is that what you would wish?"

Adiadni laughed, tears slipping down her cheeks. "Of course not. You know that."

The fisherman swallowed. "Of course, we retain our hope in your father's Healers..."

"We do. Yet, I do not have the luxury of refraining from considering the alternative."

"Right," Uritus hesitated, not sure what to say. "Are you all right?"

The princess shrugged. "I am trying to be."

Uritus felt his emotion clawing at his throat but swallowed it down again. "Well, it isn't a long road from here to Suscundos. It will be strange not having you with us, but... we will be reunited soon enough."

Adiadni blinked, hands forming and releasing fists. "Is that all?"

He furrowed his brow. "What do you mean—"

"It doesn't matter." Her hands found one another. "I suppose I thought you might try to convince me to stay…"

The fisherman didn't understand. "I could never ask you to forsake your family or your duties for what I would wish…"

"But you do wish it?"

He shook his head. "What I would wish, what I would think… it doesn't matter."

"It matters to me."

The gentle note of sorrow in her voice brought tears to his eyes.

"You are my friend," she said, voice breaking again. "My confidante, my most trusted advisor. It matters very much to me what you think."

He hesitated, turning his words over in his mind. "I only mean that your fate should be in no one's hands but your own. I do not really understand the nature of the politics of the whole ordeal, if you are unquestionably bound to your commitment…"

"I am not. It is just… with the influence that the Dagious house holds in the East, I am stepping on precarious ground if I dare to upset them. Especially during such delicate times."

"I understand."

She sighed frustratedly. "I appreciate your understanding, but it isn't particularly helpful at the moment."

"What would be?"

"I don't know…"

She chewed on her lip and he looked at her with pain in his heart. Finally, he crossed the room to stand in front of her and took her hands in his own. "You have proven yourself to be capable of so much more than you ever fathomed in the past weeks alone. You are smart and you are wise and there is no one better suited to carve your path than you. No one else can know what is right for you, not like you can know it for yourself."

She processed his words silently, moving her head back and forth, hands still clinging to his. She released them, stepped back, and brought her palms to press against her temples. "I just… need to know… what you think is the right choice."

He shook his head. "It isn't my place to—"

"Fuck this arbitrary concept of your *place*, Uritus, what would you have me do?"

"*Why* does it *matter*?"

"Do you not know?"

These last few words were frail and thin as if they could shatter. Silence claimed the space between them. Uritus felt his breath grow uneven. Adiadni closed her eyes, pressed her hands to them, shook her head back and forth.

Finally, she moved her arms to cross over herself and set her gaze on the door. "It doesn't matter."

Her voice was small and his head ached as his heart did.

"You're right," she dried her face. "The rest of you won't be long. I just, um..." She blinked tearfully and lifted her eyes to meet his a final time, "I just couldn't leave without telling you first."

And then, like a ghost, she was gone, and Uritus was alone, a heavy pit making a home in his stomach.

***

When Perplexus found him there, an hour later, the fisherman lay with his back flat against the floor.

"I came to ask if you know Adi left... I'd be willing to wager that you do."

Uritus rubbed his hands across his eyes, the pressure behind them squeezing a permanent frown into his brow. "The king is ill. They fear he may be dying..."

"Uriah told me." The navigator moved across the room and brought himself down to sit on the cool stone beside his friend. "I'm here to see how you're feeling."

The fisherman raised himself up and brought his arms to rest on his knees. "I've been grappling for words to try to express what I am feeling for days."

Perplexus sighed and allowed quiet to linger between them. He never wished to rush his friend through what he felt, but at that moment, urgency pressed on his chest. "You know that if the king does not recover... it will not be long before she is forced to marry that perfumed pile of horse shit..."

"Of course I know that. We talked about it."

"You talked about it? When?"

"She came to tell me she was leaving."

Perplexus leapt to his feet. "She came to see you before she left and you didn't go with her?"

Uritus blinked, standing. "She never asked me to go with her..."

"She may as well have!"

Uritus laughed and shook his head. "You have no idea what you're talking about, you weren't even—"

"She came to you..." Perplexus spoke slowly, gesturing with hands pressed against one another, "...knowing that she was going to be leaving, talked with you about the nature of the marriage she must soon be forced to face, and you... what?" He blinked confoundedly, throwing his hands out to his sides. "You didn't offer to go with her? You just... wished her well and sent her on her way?"

341

Uritus shook his head again.

She is not...

"What would you have had me do? She only came to say goodbye..."

"She came to you because she *loves* you!" The navigator threw his hands up in his frustration. "She *loves* you and she came to ask if you love her as well so that she might have a reason to justify leaving him."

The fisherman forced a laugh. "That is a mighty assumption about the nature of a conversation you were not privy to."

"Please, you are *enraptured* with one another. *Everyone* has seen it so plainly since the night we arrived in Suscundos. You push each other and encourage each other and feel safe with one another. When you look at her, it is as if everything that has ever hurt you has simply turned to vapor. When she looks at you... it is as if her sky has opened."

Uritus shook his head harder, squeezed his eyes and fists shut, beat back against the current... "But what does any of that even matter?"

Lex paused at the intensity of his friend's tone. "It matters very much," he finally said, his voice soft. "Uritus, I do not know much, but I *do* know love, and I know that the two of you share the rarest kind. You've fallen into each other with such ease, such grace. You must not forsake what a gift that is."

Uritus sighed, softened, exhausted tears in his eyes. "She has an entire life far beyond the scope of my understanding. She has duties and responsibilities, for herself and for the Free People."

"And such duty to herself brought her here. To *you.*"

The fisherman raised his gaze to the ceiling.

"I do not understand how you can deny her. She's captivated you since the moment you met."

She is not...

"Because she is not mine to have!"

"According to who? You?"

Uritus closed his eyes and pressed his hands against them.

Perplexus took a breath. "You were with me when Lys left. You saw what happened. My sky went black."

Uritus looked to his friend with compassion.

"I couldn't be consoled. Were it not for Havian to commiserate... I don't know what would have happened to me." The navigator dried his eyes. "Even then, I knew that Lys was not for me, that his path only ever overlapped with mine. But still, the loss was difficult to bear. I don't want that to happen to you. I don't want that to happen to Adiadni. If love like *this*, so precious and weightless and endless and solid, is just out of your grasp and you choose not to reach out to it, I can promise you that you will bear the weight of that choice for the rest of your days."

The fisherman set a hand against his chest as he took several long breaths. He felt like he was sunken amongst the reeds in a murky pond, gazing up at the light above him, too tangled to try to swim up to it. "It is not for a lack of feeling that I refrain from pursuing what you say is so plainly apparent. It is not even solely because of her duties as a royal or a diplomat, though I suppose, in that, I have found a convenient excuse to hide behind. It is just..." He paused, another breath in and slowly out. "Every single life, every single person I loved in my formative years was taken from me. I am wise enough now not to see such a thing as a pattern, but the fear lingers all the same, a hole in my gut, ripped open again when Havian died."

Perplexus felt the crush of this immense burden as if it were his own.

Uritus tearfully went on, "I witnessed... my father, in the months and years after my mother passed, and though he was strong and though he was resilient and though he was the anchor for all of us... he was destroyed. If I might spare her the fate that claimed the lives of my family... If I might at least spare her the weight of so soul-crushing a loss..."

Perplexus rushed to embrace him as he trailed off. The navigator moved both hands to lift his friend's face, tears staining their eyes. "People will miss you when you are gone whether you try to distance yourself from us or not."

Uritus sighed deeply.

"We will mourn your end just as we have Havian's. You cannot shut yourself off from love, and you *certainly* cannot shut yourself off from the people who love you. That is the most purposeless way to live and I will not allow it for you. You are the most brilliant, most compassionate, bravest man I know. You deserve to crash into someone who will catch you. Consequences be damned."

A smile lit the fisherman's eyes. He felt as though he could breathe again for the first time in days. "I love you for your wisdom as much as I do for your exceptional ability to kick my ass when I need it."

Lex chuckled. "And I love you, Old Boy."

"...But Adiadni has already left. Even if I ride ahead of you, it'll be days before I catch up with her, and who knows what could happen by then."

"Send a raven..."

"I cannot express such a thing to her in a hastily scrawled note."

Perplexus raised an eyebrow in thought. "Call your dragon."

Uritus shook his head fiercely. "Not for this."

"You may well need to reconsider your anti-riding stance soon..."

"I'm well aware of that. My refusal to call him isn't solely due to stubbornness. I do not wish to draw unnecessary attention to him, and I am firm on that. He values his solitude. I will not ask him to sacrifice that unless circumstances become quite dire."

Perplexus nodded slowly in understanding. Both men felt at a loss. The seconds ticked on in their desperate silence, each of them gradually slipping into the acceptance that they may be out of options. And then, the very faintest of sounds drifted through the windowpane to meet the fisherman's ears, and at that moment, he knew what he needed to do.

***

Adiadni retreated to the safety of her chambers, trying and failing to calm her heaving breaths. It was late and Suscundos slept, but her mind was abuzz with dizzying anxiety. Her balcony door opened and a figure in seafoam silk entered the room.

She turned to regard it. "Jasch…"

"Star said you were coming home, I didn't believe it. Didn't expect to find you here either, I thought you'd be with…"

"My father sleeps," spoke the princess tiredly. "As he should. Apparently, everyone knew he was unwell except me. Now I will have to wait until morning to see him…"

"Tef and Fifi will be here soon," said the redheaded woman as she crossed the room. "I suppose I should have considered that you will want your sleep before I told them to come, but… we've just really missed you."

"I've missed you too," Adi replied sadly. "In truth, I think it would benefit me to have company tonight."

Jasch's face lit up. "Oh good. We're desperate to hear about your journey. How are the others? How's Uritus?" She paused, a coy smile moving across her lips. "How's Havian?"

Adiadni's face crumpled as she burst into tears and her friend hurried to embrace her.

***

The soft sounds and smells of the stable that met Uritus as he entered made him feel all the more spurred on toward his aim. Cool blue moonlight spilled into the space from the open doors as the fisherman eagerly approached his horse. Moonracer whinnied upon his arrival, visibly excited to see him again.

"I missed you too, Old Friend. Though I am glad you were not present to witness the things I did in the past weeks, the time spent without you has made me eager for one of our adventures again." He pulled open the door of the stall and began readying his tack. "Now, there is something urgent that I must do, but I won't be able to do it without your help, so… I thought we might make good on an old dream. Does that sound like something you'd like to do?"

Moonracer whinnied and eagerly dragged a hoof along the floor of his stall.

The next thing they knew, the man and the horse were on their way, flying through the landscape of the mountains. In his hurry to leave, Uritus brought with him no armor, no sword, no bag, no water skin. The brisk air of the night beat against his skin as he rode out of the mountains, beyond the Lake Provinces, across the bridge. Every beat of the horse's hooves pounded in the fisherman's chest, strengthening his resolve. The land sailed by them and the sky remained unchanging, twinkling stars and silver moon lighting their way. As

344

they had since their time in Tosh, the two joined into a singular united thing, one unstoppable force like a zephyr tearing through the grass. This ride felt to Uritus no different than any he had ever taken in the sky.

Together, they soared ever onward, the boy from the fishing village and the horse who would race the moon.

***

In the middle of the princess's bedchamber, a collection of colorful skirts huddled in a pile on the floor. Adiadni's friends listened to her, held her, comforted her, helped her change, braided her hair, brought her fruit and tea and lethaa. Though her heart was deeply grieved, she acknowledged still, head in Friya's lap, that she felt significantly better.

"I know it is not helpful—and you will probably curse me for saying it—but I am still strongly in favor of you taking a lover should the worst-case scenario take place."

"*Jasch…*" Adiadni's tone was exaggeratedly tired but playful.

"Hush, Bluejay, we are *not* entertaining the idea of any such thing," said Kristefani. "Adi will have a real love. Nothing less is good enough for her."

"I wish the belief of such a thing was enough," spoke the princess dejectedly. "Truthfully, I do not think I see a way out."

"I'm sorry, are you not the woman who led a troop of soldiers beyond enemy lines and back?" Friya questioned, her voice passionate. "Are you not the woman who slayed the unkillable beast? Who raised a man from the dead?"

Adi raised herself to a seat. "You're exaggerating, Fifi."

"Maybe a little, but she's still right."

Jasch nodded aggressively. "You looked your enemy square in the face and dared him to kill you. There is nothing you cannot do. Basil is but an anthill compared to the mountains you've summited."

"You owe it to yourself, Adi," Kristefani's voice was gentle and serious. "And to the man you truly want."

"But if he doesn't want *me* then why does it even matter?"

A knock, a creak, a pivoting of heads, and the princess hurriedly stood to her feet.

The fisherman halted just within the doorway. The sight of her made his heart soar. The braid over her shoulder, the pink of her lips, the light in her eyes. She was the realest thing he had ever known and it was finally clear as day: every stumble, every step had led him straight here to her.

She is…

"Uritus…?"

Her friends looked at one another with open mouths at the sight of the windswept man who entered.

"I don't understand… How did you—"

345

"I'll explain it all, I promise. I just… I couldn't bear how our conversation ended, and… I had to see you."

A silent, anticipatory moment lapsed, the fisherman and the princess each staring at one another. The three excitable elvish women rose and filed quietly out of the room.

"I do not understand how—"

"I cannot bear to be parted from you."

Adiadni's breath caught in her throat.

"I know that is irrational… but it is true. The past days I have spent with you have shown me what it could look like to live a life at your side and I am blind to anything and everything else. When I am tossed about carelessly by life's waves and I feel I will capsize, it is you who is my rudder, my lighthouse, my shining North star. It is you whom I can turn my focus to when all else goes black, it is you who inspires me to continue."

Adiadni blinked, lashes again heavy with tears.

"You said you want to know what I think…" He took a step closer to her. "I think you are spirited and vibrant and positively bursting with life. I think you are stubborn and tenacious and gorgeous and strong. I think the way that you love your people is awe-inspiring and a clear reminder of the reason why we are all here. I think you are brave…" He set a hand against his sternum. "So undoubtedly brave that when I look to the days ahead, to the turmoil and the storms, I cannot help but also see the Light just beyond the clouds. And it is for this, Adiadni, that when I take up my sword and fulfill my destiny just as you did yours, it will be only to clear the path so that you might again lead us onward into brighter days."

He paused and took a final deep breath. "I am but a humble tradesman from a village that no longer exists. But because of you, I have begun to understand that I am more than that as well. And I know that your life is burdened with weighty decisions and heavy consequences and that I often will not know the right thing to do to help you along. But I have tasted the sweetness of existence with you and I never wish for anything else to pass beyond my lips again.

"I stand by what I said before, I cannot make your decisions for you. Your life should be in your hands alone. But if you would allow me…" He paused as he looked at her, his eyes as blue and hers as warm as the day they first met. "Then I would wish to make good on the promise that I made you long ago: that I will go by your side for as long as you would have me. I wish to remain your advisor, your confidante, your friend. Whether you would have me lead your armies or serve on your councils or if, by some miracle, you would allow me to someday stand proudly and adoringly at your left hand… know that I would. Gladly. Exuberantly. Because the truth is that a life with you is the only kind I ever wish to live. The truth is… that I love you, and I am sorry that it took me until now to find the courage to let you know.

The quiet chorus of crickets outside met with the rustling of fabric as Adiadni rushed forward and was caught up in his arms.

A flickering of light, a waft of wind, a silent symphony.

The fisherman cupped her face in his hands and kissed her.

And then gone were their worries and gone were their fears. Gone were the days which had led to this one and gone were those which had not yet come to pass. The weight of their burdens, individual and collective, were torn down and stripped away until all that remained was all that had ever truly mattered:

Their blood and their breath and the cold light of the moon.

Book Three:

The War

Chapter Twenty-Three

"A Brief Respite"

The 26th of July

"A dda?"

When Adiadni entered Agamemnon's study at morning's first light, she was surprised to find him already there, dressed and on his feet. He and Betina turned from the windows to regard their child, bright smiles moving across their faces at the sight of her. The princess hastened forward and fell into their arms.

"I do not understand," she said, pulling back from the king's embrace. "Ama's note made me fear that your condition was quite dire…"

Agamemnon waved a hand in the air dismissively, "Nonsense. I am perfectly —" The same casual hand abruptly formed a fist which flew up to the king's mouth as he was taken by a series of coughs.

His wife and daughter watched him with concern. "The cough arrived shortly after you left," Betina explained. "And regardless of what your father says, it has only grown worse since."

"I do not deny that," replied the king. "I merely felt it unnecessary to worry you when you've undoubtedly had enough to fill your mind." He coughed again with less severity this time. "But that is more than enough about me. How was your journey, my child? I wish to hear everything."

As Adiadni regarded the joy and anticipation on her parents' faces, she felt at a loss for words. "Well… we found the sword."

"That is excellent news!"

"…But it was not without a great deal of spilled blood."

The room became suddenly serious. "Yes," spoke the king. "Unorthodox though it was, sending the bodies of the goblins down Tuvibati was a clever means of communication."

"Oripidus's idea… But I speak not only of the blood of our enemies." Adi regarded the silent looks of compassion on her parents' faces before taking a deep breath and pushing on, "We lost Havian."

"Oh, Love…"

"I am deeply sorry to hear this news," said Agamemnon. "He fell during your clash with the goblins?"

Adiadni shook her head. "To Idor."

"Idor... That is—" The king's cough took him again. The queen set a loving hand upon his back and the other on his arm.

Adiadni regarded him anxiously as his breath returned to its normal pattern, tears pricking her eyes. "Won't you come sit down?" With one hand she gestured to the teal settee, her voice delicate.

"Come now, that won't be necessary..." But the coughing came once more and the princess tearfully met her mother's eye.

"I'm sure you understand now why I sent for you," said Betina.

"It is but a minor affliction..." Agamemnon argued.

"Had Healers not already tended to you to no avail, I might be more inclined to believe you."

Adiadni felt her stomach twist in her fear for her father's wellbeing. "Adda, no one doubts that you are strong and capable. But I wish to remind you that your father met an unusually early end..."

"My father succumbed to the weakness of his heart. Not his lungs."

"Yes, but..." Adi hesitated a moment before taking a deep breath. "I have been made aware in these past weeks how sheltered I have been from loss, and then suddenly forced to my knees in my grief for my first taste of the grisliest kind of it. I am aware also that the coming days will only lead to more, and I am coming to grips with that, but..." She looked up into the caring eyes of her father, lower lip trembling, "I am certain that I cannot face them without you. Please, just... come sit down."

The fear worn plainly on the face of the child he adored was enough to make the king relent. Together, the family moved to a seat where Adiadni recalled for her parents the details of her time away from home. She told them of Idor and their rescue mission and Sigmount, of the growth of her gifts and her healing of Uritus and slaying of the Shadow Beast. She witnessed the shock on their faces as she informed them of the fate of the Lake Provinces and the lake itself, the wonder as they heard of the miracles committed by her hand. They did not speak at great length of the final enemies she and her company had come to face, though she told them what little she understood of their motivations and that her party, once they arrived, would have more information to share.

"Uriah says they were able to gather a bit of intel while we were being held at the Ashen Keep. The most important thing that we know is Velup's plan to attack Judii and Lorethh. I suppose I should have gathered more details from him, I was a bit flustered in my hurry to get here..."

"You have done more than enough," Agamemnon assured her. "Now that we know the enemy's plan of attack, we may more efficiently utilize our resources to prepare for the days ahead."

Betina kept an arm wrapped around her daughter, the other lovingly stroking her hair. "We're so proud of you, Love."

Adi sighed heavily. A wave of sorrow passed over the settee as her parents observed how she was deeply tired. "I know," the princess responded. "I do not deny my achievements, though I will always redirect those who point them out to those who went with me, as none of it would have been possible without them. But truthfully…" She sat up, took a breath. "I was right before when I said I was not ready. I know now that it did not matter, that the war is upon us and we are all but at the mercy of it. I just cannot help but wonder if I *had* been ready… how some things might have turned out differently."

Though she did not say it directly, it was clear to the king and queen that their daughter still felt responsible for how her companion met his sudden end. Their eyes filled with tears and Agamemnon moved a hand to comfortingly grip Adiadni's, "I am sorry for how you have been thrust so forcefully into such turmoil. You are young and you deserve, as all young people do, to be free to explore your life and your passions in pursuit of what moves your heart to swell. Your path was paved for you long before you were ever born. You have not been allowed the same freedom of choice as your peers, and I feel sorrow for that, for you. How many times over your years I have wished your burden had fallen to me instead…

"Of course… it has not. And none of us can say why such events play out the way they do. But I tell you with utmost certainty—what you have done, what you will do… it is far greater than anything I could ever possibly achieve. You *are* the Way-Maker… that has been clear since your earliest days. I will always feel guilt for how I have not been able to do the plainest thing a father should: protect his child from how the world might wish to harm her. But it is you whom I have always known will come to protect us all. You have the heart of the eagle and the spirit of the songbird. And, in whatever meager ways I can, I *will* still protect you. I am nothing if not the place you can go for shelter."

Adiadni's eyes brimmed with tears again and, rather than searching for her words, leaned forward into her father's warm embrace. Betina wrapped her arms around both of them and the princess felt her mother's heartbeat as it pressed against her back, steady, unwavering. But the gentle moment shared by the little family was cut off abruptly as Agamemnon's body was wracked once more by his mysterious ailment.

"I'm fine," he sputtered between labored coughs. His wife and daughter shared an uncertain glance.

"Perhaps we might conclude this conversation this afternoon? I think it would be best if your father got some rest."

Adi nodded, and Agamemnon, his breath stabilizing once more, did not object. "Of course," responded the princess. "That's all of it, really. There will be much more to go over when the others arrive."

"Certainly. Try to get some rest as well, Love. You deserve it."

The princess nodded again and rose and took a few steps toward the door. But then she stopped and turned around, touching her fingertips to one another lightly as she gathered her courage. "Actually, there is one more thing."

The king and queen stood, regarding her patiently.

Adiadni closed her eyes and drew in a long breath, the comforting image of her counterpart materializing in her mind. She opened her eyes and dropped her hands to her sides. "I cannot marry Basil."

Betina moved her head slowly up and down. Agamemnon did not immediately react.

Adiadni steeled her nerves. "I know you offered me a way out before. I regret that I didn't take it then. Of course, I understand that this complicates things politically, strategically…"

"Never mind any of that," spoke the king with a firm shake of his head. She was not wrong, but such consequences were the furthest thing from Agamemnon's mind. The days since Basil's first violent outburst had pushed the king ever deeper into his guilt for subjecting his daughter to the whims of such a cruel family. She had remained loyal to her betrothed solely out of her sense of duty for her people, so to see her now abandon such a burden with confidence and surety made his heart swell with pride. "You have not had the freedom to decide much in your life, you *will* have the choice of the one you will bind yourself to. I am sorry that my selection was not the right match."

Adi's feeling of relief was cold and sweet in her stomach. "You did the best you could. None of us could have known that he would turn out to be so…" she trailed off. "I suppose in the past, I tried to dream, tried to hope for the love which might grow between us but… it never did. Before I left, I prioritized my duty rather than my heart and, I suppose as well, my dreams of love for fear of what the pursuit of it might mean for… well… everyone else. But now I… I know love. I didn't look for it, but it found me all the same, and now its face is as familiar to me as the sun which warms the sky and… I simply cannot fathom settling for anything less than that ever again."

Agamemnon nodded slowly. "You are saying that…"

"I love Uritus," spoke the princess plainly. Betina's hands flew up to cover her mouth though her smile was visible in her eyes. "And he loves me."

The king's happiness for his daughter showed on his face. "I am glad for you both," he spoke seriously before pausing a moment. "I would be happy to arrange for your return to your party if you wish to join them on their journey back here. I am sorry we had to separate the two of you in the first place…"

"You needn't worry about it, he's here."

"In Suscundos?"

"Yes. He came after me when I left. It's a long story, I'll spare you the details of it now. But he followed me here and we talked about it and I can no longer put off the thing that I know I must do." She tugged at the ring on her left hand, feeling as though the skin beneath it had begun to itch.

"Of course. Basil will shortly make his return to Suscundos along with his recruited swords. We will stand with you as you return his ring if you wish. But for now, enjoy these next few days in peace. Your mother and I are glad for you both."

Betina took this cue to hurry toward her daughter and embrace her. "So very, very glad."

***

354

On the cool stone floor of the princess's chamber just within the open balcony doors, Uritus lay on his back and allowed the morning sun to warm his bones. One hand rested on his stomach, a cup of warm tea held in it. The other cradled his head. He had not been surprised when he had awoken to find that Adiadni was already gone. Part of him had considered taking a stroll through the gardens or going to visit Moonracer in the stables, excited to have returned to this city he loved. But, knowing that his presence in Suscundos would draw a significant bit of attention, and still knowing not the state of the king's health, he had elected to wait here for the princess's return.

He was grateful for the peaceful morning, having almost forgotten what it was like to awaken with no tasks to immediately attend to, no journey that beckoned him onward. Strange as well was it to be parted from his family—something he had never really been since first finding them. But the novelty of the situation felt fresh rather than disorienting, quiet and calm and hopeful but mostly content. The joyful sounds of the city, its nature and its inhabitants, drifted up on the breeze to meet his ears and he breathed in the sweet smell of the Summer.

He wasn't sure how long he'd been lying there by the time Adiadni returned, and she entered and crossed the room so swiftly that he didn't have the chance to rise and greet her before she met him on the ground and pressed her lips against his. Her kiss was fervent and prolonged and when finally she pulled her face back and he got his first real look at her, he was pleased to see her bright smile. "How is he?"

She bit her lip and moved her head from one side to the other as she considered how to answer. "He is ill, that is clear, but he is far better off than I feared. It's a respiratory ailment, baffles his Healers and physicians. He is stubborn in his insistence that it will simply pass. Of course, it would be wonderful if he turned out to be right."

"I am glad to hear that," replied the fisherman with a smile.

"I told them about us."

Uritus brought himself up to his elbows. "About…"

"That you are here. And that I love you."

The words sang in his ears. "And that I love *you,* no doubt…"

She giggled. "That too. And that such love bars me from following through with my commitment. They understand. Truthfully, they are quite happy."

A smile danced in the eyes of the fisherman. "I am glad to hear that."

"As was I. I'm not sure why I was nervous. They've always affirmed my authority over my own life. They offered to join me when I call an end to my relationship with Basil but I do think it is something that I should do on my own."

A wave of uncertainty moved over Uritus's face as he considered her betrothed's inclination to violence.

She saw this and hurried to ease his fears, "I do not think I will be in danger. Basil has a temper but he has never sought to hurt me. If it makes you feel better, I can see to it that I have a guard nearby."

"It would make me feel better if I went with you. Though I know that would certainly not be best." He set his cup down and moved his hand to hold her face. "Honestly, I am not worried about you. I know who you are and I know what you are capable of. And I love you for it."

The corners of Adiadni's mouth curled into a smile, and she stared at him with an adoring, warm gaze that made his heart's beat feel solid in his chest. She sat up a bit—the way she always did when she grew serious. "My parents think, for the time being, that it's best I keep wearing this," she lifted her left hand and waved it vaguely in the air.

"I understand. Honestly, I often forget it is there."

"Well, *that's* certainly apparent."

He laughed. "I am sure you will be glad to be free of it."

"I will. Gratefully for both of us, Basil is not scheduled to be here for at least a few days. Though, I suppose that *does* leave me time to stew and become nervous about it…" She paused for a moment, lips parted as her eyes drifted down to his. "But I have a feeling that will not be the case."

Uritus laughed again and moved to brush away from her face the locks tossed there by the wind. "I've never been called distracting before but I'm happy to be that if it helps you. Before I get to that though, is there anything we're tasked to do over the next few days? Any official business we must see to?"

The princess shook her head. "We'll join my family for supper tonight but other than that, no, none at all. Preparations are underway for the welcome celebration but that is not scheduled to take place until the others return. There's nothing else. They've encouraged us to relax," she said, leaning forward to rest with one hand on the rug. "If we can remember how to do that."

He laughed again. "I actually think I'm pretty good at that. I'd be happy to give you lessons if you need them."

She smiled, eyes moving to his lips once more. "I think I'll manage."

He moved a hand to cup her chin and pulled her face to his but the door slammed open before their lips could meet. They sprang apart in their surprise.

"Adiiiiiiiii!" Fennispar came sprinting across the room and fell into their laps as he threw his arms around the princess. "And Uritus!" He spun around to embrace the Adalos. "I didn't know you were here too!"

"It is lovely to see you again, Good Sir."

"How have you been, Darling?" Adi asked, affectionately stroking the boy's hair. "I trust Suscundos has been safe in your care."

"Certainly, my dear," Fennispar drawled in a mock-serious tone. "And now, I return the city's flag to your capable hands." The imaginary flag held reverently in the fists of the young boy was extended to the princess before Fennispar pulled it back in a brief hesitation. Turning his body toward Uritus, he spoke again, "Or, actually, I suppose now is when it gets passed to you?"

Uritus looked down at the boy's hands, at the invisible symbol held in them. He lifted his eyes to the princess with a questioning glance.

She gave him a little nod. "He's right. Once the Way-Maker has opened the door, the burden of protection passes to the Hero."

The Adalos knew this. But in the chaos of the end of their journey and then his rush to get back to Suscundos, he had nearly forgotten. The official moment which marked their transfer of leadership had been cut short, and now, Uritus came to realize that he had not truly thought about it. He held out his hands graciously and Fennispar passed the imaginary flag into them. He gripped the pole and held it up and lifted his gaze to the place the fabric would be dangling.

The boy gave him a nod of approval. "It looks good in your hands," he said. "It matches your eyes."

Uritus laughed. "Thank you, Good Sir. I will do my best to be worthy of it."

"You don't have to *be worthy* of it. You just have to hold it."

Adiadni pressed a hand to her mouth to stifle her giggle and Uritus nodded sagely. Fennispar was right. *You just have to hold it.*

"But come on, they're going to be wanting to see you." The boy moved to his feet and held a hand out to Adi to help her do the same.

"Who is?"

"Everyone!"

The princess and fisherman shared a glance and a smile before they were whisked away.

***

Fennispar dragged them all over the palace, announcing to everyone they came upon that *the Suvah and Adalos are back and isn't that wonderful?* They found Pressio and Digtrision and the king's Keepers. They visited Winchells and Exstarferus in the kitchen where they were joined by Adi's friends. Fennispar insisted on giving Uritus a lesson in the sacred art of lethaa dough folding. Adiadni looked on with an adoring smile, feeling her heart swell to be surrounded by so many she had missed. Uritus, though he tried earnestly, could not quite master the manipulation of the stretchy dough, but he was fascinated to watch the pair of cooks as they went about their work. Adi regaled her friends with the story of the night prior. Though they spoke closely and in hushed tones, the girls simply could not contain their squeals of excitement for the realization of the princess's love. They teased her about how they had known all along that things would end up this way, and though she playfully protested, she did not mind.

Adiadni explained to Fennispar when they left the kitchen that she and Uritus wished to avoid especially public spaces until the rest of their companions arrived. Even so, they were happy to journey with him to the stables to introduce him to the fisherman's horse. Fennispar stroked the stallion's shiny black coat as Uritus told him the *Legend of the Moonracer* and the boy regarded the animal with sparkling, wonder-filled eyes. By evening's end, when their meal had concluded, the dwarf child was exhausted and went eagerly to bed.

357

The few days after that sucked the fisherman and princess into a blissful state of rest and closeness during which they were seldom apart. He joined her when she saw her family, when Agamemnon was up and about or resting in his chambers. They would play games or indulge Fennispar and Pressio when they wanted to hear the tales of their journey. All the while, it was clear to Uritus just how intentionally Adi's family sought to make him feel welcome and better get to know him. They asked earnest questions about his life, his work, his interests, and he answered them honestly, noticing also how they refrained from directly asking him anything about Erclidus, which he appreciated.

It wasn't long before the fisherman found himself feeling quite at home here, in this city, with these people around him. And though he remained committed to spending these days focused *only* on these days rather than the ones ahead, he could not help but occasionally wonder about where he would end up once the war had reached its end.

Other than the mornings or afternoons spent with Adiadni's family and friends, the pair's time was their own, and they melted into it. They passed hours in the gardens and libraries and orchard talking, laughing, sharing food and drink, reading aloud stories to one another. Their connection deepened and their love and friendship grew, and by the time their companions arrived once more in Suscundos, Uritus and Adiadni had all but forgotten what life was like before they found each other.

***

The party returned to trumpets and fanfare. The Suvah and Adalos watched the colorful petals and fronds spiraling joyfully through the air from where they stood on the steps in front of the palace. Though they hadn't intended the arrival to happen this way, they were glad that at this moment, the praises of the city were directed to those who had gone beside them on their journey. They deserved just as much recognition for the astounding feat they had accomplished as the two who had led them. They extended their hands in thanks as they wound their way through the streets and came to a stop in front of the palace. Perplexus looked to be the proudest of all of them as he waved to the crowd and then smoothly dismounted. He hastened up the steps to embrace his friends there, a flower caught on his belt and another dangling from his pauldron.

"Thank you for bringing Swadalla back safely," Adiadni said gratefully as she pulled back from his hug. "Did she mind the river?"

"The rafts were wide and slow-moving. I don't think she even realized she was on the water."

The princess laughed and the navigator turned to Uritus, "I brought something of yours too." He reached a hand behind his back and from under his green cape, he produced the Sword of Fire and held it out proudly to his friend.

The Adalos smiled as he saw the gleam of gold and lifted his eyes to Perplexus as he took it from him.,"Thank you. I am glad to have both of you back at my side again."

"Hand to the sky, Hero," Lex replied, running his eyes over the gathered masses. "They look to you now."

Uritus did not need to turn his head to know that this was true. He tightened his grip around the sheath clutched in his right hand and thrust it proudly above his head. His smile met his friend's as thunderous applause rose in response.

***

"I am exceedingly glad for your safe and successful return to our fair city and I wish to extend my gratitude to each of you. You have exceeded all expectations, protected my daughter, returned with the sacred weapon, and collected vital intelligence about the enemies we prepare to face. Myself and my bloodline and the whole of this precious nation we call home are forever in your debt," Agamemnon addressed the travelers on the veranda where they gathered. "I also wish to offer you my condolences for your fallen comrade. I know that Havian was close to you. I was sorry to learn of his death."

The companions lowered their heads in acknowledgment and sorrow.

"Adiadni tells me he fell to the Forest of Idor."

Uriah nodded affirmatively. "We were met with resistance when we attempted to pass through the forest. In his endeavor to push back against it, he met his end."

The king sighed sadly. "I am sorry to hear that. Most of all, I am sorry that I did not amend the map on my own and simply send you around the forest to begin with. Of course the breaking of the treaty would be met with resistance. I wished only to avoid making decisions that were not mine to make, but such a decision was, itself, the wrong one. I ask your forgiveness for how I failed you and him."

"Havian would ultimately fall due to the consequences of his own decisions, but we appreciate your compassion," said Punznes. "We do not fault you for his death and neither would he."

The king nodded graciously. "Even so, know that your friend will be memorialized. When future generations tell stories of these times, Havian's name will be spoken along with the rest of yours. Now, before we proceed to the main purpose of our gathering," he turned his attention to the newcomer, "I wish to welcome you, Alidistris, to Suscundos. My family and I are honored to have you as a guest in our home. My daughter tells me you displayed great bravery in defiance of your leaders."

He paused and the attention of the others turned to the woman from the West. She looked to Mikka who nodded encouragingly, and then stood to address the king, "Thank you, your highness, but… if I may speak freely…" She hesitated and he gave her a nod, a patient expression worn on his face. "Velup and Erclidus were not my leaders. If anything… they were my captors."

Agamemnon nodded again. "I understand. I am glad that you are now free of them. Know that here, you hold the reins to your life's bridle. While we will offer you all the support you may need to begin such a new life for yourself, you are welcome to create your home wherever and however you please. Your courage, free will, and boldness are emblematic of the spirit of the Free People. You are one of us, if you would wish to be."

A smile bloomed on Alidistris's face. "Thank you, I think I would."

The newest companion returned to her seat and the king gestured to the pedestal standing in the center of the veranda. "Now we may—" He sputtered, doubling over as his mysterious ailment wracked his body. Adi sprang to her feet and set a hand against his back. "I'm all right," he assured her. "My apologies."

"You can sit, Aggie…" Betina's voice was thin and laced with worry.

"Nonsense…"

"You must mind your wife's instincts, Agamemnon," spoke Aurena from the place she stood behind the king. "Be wise about how you choose to expend your strength."

"It's all right, Adda."

The plea of his daughter led Agamemnon to return to his seat with a sigh. "Thank you, my dear," he said to her gratefully, moving his left hand to take his wife's.

"I can speak for you," she said, her voice low.

He nodded, turning his attention to the man directly across from him, "Uritus, would you be willing to partner with Adiadni in leading this council in my stead?"

The Adalos stood, lowering his head in a humble bow. "I would."

"Very well."

The king nodded to the princess and she proceeded, "I have already informed my father of Velup's plan to attack the Mirrored Cities. He has begun organizing the movement of soldiers to the Western Provinces as well as the evacuation of those who will be most at risk. I understand some of you found material evidence of this plan in the Ashen Keep?"

Perplexus stood and proceeded to the pedestal where he placed the annotated map he had found with Punznes. "We did. They intend to march straight from the Western front to Judii and Lorethh, split their forces in half, and lay siege upon both cities at once. Unfortunately, the map shows us only a general plan of attack, but Mik, Rip, and Laiv found more which confirms this theory."

The navigator returned to his seat and Laivar approached the pedestal. He set upon it a pair of sketches, one of Lorethh and one of Judii, each of them an overhead view of the city and its anatomy. "We found these in the study of Octrusial, the Seer on the council of Velup's most trusted. There were many more there. He seems to have been using his abilities to map out the cities and their weak points. There were sketches of Suscundos as well, though not as many. We tried not to take too much with us for fear that they may alter their plans if they know we've found out about them, but…" The bard hesitated before producing another piece of paper from the inner pocket of his vest. "There is something else…"

He set the paper, weathered and torn, upon the pedestal. The king and princess leaned forward to regard it.

"It's a partial letter, its salutation naming Octrusial. It is mostly illegible as it is water-damaged and faded, and the second half is missing so we do not know who it is from, but it appears to speak of a curse directed toward... you, king Agamemnon."

Both Uritus and Adiadni were surprised by this. They turned to the king with expressions of shock.

"We believe Velup to be responsible for both the drought and the plague which ravaged the Lake Provinces," Uriah explained as Laivar returned to his seat. "The letter may be from Velup; however, if there is a curse set upon you, I am confident that he is not the one who sent it."

"What do you mean?" questioned Adiadni.

"Sorcerers have limits to their power just as Wizards do. Velup can manipulate matter—physical objects—but he has no power over living beings."

"It is true," affirmed Veldis from his place against the palace wall. "If a curse has been sent from the West, it is from an Alchemist."

The air grew thick with the seriousness of the matter.

Uritus looked to Alidistris, "Have you any knowledge of an Alchemist amongst Velup's ranks?"

"I... might..." She hesitated before standing to her feet. "That is... I think I've heard of him, but I have never seen him before and so doubt he resides at the Ashen Keep."

"Do you know his name?"

"I believe it is Ouro. But I don't know anything else about him, I'm afraid..."

"That's all right," Adiadni assured her. "A name is a helpful start."

"Are you able to divine things about him? About your enemies?"

"Yes and no," replied Olythia to the newcomer. Their hood was set further back on their head than it had been the first time Uritus had met the Prophet, allowing him to see the sharp curves of their facial features. "Knowing his name now—even knowing just that such an Alchemist exists—myself and the other Prophets will pray to the Divine and ask them to reveal him to us. But that is all. We have no control over what is revealed. We see what we are given and we do what we can with that."

"I see... So your power, your *sight* is... different from Octrusial's?"

"Indeed. A Seer—like an Alchemist, like a Sorcerer—does not partner with the energy. They take from it in search of personal or material gain. This is why we call them Thieves. Such practices offer them the appearance of control over their... *abilities*... In Octrusial's case, the ability to spy on the Free World whenever he wishes. But because the energy does not pass freely into their hands, their shade of Magic is tainted. It steals from them just as they steal from it."

Alidistris tilted her head. "What do you mean by that?"

"Olythia speaks of how those who seek to profit off of the Source face consequences for it, though they are often blind to them," replied Uriah. "While Octrusial can observe the goings-on of our homeland, he cannot see anything that directly relates to himself or his fate. He is also blind to discerning if anything he sees is inaccurate or false. I have seen firsthand the consequences of Velup's centuries of service to himself. His old age has made him frail and it requires much of his power to simply sustain his life. And for Ouro…"

"He is plagued by an ailment," spoke Aurena. "Festering and incurable. The more energy he directs in attempt to heal himself, the more it will grow."

The woman from the West nodded as she internalized this. "It is quite confidence-inducing to know that my new allies have such a clear advantage over those from the place I grew up."

"There are many benefits to allowing the Mother to move through you rather than trying to cut off a piece of her for yourself. Nevertheless, we must remain vigilant. There is much still to do."

The others on the veranda nodded solemnly and Uritus turned again to address Alidistris, "Is there anything else you can tell us about the land to the West or Velup's council?"

She thought for a moment before she answered, "I spent most of my life at the Ashen Keep, working in Velup's home, but I was not born there. I came from a village just a few miles South of it. To my knowledge, there are three more like villages along the front, though I cannot say exactly where. My village was run by a gruff man, not a wielder of Magic, just a general named Trugstar. I would reckon that the other villages have, each of them, a similar overseer as well."

"What goes on in the villages?"

"Labor, mostly. They are walled fortresses with crowded shacks for living quarters. As soon as the children are old enough to grasp how to use tools, they are put to work. My village primarily forged weapons and armor, all sorts of metal fabrication. I detested it. That's how I ended up moving to the keep. They needed more hands to labor in the house so I volunteered…" She paused, becoming suddenly teary-eyed as she turned her attention to the king. "There are good people there still…" she said. "In my home village and the keep. They suffer daily for the sins of their ancestors, they do not deserve such a fate. I do not wish for them to be exterminated as a product of this great conflict."

King Agamemnon nodded compassionately. "I assure you, we do not quarrel with any who are being held against their will. We will stand to face all who rise against us, but when the Shadow has been vanquished and this is over, we will assure your people's safe passage into our land for all who would wish it."

"Thank you," she nodded gratefully, returning to her seat. "That is all I ask."

The king lowered his head to her before turning to address the rest of the group, "Now, it will not be long before our allies from the East join us in Suscundos. When they do, I will swiftly send them on. You all have done vital work to further our cause and, while I will not fault you if you wish to go now and seek your peace, I tell you that the crown could benefit greatly from your continued partnership."

"Say no more, we are with you," Perplexus declared, and the others nodded affirmatively. "We will gladly do whatever it takes to see that this conflict reaches a swift and victorious end."

"Very well," Agamemnon lowered his head graciously. "I will find suitable positions for each of you amongst my troops and send you also to defend the Mirrored Cities when the time comes. However..."

He paused for a moment, lifting his eyes to Adiadni. She nodded, proceeding with the rest of his thought, "After much discussion, my father has begrudgingly relented to my insistence that he not take up his sword alongside us for our next battle."

The others nodded solemnly as they considered the gravity of the king's condition.

"I have told him what I am sure you all will agree with—that he is no use to us if he is dead and that we will need his wisdom and guidance in the coming days. Now that we know his ailment may be due to a curse, my father's Healers may have a better chance to protect him."

Aurena nodded in agreement. "We may redirect our energy to fighting against its source rather than the ailment itself."

Adiadni went on, "Hopefully, he will soon be well enough to join us in battle. Until then, I will go in his stead. Vindellas have protected this land for hundreds of years and such a charge will not die with me."

"Thank you, my dear," the king said before turning to the Adalos. "The hour of your destiny is nigh," he spoke seriously. "That blade you wear on your hip is the key to our liberation, but so is the courage which resides in your heart. I know the events that have led you here have been sudden and jarring, as well as the personal nature of this whole ordeal and how it relates to you. I ask you this not as your king, but as a citizen of this land we both love... will you take up your sword and lead our people to victory?"

"I will." Uritus did not hesitate. "Though I know not what I am doing, though I do not feel worthy of the charge, I have followed it thus far. I will see it through to the end."

"Very well," Agamemnon gave him an appreciative nod. "I believe that concludes our business..."

"There's actually one more thing..."

The others turned to regard the fisherman with curious expressions.

He proceeded, "When I saw Erclidus, he spoke about having seen things regarding the coming days. I'm sure he meant that Octrusial had, but he also said they hadn't been able to see me. My arrival in the West was a surprise to him. I didn't get the chance to ask what he meant by it, but... he thought the reason why was due to this..." He lifted a hand to the ornament around his neck gifted to him by his father.

"Amonii is a protective agent," Aurena confirmed. "It wards against that which might try to harm you. It would seem that includes watchful eyes. Thank you, Uritus, this is very helpful. Amonii is rare, but we have some in Suscundos.

I can reach out to Healers in other regions to see if they do as well. Keep it with you always," she said seriously. "Your invisibility is a great advantage for us. We will fashion tokens for the rest of you before you set out again."

"Thank you, Aurena, that will be a great help." The king once more regarded those gathered before him. "For tonight, enjoy yourselves as best you can. The celebration is for you. Drink and dine and dance while you are able. The days to come will prove challenging, but for now, rest and refresh your spirits."

The council concluded, the companions departed from the veranda.

Chapter Twenty-Four

"Hope Has Wings"

The 30th of July

The home of celebrants took such a reputation very seriously, and that night was no exception. The victorious travelers threw themselves into vivid color and vibrant mirth. They made merry and told stories and reconnected with the Suscundos natives they had come to know when last they were here. Though nothing could make them forget the things they had seen and those they were still to face, they welcomed the friendly distraction all the same.

They were glad to be reminded of what it was they were fighting for, this freedom and joy and sense of community. The food energized them and the ale warmed their bellies and Laivar sang loudly and proudly of the tales of their journey. The others found it amusing that their bard had amassed somewhat of a following in the capital and they jokingly warned him not to let such fame go to his head.

They couldn't help but marvel when reminded that *they* were the cause for such celebration. Though they were well aware of the great feats they had accomplished, it was still hard to comprehend that they would continue to be celebrated for them until the end of time. They kept one another pointed toward humility, chiding each other when they attempted to downplay their victories. The night grew long and the party continued and even Uriah joined the others in a few rounds of Kepu and later, Frali, with the deck Perplexus had obtained in Ehjonadi.

It felt strange for Uritus and Adiadni to need to revert to behaving as though they were merely friends and comrades. Those within the palace and the princess's inner circle already knew of the progression in their relationship, as did their traveling companions. But with the engagement not yet formally broken off, the pair became particularly mindful of their appearances. The citizens of Suscundos would likely have neither noticed nor cared if the Suvah and Adalos appeared to be more affectionate with one another than they had been before. But such delicate times called for increased vigilance all the same.

Adiadni joined the man who had unintentionally become her dance partner for a spin around the floor, and Uritus looked on. He was sad to have not yet gotten the chance to engage with her in the activity that so stirred her heart and resolved that once this was all over, he would not miss the opportunity.

His friends, eager to hear the tale of what happened upon his arrival in Suscundos, were wise enough not to bring it up in this setting. Instead, they shot the fisherman amused, knowing glances from time to time. Perplexus had pried for details in the brief period he had gotten alone with Uritus in their chamber before the celebration, and Uritus had been glad to indulge him. The navigator felt a considerable amount of pride for how he had pushed him to go after the woman he loved, and the fisherman affirmed that the happiness he now felt was in no small part due to his friend's insistence. Now, in the thick of the festivities, Perplexus had passed on the things he had learned to the others, and they were overjoyed to hear of the realization of the relationship they had already known would end up this way.

The night waned on and Suscundos's Wizards began to arrange the fireworks display and Adiadni found Uritus's eyes from across the common room of The Horse and Rider. Her gaze was heavy-lidded, warm like sweet brandy, and it communicated to him that she was tired and electing to turn in for the night. He nodded and she smiled, pressing her hands to one another as she approached the door and giving him a tiny, hardly perceivable bow.

His eyes lingered on the open space beyond the frame when she left. He found it endearing how she always dipped out of gatherings quietly, never drawing attention to herself, never disrupting the flow of the event. No doubt, now that she was home with curious eyes on her once more, she was eager to enjoy a more peaceful environment before she drifted off to sleep. He took a couple of minutes to finish his ale and then headed for the door.

She was waiting for him in the palace entryway at the base of one of the curved staircases and her face lit into a smile when she saw him. Somehow, in the time it took him to get there, she had managed to remove her tiara and jewels and change into a more casual dress. He crossed the room, wrapped his arms over her shoulders, and pulled her into his embrace. He was enveloped in a cloud of her fragrance, bright and sweet and effervescent. He could not help but note the way she fit perfectly in his arms. He pulled back a bit, took her face in his hand, and allowed a silent moment to pass as he gazed at her, mesmerized by her beauty. "How did you enjoy the evening?"

She smiled. "Very much. Of course, it is impossible to fully forget the increasingly dire circumstances that surround us on all sides, but... it is wonderful to be home again. Although..." She looked up at him as she paused, an expression of longing in her eyes. "It is far less wonderful to have to force myself to be distant from you."

He chuckled, running a thumb along the smooth skin of her cheek. "At least it's not *too* distant..."

"Any length of distance between us is too much," she breathed, gripping his shirt with desperate hands in an attempt to pull him closer. "I want your hands on my skin, I want your breath in my lungs. I feel mad for how fully you consume my mind."

He moved his second hand to her face and leaned down to press his forehead to hers, "There is nothing at this point that can truly separate us. I know this period of in-between is far from ideal, and I eagerly await its end just as you do. But in the times that we must be parted, I find solace when I may merely close my eyes and find you there, your smile bright as day, your skin smooth as silk. Know that there is no breadth of space I will not traverse to be beside you again."

She opened her mouth and swallowed the last of his words and he melted into her kiss. She tasted like wine, dark and sweet, and he was swept up in the lushness of her lips. Her cheeks were flushed with heat and her fingers clawed at his chest and their mutual desperation swelled until the moment suddenly burst, punctured as the door to the palace was pulled open. They sprang apart urgently but did not make it far. They turned to the open door, attempting to neutralize their expressions as they came to regard the man who stood there.

Basil.

"What is going on here...?" The man in the swishing red cape entered the palace fully and shut the door behind him.

"Basil! I... didn't realize you'd returned. How was—"

Basil lifted a single gloved hand and Adiadni stopped speaking. "I asked you a question."

"I was just telling Adiadni goodnight."

The princess's betrothed looked to the fisherman with narrowed eyes, "I was not asking *you*."

Uritus clenched his jaw and Adi took a small step forward. "Basil, might you and I go someplace where we can talk...?"

The man in the red cape snorted, a half-laugh. "This is why you sent me away, isn't it? So you could have your fun with your new paramour without fear of consequence?"

"I don't know what you think is—"

"Oh, do not patronize me, my dear. I know what I saw!"

His voice grew loud on these last words and Adiadni shrank back slightly. Uritus's body tensed. Wishing to allow her the opportunity to fight her own battle, he clenched his hands into fists.

Adi took another step forward, steeling her resolve. "I must insist that we go somewhere else where we can have a proper conversation."

Basil chuckled, shaking his head back and forth. "So this is what I get?" He held his arms out at his sides. "I devote my life to you and you give yourself away to this? A fishmonger from Tosh of all places!"

"Fisherman."

He blinked incredulously at her. "I beg your pardon?"

She raised her chin. "Uritus is a fisherman. Not a fishmonger. You know that."

Silence choked the room. The princess saw Basil's eye twitch.

"You do not deny it then?"

Adiadni hesitated a moment, but only a moment. "I do not."

Basil appeared dumbfounded. It was clear on his face that he had expected her to argue, to fight back against his accusation and plead with him to understand, but this... This was far worse an outcome than he had anticipated.

"You were *never* worthy of this!" He reached out and snatched her left wrist but his hand was ripped away from her in a sudden flurry of movement before she could gasp.

Uritus lunged forward, grabbed Basil by the breastplate, and shoved him back several paces. "Don't *fucking* touch her," he spat.

Basil stumbled back, finding his feet as Uritus planted himself directly in front of Adiadni. Basil's face split into an expression of rage. He rushed forward, one hand moving for his sword.

"No!"

Adi yanked Uritus behind her by the fabric of his shirt and raised a hand to Basil. A light shock wave traveled through the air from her fingers to meet his chest and he staggered back.

"Drop your sword!"

Through the palace doors suddenly swarmed a small group of soldiers who hurried to Basil, disarmed him, and bound his hands behind his back. Adi took a pair of backward steps, relaxing just slightly when she bumped into Uritus's sturdy frame.

Basil did not fight against the men who restrained him, but his pride would not allow him to remain silent as they began to lead him forward, "Adiadni, I swear it on the Divine, you will rue the day you betrayed me!"

A chill ran up the princess's spine and the guards led Basil away. Adiadni buried her face in her counterpart's shirt and wept.

***

"I feel it unnecessary to brush my words with honey. Adiadni…"

Agamemnon looked down at his daughter and sighed. She knew what she had done. She knew that the consequences were grave. Now, she—feeling already guilty and frightened—awaited humbly the judgment to be passed down upon her. It would do no good to seek to humble her further. She needed a father more than she did a king.

"…This will be… difficult to reckon with."

The princess clenched her lip between her teeth. Her father was right.

"I do not fault you for his violence. Neither of you," Agamemnon looked from his daughter to the man beside her and back. "But surely I do not need to reiterate the gravity of the situation we now find ourselves in."

The royal family and the Adalos were joined in the king's study by Agamemnon's Keepers, Digtrision, and Pressio, as well as Uriah and Perplexus. The light in the solemn room grew and faded with the rhythm of the fireworks outside.

"I take responsibility for my lack of judgment," spoke the princess.

"As do I."

"I hear you both," replied the king. "But we must now leave the past where it belongs and look ahead to our next steps. This is hardly a convenient time to arrange a trial."

"The hired swords lord Dagious led to Suscundos are loyal to him," Digtrision confirmed what they all feared. "I can see in the morning if there are any amongst them who wish to enroll in our armed forces, but he offered a hefty weight of coin to get them here. I would surmise that the majority will maintain their prior loyalty."

"We really should be sending them on to the Mirrored Cities in the morning. We know not when Velup plans to launch his attack and every additional hour of delay lessens our chances of being able to defend them," Pressio reminded the room of the urgency of the matter.

"I will send you on, Pressio, in the morning with the last of the city's soldiers regardless of whether any from Basil's company join you. Digtrision will follow shortly when the recruits from Cropidea arrive. But I cannot conduct a proper trial without the pair of you here," Agamemnon addressed Uritus and Adiadni. "And I certainly cannot keep you away from the front, where you are needed far more. I have no choice but to hold Basil here until you return and conduct his trial then."

"And if his swords refuse to go on without him?"

The king looked at his nephew with a sigh, "I will respect their autonomy."

"I wish not to question your judgment, Agamemnon," spoke the cropidus, "...but such a choice could be disastrous to our cause."

"Even so, my hands are bound."

Those in the room grew deeply solemn.

"I've heard much discussion about the recruits from the East and South," noted Perplexus. "But have you sought aid from the people in the West?"

"Far fewer are those who dwell in the West. Many are farmers or laborers whose contributions to the Free World are too necessary to do without."

"What about Tila?"

All turned to regard Adiadni.

"There is a centaur clan in the forest, yes? Ogres there too. I know they generally prefer to keep to themselves, but perhaps, given the circumstances, they might be willing to ally with us."

"There are some as well in the North. Miners and ice fishers. Some will need to stay behind, of course, but I know that many would gladly rise to defend this land," added Perplexus assuredly.

Agamemnon nodded. "Both are good suggestions, but we simply do not have the means to get word to them in time. Ravens and horsemen will take too long and all four gryphons and their riders have already departed to ensure the organization of the Mirrored Cities and evacuation of civilians. I do not see any other way..."

"I have a dragon."

The council looked to Uritus in stunned silence. Perplexus smiled with a corner of his mouth.

"Well… to say that I *have* him is an inaccurate description of our relationship —he does not belong to me. But he *is* loyal to me, and I am certain that he will give me his aid if I ask it of him."

"I see," Agamemnon spoke slowly, attempting to organize his thoughts. "And you have ridden before?"

"I have, many times as a teenager. Never since then, though I am confident that I can remember how."

"Very well," said the king with a gracious nod. "Do you think you will be ready to leave by late morning?"

"Yes, though… I may seek to depart before daybreak. I wish to draw as little attention to Milion as I can."

"That is his name?"

"Milion, yes."

Agamemnon nodded once more. "Thank you, Uritus. You must extend my thanks to Milion as well. Such help may be just the thing we need to reign victorious. The Heart of Heimar is apparent within you."

The Adalos touched a hand to his chest and lowered his head with gratitude. "Thank you, I appreciate that. There is just one thing I would ask…"

"Anything."

"I, uh…" Uritus paused, trying to identify the root of his apprehension. "I suppose, I've never led anyone before. Not other than the people whom I consider to be family. And I… Well, I don't know that I know the words to inspire people to something as grim as war."

"I understand," replied the king. "Those who dwell in the Forest of Tila know of the prophecy, as should those in the White Mountains and North of them. Take up your sword and they will follow you."

The fisherman considered this. "I am sure you are correct… But I suppose the thing I truly wish to request is greater still…"

***

The area beneath the palace was used primarily for storage of the city's resources, with a few rooms available for miscellaneous purposes. But there was still a small portion of the space that served as a row of holding cells for prisoners who awaited trial. The single hall, lined with barred chambers on either side—which almost always remained unutilized—now housed the first person to be kept there in years. Basil Dagious did not hear the visitor who approached his door.

"You really should have indulged me when I requested a private audience with you."

The man from Vindellaria rose to his feet and looked to the door, surprised to see the familiar frame that stood there. "Did you come merely to mock me?"

"I did not." The princess stepped forward into the torchlight. "I still seek the audience."

"Go on then. Say what you will."

Adi looked Basil over with a sigh. They had known one another since childhood. How they had ended up taking such entirely different paths baffled her. "I prepare, as do the rest of the soldiers in Suscundos, to make my way to defend Judii and Lorethh. I regret that you will not be joining us."

Basil scoffed. "I assure you, if you mean to make me feel apologetic for what I have done, you are wasting your time."

"No, I would not assume you would be."

The man in the red cape did not respond.

Adiadni took a breath. "I do not deny that the nature of my relationship with my counterpart has turned romantic…"

"I do *not* wish to hear of this."

"But you will hear me all the same." She allowed him a silent moment to object once more. He did not. She took another breath. "Now, I know you will not believe me, but I was being honest with you after the trials when I said that he and I were merely friends. Perhaps I was attracted to him even then. Perhaps he was to me, but neither of us considered acting on such a thing. That said, over the course of the journey we undertook together, such feelings grew to be so strikingly obvious that we could no longer ignore them. If I am brutally honest with you, then I must tell you that Uritus and I are deeply in love, and such emotion is inexplicably more tangible and fulfilling than anything that I have ever felt for you.

"Now, I don't know if you ever did love me, or if rather you merely felt excitement for the knowledge of what lifelong relationship with me would grant you. Of course, I do not mean to minimize any true feelings that you did have, for there was a time when I would have considered you my friend. Nor do I wish to dangle this love that I have found in front of you to taunt you. Truthfully, I *have* been unfaithful to you. These past days since Uritus and I discovered this new layer of our relationship, I have considered my relationship with *you* to be over. I know that it was not, that you knew of none of this. You have every reason to be upset about how I have blindsided you. That said, I do not regret what I have done, and though I am sure that I owed you at least the decency of a formal end before I fell into another, given the opportunity, I cannot say that I would choose any differently. I am sorry for that."

Basil clenched and unclenched his fists, remaining silent where he stood in the center of his cell.

Adiadni continued, "Now that I have explained all of that, I need to make one thing abundantly clear: my choice to call an end to our engagement is not because of Uritus. It is not because of anyone but you." She could see a wash of anger move across his face but still, he said nothing. "There was a time when I could have loved you, when I desperately wished that I would. But when we reached adulthood, you began to change in ways that became increasingly more difficult to reconcile with. You have become a slave to your ego, blind to everything other than your self-preservation. I have never felt like anything more than a means to an end to you, and it took me until now to understand that I need more than that. That I will not settle for anything less than I deserve."

The jailed man sighed agitatedly and shook his head back and forth. "I am certain you cannot be reasoned with at this point, but I assure you, you are making a terrible mistake. I would have gone to the end of the earth for you."

"Someone already did," she replied flatly. "There are many who have, and their doing so was never contingent upon the crown which might grace their heads as a reward for it."

He scoffed. "You think you can use me like this? Rely on my gold and my influence and then toss me to the side once I've delivered what I promised? Perhaps I should allow your city to burn."

Adiadni looked him up and down, sighing sadly. "If your loyalty to the Free World hinges upon the status of your relationship with me, then that only affirms to me that I have made the correct decision."

Basil shook his head in disbelief. "What could a meager fisherman have to offer you? He has no power, no status, no skill as a commander. You are tossing your future to the wayside. I do not understand."

"You do not need to understand my choices." The princess took a small step forward and extended her hand to the bars of the cell door. "But you do need to respect them." She turned then and departed with a hasty brush of wind, the silver ring that balanced on the bar the only sign that she had been there at all.

***

Cool blue dawn stretched across the horizon from Uritus's vantage point just outside Suscundos's walls. He regarded the scene in silent wonder, realizing that this was the furthest he had ever traveled East, here on the cliffs beside roaring Tuvibati Falls. The morning was warm but the cool mist chilled his skin as it drifted into the air. The sun was preparing to rise and the fisherman lifted his eyes to the sky in eager anticipation of what was to come.

At that moment sounded the faintest distant whooshing noise, and a smile spread across Uritus's face.

When he spotted Milion, it was as a faint silhouette in the Southern sky. The dragon soared in a wide, graceful loop around the city, descending as he spiraled until he came to a stop atop the rocky cliffs and folded his wings neatly against his back. Uritus turned to regard the wide-mouthed woman who stood at his side, utterly spellbound by the creature he called friend. He smiled, nearly overwhelmed by the depth of the love he felt for her, then moved along the cliff to come to stand in front of the dragon.

He extended a hand to touch Milion's face as he reached him and Milion moved to meet it. "Thank you for coming all this way. How does it feel to be in Suscundos for the first time?"

The dragon huffed, a sound Uritus knew to be one of disagreement.

"You've been here before?" He let out a breathy laugh at the revelation. "I don't know why that's a surprise to me, you can go anywhere you would like. Have you soared over all of the Free World?"

Another warm huff of breath.

"Well, perhaps we can together sometime. But I've called you here today for another purpose. A more serious one, I'm afraid."

Milion snorted lightly and Uritus continued, "This land we love is in danger. I intend to do what I can to try to save it, and right now, the most valuable thing I can do is seek out others who also might be able to help. I need to get to Tila Forest as soon as I can and then to the White Mountains after that. Would you be willing to take me there?"

The dragon lifted his head and lowered it again, a deep rumble traveling up from his belly.

Uritus smiled. "Thank you, my friend. I should let you know before we go that there is a likelihood that people might see you…"

Milion snorted again to communicate that he didn't mind.

"All right then. You are doing a great thing. The Free World is grateful to you just as I am." The Adalos paused, running his eyes over the smooth sheen of the dragon's scales. "Before we leave though, I have one more request. This woman who stands behind me is named Adiadni."

Milion moved his head to the side to regard her and the princess's hands found one another as she waited.

"She's very important to me. But she is also incredibly important to the Free World, and having her along with me as I seek the aid of others would be most helpful. I know that I'm the only one who has ever flown with you, and I understand if you would prefer to keep it that way—"

The end of Uritus's sentence was cut off by one of Milion's affirmative rumbles.

Uritus paused in his surprise, a smile spreading across his face. "Are you certain?"

A second rumble.

"Thank you, my friend. Can I invite her over to say hello?"

The dragon raised his head with a snort.

Uritus turned to look over his shoulder and moved his hand from Milion's face to extend toward Adiadni. "He wants to meet you."

The princess swallowed her intimidation and stepped slowly forward. This creature was regal and proud, but he had an air of gentleness about him which made her feel decidedly more at ease. She tried not to think too hard about how they would soon be skybound.

Uritus took her hand as she arrived beside him and, with an encouraging smile, guided it to come to rest on Milion's face. She relaxed a bit more, feeling the bumps of smooth, tightly packed scales beneath her fingertips. She was amazed at how the size of the dragon's face made her hand appear tiny as she had more than enough room to stretch out her fingers in the space between his eyes. He rumbled and snorted and gave his head a little shake. She startled at the sound and leapt back a bit, nervously giggling as she again brought her hand to touch him.

"It's all right," Uritus assured her, bringing a loving hand to rest against her back. "You have no reason to fear him, just as he has no reason to fear you."

She nodded as she relaxed further. "You are magnificent," she proclaimed, and the dragon's low rumble met her in response. "I am honored to meet you, as I will be to fly with you."

Uritus could not help but smile as he watched the interaction between the two he loved. Adi giggled as Milion nuzzled her hand with his nose, adoringly pouring affirmations over him the way she did with everyone she came into contact with. Seeing her now, one would never guess that she had been nervous. She was Heimar's descendant, after all. Of course she would be a natural with a dragon. Uritus lifted his eyes to the Eastern sky and saw the soft golden glow of morning begin to breach the horizon.

"If it's all right with the two of you, we should probably be on our way."

Milion snorted and raised his head, moving so his left shoulder was oriented toward his rider. The Adalos turned to his counterpart, "Ready?"

She gave him a little nod, anxious but excited. He smiled and took her chin in his hand and kissed her before turning to mount the dragon. She watched him with fascinated eyes. Milion moved his left foot away from his body, lowering his shoulder so Uritus could reach him. Uritus approached and raised his hands, setting one on the joint where Milion's wing met his back and gripping the other around one of the spines that sprouted from the back of his neck. Raising his left foot to step onto Milion's leg, he lifted himself up and swung his other leg over, mounting the dragon with as much ease as he did his horse.

Adiadni stood for a silent moment, lips parted, in awe of the casual capability of the man she loved. He had asked her to come with him because he feared that his words would not be enough, and she knew that he was worried that his lack of a title or leadership experience or his unrecognizable name might serve as a barrier between himself and those he hoped to inspire to follow him. But every time he moved, every time he tended to a task, every time he sprang to action, she saw so much clearer how no one could wear his boots but him. It was as plain to her as it was to everyone else that the fisherman was exactly where he needed to be, and none of them—not his family, nor hers, nor the citizens of Suscundos—had a shadow of a doubt of the victory he would lead them to. He didn't need words. The person he was was enough.

"Do you trust me?"

She looked at his outstretched hand with a bright smile and a light laugh. "I do. Unequivocally."

"Come on then. We'll keep you safe."

She stepped forward, took his hand, and pulled herself up to sit behind him on Milion's back. The dragon raised himself and brought his foot beneath him again, and Adi shrieked at the sudden movement and tightly wound her arms around Uritus.

"You're all right." The fisherman touched his left hand to both of hers, holding them soothingly. "It's safer than it seems. I've never fallen, not once. He knows we're here. We can trust him."

The princess nodded and leaned forward to rest her cheek against his back. She took in a series of slow breaths and he breathed with her. The skin of his hand warmed hers and she felt the steady rocking of his body with his breath. Any remaining apprehension she felt melted away like butter on bread.

"Ready?"

"Ready."

He smiled and let go of her hand to grip the second spine at the base of the two rows that stretched along Milion's neck. "Take to the wind when you'd like."

The dragon stretched out his wings and raised himself onto his hind legs. With a pair of powerful flaps, he lifted off toward the sky.

Adi kept her arms fast around Uritus's torso and squeezed her legs on either side of Milion's spine, trying to remind herself to steady her breaths. She turned her head to the right and saw Suscundos from overhead, watching in awe as the city she adored shrank and then vanished as Milion's path of flight lifted them above the clouds. The sky had brightened with the break of day and all around them spun a sea of golden, cottony wisps, stretching thin enough in places that they could still see the topography of the Free World from above. The sight took Adiadni's breath away.

Uritus had not forgotten the joy of the way the wind beat against his chest up here, and the thrill felt just as fulfilling as it ever had. Milion moved with such grace, powerful wings spread wide to float along with the wind. It was Uriah who had taught the fisherman that, while flyers find homes for themselves when they reach maturity, they can go for days or even weeks without touching land. The idea of such a life exhilarated Uritus, and he was deeply grateful for every chance he got to taste it.

"How are you feeling?" he called to his counterpart who had slightly loosened her grip around his body.

She responded with a delighted laugh and a shout, "Alive!"

He laughed along with her, oblivious to the ache in his brow. "This is my favorite part!" The Adalos released his hold on one of the spines, raising one arm high in the air and then doing the same with the other. Arms stretched wide, he threw his head back and loudly whooped, an excited sound that traveled up from his belly.

His joyful cry was met by the dragon's roar, and Adiadni joined in with a passionate scream and they soared on, bound South-and-West for Tila Forest.

***

Uritus spotted a clearing tucked within the sprawling treescape and directed Milion to let them down there. The dragon obliged, coming to an elegant stop, and his rider thanked him and dismounted. Several centaurs and ogres were already scattered throughout the field and more curious faces appeared from the treeline at the dramatic arrival of the dragon who carried the travelers. Uritus regarded them briefly before turning back to Milion and lifting Adiadni down.

"I'm not sure how long we'll be, but I'll call you when we're ready to travel on again," spoke the Adalos to the dragon. "Thank you for getting us here."

Milion snorted, spread his wings, and soared up into the sky and out of sight. Adi watched him leave, and when she moved her eyes back to the earth again, she saw that many had gathered there. A centaur woman stepped forward, tall, strong, bronze-complected, with thick, wild, chestnut waves the same shade as her coat. She wore a fine-crafted caramel leather bodice with many jeweled rings on her hands and a broadsword strapped to her back.

"A captivating entrance," she addressed them, her voice powerful. "I am Xinna, commander of this clan. You have our attention."

"Uritus Subian," the fisherman touched his right hand to his chest. "I hail from Tosh but... well, now..." he trailed off, finding himself lost for words, and looked to Adiadni with uncertainty.

She took a step forward. "I am Adiadni Vindella, daughter and heir to our king, Agamemnon Vindella, and the prophesied Way-Maker." Adi's dress and armor left her birthmark visible to all who regarded her. "My counterpart is the general of our king's armed forces, the prophesied Hero who bears the Sword of Fire. We seek an audience with your head council."

Xinna nodded in understanding. "The princess and the general? I would surmise that you do not travel all this way for merely a casual visit."

"We do not, I am afraid."

"Mmm." The centaur paused and turned her head to the right and the gathered crowd parted to make way for another centaur and an ogre.

"I am Azanthien, Xinna's brother and second commander of the centaurs in Tila." Azanthien had richly colored skin, hair, and eyes, and bore a similar broadsword to his sister's, positioned on his back for a left-handed grip.

"And I am Vulsdon, speaker for the ogre colony." Vulsdon stood almost as tall as the centaurs, his broad frame hunched slightly at the shoulders. His skin was mostly blueish-gray, speckled, fading in some places to a light beige, and the armor that plated his body was thin and flexible. He spoke again, his voice a deep growl, "What is it you would ask of us?"

Uritus looked to Adiadni and she nodded her encouragement. The Adalos took a breath. "We have been sent by king Agamemnon in search of recruits for the impending war. Myself and Adiadni have been West of the Looming Mountains and we have met those who intend to lay siege on the Free World. They are preparing to march on Judii and Lorethh as we speak."

"Long have we awaited the return of the foreseen Shadow, as we have the two who would rise to vanquish it. Our ancestors saw the war that preceded this one.

Stories of its horrors pass down to this day. Why should we leave the safety of the forest to face such horrors again?"

"When our enemy comes, he will not stop until he has conquered every corner of this map. The sooner we might lay this threat to rest, the better. We'll have a far greater chance if all our peoples can unite."

"You are correct about that. But you misunderstand me—Tila cannot be touched. Not by anyone who would wish to harm her. She is a Conduit, like the White Mountains, like the Eldest Forest, like Idor. The concentration of Divine energy is high enough here that the forest will be protected, and we with it."

"We are not denying your request," Azanthien clarified. "We wish simply to gather all the facts before we make such a heavy decision. We must do what is best for those we are charged to protect."

"We understand," Uritus replied. "As must we. We would not ask such a thing of you were the circumstances anything but dire."

"Surely, the king has had much time to prepare for this impending conflict. Has he anything to say for why he does not appear before us himself?"

Uritus's mouth tried to form words to answer Vulsdon's question but found none. Adiadni spoke for him, "My father has succumbed to a mystery illness—a curse we believe to have been sent by an Alchemist on the council of Velup the Sorcerer."

"I am sorry to hear that," Azanthien replied.

"As for the rest, well… an ally of ours that we were counting on has threatened to rescind his support due to complications of a personal nature. We are hopeful that some of his troops will be willing to join our armed forces, but we cannot count on it. The future of this nation depends on our victory."

"We are willing to consider an allyship," spoke Azanthien again, "...but we do not have any intention of joining an army. When this conflict is done, we will wish to return to our life as swiftly as we can."

"We understand. My father is willing to pay any contracted swords who will stand alongside us. You will retain command over your ranks and be under no obligation to continue to fight any longer than you would wish."

Xinna lowered her head to the princess. "A fair proposal. We will convene to discuss it. You are welcome to rest here in the meadow until we determine our answer."

Adiadni pressed her hands to one another and bowed her head to the council. "Thank you. We are grateful for your hospitality."

***

The travelers were led to a resting place beside a large fire and offered food and drink while the community's leaders gathered in a crimson tent at the edge of the meadow. Adi and Uritus accepted the offerings graciously. They were glad for the warm meal, a hearty stew in a thick, salty gravy abundant with meat and vegetables. They were also given warm, crusty bread to be eaten with butter, honey, and herbs, and mugs of cold raspberry mead. They engaged with the people who approached—mostly children—who questioned them about their journey and the dragon they had ridden to get here. So vibrant was the life that bloomed in Tila, and both the Adalos and the Suvah felt sad for how they had to interrupt it.

The day stretched to evening and still, the young people waited, Uritus lying on his back with his head in Adiadni's lap. She ran a hand through his hair, seeking to comfort him for how he felt discouraged by his tongue-tie. "Everything you say is so eloquent and clear," he said. "You always know the right words. I intend to keep trying, but I cannot imagine a world where I could ever find them the way you can."

She shook her head at him. "I was not born knowing the right thing to say. I have learned much from my father and the other mentors in my life. You cannot fault yourself for being imperfect at something you've only just tried. You will find your voice. I am sure of it."

She leaned down and placed a gentle kiss upon his forehead as the flap of the crimson tent was pushed to the side to make way for the council. Adi and Uritus stood to their feet. It was Xinna who stepped forward and spoke, "After much deliberation, we have concluded that we will grant your request. Myself and my brother can offer three thousand swords."

Vulsdon added, "And I will lead a thousand."

The king's messengers lowered their heads in thanks.

"We will, however, need something from you in return."

"What is your ask?" questioned the fisherman.

Xinna proceeded, "We will need to swiftly make ready to depart North for the Mirrored Cities, and doing so will require the organization of weapons and supplies. Such a thing is costly, and while we are sure you did not travel with much coin, any assistance you can provide would be a great help."

Adiadni snatched her golden tiara off her head and tossed it to the centaur who caught it in mid-air. "Take that. Let it serve as an advance payment."

Xinna held the shiny headpiece out in her hand, attempting to calculate its value. "This helps, but it is not quite enough. If it is all you have, we are willing to make do, we just will not be able to bring as many."

Adi bit her lip and looked down at her person. She carried with her nothing else of any value, nothing but her sword and armor which she could not be parted with. In a sudden flash of memory, Uritus reached for his bag. He rifled through it for a moment before he found what he sought, a silver object which he also tossed to the council. Vulsdon caught it and held it up to examine it. Adiadni's hand fluttered to her mouth as she realized what it was: a silver tiara inlaid with smooth jade stones that had remained in Uritus's possession since the first night of the Summer festival.

"This will do," affirmed the ogre. "We will make haste and arrive in Lorethh as soon as we can."

The pair thanked them for their allyship and gratefully declined their offer of beds for the night as they had to be on to their next destination. The meadow was cleared so there was space enough for Milion to comfortably return, though Tila's citizens remained at the treeline, eagerly waiting to catch a glimpse of the majestic beast. The Adalos and Suvah parted with warm goodbyes and the dragon took them away into the sky.

The sun had begun to dip toward the Western horizon as they soared North to the White Mountains and all around them spun clouds of orange, purple, and pink. Above was the endless sky, warm and blue.

Both riders let the victorious feeling that gripped their hearts fully consume them. This time, when Uritus spread his arms wide to feel as though he was the one with wings, Adiadni did the same, wind ripping through her hair, fearless fists plunged toward the sky. Uritus's whoops of joy evolved to become an exuberant laugh. He reached his right hand to his side, drew his sword, and thrust it proudly above him.

Adiadni shed a grateful tear for the scene set before her. Of all the places she'd been, all the things she'd seen, it was this that felt the most like home: Uritus, his sword in his hand, a clear, open sky above him.

Chapter Twenty-Five

"Be Smart, Be Safe"

The 5th of August

The Mirrored Cities came by such a name due to their layouts, symmetrically designed to be the exact mirror image of the other. They were square cities, each shielded by a thick stone wall and separated from one another by less than a half-mile, Judii residing North of Lorethh. Each had four wide gates to allow easy access to travelers who journeyed from all directions, but now, those who kept watch in the Western gatehouses saw to their duties with a heightened sense of vigilance.

The sound of white stone under his boots grounded Uritus as he moved through Judii's city center, eyes roving over the soldiers gathered there. The company led by Digtrision had just arrived—the last of the Eastern recruits—and having been given their assignments, split up into two groups which now were being outfitted and prepared for battle. The Adalos attempted to quiet the anxious whisperings in his mind, but every time his eyes met with those of one of his soldiers, he could think only of the devastating reality that many of those who followed him would do so to their deaths. His attempts to shut down such thoughts proving futile, he shifted his focus to aiding the organizers however he could, only to find that such duties were, apparently, far beneath the general.

Overall, he did feel in a much better mental place after the journey he took with Adiadni in search of their last recruits. They had arrived in the White Mountains to find that the Northern people had already begun to organize themselves to join the war effort, aided by Zaphron and Robalto. Perplexus had been right that the Northerners would be glad to take up their swords. Twenty-five hundred more recruits arrived at the front a mere few days after the Suvah and Adalos. But now, the two were separated again, each of them a general tasked with the safekeeping of one of the two cities, and Uritus found himself feeling somewhat lost without her example to look to.

Meanwhile, in her chamber in Lorethh's city center, Adiadni donned a new uniform. The wispy dress she ordinarily wore beneath soft leather armor felt to her better suited for public appearances than for battle, even after having seen combat while wearing it once before. This new outfit—crafted especially for her and enchanted by Veldis with a protective spell—was practical and comfortable with elements that resembled the uniform frequently worn by the Healers. Lightweight, deep purple trousers covered her bottom half, cinched at the waist and ankles, and on top, a white shirt, sleeveless, which she found she quite liked. Her armor adorned her torso, arms, and legs, and her boots fit snugly on her feet, well worn in now thanks to the journey they had taken with her. Her hair was tied up on the back of her head, a curly tail that hung against her back, and a simple gold band crowned her head. Save for her stone talisman, she wore no ornaments.

"How do you feel? Can you move well enough?"

The princess nodded at the Healer's reflection in the looking glass. "I feel… ready?" She chewed on her lip as she contemplated this. "I mean, I'm not, of course, I don't know how one ever could be. But I feel almost like… Like I can be sure that my body will do what it must even if my mind cannot keep up."

Aurena chuckled softly. "You've become quite adept at trusting your instincts. They will serve you well." She turned to open a small chest that sat atop a dresser. "One more thing though, and arguably the most important…" From the chest, she produced a pair of golden armbands, not unlike the ones she wore herself. She approached Adiadni, holding the bands out so she could see them clearly, and the princess caught a glimpse of the shimmering material lining the inner part of each. "Now when the watchful eyes of the enemy look for you, they will see nothing but the darkness of their souls."

Adi removed her gauntlets and held out her arms so Aurena could fasten the bands to her wrists, feeling the cool pressure of metal and shell as it wrapped around her skin.

"They'll ground you too," the Healer went on. "Sharpen your intuition, clear your mind. Not like you need it." She stepped back to get a proper look at the girl she loved, clasping her hands together with a proud smile. "*Now* you're ready."

Adiadni turned to the looking glass once more and lowered her gaze to regard the golden bands. "I don't think I ever expected to have a token of my own."

Aurena chuckled again. "Olythia, Veldis, and I always anticipated the arrival of such a day. The debate was just a matter of which one it would be. Naturally, I feel quite smug to be the one who gets to adorn you with yours, though, from what I've heard, the Prophet's ring or Wizard's staff could have been equally apt for you."

The princess shrugged dismissively. "I am far from well-learned in any of the Magical practices…"

The Healer clucked her tongue and stepped forward, cupping a hand beneath the younger woman's chin to lift her face. "The experience you have gained in the real world is far more valuable than anything I could teach you at the Academy. It is *you*, Adiadni, who have been chosen, and whether it be Mother or Source or Divine that calls to you, know that you have all you need. If you need a reminder, look here." With her second hand, Aurena took Adi's and lifted it to press against the princess's chest.

Adiadni felt her heart's beat, calm and steady, and nodded her head.

"And if you do get overwhelmed, don't worry. We'll be with you the whole time."

"I know. Thank you. I don't like having to keep you away from Adda, but I am glad to have you here."

Aurena sighed understandingly. "Both Agamemnon and I agreed that I can be of far greater help here than in Suscundos. But he is not alone. He has an entire company of physicians and Healers with him, many of them more skilled than I. We may well return to find him in full health yet again."

Adi nodded. "I hope you are right. I suppose I just find it hard to focus on what I am here to do when I am so achingly worried about him."

"I know. I am sorry I cannot quiet your mind."

"Perhaps I can, even if only temporarily."

Adiadni's head snapped to the door and her jaw dropped as she regarded the person who had managed to enter the room without a sound—tall, raven-headed, dressed as though she was ready for battle. "Crys!"

"Hi, Birdie."

The princess squealed as she raced forward, throwing her arms around her cousin's neck and squeezing her tightly. Crystella returned her embrace with a laugh and Aurena made her way to the door. "I'll leave the two of you be. Find me, Adiadni, when you're finished, for the last of your tools." Adi nodded and the Healer departed from the room.

"It's about time you arrived! I began to wonder if you'd show your face at all."

Adi's comment was clearly said in jest but Crystella clutched a hand to her heart and stumbled back as if she had been fatally wounded. "You insult me! I'll have you know, it took Diggie and me only *four days* to lead a company of fifteen hundred here from Suscundos. Such a thing is unheard of!"

The princess giggled. "Does he know you still call him that?"

"Never to his face, he'd have my head. But he'll always be Diggie in my heart."

"I take it your presence in Lorethh means that you are my second general?"

"That I am… Why? Would you prefer Diggie?"

"You're ridiculous, I'm overjoyed that it's you! If I am honest though, I still cannot believe that it is not you who will be leading *me*."

"Nonsense, you've gone to battle."

"So have you!"

"Tell me Birdie, what's worse, bandits or goblins?"

"Well… I suppose if I ever face any bandits, I will have to let you know."

Crystella laughed and shook her head. "You say that I am the ridiculous one and yet, here you are, victorious in ways this world has never before seen and *still* minimizing your qualifications."

"A few weeks of experience is hardly a *qualification…*"

"Nonononono *fuck* that," Crystella waved her hand in the air and Adiadni bit her tongue. "Perhaps there are some who have the right to such fears, but not you, not after all you've done. You need to cut thoughts like that off at their source and you need to do it now. They're no use to you and they're certainly no use to any who follow you. You cannot take excess weight like that with you onto the battlefield. Let it go."

"You're right." The harshly delivered words were the very ones the princess needed to hear. "I suppose I just don't know how."

Her cousin gave an amused chuckle. "You managed to shed a hundred and eighty pounds before coming here. I'm sure you can find such determination again."

Adi breathed out a light laugh, shaking her head back and forth.

A smirk grew from one corner of Crystella's mouth. "On that note, I am eagerly looking forward to making acquaintance with the man who has won the unwinnable heart."

"How do you know about that already?"

The second general shrugged. "Word travels fast. Especially in Suscundos." She paused and Adi sighed. "Tell me about him."

The princess lifted her eyes to the ceiling and her countenance visibly brightened as the image of his face bloomed in her mind. "He's... rock-solid. And gentle and... compassionate and kind. He understands me, even if I feel like my own thoughts make no sense. And I've always felt so safe with him, even since the very beginning. I've never felt like I've had to hide any of myself from him. He holds space for even the ugliest parts of me."

"Oh please, *what* ugly parts?" Crystella interjected half-jokingly, and Adiadni shook her head. "I am happy for you, Birdie. And that's all beautiful and sweet and poetic and romantic but I could have assumed that much. You've *got* to give me details!"

"What kind of details?"

"I don't know, quirks, idiosyncrasies. The seemingly inane things that make you aware of your pulse."

Adi's eyes moved to the floor and she chewed on her lip as she thought. "He's got these... hands..."

"You know what, I think I'm good actually," Crystella said, her hand raised. "I'll meet him soon enough."

Adiadni sighed. "Yes, well, he's been tasked with Judii's protection so you'll have to travel a short way to find him. But that will come in time. For now, I suppose I should see that you become acquainted with our officers."

"Is Press first commander under you or do you want me to deal with him?"

"He'll be under your command."

Crystella nodded approvingly. "Just as a little brother should."

Adi laughed. "I figured that would amuse you. My first commander is someone you've met before actually, she..." the princess trailed off as a knock sounded at the door, smiling broadly when it opened.

"Sorry to interrupt, Adi, I…" Mikka dropped the end of her sentence as her eyes moved to the other person in the room. "Stell?"

"Mikie?"

"As I live and breathe…"

The old friends hurried forward and embraced, eager questions and hastily delivered answers passing back and forth as they became reacquainted with one another. Adiadni smiled at the happy reunion and slipped quietly out the door.

***

It was Punznes who ultimately offered Uritus a reprieve from his restless mind by giving him a task he could do with his hands. The fisherman moved around the infirmary, fitting thin mattresses with hastily sewn sheets. The action was repetitive in a soothing way and he was grateful for the distraction, as was he for the voices who talked and laughed with each other while they went about their tasks. In the same way that his family found comfort in their camaraderie, so did the soldiers. Uritus found it inspiring. So, needless to say, he was uplifted when his first commander found him as he placed the last of the sheets.

"Walk with me, Old Boy?"

Uritus willingly obliged. The two friends meandered side-by-side through Judii's streets, making their way vaguely in the direction of the central building which housed the officers and served as their command center. Perplexus's natural stride was confident and relaxed, effortlessly adding to his inherent charisma. He kept his shoulders back and his head high, nodding humbly to those who acknowledged them as they passed.

"I don't know how you always manage to remain so coolly collected even when we're on the brink like this," Uritus observed.

The navigator chuckled. "If you wish to know the truth, it's basically all for appearances' sake."

"What do you mean?"

"I mean that I am also a nervous wreck, on the inside. There are too many I love here whose lives are at risk, too many I don't know but love anyway who are going to die. I also know though, that in precarious situations such as this, confidence makes all the difference. Whether I command others or merely myself, I know that trying to inspire confidence in those around me will strengthen our resolve. Besides, I know who leads us and I know how this will end. When I remember that, I can't help but feel at peace."

Uritus did not respond but rather contemplated his friend's words in silence.

"I'm sure hearing such a thing only compounds the pressure you feel," Perplexus went on. "But it is the truth. All those who gather here do so not merely out of duty, but out of faith. Faith which has only been further strengthened by the fulfillment of the prophecy thus far. We know the personal risk and we all have arrived at the same conclusion that such risk is worth it if we might secure the future for those who come after us. Believe in that if you cannot believe in yourself."

Uritus sighed understandingly. "Funny how much easier it was to be the Adalos when all that meant was competing in sporting events and speaking my truth."

Perplexus laughed. "Yes, quite."

"But I do think, if I search my feelings, that I do believe in myself. At the very least, I believe in the validity of the prophecy. I did before, and now I have seen more than enough evidence of it for such belief to have been reinforced, even if I do not understand it or why it chose me. I suppose that is the underlying issue: that I do not know *why* it is me. I never would have chosen this myself..."

"Perhaps that is the very reason why."

The fisherman looked to the navigator with a questioning glance.

"The Hero could never have been the most skilled of swordsmen or most experienced of commanders. Such a person would rely too greatly on their own strength or ability. No, the Hero could only be, could only ever have been the one who embodies the spirit of the Free World. Someone who values freedom and love and togetherness above all else, someone who works with his hands, who would never view himself as superior to another because of the position he was granted. It could only have been you."

They came to a stop as they arrived before their destination and Uritus turned to his friend, "Thank you for your words. Exactly the ones needed exactly *when* needed. Now there's a skill I wish I could tap into."

Perplexus smiled. "As I've said before, I'm happy to aid you however I can. I must admit though, the chance to give an eloquent speech was not the reason I found you. Uriah requested to speak with us."

Uritus nodded and the two proceeded in and up to the Wizard's chamber. Uriah had been stubborn before in his resolve that he wished not to be granted a rank. He hated war, and while he was glad to aid the Free People however he could, he had no desire to be memorialized by future storytellers while the names of rankless foot soldiers were lost to the passage of time. But those close to the Wizard pushed back against his insistence, reminding him that he was one of few who were qualified to lead and that if he refused, he *would* be withholding some of what he could offer to their cause. He had relented, humbly accepting their correction as well as the rank of commander under Uritus.

When the younger men found him, it was with his back to the door, gazing thoughtfully out the window at the city below and puffing on his pipe. He turned when he heard them enter, "Ah, come in, my boys." The Wizard moved around his desk, tapping his pipe's contents into an ashtray and proceeding to clean it as he came to lean against the sturdy piece of wood.

"Lex said you wish to speak with us?"

"I do," he lifted his eyes to them with a smile. "Thank you for coming. I will not keep you long, I am sure you have much to attend to. I wanted to check in with you. To check on the state of your hearts."

Uritus and Perplexus looked at one another and the navigator shrugged. "Oscillating between crippling anxiety and fervent assurance of the validity of our cause," Uritus replied.

"Mmm," Uriah nodded his understanding. "It is similar for me. Though, I suppose, in place of anxiety, it is sorrow. For those we will lose on our side as well as for those forced to the front by the enemy. War is a relentless beast that feeds upon the sacrifices of the innocent, and its is a bottomless hunger. When this is all over, we must be diligent in planting fruitful seeds in the ground tilled by those we lose."

The two he addressed nodded solemnly.

"But you are correct about the validity of our cause. Turning hopeful eyes to our header will be the very thing we need to motivate ourselves onward." The Wizard set his pipe down on the desk and folded his hands as he returned his eyes to the young men, smiling softly as he studied them for a moment. "I am quite proud of you both."

"We know," Perplexus replied for both of them.

"Now… my main purpose in gathering the two of you here is to tell you that I am sorry."

They looked at him questioningly.

"Truthfully, such an apology is long overdue, and I intend to echo this sentiment to the others when I get the chance but, as I cannot see my future, I had to be certain that I told you before we see combat again."

Uritus swallowed, his mouth feeling suddenly dry at the implications of the Wizard's statement.

Uriah raised his head and went on, "I should have told you long ago the story of my brother. Especially you, Uritus. You were immediately open with me upon our first meeting about what happened to Erclidus and I could have commiserated by telling you that a similar darkness had tempted Velup. But I did not. I kept him locked away, as I have until now, and I was wrong for that. It has been hypocritical of me to encourage integrity and vulnerability in the forging of relationships while not practicing those same things myself. I hope you can forgive me."

It was Uritus this time who spoke for both of them, "We do."

The Wizard lowered his head to them. "I thank you. As I am sure you have surmised, my history with Velup is long and convoluted. The sum of it is this; when we were boys, he and I sought the tutelage of a Wizard in our hometown of Sheth. It remains uncommon for one Wizard to take on two apprentices at once, and at the time, it was all but unheard of. But both Velup and I were passionate about understanding the gifts we displayed, and so, after much discussion with our parents, he agreed to take us on. It was not until after we had been given our tokens that my brother developed a fascination with the Shadow.

"To this day, I cannot say what drove him there, but by the time I identified what was going on, it was already too late. When the Nameless Sorcerer rose to power, Velup offered him his gifts in exchange for control over one of the Seven

Kingdoms. Many times over the years I tried to reach him, but it was never enough. When the Hope War concluded and the kingdoms united, Velup, for all I was concerned, was dead. I see now that I never truly believed that, that my intuition had been trying to warn me that he was not. But living in denial of that truth was easier for me, and it was that which led to my greatest mistake. He has been allowed to rot away in his tower, all the while plotting his revenge, and now my people will suffer for it. Though I am certain that there was nothing I could have done to have prevented this conflict, I will live with that regret for the rest of my days."

"Thank you for telling us," spoke Uritus. "I understand your hesitation to share such a tale. There is a unique, sorrowful shame in being unable to reach a loved one who has taken the wrong path."

"I'm sorry you've had to carry such a thing inside for so long," Perplexus added. "That was surely an uncomfortable weight."

"You are both correct and yes, I am glad now to be free of a bit of it. What you need to know about my brother is that he is relentless in his lust for domination. People are nothing but obstacles to him and he will show no mercy. If you come upon him, you must not allow him the chance to strike."

The young men nodded seriously.

Uriah continued, "I am not truly worried about either of you, as I have seen the growth in your wisdom and skill over these years we have shared. Every moment has been a gift. I have been blessed with more years than any man deserves, and the greatest part of them has been watching the heroes you have grown up to be."

"Don't you start talking like that, Old Man," Perplexus said, his eyes growing misty. "You've got more years ahead still. We have the protection of the city on our side, you're going to be…"

The Wizard raised a patient hand and the navigator stopped speaking. "It is no use denying that which may well come to pass. All we can do is accept it and hope for the best. But you are correct, those who defend the fortress will always have the advantage over those who seek to destroy it. I trust in the strength of our resolve. And as we are sure that our enemies have no knowledge of the tunnels, if all else fails, we have an escape."

The tunnels Uriah referred to ran beneath both of the Mirrored Cities and crossed the length of the space between them. They had been originally designed for easy transportation of resources so merchants were not always required to stop at the gates. Now, in wartime, they were the easiest way for soldiers to move from one city to another, and would serve a valuable use were one of the cities to fall.

"Thank you, for meeting with me, my boys. I will join you in your last preparations soon."

The general and his commander bade farewell to the Wizard and returned to the city below.

***

Adiadni found Aurena in a small room adjacent to Lorethh's main infirmary with a pair of younger Healers. The room was stuffed full of dried herbs—baskets covering the tables and floors, bundles hanging from the walls and ceiling—and rows of jars and bottles containing colorful powders and liquids lined up neatly on shelves. To each of the younger Healers, Aurena handed a small leather pouch, and they departed to make room for the Suvah to enter, offering her bright, hopeful smiles on their way out.

"Good timing," Aurena greeted her. "I was just about to bring these up to you." From a small table, she lifted a caramel leather belt and moved to fasten it around Adiadni's waist.

Two cinched pouches hung from the belt at her right hip and she inquired as to their contents.

"One to slow bleeding, one to numb pain," the Healer pointed to the respective pouches. "The Mother may guide you to other things you may need, but these you definitely will. Use them as sparingly as you can, we need to conserve our resources for the most dire cases."

Adiadni shook her head slowly, the weight of her new role sinking in. "I do not know how I could possibly discern who deserves to be relieved of their pain and who doesn't…"

"I understand. These will not be easy decisions to make. Trust your gut."

The princess chewed on her lip as Aurena moved once more to retrieve something from the table. "Take these as well. Drink one just before battle, it'll help clear your head and sharpen your mind." She held out two small corked vials, milky-white liquid swirling inside them.

Adiadni took them, gazing down at them with contemplative eyes.

"Hey," the older Healer stepped forward to lift the younger's chin. "You cannot do everything, but everything you *can* do matters and makes a difference."

Adi nodded and offered her teacher a small smile. "Thank you."

"Adiadni!"

The voice that called the princess was laced with urgency. She rushed to the room's door. "I'm here!"

Pressio spotted her from the other end of the infirmary and hastened to her side. "The Shadow advances."

Adiadni felt her blood grow cold.

"Gryphon riders spotted enemy troops marching beyond the range. We've a few hours still, but they'll be here before evening."

"Shit."

Aurena set a comforting hand on Adiadni's shoulder before making her way out the door to find and brief the other Healers. The general and commander shared a serious glance.

"You feeling all right?"

"I, um…" The princess looked down at the two small vials still held in her hands. "I think I need to…"

"Go," Pressio urged her. "We'll hold down the fort for now. Take the tunnels, it's safer."

"I will. Thank you." Adiadni embraced her cousin and behind him spotted one of her friends.

"If you're going to Judii, I'll go with you."

Pressio departed and Adi looked to Ilya, "Of course. I'm sorry you ended up separated, I can try to have one of you reassigned if you'd rather…"

The captain of the marksmen waved her hand in the air. "We'll serve where we're needed. I'll just be glad to see him before."

"Of course." Adiadni understood. She was making her own journey North for the same purpose. "Come on then. We've no time to lose."

***

Across Lorethh's city square, in the mess hall's kitchen, Laivar portioned potato pottage into wooden bowls which were hastily carried out to feed the soldiers.

"I still think you're ridiculous," Mikka declared. "The king of the Free World offered you a title and a rank and you turned him down?"

"I was not the only one who made such a decision. Even Uriah said no—"

"Until he was reasoned with."

"Punzie too…"

"*Chief medic* is very much a title."

"One he is undeniably qualified for."

Mikka rolled her eyes. "You've been to battle already! If that doesn't qualify you—"

"I fired arrows upon enemies from a safe distance. That is all. I will take up my bow again today, even a sword if need be, but trust me when I say that no one wants me calling the shots. It's better for everyone if I don't. I am perfectly happy slinging slop and singing my silly little songs to encourage the masses."

"You're more capable than you realize…"

"On the contrary, my dear, I know *exactly* how capable I am. I don't see you chiding Alidistris for volunteering in the kitchen."

"Alidistris never saw combat." Mikka looked with caring eyes at the dark-haired woman who stood on a stool, rhythmically stirring a tall stock pot with a wooden spoon. "How are you feeling?"

"Surprisingly calm," Alidistris replied before biting her tongue. "I suppose it would be more human of me not to be…"

Mikka laughed. "Honestly, it's rather refreshing to hear that one of us has her head on straight."

Alidistris smiled, keeping her eyes on her task. "I have full confidence in the abilities of my protectors."

The first commander also smiled, returning her attention to the bard, "As your friend and your sister, I do not have the right to tell you what to do. As your commander on the other hand…"

Laivar chuckled. "I love you and your aggressive directness. Stay safe for me, all right?"

"I'll do my best. You must promise, though, if I do meet my end, you will write at least *two* ballads recalling my noble deeds."

"*Someday* when you do meet your end, Mik, I will write a thousand."

"Love you, Laiv. Every silly, stubborn fiber of you. And I love you too!"

Alidistris turned to meet Mikka's eye, a soft smile still clinging to her mouth.

"Keep the faith." The commander turned on her heel and exited the kitchen.

***

"I can take it from here. Go see to your troops. Your general needs you now more than I do."

The energy that coursed through the city of Judii became suddenly urgent as word reached them of their impending clash. Just outside the infirmary, Perplexus and Punznes boiled water to sterilize bandages.

"You're sure?"

"I am. Thank you."

Perplexus nodded and turned to set off in search of Uritus.

"Hey."

He paused, turning back to look at the physician.

"You are determined and you are fearless, just like Havian was. Just… please have the common sense that he did not. I love you and I'd hate to lose you too."

Perplexus hastened forward to embrace his friend. "I promise. I love you too. And you, silly bird."

Qibat cawed down from his perch atop the infirmary, "And you, silly boy."

The commander turned once more to depart, calling and pointing over his shoulder as he left, "And if I *do* get sliced up out there, it'd better be you who sews me back together again!"

"I will anxiously look for your face amongst the wounded and pray that I never see it."

***

Uritus stood in the city's center atop a square stone structure that surrounded the base of a tall flagpole. Judii's flag, a black background emblazoned with the image of a towering white tree, danced and twisted as the breeze caught its edges. He gazed over the soldiers who had begun to gather there, assembling in

390

their respective squadrons and receiving instructions from their commanders, knowing that they would soon be looking to him. One hand reached to touch the shell, then the stone, his left fingers moving across the smooth golden hilt at his side. He released a breath he did not realize he had been holding when he spotted the tall familiar figure who approached. He stepped down to greet him. "Cape or no cape?"

Perplexus looked him over. "No cape. You don't need the extra weight."

Uritus nodded and his first commander moved behind him to detach the piece of blue fabric from his pauldrons. "Any sign of the troops from Tila?"

"Not yet. We'll keep an eye out though. They were scheduled to get here by tonight so they can't be far." The navigator draped the cape over his arm and returned to stand in front of the fisherman, noting the way his eyes shifted fearfully over the masses. "Hey," Perplexus raised his hands to turn his friend's face toward himself. "Breathe with me for a minute."

Uritus nodded and closed his eyes, his first inhale shaky. But by his third breath out, he identified that he did feel extraordinarily better. He opened his eyes and offered Perplexus a grateful smile.

The commander lowered his hands, keeping one on the general's shoulder. "You taught me that. I've carried it since. Even as a boy, you've always intuitively known what needs to be done, exactly when. You are the solid ground we root ourselves to. I'll be yours if it helps."

"It does," Uritus raised his hand to his friend's shoulder. "I'm not glad to be here, but I am glad you're with me."

"Always."

***

"There you are, Plum. A few more minutes and I would have headed down to find you."

"I was counting on your patience. In my gut, I knew I'd find you here." Ilya stretched her arms up and over her husband's shoulders and he leaned down to meet her embrace. "How's Uritus?"

"A wreck. But Lex is with him now, so I think he'll be okay."

"Adi's here too. She came with me."

"Good. She'll help immensely."

"How are *you*?" Ilya ran a loving hand across Nadarum's face. "I like *captain of the cavalry* for you. It's quite dashing."

He smiled. "I am honored to wear the title and take it very seriously."

"Naturally."

"It is because of that, sadly, that I cannot talk for long…"

"Neither can I. I'll have to leave soon to arrange the wall."

"Are you planning on moving to the ground at all?"

"Depends. The plan right now is to always have archers up top, even if some have to fall back to infantry. But, you know, we can't say just what will happen."

"Mmm." Nadarum gazed down at his wife, his love for her and fear for what approached clear in his eyes. "You are smart and you are strong and you are utterly courageous. Please also harness that fragment of self-preservation that I know lives inside you somewhere."

Ilya threw her head back and laughed, and the sound warmed him. "I'll harness your wisdom and you can harness my courage."

"You always did have enough for the both of us."

"Ay, lovebirds!" The pair turned their heads to see Oripidus standing atop a platform as his squadron gathered below him. "Keep yer wits about ye! I can't have anythin' happenin' to either of ye!"

"Aye aye, Captain!" Nadarum shouted back.

"Hey, Rip, I'm excited you get to see your dream of being a goblin slayer come true, but don't you get tunnel vision! Mind your blind spots and *fall back* if you're ordered to!"

"I'll do my damndest," replied the blacksmith. "But only because I love ye!"

Nadarum's eyes lingered on Oripidus for a silent moment as he returned his attention to his troops. "Havian would have been an infantry captain too…"

"Hey," Ilya took her husband's face in her hands and pulled it to meet her gaze. "I love you."

He bent down to kiss her. "I love you."

"I have to get back…"

"I know. So do I. Be smart, be safe."

"You too." The archer departed to return to the Southern city and the horseman watched her leave.

***

"I guess this is it."

Uritus felt all of the tension in his body melt upon hearing the gorgeous cadence of Adiadni's voice. He turned away from Perplexus to look at her. "Fuck, I love you." They stepped toward one another and their lips met and only then did the commander depart to see that everyone was in order. "I am sorry I did not come down earlier today, I intended to…"

"Forget about that," Adi raked her hand through her counterpart's hair.

"How are you doing?"

"Fine. How about you?"

Uritus clenched his jaw as his gaze grew distant. "I'm terrified."

"I know. I am too."

392

He sighed. He didn't wish to spend the precious time he had with her dwelling on his fear. He moved her to stand arm's length away from him and got a full look at the new uniform that adorned her. "You look ready. I like these." He took her wrist in his hand and pulled it closer to get a better look at the flash of gold that peeked out from beneath her gauntlets.

"My amonii is on the inside. They're supposed to help me maintain control over my gifts." Remembering the secondary reason she came to Judii, the princess reached for the glass vial she had stowed in her belt's pouch. "Has someone given you one of these?"

He took it, observing its shimmer in the pale sunlight, and shook his head.

"Take it just before… for clarity and all that."

The fisherman nodded and tucked it into a pocket for safekeeping. Adiadni turned her head to regard the gathered crowd and he followed her gaze. "I suppose I should probably address them now…"

Adiadni regarded the worried look on his face and set a hand beside it. "You don't need to be nervous. You have all you need. You said that to me once, a long time ago. I didn't believe you at the time, but now I do. I know you don't believe me now, but in every moment that I have felt lost since I have known you, you've always known *exactly* the right thing to say."

"It's different with you…" he protested.

"Then… talk to me. Talk to Lex, Uriah… Everyone here is rooting for your success just as we are."

He nodded, thankful for the soothing quality of her presence. He dipped his face down to kiss her once more and then mounted the platform beneath the flag. The gathered soldiers began to hush and turn their eyes toward their general without any effort required on his part to draw their attention. All eagerly awaited what the Adalos had to say. He dragged his eyes across the crowd as they settled, spying more familiar faces the longer he looked—people he knew from the White Mountains and Suscundos, the three he'd competed against in the early Summer's trials amongst them. He cleared his throat and took in a deep breath.

"I do not have the right to ask any of you to be here," he began shakily. "To give of your time, your energy, your skills, your lives… But even so, you have come, and I… I feel overwhelmed as I behold you now." His eyes flicked nervously to Adiadni and she smiled at him, setting a hand against her sternum and taking an exaggerated breath.

"As those who know me are well aware, I am not usually a man of many words. I know my duty here is to inspire you, to rouse your spirits so you are encouraged to excitedly charge forward into the Shadow that seeks to destroy us. But I don't know how to do that. I don't know how to ignore the scale of the devastation that comes our way. But over these past few days, these past few weeks, this whole Summer, I have been reminded time and again of what it is about this land that I love so much—the Free People. If I am honest… it is *you* who inspire *me*.

"I am not too proud to admit that I am petrified of what is to come. But in the moments that I feel overwhelmed, when I wonder why I am even here, when I question if any of this is worth it… I raise my eyes and I see you and I remember: this love, this spirit, this joy and hope for the future, these *people* are the only things worth fighting for. I look at you and I am so proud of this imperfect but intentional world we have created and I see that even in blackest hours such as this, there is nowhere else I would rather be than here, with you. Taking up my sword alongside you to fight to defend our freedom so that the generations to come need never see hours so dark as this. For our blood and our love and our sweat and our faith and for our collective heart and for this land that houses and protects us, we will follow in the footsteps of our ancestors and we will meet the enemy head-on!"

This sentence was met with cheers. A silent, proud tear slipped down the princess's cheek as she watched the man she loved step fully into his destiny.

"We have Divine and Source and Mother to back us. We have Wizards who have offered to fight and Healers and physicians who have offered to mend. And what's more, we have the strength of the Free People, those who gather here and those who support us from afar and all those who lived before. Take heart, keep the faith, and look out for your fellow soldiers. The prophecy is on our side!" The Adalos thrust a proud fist into the air and his troops responded in kind, shouting their collective war cry with enough passion that it could be heard in Lorethh.

Uritus stepped down from the platform and the soldiers went about their duties. Adiadni met the fisherman with a kiss. "See?" She giggled, her breath on his face. "Exactly the right thing."

"Only thanks to your exhortation." He lowered his forehead to press against hers. "Thank you. I love you to a degree that I can't understand, but I'm fine if I never do."

"I love you too. I wish I didn't have to go, but…"

"I understand. I should too." He held her face in one hand, intently studying her features for a silent moment. "May the Divine protect you."

"And you." She tightened her arms around his neck in a final embrace. "Remember who you are."

Against both of their wishes, the princess stepped away and turned to leave. His eyes lingered on her back. She was dazzling and incomparable, and though he did not truly fear for her well-being, it stung him whenever they were parted. "And if I forget?" he called after her.

She turned with a laugh, her brilliance drawing the attention of those near her. "Remember your name!" she replied without a thought. "It was given to you for a reason!"

He returned her bright smile, his eyes blue with adoration, and she made her way back to Lorethh to ready her troops.

Chapter Twenty-Six

"The Battle for the Mirrored Cities"

From the place she stood on the raised rampart at Lorethh's North-and-West corner, Adiadni watched the Shadow make its slow trek across the sky. The inky blackness grew over pale blue like mold on the walls of an abandoned seaside cottage. The Suvah shivered internally but did not let those around her see her flinch. If there was one thing she was certain she could do, it was wear an immovable mask for the benefit of someone else. Even so, she could feel her heart beat hard though not fast, her breaths evenly timed but drawing up from her chest rather than her stomach. The night before—like every other night since her arrival in Lorethh—she had been visited in her sleep by the man in the black cape... by *Erclidus*.

This time when they met, it was in the seemingly endless open field between the Mirrored Cities and the Looming Mountains, positioned, as always, toward the sheer black peaks. His cape whipped around him with the wind that tugged her skirt in all directions. He turned toward her immediately as the dream began. He looked her over, his expression neutral, and spoke with a shrug, *"When two be joined by the hand of Fate..."*

"Don't. You didn't *have* to come here. Fate had nothing to do with it."

He chuckled. "Temper like embers, as usual."

"And *don't* talk to me like you know me. You don't."

"I know that you're about to watch your people die."

Adiadni's mouth snapped shut, fists tightening.

"That is... if you don't see an end to your unreasonable stubbornness."

She shook her head, scowling at him. There it was again: the trap laid out plainly for her to see. Part of her hoped that if she just waited in silence for long enough, perhaps the dream might simply bring itself to an end. But the other part—that tiny, insatiable sliver—tugged at her wrist again. *She would be a fool to waste this time.* "My stubbornness is as indelible as it is unreasonable. But if I *were* to accept your hand... what would such a bind look like? Surely, you know that I would be satisfied with nothing short of the guaranteed safety of every one of my citizens?"

"Fine. Every one."

Adiadni narrowed her eyes. "You don't mean that..."

Erclidus shrugged again. "I can be open to reasonable compromise."

She shook her head a second time. "When last I called you to back up a promise, you turned on it the second it benefitted you. You are hardly someone who inspires trust."

He raked his eyes over her and she shivered. "I don't *want* to kill anyone, Adiadni. It is simply the most effective way to send a message."

The princess clenched her jaw and swallowed. "Tell me your message then."

A smirk lifted one side of his mouth. He stepped toward her. As she had in dreams before, Adiadni felt frozen where she stood. He drew ever closer, the sounds of his steps resonating throughout the land around them until he came to a stop, his face lowered right beside her ear. "If you wish to avoid the blade that swings for your neck…" he raised a hand and dragged a single finger along the length of her jaw, "…drop to your knees."

With a sharp intake of breath, the princess had awoken. And now, eyes to the darkening sky, she struggled to shut out the words that still echoed in her mind.

***

Over time, on the ground beneath the Shadow, Uritus began to make out the shape of Vegard's advancing forces making their steady approach. The tiny charcoal wave grew until he was able to identify individual shapes, like a swarming colony of ants.

Standing their ground between the enemy and Judii's Western gate were half of the city's forces, five hundred cavalry in front and a thousand infantry behind them. The rest were positioned with their bows atop the wall or just within the outer door of the gate, armed and ready to move out when given the order.

While the Adalos had ordinarily been keen to default to the suggestions of Digtrision or Uriah or anyone else with military experience when it came to their strategizing, he pushed back against the second general's proposal that Uritus remain at his safe vantage point atop the rampart while Digtrision led the second wave of infantry onto the battlefield.

If the fisherman had his way, he would have gone out with the first wave, on foot, but none of the other officers would allow this. They needed his eye, needed his guidance, at least until it was time to send out the reserves. Uritus had ultimately argued that they needed Digtrision on the wall more, that his knowledge and experience would make him far more valuable of a commander, and that the people needed to see the Adalos on the ground amongst them, citing the protection of the prophecy as his ultimate case. He hadn't enjoyed pulling rank this way, but it had worked, and now he needed only watch the battle helplessly from afar for part of the conflict's duration rather than its vast majority. This, as well as their final defensive and offensive tools, were necessary anchoring points for the fisherman's hope.

When the cropidus had arrived with Pressio and again later, with their leader, they set to work employing their traditional practices to fortify the cities. They had little time and precious few resources at their disposal, but as Judii and Lorethh were the largest of the Western Provinces, they served as a major hub of traders and commerce. The trolls had utilized the lumber at their disposal to reinforce the Northern, Eastern, and Southern gates. Each gate consisted of two pairs of metal doors separated by a vestibule about ten feet deep. The cropidus bolstered each one so they would be nearly impossible to break through without incredible force. They did the same to the Western gate, ensuring that its defense was easy to partially dis- and reassemble when letting soldiers in or out.

Had they more time, they would have attempted to construct traps to slow their enemies as they approached, but they devoted said time instead to the construction of trebuchets, two each mounted on both cities' Western walls. Uriah in particular was unhappy to learn that the only sizable projectiles they had at their disposal were chunks of precious White Mountain rock, but in their hour of need, he did not voice dissent.

Now, the Wizard was positioned atop the rampart beside the general at Judii's South-and-West corner, and his stare remained fixed on the encroaching swarm.

The final row of goblins came into view in the distance, and both Uriah and Uritus were relieved to see that the enemy forces marched on foot, save for a few of their officers. No sooner did they observe this than the advancing army began to split into two companies, tearing a perfect line down the middle as they divided and made their way to the cities.

The Adalos located the vial of milky liquid he kept on his person and downed its contents. "How many?"

"Hmm," Uriah completed his calculations. "Eight to ten thousand in total. More than we currently have, but not by much. That is, as well, excluding those we still await."

Uritus nodded, turning his head South again with anxious eyes.

"Focus on what is here, now."

"You're right. Thank you." The general set his hand to his sternum, took a slow breath, and felt his mind begin to quiet as the elixir settled in.

***

"Nearly all goblins from what I can see, the majority of them of their ordinary stature, though a substantial number of the new generation as well. Two officers, presumably generals, mounted on horses at the back. Only one appears to be a Sorcerer."

Adiadni listened eagerly to Veldis's observations. "Does one of the mounted officers wear a black cape?"

"The Sorcerer wears a hooded robe, the other merely armor."

The princess nodded, not sure if she felt better or worse to know that Erclidus would be warring against his brother rather than her. The afternoon stretched long and the sun crawled ever onward toward the growing blackness of swirling clouds. The distant, loudening sound of rhythmic steps was becoming difficult to ignore.

"It's time."

Adi nodded to indicate that she heard her mentor and reached a hand into the pouch on her belt in search of the glass vial. She removed its cork and lifted it to

397

her lips, consuming the elixir in a single swallow, mildly sweet with a note of bitterness. She stepped forward and gripped the mounted flagpole, raising herself to stand atop the parapet, straddling one of its embrasures. She moved her right hand to her waist and drew her sword. Its sound began the turning of heads below in her direction.

"We are the Free People and we did not come about such a name during peacetime! Our ancestors would not accept defeat nor the brutal hand of their oppressor! They rose together and fought back and their legacy has bloomed into the thriving nation we call home today!"

The wind picked up speed around the Suvah as she spoke. Lorethh's flag waved above her, black tree stretching its arms across white cloth.

"Now, centuries later, the oppressor is back again. He looked at the freedom we enjoy and declared that he would take it from us. I will not presume to speak for any of you, but as for me, he will have to pry my freedom from the fingers of my rigid corpse!"

The soldiers roused to impassioned cheers, perfectly timed, long, and loud enough for the enemy to hear. Judii also let out a cry, inspired to noise by Perplexus who rallied the infantry on the ground.

"The spirit of the Free People is alive in the Mirrored Cities! We will stand to face the oppressor once more and vanquish him for good this time!" The Suvah's final sentences were punctuated by war cries of increasing fervor, "He cannot crush our spirits, and he cannot force us from our home! As is the only thing it knows how to do, the Shadow must bow to the Light!" The blade in her hand gleamed in the rays of sun that remained. The sight of the historic weapon solidified the confidence of those who witnessed it.

"Archers at the ready!"

The marksmen on the wall drew their longbows and the cropidus manning the trebuchets awaited the next command. Adiadni lowered herself to the rampart once more and nodded to Ilya to give the order.

"Fire!"

A graceful row of arrows soared into the sky, completing a uniform arc and falling upon the enemy. A wave of goblins dropped as they were struck.

"Trebuchets fire at will!"

The towering wooden contraptions launched their projectiles into the field. Chunks of white stone flattened swaths of goblins. The princess felt momentarily sick for the joy the sight brought her.

At the same moment, the gryphon riders took to the sky, carrying archers who added to the rain of arrows falling upon the hostile forces. Just a few more moments and the order would be given for the troops on the ground to charge. A sudden sound from above pulled Adiadni's attention.

She raised her eyes and gasped as she saw a ball of fire hurtling toward them. She screamed, throwing a desperate hand in the air. The faint blue sheen of the shield she produced glimmered above them, but the ball of fire burned out, extinguished before it could fall.

"I've got it," Veldis assured her. "Keep your attention on the ground."

The princess obeyed, nocking an arrow to her bow as the Shadow eclipsed the sun.

***

"Charge!"

Uritus looked on fearfully between fired arrows as the cavalry raced ahead, a powerful collective shout rising from their lungs as they collided with Vegard's army. The first wave of infantry ran after them, clashing blades with the goblins who'd managed to make it past the wall of horsemen. It did not take long for the fisherman to spot Erclidus.

Though he appeared as no more than an immovable black shape on a horse behind his troops, the Sorcerer's apprentice worked to make his presence known. One after another, he launched hot orange flames into the sky at a frequency that left Uriah and Erephus—at Judii's North end—incapable of focusing on anything beyond extinguishing them.

The gryphon riders had been instructed to concentrate their efforts on taking out the officers. They quickly found this to be impossible as their arrows slid off the invisible shield that covered the mounted men. Judii's general was frustrated but not surprised.

He wielded his bow efficiently along with the other short-range marksmen. They focused their shots on the goblins who broke through the line and raced at the city.

The soldiers on the ground made quick work of those they encountered. Still, the marksmen had to be diligent with their shots. The area just before the wall had to stay clear, at least until the second wave took the field. Their strategy continued to play out as planned. Uritus was encouraged.

On the ground, in the thick of battle, violence splattered around Perplexus. He cut down his adversaries with ease, partnering with his fellow soldiers to bring down the goblins of greater stature. He felt no fear, no hesitation, nothing but the fire of their cause burning hot in his chest.

Occasionally, he could hear Oripidus from somewhere nearby, ceaselessly taunting their enemies. The sound fueled him; seeing the Free People band together to fight for something larger than themselves fanned the flames of his zeal. The boy from the White Mountains had never dreamed of becoming a soldier, never pictured himself taking up his sword and charging into battle. But now, here in the middle of it, he saw that there was nowhere else he was meant to be. The sickening sight of watching his troops fall hardened his resolve and drove him ever onward.

It was soon clear from Uritus's vantage point that the time for the second wave drew near. The Free People continued to press deeper into the rushing river of their enemies, but as the war raged on, more and more goblins managed to break through in their attempt to swarm the city.

The Adalos stowed his bow. "I'm going down."

399

"Mmph," Uriah grunted as his hand closed to snuff out a ball of fire. "Source go with you."

Uritus nodded briskly and hurried to the ground to lead the reserves. It was clear immediately upon his arrival amongst them that their collective energy was heightened and anxious. He moved to stand ahead of them and drew his sword. This alone was enough to rally the soldiers to thundering cheers. He nodded to the few who manned the gate and they hurried to push it open.

"For Judii!"

The Adalos raced ahead of them, spotting several goblins advancing. He positioned his sword at his hip, maintaining speed, and ran through an enemy soldier who met him head-on.

All around, his troops collided with their enemies, flashes of steel and leather, sprays of blood and sweat. Uritus pushed into the fray, spurred on by the awareness of how his identity inspired the others around him. He felt his senses heightened and his mind sharp.

He submitted to his protective instinct, defending any near him who needed aid; one who did not hear the goblin approach behind him, another coming face-to-face with one too big to fell on his own. All the while, in the back of his mind, piled his grief for the Free People they had already lost. He didn't have the time to acknowledge it.

The Adalos found that the Sword of Fire moved easily with his arm, swishing and slicing through the air as though it was guiding him rather than the other way around. He saw the spark that lit in the eyes of his troops every time they caught a glimpse of a flash of gleaming gold and realized he wielded one of the most powerful symbols the Free World had ever seen.

It was light, though immeasurably strong, and Uritus noticed that when it sliced into the clothing or armor or flesh of his enemies, faint smoke emanated from the cut. Judging by the agonized cries of those unlucky enough to be bitten by it, its name was not merely a metaphor. It burned its victims just as it did those who attempted to wield it against its will.

The general kept his head down, his goal shining at the forefront of his mind. There was much still to do.

***

Adiadni watched her troops push on, irritatingly aware of the pounding of her heart. Her eyes moved back and forth across the field, spotting Pressio still on his feet, then Mikka, then searching for Pressio again.

The Free People continued to advance and continued to hold the line. Even so, the princess knew that the aid of the reinforcements would soon be necessary to maintain their advantage.

She stepped atop the parapet again and raised her sword, moving it back and forth in hopes that the light reflected from it might alert Crystella to her intent.

"I'm going out with the second wave," she told Veldis as she hopped back down to the rampart.

"Be safe. May Source move with you."

Adi called to Ilya to mind the wall and then hurried down the steps, finding herself face-to-face with her cousin when she reached the ground. "Ready?"

"To put an end to this bullshit? Damn right, I am."

The princess laughed at Crystella's blunt enthusiasm and turned to face the gate.

"Would you care to do the inspiring?"

"I did the last bit. Your turn."

"Very well," Crystella leapt back up a few of the stairs and plunged her sword above her head. "Our people united are far stronger than any force which may try to crush us!"

Shouts and whoops were the soldiers' replies.

"If anyone amongst you manages to slay that bloody Sorcerer, I'll give you a fat, wet kiss!"

The cheers were littered with laughter. The second general dropped back to the ground beside her cousin.

Adiadni shook her head and laughed, "That's one way to motivate the masses."

Crystella shrugged with a smirk. "You have your methods and I have mine."

The gate was pushed open and the soldiers roused.

"For our freedom!"

A shouting wave of impassioned warriors rolled out onto the battlefield. The hesitation Adiadni had felt the first time she clashed with goblins had fully dissolved. She looked her adversaries in the face, met them head-on, brought a swift end to every foe who rose against her. She was a Vindella; she was the Suvah. It was she who had slain the Dagamor and recovered the Sword of Fire. Clearer now than ever was it that she was a warrior of incomparable skill. The great nightmare of the West had been defeated by her hand with ease. Nothing that sought to stop her now stood any chance.

Her confidence was grounded further as it became clear that she was never fighting alone. At every turn rose another soldier who fought to protect her as she did them, to enable her in her success. They continued holding the line of defense, pushing forward against the current. The more time that passed, the better the princess felt about their chances.

While Adiadni's primary focus was on wielding her sword, she did not ignore the pull of her attention to the wounded, doling out the contents of her pouches as necessary. A bit of dried moss to tuck between the lip and gum for heightened pain tolerance; herbs to be pressed directly into wounds. She didn't have time to stop for everyone who no doubt needed aid, but she clung to Aurena's words as she battled against her mounting sense of guilt. *Everything you* can *do makes a difference.*

Deep in the thick of the fight, Mikka carved a path for her troops to follow. The events of this Summer had revealed to her that she was unquestionably skilled with her blade. She kept the spirit of her fallen brother with her as she fought, identifying just how frequently she used a move or tip she learned from him which very well saved her life and the lives of those around her. Even the largest of the goblins were no match for the fierceness of her fight. The commander raised her eyes to see that the cloaked enemy officer was not far away.

She charged, running her blade through the back of a goblin two of her soldiers defended themselves against. They looked to her in their gratitude and she called to them, "Watch my back!"

They obeyed, springing to either side of her to intercept enemies that came her way. Mikka retrieved from the ground the spear that had been dropped by the goblin she had just slain and marched forward, the soldiers moving with her.

With one hand, she swung her sword to cut down a goblin who stood in her path, and then raised the spear with the other, lining up her shot. But before she could launch the weapon through the air, the end of it was grabbed and yanked by someone behind her.

She spun around with an aggravated groan, only to find herself staring up at the largest goblin she had seen thus far.

"All right then."

She jerked her body to the side to leverage the spear, tearing it from his gasp.

At the same moment, the soldiers beside her sprang to action, both landing shallow cuts on his torso. With a pained howl, the goblin turned and swung his blade.

Mikka watched, a sick pit in her stomach, as he cut a deep gash into the chest of one of the soldiers. The man, fatally wounded, dropped to the ground with a dull thud, and the goblin returned his eye to the commander.

A gritty cry escaped the throat of the second soldier. He leapt forward, landing a substantial slice in the goblin's upper arm and drawing his attention.

Mikka responded by immediately bringing her sword down upon the other arm of their enemy. The blade cut through skin and muscle and bone, tearing through the goblin's wrist until his hand fully detached, dropping to the ground with his sword still clutched in it.

He howled again, and with one final swing, the commander cut off the sound with the head of her adversary.

Mikka glimpsed the grateful gleam in the soldier's eye before she turned once again and raised the spear. She took a half second to line up her shot and sent the weapon hurtling through the air.

It soared straight and true toward her target and collided with force into his chest, knocking him from his horse.

It took a few moments to ascertain what had happened, but eventually, the pair of Wizards on Lorethh's wall realized that the fiery projectiles shot by their enemy had ceased. This offered the Free People an unmatched advantage, as the Wizards could now shift their focus to offensive measures.

When Adiadni came to notice this change, she was stirred up all the more. Their strategy was working; the fire in the hearts of the Free People refused to be choked out. The Suvah fought and healed and pushed back against the persistence of the enemy forces and the sky continued to darken as the hours stretched on.

***

Eventually, it happened that the Adalos and the navigator came upon each other in the field, and both men were reinvigorated to see that the other fought on unharmed. The connection they shared was clear as they fell into step beside each other, Perplexus's boldness and Uritus's careful calculation working in tandem to keep them safe and efficient in their efforts. They did not speak, save for the most urgent communications, but their presence near one another was fiercely encouraging. The general knew not what the rest of the battle would bring, but for now, his friend was well, and that was enough.

Back on Judii's wall, Uriah kept his eyes on the sky as he continued to deflect against falling flames. The onslaught had not let up for even a moment since it began and the Wizard found himself growing weary.

Though the soldiers on the ground were diligent in their efforts, none had managed to come near enough to Erclidus to attempt an attack, and the young Sorcerer was relentless in his own. Needless to say, the word that traveled down the wall to reach Uriah's ears was not accepted with enthusiasm.

"Erephus has been struck by an enemy arrow! He's alive, but we had to pull him from the wall."

Uriah grunted a response as he snuffed out another flame and then hastened North along the rampart for a better vantage point.

Flame after flame he caught, suspended in the air until they choked out and extinguished. But without the other Wizard to help defend against them, Uriah was not confident in his ability to do so on his own.

His fears were soon realized. A hot ball of fire streaked down from the sky and crashed into one of Judii's trebuchets.

The contraption was instantly destroyed, splintering pieces of singed wood flying in every direction, injuring nearby soldiers and killing two of those who manned it. Uriah did not have a moment to react before he spotted another incoming projectile and thrust out his hand to catch it.

The number of falling flames began to multiply, and though they were smaller now, they were too many and too quick to be dealt with one at a time. Uriah caught one after another, arms held wide to try to bar them from completing their arcs. Despite his best efforts, several broke through, raining down upon the wall and the city's interior with relentless brutality.

The Wizard lowered his eyes to see that more of the enemy's forces had managed to make it through the line. The anguished cries of Judii's injured rose to meet his ears, mingling in a desperate chorus. The tides were turning. If he

403

couldn't maintain defense of the wall, it wouldn't matter what happened in the field below.

Uriah accessed the reserves of his strength, drawing his open hand and his staff slowly together in front of him. The suspended flames moved with his arms, joining into one. With a final burst of power, he sent them rushing away from the city, back from whence they had come.

The massive collection of blazing energy crashed into the ground at the back of Vegard's army, exploding in a firestorm that obliterated dozens of goblins and frightened Erclidus's horse. When the animal suddenly reared, his rider was thrown violently to the ground, and the flaming onslaught finally ceased.

The enemy general was momentarily stunned by this retaliation, but swiftly rose to his feet and drew his sword. The raging heat of his anger cut down everyone in his path, his right hand casting spells, stirring up dirt and wind, disarming his opponents so the blade in his left could attack. And though the Sorcerer moved now on foot, he and his army began to drive the Free People back.

When Uriah saw this, it became clear that they needed to regroup. He told Digtrision this as he urgently scanned the field for Uritus. The general agreed and hurried to organize those within the city just as the Wizard spied the Adalos deep in the thick of battle.

A caw sounded at his side and he looked with grateful eyes to the bird, "Qibat, you must find Uritus and urge him to fall back."

The raven followed the line from Uriah's pointed finger and took off into the sky. The Wizard watched him intently for a moment before beginning to aid the marksmen in felling the goblins who raced for the city.

Qibat ducked and weaved expertly through soaring arrows as he made his way for the fisherman. Uritus heard the familiar voice call out to him to fall back and lifted his eyes to see a rush of black feathers just as the order was echoed by the sounding of deep horns from within Judii.

He turned to the city and saw that the line had splintered and knew that the Free People scattered about the battlefield had no choice but to retreat if they wished to stand a chance. "Lex!"

The first commander turned to meet his eye.

"We need to fall back!" Uritus swung his sword in an upward arc, slicing a deep cut into a goblin from which poured a steaming river of rancid blood. "Get them to Judii!"

Perplexus nodded and raced away to pass on the order. Uritus continued to fight, calling all nearby troops to retreat while slowly making his way back to the gate.

Eventually, the sound of the horns made clear to the Free People the turn of the tide, and they began to hurry back to the safety of the city. Uritus heard the rhythmic pounding of hooves grow louder behind him and turned, relieved to see Nadarum.

The horseman stretched out his hand to the Adalos and Uritus caught it, swinging himself up to a seat behind his friend. He cut down their enemies as they rode, and by the time they arrived back at the gate, the space before it had been cleared by the archers on the wall.

The general dropped to the ground as they entered the city and raced up the steps to the rampart, stringing and drawing his bow. He sprang to the aid of those who fired upon the goblins, doing his part to ensure that the Free People made it safely back into Judii. The archers in the sky did the same.

Uriah pushed past his fatigue, producing flames to hurl at their enemies and sending strong gusts of wind to push swaths of them back. In the steady stream of soldiers who rushed into the city center, the occasional goblin was swept in with them—only to be quickly exterminated.

As the soldiers continued to hurry to sanctuary, so their enemies hurried after them to snuff them out.

***

Adiadni ripped her blade from the belly of a goblin and spun around in terror as the horns of retreat sounded from Judii. The urgency of the fight did not allow her attention to linger on the Northern city for long, but it was clear that Judii's army was falling back to refuge.

She felt her heart plunge into an ice-cold bath of fear as she considered for the first time since the battle began how the people she loved were in danger. She turned as she fought, scanned the battlefield for a sign of one of her officers, and spotted Crystella several yards away.

She raced to her side, cutting down a goblin who advanced toward her cousin on the way. "Crys!"

The second general turned her eyes to the North, registering the sound of the horns and looking past Adiadni to see the retreat of Judii's forces. "I'll hold the line!" she called back.

Adi sprinted to the city. The gate opened to receive her and quickly shut when she was through. She sheathed her blade and raced up to the wall to get a better view.

The Shadow crept ever forward above both of the Mirrored Cities as the army of the enemy advanced upon Judii. The princess hurriedly called down to a pair of soldiers within the wall to tell those within Lorethh to prepare for the event that Judii fell and they needed to take in their allies.

"You must ensure that the charges are lit for when the time arises," Veldis instructed her. "I cannot risk leaving my post. Find a soldier, plant him at the entrance with a torch in his hand, and tell him to await the order. If Vegard's army breaches the city, we will need to destroy the path they can take to reach us."

Adi shook her head in confusion. "Judii's forces know to light the fuse once they've made it through..."

"And if they do not make it through and the enemy uncovers the tunnels, they can just as easily take Lorethh."

"But we can't do that—"

"We will do what we must, Adiadni, stick to the plan!"

Without another word, the princess turned on her heel and hurried down to the tunnel's entrance. She did as Veldis said, positioned a soldier with a torch at its mouth, and told him to light the fuse for her order and hers alone. Adi ran down its wide steps and walked a few paces inside.

She could see four charges fixed to the roof, emitting a soft orange glow, the rest too far and faint to be observed. No light met her eye from the tunnel's far side, its doors still fashioned shut. She took a small breath to steel her nerves and made her way back to the wall.

All around her, Lorethh's forces hastened to make ready for what might come to pass. She remembered as she hurried on how they looked to her to gather a sense of how they should feel about the events that rapidly unfolded. Because of this, she did not let her mounting sense of fear show on her face, hardening her expression as she returned to her post atop the wall.

Baskets of arrows and crates of the few remaining bits of white stone were carried up to replace the empty ones, along with any other materials the city could spare to load the trebuchets. Adiadni looked to the North, to the goblins who swarmed Judii; to the sky, to the Shadow that inched forward. And then, her ears picked up a mighty approaching sound, and she turned her head to the South.

Trumpets and shouting met with thundering footsteps and hoofbeats. The allies from Tila Forest crashed into the fight.

Adi let out a breath, feeling a relieved sob squeeze her throat at the sight of them. The spirit of the Free People was alive in the Mirrored Cities and the battle was not over yet.

***

The last of Judii's forces made it safely beyond the refuge of the wall and the gates were swiftly shut and barred behind them. Several large goblins carried with them a heavy battering ram, and they set to work attempting to force their way into the city.

The archers concentrated their efforts. Many arrows were needed to fell just one, and every time one met his end, another rose to take his place.

Just inside, the soldiers reassembled, ready and awaiting their next order. Uritus joined them on the ground, the repetitive pounding in his chest not unlike that which beat against the gate.

"Uritus!"

The Adalos turned to see his first commander hastening to his side.

"You've got to get the non-armed out. Digtrision hopes the doors will hold but can't say for how long."

"I'll send someone to lead them," Uritus insisted. "If the fight breaks through, I'll remain here to meet it."

Outside the city, the young Sorcerer had made his way to the gate, and he waved aside the goblins who attempted to force it open.

The arrows loosed by the archers and flames shot by the Wizard rolled right off the invisible barrier that protected him. Uriah looked on in horror as Erclidus brought his hands together and thrust them forward, sending a forceful blast crashing into the outer gate.

The doors blew open, their braces snapped like twigs. Uriah hurried to the ground, calling to the general.

Uritus lifted his eyes, the gravity of their situation becoming suddenly clear to him as he saw the worry on the face of his mentor.

"To the tunnels, now! The city will fall, it is only a matter of when. You must get out while you can."

Uritus shook his head furiously, eyes darting to the soldiers who attempted to brace the inner gate. "I cannot leave you here—"

At that moment, an explosion. Sparks and charred wood flew through the air as the soldiers nearest the gate were blown back.

"Go, now!"

A firm hand closed around the Adalos's arm and dragged him away before he had a second to argue. He watched over his shoulder the enemies attempting to force their way into the city as he hurried away with Nadarum.

The medics, cooks, and other vulnerable citizens had begun to organize, and the two men led them to the tunnel's mouth, sending them swiftly through on horseback to safety. Uritus felt every one of his senses heightened, eyes constantly drifting back to the fight across the city.

The footsoldiers at the gate fought back against the intruders, but they were no match for the man in the black cape. It became quickly clear to all at the front that Judii had been lost.

The officers called their troops to fall back in waves, back to the tunnel, back to the safety of their sister city. Many of the Free People ignored these calls, pressing forward, fighting still to ensure the safe evacuation of the rest. At Uriah's order, Perplexus found and dragged Oripidus back from the gate, ignoring the dwarf's relentless cursing and sending him with Nadarum through to the other side. The arrows of the archers were all but spent, the single remaining trebuchet proving useless as their enemies closed in.

The goblins remaining in the Southern battlefield began to realize that, with the arrival of the reinforcements, they were vastly outnumbered. They hastened to retreat, hoping they might also find shelter in the Northern city.

Bodies continued to pile up before the gate. Uriah used the last of his strength to attempt to push back the steady inflow of foes, but his efforts and those of the soldiers on the ground proved futile. The city had fallen.

All the Wizard could do now was ensure the safety of as many as he could. He grabbed soldier after soldier by the arm, forcefully shoving them in the direction of the tunnel, wielding his staff as a weapon as he moved. A firm hand seized his arm and he turned to see the wide blue eyes of the fisherman.

"I won't leave without you! We need to—"

The last of Uritus's sentence was drowned in noise as flame and rock exploded a few feet away.

The force of the blast sent them flying back. They crashed to the ground, and when the Adalos raised his eyes, he saw his brother advance, droves of goblins moving with him.

He leapt to his feet and helped the Wizard to his own, and when the next wave of soldiers hastened to their escape, he shoved him to be swept up in the current and carried away to safety.

The general sprang back to action, partnering with those who beat back against the rush of adversaries. His first commander was soon back at his side.

Uriah stepped out of the path of the fleeing troops as they came upon the tunnel's entrance, spotting Erephus and urging him to pass through.

The injured Wizard refused, "They'll need you on the other side. I can hold the line, I'll light the fuse when it's time!"

Uriah shook his head. "We can light the fuse from Lorethh, you do not need to do this."

"But I do. Judii is my home. If she burns, I will burn with her. Protect the others. Go with Source."

With a stinging in his chest, Uriah relented and descended into the tunnel.

Uritus and Perplexus planted themselves in the space between the tunnel and their foes. Step by stubborn step, they continued to be driven back.

Uritus could see his brother making his steady approach. He had no desire to cross blades with Erclidus, Perplexus knew this well. So when the enemy general drew near enough, it was the navigator who rose to face him.

He ignored his friend's screamed objection as his blade collided with the Sorcerer's.

Erclidus was amused by the commander's fire and impressed by the skill of his blade. The two traded off attacking and parrying in a dangerous dance. Uritus, forced to react to the battle as it continued to play out around him, could do nothing but watch.

Perplexus knew he had met his match but was glad to hold his foe's attention for long enough that a few more Free People might have the chance to make their escape. Erclidus's hand was stubborn and harsh. But under the tutelage of the man he called brother, Perplexus remained steadfast. Havian's lessons echoed in his mind as though the swordsman fought beside him.

Such confidence, however, proved once again to be blinding, and in a crucial moment when the navigator should have waited, he lunged.

With a wave of his hand, Erclidus sent Perplexus's sword careening to the side and then reached out and grabbed the navigator by the throat.

The young Sorcerer chuckled darkly as he tightened his grip. "You'd think the dog would come to learn his place. I suppose some mongrels are better trained than others. One more kick ought to do it..."

But before Erclidus could deliver the fatal blow, a blade cut through fabric and then flesh at his hip.

He cried out in pain, releasing his hold on Perplexus as he turned to face the soldier who rose against him.

Dustafes Elbon leapt back, waving his blade with a flourish.

Uritus fought his way forward to help his friend to his feet and Perplexus retrieved his sword in just enough time to plunge it into an enemy who raced toward the fisherman.

Erclidus chuckled again at the audacity of the bold soldier. "You Easterners just refuse to learn."

With an angry cry, Dustafes charged, swinging his sword with all his might.

Erclidus retaliated—one strong swing to parry—and then plunged his blade into his opponent's gut.

Uritus's heart lurched as Dustafes's lifeless body dropped to the ground. He turned at an urgent tug of his arm and raced to the tunnel with Perplexus.

Many goblins had identified the route the Free People utilized to escape and it was clear from several yards off that its door was now inaccessible. Erephus stood his ground, sending bursts of flame and wind to drive their enemies back.

"Come on!"

Perplexus obeyed his friend's command and followed him up the wall. In the distance, he spotted one of the gryphon riders and furiously waved his arms in the air to get her attention.

She spotted them and hurried to land, offered her hand to the navigator, and pulled him up to a seat behind her.

"Go now!" cried the general, and then, before they could object, "That's an order!"

The gryphon took to the sky, Perplexus's screams of dissent fading into the distance as he was carried to the safety of Lorethh.

Uritus returned his eyes to the ongoing battle, his new vantage point offering him confirmation of what he already knew—that he had lost the city he sought to defend.

The violence on the ground was ceaseless. The few Free People who remained to ensure the safety of the rest were brutally cut down one by one.

There was nothing more that the Adalos could do. He could drop to the ground, give the last of his energy and his life to the cause, and die alongside the heroes who refused to surrender. But in his heart, he knew that his work was not done, that the war was not done, and that the Free World needed him to see it through to its end.

He raised his eyes to the sky in search of the second gryphon rider, black Shadow stretching its fingers out to extinguish the last of the light above Judii. Just before his heart resigned to hopelessness, he saw a blessed shape move from beyond the edge of swirling black cloud.

Milion roared as he came upon the fallen city, descending until he came to land atop the rampart.

Uritus had not called him. The dragon had sensed that his rider was in danger and come of his own accord.

Uritus raced along the wall to reach him, the Sword of Fire putting an end to the few goblins who stood in his way. He sheathed the blade as he came upon Milion, reaching out his arms to pull himself onto the dragon's back.

His escape would prove not to be so simple as a goblin of larger stature grabbed and yanked him back by his boot.

Milion whipped his neck around and clamped his teeth around the one who threatened his rider. He lifted him off the ground, swinging his head one way and then the other, and released him, sending the goblin crashing to the ground below.

Uritus settled into his spot on the dragon's back, the eyes of his enemies looking up to regard the beast on the wall.

With a final roar, Milion spread his wings, lifted into the sky, and carried the Adalos away.

***

In Lorethh's infirmary, Adiadni did as she was told, hastening from bed to bed to administer aid to the injured. Her eyes darted anxiously around, searching for a glimpse of those she loved amongst the waves of soldiers who arrived from Judii. She let out a relieved breath every time she saw one; Punznes hurrying to bandage the wounded, Oripidus cursing at Nadarum for not allowing him to remain behind and then the horseman disappearing into the arms of his wife.

A series of distant booms reached her ears, eight of them in quick succession, growing louder as they went. The tunnel had been collapsed. All who would escape to safety were already here.

She felt her heartbeat in her ears, the sickening twisting of her stomach. The urgency of her present duty did not allow her to consider her worst fears.

When Milion let Uritus down in the city's center and took off again into the sky, the fisherman felt, for the first time since the battle began, helpless and defeated. He had no skill to mend or heal, no remaining brainpower to join the ongoing fight. He wandered through the streets toward the infirmary in a fog, urging himself to remember that his attitude had a direct effect on those who looked to him as their leader. He did not observe the Shadow as it moved fully across the sky above the cities, did not hear the sound of trumpets from outside

Lorethh's wall proclaiming their victory on the battlefield. He saw only the agony of his soldiers, heard only their pained wails and devastated sobs.

When he eventually found himself in the infirmary and his eyes met Adiadni's across the room, it took every mite of remaining strength he had not to break down into tears.

The relief that rushed through the princess's body when she spied the man she loved was sweeter than any she'd ever known. She had only a moment to hold his gaze before she was pulled away to her next task, but it was enough to communicate everything that she wished to: *I love you, I'm sorry, I'm so glad you're okay.*

With the new inflow of soldiers through the gate from the battlefield, her attention was stolen and she returned to her work.

Uritus observed the soldiers tearfully embrace as they were reunited. These little bits of joy offered a small amount of relief to the unending heaviness in his heart, but even so, he was now aware of the undeniable truth in the words spoken earlier that day by his mentor.

War is a relentless beast.

Chapter Twenty-Seven

"The Hands that Bake the Bread"

The 6th of August

Uritus's wounds were seen to by one of the Healers shortly after his arrival in the infirmary—wounds he had not been aware he had sustained. They were minor, a shallow gash on one arm, another across his cheek, plus the assortment of bruises which were a natural product of any prolonged fight. He accepted the Healer's offerings with stoic gratitude, attempting to quell his irritation for how his minor injuries were prioritized over those who were in far worse shape than he. He sought out Aurena, and later, Alidistris in a desperate search to make himself useful, but was told the same thing by everyone he spoke to: *we've got it handled, you've done enough, get some rest.* Finally, once he had personally located each member of his family and ensured that they were alive and well, he relented.

He bathed and changed and then set to work meticulously cleaning his armor and weapons, knowing that lying down and attempting to rest now would prove fruitless. He did his best to remember the hopeful things he had seen that day— the unity, the heroism, the little victories. But try as he might, he could not shut out the sounds of the people's anguished cries or the images of their violent deaths, deaths which came far too soon for many of them, deaths which he had led them to. He shook his head vigorously when these thoughts surfaced, knowing they were of no use to him. Despite his belief that at this point in his life, he was a master at facing grief, in a time of such heaviness, he didn't know how to begin. The Adalos wasn't sure how much time had passed when a gentle voice at his door pulled him from his dizzying haze.

"Are you okay?"

Uritus moved to his feet and crossed the room to pull the princess into his embrace. He did not answer the question she posed, instead burying his face into the crook of her neck and holding her tightly as though she could vanish at any moment. He did not notice how the blood and dirt that still covered her soiled his clothes, thought of nothing but how unendingly grateful he was that she was still here. In the still and quiet, he released his hold on the necessity to appear strong and wept.

She wept with him. They sank to the ground, arms fast around one another. They did not speak, but in their silence communicated everything they needed to —mutual devastation and gratitude, deep sorrow intermingled with relief. And with every tear shed, each of them felt just a tiny bit lighter again. Eventually, the wells of their grief ran dry, and Uritus loosed his hold on his counterpart to get a look at her face. Even now, caked with dirt and puffy-lidded, she appeared so soft and so bright. He could not comprehend such radiance, could not fathom how, even in his darkest moments, the mere sight of her was enough to draw him back to himself again. More aggressively than he intended to, he pulled her face to his own and kissed her. And in her kiss, the breath of light, the taste of love and freedom and everything pure and good. He knew it would take the rest of his life to mourn these days and the lives they had lost. But for tonight, for this sacred moment, he was reminded of the reasons why he fought, and he held them close with the body of the woman he loved.

***

"It would appear that my brother has chosen to cower in his keep rather than fight the battle he himself ordained. I cannot say that such a thing comes as a shock to me, considering the state of his health when last we met. But such a choice on his part does prove to be a bit of a snag in our plans."

Uriah addressed the council who gathered the morning after their battle, minus a few officers who saw to the goings-on of Lorethh. Any living wounded had long since been recovered from the battlefield. Now, the Free People gathered the bodies of their dead and burned them before doing the same with those of their enemies.

"I saw with them no Alchemist and no Seer," Veldis added. "There is always a chance that such key figures may arrive later, now that their forces have opened a path. But at this point, I doubt they would choose to leave the safety of their homes."

Adiadni chewed on her lip as she considered what this could mean regarding her father's health.

Veldis continued, "Naturally, we will need to take all of this into account as we consider and map out our next moves. This morning, I…"

The council was interrupted by Mikka's arrival, her presence an indication that the fallen had been accounted for. All eyes looked to her in silent anticipation of the news she carried. The commander took a breath, "Final count: one thousand and twenty-three dead, three hundred and fifty-seven wounded, eighty-eight of them in rough enough shape to be bedridden. The rest can move out as needed."

A solemn air settled in the room, broken after a few moments by Laivar's query, "And those we know?"

Mikka's eyes, tired and red, looked across the faces of her family. "Erephus of Judii, Dustafes Elbon, Lyra and Jessop Fril, and…" She paused and swallowed, her throat tight with grief. "Seryc Tarish."

Empathy squeezed the hearts of her friends. "I'm sorry, Mik…"

She raised her hand, shook her head. "She knew the risks. As do we all."

"That may be so, but you are still allowed to grieve…"

"And I do. But I choose also to keep moving. The people look to us still. We must turn our eyes to what comes next. That endless field of broken bone and ivory stone cannot be for nothing."

They knew the commander was right. Veldis returned to his unfinished thought, "I received word this morning from Suscundos. The Prophets have foreseen that the enemy will soon proceed from Judii to lay siege on the capital. In such a case, we will need to be swift to send our soldiers ahead so we may be ready to meet them when the time comes."

"Our allies from Tila have agreed to hold Lorethh so we are free to move as needed," Digtrision shared. "I presume that the Prophets do not know exactly when the enemy will advance?"

Veldis shook his head.

"In that case, we must act quickly. We can allow the soldiers a day to rest, perhaps two for those who need it. I can be ready to lead a group on tomorrow morning."

"I'll go with you," Adiadni offered, eager to see her father again. Digtrision nodded his agreement.

"Very well," Uriah approved. "We will make our hasty return to Suscundos and begin to prepare the city to withstand the next attack. But something must be done about those who hide in Vegard."

All nodded their silent agreement.

"We cannot guarantee that Velup and his council will come out to face us themselves, and we cannot make the same mistake we did at the end of the Hope War. We mustn't allow them to flee and wait and scheme their next plan of attack. This conflict must end with us. We do not have enough soldiers that we can presently risk storming the Ashen Keep, but every hour that Velup's Alchemist is allowed to remain alive is a further risk to the health of the king. I propose that we send a small group into Vegard to find Ouro and assassinate him."

"Let me go," Mikka spoke without hesitation. "I am one of few who have been beyond the Looming Mountains. I will seek out the villages South of the keep, search them all until I find him."

"Very well," Uriah nodded to the young soldier in admiration of her courage. "I appoint you the leader of this mission."

"I'll join ye," Oripidus declared.

"As will I," said Laivar. "Mother only knows what may happen to you two without me to protect you."

Oripidus did not try to hold in his laughter, clapping a hand loudly on Laivar's back. "What indeed?"

Mikka smiled and shook her head at them from across the room. The bard, uncertain though he was of his skills as a combatant, was sure of his decision nonetheless. He could not bear the thought of what harsh fate might meet his friends behind enemy lines, and knowing that he would journey with them offered him a mite of solace. Personal risk be damned, he loved them too much to stay behind.

"I'll go too," spoke Punznes, a caw from the raven on his shoulder punctuating his sentence. "You'll need my common sense and Qibat's eye if you wish to make it there and back safely."

Uriah nodded once more. "So be it. You'll be escorted on horseback to the range under the cover of night and proceed from there on foot. The rest of us will make our way to Suscundos as soon as we are able."

Uritus had spent the duration of the council up to that point in pondering silence, but the lingering fear that itched at his brain demanded to be addressed. "I am concerned, as we do not know the planned timeline of Vegard's forces, that they intend to proceed sooner than we anticipate. They will need to reorganize, and such a thing will take time, but I hate to consider what may come to pass if they move out before we do."

"Are you suggesting that we send troops on today?"

Uritus shook his head. "They need and deserve every bit of rest we can offer them. My thought is more… steps we could take to delay our enemies. Offer the Free People a head start."

"What do you have in mind?"

The Adalos took a breath, knowing his suggestion would not be popular amongst the others, "I wish to go to Judii on my own to speak with my brother."

The room fell silent and remained that way for several seconds.

"I will ride under a white flag," he continued, "...and propose a negotiation. Erclidus is smart and strategic and will not say no if he believes there is an easier path forward."

Uriah replied, a hesitant note in his voice, "And what exactly is it you plan to propose?"

"I haven't thought that far," Uritus admitted. "Obviously, we have no intent to surrender, and I doubt that he can be persuaded to cease his campaign, but the point isn't actually to sway his mind. Rather… to pull his focus. Delay him so our people might have a chance to make it to Suscundos before he can."

Silence took the room again, each member of the council weighing in their mind the merits of this plan against its risks. It was Adiadni, in an overwhelming state of bewilderment, who spoke first, "I don't know if the rest of you refrain from objecting to this plan merely because it is our general who proposes it, but I am happy to be the singular voice of dissent. You cannot do this. It is foolish and dangerous and we cannot guarantee that it will even be successful in its intended purpose."

Uritus sighed. He had anticipated the princess's objection and knew that it would be a challenge to convince her to let him go. "You are right. But the alternative is to simply hope that we make it in time, and… as necessary as hope is, in this case, I do not think it is enough."

"And if he kills you?" The sentence was harsh, bitter in Adiadni's mouth, but she felt desperate to try to reason with him.

"I believe that I will live to see my destiny through to its completion, as you did. Erclidus had the opportunity to kill me before, could have killed any one of us in the Ashen Keep, but he didn't."

"And if he steals the Sword of Fire again?"

"I won't bring it with me."

"Are you hearing yourself?" Adi's eyes darted from one face to another, desperately searching for the one who might partner with her in persuading him to reconsider. "You intend to ride straight into the mouth of the enemy with no weapon to protect you and try to negotiate with the most hard-headed man currently in the Free World? Do not be a fool. White flag or none, we cannot assume that the enemy will abide by the rules of war. This is an unnecessary risk. Our people need you." *I need you* is what she meant to say, but the sentiment was communicated even with her chosen words.

"The Adalos has the protection of the prophecy on his side," Uriah gently attempted to reassure her. "Uritus is correct about the necessity of delaying Vegard's advance. Even half a day of a head start could make all the difference."

"So send someone else. It doesn't have to be you…"

"I will not risk anyone else." Uritus's words were gentle yet firm. "As Uriah said, the prophecy protects me and ensures my safe passage to the end of this conflict. It does not do the same for anyone else. Erclidus's heart may have been blackened by Velup's poison, but he is still my brother. I do not believe he wishes to see me die. It cannot be anyone else. I must be the one to go."

No other voices spoke up about the issue and Adiadni concluded that she had lost the debate. The discussion turned to other matters and the princess crossed her arms tightly, her fear for what might happen to her counterpart difficult to ignore. She would not speak up about the issue again, knowing well that it would do no good. A quiet storm began to brew in her head.

***

"I'm sorry."

The princess and fisherman stood in her chamber, the wide, Southern-facing window open to let in the air. Adi stood in front of it, arms wrapped around her body, eyes to the dark swirling clouds that stretched across the sky.

Uritus went on, "I mean it. I know that these circumstances are not ideal and I hate to be the source of your anxiety."

"I know," she replied. "I do not fault you for what you must do. You are far braver than I."

He shook his head, breathing an amused laugh out of his nose. "Courage is one of my better traits, I admit that. But you must know that you are the one who inspires it in me." He crossed the room to stand at her side and raised a hand to turn her face toward him. "I have witnessed with my own eyes the impossible feats you have accomplished despite your self-doubt. For every danger that I run headfirst into, know that I will make it out if only to be near you again."

416

She sighed softly as she gazed up at him. "I know. I do believe you. I just do not know how not to worry about you."

"Unfortunately, I think worry is a side effect of love."

"Well, in that case, know that I love you an incomparable amount."

He chuckled, pulled her into his arms, and buried his face in her hair, "As I do you."

There was a knock then at the door, and the pair looked up as it opened. The frame of the navigator was backlit in the doorway, bearing a clay pitcher and trio of cups. "I thought I might find you two here. I hope I'm not interrupting…"

"Not at all," the princess crossed the room and took a pair of the cups into her hands. "I realize now that I haven't gotten the chance to spend time with you since last we were in Suscundos."

"I realized that too," he replied, filling the cups one by one with red wine from the pitcher. "Not since we celebrated our return. Of course, celebration now would neither be appropriate nor beneficial, despite the victory we secured yesterday. But since we're all about to split up to some degree, I thought a gathering might enliven our spirits. I told the others we'd be here. I hope you don't mind."

Adi shook her head and handed one of the cups to Uritus as he moved to stand beside them. The fisherman raised his vessel and the other two did the same, touching them to one another before lifting them to their lips to drink. The wine was thin but warm and satisfying, and they were grateful for it. Uritus came to realize that he had taken for granted the simple luxury of sharing drink with the people he loved, and he voiced this to his friends. "It was a nightly event back home in the Alabaster Keep, a communal joy that was such a natural part of our ordinary lives, I didn't recognize its significance until now. I know I've said it many times already, but I am flushed with gratitude when I remember how lucky we are to have the opportunity to again. All of us. Except…"

He trailed off and the princess and navigator hurried to embrace him. The family was not the same without Havian and it never would be again. The heaviness in the room settled somewhat when Nadarum and Ilya arrived, mugs in hand, and Perplexus filled them.

"Did you know Mikka was the one who slayed that Sorcerer yesterday? Plum was just telling me."

"Spear straight through the chest," Ilya shared with a nod of her head. "She's unstoppable, that one. No one better to lead the mission out West."

"I wonder if she got that kiss…" Adiadni muttered under her breath.

"Kiss?"

The princess laughed. "Before Crys and I moved out with the second wave, she promised the soldiers that she would reward whoever felled the Sorcerer with a kiss. Mik wasn't there, of course, she was out on the ground already, so she didn't know about the bounty, but…"

"Hmm," Ilya lifted her eyes to the ceiling with an amused smile. "I can't say I would have considered putting the two of them together…"

"I'm sure that's the last thing on Mikka's mind at the moment. What with Seryc's death…"

The room grew somber at Nadarum's comment but lightened again moments later when Oripidus loudly entered the room with Punznes on his heels, "I hear ye've found a bit o' drink. Give it here."

The blacksmith and physician had not brought their own drinking vessels. Perplexus crossed the room to fetch a pair of glasses which he filled and handed off to them. "Ilya was just gracing us with the tale of one of Mik's victories yesterday."

"The Sorcerer?" Punznes asked, and the navigator nodded. "A remarkable feat which I'm sure none of us were surprised to hear of. That woman's determination is unmatched. I believe strongly that such an act played a mighty role in Lorethh's victory."

The others nodded their heads.

"I hate to give credit to a monster of a man," said Oripidus. "But our Adalos's brother is a force to be reckoned with. None of us managed to come at all close to slowin' him down, let alone stoppin' him."

"Lex did."

All eyes turned to Uritus and then Perplexus. "When was this?"

"Toward the end, just before we evacuated. Courageous bastard almost got himself killed."

"Were Erclidus a right-handed sword fighter, I may have stood a chance."

"That very well may be true. But the fact is that you attempted an attack when you should have waited. Not that I am trying to cast doubt on your unquestionable skill. But I couldn't reach you, and were it not for Dustafes, you surely would have died."

"Who's this that nearly died?" Laivar entered the room with Mikka on this last sentence.

"I did," Perplexus replied, taking up and filling a pair of teacups for the new arrivals. "At the hand of Velup's apprentice. Dustafes Elbon gave his life for mine. A hero in his own right." Solemnly, the navigator raised his cup and the others did the same, sharing a drink in honor of the fallen one.

"The more I hear you lot share of the things you experienced on the field, the more grateful I am to have been allowed to do my part atop the wall," the poet admitted. "I tell you assuredly that I was made for softness, for luxury, and for art. I was certainly *not* made for such brutality."

"None of us were," Mikka affirmed. "We'd be far different people if we took up our swords for the joy of it. Even Havian would be disheartened had he lived to witness the things we have."

"Never did I question why Uriah has such a deep hatred of war, but now that I have taken part in it myself, I feel that hate is not strong enough a word," Ilya shared, and the others nodded their agreement.

"I'm sure such circumstances were not the kind you had hoped would pull you back to the place of your birth," said Oripidus to Punznes.

"Indeed. I am glad, of course, that she still stands. But I cannot deny that the Lorethh we see now is merely a skeleton of the one I knew in my youth. Truthfully, I'm glad Hav didn't have to see her this way. She is not herself without the sun to warm her."

Adi turned again to the window, to the inky black sky that stretched as far as she could see. The others in the room continued to share their stories of fights won and lost. Though she tried her best to put her anxieties aside, she felt the storm in her mind again begin to stir.

"You all right, Love?"

Laivar's inquiry caught the attention of the others who quieted and turned their eyes to the princess. Uritus looped an arm around her and she looked from one face to another. She didn't wish to bring them down, but had suddenly become overwhelmed by awareness of the days to come. In these last hours that the loving community shared before they split up, she wished to find a way to redirect them to the Light. "Might we… speak of joy?"

Enthusiastic nods met her in response.

"When I was a boy, probably five or six years of age, I remember being devastated to learn that all the fireflies I saw in the dim light of dusk would be dead by the end of the season." The deep, gentle voice of the horseman warmed the blood of the others who sat in chairs and settled onto the ground supported by cushions to listen to his tale. "It was one of my brothers who told me. He didn't intend it as a harshness, merely as a fact, but even so, I was inconsolable. I thought it unfair that such pure and precious creatures existed only to light the world for a few short months, sire the next generation, and then return to the dirt. My father found me outside, lost in my tears, and he picked me up and set me in his lap.

"He did not speak for some time, rather waited for my breaths to return to their ordinary pattern. And then he reached his hand to the sky, plucked one of them from where it lazily drifted through the air, and brought it down to cup in my hands. I watched it blink, once, twice, until it rose into the air and fluttered back to the cornfield, flashing golden light as it left. *Everything has its time*, he told me. *Like the corn, born to grow and fruit and nourish our bodies and then wilt once it's served its purpose. Like the sun and the storms and each one of us who is blessed to walk this earth. We are born, we grow, we die. And when our bodies rot and become one with the earth again, new life grows. Nothing ever truly dies*, he said, *not if we don't want it to. We will live on long after we've passed from this place, in story, in memory, in the faces of our youth, in the mushrooms which sprout from our flesh.*"

Nadarum cleared his throat and Ilya scooted closer under the crook of his arm. "I never forgot that. And while I am still saddened by each life, great and small, that I witness pass on, I attribute his words that day to the reason why I do not fear death, not really. Our bodies are finite, but our spirits are not, and when I leave this realm, something new will grow in my place. And while a part of me will always be the twenty-year-old whom my father rejected, part of me still is five or six, safe in his lap, watching the fireflies blink their last as the sun goes down. Each one of us, so small and so frail. Each one of us, infinite in our own right."

In the room, a chorus of quiet sniffles. The pitcher of wine was passed around to fill cups as they emptied.

"All right, my turn," Laivar proclaimed, standing to his feet. "There once was an elvish girl named Fariya, an orphan raised by her maternal aunt in a manor by the sea. She had been too young to remember her parents after they passed, so she beseeched her aunt to tell her about them. And her aunt, earnestly wishing to offer the child her peace, obliged. She told her of her mother, sharp, wise beyond her years, and of her father, patient and unendingly kind. Over and over, Fariya pleaded to hear the stories of the people she had come from, and again and again, her aunt shared them. As she grew, the girl kept these stories close to her chest, clutching them as though they might be ripped from her hands by a sudden gust of wind. Though her aunt tried to bring her solace, to teach, guide, nourish, and comfort her, still Fariya was deeply sad and drifted about the grounds of the manor as though a part of herself was missing.

"There was, however, one thing that brought the girl joy, one blessed thing that caused the stars in her eyes to twinkle, and that thing was the moon. She adored it through all of its phases be they sliver or whole, loved it most when it was full and glowing peachy-golden light. She was old enough to understand that it was a permanent fixture of the sky, not to be held by mortal hands. But as time passed, this too, made her sad. So her aunt, creative and clever, began to construct a plan.

"On Fariya's tenth birthday, she went with her aunt to the cliffs by the sea to watch the moonrise as they did most nights. On this particular evening, it happened that the moon was golden and full, just as the girl liked it. It grew ever smaller as it stretched toward the sky, and before Fariya had the chance to feel the melancholy that stems from being separated from what one loves, her aunt set gentle hands on her shoulders and directed the girl toward the gift she'd had made for her. There, in the garden, stood a wide stone basin, shallow and filled to the brim with still water, silver inlaid in the bowl to better reflect the light. She encouraged her niece to move to its edge, to gaze into it and tell her what she saw.

"Fariya did as she was instructed, approached the basin and peered inside, and a smile lit on her face as she saw her reflection staring back up at her, the moon just next to her face. *I know this won't truly make up for how you cannot be together*, her aunt said. *But I hope it can bring you a bit of the closeness you crave, and that such closeness brings you joy.* She took the girl's hand in her own and touched it to the image of the moon, soft ripples of golden light rolling out to the basin's edge. As the water settled and the reflected image became clear once more, Fariya saw them all there, herself and the moon and the woman who loved her, and she came to realize that she had everything she had ever truly needed.

"She would still feel sorrow for what she had lost, but the empty space in her chest that she'd tried to fill with constructed memories opened and she began to tuck into it new things. Lessons from her aunt and adventures they shared, the joy of tending to the earth with her hands, and eventually, love for a boy who lived in a cottage across town and the children she would raise with him. And one day, Fariya will go to her aunt to find that she too has passed on, and the space she leaves behind will ache in a way the girl had all but forgotten. But she will go again down to the garden by the sea and watch the moon lift into the sky. She will look into the pool of the basin crafted of the purest love and she will see there her reflection and the moon beside her face, and in its light, the face of the one who loved her. And while it will not truly make up for the closeness that she craves, it will bring her joy. Still shining, still golden, still alive."

The bard returned to his seat, the glistening tears on the cheeks of his friends an affirmation of his gifts.

"Is that a true story?" Punznes asked.

"Does it matter?"

The physician chuckled, "No, I suppose not."

"I guess I should apologize, Adiadni, you asked for joy and received two sad stories in response."

The princess shook her head. "Joy is still joy even when mingled with grief. We know that well by now."

"Hear, hear!" Oripidus raised his glass and the others mirrored this action.

"You are correct," Laivar affirmed. "Joy rises and recedes like the tide along the shore. There is solace in knowing that it will always return."

Ilya tipped the last of the drink into the poet's cup and Mikka offered to go fetch more. She took up the clay pitcher and departed from the room, the chattering and laughter of her friends bringing a smile to her face as she returned to the city below. The pitcher was filled for her by a worker in the mess hall, and as she waited, her eyes drifted over the masses there. They too shared food and drink and stories and laughter, and she felt herself choke up a bit as she observed them. They were resilient even in the face of their defeat. The hope of the Free People was alive still in Lorethh. She thanked the worker as the pitcher was returned to her hands and made her way to the door.

"Mikka!"

She turned her head as she stepped through the doorway in search of the one who had called her name and spotted Alidistris hastening to her side.

The woman from the West paused to catch her breath. "Laivar said you're leaving?"

The soldier nodded. "Tonight. I'll be leading a small group back beyond the mountains in search of the Alchemist who has cursed the king."

Alidistris chewed on her cheek a moment before declaring, "I want to come with you."

Mikka blinked in surprise, her head tipping over one shoulder. "Are you sure? It will be a tedious trek, a dangerous mission."

"I know. I…" The former attendant paused, trying to gather her thoughts. "I just… I want to help. Everyone here has the chance to dedicate their skills to the cause. I do not know how to fight, though I am a fast learner. And of course, I do not wish to saddle you with the burden of my protection, and if it would be easier for you to go without me, I will understand. But I know the people back in Vegard. While I don't know exactly how I might be of assistance, perhaps I can—"

"All right."

Alidistris blinked, a smile creeping across her face. "Are you certain?"

"Yes. Were it not for you, we might never have made it out of the Ashen Keep. I understand well the desire to do one's part. We'll be glad to have you along with us." The dark-haired woman's smile bloomed to fullness, spreading also to Mikka's face. "If you want, you can come with me now. We are sharing drink and speaking of joy. Trying to make the most of the last hours we have before we part."

"Oh, I don't wish to intrude…"

"Nonsense. You are always welcome. We are a collection of misfits, my family and I, sad stories who refused to give up on hope and who found each other because of it. You are one of us, if you wish to be."

Alidistris smiled again, soft and grateful, and the two proceeded to the princess's chamber. They could hear the loud, raucous laughter as they approached, the scratchy voice of the raven repeating a word that Alidistris could not immediately understand that made Mikka chuckle.

"Wal*nut*, wal*nut!*"

Qibat's emphasis on the word's second syllable was the silliest thing that never failed to make the group devolve into hysterics. He did not always say it this way, and they suspected that the reason he did was because he knew the reaction it would elicit. The two entered the room just as Punznes offered the bird the precious treat. Mikka was glad to see that Uriah had joined them there. Laivar stood to retrieve the last of the teacups for the newcomer and the pitcher was again passed around the room.

"Aye, Qibat, but not merely wal*nuts*. All food and all drink. And I know what yer thinkin'—of course the dwarf loves food, what a classic stereotype that is. But listen here, I speak not merely of consumption, but of the hands which make such a thing possible."

Fragrant smoke drifted into the air from the pipes in the mouths of the Wizard and the navigator and a gentle breeze wafted into the room from the open window. In the time the commander had been gone, the candles scattered about the space had been lit, and they offered the room a cozy warmth. Mikka and Alidistris settled down on the ground amongst the others, listening as Oripidus continued speaking.

"Picture with me, for a moment, the hands which till the earth, plant the seeds, nurture and harvest the wheat for our bread. How many more hands then, mill the flour, deliver it to bakeries, mix it with water and salt and bake it before the risin' of the sun so we might have it fresh when we break our fast? And that's just the bread. More hands still milk the cows, churn the butter, raise and butcher and preserve the meat, grow and dry the spices, grind them with salt so we might have the luxury of flavor."

"That's quite poetic," Laivar teased.

"Perhaps. But the point is this: we are all intrinsically connected to one another. We cannot exist, at least not as we do, without the hundreds and even thousands of hands that make such a thing possible. So to conclude, yes, the eatin' of food and drinkin' of wine are among life's purest joys. But awareness of exactly where our food and wine comes from… that is greater still."

"That's a lovely sentiment, Rip," said Perplexus. "Where would any of us be without the aid of the rest?"

"What about you, Uriah?" Ilya asked. "What brings you joy?"

The Wizard chuckled softly. "Why, your smiling faces, of course." His eyes moved to meet each pair that stared back at him. "I have been around a long time, known and loved many individuals. I do not deny that at times, the life I have led has been quite lonely. I endured long seasons during which I felt afraid to be close to another, knowing that one day, I would very well live to see their end. I carry thousands of stories near to my heart, though many of the faces have long since faded from my memory. But now I see, clearer than I ever have, that the purpose of all of this, of existence as we know it, is right here." He gestured to the room, and the family looked around at one another. "Whatever may happen to me next, whether this war claims my life or I live to witness each one of you pass on to the next phase, I can rest knowing that I have tasted the sweetest treasures that life has to offer: love and unity and stories shared by candlelight. As for the rest…" he chuckled, shrugged, "…a dusting of sugar atop the divinest of cakes."

Uritus sighed contentedly, his cheek nestled against the head of his counterpart who warmed his side. How grateful he was for these people he called home.

Chapter Twenty-Eight

"Freedom is a Deafening Cry" and "Freedom is a Whisper"

The 7th of August

The city of Lorethh bustled with activity as the sun made its ascent in the Eastern sky. All the king's troops who were able to travel were setting out that day, one company in the morning led by Digtrision and Adiadni, the other that night, with Crystella and Pressio. The wounded would remain behind with a small number of physicians under the protection of the hired swords from Tila. On the rampart above the city's Northern wall, the Suvah bid the Adalos farewell.

"I don't like this." Adiadni gazed through the fog at the ominous shape of the enemy-occupied city in the distance. "I trust you, of course, and I trust the prophecy. But I do *not* trust *him*…"

Uritus moved his hands soothingly across her shoulders from where he stood behind her. "I know. I can't say that I do either. But I knew him once. And he knew me. And he loved me just as I did… *do* him. I saw the flicker in his eyes when I told him about the death of our father. I believe the one I knew is still in there, somewhere. Even if I have to do a bit of digging to unearth him."

The princess gave a little nod and turned to press her face against his chest. He still refused to bring with him any weaponry, though he had donned his armor at her insistence along with his blue cape. His body shielded her from the bitter wind that had arrived with the Shadow. She heard its whistling, the fabric of the flags atop the wall as they whipped back and forth, the voices of the busy people below. But she also found that if she focused with eyes tightly shut, she could still hear his heartbeat beneath the leather barrier that separated her from his skin. She stepped back so she could look up at him, at the steady, unwavering amber of his eyes.

"I love you," she said. "I'll see you soon."

A tiny note of grief on this last word prompted Uritus to pull her into his arms once more. "Sooner than you think. I love you too."

He cupped a hand beneath her chin to raise her face to meet his kiss, then hastened up the wall to mount the gryphon whose rider would deliver him behind enemy lines. He took up the flag that had been set aside for him—a hastily fashioned square of white fabric on a crooked wooden stick—and they took to the sky. Adi watched him disappear into the mist, a hand drifting up to touch the stone carving that lay against her chest, and the fisherman felt a cold spot where his own rested.

The journey from Lorethh to Judii happened so swiftly that many of the goblins who meandered about did not notice when the Adalos was let down in the city's center. Naturally, of course, some of them did, and those alerted others who spread the news of this sudden event. It took only a few moments for the fisherman to be grabbed, white flag ripped out of his hands, and forced to his knees. One of the goblins—larger, appearing to hold some sort of leadership position—struck him, a quick backhand across the face, a kick to the stomach. Uritus doubled over in his pain but did not cry out. Jeers in gish and garbled common tongue grated in his ears.

"What do we have here?"

The fisherman saw the crowd begin to part, heard the clicking of silver spurs before he saw the boots they adorned. He raised his eyes as the dark shape of his brother appeared before him.

Erclidus chuckled, a cruel sound, almost a pitying one. "Come to surrender already, little brother? That's quite disappointing. I thought we were having fun."

Uritus gritted his teeth, choosing not to react as Erclidus clearly wanted. "Not to surrender. To talk."

"Of course. Come to fill my ear with moans about the lives I have wasted. Such a bore." One thing remained true about the elder Subian: he knew all the right threads to tug at.

"I seek only a peaceful audience with intent to find a solution. It doesn't have to be this way."

The man in the black cape looked down at the one in blue, his pensive expression making it impossible to determine what he was thinking. "All right," he said finally. "Release him."

The goblins begrudgingly obeyed, shoving Uritus so he stumbled as he tried to rise to his feet. The crowd that had gathered dispersed with a wave of their general's hand and Uritus looked to his brother with a note of surprise on his face. "Just like that?"

The elder man shrugged. "You may think of me as a monster, but I am still respectful of some level of decorum. You arrived under a white flag, and wise enough to keep the sword out of my grasp. Besides, I do not think you are capable of hurting me. Not even if you wished for it. You're far too *good* for that."

"You'd be right. I would not wish it."

Erclidus jutted his head sharply in one direction and then turned and began to walk. Uritus took this as permission to follow. The men did not speak as they made their way to the command center. Uritus took this time to look around at the state of the city. He could see the scorched earth and blackened marks on the walls where fiery projectiles had struck. Other than this, there was little about Judii which looked all that different from Lorethh. But there was a heaviness here, a sinister darkness that did not exist in the Southern city. The Adalos felt it in his bones and stilled himself against its chill.

Before long, the two brothers arrived in Erclidus's chamber, the room which only a couple of days before had been inhabited by Uriah. Uritus lingered near the doorway as the young Sorcerer crossed the room, offering him a cup of tea as he set to prepare one for himself. Uritus refused.

"I'd ask what that caused you to become so stiff but, to my recollection, you've always been this way."

Uritus did not dignify this attempt at a slight with a response. It was true that the elder Subian had always been the bolder of the two, more outspoken, more curious, more rash. Uritus was the thoughtful one, cautious and prone to trusting and taking the advice of those who taught and guided him. Erclidus, who wished to learn his lessons on his own to better understand them, had grown to interpret his younger brother's preference for having his boots on stable ground as a threat, a barrier to his thirst for freedom of exploration. So even now, with over a decade having lapsed since the two had really known each other, each found himself clinging to his perceptions of who the other still was. Uritus attempted to release his hold on his own with a long breath out.

"What would it take for you to cease this campaign?" The Adalos had spent the night deep in thought of how to go about broaching the issue but at this moment saw no use for anything but straightforwardness.

Erclidus chuckled, setting down a teaspoon after stirring a cube of sugar and a dash of cream into his cup. "Let's see…" He reached a hand to his neck and undid the clasp that held his cape around his shoulders, draping the piece of thick fabric over the dressing screen before strolling the length of the room. Uritus spied the neatly stitched row that repaired the cape where it had been torn by Dustafes's blade, hardly noticeable. If the cut had done any lasting damage to the man in black's hip, he did not let it show.

"Contrary to what you may believe, I do not seek wealth," Erclidus went on. "Neither do I seek destruction, though I am not opposed to taking whatever path necessary to lead this land toward her future. Times change, Uritus. And if the systems at play cannot change along with them, they naturally should be disassembled and replaced."

Uritus sought to understand, "You take issue with king Agamemnon's leadership?"

"You don't?"

"The king is as I believe all men to be: imperfect and doing his best with what he has been given."

"Of course." The elder man paused his walk, sipped his tea. "But the fact remains that the crown has fallen short, time and again, to prevent the disasters that have befallen the people; in many cases, even to provide aid during said disasters."

Uritus frowned. "You would fault the one who knew not of certain tragedies for failing to act and yet… align yourself with the one who himself committed those tragedies?"

Erclidus shrugged. "Velup is a man of action, much like myself. As brutal as you may believe his tactics to be, you cannot say that he does not do what he must for his people."

Uritus made a sound that could only be interpreted as a scoff and his brother glared at him. "Do you truly believe that?"

The man in black did not respond.

"If Velup would force his people to submit to his will, it cannot be said that he is motivated by their needs and wishes. He seeks now to force the Free People to submission just as he does those in Vegard."

"You do not know him."

"Do you?"

Again, Erclidus fell silent.

Uritus took a breath. "I am just trying to understand. I do not deem you to be evil, just misled. I am speaking genuinely when I tell you that I will do whatever I can to reach a peaceful agreement. But if the only thing that would appease you is the dissolving of the crown, then I tell you that it cannot be done. Not by me, at least. The people chose the line of Vindella as their guardians long ago, I do not get to decide that now is the time to change that. Even if I did, a new power would naturally rise to take its place. Do you wish me to advocate for that power to be given to Velup, to you... despite how you will burn any who resist?"

Erclidus swallowed the last of his tea and crossed the room to refill his cup. He took into his hand this time not the teapot, but a heavy glass decanter with a sharp, glittering stopper. He poured the cup full of rich, golden liquor and then turned piercing eyes to his brother once more.

The question in them was clear, *are you sure you do not wish to indulge?* Uritus wondered if the dark-haired man did not speak the inquiry because he did not wish to again be rejected. After the briefest of hesitant breaths, the Adalos nodded his head, and a cup was prepared and handed to him before the decanter was returned to its shelf.

"I do not lead my campaign merely due to disdain for the crown. You have set foot in Vegard. You've seen the lack. You may have your doubts as to Velup's character, and you've no doubt been fed all kinds of tall tales by the woman you kidnapped from the keep, but by reclaiming the land which was stolen from our forefather, our people will have the opportunity to thrive in ways they never could if forced to remain in the desert of the West."

Uritus drank from his cup only after watching his brother do the same, a subconscious action that hinted that he may not have trusted Erclidus as much as he had previously thought. The whiskey was warm and sharp, settling into his belly lazily like a nearly-forgotten dream. "I understand. We do not wish for those in Vegard to suffer. We would be happy to welcome you into the Free World, to incorporate you into our land. Of course, only if such a thing can be arranged peacefully."

Erclidus clucked his tongue. "I acknowledge that you wish to help, but I assure you that your efforts are futile if you cannot guarantee the dethroning of the king and building of the new empire. You are smart… in an academic sort of way. I'm sure I could find a rank that would suit your talents. Even the line of Vindella could be spared. I see no reason why a woman as charming and capable as Adiadni need meet the same fate as her father. Something will need to be done about that temper, of course, and that glaring stubbornness. But the transition would be all the smoother if I oversaw it with her on my arm."

Uritus clenched his jaw for the briefest of moments before quickly relaxing it again. His brother had found it, *the* thread to pull which would lead to the younger man's unraveling, and the Adalos knew that it was dangerous to make this known. He tipped his head back and finished the last of the drink in his cup. "Adiadni is not a token of bargaining and neither is her father. I will not grant you the luxury of determining who must die and who may be spared. Such decisions should be made by no man. I tell you again, I am willing to debate, willing even to compromise. But I will not barter with anyone's life. I do not have the right and neither do you. If that means that we are at a stalemate… so be it."

The young Sorcerer clucked his tongue again with a small shake of his head, but his expression remained neutral. Uritus felt his face grow warm from whiskey or frustration or both. He couldn't comprehend how it had come to this, how he was forced to attempt to convince his own blood that it was wrong to kill one person, let alone many, for any reason but especially for one's personal gain. The two brothers had been raised in the same home, in the same town, by the same parents, and taught the same lessons. But now, one was here, desperately begging the other to take the peaceful path, the *easiest* path, and slowly arriving at the conclusion that his words, impassioned and reasonable as they were, meant nothing. He couldn't reach him, and as it did twelve years ago and as it had again and again in memory ever since, his heart broke for the man whom he could not save from himself.

Erclidus finished the last of the drink in his cup and set it down on the table beside the teapot. He clasped his hands behind his back and approached the window, looking out silently over those who went about their business in Judii. Uritus clenched and released one fist, waiting in agonized silence for his brother to speak what was on his mind. He did not know whether Erclidus would seek to deny the atrocities committed by his hand or justify them.

"Do you believe in destiny, Uritus?"

The younger man blinked. "I do."

"Of course. How could you not? No doubt you've had thousands shower you with praises and treasures for who they believe you to be. Tell me, what have they promised you in exchange for embodying their cause and blindly leading their people into oblivion? Wealth? Status? Protection and whichever women you want and a castle on a hill?"

Uritus frowned. "They have offered me nothing and I have asked for nothing."

This caused Erclidus to turn, incredulous. "You offer yourself freely as a tool to spread Agamemnon's propaganda? Perhaps you are not as smart as I thought."

Uritus ignored the insult. "I take it you do not believe in destiny?"

"On the contrary, I believe the hand of fate plays a great role in what becomes of us. I also believe, however, that we do have a say in what happens to us; that if a path is laid out that we do not wish to take, there is nothing that can force us to take it."

Erclidus began his slow walk back toward his brother and Uritus became suddenly aware of a dryness in his mouth, slick sweat which had begun to gather on his palms.

The older man continued, "In our youth, we were forced to sit and watch the cruel hand of fate wreak havoc on those we loved, helpless to do anything to prevent it. But as I grew older and came to understand my gifts, I learned that it does not have to be that way. I do not need to sit idly by and allow life to happen to me. Never again will my fate be a cruel and untethered thing, no, now she must bend to my will. As must all those who stand in my way."

Uritus's vision blurred. He blinked several times, waiting for it to clear again as his eyes made their change. But his sight remained fuzzy and no headache arose behind his eyes. He looked down at his hands, at the delicate pattern painted on the teacup still held in one of them, trying to focus on its details. "What have you done?"

"I can't let you go back to your camp, Uritus. You are too vital to the enemy cause. I am sad that it has come to this, but you leave me no choice. You simply refuse to listen to reason."

The Adalos felt his stomach lurch and the cup slipped out of his hands, shattering as it crashed to the stone floor. He reached behind himself desperately for the back of the sofa that rested there, but all at once, his knees buckled and he collapsed to the floor alongside the porcelain shards. "Erclidus…"

"Hush now," the man in black squatted down beside his brother. "You needn't worry, you will not be meeting your end just yet. You may still prove useful to me."

Uritus could not move, and though he fought to stay awake, his eyes drifted shut and he disappeared into the dark.

＊

It was still night when the party led by Mikka emerged from the Looming Mountains and they spied, at the base of the range, one of the four villages where Vegard's citizens were kept. There was a brief debate amongst them about whether it made the most sense to approach under the cover of night and look for signs of Ouro's presence or to get their rest and strategize in the morning. They ultimately determined that it was best to wait, to act only once they were at full strength, so they assembled a small camp where the light of their fire would be hidden by one of the towering peaks.

In the morning, they quickly set to work strategizing their approach. Qibat flew ahead to scope out the village from the sky and informed them when he returned that there were guards positioned atop each of the watchtowers at the village's four corners and more patrolling the ground.

Mikka grew frustrated when it became clear that there was no way to make their approach without the risk of being seen. The mission she had been excited to lead was requiring more patience than she had been prepared for. Ultimately, it was Alidistris who proposed a solution.

"This is the place I am from," she reminded them. "It will be difficult to sneak our entire party inside without being spotted, and if the village is as I remember it, there will be scant few places for us to hide once we've made it within the wall. But I… I know these people. I am sure that I can slip in quietly and go unnoticed, at least for long enough to gather information."

The others looked at one another, silently weighing this option.

"I *will* have to leave my armor behind…" Alidistris continued, looking to the place where it lay beside the remains of their fire. "Stain my clothes so that I may blend in easier."

"You do not think they will be suspicious why you travel there on your own?" Mikka knew this plan was the only one with any potential, but she was hesitant to send any individual to see to a task unarmed.

"There is a place in the wall where the boards are loose. I should be able to enter through there and avoid the gate. If they spot me ahead of time, I can tell them that I was taken from the Ashen Keep but I escaped my captors."

"What will you do when you are inside?" Punznes asked. "If you happen upon Ouro, you must not seek to assassinate him on your own. You could risk getting caught, and then your life would be in danger. We do not have the numbers necessary to rescue you."

"I understand. I am not someone who ordinarily would take such a risk, but I'm not sure what other choice we have. When I make it inside, I will seek out the people I know, see if anyone has heard anything about Ouro. I cannot speak for all who live in the village, but I know for a fact that there are many who wish to see Velup fall. Generations have lived and died with this hope in their hearts. They can help us, I'll stake my own life on it."

Punznes looked to Mikka and the soldier sighed. "All right. You may go. We'll send Qibat with you. Send him back to us if you are in danger or if you have news to convey. If you are not back by nightfall, we will assume something has happened to you and begin to orchestrate your rescue. But I cannot let you go without any means of self-defense. Take this with you." From her belt, Mikka retrieved a small single-edged knife.

Alidistris accepted the offering with a grateful nod and tucked it safely into her boot. From the pit that had housed their fire, she took up a piece of blackened wood and used its ash to dirty her clothing and her skin.

When she finished, she looked at the village and then returned her attention to the four who accompanied her, "Whatever happens next… thank you for what you are doing. Knowing that there exist people like you, selfless and brave and determined... it gives me hope for the rest of us." With that, she turned and made her descent to the village below, and Qibat flew ahead of her.

Mikka watched them leave. Anxious heart beating in her chest, she kept her eyes fixed on the slowly shrinking form until she disappeared around the Northern side of the village.

"She'll be all right, Mik," Laivar sought to comfort her. "Remember how she joined us in the first place. She may just be scrappier than you think."

"I do not doubt her cunning or her capability. But I will always feel hesitant to send a civilian to do a soldier's job."

"No greater of a spy do we have than one who spent her life in enemy territory," Oripidus remarked.

Mikka replied, "I'm sure you are right," and then settled down to the ground to await Alidistris's return.

***

The space between the wall's loose boards was tighter than the Western-born woman had remembered, and the jagged wood tore the fabric of her shirt as she forced her way through. She looked around for the patrolling guards, spotting a few—clubs and whips in hand—who meandered amongst the workers. Shortly, a small group transporting scrap metal passed by the place she hid, and she dashed around the side of the shack that had sheltered her to join their ranks. A few heads looked up curiously, but they did not acknowledge her besides this. She breathed a tiny sigh of relief for having made it in undetected.

She took stock of the village as she moved with the group and found that it was, for the most part, as she remembered it to be. The dilapidated shacks which served as housing for the workers lined the perimeter of the space, the town's center utilized entirely for the crafting of metal goods—weapons and armor and horseshoes and nails—with only a small area designated for the workers to rest in shifts while they ate. There was a small stable that housed a half dozen horses, kept only by the guards and used only to transport resources from one village to another. In the town's center, a tall, sturdy building, far better built and maintained than any of the others, where the guards were housed. If the Alchemist was here, that was where he would be.

The group she moved with came to a stop when they reached the smithy and she spotted a large pile of nails of various sizes being sorted by a cluster of women huddled beside a small fire. Alidistris recognized one of the women there as someone she had known and trusted in her girlhood. She quickly came to squat down across from her and began transferring nails into buckets. The woman, called Kala, lifted her head immediately and her face scrunched up into an expression of surprise. "Alidistris...?"

The spy gestured to her to keep quiet. Kala began to nod, and then her eyes darted up and dropped down again and Alidistris became aware of the guard who approached just behind her. She ducked her chin down, eyes fixed on the nails that passed through her hands. She felt the gaze of the guard burning the back of her neck. Periodic waves of heat rolled out from the smithy as bellows strengthened the fire burning in the forge. Alidistris suddenly wished that she still had her long hair to hide her face.

A moment before the spy had the chance to panic that she'd been identified as an intruder, one of the other women stood to her feet. She took hold of two of the buckets, each of which had been filled to their brim, and moved to transfer their contents to the larger receptacles where they would be stored for use. When she returned and set the buckets down again, Alidistris looked once more at the woman on the opposite side of the fire. Kala's gaze moved slowly, tracking the path of the guard as he departed, and then met Alidistris's eyes when he was finally out of earshot.

"What are you doing here?" she asked, her voice low. "Were you transferred back from the keep...?"

"I don't have time to explain everything," Alidistris replied. "We are looking for the Alchemist called Ouro. Do you know if he is here?"

"We?"

Alidistris opened her mouth to speak but quickly shut it when she was nudged by one of the women next to her. She lowered her head again, tracking the passing guard in the corner of her vision. She looked up once he had gone and the others continued to keep silent watch. "I have allied with the Easterners," Alidistris explained. "There is a small group of them traveling with me. Ouro has cursed their king, and we seek to take him out so the king might return to full health."

The spy could not immediately tell from Kala's face how she felt about this information. "Have you... brought the war to us?"

"No, no, you are safe. At least... to the degree that you already are. The Easterners have no quarrel with us, only with Velup, and once he is defeated, all will be welcome to peacefully integrate into their land. The king himself has promised me this. I have seen it, Kala, the Free World East of here. There is abundance and prosperity and joy. We can have a future there."

Kala's eyes, fearful, thoughtful, and then suddenly hopeful, brimmed with tears, and she nodded to her old friend the affirmation of her desire for such a future. "You will not find Ouro here," spoke one of the women without looking up. "Perhaps at one of the other villages. There are maps and correspondence in the main house, but you will have a hard time getting in there unseen."

"I'll find a way." Alidistris turned her head toward the town's central structure, observing her surroundings in an attempt to map out her path.

"Be careful," urged Kala. "There are not many of them, but they are watchful. Each one."

The spy nodded her thanks and stood to her feet, taking hold of a pair of nearly full buckets as she rose. She emptied them where she had seen the other woman do the same, set them on the ground, and took up a box filled with arrowheads. With a tiny breath to solidify her confidence, she proceeded to the main house. She spotted Qibat nearby, perched atop the wall where he kept watch. The workers moved about the village as usual, not acknowledging Alidistris as she passed. She was grateful for this. She was not a warrior like her allies, but if there was one skill she knew she had, it was the ability to blend in. She did not, however, make it even halfway to her intended destination before she was stopped.

"Where are you headed with those?"

Alidistris hesitated the briefest of seconds as she scrambled for a believable answer. It was still too much.

The guard grumbled and tightened his grip on the many-tailed whip held in his fist. "Where are you assigned?"

"Oh, well, I had been... um..." The spy realized mid-sentence that she didn't wish for her friend also to be punished, so she dropped it rather than proceeding to its end.

"Can't remember, eh?"

She offered him a tiny shake of her head.

"Predictable, you lot. Tell you what, I feel generous today. Ten lashes and I'll let you get back to work."

Her fingers gripped the edges of the box and her body stiffened. Two decades had passed since she had been subject to the brutal violence of her home village and she suddenly remembered why she had been so keen to move to the keep. She hesitated again, clinging to the box like a shield. She could not fight, she had drawn enough attention to herself as it was.

"Come on then," the guard barked. "Let's get this over with."

Alidistris swallowed and bit her tongue, fighting back against the tears that gathered in her eyes and threatened to spill over at any moment. She set the box gently on the ground.

"She was working with us."

Kala.

Alidistris turned with panicked eyes to her friend as she stood to her feet.

"She was just bringing those to the fletchers, they asked us to send some when they were finished."

The goblin grunted with annoyance and took several steps toward Kala. "I don't remember asking you. Get back to work!"

"Of course... Just... let her off for this one? She hasn't been sleeping well. We'll keep her in line..."

By this point, the confrontation had drawn the attention of those nearby. Their work slowed as they watched, eventually coming to a halt. Alidistris realized that she should have taken this moment to flee, to try to break into the main house or to return to the safety of her party at the top of the front.

The guard's irritation was apparent. He took another few steps toward the defiant one. "I don't take kindly to sniveling. Twenty lashes ought to do it. On your knees!"

Kala's mouth snapped shut in her fear but she didn't move otherwise.

"I said *on your knees*!" The guard stormed forward and raised his hand to strike.

"No!"

Alidistris reacted before she knew what she was doing. She leapt forward, retrieved Mikka's knife from her boot, brought the weapon up, and drew it in a quick slice across the goblin's neck. He dropped to his knees and crashed face-first into the dirt, sputtering, choking on thick blood until he died.

For a moment, the entire village froze and not a sound was uttered. But the stunned pause did not last long.

Other guards quickly caught wind that something had happened. Two of them looked to see the one who had fallen to the ground and hurried to the scene of the event.

Alidistris began to panic. She had endangered herself and the others nearby and possibly, the entire mission.

Suddenly, just as the approaching goblins drew near, a brave young blacksmith took up a half-finished sword and, with an impassioned cry, plunged it through the heart of the nearest one.

This act of courage, obviously inspired by Alidistris's own, stirred up the rest of the workers to seize whatever weapons they could find and attack the remaining guards. The spy had hardly a second to think before a full-fledged clash broke out.

The sounds of battle rose up from the small village and Mikka leapt to her feet when they reached her ears. "Fuck, something's wrong. Come on!"

"To do what?" Punznes called after her as she raced down the front.

"Anything other than sit here!"

The other three took up their weapons and followed her to join the action. Qibat took flight back to the camp immediately as the violence began and doubled back around when he spotted the others already on their way. He led them to the place in the wall where Alidistris had entered and Oripidus split the loose boards with his hammer to make space for them to squeeze in. But by the time they made it inside, the conflict had reached its end, and the villagers stood amongst the corpses of their captors in a collective state of shock.

Alidistris raced to embrace her friends when she spotted them.

"What in Shadow happened?"

The spy turned to regard the wreckage, the bloodied weapons in the hands of her peers. "I think the village just freed itself."

***

At the front of a long caravan of traveling soldiers, Adiadni rode in pensive silence. They were making good time, spurred on by urgency, but she could think of nothing but fear that the man she loved had taken an unnecessary risk by seeking a negotiation with the enemy. Leading the caravan alongside her were Nadarum and Ilya who had not ceased their friendly conversation with the members of the cavalry since they'd set out again after their brief midday rest. Digtrision made up the caravan's tail, keeping watch alongside his officers to ensure that they were not being pursued.

Eventually, Ilya came to notice the Suvah's silence and gently inquired about it, "I will not press if quiet contemplation is more helpful to you at the moment, but would I be right to assume that the source of your worries is... back in the Mirrored Cities?"

"You would." Adi did not elaborate, fearing that she'd drown in the inevitable river of tears if she spoke on it further.

The archer and her husband met each other's eyes. "May I tell you, Adi, about the days that led to my falling for Plum?" asked the horseman.

A smile grew across Adi's face. "The love shared by the two of you is a radiant beacon. I would be glad to hold as much of its legacy as you would entrust me with."

"You honor us," Nadarum chuckled. "Now, you already know that we grew up near each other. The steady comfort of our friendship provided the stable base upon which we've been able to build our committed partnership. But were it not for the... shaking of that base, were it not for the days when our friendship first became challenged, I may never have realized the truth of what I wanted. Ilya's family was... well, do you want to tell this part, Plum?"

"There's not much to tell. They didn't like that I wanted to travel, and they especially didn't like that I had no interest in marrying a man from the Fifth. There was nothing wrong with him, really. He was just entirely too dull for my tastes *and* I was young, only nineteen. I didn't know what I wanted for my life yet and I was eager to explore in my state of not-knowing."

"Her curiosity and open-mindedness were two of the things I admired most about her," Nadarum went on. "But when she told me that she planned to leave —particularly when she told me that she *was* leaving with no plan at all—I grew fearful. I recognize now that my true fear was of being parted from her, but in the foolishness of my youth, I responded to feelings I did not understand by trying to convince her that she was making a mistake."

"I was rather blindsided by this," Ilya shared. "Here was this man whom I'd come to know as my greatest supporter suddenly trying to sway me from my heart's true desires. I had told him of such dreams before and he had always encouraged me to keep dreaming. But now that I had grown past merely dreaming and sought to take action, he was behaving just as my parents were— as a boulder in my path. Eventually, the conflict with my parents came to a head and their patience reached its limit. They told me that I had to make a choice. I could release my stubborn hold on this *fantasy* of a far-off somewhere, or I could leave. So I left. And though I was still infuriated with him, I could think of no one else to go to than Nadarum."

The horseman sighed as he visualized the memory. "She showed up at my door, soaked from the rain, bow and quiver on her back, an overstuffed bag held in one hand. And when she told me what had happened, I immediately came to understand how wrong I had been. She was a courageous spirit, the brightest star I had ever seen. How dare I try to smother that spark? If I loved her as I knew I did, it was my duty to nurture it, not to snuff it out. I begged for her forgiveness and told her I would follow her anywhere she went, never again to try to keep her tethered."

"I forgave him, of course," said the archer with a smile. "I made it clear that while I cared for him and was glad to have him along, I still did not wish to commit to any future, at least not for a while. Our courtship would need to proceed with the same open-endedness as our adventure. But when he agreed to that, I was sure of the future I wanted. This man whom I already loved and trusted was willing to change his mind, to compromise, and to admit when he was wrong. What more could I possibly want in a partner? I held out for two months before I agreed to marry him."

"The relationship-ending conflict with my family would take place a few days after her own. We took a pair of horses and left after that," Nadarum drew the story to its close. "I was quite terrified to leave what I had known, even with the knowledge that it was no longer for me. But falling into step beside this woman, watching how she always kept her eyes fixed straight ahead has strengthened my heart ever since. She may still be a bit blind to danger at times, but I'm happy to keep an eye out for the both of us."

"The Mother only knows how many times I'd've met my end if not for this one," Ilya added. "We strike the perfect balance, he and I."

"I wish I could say that there was a point to telling this story, Adi, save for offering you a pleasant distraction from that which weighs heavy on your mind."

"It did succeed at that, thank you."

They rode in silence while Adi attempted to seek out the root of her concern. "You know those stories," she eventually began, "...of people who are granted a wish, or who have their futures foreseen? But then you get to the end, and you find out that the wish was... *twisted* somehow... as a cruel turn of fate?"

The couple beside the princess looked at her with compassion in their eyes.

"It is not that I think that Uritus is incapable or rash. He considers things very intently. He is both patient and wise. What I fear is that..." Adi paused for a moment with a bite of her lip and a breath. "The prophecy says that the Adalos will banish the Shadow, but... it does not say how. I want to believe that it will protect him as it did me, that he will be safe. But I cannot help but fear that, perhaps by some cruel twist of destiny, his *death* is the thing that inspires the Free People to their victory. That his legacy, not his leadership, is the thing which will lead us on."

Ilya reached a hand to take the princess's as tears streamed down their faces.

"I feel horrible for voicing this..." Adiadni admitted. "Like I don't believe in him the way he deserves..."

"Uritus never would have been bold enough to step fully into his identity if not for your belief in him."

The princess nodded her acknowledgment of Nadarum's reminder.

The horseman continued, "You are young and you have undergone a devastating amount of trauma in a very short period. It is completely rational for you to be afraid, especially concerning the ones you love. Every one of us is afraid right now, even Plum."

The archer nodded vigorously. "It's true. I'm terrified."

"There is nothing wrong with being afraid, and fear can even do us a service by reminding us to be mindful. But once we have felt it and acknowledged it, we must be diligent to turn our focus away from it. It will consume us if we do not."

"None of us can know how things will end, save for the luckiest of Prophets," said Ilya with a shrug. "It gets easier when you remember that. We all believe in and hope for the very best for our boy. That's all we can do, really."

Adiadni smiled and squeezed the hand that clutched hers. "Thank you. Both of you. Your love inspires me. I hope I can be as good to him as the two of you are to each other."

"You are," Nadarum assured her. "There's no doubt about that."

***

Uritus's head ached when he finally woke, still blurry-eyed. His fingertips identified the cold stone upon which he lay and he pushed himself up to a seat. Looking around, he found himself to be in a cell.

"Good afternoon."

The fisherman's head jerked to the side. His vision slowly began to regain clarity, but still, his brother was difficult to see, all-black uniform allowing him to become one with the shadows that made a home in most of the space beneath the city.

"You should have had the tea."

Uritus stood to his feet. "What do you want from me?"

Erclidus chuckled, stepping a few paces forward from the wall he'd been leaning against. "I want you to stay out of my way."

Uritus clenched his fists.

"You were an annoyance as a boy and an inconvenience when you showed up in Vegard with Adiadni. I have taken the liberty of preventing you from becoming something worse."

Uritus frowned, his mind becoming clear as his sight did. "You forgot about the second half of the prophecy."

It wasn't a question. Had Erclidus recalled the whole of the legend, he would have expected to meet the Adalos when he did.

"A crucial mistake on my part. One that has caused me a sizable amount of frustration. But now that you are dealt with, I may move on. I have an appointment at the capital."

"So that's it? You're just going to keep me here until… what?"

"Perhaps if I ever need it, I might seek to get information out of you. But unless that day ever comes, you will remain in here, yes, at least till the end of the war. By then, perhaps you will have learned to understand the value of partnering with me rather than serving as a thorn in my side."

Uritus sighed, the confirmation that his brother did not wish to kill him offering no alleviation from the sorrow he felt on his behalf.

"For now, I must bid you farewell. I've much to see to. I doubt I'll get the chance to pay you another visit before I make my glorious journey onward, but don't fret. You'll be well taken care of." Erclidus turned on his heel and proceeded toward the stair to Uritus's right. "You're the blood of this land's new leader, after all. Nothing but princely treatment for the prince."

The younger man stepped forward, touching hands to steel bars. "Was I only ever an annoyance to you?"

Erclidus stopped walking, hesitating with his back to his brother. Finally, he turned halfway over one shoulder, "You were a companion. A comforting presence during my darker days. I am grateful to you for that." He proceeded onward and Uritus listened to the sounds of his spurs as he departed.

The fisherman sighed, tired, frustrated, his head still aching dully. His desire to remain open-minded about Erclidus had proven to be a grave mistake, and he was annoyed with himself for not heeding Adiadni's warnings.

He looked around at the space that housed him. The fair stone looked markedly different down here in the dark. There were dim torches lining the wall opposite the cells but no light other than this save for that which peeked through the small window only some of the cells were outfitted with—small, barred, and far out of reach. There was a rectangular stone platform in the cell's back corner, a crude straw mat lying atop it, intended to serve as a bed. Save for this, the cell was bare, and after spending a few moments tugging on the bars, Uritus resigned to a seat on the mat. It was cold down here, even with his heavy armor and cape.

Abandoned were any thoughts of trying to work out an escape plan. If he made it out of here, he'd have to find a way out of the city unarmed, a feat which at present felt entirely impossible. In his mind grew a cloud that he had felt only once in his life and had all but forgotten since.

Hopelessness.

He rested his head against the wall and reached a hand to pull the white stone out from behind his breastplate and clutched it.

Miles away, Adiadni felt the cold spot form on her chest, and her hand flew up to grab onto her talisman with a gasp. Uritus was alive, at least for now. That was enough.

When the ornament grew cool in the hand of the Adalos, the stone against his back did the same, and he was suddenly reminded of what surrounded him on all sides. Fragments of his home in the mountains. He breathed out a weighty sigh and the cloud dissipated.

"Wait," spoke the Voice, still and quiet and undeniable as ever.

Uritus took another breath and did.

Chapter Twenty-Nine

"Your Neighbor is Your Liberator"

"They're all dead?"

"Every last one." The blacksmith from the Vegardian village looked over his shoulder at the central building. "Unless any hide in there… But we could easily overpower them too."

A large crowd of townspeople had come to gather around Alidistris and her friends, their curiosity piqued at the sight of the armored Easterners. Mikka, having been filled in on the events that had led to the fight, was trying to determine what to do about this unexpected development. "How many are you?"

"Eight-hundred and fifty-three!" replied one of them proudly.

"Fifty-two."

"Eight-hundred and… fifty-two."

Collectively, the group lowered their heads, touching right hands to their chests. The foreigners mimicked this show of respect for the fallen.

"Why have you come?"

Mikka lifted her head to regard the questioning laborer.

"Alidistris says that you fight for the other side."

The commander moved her eyes across the gathered faces, observing that they appeared neither threatened nor relieved. "We fight for all who have been endangered by Velup the Sorcerer's cruel hand," she spoke loudly. "His army has invaded the Free World. We stand to face him. Our intent, once this has all concluded, has been to free all he has kept captive, but… it seems you do not need our help to do that."

It brought a smile to Alidistris's face and tears to her eyes to consider the sky which now opened above her birthplace.

"Even so, we will help you in whatever ways we are able. Our primary purpose on this particular mission is the location and assassination of Ouro the Alchemist. But if we might provide you aid or protection, know that we will do all we can."

Punznes had already begun to see to those who had sustained injuries during the clash, delegating tasks to nearby workers to ensure that everyone was taken care of.

"Alidistris trusts you, and for this, so do we," Kala declared, and the others murmured their affirmation of this. "She says that there is a place for us… in your land?"

Mikka nodded assuredly at the array of hopeful faces. "There is. I will not lie to you, the Free World's Western Provinces are presently wrought in Shadow, and it may be some time before the light returns."

"Anything at all would be better than this."

The commander nodded again, chewing on her cheek. "I do not wish to subject any of you to violence, but in a time like this, we must be prepared for when it may come to face us. Who amongst you can fight? Or rather... who amongst you is willing?"

A wave of hands lifted, gently at first and then growing in confidence. More than half.

Mikka turned to Laivar and Oripidus, "Try to find a map. All information you can gather about the other villages and any clues as to Ouro's location."

The elf and dwarf hurried to see to this task.

"If it sounds all right with you," the soldier returned her attention to the crowd. "We'll have some of you join us on our search. We're far more powerful in numbers. The rest of you will be safe here, at least for now. Once Ouro is dealt with, we will organize your safe passage to our Westmost base. For now, begin arming yourselves. We've a long road ahead, but with your allyship, I reckon it just got a lot easier."

***

Uritus continued waiting on the cold stone platform long after the sun departed. A meal had been brought for him, roast chicken with potatoes and peas served alongside a pot of hot, fragrant tea. He ate and—after a bit of deliberation —drank. They had him trapped here already, there would be no purpose to sedate him again. A goblin came to collect the tray, not even looking up at the prisoner as he did. The half-alive wanted for nothing save for the minute amount of fuel required to keep them alive. They were an efficient tool in this way, desireless, expendable. They craved only violence, paid little mind to pain, wept not when watching their kin fall. Sorcery's ultimate creation—purposeless except to destroy.

The entroleps had seemed different, though at this point Uritus was all but certain that he would never know if they truly were. Yider had seemed different. He, unlike the goblins, felt fear. He had bargained for his life and been smart enough to know how to do it effectively. His had been a lonely existence despite how he was supposedly one of many of his kind. Uritus wondered if any part of Adiadni had mourned him when he died.

In due time, he came to realize that he resented his brother for this just as much as the rest—for the needless cruelty of fabricating scores of beings for no purpose other than to await their inevitable deaths. Perhaps the goblins could not feel, and perhaps they were better for it. But Yider had not been an object of war, merely a sadistic exercise in power. If any shard of the old Erclidus still existed, he was both bound and gagged.

Sounds of busy enemy soldiers—heavy footsteps and clanking metal— traveled down from the small window. The fisherman felt he had not been very successful at delaying the departure of Vegard's army. While he sincerely hoped that the second company had set out from Lorethh already, in his heart, he knew they would not leave without him. If his coming here delayed them too much, they very well ran the risk of losing the capital. One misguided decision and the fate of the entire land was at risk. Uritus attempted to shake this sense of guilt away. With nothing to do here but sit quietly with his thoughts, it began to happen more frequently that the most stifling ones fought to be acknowledged.

Eventually, he came to notice a faint sound—sometimes a scraping and sometimes a tapping—coming from somewhere in the cell block. Rats, probably, the prisoner had not observed any others being held down here. Save for the wall of bars on one end of the cell where the door was, everything else was made of stone, so it was difficult for him to see much of anything beyond the length of the walkway when he pressed his face between cool lengths of iron. He had been surprised by the realization that no guards were stationed down here to keep an eye on him. With the exception of the one who had brought him his dinner, he had seen none of the armored goblins since he first arrived in Judii that morning. There was a stair at the end of the walkway which curved to the right as it ascended, the only way in or out. He kept his ears open for any other signs that he was not alone.

The scrape-tapping persisted, never growing louder, never seeming to move. Uritus frowned and closed his eyes in an attempt to ascertain its origin. Eventually, he gave up, and it faded to the background along with the noise from outside. He sighed frustratedly and set his head back against the smooth stone. As patient and thoughtful and intentional of a person he was, it pained him now to wait. In moments of crisis, the fisherman instinctively leapt to action; he was not one who merely sat and let life happen to him, regardless of Erclidus's recollection of their youth. When the plague came, they hardly slept, prioritizing the care of the younger ones over everything else. When his family was gone, Uritus sought out a new home for himself. When the king called for traveling companions for his daughter, when Nadarum and Ilya were captured, when an army of Shadow laid siege on his homeland, the Adalos rose to his feet and did what needed to be done. And none of it had been nearly as difficult as the moments when he was expected to sit still and do nothing.

He contemplated why such stillness bothered him so much. He did not consider himself to be someone who had a hard time relinquishing control, nor did he lack trust in the capability of those who worked while he was waiting. Rather, he came to realize, it was the anxious whirring of his mind that would not allow him to stand aside when there were things that needed to be done. *Was this a bad thing?* The Hero *should* be a man of action, one motivated and driven and willing to devote all of himself to the cause. But it was not merely his labor, his devotion which would deliver them from the Shadow—it was all of them. Each selfless soul who willingly made sacrifices for the greater good, it was the sum of all of their efforts that would save them in the end. He needed only point the way.

Suddenly, a loud crack.

The fisherman leapt to his feet.

The scraping grew to the undeniable grinding of stone and Uritus watched as a portion of the wall across from his cell was pushed open, releasing his breath only upon seeing the face that appeared from the other side. He stammered in his disbelief, "What the… how are you—"

"Blessed Source, I'm glad you're in here. Would have been a royal pain in my ass to try to find the other holding area." Perplexus stepped into the dim torchlight of the walkway. "You don't look too bad at all. I was worried I might have to carry you out of here."

Uritus shook his head, open-mouthed, still not comprehending. "Explain."

"Gladly," the navigator stepped to the door of the cell and produced from his pocket a set of lock-picking tools. "There is a council presently discussing what to do about the fact that you haven't yet returned, dancing around saying that they fear you might be dead. Adi made me promise that I'd get you back if something went wrong, so I spent my day perusing Lorethh's archives. I found blueprints of the city, maps of the tunnel systems, and identified several we hadn't found, abandoned by the cities long ago for the larger and better-constructed ones."

Uritus looked to the dark space beyond the sliding stone door. "Are they safe to use?"

"Probably not." Perplexus continued fidgeting with the lock.

"And I take it no one else knows you're here?"

The rescuer breathed out a laugh. "Wasn't worth the time arguing with them about letting me go. Better I took the situation into my own hands and…" The lock made a satisfying click and the door was pulled open. "We'll be back before their discussion has reached its end."

"You are senselessly bold and I have never been more grateful for that." Uritus emerged from the cell and embraced him.

"For you."

Into the fisherman's hands were placed his belt and knife. He strapped them to his waist, nodding approvingly at the navigator's decision to leave the Sword of Fire behind. "Did you ever consider that I might be dead?"

Perplexus shook his head. "Not once. You said you didn't believe he wanted to kill you. I trust you know him far better than the rest of us. Now, come on, we've got to…"

Uritus felt his stomach drop the instant his friend fell quiet. He spun around to regard what had captured Lex's attention.

Standing there, at the base of the steps, was a wide-eyed attendant—a human man, frozen in shock. They stared silently at one another for what felt like a short lifetime. Under one arm, the man carried a thin wool blanket, in his hands, a tray with another pot of tea. Uritus saw the flickering in his eyes change to surprise, then fear, then urgency.

"Wait…"

The man dropped the tray and raced for the stairs.

The fisherman cursed and sprang to action. He overtook the attendant, took hold of his arm, and yanked him back to the ground.

"Please," he spun him around, taking his shoulders in his hands. "Just wait…"

A fearful flame lit in the man's eyes again and he hesitated for only a second before he opened his mouth to scream.

Uritus's heart leapt into his throat. This could be the end, they stood no chance to fight their way out of Judii.

Before he knew it, his dagger was in his hand, its blade buried deep in the man's gut.

The man did not scream, made no sound but a sharp exhale and then a gargling as he choked on his blood. Uritus pulled his knife from the attendant's belly and lowered him gently to the ground. Dark blood pooled in the place the man's hands clutched, and when finally he stopped choking and succumbed to the wound, his fearful eyes remained fixed on the one who had killed him. Uritus pushed his eyelids closed with shaky hands, muttering a devastated prayer.

"We need to go."

Footsteps from atop the stair. No doubt someone had heard the tray crash to the floor.

Perplexus took up the knife, grabbed hold of his friend's arm, and yanked him to his feet. They hastened for the tunnel and pulled its door shut behind them. From his bag, Perplexus produced a jar full of a dark, thick paste which he scooped out with his hands and began applying liberally to seal the cracks.

All the while, Uritus's head continued spinning. He felt feverish and sick to his stomach, shaking as though he had caught a chill, sweat gathering on his hands and brow and collar. He breathed heavily, pacing back and forth until Perplexus finished his task, took up a torch, and urged him to follow.

The tunnel was small and dark, lit by a single torch every several yards. Perplexus explained that he was glad to have found them already down here. Uritus didn't hear him.

In some places, the beams supporting the roof were positioned low enough that they were forced to duck beneath them. The ground was rocky and uneven, and Uritus tripped several times as they hurried on. Eventually, they came to a fork where their tunnel met a larger one, stretching wide arms out in both directions. The navigator led them to the left.

The fisherman followed, making it only a few more steps before his foot caught and he stumbled to the ground. The rocky dirt scraped his palms as he caught himself, and all at once, any shred that was left of his composure was gone.

"I can't keep doing this, Lex."

The navigator turned and brought himself down to a knee beside his friend. "It's not much further, I promise. I can help you. I'll carry you if I have to…"

"Not the walk," Uritus pushed himself up to a seat against one of the tunnel walls.

"What then?"

The Adalos shook his head exhaustedly. "I can't do any of this."

Perplexus waited patiently for him to continue, knowing already by the look in his eyes what he meant.

"He had a future," spoke Uritus through tears. "Dreams. A whole identity beyond just being a Vegardian. I had no right to take that away."

"You know as well as I do that in that moment, it was his life or ours."

"You cannot say that for sure…"

"You stopped him from running up the steps to alert the guards."

"He could have been running for his life. I thought he was going to scream… What if he meant only to plead with me for mercy? I did not allow him that chance."

"You can't know any of that," Lex sought a way to proceed gently. "The scale of things now… it is far greater than one life. It affects all of us—"

"Fuck, do you not grow tired of bargaining?"

The navigator fell silent.

"This life or that one, fight or die, spill blood without question or watch helplessly as it spills anyway, who the fuck am I to decide? I was asked before this all began if I would be willing, should the time arise, to abandon all else for the sake of Adiadni's safety. I pictured her and I pictured you, each in danger, tried to be honest with myself about which of you I would save if I could only save one, and I didn't know how I could possibly choose. I've thought about it every day since and I still don't.

"We say we're doing this for the Free World, for the future… Whose future? Scores of lives already cut short, they had a future too. I don't know how I'm ever supposed to be at peace with this, to feel anything but sick about it. When this is all over, I'll be praised for my victories, honored and memorialized in myth and legend, and absolved of all sins I must commit as I make my way. That isn't fair. It isn't right. I'll be remembered for my courage while the truly brave ones, the individuals with nothing to gain in exchange for their offerings, they'll be forgotten, written about only in numbers and never names. I'm tired of sacrifices and rationalization. I'm so damn tired, Lex."

The dark-haired man sighed sadly and brought himself to a seat beside his friend. "I am too." They stayed there in silence for a time, Uritus trying and failing to regulate his breath and body, Perplexus racking his brain for how he might be of any help at all. "I don't like the way I've learned to shove aside my feelings for the sake of the *greater good*," he finally admitted. "I used to bait short-tempered men into fighting me. Never with the intention of fighting back, just to see how much I could stoke the flames before they raged. Looking back now, I'm not sure how I managed to be so casual about such a thing. If I never have to be a part of a violent altercation again, it'll be too soon."

Uritus felt sorry for having snapped at him and set a loving hand on his knee.

"Despite all of that," Perplexus continued, "...despite the exhaustion and the frustration and the overall gut-wrenching nature of the whole thing... I know that my work here is still not done. I have a responsibility to this land and her people—all of her people—one which is far bigger than me. I don't understand it and I don't like it, but I know what will happen if I give up. And at the end of all things, it is simply not who I am to cower from my duty. It's not who you are either.

"I know that this has been a difficult road to walk. For everyone, but for you especially. I cannot fathom the weight that is on your shoulders and I know that there is little I can do to alleviate it. I'm sorry for that. But there is something that you need to understand: the Free People are not helpless innocents incapable of speaking for themselves. They have chosen to be here for the same reasons that we have, for the same love and protectiveness and sense of responsibility. They know the risks, they know what they could lose. And they know just as much what they will gain, what we *all* will gain once all this has been said and done. Damn the personal risk. I know that this may sound harsh, and perhaps it should, but Uritus, this isn't about you.

"Each of us is willing to do our part, from the warriors to the Keepers to the medics to the laborers. Each one willing to stand, willing to act, willing to sacrifice. For the future, yes, one where there will again be born generations who will live and die and never have to know the horrors of war. You cannot abandon them now. You cannot leave your post. You must do what we all must —you must stay your course."

Uritus let out a long breath, allowing the words to wash over him and take root in his heart and his mind. Then he stood to his feet, helped Perplexus to his own, and proceeded down the tunnel.

***

"You're doing well, but you need to mind your feet."

Alidistris, sword in hand, listened attentively to Mikka's advice.

"Don't plant yourself and attempt to hold your ground, be ready to move at all times. Light and quick."

The student of swordsmanship nodded and looked down at her boots.

Mikka chuckled, tucked the flat of her blade beneath the Westerner's chin, and lifted her face. "Ideally, you'll want to know how to move around while also keeping your eyes at attention. There are exercises you can practice to stretch and strengthen your ankles. It'll make a world of difference, you'll be able to move with far more confidence on uneven terrain."

Alidistris blushed, feeling mildly embarrassed for her lack of inherent skill.

"You *are* doing well though," the soldier assured her, sheathing her sword. "Especially for your first day. You'll be a proper warrior in no time."

The former attendant also stowed her blade and followed Mikka to rejoin their friends beside their fire. Some of the people in the village had raided the food stashes and set to work preparing a feast to celebrate their liberation. Others fitted one another with armor and chose weapons, sparring to get a feel for what they would face the next day. A hundred and fifty brave volunteers would be proceeding South with the Easterners to liberate the second village and continue their search for the elusive Alchemist. Oripidus and Laivar had found an abundance of information in the main house, but none which conclusively confirmed where Ouro might be found.

They had learned that the villages were numbered rather than named—*enk, onnuk, dersh,* and *nott,* the gish words for numbers one through four—and that they were arranged as Alidistris had thought, in a straight row along the Western front of the Looming Mountains. There was no evidence to suggest that Ouro had recently made his way to the keep, so they would continue on their journey, entrusting Enk's safekeeping to the villagers who, for the time being, would remain behind.

Oripidus lounged with his head back, puffing on a pipe that one of the villagers had offered to him.

"Thought you gave that up years ago, Rip."

He shrugged at Mikka's comment. "Of all the things that presently seek to do my body harm, I'd wager that smoke is the least of my worries."

Mikka chuckled as she and Alidistris found their seats.

"Ye know, I find it mighty curious the way Velup proclaims the glory of the Shadow and yet cannot even be bothered to conjure it any further West than the peaks."

Laivar's eyes jerked to the sky, his mouth falling slightly open as he regarded it. "By my pen… You can almost see the stars."

Though the clouds above Vegard remained stale and gray, through them, the heavens demanded to be recognized.

"Velup may seem blinded by his hunger to conquer, but he is no fool. He knows the merits of the sun," said Punznes.

"So it's a tool of war then," Laivar concluded. "Designed to strike fear into the hearts of those it covers."

"Quite," said Punznes. "But it's more practical than that even still. You said it yourself, it's a weapon of war. No light…"

"No food…" Mikka felt her stomach grow cold as she considered those in the Western Provinces who were already blanketed by the dark.

Laivar shuddered and then, determined to shift the gaze of their focus, turned his attention to Alidistris, "How does it feel to be back?"

She looked around. "Markedly different from when I left. There's something in the air… something that wasn't here when I was before."

"That, Dear, would be hope, and it is sweet in the lungs." Oripidus's remark caused the rest to lean their heads back and breathe deeply.

"It is," Alidistris affirmed. "There burns here a determined fire, unlike anything I'd ever seen before meeting the lot of you. As if the people have laid in waiting for long enough and are ready now to act."

"It would be fair to say that you were the Catalyst that lit the spark," Mikka observed.

"Oh, I'm sure that isn't true…"

"'Twas ye who spilled first blood," argued Oripidus.

"Acknowledging the important feats you have accomplished takes nothing away from the valuable contributions of others," Laivar reminded her. "The spirit of revolution has been quietly moving here for some time, but it *was* your boldness that inspired the rest. It's all right to be proud of yourself for that."

Alidistris nodded graciously. Just within Enk's Southern gate, a wooden cart had been loaded with the bodies of the dead goblins. They would be taken out and buried in a shallow ditch outside the village rather than burned, as they feared that too much smoke might draw the attention of Onnuk or the Ashen Keep. Within the town's center, a singular smoldering pyre burned its last—the sendoff of the laborer who had given her life to the cause.

"Is it ordinary for there to be so few guards stationed here?" asked the physician.

Alidistris frowned as she tried to remember. "There were never very many, but I do believe there used to be more. Presumably, the rest were called to the front. Trugstar, the village commander, is gone too. Seems strange that Velup would send them away…"

"He underestimates the will of the collective," replied Punznes. "It'll lead to his downfall in the end."

"I'll drink to that," declared Oripidus, taking a swig from a flask and passing it around the fire.

The party was encouraged by the events of the day but still deeply tired, so their energy was quiet and subdued in contrast with the celebration around them. Mikka felt further rooted in her resolve after witnessing the passionate action of the Vegardians. There was no way to be sure that they would be granted similar ease as they continued, but the soldier felt that it didn't matter. They had already accomplished far more than they had expected to, thanks to the boldness of the newcomer who didn't even consider herself a warrior.

Mikka gazed proudly at the dark-haired woman across the fire. Alidistris had grown at an impressive rate since she'd joined them, her courage and conviction flowering with every passing day. Her instincts and willingness to follow her heart had saved countless lives thus far, including the party's own. It hurt the soldier's heart to see the melancholy that pooled in her dark eyes.

"I'm not really sure that I know who I am," Alidistris answered before Mikka could ask.

Punznes offered a walnut to the raven who sat beside him. "What do you mean by that?"

"I mean…" the Western-born woman lifted her eyes to the darkening sky with a sigh. "I grew up here, but… this place never felt like home. I didn't know who my parents were… None of us do. There were workers assigned to the caretaking of the younger ones, but we didn't live as families. To be honest… the concept of a *family* was wholly foreign to me until, well, until I met you."

"Sweet Divine that's… fucked." Mikka voiced the shock on everyone's mind.

Alidistris shrugged. "I didn't know any better. I didn't know I was missing anything."

"Do you think you might be able to find them now that the village is free?"

"I might. When we finally get the chance to breathe again, I do intend to try. They keep… *kept* us here this way no doubt because it makes us easier to control. We have little opportunity to form bonds when we're worked from sunup to sundown. The keep was quieter at least, but I felt far lonelier there than I ever did here. But when you showed up…" A smile crinkled her eyes. "You spoke to me like I was an equal. I knew then that the tales of how you were a brutal people who wished to dominate couldn't be true. I felt safe in your presence. That's why I went with you. Because I knew you were good."

Mikka rose to her feet, moved around the fire, descended to her knees, and took Alidistris's hands into her own. "You deserved better than the way you were treated here," she said. "I sincerely hope that we can make up for the love you were robbed of. You may not feel that you know who you are, and perhaps it'll take you some time to figure it out, but I do. You are a force of nature. You are a rebel and a soldier and a spy. You are a revolutionary with a lion's heart and an unbreakable spirit. You are a Free Person," she gestured with one hand to the people who moved around them, "…they are Free People now, because of *you*. The rest will come in time." Mikka leaned forward to plant a warm kiss atop her new friend's head and brought herself down to a seat at her side.

Laivar took up his lute and began to play. "How might we help you better get to know yourself, Alidistris?"

She considered this. "I wish to find a way to symbolize my departure from my past," she finally replied. "Standing up to Erclidus, cutting my hair, devoting myself to a cause I believe in, these were all steps in the right direction. Perhaps it is being again in the place of my birth, but I feel this is as good a time as any to shake the dust from my feet and be done with it."

The group fell to silence as they pondered this and the flask was passed around once more. The rebel's dark eyes drifted across the village and came to a stop when they landed on the blackened pyre which had all but burned out. "I didn't know her name."

The others turned their heads to follow her gaze.

"I didn't recognize her. She was older than me so could have known me as a girl. I don't like the feeling that her death is because of me…"

"You can't do that," Mikka said gently, and Alidistris dropped her head to rest on her shoulder. "You are responsible for your actions alone. Her death is a tragedy and it is not your fault."

Alidistris nodded slowly, chewing on her cheek for a prolonged moment. "Because we don't have families… we don't have surnames. I have only ever been called Alidistris. Perhaps that's the thing I need to leave behind."

"There's a deep significance to one's name," spoke Oripidus. "I think that's a fine idea."

"What would you choose to call yourself?" asked Punznes with a smile.

"I don't know." She sat up and folded her hands in her lap, thinking seriously. "There are so many beautiful names, even ones that I've just learned in these past weeks. I don't know how I could choose."

"Perhaps we can help," Laivar offered. "It is usually family who give one their name."

"What would you call me?"

The bard strummed as he thought. "If choosing a name out of thousands seems too daunting, the next thing to try is a variation of one's name. Lob a part of it off, like you did your hair."

"What would ye say to being called *Ali*?" suggested Oripidus.

A smile lit in the rebel's eyes. "I like that. It's quite lovely. And I like the symbolism behind keeping a piece of the old name. I am who I am in part because of my past. I do worry, though, that it's a bit too much like *Adi*."

"What about *Tris*?"

Dark eyes met Mikka's blue ones, narrowing further as her smile grew. "Tris… I quite love that."

"Welcome to the family, Tris." Punznes lifted his water skin in their newest party member's direction and the others mimicked this, toasting to her honor.

Tris giggled and sighed contentedly. "Thank you all, for everything. I am glad to have you with me." With that, she stood and departed to offer her time to the villagers. Mikka's eyes lingered on her as she shrank away into the crowd.

Laivar cleared his throat, loudly, intentionally, and Mikka's gaze snapped back to meet his, "What?"

The bard did not reply, rather shrugging casually while continuing to play his instrument, a sly smile grazing his mouth.

"Oh, shut up."

"I don't remember saying anything. Punzie, did you hear me say anything?"

"Not a word."

"What about you, Rip?"

"Can't say that I did."

Mikka rolled her eyes. "You know what I mean."

"It's been a while, Mik," Laivar shrugged again. "You cannot deny that she is quite lovely."

"Quite lovely."

Punznes chuckled and offered Qibat another treat.

"And why would I ever deny that?"

"All I mean to say is that no one would blame you if you fancied her."

Mikka shook her head at Laivar, leaned back on her hands, and sighed. "The four of you are a monumental pain in my side, do you know that?"

"Tell ye what, Mik, we'll leave it be if ye answer us one simple question."

Mikka narrowed her eyes at the dwarf, "Go on then."

"Why do ye look at her like that?"

The three men laughed uproariously and their commander shook her head as she chuckled at them. She sat up when they finally quieted, "Listen, I do not deny that I feel bonded to her in a way not unlike how I feel bonded to each of you. I also do not deny that I find her to be attractive. She is beautiful and resourceful and driven. But I need you all to hear this next part clearly: when I say that I have no wish to pursue or even recognize a romantic connection at least until this war is done, I mean it."

The others nodded as they listened.

"I am constantly afraid of finding out whom I will lose next," she admitted, her throat catching. "The weight of that is too much to balance already without giving more love away. When Seryc died, it was reaffirmed for me. I will not explore something like that until this is through. I cannot."

Laivar set his lute down and moved to wrap an arm around his friend. "We hear you. Romance will woo you again one day, my dear, but she is a patient lover. She will be happy to wait until you are ready."

Mikka knew this to be true.

***

A wave of sound rose into the air—the sound of cheering, Adiadni came to realize—and when she lifted her eyes to the sky above the camped convoy, she quickly understood why. Tears glistened in her eyes as she spotted the silver belly of the soaring dragon. The Hero had returned. Milion came to land several yards South of the camp and the princess began running to meet him before Uritus had the chance to dismount. He broached the last of the space that separated them, catching her up in his arms as the dragon departed again beyond the clouds.

"I'm so sorry I left," he spoke, his lips wet with her tears. "I should have listened to you."

"Damn all of that," she set her hands on the sides of his face and paused as she gazed into his eyes. "I care only that you are alive and well and back with me again."

He held her tightly to himself and kissed her. "I see now that you were right about Erclidus. I should never have trusted him. Thanks to Lex, I'm fine, but my brother is proving to be a formidable foe."

"How was the city when you left?"

"We've left Lorethh in good hands," he assured her. "One of the gryphons has stayed so they might have a swift means of communication while we are gone. I assured that the second company had departed safely before I made my way here. All we can do now is hope that the delay I caused was enough."

Adiadni nodded, smiling softly. "You've done well, Adalos."

Uritus returned her smile, holding her chin gently in one hand. "Thanks to you, Suvah."

He kissed her once more, her mouth an anchor for his anxious mind. These days were grueling and tough, and Uritus knew that it would be some time still until their mountain of a challenge would be summited. But with a moment now to breathe, to gaze into her sparkling eyes and feel the locks of her dark hair tangled into his fingers, he was reminded all over again why he was here. He pulled her close to sink into her scent and the two made their way together back to the camp.

Chapter Thirty

"The Battle for Nott" and "Visions in the Dark"

The 11th of August

By the time the king's army had returned to Suscundos, the capital was deep in preparation for the anticipated battle. The cropidus set to work fortifying the city and constructing traps for the invaders, and many citizens began to evacuate. The soldiers were offered praise and gratitude upon their arrival, but the overall mood of the place of Adiadni's birth was heavy and serious. Everyone knew what was coming, everyone did their part, eyes flicking compulsively to the Western sky as they awaited the enemy's approach. Adi quickly made her way back to the palace upon their return.

When she arrived in the foyer, she paused, looking up and around at the many who hurried about there. The sense of urgency she held at all times was carried not only by her. Her ears caught the sound of a familiar voice, distressed. She turned her head, Fennispar arguing furiously with Gwynn about something she couldn't make out. The princess made her way to his side.

"Adi!" The boy flung his arms around her the second she arrived.

She returned his embrace, lifting her eyes to regard the attendant, "What's the matter?"

Gwynn sighed sadly. "The young sir doesn't feel much like traveling at the moment."

"*Not* just at the moment. I don't want to go at *all*."

Adi nodded to Gwynn and the attendant departed. The princess crouched down to be at eye level with Fennispar, "Talk to me. What's bothering you?"

"It's not fair," he replied, sniffling.

"What's not fair?"

"That everyone else gets to stay here and I have to go somewhere new where I'll be all alone!"

The princess's heart broke for the boy she loved. "You won't be alone," she assured him. "Gwynn is going with you now and Ama will be close behind…"

"I know that Betina is coming and I know that Agamemnon has to stay… But why do *you* have to stay?" Fennispar's lower lip trembled and Adiadni pulled him into the tight squeeze of her arms.

"I am sorry that I cannot go with you," she began, pulling back to look at him. "With Adda not at full strength, it is up to me to take up the mantle of my namesake. The duty of the line of Vindella in the Free World is to defend the people in such a time as this. I am not only the Free World's next guardian, I am also the Suvah. This is my purpose. Suscundos will not fall if I have anything to say about it."

Fennispar's head drooped toward the floor. "You'd let me stay if *I* was a Vindella."

"Hey," Adi lifted his chin to look into his sparkling dark eyes. "You *are* a Vindella."

"Not by blood."

"By spirit then. You are the most fiery-hearted of all of us."

"Then why can I not also do my part? I care for Suscundos just as much as you do."

The princess sighed. "I am sure this answer will not be satisfying to you and I am sorry for that, but you are too young. I would not have been permitted to go to battle at your age and neither would have Adda. But Fenn, I need you to hear me when I say that you do not wish to fight. None of us do."

The boy nodded, growing serious.

"I take my place on the battlefield with the fierce hope in my heart that you will never have to. I'm the Way-Maker, remember? I exist to lead you to a brighter future, one free of war. This is how I must do my part. You must do yours by staying safe so you can lead those who come next. Can you do that for me?"

Fennispar nodded again and then sighed and shrugged with a shake of his head. "I just wish I could do something to help."

Adi bit her lip, racking her brain for an offering. "You know what you can do?"

"What?"

"You can inspire hope." The princess took the boy's hands into her own, "The most important thing any of us can do at a time like this is hope. It is the brightest of Light beneath the heaviest of Shadow."

"But how do I do that?"

"Keep your eyes open for joy. Pay special attention to every beautiful thing you see, every lively song you hear, every delicious morsel you eat, every rousing game of Kepu you play. Pay attention to the way people look and sound when they laugh. Give thanks to everyone who does something kind to you. Identify how you feel when they do and then pass that feeling on to someone else. Tell stories. Share the tales that I've told you, the ones about great victories *and* the ones about living softly, about the delight of sharing a piece of fruit with someone you love under the bright Summer sun. We'll be together again before you know it." Fennispar stretched his arms around Adi's neck and she held him tightly. "I love you, brave boy."

"I love you too," he said, stepping back. "Remember that we share the same moon if you ever feel alone."

Adiadni swallowed, tears pricking her eyes. "I always remember. But you needn't worry, I'm not alone..." She lifted her eyes as a group of officers entered the foyer, Uritus amongst them. He made his way to her side upon seeing her and she returned her gaze to Fennispar, "And neither are you."

"Headed on your own adventure, are you?"

"Uritus!" The boy hastened to embrace the Adalos. Adi rose to her feet as her counterpart descended to his knee. "Yours is the last goodbye I have to say before I leave," spoke Fennispar.

"You honor me, Good Sir."

"I'm sorry you have to fight but… I know that you are strong."

"Thank you," Uritus said with a gracious nod. "As are you."

Gwynn returned and Adiadni embraced her. "Thank you for watching after him. You stay safe." The princess turned and dipped her head to plant a kiss atop Fennispar's chestnut curls. "Safe travels, Fenn. Mother protect you."

"And you."

She gave the boy a final embrace and then left him with Uritus and hastened up the stairs to see her father.

***

"More than before," Qibat returned from his latest mission as a scout, confirming what they suspected.

Punznes rewarded the bird with a treat and Mikka nodded her head slowly. Though her confidence in their company had grown as their numbers had over the past few days, it still made her anxious whenever the time arose to lead them into battle. They had faced little resistance when they freed Onnuk and Dersh, finding the second village to be the producer of textiles and the third of leather goods. The laborers there proved to be as enthusiastic of revolutionaries as those in Enk, and three hundred volunteers now journeyed with the Easterners, eager to liberate their brethren. Ouro remained elusive, and Mikka did not wish to consider how their plan would need to change if they did not find him in Nott.

They had stopped about a mile North of the final village as it came into view through the early morning fog. It was the largest of the fortresses, housing within its walls the agriculture that fed all of Vegard's citizens save for those at the Ashen Keep. A wave of anticipatory energy rolled through the revolutionaries. Mikka felt it approach from behind and then wash over herself and her friends. One more village, one more battle, Divine willing. When this was done, the Vegardians would be free.

"Ready?"

Mikka looked at Tris with a nod and a small smile, "Let's end this."

A pair of horses had been hitched to a wagon, two laborers clad head to toe in the armor worn by the guards waiting on its seat. Four more disguised rebels would go with the wagon to the gate under the guise of delivering goods from Dersh. The Easterners climbed into the wagon bed along with another half-dozen of their allies. The idea for the ambush had been conceived by the minds of the rebels and had proven to be an efficient plan. Once the gate had been opened and the guards startled by the ambuscade, the rest of the company would

455

storm the village. The goblins never had any reason to be suspicious and the battles had been swiftly fought and won.

A tarp was draped over the wagon bed once the revolutionaries had settled into place. This was the part that always made Tris acutely aware of her heartbeat. She had surprised herself with how quickly she had learned to wield a blade, but the courage that appeared to come so naturally to her comrades seemed to evade her. She took a shaky breath to steel her nerves and the wagon rolled forward as the rebellion proceeded to Nott.

Qibat flew ahead of them, bringing himself to perch atop the Northern wall where he would wait until the gate had been opened to rally the others. The trek to the village seemed to take an age. They came to a stop and Tris clutched a hand to her rapidly beating heart. She heard a question posed in gish, no doubt about the nature of their delivery. The volunteers disguised as guards were among the most proficient in the goblins' tongue. A few short sentences were exchanged before the gate's wooden doors creaked as they were pulled open and the wagon lurched forward again.

Mikka moved her hand to her sword. The others followed suit. Tris lowered her head, her energy entirely devoted to deepening her shallow breaths. A hand reached to brush hers. She opened her eyes, seeing nothing but warmth and surety in Mikka's. She nodded her head. She could do this.

The wagon came to an abrupt halt and the tarp was ripped from its bed. The revolutionaries sprang to action.

Tris leapt to the ground with a shout just in time to see a flurry of black feathers vanish beyond the wall. She ran at and impaled one of the goblins. All around, she heard the battle cries of her allies, the clashing of steel. She looked only briefly at her feet before raising her eyes and charging for another of the guards. The battle for Nott had begun.

***

"What's the matter? Is he all right?" Uritus hurried down the hall toward the king's chambers as he saw Adiadni emerge with tear-stained cheeks.

She ran to meet him, holding her arms tightly around his body for a prolonged moment before she answered, "He's still alive, thank the Mother. But his condition has worsened. He is confined to his bed."

The Adalos struggled as he searched for words to comfort her.

Adi used her sleeves to dry her eyes. "My mother does not wish to leave him. I told her she must, at least for Fenn, if she cares not for her own safety. His, um…" She paused, took a breath. "His cough has begun to produce blood."

Aurena appeared then around the corner at the end of the hall. "How is he?"

The princess sighed. "Alive but worse."

The Healer nodded thoughtfully. "Alive is good. How are you?"

Adi shrugged. "I'd be better if he was."

"Of course. I'll do my best to help." Aurena set a loving hand briefly on Adiadni's shoulder and made her way to see the king.

456

Adiadni returned her attention to Uritus, "I'm trying my best to have faith in our friends who've gone to Vegard. It is not an easy task we've entrusted them with."

He tucked a rogue curl behind her ear and kept his hand there, feeling her cheek so cold beneath his palm. "I believe in their determination and resourcefulness more than most anything. They'll get it done, I've no doubt in my mind. We just need to spare them a bit of patience. A task as daunting as theirs takes time."

She nodded. "I know. There's just... no saying how much he has left." The princess sighed and straightened herself. "Of course, I am not giving up hope. But at least for now, until he is well enough to resume his ordinary duties... I will need to behave as though his role is mine."

This was a heavy new responsibility. "How do you feel about that?"

Adi shrugged. "This is far sooner than I had hoped to act as queen, but I know I can do it."

Uritus smiled proudly at this significant increase in confidence.

"On that note, I think we need to gather some of our leaders for council. We received word from Lorethh this morning that Vegard has begun their journey here."

"I can gather them. Who do you need?"

"Uriah, of course, Crystella if she's able... Anyone who doesn't have more important things to see to."

"Your efforts are irreplaceable in their importance, Adiadni."

She looked down as she blushed.

"Hey," he cupped a hand beneath her chin to lift her face, "I'll help you however I can."

She smiled. "I know."

"I'll have everyone meet on the veranda?"

"No, that's far too... *formal*. Meet me in my father's study instead." She paused, biting her lip. "Though, I suppose that also feels..."

Uritus leaned down to kiss her forehead. "He's going to be fine. So are you."

She nodded with a small smile and then pressed her lips to his. "Thank you for all your help."

He returned her smile, running his thumb across her cheekbone, and departed to gather the others. Adiadni made her way immediately to the study. Ordinarily, after such a long journey, the princess would be quick to seek out a bath and a change of clothes. Under the present circumstances, however, she had far too much on her mind to even remember that that was what she wanted.

She paced back and forth in front of her father's desk. He looked different when she saw him, paler, thinner, weaker than he ever had. She felt guilt, as though her worrying about him in some way meant that she didn't trust her friends would be successful on their mission. She did trust them. She was, though, profoundly aware of just how seemingly impossible the task they'd been given was—to explore a land they knew all but nothing about with naught but the approximate location of a village and a healthy dose of pluck. Worried as she was, Adiadni knew that she would need to put her fears aside, at least for the next hour. The next battle was coming whether they were ready for it or not, and now she had to try to find a way to fit into her father's boots.

She stopped pacing, becoming suddenly aware that the room had grown quite warm. She crossed to the balcony doors and flung them wide, gasping in fresh air as she stepped out into the day. Her hands caught the balustrade as she reached the balcony's edge. She took several panicked breaths, looking down across the orchard as she attempted to steady her heart. *Their spirits are with you,* she tried to remind herself. *Adda is with you, in spirit* and *on earth. You were born for this. There is nothing you cannot handle. You've done far—*

"Adiadni?"

The princess turned abruptly, one hand still on the balustrade.

"Everyone's assembled. Whenever you're ready."

She nodded, offering a small smile to her counterpart, and returned to the study. Gathered there were Uriah, Perplexus, Olythia, Crystella, and Pressio. More than she had expected. They naturally assembled into a half circle and she brought herself to stand in front of them, Uritus shutting the balcony doors and moving to stand beside her. The study door opened before Adiadni could begin to address them.

"Forgive me, Love… Have you begun already?"

"No, Ama, come in."

The queen shut the door behind her and crossed the room to take her place beside her daughter. Adi was glad to have her there. Betina looked weary; no doubt she had lost a significant amount of sleep with her husband in such a poor state. The princess's right hand reached for her mother's as she arrived at her side and the queen offered her an encouraging squeeze.

"Some of you may have heard already that our enemy has proceeded from Judii to Suscundos," Adiadni began. "We'll hold a more official meeting tomorrow to discuss strategy. For now, I wish to, um… I wish to determine how we might best use our time before they arrive. Hopefully, we have five or even six days to prepare, but we must behave as though we have only three or four."

The others nodded in agreement. "The city's defenses will be completed by tomorrow evening," Pressio shared. "All the vulnerable citizens should be evacuated by then too."

"Good."

"There is still, however, the matter of Basil's hired swords."

"They're still in Suscundos?"

"They are."

"And they still refuse to fight without him?"

He nodded.

"Of course." Adiadni sighed. "How many soldiers do we have presently?"

"With the recruits who've joined the cause since we were away, just shy of five thousand," Crystella replied. "Strong numbers, more than we'd hoped for at this point. Healers are seeing to those who sustained injuries in the Mirrored Cities in hopes that they'll be well enough to join us in the next battle."

The princess nodded, grateful for the leadership training her cousins had undergone since their youth. She did not have her father to lean on at present, but she did have them. "We cannot conduct Basil's trial until my father is well again, so I believe it wisest to behave as though we will not have the aid of his swords. We will almost certainly be outnumbered... but we must retain our hold on hope. Unless you suspect, Uriah, that Velup will join them on their way here, we will only need to face one Sorcerer."

The Wizard shook his head. "If there is one thing I know for certain about my brother, it is that he will always prioritize his own well-being above everything else. He is old and weak. If he did not see it fit to accompany his troops to the front the first time, he certainly will not change his mind now."

Confirmation of this eased the minds of the council.

"Nevertheless, it would be unwise to underestimate Erclidus. He has a greater hold on his ability than most experienced Sorcerers I have faced."

"I do not understand his strength," spoke Perplexus with a shake of his head. "Twelve years of tutelage under even the most proficient Sorcerer should not be enough for anyone to display the power he has."

"I have considered this as well," Uriah replied. "What one takes from the Source must be repaid in full, and Erclidus appears to be at peak physical strength. I do not believe he is capable of bypassing Magic's natural laws and so, I suspect that Velup may be diverting some of his own power to his apprentice."

"Can he do that?" Adiadni had never heard of such a thing.

"He can. But not without a token."

"Erclidus does not bear a staff..."

"Nor does Velup. The Thieves rely heavily on what they believe to be their ability, feeling that they do not need a grounding agent to display great power. This is one of the most significant dangers of Stolen Magic. They do not know their limits and therefore run the risk of harming themselves each time they cast. But if Velup is doing what I believe, both he and Erclidus will require a token for it to be possible."

"Do you know what Erclidus's token might be?"

"The unfortunate thing is that a token can be any object one keeps on their person."

Adi nodded slowly, chewing on her lip as an idea began to take shape in her mind. "I don't expect any of you to be very keen on this, but... I believe I may be able to find out what it is."

The others waited in silent anticipation.

The princess took a breath before continuing, "In the times that I have spoken to Erclidus, he has been persistent in trying to persuade me to join him. To partner with him to usher in the *new age*."

"Times?"

Adi turned to Uritus.

"When have you spoken to him since the Ashen Keep?"

"Well… perhaps it wasn't *him*, exactly. But my dreams of the man in the black cape returned when we were in Sigmount. When they come, I try my best to pry for information. Or at least… to attempt to convince him to stop."

Uritus nodded briskly, not sure why he was surprised.

"I believe your dreams come from two different sources," Olythia addressed the princess. "The first, of course, is your natural proclivity to prophecy. The Divine's way of warning you of what is to come. The second—which is only a hunch—is that Octrusial has sent you projections of Erclidus. We know that he was keeping an eye on you during your journey. It seems likely that our enemies would wish to get into your head as much as they are able."

Adiadni did not understand. "We saw no sign of Octrusial in the Mirrored Cities…"

"He does not need to be with Erclidus to project him to you. He needs only something that belongs to him—a book, a pair of boots, a lock of his hair. Have you had any similar dreams since Aurena gave you your token?"

The princess shook her head.

"Good. The amonii seems to be working."

"You said he's tried to persuade you to join him…" Uritus returned the conversation to its beginning. "What has he said?"

Adi shivered as she recalled her dreams. "Nothing especially interesting. He claims to believe that we can help each other, he and I. I think he views me as a tool that he might use to more easily conquer the Free World. In return for my partnership, he has offered to be merciful in his conquering, whatever the fuck that means. Of course, I am not particularly inclined to believe him."

"And what have you said to him?"

The princess hesitated. "I've told him that I will always put my people first and that the only thing I would consider accepting in exchange for my partnership is their guaranteed safety. He did agree to this, though I do not trust that he would keep his word. And while I have made clear my feelings on the matter, I believe that in my search for information, I've left a window ajar. He believes that I *can* be persuaded, and I wish to use this against him."

"How?"

"By going to him and telling him that I have changed my mind."

The king's study fell silent and Adiadni felt the energy in the room shift. She was prepared to face their resistance.

"Do you mean to go on your own?" Betina was the first to speak.

"I do. I would not subject another to unnecessary danger."

"So you admit that this would be a needless risk?" Uritus, who up to this point had been content offering Adiadni his silent support, suddenly felt himself grow hot with dissent.

"If I cannot identify his token, I might at least be able to buy us some time. It was not needless when you went to Judii to negotiate with him."

"That was different. I had an entire army a quarter-mile away."

"Even so, you went alone, defenseless, straight into the heart of the enemy despite the risk you knew it posed. I have faced greater foes than he."

This was true and Uritus knew it, but still, he pushed back, "I was a fool for believing that my going to him was a good idea. The fire of his determination burns hot and wild and it is not lost on me how lucky I am that I was not burned by it. If Erclidus has the opportunity to take something he wants, he will not hesitate. He views me as an obstacle to overcome; you, by your own admission and his, as something he might possess to make his path all the easier to walk. You cannot go to him, not on your own and not with a thousand soldiers to back you. I will not permit it."

"Permit it?" Adiadni laughed, incredulous. "Are you under the impression that I need your permission to do anything at all?"

"There may be another way."

All eyes turned to regard Olythia.

The Prophet explained, "Just as Octrusial has projected Erclidus to you, with the help of a few more Keepers, I should be able to project you to him."

The Suvah was intrigued by this prospect. "How does it work?"

"You'll be put to sleep. It'll be just like a dream, for both you and him."

"Is it safe?" It pained Betina to consider sending Adi again into danger.

"He will not be able to harm her," Olythia replied. "Not with anything but words."

"Fine," said Adiadni. "How soon can you make this happen?"

"I can have everything prepared by tonight."

"Very well, that will do. That's everything for now, thank you all for meeting with me. I'll send for you if I need anything else." With that, the princess turned and made her way again out to the balcony.

The others lingered for only a moment before filing one by one out of the room until only the queen and the fisherman remained. They met one another's eyes and she smiled at him sadly and made her way back to check on her husband. Uritus looked at his reflection in the large mirror above the settee and sighed. He did not wish for the intensity of the present days to weigh on his relationships, and it was clear that he had pushed too hard. He moved to the balcony, hesitating when he reached the doorway. "Adiadni…"

"I just need a moment alone please."

Her voice was strained and she did not turn to face him. Hesitating only another moment, he departed from the study. Adiadni crouched down to set her forehead against the balustrade and wept.

***

It became quickly clear to the revolutionaries in Nott that they had their work cut out for them.

The goblins who guarded the village—at least three times as many as they had faced in their prior battles—swarmed the Northern gate when they became aware that they were under attack. The sound of pounding boots and gritty cries grew steadily as the rebellion raced for the town.

Mikka knew they needed only hold out a few moments more before their victory was guaranteed. The soldier parried an attack made by a guard once, twice, and dropped to a knee as he launched a third attack. With a wide swing of her arm, her sword sliced into the goblin's belly.

He howled as his blood spilled onto the ground along with a pile of intestines. Mikka cut off his head as she leapt back to her feet and saw four guards working to push the doors of the town shut.

"Rip!" she cried, raising her blade to block another attack. "The gate!"

Oripidus acted immediately. He raced to the doors, driving the spike of his war hammer into the back of one of the guard's necks, killing him instantly.

The guard beside him turned with a grunt, only to be slain before he had a moment to react.

Hastening to close the second door was one of the larger goblins, but the dwarf did not hesitate to face him. He sent his hammer crashing into the guard's knee, killing him with a swift strike to the jaw as he dropped to the ground.

Oripidus leapt back as the final goblin sought to strike him down. "Come on then, ye worthless assembly o' bones! Finish me!" he taunted.

The guard took the bait, raising his sword in the air as he approached the dwarf. Oripidus seized the moment.

With an upward swing, he delivered a swift blow to the goblin's groin, and when he doubled over in pain, Oripidus sent his hammer crashing down into the back of his skull.

He hurried then to pull open the door of the gate and the rest of the rebels poured into the village.

Mikka breathed a sigh of relief at the arrival of their allies. She spun around, scanning the town for the place Ouro might seek to hide, and saw a wisp of dark fabric disappear into the central building. She cut down a goblin who charged for her and raced to the main house.

All around, the town's laborers fled, seeking shelter from the fight. One of them tripped, crashing to the ground.

Mikka diverted her course to help him up.

462

He cowered when he saw her approach, dragging himself back along the ground. "Please!" he cried. "Have mercy!"

"We're not here to hurt you," she replied, taking him by the arm and dragging him to his feet. "We're here to free you!"

He looked at her with gratitude and confusion, "Are you from the East?"

Mikka ignored his question, "Ouro the Alchemist. Is he here?"

The man nodded, lifting a finger to point to the main house, and Mikka hurried away.

The door to the building was ajar. She entered, finding it to be dark and cold. The atrium was tall and open, with visible stairways leading up to the second and third floors.

The soldier cursed under her breath, not sure where to begin searching. She paused, racking her brain, and then touched the tip of her sword to the ground, took a knee, and bowed her head.

She breathed slowly as she attempted to shut out the sounds of the battle outside and the stifling quiet that surrounded her. It was only a few moments before she could hear, clearer than anything else, her heartbeat, and then...

"Down."

She frowned, scanning the room once more as she stood to her feet, and spotted against the wall ahead of her another door, open just a crack. She ran to it and flung it open, finding a narrow staircase.

When she reached the bottom, she found herself in a large room lit by torchlight. Three wide steps led down into the main space where the ceiling was so high she could not see it. Lining the walls were cabinets and open shelves, each one buckling under the weight of jars and bottles and boxes and vials. Multiple large tables were set up in the room's center, covered with glassware and colorful potions, some of which glowed in the dim light. There was a strange smell about this place, stale, musty, with an undeniable note of something unnatural, metallic, nauseating. Scattered across the floor and piled into every nook were trinkets and coins of glimmering gold.

Mikka gripped her sword as she proceeded slowly into the main area, eyes darting back and forth. She was careful not to bump anything as she weaved between tables, uncertain what was in the glassware and not wishing to find out.

"Ouro!" her voice echoed up into the dark. "I know you're here. Show yourself!"

Silence for a prolonged moment and then, "To what do I owe this unwelcome intrusion?"

Mikka turned, raising her sword as a cloaked figure emerged from the shadows. "The people of Vegard have been liberated of their shackles and now, I have come for you."

"And just who might you be?" Ouro stepped further into the light. The fabric that shrouded him was pulled low to cover his face, but still, Mikka could see the blistering sores that peeked out from the edges of his collar and sleeves.

"A reckoning," she replied, voice deep and strong. "For your crimes committed against king Agamemnon and the Free World."

"Mmm. So I take it the curse has been successful?" He snaked around one of the tables and Mikka watched him intently, making sure to keep some distance between them. "It was a waste of time coming here. By now, his ailment will have taken full effect. You have failed."

"We'll see about that."

Ouro touched his hand lightly to the corner of a table and Mikka clenched her teeth. "Too late to save the king, too late to save your homeland. Tell me, what will you do when the East has fallen, take your own life or cower and wait for it to be taken from you?"

"The West *has* fallen. Your citizens have chosen to rise against you. And now, it is you who cowers down here in the dark."

"Foolish girl," the Alchemist spat. "The Shadow will not be stopped. Kill me now, it will make no difference. The land of your birth will know nothing but plague and famine and drought. You will watch helplessly as every last one of your loved ones is slain before your eyes. And then, when you have nothing left, when your world has turned to ash and your sky has blackened, only then will you realize how your efforts were all in vain, and you will die, hopeless and alone."

Ouro seized a small bottle from a table and cast it against the ground.

Mikka staggered back, covering her face at the sudden appearance of black smoke and dust. The vapors stung her eyes and her lungs filled with a scent all too similar to that of burning flesh. She heard footsteps as her enemy began to flee, and then a crash and a thud.

The soldier opened her eyes, and as the smoke dissipated, she saw Ouro, a puddle of fluorescent green liquid all around him, and behind him, Punznes, the jagged neck of a glass bottle still held in his right hand.

"Get away from that!"

The physician dropped the bottleneck and leapt up one of the steps. The corrosive liquid began to sizzle and steam.

Ouro cried out as it ate through his clothing and then his flesh. "You're already dead!" he choked out. "You will never be free!"

"We're free of you now." The bright green turned quickly black as the liquid thickened and dried up. Mikka moved to stand above him, raised her sword, and plunged it into his heart. "May you find all the peace you deserve."

With a final ragged breath, Ouro died. Mikka pulled her sword from his shriveled corpse and wiped it clean.

"Are you all right?" she asked, lifting her eyes to Punznes.

He looked down at his person for any signs of having been burned. "It would appear so. You?"

She took a deep breath to assess the health of her lungs and then nodded. "I'd like to think I had a handle on things, but who knows what might have happened if you hadn't arrived when you did. Thank you for that. Interesting choice of weapon though," she remarked with a smirk, looking to the bow and quiver slung against his back.

"I suppose I acted on impulse," he said with a chuckle. "I'm a fine marksman, but slow to the draw. And of course, far greater of a healer than a fighter."

"Well, your fighting may well have healed the king." Mikka paused, looking down at the lifeless body of the Alchemist.

"What's wrong?"

The soldier shook her head. "When I spoke with him, he said it was too late. That the king was already dead, that all of us were."

"Lying to save his skin."

"Maybe. But can we be sure that by killing him, we broke his curse?"

Punznes looked across the various bubbling potions on the tables. "I suppose we can't. I don't know how this all works."

Mikka chewed on her cheek as she thought. "The village has been won?"

"Yes. I ensured that the last of the guards had been slain before I came looking for you."

"Good."

"What are you thinking?"

The soldier looked once more around the room and sheathed her sword. "Have the laborers take all they would wish from the fields."

"Very well."

"We'll head back to Dersh tonight. Once everyone's out of the village, burn it. Nothing left behind."

Punznes nodded in agreement and the two made their way together back up the stair.

***

Beneath the palace in Suscundos, Adiadni waited anxiously outside the room being prepared by Olythia. Uritus waited with her, leaning against the wall of the hallway where she paced back and forth. His tired eyes moved with her as she trod her weary path. They had not spoken about their argument earlier that day, as the princess did not seem to wish to, overwhelmed by burden upon burden and coping by putting her head down and doing the work she needed to. But the regret he felt for the things he said weighed heavy on his heart and he knew that he could not let her see to this next crucial task without telling her so.

He stepped into her path before she could pace by him again and took her shoulders gently in his hands, "If you do not wish to discuss it, I will understand. But I must tell you how deeply sorry I am for the way I behaved in our council this afternoon."

She sighed, raising her eyes to behold the look of remorse on his face.

"I allowed my fear to get the better of me. That was wrong. You are right that you do not need my permission to do what you must. You are the radiant light and heat of the sun. You cannot and should not be controlled, and I have no desire to try. I am still learning what it means to be beholden to your majesty and I am sorry for falling short of what you deserve. I hope you can forgive me."

"Of course I do." Adi stepped forward to embrace him and melted as strong arms wrapped around her shoulders. "I'm sorry for how I may have taken my frustrations out on you. You've been nothing but kind and patient with me since our first meeting. I just feel so…" She trailed off, unsure exactly what she felt.

"I know," he said. "You've handled your responsibilities with such strength and grace. I do not understand how you manage."

She shrugged. "I've been trained my whole life for the role that will one day be mine. I just wish it didn't need to come so soon…"

"Hey," he touched her face, lifting it so he could look into her eyes. "It's not over yet."

She sighed, willing herself to believe him. The door to the room opened and Olythia appeared. "We're ready when you are."

Adiadni nodded, looking from the Prophet to Uritus and back. "Can he come with me?"

"Of course." Olythia made their way into the darkened chamber and the young people followed.

This room was not unlike the one where Uritus had undergone his character assessment, just slightly better lit. A chaise had been positioned in the center beneath a dim light that beamed down from the ceiling. Against one wall stood two more Prophets and Olythia gestured for Uritus to wait beside them. Now that she was here, the gravity of what Adiadni was about to do began to set in. She took a long breath to steady herself.

"I'll need to remove these," Olythia said, touching their hands to the gold bands on Adi's arms. She nodded and the Prophet took the tokens, handing them to one of the others. "Come take a seat."

Adiadni did as she was told, bringing herself down to the chaise. Olythia turned to the second Prophet, taking from him a small vial which they carried back and handed to the princess.

Adi took it, observing the shimmering flecks of silver that swirled through rich purple liquid. "What is it?"

"Aurena's. It'll put you to sleep. You'll be able to wake yourself whenever you are ready, but if I sense that you are in distress, I will do so myself."

Adi nodded, taking in another breath.

"Know that while you are there, everything you experience will feel real to you. There is a small chance that you may forget you are asleep."

"Like yuzh," the princess whispered under her breath.

Olythia breathed out a small laugh. "Yes, much like that. There's a bit of kuffa in the potion."

"What will it be like for Erclidus?"

"If he sleeps, it will be as a dream, if he is awake, as a vision. It will feel as real for him as it does for you." They paused as the princess looked again at the small vial. "I must remind you that while you are without your amonii, you will be vulnerable. He will no doubt pry for information as you do. Stay sharp. Don't give away anything that he may use against us. How do you feel?"

Adi sighed. "Afraid. Though I don't really know why…"

Olythia hesitated. "You do not need to do this if you don't want to. No one will blame you if you change your mind."

"I do want to." The princess raised her eyes to meet the Prophet's, a determined spark flickering in them.

"Very well," Olythia knelt to a seat at her side. "You will be safe. I promise."

Adiadni nodded once more, looking across the room to Uritus. He offered her a soothing smile as he raised his hand to his chest, and her talisman grew cold. With a final breath to solidify her courage, she removed the cork from the vial and drank the potion, finding it to be milky and sweet like a mild tea. She laid back on the chaise and took Olythia's hand, blinking a few times before she drifted off to sleep.

***

When the princess opened her eyes, she found herself standing in the middle of a large tent, layers of patterned rugs beneath her feet. She turned to regard the space around her. On one end, partially concealed by an ornate wooden screen, she could see a pile of cushions and blankets on what she presumed to be a low bed. There was a sitting area near the tent flap consisting of a sofa, a low table, and a pair of round ottomans, with a copper tub to one side behind a dressing screen. All around were heavy chests and vases filled with scrolls. Everything in the tent was colored in deep, rich tones, luxurious but not opulent, comfortable but not at all welcoming. Outside, she could hear the sounds of Vegard's camp.

The tent flap lifted and Erclidus entered, halting as he beheld the vision in deep violet silk who stood there. His light startle quickly made way for an amused satisfaction. "This is a lovely surprise," he said, looking her up and down. "To what do I owe the pleasure?"

She hesitated, arms crossed over her body, and reminded herself of the reason she was here. "I've been thinking, and… while I am committing to nothing right now… I wish to consider the possibility of allying with you so that this war might come to an end."

A corner of his mouth lifted into a smirk. "I knew you were the one who could be reasoned with." He strolled to the dressing screen, spurs clicking clearly with every step.

Adi dropped her eyes to them, remembering the things Uriah said might help her identify his token. It would be something that could not be easily taken from him, so probably not his sword. There was also a great chance that the token was made of a natural material—metal or jewel or some kind of stone. Cloth would be too fragile, the Wizard had said, so when Erclidus removed his cape and draped it across the screen, the princess determined that she could also rule that out.

"What did they say when you told them of your change in heart? I'm surprised they let you come here."

"I didn't tell them," she lied. "You're right, they wouldn't understand."

He chuckled as he turned again to face her. "Perhaps your defiance *is* one of your more attractive qualities." The man in black made his way toward her, hands clasped behind his back. He came to a stop, eyes raking her over from head to toe, and then gestured with one hand to the sitting area. "Come," he said. "Make yourself comfortable. Let's talk."

Adi reluctantly obeyed, bringing herself to perch on the edge of one of the ottomans.

Erclidus took a seat on the sofa and reached for the tea set atop the small table. "Care for a drink?"

Adiadni's eyes flicked to his hands as he began preparing himself a cup. They moved slowly, tenderly, as he selected a sugar cube from its bowl and dropped it into the teacup with a satisfying clink. The sweet gem melted, dissolving entirely as hot red liquid consumed it. Steam spun in alluring ribbons as a small silver spoon stirred in a light cloud of cream. The simple band on Erclidus's index finger was the only visible piece of jewelry he wore.

"I heard about what your hospitality did to Uritus. I think I'll refrain."

He chuckled, sitting back and bringing one boot to rest on the table. "Had Uritus taken the tea—and the antidote with it—he'd never have succumbed to the effects of the liquor. Such a choice was his alone."

"And I'm sure you would have allowed him to return safely to Lorethh if he had? Spare me your pretense, Erclidus. I am here to bargain, *not* to be trifled with."

He raised an eyebrow and smirked. "Have I told you how I love that raging fire in your belly?"

Adiadni did not respond, glaring at him instead through narrowed eyes.

"Oh, all right." The man in black returned his boot to the ground and took a sip of his tea. "Bargaining it is. Tell me, what was it that made you change your mind?"

"Far too many have died already," her voice hitched as she answered him. "Far too many more *will* die if this goes on. If I might wield my position to protect those who remain, I will... however I can."

"Smart girl," he said, looking her over again.

Adi steeled herself against the chills that pricked her arms. "The last time I dreamed of you, you promised me that in exchange for my partnership, you would guarantee the safety of the Free People. Was that you, or merely a figment of my mind?"

He smiled. "That was me. I meant it. If you can be willing to compromise, so can I."

"I'd like to be able to take your word for it, but surely you understand why I cannot. How can I be sure that you are telling the truth and not merely deceiving me so you might have your way?"

"What would it take to convince you of my intent?"

She shook her head slowly. "Short of withdrawing your troops from the Free World, I can think of nothing."

Erclidus nodded thoughtfully before leaning forward to set his cup on the table. He rose, moved to stand before her, and drew from his belt a thin silver dagger with a ruby inlaid in the handle. He held out to her. She took it hesitantly, turning it over for a moment in her hands. "What am I to do with this?"

"If I go back on my word, kill me with it."

His casual tone startled her. She looked down at the weapon and then returned her eyes to his and held it out to him. "I do not wish to kill you, Erclidus."

"I don't believe you."

He took the dagger back from her and crossed the tent, retrieving a scroll from one of the vases and laying it flat on a table that bore an inkwell. "But have it your way. Blood is blood, there's nothing better for the sealing of an oath. It's all the same to me." He set the dagger aside on the table and drew the quill from the inkwell. "I, Erclidus of Vegard, hereby declare that no harm shall befall the citizens of this land, so long as Adiadni Vindella fulfills her part of the bargain."

He signed his name upon the parchment with a flourish and returned the quill to its home. Then, taking up the dagger, he pierced his left thumb with the tip of the blade and smeared a streak of dark blood across the letters of his name.

He turned, extending the weapon's handle in her direction, "Your turn."

Adiadni rose, taking a few small steps toward the table to regard the scroll. Its words were as he had said them, elegantly scrawled and vague. "What exactly *is* my part of the bargain? I'd much prefer to know what will be expected of me before I agree to it."

His brow twitched—a tiny, hardly perceptible note of irritation. He brought the flat of the blade to tap against his fingers. "Perfectly reasonable." He set his hands again behind his back and began to walk the length of the tent. "You will be expected to take on all the ordinary duties of a ruler. Just... at my side."

"As a secondary to your kingship?"

He chuckled. "We can certainly rule as equals. I quite like the idea of calling you my queen. Of course, only once such a relationship develops on its own. I would not be so presumptuous to assume that that is something you can be forced into. But that's all right. I am willing to put in the work to win you over." He stopped as he arrived in front of her again, taking her left hand into his right and running his thumb over her knuckles. "It would seem the last one who tried has been done away with."

She snatched her hand away from him and rubbed it with her other, unsure if it was merely perception or reality that the heat of his own had burned her.

Erclidus chuckled again, returning to stand in front of the table that bore the scroll. "What was it he did to fall out of favor with you?"

Adiadni balled her hands into fists and set them at her sides. "He viewed me as something to be possessed. As a means to an end."

"Hmm." The man in black turned, leaning back against the table. "Do you feel you are that to me?"

She clenched and unclenched her jaw. "It's difficult not to, considering the circumstances."

He nodded, remaining silent for a prolonged moment before approaching her again. "I had hoped that our relationship would have a smoother start than it has. But I still hold out hope for its future. I think you'll find that I'm not as much of a monster as you believe me to be." He set his hand beside her face and ran his thumb lightly across her cheek and she flinched. He dropped his hand, returning it behind his back. "But I am happy to allow that to happen in time."

She moved her arms again to cross over her body, trying not to panic as she came to realize that she didn't remember how she had ended up here.

"What more do you want to know?"

The princess racked her brain for an answer or a clue. Finding none, she continued stalling for time, "You told me when we met that you had dreamed of me as I have of you. What took place in your dreams?"

Erclidus's mouth curled into a smile. He replaced the small knife in its home on his belt. "They were always the same," he began. "I would walk a narrow path, bound for what I knew to be my future. But before I could arrive there, I would happen upon you, feet firmly planted, directly in my way. *I cannot let you pass*, you would tell me. *It is my duty to guard this place*. You were firm in your resolve, but so was I. I would tell you of the vision I had of a world where I need never fear nor lack. I would tell you that if you came with me, the same could also be for you." He paused, moving his eyes across the soft features of her face. "In most every case, you remained stubborn and immovable, and I would wake shortly thereafter. But sometimes... you would hesitate, turn to look over your shoulder in an attempt to glimpse what I saw. I knew then that you long for the same things I do."

Adiadni breathed in shakily, trying not to show her intimidation.

"That was when I would approach you..." he continued, taking another step closer to her, "...take your hand in mine, and lead you on." He brought the fingers of his right hand to intertwine with her left, his face now so close to hers that she could feel the heat of his breath as he lowered his voice to a whisper, "I could lead you that way if you'd let me, Adiadni. You would never want for anything ever again."

Adi swallowed hard, heart pounding, all of her body's alarm bells ringing in her ears. "And what would become of my friends?"

He withdrew his face from hers, standing taller again. "Friends?"

The princess dug through the archives of her memory, scrambling her brain all the more as she tried to discern what was wrong. "Well, yes, you... You promise contentment for me and protection for my citizens. What would become of those closest to me?"

Erclidus moved his head from one side to the other as though he was weighing options. "They would be spared as well... provided that they surrendered willingly."

"And if they don't?"

"Don't?"

"Surrender..." Adi felt her hand and face grow warm.

The man in black gave a casual shrug. "Then I suppose they would need to be punished."

"Punished how?" Adiadni began to squirm, attempting to wriggle her hand out of his.

Erclidus's grasp remained fast. "In a manner equivalent to their defiance."

"And my family?" The princess's voice cracked as she began to panic.

"Adiadni."

"They could come with us, as long as they come peacefully. Your father, though..."

Adiadni's fear shifted to rage. "What about my father?"

"His way is... tired. Outdated. You and I cannot build a new empire until the old one has been destroyed."

With force, she managed to rip her hand out of his. "You cannot believe that I will stand for this."

"You said you would do whatever it takes. Why would I assume you meant otherwise?"

"You would do away with my father, my friends, anyone who defies you. Why would I ever feel safe to speak my mind? One disagreement and it'll be off with my head too."

"Adiadni."

Erclidus laughed and shook his head. "There cannot be order if there is no punishment, Adiadni. How could anyone take me seriously as a leader if they do not bow to the strength of my hand?"

"Everyone? *Everyone* must bow? Even Velup?"

The young Sorcerer curled his hand to regard his fingers. "Even he will take his rightful place in time."

Adi began to feel sick. "So should my mother defy you... or my little brother?"

"This isn't real."

He shrugged and her blood boiled. "All who stand in the way of the future must be dealt with."

She inhaled sharply and felt herself grow internally cold. "...And Uritus?"

He frowned slightly, bringing himself to his full height. "Uritus?"

Adi froze, only now becoming aware of the precipice on which she stood. "You would kill your own brother if it came to it?"

Erclidus did not answer, but rather stared down at the princess, the cold, dark blue of his eyes feeling as though it would burn right through her.

"Adiadni."

And then, something changed in his face—something sinister—and Adiadni's heart dropped to her stomach as she realized what she had done.

"That's why you did away with the ring..." He seized her hand again and looked down at it. "And why he is always so bothered whenever I bring you up. I can't believe I didn't see it before, to be honest. My hope in you has blinded me."

"Let go of me..." Adi tore her hand away again and then yelped as he forcefully grabbed her face.

"And here I thought you were better than him. I was a damn fool."

Her fingers clawed at his arm and wrist as the heat of his hand began to burn her cheek. "Let me go!"

He clucked his tongue with a shake of his head. "I can't do that now, little bird. You're not serious about our partnership yet, but that's all right. I have ways of making you yield."

"He can't hurt you... "

"And now I know the first who must go in order to clear our path."

"You're not awake... "

With a gasp and a jolt, Adiadni sat up straight on the chaise, panting desperately and heaving with fear.

"You're all right!" In an instant, Uritus was at her side, holding her tightly and stroking her hair. "You're all right. You're safe. He can't hurt you, I'm here."

"Adi, are you okay?"

The princess noticed Olythia there in the same place they had been the whole time.

"What happened?"

All at once, her memory flooded back to her. "He has a token," she spoke between gasps. "A silver ring on the hand he uses to cast."

"You are certain?"

"I am. It burned me..."

Uritus took her face in his hands and moved it to regard the place she touched on her cheek. "There's no mark. You're safe. It was only a dream."

She nodded shakily and leaned forward to bury her face in his shoulder.

***

Eventually, with Uritus's help, Adiadni regained control of her breathing, and Olythia departed with the other Prophets to pass on what she had learned. The princess again donned her golden armbands, feeling her sense of security return with them. The Suvah and Adalos walked arm-in-arm together back to the hall, and Adi came to an abrupt halt when she laid eyes on the figure who approached them.

"Adda...?"

The king smiled warmly, spreading his arms wide. "My child."

The princess ran into his embrace, tears streaming down her cheeks. "You're all right..." She pulled back to look at him, finding him to be as strong as she had ever seen him. "What happened?"

"I felt as if a weight had been lifted from my chest, and then, all at once, I could breathe deeply again."

She shook her head in wonder, running a hand across his face. "A bloody miracle."

Agamemnon laughed. "I believe we have your friends to thank for that."

"I'll kiss the ground they walk on when I see them again."

The king paused, looking caringly down at his daughter. "How are you feeling, Adiadni? When I saw Olythia, they said you were quite shaken up."

She shook her head. "I've all but forgotten that now. I am just glad to have you back again."

Together, they returned to the palace above. Adiadni retired to bed that night feeling lighter than she had in weeks. But all the while, as she slept, she was repeatedly agitated by a phantom sensation on her left cheek.

Chapter Thirty-One

"The Trial of Basil Dagious"

The 15th of August

It took a bit of time, but Adiadni did eventually share with Uritus the harrowing details of her discussion with the man in black. She wept as she recalled them, deeply remorseful for how she had inadvertently shared with the enemy her greatest weakness. The Adalos did his best to soothe her fears, reminding her that it made no difference if his brother knew of the love they shared, that he would proceed with his campaign whether he knew or not. Adi knew this to be true, but still, it did little to ease her anxious mind. Erclidus was aware now of the primary barrier he faced in both conquering the Free World and winning over the woman he believed to be his destiny. If there had been any part of him that was unwilling to cause his younger brother harm, surely now it was long gone.

Though Uritus did not say it, his worry that Erclidus would seek to harm Adiadni in an attempt to get to him was difficult to ignore.

With king Agamemnon again at full health, the energy in Suscundos was rejuvenated and the people felt all the more optimistic as they awaited the coming battle. Gryphon riders continued to track the progress of the advancing forces, and the last of the city's defense systems were completed and ready for use. Queen Betina was at peace leaving with the last group of evacuees now that one of her greatest concerns had been alleviated. She and Adiadni met for a final tearful goodbye on the steps of the palace.

"I feel I should offer you a bit of sage advice before I depart, but at the moment, I can think of nothing that you do not already know."

Adi laughed. "I owe most of what I know to you, Ama. The greatest gift you can give me is the assurance of your safety."

"I am so very proud of you, Love." Betina pulled her daughter close and kissed the top of her head before stepping back and looking at her seriously, "Do you feel okay heading into this afternoon? I regret that I cannot be here to offer you my support."

With just over a day and a half before the enemy was expected to arrive and the preparations for battle complete, the time had come to conduct Basil's trial.

"I feel… tired, mostly," replied the princess with a shrug. "But I'll be fine. I will be happy to know that you and Fenn are both safe."

"Adi!"

The queen and her daughter turned to regard the two women who hurried up the steps toward them.

"Oh, good," said Adiadni as she embraced them. "I was just beginning to wonder where I might need to look for you. But where's Jasch?"

"Has she not told you?" Friya and Kristefani shared a glance. "Jasch is—"

"Staying behind to do her part." The fourth member of the group of friends made her way to join the rest, smooth, supple armor plating her body.

Adi's mouth curled into a smile when she saw her. "How very like you."

The sound of a trumpet announced the assembly for the departure of the evacuees. Betina embraced her daughter a final time and then did the same to Jasch, whispering to them both to keep themselves safe. Friya and Kristefani tearfully bid their friends farewell, promising Adi that they would look after her mother and Fennispar and urging Jasch to keep her head on straight and mind the orders she was given. The three departed together, leaving the princess and the soldier together on the steps.

"I half expected you to try to make me go with them," Jasch remarked.

Adi giggled. "Seems like a waste of time. You wouldn't listen to me even if I did."

The fiery-haired woman threw back her head and laughed. "You'd be right. You know me too well."

"Honestly, I'll be glad to have you with me. You're exactly the sort we need fighting for our continued freedom."

"Brave in a blind sort of way?"

Adiadni chuckled with a shake of her head. "Passionate and devoted, to this land and your convictions."

"That's a much nicer way of putting it."

"Where have you been assigned?"

"Infantry. First wave."

The princess nodded her approval. "Good. We'll go out together then."

"I'll be honored to accompany the Suvah into battle," said Jasch, touching a hand to her heart. "We'll take up swords together just like we always said we would."

Adi embraced her friend, speaking a silent prayer of protection over her, and then made her way back into the palace to seek out Uritus.

***

Come midday, the king and his council had assembled in the courtroom for the trial of Basil Dagious.

Agamemnon took his place on the highest seat of the court, where he would act as mediator and judge. His Keepers stood against the wall to his left, behind the pair of seats designated for the victims of the attempted crime.

Uritus's hand found Adiadni's as they waited for the hearing to begin.

To the king's right sat the accused. The flat expression on Basil's face did little to hide his irritation with being humiliated in this way.

Every seat in the courthouse intended for citizens who wished to observe the adjudication was filled, with more of the Free People gathered in the square outside. It made sense that those remaining in Suscundos would seek out a distraction from the impending doom of the Shadow, particularly for a trial of such historical significance. Adiadni didn't know why she had expected anything less.

The doors to the courtroom were shut and the people fell silent as Agamemnon stood to his feet.

"Citizens of the Free World," he addressed them, "We are gathered here to seek justice on behalf of the victims of an attempted crime. As your king, guardian, and presider over this court, I hereby swear to remain unbiased and faithful in my pursuit of appropriate justice so that we all may continue to live peacefully and free of fear. Let us begin." Agamemnon returned to his seat and Adiadni shifted in her own. The courtroom felt unnaturally warm, even for the Summer.

"I present to you the accused, lord Basil Dagious of Vindellaria," the king gestured to the man on his right, who reluctantly rose. "Do you swear, on life and legacy, to behave appropriately, speak honestly, and accept humbly the judgment passed down to you today?"

Basil's cold glare lingered on the princess and the fisherman for a moment before he responded, "I do."

"So be it."

The accused sat and Agamemnon turned his attention to the other side of the courtroom, "I present to you the victims, princess Adiadni Vindella, the Suvah and heir to the throne of the Free World; and Uritus Subian, the Adalos and first general of the Free World's armed forces."

The young people dropped each other's hands before standing.

"Do you swear, on life and legacy, to behave appropriately, uphold integrity, and lead with grace as you pursue justice for the crimes committed against you?"

Both responded affirmatively and returned to their seats.

"So be it. Let the trial begin. May the precedents set today make way for a fairer and safer future for us all. Basil."

"Your highness."

"You have been accused of the attempted assault of both Adiadni and Uritus, with the intent of taking Uritus's life. Do you contest these accusations?"

Basil's eyes flicked once more to the princess before he replied, "I made no attempt, in action or in will, to cause any harm to Adiadni. But as for the rest, no, I do not contest."

Admission of this was not something Uritus had anticipated. Though he already knew it to be true, the confirmation of Basil's wish for his death settled into his bones with unease. There were many now who wanted the Adalos dead —thousands who presently made their way to Suscundos, his last living blood relative amongst them. Their motivations he could understand—the inherent bloodthirstiness stitched into the very fabric of the half-alive soldiers, the slow poisoning of the mind of a boy who longed only for a sense of security.

But Basil was no fool, and he knew without question that seeking to cause harm to the one Adiadni loved would do nothing to help return her affection to him. No, his aggression stemmed only from a fit of rage at being robbed of something he felt entitled to. This man, who had never wanted for anything, who had only ever been held in the highest of regard in the eyes of the people and the royal family had been willing to sacrifice all of that for the sake of his bloody revenge. And though he did not truly fear either of them, Uritus became suddenly aware that men like Basil were far more of a threat to the continued peace and safety of this land than Erclidus ever was.

The fisherman recalled the solitary pilgrims he had come across when first journeying into the White Mountains as a boy. So relieved had he been to happen upon another wandering soul, having been so alone since leaving Tosh, save for the company of his horse. He had not understood their cold faces or why they preferred not to have any company on their travels. Uriah would later explain to him that many of the voyagers came there because they were searching for something, just as Uritus was. But while the boy had sought out the mountains in the hope of finding a community and a place where he might again put down roots, in many cases, the pilgrims sought only what they believed the mythical range might have to offer them. In their search for personal power, they rejected the only things that had any true value, and for this, they would always be empty and alone. Uritus wondered if they would ever realize this, if Basil would ever grow to understand where he had gone wrong or if he too was destined to wander aimlessly, a hollow hunger ceaselessly gnawing at his stomach which no amount of gold or influence ever stood a chance to fill.

The Adalos returned to attention as Adiadni stood to her feet beside him, prompted by the king to share her testimony. The princess moved her eyes across the faces in the crowd—Perplexus, Uriah, Nadarum and Ilya, Jasch, Pressio, Winchells and Exstarferus. Crystella and Digtrision would also have appeared if they hadn't needed to see to all five generals' duties. Many more as well would have attended the proceedings to show their support had they not been forced to leave in search of sanctuary. Dozens, hundreds, *thousands* who wished only the best for her, for her safety, for her happiness, for justice on her behalf. When she was able, in precious, fleeting moments, to forget the war, she was reminded again and again how she had everything she could ever want. She looked at Basil and felt a sudden sting in her chest. His father was not here. Suprafalo, like many, had chosen to stay far away from the path of the Shadow. Even if he had been informed as to the whereabouts of his son, it was unlikely that, in such a time, he would have bothered to make the journey. And so this man whom she had once called friend, whose ring had so briefly clung to her finger was entirely alone, and in spite of her anger, she felt sorrow for him.

"Adiadni?"

Her father prompted her a second time to begin. She cleared her throat. "The evening Basil arrived in Suscundos with his company of hired swords, he happened upon Uritus and I together in a moment of intimacy. At this time, Basil and I were, by all accounts, still engaged to be wed. Naturally, he was angered by this, and in his anger, he grabbed my arm. Uritus was quick to come to my defense, bringing himself to stand between us. It was then that..." Adiadni paused as she remembered the fear she felt during the altercation. "It was then that Basil drew his sword. He began to approach. I pulled Uritus behind me, and... accessed the Source energy that goes with me to push him back. Guards arrived then, four of them returning from the celebration," she gestured to the witnesses seated in the first row. "The rest happened quickly. They took him away. He shouted at me. I don't remember what he said."

Agamemnon nodded and turned to his right, "Basil, do you take issue with any of Adiadni's testimony?"

Basil remained silent for a moment, he and the princess sharing a prolonged glance. "I do not," he finally said.

"Very well. Uritus..."

"Wait."

The king paused, looking at his daughter, "Have you remembered something else?"

"Not exactly, I..." Another brief moment of silence. "I just wish to say that Basil and I *were* friends in our youth. We dreamed of going to battle together, of positively affecting this world together. Of course, as we have grown, we have developed our differences in values and opinions, and he has done many things that I believe to be quite detestable." The gaze of the victim did not waver from that of the accused as she made her speech, "But I do believe, in my heart of hearts, that he has never wished and still does not wish to hurt me. I admit that I have done wrong by him, and while no degree of wrongdoing could ever warrant such a barbaric response, I do not believe that I am the one who has cause for grief today. And so... I wish to rescind my case."

Hushed gasps from the crowd. A note of confusion which moved across Uritus's face. Her father hesitated only a moment before asking, "You are certain?"

She nodded confidently. "I am. The aggression Basil displayed was solely against Uritus. It is he who has the right to pursue justice for this incident. Perhaps I do as well, but..." She paused, met Basil's eye across the courtroom once more. "In light of recent events, I do not feel it particularly worthwhile to seek it."

With that, she returned to her seat, and the king nodded slowly. "Very well. Let it be known that princess Adiadni Vindella has withdrawn her case against lord Basil Dagious. So be it."

The voices of the seated observers responded, "And so it is."

Adi whispered this seal as well, sneaking another glance at the man from Vindellaria. His expression remained unmoving.

"Uritus."

"Your highness."

"Have you anything to add to Adiadni's testimony?"

He shook his head. "She has recalled everything that I remember."

"Let us then proceed to questioning."

Uritus gave a singular nod and stood. Adi moved her hand to toy with the ornament around her neck.

"The incident after the celebration was not the first time Basil has sought to harm you, is that correct?"

Uritus hesitated. He didn't know why. "Yes, that is correct."

"On how many occasions would you say he physically threatened you?"

"Only twice. Once, earlier this Summer, after the conclusion of the physical trials during the search for the Adalos, and the second time after the celebration of our return."

"Would you recall for us the events of the first incident?"

The fisherman nodded briskly, ignoring the mounting pressure from Basil's unwavering glare. "It was not entirely dissimilar to the events of the second. Adiadni sought me out after my third victory in the stable, where I was visiting my horse with my friend, Perplexus Everstone. She wished to congratulate me. Basil arrived then and, upon seeing us share an embrace... he attacked me."

News of this event had somehow, miraculously, remained out of the awareness of the public. Uritus was reminded of this as again the onlookers gasped and began silently murmuring amongst themselves until Agamemnon brought them to silence with a raise of his hand. "I understand, of course, if you do not remember the specifics of the attack, but will you share, please, the details that you do?"

Uritus hesitated again, looking briefly at Basil. "I will... Though I wish to say that, as I elected not to bring a case against Basil at the time of the first incident, I have no intention of dredging up the past and seeking vengeance now."

"Of course. I need only a record of all the evidence for the sake of arriving at a just conclusion."

"Right," the Adalos took a breath. "To my recollection... Basil grabbed me and shoved me back against the door of one of the stalls. I did my best to fight him off, but it did not take him long to get me on the ground. When he did, he fastened his hands around my throat to choke me. Adiadni tried to get him off, though she was not successful. The next thing I knew, Perplexus was back—returned after having gone for help—and guards were leading Basil away."

The king nodded and turned his attention to the accused as Uritus sat. "Basil, do you take issue with any of Uritus's testimony?"

"My accuser leaves out the part when an invisible force cast me back and away from him. I was left with a substantial bruise in its wake. Other than that, I have no addendums."

"Very well. Adiadni, as the sole witness to this event, did you observe this force that Basil recalls?"

"I did," replied the princess. "It was I who was the cause of it."

"Explain, please, what you mean."

"I mean that… while I am by no means a Wizard, and am unsure whether it even feels right to call myself a *Keeper*… as I said before, the Source goes with me. While I did not mean for anything to happen, in my fear and desire to affect the situation, it was I who caused the concussive wind that drove Basil away from Uritus. And while I'm glad I did, it was not my intention to cause Basil harm. I am remorseful for that."

"I see." Agamemnon nodded and looked again to Basil, "You may now make a case in your defense."

Basil appeared to mull over it for a moment before rising to his feet. "I see no use in denying any of the accusations made against me. These are all things I have done, and most of them I feel no regret for doing. I do, of course, feel sorry for the pain that Adiadni has been caused as a result of these events, but by her admission, I was wronged. It is not worth the effort to claim that I was justified in doing the things I did—I know the values I hold of honor and dignity are not highly valued in this court. And so, I have no defense. Imprison me, banish me, kill me if you wish. I have only done what I believe to be reasonable and I will maintain my hold on that belief."

The king nodded slowly as Basil sat and then turned once more to Uritus, "Is there anything else that you wish for me to take into consideration before I begin deliberation with my council?"

Uritus considered this. He looked from Agamemnon to the assembly of onlookers, from his friends in the crowd to the man who wished him harm. And then he looked to Adiadni, and as he did, the fog in his mind dissipated. The Adalos took a deep breath and stood. "On more than one occasion, Basil has attempted to claim my life, and in so doing, he has subjected Adiadni to danger. There is no question in anyone's mind that I am owed justice, or, at the very least, peace. If I am honest, then I must say that I am not truly afraid of Basil and I never have been. I do not view him as my enemy, merely as a man who believes himself to be cheated. Such belief has led him to behave wrongly, but I cannot say that I feel such wrongs make him undeserving of the same grace that each of us is.

"I have done… dreadful things… in my pursuit of freedom and peace for this land I love. Perhaps my actions *are* justifiable, and perhaps his are not. But I have witnessed things in these past days… horrible things. Things which may well haunt me for the rest of my days. And I tell you, I do not desire to inflict any more misery. I have seen my fair share and I wish for no part in it. My wish is for everyone… *everyone*… to be safe. Perhaps Basil still wishes me dead, but when this trial concludes, however it concludes, I will walk out of here straight to the barracks, and tomorrow straight to the battlefield, straight into the jaws of nine thousand more who also wish me dead. I do not fear death, merely a world in which men feel they have the right to bring it upon another. Determine his fate however you deem to be fair. I have greater matters on my mind than he."

"I will take all into consideration," spoke Agamemnon as Uritus returned to his seat once again. "Is there anything else anyone might wish to add?"

No one stood, and the courtroom remained silent.

"Very well. I will now convene with my council to determine an appropriate verdict." With that, the king made his way out to the veranda, the three Keepers following in a straight row behind him.

Uritus sighed tiredly and relaxed in his seat.

"I don't ever want to hear again that you are not a good speaker," Adiadni whispered.

He smiled. "I've learned a lot from you."

***

The deliberation was short. Eagerly, the people returned to attention as Agamemnon took his seat and the Keepers reclaimed their place on the wall.

The king looked across the members of the court, from the victims to the accused, and settled on the audience, "My verdict is this…"

The onlookers leaned forward in their anticipation.

"Lord Basil Dagious, guilty of all charges raised against him by his own admission, and extended grace by the victim of his crimes, shall be absolved of the burden of his guilt and released from his imprisonment. The conditions of release shall be probation from now until the end of his days. Should Basil again display physical aggression toward or intend to cause harm to Uritus Subian, he will be arrested, stripped of all ranks and titles, and imprisoned for a minimum of three years." Agamemnon turned his head to regard Uritus. "Do you accept this verdict?"

The Adalos nodded once. "I do."

"Very well." Once more, the king looked at Basil. "This is the judgment of this court. Go now in search of peace and self-improvement. May you find a steady path as you make your way home. So be it."

"And so it is."

Basil rose to his feet and made his way out of the courtroom before the seal of the people had been spoken. The doors were opened as he approached, and he departed through them without looking back.

Adiadni hastened after him. He was nearly down the stair by the time she reached the landing. "Basil!"

He ignored her, proceeding briskly to the doors of the palace.

She gathered the hem of her skirt and hurried to catch up to him. "Basil!" She raced out the door, finding him at the base of the first tier of steps with no intention of stopping. "Basil, wait."

To her surprise, he came to a stop, though he still did not turn to face her.

"Just wait a minute…" She stepped in front of him to look him in the face. She hesitated as their eyes met, searching his for a glimpse of emotion. "I know

481

you are still angry with me. I know that you probably always will be. There's nothing I can do about that. And of course, you have every right now to go and live in peace…"

"I certainly do. Now get out of my way so I might begin."

He brushed past her to continue down the steps. In the square were gathered hundreds, maybe thousands, curious about the conclusion of the trial. The palace doors opened again to make way for Uritus, who came to a stop when he saw the scene unfolding below.

"Wait!"

Basil halted again, raising his face to the clouds and sighing with irritation.

The princess bit her tongue, her mind a rushing blur. "All I ask is that you consider what is at stake." She took another couple of steps toward him. "You have not seen what we are up against, but I have. I have looked our enemy in the face, seen his sharpened teeth, felt his hot breath against my skin. I know what will happen if he is not stopped, and I know that we have a far greater chance of stopping him with the aid of your hired swords."

The moment of pause that followed had Adiadni feeling as though she might burst. Basil turned his head over his shoulder to regard her, "I do not owe this to you."

"Not to me. To them," she nodded her head to the crowd assembled below. "To the Free World and the Free People. The quality of life you enjoy, the security, you would have none of it if not for them." She saw the muscles of his jaw clench in his frustration. "I would not ask you to do this for me, but I implore you to do it for them."

To her surprise, the man from Vindellaria turned fully, lifting his head to regard her. He lingered there in silence for a moment, almost as if he was deliberating with himself the best course of action to take. Then, slowly, he climbed the steps, one after another until he stood right in front of her. "You told your father that you did not remember what I said to you when the guards took me away that night," he said. "Perhaps you were telling the truth. But I *do* remember, and I'm happy to enlighten you."

Adi swallowed, waiting in silence. Uritus felt the sudden urge to run to her and pull her away from him. He resisted.

"I told you that you would rue the day you betrayed me. Look around, Adiadni, at the bricks that construct the fair city you call home, at the blue of the sky, at the hopeful faces of the people you claim to so dearly love. The hour of your regret is nigh. When Suscundos crumbles and its people with it, when the clouds turn black and your freedom is ripped violently from your fingers, I want you to remember my face," he snarled. "Remember what you did to me. Remember the day that you made an enemy out of your greatest ally, and know that if the Free World falls, you are solely to blame for its destruction."

He turned and made his way down and away from her.

Adiadni began to feel the cold fear of failure take root in her body. Her mind swam, images of battles she'd seen and of those still to come, of bloodshed, of destruction, of Shadow, of Erclidus.

Desperate, she took one more step toward the square, shouting after him, "And if Vegard reaches the East?" Her voice was tired, gritty with emotion. "What then?"

Basil reached the bottom of the stair, holding his arms wide as he turned a final time to look at her. "Then I will stand to face them. But you're on your own, Adiadni. You will learn the things that happen when you betray the ones who love you." His crimson cape swished as he turned on his heel and vanished into the crowd.

"Basil!"

"Let him go."

Adi lifted her eyes to Uritus at the soothing touch of his hand on her arm.

"We don't need him. We've beaten the odds before."

The princess shook her head, pain steadily rising in her temples as her stress laid claim to her body. "It is not enough to assume that such a pattern will continue. Every single sword counts for something, and we just lost two thousand of them. We have no advantage, no edge. Our enemy is set to be here by tomorrow and I do not wish to consider what this land will become if Suscundos should fall..."

In the square below, the people had begun to murmur about the confrontation they had just witnessed. The masses who had filled the courtroom now began to file out of the palace to return to their duties. Adiadni looked over them all, turning her head West to regard the sky.

Uritus took a small step toward her, setting warm hands to rest firmly on her shoulders. "Suscundos will not fall," he spoke gently. "I will not allow it. I know the desire to safeguard the Free World is intrinsic to who you are. It is one of my very favorite things about you. But I remind you that the burden of this land's protection now falls to me. I will, of course, never dare to diminish the vital role you have played and will continue to play in all of this. But saving Suscundos is my responsibility now, not yours. Though I do not know how, I *will* lead her through to the break of day. The sanctity of this land will not be destroyed, not as long as I still breathe."

Adiadni pushed a long breath out through pursed lips and nodded. "You're right. You are our long-awaited Hero. Forgive me for succumbing to my fear, it was never my intention to cast doubt on your capability."

"Forget about that," he said, brushing her long hair behind her shoulders. "We're all afraid and we all do foolish things because of it at times. I may never know what guided me into the mountains, what led me to Milion and Uriah, to Suscundos, to you, what brought me back from the brink of death and allowed me to escape its clutches again and again, but I know that it will not fail me now. I love you and *I* will not fail *you*. And I am unendingly grateful for your contributions to our cause. We will see the light of dawn again, Adiadni, I swear it."

The princess lifted her face to his and kissed him, the taste of his lips like an old, familiar song. "You are the kind of man people tell stories about," she whispered. "If there is anyone who can do the impossible, it is you. As for me, I will continue to contribute however I might." She paused, looking again over her right shoulder and then returning her gaze to his once more, "I think I know what I must do."

***

The Western gate of Lorethh opened to receive the traveling soldiers who made their return from beyond the Looming Mountains. With them were thirty-nine hundred Vegardians, four dozen livestock, two dozen horses, and a dozen wagons piled high with material goods and harvested crops. The Free People were glad to welcome their new allies. While the newcomers and their spoils were seen to, Mikka and Oripidus hastened through the city in search of its commanders. They found them shortly, and the small group gathered outside the command center to overlook the goings-on of the arrival. Vulsdon, Xinna, and Azanthien were informed of the most notable events of the expedition, but Mikka had something more pressing on her mind.

"Let me begin by saying that I know I am not your general. I also have not had the opportunity to run this idea up my chain of command as my past week has been quite eventful. Know that it comes solely from me."

"And, if ye like it, from myself as well," Oripidus added.

Mikka abandoned her intention to find a smooth way to proceed, "I wish to take back Judii."

The three commanders looked at one another and Xinna chuckled, "That's quite an ask, but I like your spunk. Go on, make your case."

The soldier let out the tiniest of relieved breaths. "I have learned since returning that Vegard has advanced. That means Erclidus has gone, along with everyone of notable strength and importance. They will expect that Lorethh is the same. They do not perceive us as a threat. They do not think we have the numbers and they wouldn't assume that we'd take the unnecessary risk."

"*Do* we have the numbers?" Vulsdon asked.

"I believe we do, yes," replied Mikka confidently. "With all of yours plus the Vegardian rebels, we have over six thousand. That's more than enough, even if they send reinforcements. I cannot say how many reserves might live at the Ashen Keep, but it cannot be many. We've been there, there isn't much space, and what there is is mostly a home about half as big as Velup's ego."

"These rebels…" spoke Xinna. "They are not soldiers. They are not trained. What makes you think they will be a valuable asset in such a battle?"

The commander considered this carefully. "To speak candidly with you, I would not consider them *assets*. They are people, as noble and stouthearted as we, and they have endured much in their long wait for freedom. There was once a time when the Free People were similarly kept in a state of lack so they might remain docile. But their time has come, as has ours once again. I watched them strategize, act, organize, fight back against the hand that beats them, I watched

484

them crush it entirely. I have seen their ability. More than that I have seen their courage, and I tell you with my hand to the Divine that there are none to whom I would sooner trust my life.”

Oripidus loudly cleared his throat and Mikka chuckled. “Except for this one and the rest of our family.”

The centaur nodded gracefully. “Very well. And how might you propose we make our attack? We have little artillery at our disposal. Breaching a fortified city is not a simple task.”

“We can find something in Lorethh that can serve as a battering ram. I am under the impression that the ogres are quite strong.”

Vulsdon chuckled and offered Mikka an approving nod.

“We know it is a lot to ask,” said Oripidus. “But we’ve faced these bastards many times now. The rebels are excited, hungry to see the Light again. Let us use the inherent bloodlust of the half-alive against them. Let us draw them out and crush them while we can.”

“When this war ends, it needs to end for good,” Mikka concluded. “Not for merely five hundred more years, for *good*. Either we take out the goblins now or allow them the opportunity to retreat to Vegard when they realize they’ve lost, and I assure you, hunting them down then will be far more challenging than one more battle in the morning.”

Azanthien laughed and nodded his head. “You make a compelling case. I presume my sister will wish to take some time to discuss it…”

“No,” Xinna interrupted. “Our friends are right. We came here to contribute to the war. Let’s. If our strength is as impressive as your spirit, we may see the light of day again soon. We will go to battle with you. That is… if you would lead us. General.”

Mikka weighed the heavy title in her hand for a moment before nodding confidently. “I will. As long as I have you as my second.”

Xinna lowered her head graciously. Mikka and Oripidus shared an excited glance and hurried to pass on the news.

***

“You’re sure you don’t want me to go with you?” Pressio asked as the Sword of Light was passed into his apprehensive hands.

“I’m sure,” replied the princess. “I must do this on my own.”

Adiadni tilted her head back to regard the crowns of the dancing trees. Idor seemed taller now than it had when last she had come here.

Her cousin studied her face silently. “No one has asked you to do this…” he reminded her. “I certainly will not blame you should you elect to change your mind.”

She shook her head slowly, eyes still fixed on the towering forest. “I’ve said that I will do all I can to save us. I mean it.”

“Do you feel safe?”

She hesitated. "I do not feel that I will be in danger, but I suppose I cannot say that *safe* is the thing I do feel. But I'll be all right." She turned to face him. "When they see that I do not wish to hurt them, they will not wish to hurt me. They're misunderstood, not violent."

Pressio nodded. "I'm not worried about you. I know you are strong. I am just sorry that you have to be."

Adi furrowed her brow. "What do you mean?"

"I mean that..." The soldier sighed. "You've always been strong. Fierce. An unstoppable force of nature. But I know that those are not what you were meant to be. At least... not all."

Adiadni did not understand.

"Do not mishear me, those are intrinsic parts of you, and they are as profoundly beautiful as the rest. But I've known you your whole life, Birdie. I know that your natural state is soft and gentle and romantic and sweet. You were meant to lie in the sun and read poetry, to dance and laugh with your friends. These recent days have robbed you of that, forced you to develop calluses so you might be more resilient to face your challenges as they come. I'm sorry for that. The way you have managed to retain that softness is a wonder to me. I dream of the day that you might return to it in full."

Adi reached her arms over her cousin's shoulders to embrace him. "I love you, Press," she whispered. "This world is better with you as a part of it. So am I." She stepped back, looking again up at the whispering trees. "I don't expect to be gone long. But if I don't make it back... tell Uritus—"

"You can tell him yourself," he cut her off. "I'll see you again shortly."

She gave him a little nod in response and then stepped beyond the treeline. The Forest of Idor was as colorful and enchanting as she had remembered it to be, and her heart beat with the same energetic intensity that it had when she entered the first time. The sounds of snapping trees and rustling leaves did little to pull her attention; she offered the sudden movement of the animals startled by her presence little more than a glance. The princess had come here for one purpose and her mind was devoted solely to it. She did not walk far into the forest, knowing that however this ended, she would need to easily find her way back and out. She went only far enough that when she turned back over her shoulder, she could no longer see Pressio and their horses where they awaited her return.

She turned back around, eyes scanning the ground in front of her, identifying several clearly marked faen rings. She had promised Uritus that she would not cross into one of them unless she felt she had no other choice, and though she carried with her a message that needed to be delivered, she intended to keep such a promise.

Raising her eyes once more to the trees, Adiadni called out the name of the one she sought, "Syv!"

She waited, holding her breath and standing perfectly still. Several moments passed and the forest remained unchanging around her. "Syv!" she cried again. "I need to speak with you!"

"Well, this is an interesting surprise."

The princess spun around to see the silver-headed fae behind her.

"I admit, I did not expect to see you again after I put your friend to sleep. I take it you are here to finish what he started?"

Adi shook her head, turning slowly as Syv circled her. "I am unarmed," she told them honestly. "And while I am still devastated by Havian's loss... I have not come here to avenge him. Nor even to defend him. His fear took hold of his heart and urged him to do a foolish thing. I understand that you did only what you felt you must to protect yourself and Idor's inhabitants."

Syv chuckled, amused. "Well, if you are not here to kill me, then I take it you are a fool. You have broken the treaty once already, little princess. What could possibly constitute a second time?"

Adiadni took a breath. "I am sure you can understand that I would not be here if circumstances had not grown quite dire. The army of Shadow is proceeding to Suscundos as we speak."

"Ah, yes," the fae mused. "They attempted two days ago to breach our Western border. To no avail, of course."

"Right. It came to my attention recently that Conduits like Idor are safe from the destruction of our enemies. I am glad for that."

"Are you?"

"Yes. Everyone deserves to be free and protected. Fae and nevyn alike."

Syv ceased their circling, looking her over from head to toe as they came to a stop. "Out with it then. What have you come to ask?"

Adi took in another long breath to solidify her confidence. "By tomorrow evening, the forces that seek to destroy us will arrive before the capital city. Myself and thousands of other Free People will choose to stand in their way and fight to put a stop to this siege of our home. I know that I haven't the right to ask it, but nevertheless, I come before you as a fellow lover of this land and implore you to rise with us."

Syv remained silent for a moment before their mouth split into a cruel smile. Their laughter filled the air, spiraling up into the treetops and causing her to shiver at the fearful memories its sound carried.

"So very desperate you must be..." Syv mocked, "...to dare broach our borders again after what happened the first time. So bold to ask something as unreasonable as this..."

"I do not ask, I beg," Adiadni's voice broke as she dropped to her knees. "I know that what may happen to myself and my kin is of no concern to you. But I also know that you love this earth just as much as I do and that, though you distance yourselves from us, you do not wish to see the Free World fall."

Syv clucked their tongue, shaking their head as they regarded the desperate girl who knelt in the dirt of the forest path. "Even in an hour as dire as this, still the Free World's king cowers behind a naive child."

"He doesn't know I'm here," she admitted. "Had I told him of my plan, he would have insisted on coming in my stead. But it was I who broke the treaty and I who was foolish enough not to turn back when we had the chance. I am the one who has seen with my own eyes what we are up against. It should be no one but me who pleads with you for your forgiveness and your aid."

The silver-headed one allowed silence to settle there for a time. Adi remained on her knees, fists clenched at her sides. The fae appeared to deliberate with themself, trees rustling, birds singing, bugs buzzing around them all the while. The princess felt her heart pound in her chest and her head. Silently, she pleaded with the Divine to soften the one who held their fate in the balance. As contrary as it was to her very being, she did not allow herself to hold out hope.

"Go," Syv finally said. "Leave this place and take your war with you. Know that there will be devastating consequences if you dare return."

They vanished without a trace. Adiadni's eyes scanned the forest for the silver dragonfly, but they were nowhere to be seen. The princess had anticipated such an outcome, but still, her devastation squeezed at her heart as she rose to her feet and began to make her way out of Idor.

"Wait."

Adi turned, a startled gasp escaping her lips as she beheld those now behind her. There, where Syv had been, a row of faen beings hovered a foot above the forest floor. A dozen of them, each as radiant and stunning and ethereal as the next. "Who are you?" she asked, hesitation clear in her voice.

"We are the Fae Court," one of them replied. Her skin was as rich and deep as her voice. Tight, golden coils of hair crowned her head, the same shade as the wispy, shimmering fabric of her dress. "We have heard your plea," she continued. "Regardless of what Syv may have led you to believe, they are not the only one who speaks for the forest."

The princess looked over the Court, feeling profoundly safer with them than she ever had in Idor. "What can I do for you?"

"We believe your heart and intentions to be pure. While we will always devote ourselves first to the safekeeping of the Forest, we know that Idor cannot truly be free unless the nevyn are as well. What is it you would have us do?"

Adiadni hesitated, dumbfounded. She had not expected to make it this far. "I would not ask you to leave the safety of your home," she began. "Our enemy is fearsome and brutal. I will fight along with my people, and when the Adalos leads us to victory… no doubt, the goblins who remain will try to flee. I ask only that you stop them before they can. We cannot chance that a few of them return to a place where they might bide their time before their next attack."

The golden-headed one nodded understandingly and turned to the other members of the Court, silently communicating with them as they attempted to reach a verdict. Suddenly, there was a flash of white light, and Syv reappeared amongst the rest.

"Do not let this one's innocent face fool you," they spat. "It was she who led here the swordsman who threatened our safety."

"You know as well as we do, Syv, that you were never in any danger. Had the nevyn truly desired to cause us harm, they would have been barred from entry. Luring him into a fight he could not win was an act in direct defiance of our values."

Syv was visibly angry. "It was they who defiled the sanctity of the treaty. Do not pity them now that they have made enemies stronger than they."

"The enemy of the Free World is the enemy of us all. What good is an idyllic separatist society if all that surrounds us should turn to ash?"

Syv scoffed. "All the nevyn do is bring destruction."

"Perhaps. Nevertheless, we will settle this matter as we always do—by putting it to a vote." The voice of the Fae Court turned her attention to the rest, "All those in favor of offering the Free World our aid..."

Tears gathered in the eyes of the princess as twelve sure hands rose into the air.

"And those opposed..."

All turned to Syv. They shook their head frustratedly and rather than responding, transformed into the shape of the swift silver bug and darted away.

"The vote is affirmative," declared the golden-headed one. "When the enemy seeks to make their retreat, Idor will stand in their way."

"Thank you," Adiadni breathed. "I will not forget this. May you be abundantly blessed from this day forward."

The fae lowered her head to the princess and then she and the rest of the Court disappeared as though they were never there. With joyous tears streaking down her face, Adiadni departed from the forest.

***

"What's the matter with you?"

Mikka looked up suddenly at Punznes, who sat on the opposite side of a long wooden table. She shook her head. "Nothing's the matter..."

"Bullshit."

"Bullshit," parroted the raven.

"You've been off since Nott. What's bothering you?"

The mess hall was noisy around them, full of anxious soldiers who awaited the battle that would take place at dawn. Mikka sighed, knowing that even if she tried, she had no chance of convincing the physician that his instincts were incorrect. "It's trivial. But try as I might, I cannot stop thinking about what Ouro said when I spoke to him."

The conversation drew Tris's attention from where she sat to Mikka's right. "What did he say?"

Mikka sighed again, not wishing to revisit the words that had haunted her since then. "This might be silly..." she began tentatively. "But I feel as though... he cursed me."

Tris took in a frightened breath and Punznes furrowed his brow. "What do you mean?"

"I mean…" Mikka threw her head back dramatically and stared up at the ceiling. "I mean…" She lowered it again, eyes passing over the soldiers and family who surrounded her. "He spoke to me as though he *was* cursing me."

"What did he say?" Tris asked gently.

"I don't remember exactly. He said that bad things would befall both myself and the Free World. That everyone I love will die and then I will with them."

The dark-haired woman reached out a caring hand and set it atop hers.

"You killed him, Mik…" Punznes reminded her.

"*We* did."

"Right. *We* killed him, and then we burned the village to the ground. We left nothing untouched, not on the grounds and not in his laboratory. When we did that, the curse on Agamemnon was broken."

"Who told you that?"

"Azanthien. But listen: if a curse as strong and unshakable as that was broken, they *all* were broken. Ouro cannot touch you from beyond the grave."

Mikka nodded as though she were trying to convince herself. "You're right. And I want that to be enough, Punzie, I do, but…" she trailed off, bringing her left hand to pinch the bridge of her nose.

Tris and Punznes shared a glance and the rebel scooted closer to the general, bringing her free hand to rest on her back. "It's perfectly reasonable to feel such fears at a time like this," she spoke soothingly. "You've been so strong for all of us. And while you may not be right about the curse, you *are* correct to be afraid of the many who seek to take your life. I'm still learning how to be at peace, even in the quieter moments. It will likely take years for any of us to be able to shake the grips of such trauma. But brighter days *will* come again, Mikka. I didn't believe that before I met you, but I do now. And now I cannot let you forget."

The general smiled, raised her friend's hand, and kissed it, thanking her.

"And Mik…" The physician reached a hand across the table to hold Mikka's other. "If we die… *When* we die… we just become part of all this…" He waved his free hand vaguely around the air above the room. "When you remember that, there's nothing to be afraid of, really."

Mikka smiled at him and squeezed his hand. By this point, Laivar and Oripidus had become aware of the conversation and the state of their general's heart. They looked at each other, silently deliberating how they might help. Oripidus nodded his head toward the room and Laivar looked around. The rebels were tired, the others, nervous. And why wouldn't they be? The eve of battle was never a particularly jovial event. Laivar knew the privilege he had as an archer who would remain on the wall, far away from the heart of the fight. At this moment, he wished more than anything to alleviate the burdens of those around him. So, in true bardic fashion, he wiped his mouth with a cloth, climbed up to stand atop the table, and began to wax,

"On the eve of destruction
In this fair sky of ours,
Hidden sun, blackened moon, bits of coal for our stars.
Bravest heroes would wonder,
Could it all be for naught?
But something far greater they had all but forgot.

Purple crocus in springtime,
Golden harvest in June,
And when the skies clear, oh, the sight of the moon!
Treasures just out of reach
Like the warmth of the sun
But in heroes' hearts, something new has begun.

Hot sparks have been lit
Like the flick of a match.
Twinkling like fireflies eager to be catch'd.
Just the warm breath of life
And some fodder for kindling,
And all at once, wildfire is only beginning.

Let it burn white and hot,
Let it burn villains down.
When it's done, what remains is the fertile new ground.
Plant the seeds of your brother,
Water them with warm blood.
May the harvest be rich like a heavenly flood.

Then heroes will remember
What they came here for,
To banish the Shadow, shut and bar the door.
We'll look around then,
Beaten hearts in our hands,
And strangely enough, we will begin to dance.

There'll be snow in December,
Wildflowers in May.
We'll forget all about when dark threatened the day.
A new generation
Of heroes shall bloom.
In their sparkling bright eyes, we'll see light of the moon.

With sun on our faces
And wind at our backs,
We'll polish our porcelain, lay gold in its cracks.
Our heart's map will
Guide our feet on straight and true.
We'll tell stories, share peaches, someday feel brand new.

Though Shadow tried to stop us
We never would break.
We are light reflecting from the shimmering lake.
And we'd relive each moment,
Be they battered or scarred,
For our blood and our breath and the light of the stars."

Chapter Thirty-Two

"Adalos"

Cold water dripped from Uritus's face and trickled down his arms as he gripped the edges of his washbasin. The night before, he had reluctantly accepted a sleeping potion from Aurena. It worked some, but only for a few hours, and the Adalos found himself wide awake long before the sun or the rest of Suscundos. He'd saddled Moonracer and gone on a long ride South, no particular destination in mind. The morning air and company of his horse did help clear his head a bit. When they returned to the stable, Uritus took his time brushing Moonracer's shiny coat. The animal could tell that something was wrong, and the man tried to soothe him and assure him that he had nothing to fear.

"You will be safe here with the others," he told him. "I'm sure it would do much for my confidence if I had you with me. But you are not a war horse and I do not wish for you to be one. We can ride anywhere you want once this is done."

Now, again in his chamber, the Adalos struggled to get a grip. *They're counting on you*, he reminded himself. *They look to your example.* But no attempt at self-motivation could change the fact that Uritus was no more a creature of war than his horse. While he would continue to persevere through all that was thrown at him, if he was honest with himself, he didn't know how much more he could take.

The door to his chamber opened and shut with hardly a sound. He lifted his head at the faint click of the latch. *Perplexus.* They greeted one another with silent nods and the fisherman found a towel to dry his face.

"The Shadow can be seen from the wall," spoke Perplexus after a time. "They'll be here shortly after sundown."

Uritus nodded, not sure what to say. He crossed the room and pulled his shirt over his head, his mind swimming. Acting as first general was intimidating enough without the king there to bear witness to his victories and defeats. The battlefield would be a waking nightmare even without his brother on the other side. The fisherman was halfway through lacing up his second boot when he became aware of how stiflingly silent the room was. This would not have been out of the ordinary were it not for his best friend's presence there with him; everyone who knew and loved Perplexus was well aware of his difficulty remaining still and silent.

"Are you feeling okay?" Uritus lifted his head to regard the navigator where he leaned with his back against the door.

Perplexus shrugged and forced a smile, but his glassy eyes betrayed the state of his heart. "Oh, you know… Never gets easier."

The crack in his voice mirrored the state of Uritus's heart, and he hurried to wrap his arms around his friend. "Of course it doesn't," he said sadly. "You've been so rock-solid through all of this. I don't know how you do it."

"*Unshakable* is my surname," replied the navigator with a chuckle. "Seriously though… it's because of you. *For* you, really. I said long ago that I would do all I could to help you. I meant it. Even if that means being delusional in my belief that we'll make it through."

"You're a good man, Lex," Uritus said, one hand holding the back of Perplexus's neck. "And an even better friend, somehow. Every victory I lay claim to is yours as much as it is mine."

The commander and general shared a smile and Perplexus set his hand atop Uritus's shoulder with a sigh. "I can't imagine how hard this is for you. The responsibility, the visibility, the exhaustion, the fear. You are as resilient as they come. You've witnessed so much, felt so much, for yourself and all those beneath you. And having to do it all with the knowledge that the enemy is your brother…"

"*You* are my brother," spoke Uritus ardently. "It is you who have been at my side this whole time, it is *you* who has never left. How could I feel anything but sure when I have you with me?"

The door to the room pushed open and bumped into the navigator's back.

"Sorry… I can come back later—"

Perplexus laughed, opened the door all the way, pulled Adiadni into the room with them, and kicked it shut again. "You've come just in time. We're being emotional."

"Perfect," she replied, wrapping her arms around their backs as they did the same to her. "I am here for just the same purpose."

Uritus planted a soft kiss atop her head. "I must admit, I feel quite nervous to act as general a rank above your father."

"You needn't. He knows his place, and yours. I've no doubt he had a far harder time passing off responsibility to me than to you."

"How did he take it when you told him of your little excursion yesterday?"

Adi winced comically and the two men laughed. "He was not happy to hear that I went on my own, though the positive result of my brief adventure softened the news. But how are the two of you? Still holding on?"

Uritus looked at Perplexus and the navigator shrugged, "I consider the fireworks that will light the sky upon our victory, the music we will enjoy, the food we will share. Holding out hope for the return of little joys helps, I think."

"That, and the recognition of the little joys already in our grasp," added Uritus, squeezing his friends tighter. "Like this one."

Adiadni made a satisfied sound and Perplexus asked her, "What about you?"

"Little joys help," she confirmed. "The thing which will make the biggest difference today, though, is staying far away from the Eastern gate."

"Has Basil's company left yet?"

"Not quite, though they've begun to assemble. Winchells expects they'll be on their way once they've had their midday meal. And good, I want them to be well-fed before their journey. I just… don't wish to see them, if I can avoid it."

The two men nodded understandingly.

"But I also do not wish to be consumed by my anger with Basil. There are far more valuable things fighting for my attention. On that note," she stepped back from their tight circle, taking their hands in her own. "Are we ready to face the day?"

Perplexus looked at the Adalos who gave a confident nod, and the three friends departed from the room.

***

"Occupants of Judii! The hour of your end is nigh! Come out and face us or prepare to be besieged!"

Xinna's voice remained powerful and clear despite having repeated this call for over an hour. She stood with her brother at the front of their company, two thousand centaurs and ogres armed and ready to fight. They were certain that those in Judii were aware of their threats.

Periodically, new goblins would peer over the wall only to vanish again without speaking a word. Those who patrolled along the rampart did not move from their posts, though they did turn to regard the Free People every time the second general sent up her call.

Mikka kept watch from her place on Lorethh's wall, not yet willing to accept that they may need to adjust their approach.

"Just let me go," Oripidus urged her. "We've given them long enough!"

The general sighed, annoyed with herself for not deciding beforehand how long they would wait before enacting their backup plan. "Not just yet…"

The commander grumbled, anxious to reclaim the land that had been stolen from them. "The longer we wait, the more time we allow them to organize their counterstrike. Let us rather take them by surprise!"

Mikka chewed on her cheek, knowing he had a point. "Just a few more minutes," she assured him. "I believe that if we are patient, it will…"

She dropped the last of her sentence and squinted as she tried to determine whether Judii's gate was truly opening or if it was merely her imagination. A few more seconds proved her right—finally, Vegard had chosen to respond.

A wave of energy moved through the fighters on the ground. Xinna raised her hand to tell them to wait. Out of Judii's Southern gate poured a stream of foul-smelling gray-skinned soldiers who assembled in rows opposite the Free People. A mounted general exited last.

The gate was shut, and the three officers on the ground squinted as they regarded him. They could not be sure, as he was plated in armor from head to toe, but Xinna and Vulsdon and Azanthien each would have been willing to swear that he was a human.

Mikka addressed the rider who landed on the rampart, "How many?"

"About thirteen hundred on the ground, more still in Judii," he replied. "It's difficult to say the exact amount, but I'd wager they've no more than a thousand reserves. We far outnumber them."

The general nodded approvingly, glad for this confirmation of what they had suspected. She turned to Oripidus, "Go down and make ready. I'll send word when it's time."

He nodded and descended from the rampart to join his squadron.

When the last of the goblins had assembled, Xinna drew her sword and thrust it proudly above her head. "Invaders of the Free World!"

The centaurs drew their swords and scraped their hooves against the ground and the ogres clutched their clubs and hammers and axes.

"In the name of king Agamemnon Vindella and this land we call home, we banish you to the grave!"

Azanthien called the charge. With a deafening cry, the Free People stormed forward into battle. The goblins charged as well, and the two opposing forces collided with the sound of thundering steps and clashing steel.

Mikka set a hand against her chest and took in a shaky breath.

***

As the Shadow drew ever nearer to the setting sun, Uritus climbed the steps to join Uriah atop the North-and-West tower of Suscundos's outer wall.

The first wave of the king's army assembled in the Clearing—the king and princess with them—and the rest took their places within and atop the outer wall. It had been a long day of anxious anticipation which only intensified when it was announced that the Shadow was nearing the Eastern border of the Forest of Idor. The Adalos looked on, pounding heart, pounding head, as the first of the enemy soldiers came into view around the treeline.

"It is time," said Uriah seriously.

Uritus nodded, his attempts at steady breathing proving futile.

The Wizard's hand found its way to his pupil's shoulder and the two met eyes. "You are the very best of this world," Uriah spoke with a loving smile. "New generations will be born of those you save. Years from now, when you and I are long gone, the stories they tell of you will capture only a fragment of your goodness and bravery. I am honored to witness your legacy as it is written and I am honored to fight at your side."

The fisherman returned his smile. "I wish I had words to express how grateful I am to you for—"

Uriah cut him off with a gentle shake of his head. "I know your gratitude. You can tell me later. It is they who need your words most now."

The Wizard turned his gaze to the people below and Uritus did the same. He nodded slowly as he looked them over, silently considering how to best encourage them. He moved to the rampart's edge and reached for one of the erect flags. Taking it in his hand, he raised himself to mount the parapet, one foot in its embrasure, the other set atop the coping. He did not see it, but behind him, Uriah raised his staff to produce a bright white light, and this drew the eyes of the soldiers on the ground. Uritus did not notice when the sun dipped behind the dark.

"When I was just a boy, still living in Tosh, I dreamed of coming to Suscundos one day."

The echo of his voice called to attention the last of the Free People.

"I wasn't sure if I would ever make it here," he continued. "But when I finally did, I was astounded to learn that this fair city is everything and more than I had read of in books. The people here are brilliant, generous, and kind. I was welcomed with open arms and I quickly discovered that your hospitality extends to all those who are welcomed into your gates. It was in Suscundos that I chose to step fully into my destiny as the Adalos. It was in Suscundos that I met the other part of myself."

On the ground, teary-eyed Adiadni smiled and touched a hand to her heart.

"Though I have not known this city for long, I love her with every breath I have to give. She is the steady beating heart of this gorgeous land of ours and I will protect her until the heart in my chest becomes still!"

Rousing cheers met him. When they subsided, the sound of marching footsteps could be heard growing ever closer.

"I am afraid today. And I know you are as well. These days of suffocating darkness have challenged us all. In many ways, they have revealed to us who we truly are. And while we are tired and anxious and bloody terrified, we are more than that even still. We are compassionate and creative. We share all we have, as little as it may be. We lay down our pride and our stubbornness for the sake of our brethren, and even when we have all but nothing left to give, still we give anyway. I have seen the ways the Free People have responded in the face of such terror, and my heart swells with pride when I consider how nothing, not Shadow nor bloodshed nor famine nor drought has come anywhere close to breaking our indelible spirit.

"Now, Shadow is here, and it will seek, as it has, to wipe us out. Every one of us, down to our last spark. But I have gone to the hopeless place and friends, I tell you that even there, I have seen the Light. I have held it in the palm of my hand; followed it into the dark. Though I am finite of body and fickle of faith, still I have chosen to trust it. And it burns and it burns and it burns, hot and fearless, determined and wild, and *nothing*—not even the cruel hand of the enemy—stands a chance of stopping it. It will continue to burn long after we are gone. And those of us who will go forth today and depart from this mortal plane will be wrapped in it, and it will burn all the brighter, fueled by the love which drove our sacrifice."

The enemy forces grew steadily nearer. The Adalos kept his focus on his people, Suscundos's blue flag whipping in the air above him all the while.

"My name means courage. I've always known that. But until I came here, I never considered what that meant for me. I do not feel brave most days. But my father once told me that courage is not the absence of fear. Courage is daring to look your fear straight in the face and tell it that it does not own you. Shadow does not own me!" The soldiers roused and Uritus drew his sword and thrust it toward the sky. "Vegard does not own me! Fear does not own me! And though its grip on my heart may grow all the more crushing, still I will stand! Still, I will fight! And still, I will give all that I am able for the sake of this land and this people without whom I would be nothing!

"Friends, our midnight is here. And I cannot say how long it will last, but I swear to you that the Light *will* find us again. Our children will bathe in it, drink it up like water, know its face with the same familiarity as their family and their friends. One day, the Shadow will be all but a distant memory; one day, nothing more than the villain of a bedtime story. Our legacy will be that of a people who shine with all the radiance and color of the dawn. Cling to hope, keep the faith, stay your steady course. And hold on till sunrise."

As the Adalos descended to the rampart, he was bathed in glorious noise. The Free People were hungry for their liberation and it was clear in their zealous cry. Uritus sheathed his sword and drew his bow as he turned his attention to the encroaching horde. Any moment now.

The soldiers on the ground could feel the faint rumbling of goblins' boots as they drew near. The horses began to grow restless. Nadarum spoke gentle words to his stallion from his place on the frontline and stroked his neck. All those who made up the first wave felt as though their breaths were collective, and each one found a bit of solace in this.

"Draw your weapons!"

The army responded to the command of the king. Emipera felt light and dynamic in Adiadni's grasp, and the sense-memory of making ready for battle caused her heart to pick up speed.

"Stay near me," she urged her father and Jasch behind her. "I'm stronger with my tokens. I'll be able to protect you."

Agamemnon turned his head to smile down at his child. "You are hope embodied. Watching you as you have learned and grown has been the great joy of my life."

Adiadni swallowed, her throat tight. "There are many joys still to come. You cannot leave yet. I need you here still."

"We're not going anywhere," Jasch assured her. "Nowhere but into the glorious future you pave for us."

"We will keep you safe just as you will us," said the king. "The only way any of us get out of this is with each other."

The princess nodded and readied herself for the charge.

The last of the enemy soldiers came into view from beyond the trees. Erclidus was their only general, sitting tall in the saddle of his powerful black horse. The goblins assembled in rows and came to a stop before emitting a wretched cry of war.

The Free People responded in kind, shouting without prompt from their leaders. The sound of them shook the earth, and when the noise subsided, deep peals of thunder cracked overhead. There passed a strained breath of anticipatory quiet.

The army of Shadow charged.

Uritus watched intently, waiting for the right moment to give the order. He felt his heart in his throat, the aching of the viraglas in his eyes. The enemy closed in on the Free People but still, the Adalos waited, relying on his instinct to make clear the opportune moment.

"Now."

"Do it now!"

This call echoed down the wall to the South-and-West tower, and both Veldis and Uriah were quick to respond. Two bright balls of flame soared into the sky and then barreled down hot and fast to the edges of the battlefield. As they crashed to the ground, the first of the traps laid out for the invaders was activated.

A series of small explosions rang out and the earth gave way, a long strip of land collapsing into a wide ditch. The bottom of this ditch was lined with rows of long, wooden spikes. As the momentum of the goblins carried them forward, those unfortunate enough to be caught behind the ditch fell into it and were impaled. In the subsequent chaos, the enemy became disoriented, over half of them forced to stop behind the Cropidean trap.

King Agamemnon seized this moment to call the Free People to action. They rushed forward, the cavalry leading the charge. Suscundos's soldiers crashed into the swarm of invaders like a wave upon the sand, and just like that, the battle for the capital began.

The infantry slowed as they drew near to the fight, waiting to meet the goblins who squeezed through the line. Adiadni felt the effects of Aurena's pre-war elixir coursing through her veins. When she spotted the first of the half-alive who raced toward her, she did not hesitate to meet them.

The Sword of Light swished through the air with speed and grace. After each body she slayed, the princess's eyes darted to her father and her friend, keeping watch on them always to ensure that they were safe. Agamemnon and Jasch had never before seen battle, but both had trained extensively for this very purpose and both were as skilled of warriors as anyone would have expected them to be.

This diversion in Adiadni's attention, however—as fleeting as it was—quickly proved to be a threat to her safety. With a swift parry and a strong backhand, a large goblin sent the princess flailing to the ground.

She crawled forward to retrieve her sword and flipped herself onto her back. Before she could raise her blade to defend herself, another burst through the armor on the goblin's chest.

He collapsed to the ground with a howl and died, and in his wake, Adiadni saw her father.

He helped her to her feet. "We'll be all right. Keep your gaze ahead."

The princess nodded and rushed back into the fray.

The stall of the advance of his army drew Erclidus to the front of the line where he cursed when he observed the cause of the delay. The ditch was deep and wide, stretching from North to South as far as he could see. Some of the goblins had already begun to hasten around the great barrier, but the young general knew that to send all of them this way would be an unnecessary waste of time.

Remaining in his saddle, Erclidus stretched his arms out at his sides. He focused his energy, rotated his hands to face the Shadow above, and, with a laborious cry, raised them upward.

The ground in the ditch moved as his arms did, rumbling and rising until it was level with the rest of the Clearing. Most of the spikes were covered by the dirt and rock; the rest rose and toppled to the ground as the earth settled into place. The corpses of the goblins impaled at the bottom of the ditch were buried in the rubble. When Erclidus's task was done, the rest of the half-alive charged forth.

Uritus witnessed this with gritted teeth. Fearfully, his eyes scanned the Clearing in search of Adiadni. He spotted her cutting through the rotten river like she had been a fighter for a hundred years.

Ilya called orders to the marksmen who expertly shot down any goblins who drew near to the wall. The battle raged on, Suscundos's army beating back against the persistent onslaught.

In time, the Adalos saw them begin to be driven back.

"I'm going out," he called to Uriah, hastening down the rampart for the stairs.

This call was passed along the wall, and when he reached the ground where the second wave was gathered, Perplexus was waiting there for him alongside Crystella and Pressio. The navigator offered him a bright smile. He returned it, feeling his heart somewhat comforted.

"Noble warriors!" he cried out as he drew his sword. "This is the hour we have long awaited! Let us follow in the footsteps of our ancestors and crush the oppressor where he stands! Let us show them the true spirit of the Free People!"

The sound of the opening gate was drowned out by the earth-shaking war cry sent up by the soldiers. Uritus and Perplexus shared a final grounding glance and the Adalos led the charge out to the field.

The Wizards on the wall realized that the fiery onslaught they had fought off in the Mirrored Cities showed no sign of arriving now. Both Veldis and Uriah lowered their defenses and set to work activating the next of their planned tricks.

Sudden flashes of color above her head brought a smile to Adiadni's face and strengthened her resolve. Dozens of vibrant projections sprang to life on the battlefield. The goblins didn't know what hit them.

The figures were varied in color, shape, and size, and they burned when they struck their targets. In truth, these projections did no more lasting harm to the enemy than they had to the contestants during the Trial of the Arrow, but the pain was all the same, and the disorientation that the flashes of bright dust caused amongst Vegard's forces offered the Free People a crucial advantage.

The soldiers cheered as the rainbow of relief appeared and the second wave rushed into the fight with a heightened sense of vigor.

The blade in Uritus's hand carved the way. The Adalos fought like a true champion, wasting no time felling each enemy in his path with ease. The cavalry and infantry already in the field fought on with renewed strength as they glimpsed the golden flashes of light glinting off the Sword of Fire.

The goblins continued to close in, but the Free People held their ground. They had a long night ahead of them, but they clung to their faith, emboldened by the hope of the future that would bloom from this hallowed ground. Another deep rumble of thunder sounded from above. In a sudden torrent, it began to rain.

***

"I'm going out with the second wave. When you see that our victory is imminent, send word down to Rip and the reserves."

Laivar nodded to the general between fired shots. "Stay safe out there. I don't want you getting overconfident and taking needless risks."

Mikka grinned. "You know me too well, Laiv. I promise to keep my wits about me. I'll see you soon."

She vanished down the steps and the poet sighed shakily as he attempted to focus. From the ground below, he could hear Mikka's cries of passion, stirring up the warriors who would charge into the fight with her. The general was one of the most dauntless and determined people he knew. Again and again since they departed from home, she jumped fearlessly headfirst into each challenge that came their way, proving time after time that, though she had left the king's army years before, she had never ceased being a soldier. And now, she was here, the truest iteration of herself, a force, a leader, a golden-hearted victor, and still it made his stomach churn every time she left him to engage in the fight. Laivar prayed to the Mother for her protection as Lorethh's gate opened and Mikka led the second wave onto the battlefield.

Tris was immediately overwhelmed by the scale of the conflict, but she put her head down and kept her focus on her goal.

One foe at a time.

Once in the thick of the fight, she was comforted by the presence and strength of the warriors from Tila. Joining the first wave were the remaining five hundred ogres along with five hundred centaurs and five hundred Vegardian rebels. The stronger fighters kept the novices safe, and the people from the West,

501

inexperienced as they were, were fueled by their devotion to one another and this new land that had welcomed them with open arms.

But the king's forces were not the only ones with new swords to spare. Shortly after the newcomers settled into their stride, Judii's gate opened and a flood of bloodthirsty goblins raced to join the action.

Mikka cursed when she saw them, more rotten soldiers than she would have expected Vegard to have to spare. Furiously, she fought her way to the wall, and her nearby troops followed her example.

The goblins on the rampart fired down a steady stream of arrows as the Free People drew near, inconsistent in their accuracy but numerous enough to still prove a hindrance. The general did not allow this to discourage her. They were so close to their victory that she could feel it in her bones, the taste of it as cool and sweet as spring water.

She felt no pain despite the numerous strikes dealt to her body by her enemies. There was much still to be done, but witnessing the fall of goblin after goblin fanned the flames of her determination. Mikka felt invincible, and such confidence drove her further into the thick of battle.

Then, something sounded overhead, a whoosh of wind, a crash.

The Free People lifted their eyes to witness the hurtling of projectiles from Judii's wall. Laivar watched in horror as the trebuchet was engaged. They had been foolish not to consider that the enemy would seek to utilize the offensive tools left behind in the wake of Judii's fall.

The bard felt helpless as he watched bits of wood, rock, and metal crash down upon the people who waged war on the battlefield. He continued wielding his bow, firing arrows at the half-alive only when his shot was undeniably clear, muttering prayers for protection over his people all the while.

An ogre was quick to yank Tris out of the way of a hurtling hunk of stone and she screamed as the projectile bashed in the head of an advancing goblin.

The steady pelt of debris from above added a new level to the chaos and disorientation of the fight. All she could do was react to the dangers that came her way.

Suddenly, her focus shifted from furthering the cause to simply fighting to survive. A goblin launched a spear in her direction. She leapt out of the way only to be immediately forced to parry an incoming blade.

Three times she defended herself against this assault before she was finally able to slay her adversary.

This pattern continued, repeating like the choreographed steps of a dance, and the rebel felt herself grow weary. Every muscle in her body ached, her brain nearly overwhelmed by the brutal violence exploding all around her. Still, she fought on, knowing that no matter how this concluded, there was no other cause to which she would more willingly give her life.

Mikka's frustration with the apparent turn of the tide made her an even more aggressive fighter. While Vegard had not succeeded in pushing the Free People back, they had put a stop to the steady crawl of their approach with the addition of the new soldiers and the cropidus-built weapon.

The ogres who bore the heavy stone column that they would use to bash in the gate had made little progress. Every few steps they took, they were forced to halt and confront the swarms of goblins who sought to stop them. The mental connection shared by the half-alive ensured that every time one of them was slain, another rose to take their place. They were not intelligent creatures, but they were built for war. Try as they might, the ogres struggled to make it past their regenerative blockade.

Mikka saw this and called to Azanthien, "We need to clear their path!"

The centaur responded immediately, racing to meet the general ahead of the column-bearers. He wielded his greatsword with strength and ease. With his help, and that of several others who caught wind of the general's plan, the ogres began to move steadily forward. Mikka felt reinvigorated by their progress and clung to her faith that the end was in sight.

Finally, after what felt like hours of ceaseless attacks, Tris withdrew her sword from the body of a goblin and found herself with a moment to rest. She whipped her head around in search of her next target and her eyes landed on an intense conflict not far away.

A crash of falling debris exploded on the ground, and when the dust cleared, the rebel watched as an arrow, loosed from the bow of one of her comrades, pierced through the upper arm of Vegard's mounted general.

The force of the blow knocked him from his saddle. He hit the ground, helmet tumbling from his head. Tris squinted, and as he rose to his feet, she saw that her suspicion had been correct.

Vegard's general was none other than Trugstar, the man who had ruled over her home village with a brutal, crushing fist.

The fire of rage roared in her chest. Before she knew what was happening, she found herself barreling across the battlefield toward him.

With an ear-splitting cry, she raised her sword and swung it down at him with all the force she could muster.

Trugstar raised his own just in time to deflect her blow.

The rebel was relentless, launching attack after attack, her fury growing with each slash of her blade. The beatings he had inflicted on her and his other captives were as fresh and vivid in her mind as they had ever been. The scale of the misery he caused was too great for her to quantify. The mighty craving for vengeance pushed her harder, made her stronger. Trugstar stood no chance.

With an elegant swing of her blade, Tris knocked his from his hand, and one final flourish plunged it deep into his chest.

He sucked in a breath, eyes widening as the life drained from his face.

"For the people of Enk," she spat. "May your suffering be tenfold what you dealt upon us."

The rebel yanked her sword from his ribcage and Trugstar collapsed into a lifeless heap in the dirt.

Tris released a shaky sigh, stunned by her strength.

But her moment of silent victory was cut abruptly short. She felt a pain, searing, sharp, pierce through her back, and she gasped, breath knocked out of her lungs. The grip of her fingers around her hilt loosed and her sword dropped from her hand.

She lowered her head to regard her body and saw, protruding from her stomach, the unmistakable point of an enemy arrow.

Her mind became suddenly a white, dizzying haze. She managed to take only a single step before her legs gave out and she dropped face-down upon the battlefield.

The scream emitted from the depths of Mikka's belly as she witnessed Tris's fall tore her throat and split the ears of all near her.

Desperately, she fought her way to her, caring not that she was forced to abandon her post. She dropped to her knees as she reached Tris's side, tears coursing down her cheeks, pleading with the rebel to be all right. She rolled her onto her side and pushed her dark hair away from her face with shaky, tender hands.

"You've got to wake up," she said through tears. "You can't leave us yet, Tris, we need you too much."

Tris did not respond and, frighteningly close to hopelessness, Mikka lifted her body into her arms and began to carry her back to Lorethh. The soldiers around her paved her way, slaying all enemies who sought to take her down. The general paid no mind to the arrows that whizzed past her head, the explosions of dirt and rock as flying projectiles struck the ground. She kept her eyes fixed fast on the city as she drew nearer, trying and failing to regulate her breath as the limp body of her friend grew ever colder in her arms.

Laivar called for the gate to be opened as he spotted the general making her steady approach, and he hurried down to meet her.

Two medic's assistants were there when Mikka entered, and they took Tris's body out of her arms and rushed her to the infirmary.

Mikka watched them leave, tears burning in her eyes, breaths catching in her throat. She collapsed to her knees as the bard reached the ground and called her name.

"I can't do it anymore, Laiv," she sobbed, breaths frighteningly short. "Havian alone was too great of a loss. Then Seryc and now Tris…"

"She'll be fine," he tried desperately to reassure her. "Let Punzie do his part, he won't let her die."

"It isn't up to him!" Mikka cried, inconsolable. "It doesn't matter what he does, what I do, what any of us do. The Free People are bleeding and we can't do *anything* but sit here and watch…"

"Snap out of it!" Laivar shouted, taking her by the shoulders. "It doesn't help anyone to give in to your hopelessness!"

She met his eyes, sorrowfully shaking her head. "I don't have it in me to watch any more die."

"Then don't simply watch. Get on your fucking feet and do something about it!"

"But nothing that I do is ever enough…"

"Fuck that, Mik. Nothing any one of us does could ever be enough. Do you think I don't feel bloody helpless witnessing our soldiers drop in droves? If we submit to the fickle fragility of our feelings then we may as well just lay down and let Shadow lay claim to all we hold dear. Damn our feelings and damn our fear. Our work is not done and I'll be damned before I let you surrender to the dark." Laivar rose and extended an open palm to his friend. "Now. On your fucking feet."

With a pained sigh, Mikka took his hand and allowed him to help her up and the two hastened together back through the gate and onto the battlefield.

***

Uritus feared the way the storm would add to the difficulty of the fight, but the Sword of Fire remained strong and true in his right hand.

Even the largest of the goblins were no match for the sacred weapon, and he soon noticed that the enemy soldiers had ceased coming after him, rather electing to stay out of his way. This freed the Adalos to devote himself fully to the offensive and he dove into this opportunity as if he were invincible.

With each soldier he saved from an attack they did not see coming, he stepped further into his calling. Though he did not imagine that he would ever feel bold enough to call himself a *Hero*, as the eyes of his troops looked to him with gratitude, he came to realize that he undoubtedly was.

Pressio and Perplexus discovered that together, they made an effective team. The foresight of Crystella's first commander balanced the unchecked fearlessness of Uritus's, and they were emboldened by their collective success as they fought their way across the battlefield.

Pressio called to Perplexus to duck, knocking an incoming spear away just in time; Perplexus ran for a goblin who charged toward them, sliding forward on his knees and swinging his sword in a broad arc to slice into his gut. Together, the two men were unbeatable, and they allowed this knowledge to spur them on.

As Nadarum rode deeper into the thick of enemy forces, he identified that Erclidus was not advancing with the rest of them, neither fighting nor defending but rather looking over the battle as it played out from his seat high up in his saddle. The horseman wasn't sure why the general was electing not to get involved, not to rain down a firestorm upon Suscundos the way he had in Judii. Presumably, he was merely saving his power until the time came to unleash it, but the reasoning didn't matter. He was near enough and vulnerable, and Nadarum had a clear shot.

He urged his horse forward, snatching up a spear from the hands of a goblin as he went. The horseman raised the weapon, harnessed all his strength, and launched it across the Clearing toward his target.

Erclidus, heightened of senses and perception, became aware of the hurtling spear a split second before it arrived.

He was quick to react, deflecting the powerful weapon with a flick of his wrist.

But the sudden shock of this, as well as an explosion of colorful dust on the ground just ahead of him, startled the general's great black horse, and as he reared, Erclidus was cast to the ground anyway.

The fight grew dense around Nadarum, forcing him to stop his advance, but he smirked to himself, knowing that though the throw of the spear had failed, he had succeeded in his goal nonetheless.

Erclidus rose to his feet with an aggravated groan and drew his sword. With one brutal hand, he wielded his blade, with the other, he cast his wicked spells. Fire and shockwaves spilled from his fingertips. Easily, he disarmed any who dared rise against him. His army of half-alive fought on around him, excited by the destruction he wrought.

Agamemnon became aware of this advance, turning his head as he heard the terrified screams of his soldiers and catching his first glimpse of the fabled foe who had caused endless torment to his daughter and his people.

He swished his longsword this way and that, a deep gash cut into the back of one goblin, the decapitation of another. With the courage of his ancestors fueling his heart, the king made his steady advance toward the enemy.

Adiadni saw him move, discerned his intentions, and screamed at him to stop. Whether he simply did not hear her or chose to ignore her, she did not know. But certain that her father was underestimating what he was up against, she dodged the aggressive swing of a club and raced across the Clearing to beat him there.

Agamemnon soon came upon his target. He bided his time for several moments, slaying goblins as he studied the way the Sorcerer's apprentice fought.

Erclidus would cast to disarm or disorient and then immediately strike with his blade, a repeating pattern that seemed to come as naturally to him as breathing. A charge of brave soldiers drew his attention. With Erclidus's back now turned, the king seized his chance.

He sprang forward, sword poised to kill.

Erclidus knocked the incoming soldiers away with a sudden blast of wind and whipped around just in time to catch Agamemnon's blade with his own.

He smirked maliciously as their eyes met. "I'd been wondering when I'd finally get the chance to meet you. I'd say it's a pleasure but, well, it isn't."

The king pushed back against his block and launched a second attack.

Erclidus parried with ease, ripped Agamemnon's sword away with a casual cast, balled up his right fist, and punched him square in the nose.

Agamemnon was knocked flat on his back, stunned, warm blood streaming down his face. He fumbled for his dagger, but this too was knocked away.

Erclidus laughed as he stood above him. "Nobility is a fruitless virtue," he growled. "See now what your blindness has brought you."

The Sorcerer's apprentice raised his sword. The king did not look away.

But when Erclidus brought his hand down to strike the fatal blow, he found that he could not. He frowned, pulling the weapon with all his might, but it refused to budge.

Erclidus turned to look over his shoulder, Agamemnon followed his gaze, and both men saw Adiadni standing several yards away, hand outstretched to prevent the blade from falling upon her father. The king was pulled to his feet by a pair of his soldiers who dragged him away from Vegard's general despite his shouted protests.

Erclidus chuckled as he turned his body toward the princess. She had grown stronger since last they had met.

Her hand began to shake as she struggled to pull the sword from his own. He watched her for a moment, allowing her to struggle against him before suddenly, he let it go.

Adi screamed and dove out of the way as it flew toward her. She scrambled to her feet and prepared to face him.

Erclidus drew both of his hands together and thrust them forward. An explosion of fire and mud sent Adiadni and all other nearby soldiers flailing. The spark of his fury had been lit. The young Sorcerer unleashed a rain of fiery terror upon all in his path.

Veldis and Uriah abandoned the conjuring of colorful projections in favor of flame. They struck down swaths of goblins whenever they had the chance, but with Erclidus now fully engaged in the fight, it was clear that the Free People on the ground were at a disadvantage.

Uriah looked on fearfully as the half-alive army closed in around Suscundos's soldiers, steadily driving them back toward the city. The longer they waited to reconvene, the more the enemy had the opportunity to thin their ranks.

The Wizard raised his staff and waved it back and forth, emitting the bright light that called for their retreat.

Uritus spotted the light as the horns sounded from the wall and he hastened to urge the soldiers around him to fall back.

The other officers did the same, making their way to the safety of the city as they fought to ensure that their troops had the same opportunity.

Adiadni ran to Jasch when she spotted her caught between two attacking goblins. The princess made quick work of one and then the other.

Jasch laughed as she beheld the sight of her rescuer. "My queen!"

"We need to get back to Suscundos—" Adi cried.

But she was cut off suddenly as Jasch let out a harrowing scream, pierced through the shoulder by an enemy arrow.

She sank to her knees and the princess swore, dropping down with her.

"I'm okay!" Jasch insisted. "It's hardly fatal."

The body of a goblin crashed to the ground just beside them, and Adiadni lifted her eyes to see Crystella.

"Is she all right?"

"Fine. I can get her back, make sure my father does too!"

Crystella nodded and raced away.

Adi moved quickly, slinging Jasch's arm over her shoulder and dragging her back to the safety of the wall.

Uritus halted his retreat when he drew near the city, as did Perplexus and Pressio. The three men warred with the goblins that advanced, buying time for the last of the Free People to make it safely to the gate.

The king fought back against his niece's insistence that he retreat with them. She shouted at him that he needed to, for Adiadni if nothing else, and he begrudgingly relented.

The Wizards did their part to stall the encroaching goblins, free to increase the power of their strikes with the Free People out of the way. Uriah scanned the field, waiting for the last of the soldiers to move beyond an invisible line before he activated the next means of defense.

He thrust both arms out and raised them up, and through the ground burst forth the cropidus's second trap. Two densely packed rows of tall metal bars exploded up from the earth, impaling several goblins as they stretched toward the sky. Digtrision cheered loudly from his place on the wall.

The bars were too close together for any trapped behind them to squeeze through, and the few who had managed to make it beyond them were quickly slain by the officers who held the line for their comrades. The rows of metal stakes extended well beyond the edges of the enemy horde, from Tuvibati to several yards South of where Suscundos's wall ended. Veldis was swift to incinerate all who dared try to make it around their edge. The archers rained down a storm of arrows upon the invaders trapped behind the great barrier.

Nadarum and the cavalry were the last to arrive back in Suscundos, and Uritus took their arrival as permission to retreat. The Adalos was the last to return through the gate. It was quickly shut and barred behind him.

Uritus hurried up the wall to join Uriah on the tower. They looked over the field, assessing their next steps. Even with the aid of the barrier and the assault rained down by Veldis and the marksmen, the Free People were greatly outnumbered. And even with the opportunity to reconvene, the battle from here on would be hard fought with no guarantee of victory.

Shortly, the general spotted his brother steadily approaching the wall of spikes. Uriah sent down shot after shot of hot flame in an attempt to slow him down, but the young Sorcerer remained mostly undeterred.

"We haven't much time before he arrives," said the Wizard. "I will do all I can to stop him, but if he breaks through the barrier, they will be here in an instant and we'll have no chance of making another attack."

Uritus clenched his fists, knowing his mentor spoke the truth. Erclidus was too strong. If he had the chance to reach the gate, it would be only a matter of time before the city was breached. They had lost many of their troops already, and though they would stand again to fight no matter what, the Adalos feared that they did not have enough to reign victorious on this day. Still, the rain pelted down upon them and thunder roared ferociously.

"What are you thinking?"

Uritus took a breath. "I'm going to assemble them for the next advance. Hold him off as long as you can. I think I know what needs to be done. It's a long shot, but we need to try everything we can."

Uriah nodded and the Adalos hurried back to the ground.

Adiadni lowered Jasch to a seat against the inner wall as its gate opened and a flood of physicians and Healers rushed out to tend to the wounded.

"This is going to hurt," said the princess to her friend, snapping the arrowhead from its shaft.

"Do it."

"Okay. Deep breath in."

Jasch obeyed.

"And out…"

She did as she was told, crying out in pain as her friend removed the shaft from the wound.

"You're okay, take this." Adi retrieved the dried moss from the pouch on her belt and tucked it into Jasch's mouth to alleviate her pain. She took a pinch of herbs from the other pouch and pressed them to the wound, keeping her hand there for a moment as she muttered a prayer to the Mother. Medics arrived then and quickly took Jasch away to stitch her up.

Adiadni rose to her feet and looked around at the masses, eagerly searching for the faces of those she knew. She spotted her father, her cousins, Nadarum, Perplexus…

"Adiadni!"

She spun around.

Uritus.

Tears gathered in her eyes as she sank into his embrace.

"I need you to do something for me." He took her by the arm and led her through the inner gate.

"Anything."

They came to a stop where they would not be in the way, far enough that none could hear their conversation. He lifted his eyes to the swirling Shadow and then lowered them to regard her face with a deep breath, "I need you to go with Milion to beg the aid of Basil's hired swords."

"What?" Adiadni shook her head, incredulous. "Alone…?"

"Yes. I need to lead the rest back onto the field before Vegard can reach the wall. I cannot leave now, it will look like I am abandoning them."

The princess stood, mouth agape, head still shaking back and forth as she tried to comprehend just what he was asking of her. "I cannot do this…"

"I would not ask you if I felt I had any other choice. But Adiadni, we don't have enough men, and if we don't at least try, this could very well be the end of the Free World as we know it."

Tears spilled onto her cheeks, mingling with drops of rainwater. "They won't listen to me…"

"They will. You are their leader, the most inspiring force I have ever known. They will hear your plea."

"Uritus, I cannot ride a bloody dragon! I don't know how…"

"You don't need to. He does. He'll keep you safe, I promise."

At that moment, they heard the flapping of mighty wings above their heads. They looked up to see the shimmering belly of the great beast as he descended to land within the city.

Adiadni lowered her gaze to his, her vision blurring as her tears fell faster. "I don't want to leave you…"

The fear worn plainly in her eyes broke his heart. He took her face firmly in his hands and kissed her. "You are the only one who can do this," he whispered, inches from her face. "Remember who you are. Remember what you have done. Remember why we are doing any of this at all."

Adi took several ragged breaths. He was right. She had said a hundred times that she would do whatever it took to liberate her people. This was her chance. The soldiers would willingly storm out from here back onto the field with no regard for their safety, caring only for the good of the collective.

With a deep, shaky sigh, the princess nodded. "Okay."

"Okay." Uritus pressed his lips to hers once more, drinking in the taste of her breath, the smoothness of her skin, her invigorating scent of juniper and rosewater. "I love you."

"I love you too."

And just like that, he was gone, and the princess found herself standing alone in the rain as the troops made ready to return to the battlefield. Adiadni took a final breath to steady herself and then turned and hastened to the place where Milion waited.

Chapter Thirty-Three

"Sunrise"

"Hello, Friend," the Suvah set a soft hand on the dragon's face, relieved when he leaned into it. "I know you were expecting Uritus... To be honest, this is a surprise to me too. But the Free World is in dire need of our aid. If you would be so kind as to give it to me, I could really use your help."

Milion snorted and she felt his hot breath against her face.

She relaxed. This was a proud, powerful creature, but with him, she had never felt anything less than safe, just as she did with Uritus. "There is a company of fighters just East of here," she explained. "I need you to take me there. Uritus believes that if I ask it of them, they will return to Suscundos to join us in defending her. He would go himself, but..." She trailed off, not knowing how to explain the gravity of the situation the Adalos faced.

A rumbling sounded from the dragon's belly, deep and strong like the thunder that growled from above. He stepped back from her, turning his body and lowering himself so the princess might easily mount him.

She planted a grateful kiss on his face. "Thank you, Friend."

She took in a shaky breath as she lifted her eyes to regard just how high of a climb it was to claim her seat on his back. She went inside herself in an attempt to channel her counterpart, remembering how he made ready to take flight with such ease. Timidly, she approached Milion's side and raised her hands, one to rest on the joint of his wing, one to grasp the spine that sprouted from the back of his neck. Raising one boot to set it atop his leg, she pulled herself up and settled into place. She let out a small laugh as she arrived at her seat and gripped her fingers tightly around his spines.

"All right, Milion," she said, harnessing every last drop of courage in her body. "Whenever you're ready."

The dragon raised himself up, spread his wings, and lifted into the sky.

Adiadni felt her heart beat faster with his every wingbeat. In a matter of seconds, they were soaring high over Suscundos, Eastbound in search of the journeying swordsmen.

The princess was surprised to find that the higher into the air they climbed, the more at ease she felt. The rain began to dissipate as they departed from the city, ceasing entirely as they left it behind. It was not long before Adiadni spotted the glowing fires of the travelers' camp.

She urged the dragon down and he descended, drawing the attention of those who still lingered outside their tents. The sound of the approaching beast and the wind stirred up by his wings alerted the rest of his presence. By the time Milion came to land in their midst, a sizable crowd had assembled to behold him.

Adiadni looked at the gathered masses, seeing them stunned by the sight of the beautiful creature and yet still maintaining their distance from him.

The flap of the largest nearby tent was pushed open and Basil emerged, stopping in his tracks when he saw the dragon and his rider.

"Adiadni? Wh… what is the meaning of this?"

The Suvah did not descend from her seat. She waited another moment for the last of her audience to assemble and then drew her sword and raised it high in the air. "Swordsmen of the East! I call upon you to take up arms and rise to the aid of the Free World!"

Basil scoffed. "Truly, a remarkable show of power. Do you come to us on a dragon in the hopes of intimidating us into acting as you would wish?"

Adi ignored him. "Right now, the army of Shadow seeks to bring an end to this land as we know it. They lay siege on Suscundos as we speak. We are doing all we can to hold them off, but if I speak the truth, then I must tell you that we are on the brink. If the capital falls and Vegard is allowed to proceed with their brutal campaign, there will be no one to stand in their way, and a new age of darkness will rise."

Basil laughed loudly. "You had your chance, Adiadni. These men have made their choice. You may seek to force us into submission, but know that we will not go without a fight!" He took several steps forward in his anger, stopping only when Milion turned his head to face him and growled.

"I know that I cannot force your hand," the princess continued. "I will not try to. I know as well that Basil has agreed to pay you more than we are able. If you choose to stand with us, know that you will be compensated as fairly as all our other hired swords. But if gold is the sole thing that stands between you and your duty to your homeland and your brothers, I must implore you to reconsider your priorities."

Adiadni saw several of them exchange glances. She took a breath and made her final case, "Every last soldier up there takes to the battlefield fueled by the love of this home we share. Whether or not you come with me, I will return from here to take my place beside them. This land is good and generous, her people even more so. Should I die defending her, my last breath will be a sigh of satisfaction for the knowledge that I have done my part. I offer you the opportunity to do the same. Will you rise to the challenge of the fight, returning to this land the love and sacrifice she has given to and for you? Will you lay down your pride and individualism, take up your swords, and fight for the Free World?"

There passed then a moment of stillness and Adiadni held her breath.

***

Punznes felt his heart drop into his stomach as he beheld the woman laid on his table. Her face was pale and cold, but still she breathed, still her heart beat though it was nearly too faint to perceive. The physician sprang to action, calling orders to his assistants as he prepared to do his work. No Healers remained in Lorethh—they had all gone with the army to stay at the heart of the war. There were only a small number of medics like himself, trained to mend the broken on their own with no Magic to aid them and so no promise of success.

Before leaving his home in the White Mountains, Punznes had never needed to mend anything greater than a shallow gash or a broken bone. During the battle for the Mirrored Cities, he had experienced the loss of his first patients, more still during his expedition through Vegard. Each one had rattled him, forced him to reckon with the fact that he was not omnipotent, that he could not save everyone no matter how much he wished to. Uritus's miraculous recovery had softened the devastation of Havian's untimely death. But even with the hours of careful work done in Sigmount by his own hands, even now, Punznes struggled to attribute the Adalos's healing to both his efforts *and* Adiadni's rather than just her own.

But the Suvah was not here now and Tris was, creeping closer to death with each passing second, and though he knew that her fate was mostly out of his hands, still he had to try. She had no one but him, no chance of survival save for his gauze and his needle and his pleas to the Mother for her deliverance. And so the physician swallowed the sickly pit of fear in his gut and set to work.

*****

Oripidus paced back and forth, growing more impatient by the minute. He could hear the distant crashes and cries of war from beyond Lorethh's wall, the war he was waiting to take part in. He didn't know how long he had been here, anxiously anticipating the order that would send him through the tunnels with the reserves. With the sun not visible through the heavy Shadow, it was hard to gauge how many hours had lapsed since the battle began. Periodically, a young soldier would call down to the commander from the wall, never with any meaningful updates to share. Eventually, he had enough. The lives of the people he loved were at risk. It was time to take matters into his own hands.

He spotted a stack of wooden crates and moved to climb atop one of them. "All right, soldiers, listen here!" He looked over the last of the centaurs and Vegardians who would join the fight, over two thousand of them. "I don't know about ye, but I've grown tired of awaitin' the call. I say we make our advance and send these bastards back to the dirt where they belong!"

The fighters sent up their cries of agreement.

He nodded to himself, pleased with their enthusiasm. "This reign of Shadowy terror ends with us!"

The documents Perplexus had left behind with Lorethh's guardians—which mapped out each of the secret tunnels between the two cities—were a precious resource that Oripidus believed held the key to their victory. The reserves had been split up into three companies: the centaurs who would take the largest of the three tunnels, and the two groups of Vegardians who would snake their way through the smaller ones. The commander had gone with a few scouts the night before to ensure that the tunnels led where the maps said they would and that they were stable enough to be trusted.

513

Now, the time for the ambush had come, and Oripidus called the charge. The companies split off from one another to enter their respective tunnels and the reserves stormed to their victory.

Oripidus led the advance of his squadron, instructing a pair of soldiers to light the torches as they made their way. They traveled quickly, but still, he cautiously inspected the support beams as he came upon them, ensuring once more that they were stable and strong. Eager as he was to play his part in the battle, he was resolved to never again lose anyone to a cave-in.

In due time, they arrived at the tunnel's end, and with the aid of a few other soldiers, he scraped away all that was left of the door's seal and slid it open. They emerged into a small underground chamber, white stone lining all its surfaces, a few shoddy pieces of wooden furniture set up here and there. There were people in the chamber—humans dressed in rags—and Oripidus called his company to hold their attack.

These were Vegardian attendants—captives, just like Tris and his soldiers once were—and he was quick to explain that they meant them no harm. They were here to liberate them, the soldiers shared, as they had liberated themselves in the West. Though the captives were visibly fearful, they pointed the way to the city above.

The commander raced up the stair with his troops close behind, bursting through the door into the dark of day just as the other two companies did the same. Scant few were the goblins who remained within Judii's wall, and the Free People were on them in an instant.

Eventually, the cries of the dying called the rest to attention. They rushed at the invaders, paying no mind to the danger they faced. But their enthusiastic efforts proved to be in vain. The goblins were outnumbered, the Free People stirred up, and the battle steadily creeping toward its end.

The first moment that Oripidus got the chance to breathe after the attack began, he turned his attention to the trebuchet atop the wall. They had little left to be used as ammunition and had begun firing broken spear tips and arrowheads along with any other scraps they could find. But still, the great weapon was the primary danger facing those outside on the ground, and the commander was resolved to clear their way as best he could.

He called to two nearby soldiers, and together, they hastened up the steps to the rampart. Oripidus knocked aside the enemies in their way, sending them flying to the ground with a swift strike of his trusty hammer. The two soldiers aided him by slaying the nearby goblins while the commander made his way for the weapon itself.

Mustering up all his strength, he bashed his hammer into one of the sides of the trebuchet. Again and again, he beat against the beam, stopping only to confront the occasional goblin who drew too close.

One final strike forced the support to splinter and snap, disabling the mighty weapon. Oripidus looked around in search of another foe and saw that more of the Vegardian rebels had made their way up to clash with the goblins on the wall.

Laivar stayed close beside Mikka at her command, feeling no cause for fear with his friend to protect him. The poet kept his focus on wielding his bow, firing upon the enemies that Mikka was too busy to notice.

The general fought on with renewed strength and determination now that the bard had successfully shaken her awake. Her head throbbed from days of travel and battle with little sleep to make up for it, and there remained a dull aching in her chest when she remembered how her fallen friend was only one of many who sacrificed everything for the cause. But she harnessed this ache to drive her further on, scores of goblins slain by her quick sword, and she sent up a silent prayer of thanks for her lost brother, without whose tutelage none of her victories would have been possible.

With the enemy soldiers within Judii almost fully eliminated, many of the centaurs hurried to the Southern gate. They disassembled the locking mechanism, pushed open its doors, and poured onto the battlefield to attack the rear of Vegard's army.

The soldiers already on the ground cheered when they saw this, and their cheers alerted Mikka and Laivar of the approach of their victory.

"Atta boy, Rip!" cried the poet with glee.

A stimulating surge of energy took hold of the Free People. The end was in sight. They vastly outnumbered their enemies and they pushed forward with this in mind, knowing that the battle was all but won at this point.

It was not long before the goblins, too, became aware that their end was nigh, and many of them chose to flee to the West in a desperate search for sanctuary. Xinna had anticipated this, and her company was hot on their heels, quickly overtaking them and cutting and shooting every last one down before they could make their escape.

After a while, Mikka looked around, eyes darting back and forth in search of her next target only to find that there were none to be seen. The last remaining goblins were surrounded just outside Judii's wall; atop it, the city's flag was raised to declare that it had been won.

Her eye caught a flurry of movement overhead and she raised her gaze just in time to see Qibat soar by, calling down to her two simple words,

"She's all right."

The soldier's emotion overtook her and she began to laugh as tears spilled onto her cheeks. She turned to Laivar and the two fell into each others' arms, weeping with joy and sorrow and relief. The sounds of battle died down and were replaced by the glorious trumpeting of horns.

***

When the soldiers reassembled to take the field, Ilya passed off leadership to one of the other marksmen and descended from the wall to join them. Digtrision too, left the Wizards in command in favor of engaging in hand-to-hand combat.

Veldis continued to rain down fire on the goblins who sought to snake around the barrier to the wall. Uriah did his best to delay Erclidus's approach, though the Sorcerer's apprentice remained untouchable.

Nadarum spotted his wife as she reached the bottom of the stair, fiery determination in her eyes. She came to a stop when she met his gaze.

"I'm coming with you," she declared. "Every man on the ground counts for something and I do *not* wish to argue about it."

Nadarum laughed for the first time all day and the deep sound warmed her. "You will hear no arguments from me. I'm far safer with you than without." She returned his smile and accepted his hand, pulling herself up to settle into a seat behind him.

Uritus did not need to wait long for his soldiers to take their places. Though the Free People were battered and fatigued, they were anxious to see the war through to its end. The Adalos drew his sword once more.

"One more charge!" he cried, the enthusiasm of the masses cutting him off. "For Suscundos! For the Free World! For the return of the Light!"

The gate was opened and the cavalry led the charge, Uritus and the infantry following quickly behind. Uriah thrust his hand and staff forward to send the metal bars crashing down upon the enemy, paving the way for the king's army.

Fearlessly, they collided once more into the fight.

Nadarum rode deep into the thick of the goblin swarm, slaying many as he went, Ilya behind him rapidly firing arrows to thin their ranks.

Perplexus and Pressio were soon separated as their fighting led them separate ways, but each kept his head down and battled on with the same ferocity that they would have had they remained together.

Crystella kept one stealthy eye on Agamemnon at all times, intercepting several large goblins who sought to slay the king.

Digtrision and the cropidus were the most ferocious of them all, having waited long for their opportunity to defend their home.

The storm raged on, rain beating relentlessly down upon the tired soldiers. Though many arrows and flaming orbs hurtled toward Erclidus, still the young Sorcerer could not be touched.

Uritus was not immune to attack as he had been upon their first charge. Goblins came at him in droves. His awareness was heightened, his senses sharper than they had ever been. Again and again, he turned just in time to catch an incoming blade with his own or knock away a soaring arrow or spear. He did not know if his proficiency on the battlefield was due to his ability or the Magic of his weapon, but he didn't question it. His skill was due to his practice, yes, but also Havian, Uriah, the experience of the adventure, the sacred blade divinely entrusted to him.

Though he still did not feel brave, neither did he feel fear, far too occupied by the battle as it raged. The Sword of Fire steamed and sizzled as drops of rain splashed upon its blade.

Erclidus maintained an air of casual confidence as he cast and cut his way through swaths of soldiers at a time. Brave warriors continued to rise against him, planting themselves between the general and the capital city.

Perplexus felt as though a hammer struck him in the chest when he looked up to behold the devastating sight of soldiers blasted back by a wall of hot orange fire. The navigator knew without a shadow of a doubt that Erclidus's relentless terror had to be stopped if they wished to stand a chance of obtaining victory. The goblins alone were easily felled when the Free People worked together, but Vegard's general was too strong, too powerful as he wielded his Stolen Magic as well as that of his mentor. Rooted in his resolve, Perplexus began to fight his way to the young Sorcerer.

Ilya noticed this immediately, cursing as she did.

"You all right?"

"I need to go after Lex. He doesn't stand a chance on his own." The archer planted a kiss on the back of her husband's neck, leapt down from the back of the moving horse, and raced to catch up with the navigator.

She placed herself directly in his path. "What do you think you're doing?"

Perplexus grabbed her by the arm and yanked her aside just in time to plunge his sword through the chest of an advancing goblin. "What does it look like I'm doing? Someone needs to stop him!"

Ilya dodged an attack, thrust an arrow through the eye of her enemy, and then shot it at another. "You're right," she said. "But you're not doing it alone. I'll clear your path. Figure out a plan of attack."

The navigator nodded, slayed a final goblin, and proceeded to make his way toward his new target. Ilya moved with him, gathering and firing arrows as she went, doing her best to free him of the burden of his attackers so he had a moment to think.

Perplexus knew by now that his strength and skill were not enough to best this great foe, that Erclidus was far too quick and cunning to be defeated by willpower alone. And so, channeling the swordsman who taught him everything he knew, the commander stooped down to snatch up from the ground a length of torn fabric and wrapped it around his left arm.

Uritus caught a flurry of movement in the corner of his eye—two of his friends proceeding forward to launch an attack on his brother. He swore, his fear balling into a tight knot in his chest.

Dauntless and daring as they both were, Erclidus would not go down easily and would sooner self-destruct in a chaotic wave of obliteration than allow Perplexus and Ilya to defeat him. No, as sick as it made him feel, the Adalos knew that the only one capable of bringing an end to his brother's wretched reign was himself.

He fought to catch up to them, his progress excruciatingly slow due to the horde in his way. He felt as though the goblins were targeting him specifically, as though they had learned that the greatest threat to their success was he.

Never did his enemies manage to land a hit on him though, and he felt emboldened by the protection of the prophecy. Finally, after a series of consecutive cuts that felled three of his attackers, Uritus saw a clear path to the Sorcerer's apprentice. He took it, running as fast as his legs could carry him.

Suddenly, he was tackled to the ground.

The Adalos shook his head, located his sword several feet away in the dirt, and lunged for it. The goblin, however, was as quick as he was. He snatched him by the ankle and dragged him back.

Uritus flipped over, swinging his free foot to land a kick on his assailant's jaw. The goblin growled and released his foot but was otherwise unfazed. Uritus lurched forward to pull the club from his hand before he could land a fatal blow.

They struggled against each other, Uritus's strength a surprise even to himself. Still, the general knew that he was outmatched when it came to sheer power, and so, growing desperate, he landed a firm kick on his opponent's belly.

The goblin doubled over, releasing his hold on his weapon, but recovered in just enough time to punch the Adalos in the face.

Uritus's head seared with pain, his mind spinning so violently he did not notice when the club slipped from his fingers.

The goblin seized his opportunity to attack, fastening his fingers around his victim's neck. But before Uritus had the opportunity to consider that this might be his end, the goblin's grip loosed as he was lifted up and away from the disoriented general.

Uritus gasped for breath, shaking his head as his vision cleared. Above him, he saw his savior, Shrigmut Olar, snap the neck of his attacker and cast his lifeless body to the ground.

The half-alive responded in kind, several of them rushing to take the place of the fallen one.

Uritus snatched up the club to help defend against them, one swift swing to bash in the knee of a charging goblin, another to the side of his head, splitting his skull and killing him instantly.

But the Adalos's efforts were in vain. Just as Shrigmut decapitated one of his enemies, another drove his sword through the brave soldier's gut.

Uritus screamed and dropped the club, rushing to catch Shrigmut as he collapsed to the ground. The fisherman did not see when the assailant was slain. The man from Lorethh clutched a hand to his wound and Uritus pressed his own on top of it.

The river of dark blood flowing from his belly communicated clearly to the Adalos that this hero had met his end. Tears gathered in Uritus's eyes and his heart lurched as he was forced to face the reality that he could not save him.

"You must not let them win…" Shrigmut spoke weakly. His head dropped to the earth, his eyes drifting shut for the last time.

The Adalos dried his eyes, rose to his feet, and retrieved his sword.

When Perplexus arrived behind his intended target, he was quick to make his attack. One broad stroke slashed across Erclidus's back.

The young Sorcerer cried out in pain. He spun to face his aggressor, eyes narrowing as he beheld him.

"You again."

He cast to drive Perplexus back before he could attack again and then raised his hand to his neck and undid the clasp that held his cape in place.

The torn piece of fabric fluttered to the ground. Erclidus raised his blade to catch Perplexus's next swing. Forcefully, he shoved him back, casting this time a ball of hot flame which Perplexus deflected with the aid of his heavy, damp, makeshift shield.

"Are you too much of a coward to face me as a man?"

The navigator's taunting tone enraged his enemy, but it accomplished its purpose, and when Erclidus marched forward to launch his subsequent attacks, all came from his blade alone. Without the use of Stolen Magic, the men were equally matched.

Erclidus was quick and determined and relentless, but Perplexus was clever, wielding the piece of fabric for defense in the same way he had grown up watching Havian wield his cape. Perplexus's improvisational shield was lighter and thinner than his brother had ordinarily preferred, but the weight added by the rain made up for it. He did not successfully strike the young Sorcerer again, but he managed to deflect his flurry of furious blows with an ease that surprised him.

Step by step, Erclidus slowly drove him back. Several yards away, Ilya kept watch.

Erclidus's frustration grew as the defiant young commander continued to evade him. He was swift-moving and slick, and each missed blow drove Vegard's general further into his rage. Angrily, he lunged forward with a thrust of his sword.

Perplexus sidestepped smoothly. At the same moment, he raised the length of fabric and swished it to the side, managing to wrap it around his attacker's blade.

One strong tug ripped the sword from Erclidus's hand. The navigator seized his chance.

He leapt forward, bringing his sword down toward the Sorcerer's apprentice with impressive speed.

Erclidus's right hand came soaring toward him.

The navigator was blown back, a powerful wave of wind and water, fire and rock sending him crashing to the field several yards away.

The man in black reclaimed his sword with a light flick of his wrist and stormed forward, determined to end this conflict here and now. He did not make it more than a few steps before he was struck by one of Ilya's arrows.

He cried out in pain and rage, eyes scanning the field for the archer who had landed the hit, anger bubbling up inside him when he spotted her. The concussive blast that followed was the greatest of them all.

He swung his right hand in a wide arc across his body, casting all nearby soldiers away, his own included. Ilya hit the ground and clutched her head, writhing in pain.

Erclidus looked down at the right side of his abdomen and broke off the shaft of the arrow protruding from it with a pained grunt.

And then he heard a sound, faint but familiar, come rushing toward his head. The young Sorcerer spun around just in time to catch his brother's blade with his own.

He paused as he held back the blow, surprised for the briefest of moments to see Uritus act as the aggressor.

"So it has come to this," he growled. "Not too late to surrender and save everyone that's left."

Forcefully, he thrust Uritus back and sent a blow of wind rushing his way. Uritus rooted his feet, not allowing the spell to knock him down.

"Don't do this."

Erclidus barreled forward and brought his sword down again.

Uritus raised his own to deflect it, ducking as it spun back around.

"Erclidus, I don't want to do this!"

A ball of flame came crashing toward the Adalos, exploding in a shower of sparks when it made contact with the Sword of Fire.

Stunned, the elder Subian launched an attack again, a blow of his blade, a shot of Stolen Magic; twice more, growing more enraged every time Uritus managed to evade them. His efforts were in vain. The Hero could not be touched.

"Please don't make me do this!"

At that moment, another hero appeared, a golden-hearted warrior with the passion of a thousand suns. Perplexus sprang to life at Erclidus's side, brought his sword down with all of his strength, and sliced his great foe's right hand clean off.

It fell with a dull thud to the ground, silver token glistening in the rain.

Erclidus threw back his head and roared. The heavens roared with him, deafening peals of thunder followed by a wild torrent of rushing wind. The Sorcerer's apprentice turned to face his aggressor.

Uritus screamed as his blade swung. The Adalos felt the world slow, watched the sword's arc, saw Perplexus attempt to stumble back away from it. In the end, it was not his fear, nor his sense of duty, but his love that drove him forward.

The navigator flew back and crashed to the ground just as the Sword of Fire pierced through studded armor and emerged through Erclidus's chest.

A trail of dark, Shadowy mist escaped the wound. Erclidus sucked in a sharp breath. His sword slipped from his grasp, the burn of golden steel drawing the last of his power from his body. Uritus removed the blade and cast it aside as he dropped down to lower his brother to the ground.

Immediately, he was rocked by the weight of what he had done. Erclidus sputtered and grew pale. Uritus pressed his hands against the oozing wound, eyes searching the field for a Healer, the crushing weight of regret lessening only somewhat when he saw Ilya drag Perplexus to his feet.

"Leave it," Erclidus choked. His voice was thick and strained.

Uritus returned his eyes to his brother, sparkling blue and filled with tears. He shook his head, a solitary sob escaping his throat. "I'll get you a Healer," he insisted. "I myself was brought back from the brink of death—"

"Don't."

Uritus frowned, opened his mouth again to object.

"You've won."

The younger brother shook his head again, a rejection of the elder's surrender. "This is not a win for me," he sobbed. "I never wanted any of this. I never wanted anything but to have you back."

Above them, the rain slowed. The Adalos did not see it, but the heavy Shadow too began to dissipate.

"I don't want you to go like this. I don't want you to go at all…"

With Erclidus's every labored breath, Uritus's heart tensed all the more. Though the fate of the Free World played out around him, his own world had condensed down to the size of a single human body.

"I forgive you, you know."

Erclidus's eyes, previously fixed on the dying storm, drifted down to meet his brother's as the black above gave way for the return of cold blue. They were weary and sorrowful, but in them, Uritus recognized the very thing he had spent over a decade scanning the horizon in search of…

The return.

Erclidus did not speak, his body weakening and growing more pale with each excruciating second. But still, his spirit, fiercely stubborn as it had been all his life, fought against its inevitable eviction. His body would not allow him to speak, even if he had managed to find the words. Though their innate brotherly connection had perished long ago, somehow, in the deep of the older man's eyes, Uritus read clearly everything Erclidus wished to say,

I love you, I'm sorry, be better than I was.

His dark eyelashes fluttered closed as a final sigh left his lungs and his body grew cold beneath his brother's hands.

Uritus felt his chest burn as though his heart had been the one that was pierced. One hand quivered as he moved it to hold the side of Erclidus's face.

"There was so much I wanted to tell you."

The sounds of battle had long since faded from his awareness. Now, the knowledge that he was in the midst of a battle at all did the same. The Adalos brought his head down to rest against his brother's body and wept. He had taken the only possible course of action to return the Free People to safety. Though he knew this without a shadow of doubt, it did nothing to alleviate the immense weight of devastation and sorrow that pressed down on his shoulders. He had done all he knew to do, offered Erclidus countless opportunities to turn and face the error of his ways. The heaviness of his failure to save the last of his living kin far eclipsed the relief and satisfaction of having saved the rest of his people. The rhythmic pattern of rushing wind soon drew his eyes to the sky.

He spotted the mighty dragon and his gorgeous rider as another rising sound met his ears—pounding hoofbeats, powerful cries, and war horns. Around Suscundos's Southern edge stormed a wave of relief, two thousand Eastern swordsmen come to the rescue of their brethren. The unstoppable force crashed into the fight, the final ingredient necessary for their assured victory.

The soldiers already on the ground cried out their grateful welcome. Soon, Vegard's army came to understand that they were defeated, and began fleeing in droves to the safety of the woods at the edge of the Clearing. But there they would find no sanctuary, as out of the treeline soared one sparkling, golden projectile after another—the final defense offered by their faen allies.

Uritus released a heavy sigh and looked again for Milion, spotting the dragon coming to a graceful landing just outside the city wall. He saw him take up goblins in his teeth and dash them upon the ground before taking to the sky once more. He saw Adiadni dismount and run onto the battlefield to rejoin her troops and lay claim to their victory.

Fear knew no place in mer mind or in her body. There was nothing on the earth capable of quenching her fire. Victorious horns sounded from the city's walls as daybreak exploded over the horizon. The Suvah plunged her sword to the sky. An all-but-forgotten joy laid claim to the Adalos's tired body.

She is the sun.

***

When the company of soldiers led by Crystella arrived at the Ashen Keep, they found Velup there, dead, lying alone in his tower. There was no indication on his body as to what may have caused his timely demise, so it was assumed that the last of his energy had drained from his living corpse when Erclidus died.

The keep was easily overtaken, the captives liberated, and the last remaining goblins slain. It took some time to locate Octrusial, but eventually, some of the attendants directed their liberators to his hidden chamber, and they found him there, also dead, his throat slit by a jagged fragment of a shattered looking glass that remained loosely clutched in his hand. His body and Velup's were tossed atop the pile of corpses of the Sorcerer's creation and burned along with them.

The company scoured all of Vegard, each of the villages, traveling as well further West than the established settlements to make certain that none of their enemies remained. No more were found, and they returned to the Free World confident that any who may have still lived would not survive long wandering the wastes of the West. The light of the sun returned in full, shining brightly upon the jagged black peaks, and when Crystella again arrived in Suscundos,

522

she told Adiadni that somehow, in the light, the Looming Mountains were beautiful to behold.

Tris and Jasch made full recoveries, as did most of the wounded in the capital and the Mirrored Cities, and those who did not were honored as best as the Free People knew how. Memorials were held throughout the land, somber ones, grateful ones, joyful ones. At Uritus's insistence, the king implored his citizens to share their stories of the fallen with one another so that even in death, their legacies might live on as they deserved. The fisherman kept always the memory of Shrigmut's courage close to his chest.

The evacuees returned to their homes, reunited with their loved ones, and immediately set to work rebuilding. Agamemnon went with Adiadni when she returned to the Forest of Idor to offer the fae their immense gratitude for the service they had done. The king apologized to the Court for any grief the mission he ordained had caused and offered to draw up a renewal of the treaty so they might return to living in peaceful separation from the rest of the Free World. The Court graciously accepted this apology and declared that while they were still firm in their refusal to allow the forest's resources to be exploited, they were glad to open their borders to allow guests to visit or pass through. With this, a new treaty was born, and Idor was reintegrated into the kingdom.

The Vegardian rebels were recognized for their courage, thanked for their service, and welcomed warmly into the land that would serve as their home for generations to come.

A month to the day after the final battle at Suscundos, the city's inhabitants organized a celebration to commemorate their victory. The erecting of banners, preparing of food, playing of music, and lighting of lanterns made it feel as though the people had never left, as though the city had never been under attack at all. The valiant warriors knew that they may never again feel the same as they had before participating in the war, but surrounded by the love of their communities once again, they found their way back to quiet contentment and comforting peace anyway.

While away from home, Fennispar had rallied the children of Suscundos to craft gifts of gratitude to offer the soldiers once they returned home. Paper flowers, a rainbow of them—fashioned originally out of necessity due to the scarcity of real ones in Quabish where they sheltered—were the sweet and pure recognition of all that the noble warriors had sacrificed to protect them. The vibrant symbols of hard-fought freedom bloomed all over the city, tucked into buttonholes and shirt pockets, and pinned to lapels and capes of those who had taken the battlefield as well as those who had supported them—medics and cooks and attendants and Keepers alike.

Adiadni wore her flowers tucked into her hair, two of them a deep purple and gifted to her by Kristefani and Friya, the third, cornflower blue, the first folded by her little brother's caring hands. A canopy of star-shaped ivory and magenta blooms sheltered the princess in the peaceful Eastern garden where she rested before the festivities commenced. She breathed in their sweet fragrance as she leaned against the smooth bark of the tree, a soft smile gracing her face as the sounds of music and laughter met her ears. It was there that her father found her and joined her in her seat on the ground.

They greeted one another with a shared smile and sat in silence for a moment, taking in the sacred joy of stillness. Both the Suvah and the Adalos had insisted on not making a grand entrance at the start of the celebration, neither of them wishing to be praised above the thousands of others who had sacrificed just as much and more than they had. Agamemnon had agreed to honor their request but reminded them that they would be praised regardless, for the rest of their days and long after. It was good of them to remain humble even while being lauded as the Free World's saviors, but they could not deny that the feats they had accomplished were undoubtedly remarkable, and the king impressed upon them that they had every right to be proud of themselves.

The sun crept ever closer to the Western horizon, indicating that the festivities would soon begin. Agamemnon brought a gentle hand to rest atop his daughter's.

"I know I have told you a thousand times that I am proud of you," he said. "I will tell you a thousand more. From the moment your mother told me of her suspicion that you had begun to grow in her womb, I dreamed of the kind of person that you would become. I imagined that you would be kind, compassionate, and soft-hearted as she, bolder and braver than I could ever be myself. It was clear to me from your beginning that you would be all of that and more, and as you have grown, you have far surpassed every dream I have ever held for you. You are the very best parts of your mother and me, the culmination of the goodness of all of your ancestors. You have been, and will remain, a spectacular example for the Free People to look to."

Adiadni smiled lovingly, scooting closer to her father to rest her head on his shoulder. "I have been blessed with a wonderful example of my own."

"I will soon need to announce the start of the festivities," Agamemnon went on. "But before I do, there is something I wish to discuss with you."

The princess sat up, her curiosity piqued.

The king regarded his daughter for a moment before he proceeded, "I know that you spent much of this past year—before your journey and during—fearing that you were not ready to take on such a responsibility. As your father, it is my duty to push you forward, but also to protect you, and I am sorry for the ways I contributed to your lack of certainty in yourself. I suppose I do not believe that any one of us can ever truly be ready for a task as great as the one you undertook, and you indeed know yourself better than anyone else. But as someone who has known you your whole life and witnessed your growth, I remain firm in my belief that you are far more ready than you may think.

"You are young still, and I will take great care to never again push you into something you do not feel you are yet prepared to take on. But something you said to me before the last battle has had me thinking. You said that you do not wish for me to leave yet, that you need me here still beside you."

Adi nodded, recalling the intense emotion she felt just before they made their charge.

Agamemnon continued, "My own father's death was sudden and untimely. Though he and I had our disagreements, his loss was difficult to bear. It would have been no matter the circumstances, but needing to bury him and then immediately proceed to take his place on the throne was uniquely challenging and disorienting. I leaned heavily on your mother and my own, and their support, as well as that of countless others, contributed to shaping me into the king I am today. I am endlessly grateful for those who aided and guided me in those first months, but I cannot help but wonder, even now, how things may have been different had my father been there to walk with me through that transition, as his father had done for him, as his grandmother had done for his father.

"I do not wish for that to happen to you, to be forced to take on such a great mantle before you are ready and without me there to guide you. And so, while I will not push you into the role until you are ready, I wish to tell you that I believe you are, and I will be glad to pass my mantle down to you as soon as you feel it is time."

Adiadni's lips parted, the realization of what her father was saying settling in. "You are telling me that… that you believe I am ready to become queen?"

"I am. And I do. I am most certain of it. The people adore you. They have followed you into the dark and you have led them out of it, remaining all the while loving and gracious and just."

"Do you not think I am too young?"

Agamemnon shook his head. "Age does count for some things, but wisdom and capability can exist in anyone. Again, I will not force you into your queendom until you would wish it for yourself. You *are* young, and you should be allowed to enjoy what remains of your youth however it pleases you. But when you *are* ready, know that I am too and that I will be most glad to walk with you into this next phase of your life."

The princess reached her arms up and around her father's neck. "Thank you, Adda," she said, pulling back from their embrace. "If I am honest… I think that I *do* feel ready. Or at least, far more than I did at the start of the Spring. But… I do want more time. Just to be. I've only begun to grasp the seriousness of such a responsibility, and I owe it to our people to learn as much as I can before I take the throne. There is much of this land that I have yet to even see with my own eyes. And you are a good king. The Free People love you just as much as they do me. They deserve the blessing of your leadership for at least a while longer. Perhaps… a few years from now?"

The king chuckled and nodded in agreement. "Very well."

The distant chiming of bells met their ears—the first indication that the celebration was about to begin.

"I must go," said Agamemnon, rising to his feet. "Enjoy the festivities as much as you are able. You deserve to lose yourself in joy again."

The king departed and Adiadni sighed happily, leaning back once more against the support of the tree.

With the war concluded and the Free People at peace once again, the Adalos finally did elect to ask for something in return for his service. While the rest of the soldiers labored to recover the bodies of their own from the Clearing and dispose of those of their enemies, a single pyre was lit on the cliffs beside Tuvibati Falls. Gathered there with Uritus were the Wizard, the navigator, the archer and horseman, and the princess. Only the king and a select few trusted officers knew of the memorial held for the one who had laid siege on the Free World. Uritus knew that if he ever wished to gather up his shattered pieces and move forward, he needed to find a way to definitively close this chapter. He bade his brother a tearful goodbye, watching as his ashes were swept up and ushered away by the wind to mingle with the water as it tumbled down and rushed on.

Uritus's twenty-fourth birthday came and went with little fanfare. Ordinarily, the members of his family would plan an elaborate meal for him, leaving him be for most of the day to read or ride or relax as he wished. They understood that such a day—both the celebration of his life and the anniversary of his father's death—was complicated for him. With ten years now since Odipar's departure, Uritus was acutely aware of the tenderness of the subject. The death of Erclidus only compounded the fisherman's profound sense of grief.

But now, the Hero was overjoyed to have his companions all in the same place again. When the small group returned from Lorethh to Suscundos, Zaphron and Robalto came with them—a welcome surprise that livened the fisherman's heart. He was excited, as were the rest of them, to introduce the twins to the celebratory ways of the capital. The mirth and merriment that echoed through the city was as vibrant as the day the companions were first welcomed there.

They sat together around one of the long wooden tables in the square where they partook of the feast prepared by the palace cooks and toasted to their victory.

Uritus looked from one smiling face to the next, to the paper flowers each of them wore, his heart warming when he observed how Punznes's dark green bloom was pinned to his collar with the aid of Havian's silver pin. They shared their joyful stories of the things they had witnessed since the end of the war. Uritus was positively bursting with gratitude and admiration for these people, without whom none of what he had accomplished in the past months would have been possible.

Together, they discussed their next steps and the various opportunities they would take to aid in the reconstruction of the Free World. For the first time, Uritus considered that the family from the Alabaster Keep may never look the same as it once had, with many of its members choosing to go in separate directions, at least for a time.

"What about you, Uritus?" Robalto inquired. "I take it you're planning to make Suscundos your new home now that you've found your great love?"

The fisherman considered this quietly. "I suppose I haven't thought about it," he admitted. "I've been so devoted to the obstacles right in front of me that I've yet to consider where I'll go or what I'll do next."

"What would you do if you could do anything? I think it's fair to say that you could," Laivar remarked.

Uritus chewed slowly on a piece of lethaa and raised his eyes to the darkening sky, twinkling stars just beginning to come into view. "Honestly, the only thing I wish for is rest. Perhaps someday I will long to travel, learn a new trade, or serve in a more permanent role as a soldier. But for now... I miss stillness. I miss quiet and reading, long rides with Moonracer to nowhere in particular. I miss *this*," he paused, looking around at the people he loved. "And I suppose right now, all I wish is to be able to soak it up while it's still mine. But as for the distant future..." he trailed off with a shake of his head and a shrug.

"It is perfectly fine, not knowing," Uriah assured him. "There is honor in rest, just as there is honor in pursuing that which sets your heart alight."

The Adalos nodded, finishing his piece of flaky bread. "I suppose the one thing that I *do* know is that I can't imagine my life without Adiadni. I can't imagine my life without any of you, but her absence would always leave me feeling incomplete. I may not know what I want for myself, but I know that I'd follow her anywhere. Though... I haven't had the chance to discuss that with her yet..."

"Discuss what with whom?"

Amused smiles lit the faces of those around the table as the princess squeezed her way into a seat between the fisherman and the navigator.

Adiadni arrived with her friends in tow and room was made for them at the table. The three young elvish women excitedly made the acquaintance of the members of the family they had still yet to meet.

"I'll tell you later," Uritus whispered, wrapping an arm around her as he planted a kiss atop her head.

"We were just discussing future plans," Mikka offered with a wink at Perplexus. "No doubt you have many of your duties laid out for you already, but have you considered what you *want* to do, now that we're able to begin clawing our way back to some shade of normal?"

"Hmm..." Adiadni leaned her head back to look up at the stars. "I just want to sleep," she said with a laugh. Ilya clapped a hand to her mouth to keep from squealing with delight at this similarity to Uritus's answer. "I want to sleep and I want to read for a whole day, *two* days, without a single responsibility to interrupt me. And then, I suppose I want to go places. I want to see the parts of the Free World that I've yet to explore. And I want to visit you lot in the mountains as often as I can. That is... if you'll have me."

"There exists no world in which we would ever turn you away," said Nadarum.

"Hear, hear!"

The others followed Oripidus's example and raised their cups.

"It's unlikely that we'll all end up back there," said Zaphron sadly. "But wherever we are called, I am sure we will thrive. This group always manages to land on our feet somehow."

"I think these dark days have reminded us of the things we truly value," Punznes remarked thoughtfully.

Adi leaned forward to rest her chin on her hands. "And what's that?"

"Wal*nut*!" cawed Qibat.

The companions around the table laughed as the physician offered his bird a treat

"Love and devotion," he replied. "To the world which houses us, to one another, and to those we've still yet to meet."

"The thrill of the adventure," Ilya added.

"Cold ale and warm company." Oripidus cradled his nearly empty flagon.

Tris chimed in, "The satisfaction of laboring for something you can be proud of," and Mikka smiled.

"It would seem that our values haven't changed all that much," Nadarum noted. "We've simply become further rooted in them."

"And of course, that serious stuff is all well and good," said Perplexus. "But friends, let us not also forget the joy of revelry and celebration! Especially after surviving the things we have."

Uriah chuckled and the others murmured in agreement. Across the square, the band began to play, and Laivar retrieved his lute from its place at his feet to softly strum along.

"I can't state how glad I am that you all chose to come here," Adiadni shared, tears in her eyes. "And not just because you brought with you the long-awaited Hero who delivered us all. I've been grateful to always know love and family, friendship and community, but... it was you who showed me that it can be found anywhere. A gift as precious as that makes everything else just feel like fluff."

"You're right," said Perplexus with a sly smile. "But there's a place for the fluff too."

"You know what? You're right. What say we make our way to The Rose for a bit of Kepu?"

The companions enthusiastically agreed.

"I think that's a grand idea, but there's one more thing I want to do here first." Uritus stood to his feet and extended his hand to the woman he loved, "Dance with me."

A smile spread across Adi's face and she took his hand, also rising from the table. This time, Ilya could not hold in her glee, and it spread to the rest of the table who erupted into cheers as the fisherman led the princess beyond the fountain to the other side of the square.

Their shared dance had been a long time coming, and though the fisherman was not entirely confident in his ability, he was happy to engage with her in the activity that brought her so much joy. They shared one dance and then another, bright moon rising high above them by the time they had finished their third. Adiadni paid no mind to the curious eyes that watched her, the happy voices that spoke softly about how wonderful it was to see the princess so deeply in love. The Suvah and Adalos departed from the dance floor with fingers interlaced and proceeded together down to the city's second level to join up with their friends at the tavern.

They walked together in peaceful silence, admiring the joy that danced around them. Adi turned her head to look up into her counterpart's face, his expression soft but serious. "How's your heart today?"

He sighed and offered her a little shrug. "The pain comes and goes. Sometimes heavy, sometimes not. Little distractions have been abundant today, so that helps."

She nodded, chewing on her lip.

"Mostly, it still doesn't feel real," he went on. "I keep thinking that one day I'm going to wake up and go down to break my fast and I'll find him there, chatting with the others as though he'd never left in the first place. I don't know how to convince myself that he's really gone, that I was the one who…"

Adi stopped walking and turned to face him. "I'm sorry," she said sadly, running a hand through his soft brown locks. "Two brothers in a matter of months is too devastating a loss for me to even fathom."

He nodded, sighing again. "I keep imagining what he could have been had he come with me when I went into the White Mountains. He and Havian would have been thick as thieves. He and Lex too. I don't like that all anyone will ever know of him was the thing that he became."

"I understand."

"He was so full of life. He could have changed this entire world if he had managed to break free of the hold his fear had on him."

"I believe it. If he was anything like you…"

"He wasn't," Uritus shook his head. "He was his own man. Faced his grief in his own way. I think I will always feel guilt and sorrow for how I was powerless to bring him back. But I am beginning to accept that I did all I could. Wherever he is now… he is free. There's a quiet comfort in that." The fisherman raised a hand to dry his eyes, his other making its way to the side of the princess's beautiful face. "And in knowing that all of this, the victories and the crushing moments did their part to lead me here to you."

Adiadni smiled, admiring his sparkling blue eyes, and brought a finger to toy with the matching paper flower tucked into the pocket of his loose white shirt. "I am not glad for the pain you had to feel to arrive at this place, but I am glad that you made it here. I sometimes forget that just last season, I was drowning in the fear that I would never know romantic love."

He threw his head back and laughed. "It does seem ridiculous, doesn't it?"

She giggled and bit her lip and tilted her head over one shoulder, studying him. "Wasn't there something you were going to tell me?"

He considered this for a brief moment and then shook his head. "I will, but not now. I don't want anything at the moment but just this. No past, no future. Just right now. My hands and your voice."

"My lips and your eyes."

"The stars above us and the earth below."

"And the love of our friends just around the corner." She took a few steps forward and then turned over her shoulder to look at him, "Are you coming?"

Uritus paused for only a moment, admiring the soft glow of her skin in the moonlight, the dark curls that tumbled over her shoulders, the gentle curves of her gorgeous face. He then stepped forward and accepted her outstretched hand and the two journeyed on together, side-by-side.

Epilogue

"I thought I'd find you here."

Uritus looked up at the sound of the sweet voice and smiled. The fisherman lounged in the shade of an apple tree in the orchard behind the palace, his boots on the ground beside him, a familiar book of poetry lying open on his lap. Adiadni gathered the deep magenta hem of her skirt as she descended to sit beside him where she greeted him with a deep, prolonged kiss.

"I suppose I've grown quite predictable," he joked.

She giggled and the wind whispered through the branches above them. "This is, what, the third time you've read that one?"

He chuckled. "Something like that."

"Read me something."

He straightened his legs as she leaned back to rest her head in his lap, and he brought one hand to tangle in her hair. She looked up at him with adoring eyes as he thoughtfully turned the pages, sitting up a bit straighter and clearing his throat when he finally landed on his chosen piece.

"Somewhere in the darkness
There glows a tiny light
It's silvery and steady
Like the stars above at night
Not everyone can see it
But I think if you try
You'll find it there, a gentle glare
Sure as our blessed sky

It cannot be moved from there
It's rooted like a tree
But even so, it softly glows
For those with eyes to see
A comfort to the lost ones
It draws the wounded close
A beacon and an anchor
For all those that need it most

But still there remain others
To whom it's just a myth
A fairytale, not tangible
Not fleshy fruit, just pith

531

"I love that one," the princess hummed. "It makes me think of you."

"That's funny."

"Why?"

"I chose it because it makes me think of you."

Adiadni laughed and sat up to press another kiss to his lips. He closed the book and set it down, studying her for a quiet moment. "I have something for you."

Her face scrunched up into an expression of surprise. "For me?"

"Yes."

"What is it?"

He laughed at her enthusiasm, one hand finding his way to his pocket, the other holding hers. "I wasn't sure when I was going to give it to you, but once the festival starts we'll be tired and busy, and I don't think I can wait until after."

Her brow creased as she did her best to keep her grip on her patience.

"Close your eyes."

The princess let out a tiny, exasperated sigh and followed his instruction. She heard the shuffling of fabric and then felt it land in her outstretched hands, small and cold and surprisingly heavy.

"Open."

Again, she obeyed, and her mouth fell slightly open as she beheld it—a tiny golden ring, vines entwined with one another. "Uritus…"

"I want to say that I have no expectation for you to accept it now," he spoke before she had the chance to. "I know that there's still a bit of time before you will take the throne. And whether or not you choose to accept it at all, I will remain as I am, at your side, fully devoted to you in whatever respect you will allow me to be."

"Uritus..."

He continued, "In all honesty, the idea of claiming the title of king feels... not quite right to me. But even more than that, it would feel exceedingly not right to live my life as anything other than your partner. You are my dearest friend and I am so in awe of you that at times, it makes my heart ache. You have done and will continue to do incredible things for this land and her people, and wherever that leads you, I want to follow.

"I want to move together, to fight together, to rest and enjoy stillness together. I want to sink deeper into the sound of your voice, the pleasure of your touch, the love and joy and hope and peace that I only found once I came to know you. I want to love *you*, Adiadni, as fiercely and ardently and fully as you deserve, for the rest of my life and long after it has ended. That is... if you would have me."

Adi's open mouth curled up into a smile and then exploded into a laugh, so loud and so long that the wind stirred up and shook the trees with it.

Her joyful peals spread to Uritus's mouth, an amused chuckle. "You're beginning to make me nervous that I've made a fool of myself..."

"No no no..."

She leaned forward and kissed him deeply. When she pulled back, her hand made its way up to her neck, and she tugged on a chain that Uritus had somehow failed to notice. She pulled the chain up until it was free of her neckline and the fisherman laughed again when he saw what hung from it—a golden ring, vines entwined. She tugged it free of her neck and dropped it into his hand.

"I'm only a little bit annoyed that you beat me to it," she said. "But since you did, yes. I will have you. There is nothing that would bring me greater joy."

This time, it was he who kissed her, taking her face into his calloused hands and dipping her back until her head nearly touched the grass. Birds sang around them and wind whipped through the trees and for a blessed moment, both the fisherman and the princess forgot everything but the touch and taste and scent of one another. Such a moment came to a timely end when a loud whistle rang through the orchard.

"Should I come back later?" Perplexus stopped in his tracks several yards away.

Adi and Uritus laughed and the fisherman beckoned him over. The navigator grinned and hurried to collapse on the ground with his friends, greeting them with a warm embrace.

"Shoes off."

"Right." The dark-haired man began to remove his boots. "I must warn you, I've been traveling all day, so I highly doubt I smell very…"

He trailed off, forgetting entirely his task as his eyes landed on the glimmering gold held in each of their hands.

"Fuck. I did pick an inopportune moment to arrive, didn't I?"

The lovers laughed. "Not really," said Uritus. "It feels apt that you'd be the first to know."

Perplexus had returned after his latest journey serving as a navigator for a company of the king's soldiers. He had found joy and fulfillment in this new role, glad to have the opportunity to devote his life to adventuring across the land he loved. Mikka and Tris also had stepped into more permanent roles as soldiers, happy to offer their time to serving the Free People however they were able, under the sole condition that whenever one of them was appointed a charge, the other would be also. The rest of the companions—who all found their way back to their home in the White Mountains—placed bets with one another on how long it would take Mikka to finally admit to Tris the true nature of her feelings.

"Have the others arrived too?"

"Not yet. The family should be here in a matter of hours, Mik and Tris maybe not till tonight. But they'll be here. They wouldn't miss it."

Uritus smiled, knowing he spoke the truth. It had been months since Uritus had seen the rest of the people he called home and he was grateful to the Summer festival for bringing them all together once more.

The perpetual smile Perplexus had worn since his arrival widened significantly in the moment of silence that followed. The fisherman could not help but laugh as he observed this.

"I have a bit of news for you too. Not nearly as exciting as your own, but enough that I cannot wait until later to tell you…" With a happy sigh, he sat up and took Uritus's hand into his own. "The lake has returned."

The fisherman's mouth fell open and the princess's hand raised to her own.

"The Plentiful Lake?" Uritus could not believe it.

The navigator nodded joyously. "Saw it with my own eyes. It's beautiful, Uritus. Silver and sparkling. Apparently, the rain started again when the Shadow left. Uriah thinks it won't be long before we can rebuild the towns. Many of the Vegardians are thrilled to make their homes there."

Uritus sighed deeply, eyes drifting closed as grateful tears traveled down his face.

"*You* did that," Perplexus said. "The new life that blooms there now, that's all because of you."

"Because of *us*," Uritus corrected him, squeezing his hand and finding Adiadni's.

The navigator grinned. "You're right, of course. But that won't stop me from claiming the title of the Hero's Second at every tavern I visit for the rest of my days. Do you know that mere association with you provides me more free ale than I'm even capable of drinking most nights?"

Adiadni loudly laughed. "As outrageous as that sounds, I think I may just believe it."

"On that note, I should probably get cleaned up and changed. You two planning to be here for long?"

"Actually, I think we'll come with you," Adiadni said, sitting up. "I'll want to tell Fenn and my parents."

"Of course." Perplexus rose to his feet and helped the princess to her own.

"Wait a minute..." Uritus retrieved the book of poetry, tucked it under his arm as he stood, and then held an open palm out to Adiadni. "Give it here."

Smiling, she placed the little circle of vines into it. He took her left hand in his and Perplexus took a step back, his own hand lifting to cover his mouth as he grinned from ear to ear. Lovingly and intentionally, the fisherman slid the ring onto the princess's third finger. "To every step we have taken to get here..."

Adiadni took the other ring from him, slipped it off its chain, and placed it onto his hand. "And to every step we will take from here on."

Uritus pulled her close, kissing her once more, and the three friends proceeded back to the palace. They made it all the way out of the orchard to the stone-laid ground before the fisherman realized that he had forgotten his boots.

Acknowledgments

First, to Leo, my counterpart, none of this would have been possible without you. Without you, I would not have had the confidence, time, or wherewithal to even attempt a project of this scale. My manager, researcher, proofreader, diligent doer of technical tasks that I would rather pull my hair out than do myself, for your bottomless well of faith in me and the encouragement that flows from it—thank you will never be enough. I am who I am because you love me. Everything I create is inspired by you.

To my parents for fostering my love of writing and encouraging me to pursue it; to my mom for teaching me to read and write, for reading me abridged Shakespeare as a child so I could act out the plays with stuffed animals, and for teaching the fairytale writing class at our homeschool co-op when I was ten where I wrote the first iteration of Adiadni; and to my dad for sitting with me when I was twelve and helping me come up with names that sounded right for a fantasy setting (among them: Uritus, Perplexus, Suscundos, Agamemnon, Fennispar, and so many more). Though not all of them made it to the final version of the story (rest in peace, Fartmart), your influence will always remain. To Faith and Matthew, my lifelong companions, Ehjonadi historians, ingosoni translators, and architects of Cevyna, I am proud to be your big sister. Watching you two pursue the long-held desires of your hearts played no small part in reminding me of my own. You are my favorite jesters. To Aunt Dot, my twin, for paving the author trail for me, I love knowing that wordsmith's blood runs through my veins.

To Anthony for the book's stunning artwork and the time and care you took to bring my imaginings to life; and to Shannon for helping me fashion a clear picture of Moonracer and also for just being generally cool. The outside of the book holds just as much value to me now as the inside does, and my gratitude for that knows no bounds. To my mother-in-law, Kristin, for staying up late with us on FaceTime to bring my vision for the cover to life, it's somehow even more perfect than I imagined. To Rhys for your aid finding the right typefaces; to Acasia, Monica, Luke, and Ally for having first eyes on the story. Additionally, to Acasia for help with website design; to Luke for offering me your much needed tips as an author who has self-published before; and to Monica for all your miscellaneous notes and opinions that helped me tie everything up with a nice little bow.

To all the teachers I've had who've given me the tools necessary to grow as a writer; to everyone who has ever read my words and told me that they meant something to you; to all the hands who contributed to the book's launch and subsequent celebration; and of course, to you, my beloved Dear Reader. I wrote this story for no reason than to fulfill my own Divine-ordained destiny, but the fact that you saw something in it that made you pick it up means more than I will ever be able to say. Thank you for journeying with me. I hope to meet you again as I continue to trod my path.

Pronunciation Guide

—CHARACTERS—

Adalos: AH-duh-lohss

Adiadni Vindella: ah-dee-AHD-nee / vin-DELL-uh

Agamemnon Vindella: aag-uh-MEM-non / vin-DELL-uh

Alidistris: aal-ih-DICE-triss

Aurena: OUR-ehn-uh

Avyra: uh-VEER-uh

Azanthien: uh-ZAN-thee-in

Basil Dagious: BAA-zull / DAY-jee-us

Betina Alenvir: beh-TEE-nuh / uh-LEN-veer

Cereill Vindella: sir-ILL / vin-DELL-uh

Crystella Alenvir: krih-STELL-uh / uh-LEN-veer

Dagamor: DAG-uh-more

Digtrision: dig-TRIH-zhun

Dijonas: dih-JOE-nuss

Donlimites Subian: don-LIM-ih-teez / SOO-bee-in

Dustafes Elbon: doo-STAH-fiss / ELL-bun

Erclidus Subian: err-CLY-diss / SOO-bee-in

Erephus: AIR-eh-fuss

Ergo Vindella: AIR-goh / vinn-DELL-uh

Exstarferus: ex-TAR-fur-us

Fariya: FAR-ee-uh

Fennispar: FEN-iss-par

Friya: FREE-uh

Gwynn: GWIN

Havian Elix: HAY-vee-in / EE-lix

Heimar Vindella: HIGH-marr / vinn-DELL-uh

Iladder Qinna: EYE-lad-ur / KIN-uh

Ilya Sadieu: ILL-ee-uh / sah-DYOOH

Jasch: JAYSH

Jessop Fril: JESS-up / FRILL

Kala: KAH-luh

Kensus: KEN-zuss

Kristefani: krih-steh-FAHN-ee

Laivar Lethiel: LAY-var / LETH-ee-ehl

Lyra Fril: LIE-ruh / FRILL

Lys: LISSx

Maium Sadieu: MY-ihm / sah-DYOOH

Maja Lowwar: MAH-zhuh / LOW-arr

Meladashing: mell-uh-DASH-ing

Mikka Galinzen: MEE-kuh / guh-LIN-zen

Milion: MILL-ee-on

Moonracer: moon-RACE-ur

Nadarum Cupetati: nuh-DAHR-um / coop-ih-TAH-tee

Octrusial: oc-TROO-she-uhl

Odipar Subian: oh-DIH-par / SOO-bee-in

Olythia: oh-LITH-ee-uh

Oripidus Vengar: oh-RIP-ih-diss / VEN-gar

Ouro: ORE-oh

Perien Subian: PAIR-ee-in / SOO-bee-in

Perplexus Everstone: purr-PLEX-iss / EHV-er-stone

Pressio Alenvir: PRESS-ee-oh / uh-LEN-veer

Punznes Caen: PUHNZ-ness / KEN

Qibat: KEE-baht

Quickspa: kwik-SPUH

Robalto Hammitt: ruh-BALL-toh / HAM-it

Seryc Tarish: SAIR-ik / tuh-RISH

Shrigmut Olar: SHRIG-mutt / oh-LAR

Suprafalo Dagious: soo-PRAH-fuh-low / DAY-jee-us

Suvah: SOO-vuh

Swadalla: swuh-DOLL-uh

Syv: SIV

Tevel Subian: TEH-vull / SOO-bee-in

Trugstar: TRUG-star

Uriah: yur-EYE-uh

Uritus Subian: yur-EYE-tiss / SOO-bee-in

Velatondra: vell-uh-TAHN-druh

Veldis: VELL-dis

Velup: VELL-up

Vexol Subian: VEX-ohl / SOO-bee-in

Vulsdon: VUHLZ-dun

Winchells: WIN-chulls

Xinna: ZIN-uh

Yider: YIE-dur

Zaphron Hammitt: ZAFF-ron / HAM-it

—PLACES—

Akmen: AHK-men

Arkenn: ARR-kin

Cevyna: kev-EE-nuh

Cropidea: crop-eh-DEE-uh

Dersh: DURSH

Ehjonadi: eh-ZHON-uh-dee

Enk: EHNK

Idor: EYE-dor

Judii: JOOH-dee

Lorethh: LORE-eth

Martella: marr-TELL-uh

Myrell: mer-ELL

Nott: NOT

Onnuk: ON-nook

Quabish: KWAH-bish

Sheth: SHETH

Sigmount: SIG-mount

Suscundos: sus-KUN-duss

Tila: TEE-luh

Tosh: TAHSH

Tuvibati: too-vih-BAH-tee

Vegard: VEH-guard

Venadalis: ven-uh-DAHL-iss

Vindellaria: vin-dell-ARR-ee-uh

—OTHER—

Amonii: AM-uh-nee

Arkennish: arr-KEN-ish

Cropidus: CROP-ih-duss

Emipera: eh-mee-PAIR-uh

Eoher: AY-oh-err

Ezo: EH-zoh

Frali: FRAH-lee

Gish: GISH

Ingosoni: in-GOH-soh-nee

Kepu: KEH-poo

Kuffa: KOOH-fuh

Lethaa: LETH-uh

Melodia: meh-LOH-dee-uh

Nevyn: NEH-vin

Nevyna: NEH-vee-nuh

Viraglas: VEER-uh-glass

Yuzh: YOOZH

About the Author

Dove Segovia writes because, to her, creation is magic. She is
deeply appreciative of art in all its forms and feels immense
gratitude for the opportunity to share her own with the world. She
is a novelist, poet, and songwriter, with dreams of becoming a
screenwriter and director. Dove lives in the Shenandoah Valley
with her husband, Leo, and their ever-growing collection of stuffed
animals.